The
CLARINET
POLKA

Keith Maillard

THOMAS DUNNE BOOKS
ST. MARTIN'S GRIFFIN ✹ NEW YORK

THOMAS DUNNE BOOKS.
An imprint of St. Martin's Press.

www.stmartins.com

Library of Congress Cataloging-in-Publication Data

Maillard, Keith.
    The clarinet polka / Keith Maillard.—1st U.S. ed.
        p. cm.
    ISBN 0-312-30889-2 (hc)
    ISBN 0-312-30890-6 (pbk)
    EAN 978-0312-30890-2
    1. Vietnamese Conflict, 1961–1975—Veterans—Fiction. 2. Polish American families—Fiction. 3. West Virginia—Fiction. 4. Polka (Dance)—Fiction. 5. Bands (Music)—Fiction. 6. Young men—Fiction. I. Title.

PR9199 3.M345 C58 2003
813'.54—dc21   2002032511

First St. Martin's Griffin Edition: June 2004

10 9 8 7 6 5 4 3 2 1

More Praise for *The Clarinet Polka*

"Brilliantly resonates into the universal human condition . . . brims with life as we all live it. This is a remarkable novel from an important writer."
—Robert Olen Butler, Pulitzer Prize–winning author
of *A Good Scent from a Strange Mountain*

"Great novels immerse their readers into a world previously unknown and by that test alone, this is a great novel. . . . I promise these are people you will never forget and will be glad you got to know."
—Homer H. Hickam Jr., author of *The Keeper's Son*

"Encore! I'll play over and again in my mind this hard-edged, sweet-souled story of a heart's homecoming."
—Suzanne Strempek Shea, author of *Hoopi Shoopi Donna*

"Jimmy's irreverent voice remains strong. His descent into alcoholism and his subsequent arduous climb toward a life of purpose ring true, as do the voices of other characters who each play a part in this stylistic re-creation of a turbulent era in our history."
—*Rocky Mountain News*

"Maillard succeeds in giving Jimmy a distinctive voice, and his self-deprecating humor—he's an older but less cerebral version of J. D. Salinger's Holden Caulfield—gives the novel a lively narrative thrust. . . ."
—*West Virginia Gazette*

"This hilarious, often sentimental novel is ultimately a joyous, foot-stomping celebration of the human spirit."
—*Booklist* (starred review)

"Engrossing . . . Jimmy is a wry, down-to-earth, irresistible narrator. . . . This moving, well-drawn story of sin and redemption in a fading industry town may remind readers of Richard Russo."
—*Publishers Weekly* (starred review)

"Maillard has once again written an absolutely captivating novel, this time a warm and wonderful story of reconciliation and redemption, chock-full of memorable characters and true to its time and place."
—*Library Journal* (starred review)

"Finely rendered . . . rich in detail and incident, a story of marvelous skill and poignancy: Maillard is a national treasure."
—*Kirkus Reviews* (starred review)

Also by Keith Maillard

Gloria

Dementia Americana (poetry)

Hazard Zones

Light in the Company of Women

Motet

Cutting Through

The Knife in My Hands

Alex Driving South

Two Strand River

IN MEMORIAM

William Wayne Barringer
April 17, 1940 – August 28, 1996

George Cedric Hudacek
November 24, 1942 – December 6, 1996

*Hear my prayer, O Lord, and with thine ears consider my calling: hold not
thy peace at my tears.*
For I am a stranger with thee: and a sojourner, as all my fathers were.
*O spare me a little, that I may recover my strength: before I go hence, and be
no more seen.*

—PSALM 39

The
CLARINET
POLKA

ONE

I got out of the service in '69. The last place I was stationed was down at Eglin, and I had an old beater Chevy, so I put a picnic cooler on the passenger seat, filled it up with a case of beer and a couple fifths of Jack Daniel's, and started driving. I thought I was on my way back to Texas, but eventually it occurred to me that it might take me a while to get there. Then at some later point—I was pretty well into the second fifth by then—I'd kind of lost track of my exact location, so I figured the best thing to do was keep on driving, and wherever I was when I passed out, I should just cool out there for a few days until I figured out what to do next. I was supposed to reintegrate myself back into civilian life, right? So why shouldn't I just drive around? See America first, right? I don't remember much more than that, but my automatic pilot must have taken over because I ended up back in Raysburg feeling like shit.

That was the most miserable time of my life, and for years afterward I tried to figure out why. You know how it is—you've got to find something or somebody to blame, and the easiest thing to blame it on was the Vietnam War. But that didn't make any sense. I'd never set foot in Vietnam.

I'd been trained as an instrument technician, so damn near the first thing Old Bullet Head—that's my father—said to me was, "Okay, Jimmy, you've got a trade now, so use it." He was looking for me to start paying room and board like my sister, but I wasn't in any great hurry to do that. I wasn't in any great hurry to do much of anything. I'd done my four years in the air force, and I figured the world owed me a good time. Nobody else thought that, of course, and I couldn't figure out why they didn't. So after I'd been laying around the house for a few days, Old Bullet Head took matters into his own hands and went out and got me a job doing TV repairs with an old buddy of his, and I couldn't *not* take it, if you know what I mean.

Vick Dobranski had a little rat's-ass shop up in Center Raysburg. After running a one-man operation for years, he hired me to do the in-home repairs. That way he could stay in the shop and work on the sets that people brought in to him. That was the theory anyway. What it meant was that I got to drive around the valley all day in his panel truck, and the main thing I remember is that nothing looked right to me. Everything looked dumb and grim and, I don't know— It was like while I'd been gone, everything had shrunk.

Our neighborhood is a narrow strip from 43rd Street down to 48th Street where Millwood starts. One set of railroad tracks runs along the river, and then there's three streets and another set of railroad tracks and, bang, you're slapped up against the side of the hill. That's South Raysburg. We just called it Polish Town, but the old folks called it *Stanisławowo,* you know, after the church, and they'd got that right because St. Stanislaus was pretty much the center of everything.

You'd come out of the church at night and look south toward Millwood and the sky'd be lit up bloodred from the blast furnace, and you'd get up in the morning and you couldn't see much of anything over your head except a kind of ugly brown haze, and sometimes in the winter the air pollution would be so bad you'd get these unbelievable fogs and you couldn't see from the church down to the PAC—that's the good old Polish American Club—and every damn thing would be covered with this fine red dust from the iron ore. My mom must have spent half her life sweeping that red dust off the front porch and the front steps. Even when I was a kid, I remember thinking, hey, this can't be good for you.

The guys in South Raysburg really kept up their houses, and you'd never see one looking the least bit run-down—which was no mean feat considering that the Raysburg rain in those days was so acid it ate right into your paint job. Our house was pretty much like everybody else's. You walk in the front door and you're facing the stairs and a long hall that runs back to the kitchen. You turn to the right and you're in the living room, and it's just big enough to hold a couch and a chair and the old TV set—you know, one of the first color TVs that's so big it takes up half the room. You walk through the sliding doors and you're in the dining room, and there's my sister's piano and the long mahogany table Mom uses for company—it's her pride and joy, and if you want to die young, just scratch the top of it—and then, what with the matching chairs and everything, you've got to turn sideways to squeeze though to the kitchen where we eat dinner around the old beat-to-shit blue table, crammed in so tight we got our elbows in each other's ears half the time.

On the second floor there's a little bedroom for my parents, and a little bedroom for my sister, and a mouse-sized room that used to be Babcia Koprowski's when she was still alive, but now it's where my mom goes when she pays the bills or does her ironing, and of course our one and only bathroom's up there, and it's big enough for maybe half a midget. Then at the end of the hall you see a little door that looks like it should be in a doghouse. Crawl through it and climb up the stairs to the attic—if you've got broad shoulders, you'll be touching the walls on both sides—and you've made it up to my room, and everything there's exactly the same as it was when I left, and that just depresses the hell out of me.

It used to be the attic, and the ceiling is sloped, so if you're a tall guy like me, the only place you can stand upright is in the center of the room. There's my football trophies on a shelf, and in my closet there's a whole bunch of ridiculous clothes I must have thought looked real sharp when I bought them. The sloped ceiling is covered with all the *Playboy* centerfolds I taped up in high school, and if you can imagine anything more depressing than Miss November from 1960, then tell me about it. The picture of me and Dorothy Pliszka from the senior prom is still sitting on my dresser, and, yeah, I've got to admit that might be even more depressing than Miss November.

Except for my room, where Mom never goes—we made a deal about it when I was sixteen—the whole house is spotless, and I don't just mean clean, I mean eat-off-the-floor clean, because if one of the other moms dropped in for a cup of coffee and saw it any other way, the world would come to an end. But of course none of the other moms ever drop in for coffee because they're all too busy keeping their own houses clean in case somebody drops in. And I'm hearing the same things I heard all the time I was growing up—"Hey, Jimmy, what the hell's the matter with you? Were you born in a barn?"

So there I am at home again, paying room and board like a good son, and wiping my feet on the mat and worrying about getting flecks of toothpaste on the bathroom mirror, and I'm working for that sour old bastard Vick Dobranski for a couple cents above minimum wage, and I'm hanging out at the PAC with a bunch of old farts because the Sylvania plant's closed down and Raysburg Steel's been laying off and most of the guys I went to high school with have left town looking for work, and when I crash out in the living room to watch the tube, what I see is Vietnam and Vietnam protesters and tricky Dick Nixon lying to us. Are you getting the picture? It's funny what can really get to you, but the last straw is my sister's learning to play the trumpet.

All her life Linda's played the piano, and I'm used to that. I even enjoy it. She was so good on the piano, she won a scholarship to go down to Morgantown and get herself a B.Mus., and, like Old Bullet Head must have told her about a million times while she was getting it, a B.Mus. adds up to absolutely nothing, so she's working as a receptionist for some dentist in Bridgeport, a job she could have got straight out of high school. She's also teaching piano to a bunch of little kids on Saturdays, and she already had piano students before she ever got the B.Mus. But, hell, she's certified musical, right, and she's got the degree to prove it. But no matter how musical you are, the trumpet is not an instrument you just pick up and play. At that point she's maybe a notch above "Mary Had a Little Lamb."

I don't know if you've ever lived in the same house with somebody who's learning to play the trumpet. Linda comes home, goes in her room, shuts her door—for all the good that does—and it's BLAT, BLAT, BLAT for a couple hours. She carries her trumpet mouthpiece around, and when you're trying to have a conversation with her, you look up and she's got the mouthpiece up to her lips going BUZZ, BUZZ, BUZZ like a mosquito. When she's not playing the trumpet, she's sitting at the piano singing songs in Polish. When she's not doing that, she's playing polkas on the stereo. *Polkas?* Yeah, polkas. How about a little variety? The Jefferson Airplane might be too much to ask for, but how about a Beatles record? Or even Frank Sinatra? No way. Just more polkas. "What's with Linda?" I say to my mom. "Is every day around here Pulaski Day or what?"

Mom just shakes her head. "You think *I* know?" It seems like ever since Linda came home with her B.Mus. she hasn't had a single date, and the way Mom sees it, Linda is aging rapidly—she's twenty-one, for Christ's sake—and so she's in serious danger of ending up an old maid. "I don't know about your sister," my mom says. "She's turned out even crazier than you are."

There's one thing you learn in the service, and that's when you think things can't get any worse, they get worse. So I come home from the shop, walk in the house, look down at the shelf where the mail goes, and I've got a letter. It's one of those flimsy airmail things like you get in the service. I rip it open, and it's from my buddy Jeff Doren in Da Nang, and he's telling me that Ron Jacobson has bought it. Now me and Doren and Jacobson were real tight. Shit, we were like the Three Musketeers. And except for Georgie Mondrowski who I grew up with, Ron Jacobson was just about the best friend I had in the world. And I'm standing there reading the letter, and I'm going, oh no, this can't be real.

There'd been a night raid, you know, mortar fire. Jacobson had his right arm blown off and part of his face. They rushed him to the hospital, and he hung on until the next afternoon. A couple other guys we knew from Carswell got killed too—Tom Foley and Dick Hewitt. You never know how you're going to react to something till it happens. I'm reading this shit, and I'm just crying like a baby.

My mom comes running in yelling, "Jimmy, Jimmy, what's the matter?" I yell back at her, "I'm okay, Mom, just leave me alone, okay," and I go tearing out of the house just like I used to do in high school and head straight down to the river. Just sit there on the bank, and I'm really hurting, you know what I mean?

I couldn't stop reading that letter over. "As soon as I finish writing this, I'm going to go get totally shitfaced," Doren said, "but I thought you'd want to know about it right away, and I thought you'd want to know exactly how it happened," and he was right about that.

"Things were real harsh around here for a while," he said, "but anyhow, it's down to you and me, so listen up, asshole, we got a date in the Soap Creek Saloon. We'll drink to Ron Jacobson, just about the nicest guy I ever knew."

I didn't want to go home because I wasn't ready to talk about it, so I started hitting the bars. I ended up in the PAC bullshitting with Bobby Burdalski, asking him about the girls, who's got married and who's still available—and, of course, which of the girls I should call up if I'm looking for a little action. You know, just talking about anything to distract myself. By closing time, I was pretty well loaded but not quite loaded enough, so I slipped Bobby a bill and he slipped me a pint of Four Roses out the back door.

I sat on the riverbank and drank it. I had enough sense to go home while I could still walk. You can imagine how nice and cool it was up in my room right under the roof where the sun's been beating down all day long. I lay there sweating like a pig and killed the rest of the bottle.

I was doing my best to pass out, and I did eventually, but I woke up again around four—totally wide awake with the kind of hangover you think death might be preferable—and, God, did I ever want another drink. There was nothing in the house but a six-pack I'd stashed in the icebox, but I was afraid if I went down to get it, I'd wake up Old Bullet Head, so I just lay there trying to get back to sleep, but every time I'd start to drift off, I'd be seeing Jacobson.

He was a huge guy, kind of sandy colored. Over six feet. Not fat, you know, just big. And strong? Hell, I once saw him walk up five flights of stairs with a refrigerator strapped to his back. He said it was the easiest way to get it up there. He used to say, "My strength is the strength of ten because my heart is pure," and it was true. His heart *was* pure. I never heard him bad-mouth anybody. Even the biggest prick in the world, Ron Jacobson would find something nice to say about him.

Doren and Jacobson and I got to be tight at Carswell, and out there in Texas—you know, among the young bucks—duking it out is considered a pleasant way to pass the time, about on a par with shooting pool. But Jacobson just plain hated fighting. He even hated seeing other guys fighting. A man would have to be a total fool to try to break up a fight in a Fort Worth bar, but I've seen Jacobson do it.

Back in Wisconsin, he'd been his high school's heavyweight wrestling champ, and I've seen, oh, five or six guys take a swing at him, but I never saw one of them connect. Something magical would always happen and they'd end up sailing through the air. He was so good he could land them easy or he could land them hard; he always started off landing them easy. Then he'd go, "Hey, come on, buddy, we don't want to be doing this shit. We're just wasting good drinking time." It was really weird, and you had to be there to believe it, but he could get two guys who'd been trying to kill each other—and to kill *him*, for that matter— He could somehow get those guys calmed down again, drinking a beer, and laughing at some silly story he's telling them.

Jacobson and Doren volunteered for Vietnam. Now with Doren I could sort of see it. He about half believed in the war—like maybe three days out of seven he believed in it. But Jacobson's opinion on the topic never changed a bit, and it was real simple. "We got no business in Vietnam whatsoever," he'd say. "It's not our country." He'd joined the air force to get *out* of going to Vietnam, so when I heard he'd volunteered, I just couldn't believe it. I said, "You idiot, what the hell'd you do that for?"

"Well, you know, Jimmy," he said, "it's what's coming down, and I figure I ought to catch my share of it."

And remembering that, I was so mad at him, if he hadn't been dead already, I could have killed him myself. You goddamn stupid son of a bitch, I was thinking, look where it got you.

Finally I checked my watch, and it was after five, and I thought, to hell with this.

I lurched down to the kitchen and sucked back a couple cans of beer and then carried the rest into the living room and sat there nursing the next one because once I'd killed the six-pack, there'd be no way to get anything more until the stores opened. About five minutes later, there's my sister in her bathrobe. She goes, "What's the matter, Jimmy?" you know, whispering it.

I've still got the letter in my pocket, so I just hand it to her. She reads it and says, "Oh, I'm so sorry."

"You want to talk about it?" she says, and I just shake my head.

"Is there anything I can do?" she says, and there's nothing she can do, but I don't want her to feel bad, so I say, "Just sit here awhile, okay? Keep me company."

I don't remember much what we talked about, but every time I closed my eyes, I could see Jacobson clear as if he was standing in front of me, and finally I kind of snapped—like, "Fuck this goddamn war. Just fuck it, fuck it, fuck it."

I look over at Linda, and she's got her glasses off, wiping the tears away, and then it hits me—hey, that's my little sister, my number-one fan. She isn't just being nice, she really cares about me, and I'd been home for damn near a month and I hadn't paid the least bit of attention to her except to get pissed off at her for playing her trumpet.

Linda and I have always been close. It's not like we hung out together or anything like that. I'm four years older, and we had a totally different set of friends, totally different interests, but we were—I don't know how to say this— I guess like a two-person team. We could always tell each other anything, and no matter what went wrong, we always had each other. So it just starts pouring out of me, and I'm telling her about being in the service and all that.

Jeff Doren was from Austin, and four times he took us home with him, and we just plain fell in love with the place. Then, lo and behold, we found ourselves on the delightful Isle of Guam, and there's nothing to do on Guam but drink, and that's the whole story, alpha to omega. So that's what the three of us did, and naturally we shot the shit a lot, and, I guess you could say, peered deeply into each other's souls.

All his life Ron Jacobson wanted to get off the farm. "You bust your ass for nothing," he said. "The bank owns everything you've got." And by that time, I'd figured out that maybe I didn't want to spend the rest of my life in the crazy Ohio Valley. And Doren kept saying, "Come to Austin, come to Austin. You can always get work in Austin." So that's how we cooked up the scheme that after they let us out of the war effort, we were going to have a big reunion in the

Soap Creek Saloon, and we were going to rent us a little house in Austin and just basically party on.

What I was supposed to do when I got out was go straight to Austin and warm it up for them—and talking about all this, I just can't see Jacobson dead. I just can't. He seems so real. I can close my eyes and see him, you know, as alive as anybody. "Koprowski," he used to say, "you got the greatest laugh I ever heard in my life. I hear you laugh, it always makes me feel good." Shit, I can almost hear him saying it.

"It's weird," I told Linda, "how you keep wishing there was something you could do for him, and there's nothing. When somebody's dead, they're dead. But it keeps popping into my head I should have a Mass said for him—maybe because it's the only thing I can think of. That's really stupid, huh? He wasn't even Catholic."

"It's not stupid," she says. "Go ahead and do it. God won't mind that he wasn't Catholic." Even before Pope John, Linda's theology was always, I guess you could say, liberal. I don't know where she could have got it from. It sure wasn't from the nuns.

"Aw, Linny," I say, "I don't know if I believe any of that shit anymore."

She lets that one go, and we talk awhile longer, and then she asks me if I've been to confession. "Oh, hell, no," I tell her. "Not in years." It's been maybe three years since I've even been to Mass.

"You ought to go. You'll feel better."

"Yeah, yeah, yeah."

"No, I mean it. It'll really take a weight off you. You'll feel a million times better."

"Yeah, maybe." I was humoring her. I didn't have the slightest inclination to go to confession. If Father Joe was still around, maybe, but with this new priest they'd got in there, forget it.

It's broad daylight by then, and all of a sudden we hear Old Bullet Head's alarm go off. We don't say another word, just jump up and go scurrying back to our rooms. And poor Linda's got to pull herself together and drag herself in to work, but I'd pretty well said piss on it by then, so I grabbed a few Z's and drifted into the shop around two. Of course I had to listen to Vick going, "Hey, Koprowski, you dipshit, are you working for me or are you working for me?"

When I got off that day, the first thing I did was go in the PAC and write a letter to Doren. "You watch your ass, buddy," I said. "You and me got that date in the Soap Creek Saloon." And then on the way home I bought four gallons of Paisano Red and four fifths of Jack Daniel's and stashed them in my closet because I sure as hell was never going to get caught in an emergency like that again with nothing in the house.

Okay, so living in South Raysburg is like living in a fishbowl—everybody knows everybody's business—and we're having dinner a day or so later and Old Bullet Head says to me, "I hear from Vick you ain't exactly responsible."

The old man could piss me off faster than anybody alive. "What the hell's he talking about? I missed half a day's work? Big deal."

"You know something about working, Jimmy? I'll tell you a secret. The main thing about working is you show up."

Then, just like she's done for years, there's Linda interceding on my behalf. "Come on, Dad. He got real bad news the day before."

Old Bullet Head looks at me. "Oh, yeah? Is that right?"

But I'll be damned if *I'll* tell him. Mom goes, "A buddy of his got killed—in Vietnam." Now I've got both Linda and my mom lined up on my side, so I'm in pretty good shape.

"Oh, yeah?" the old man says. "That's rough. Yeah, that's really rough. But hell, Jimmy, you could have called in. That's just common courtesy," but I can't even give him that—that's how mad at him I am.

I don't know when I started calling him Old Bullet Head—probably in high school and never to his face. He always wore his hair in a real short buzz cut, and he has one of these heads that narrows in at the top and widens out at the jaw, and he's got no neck at all, just a big head that goes straight down to these enormous shoulders like an ape, and if you look at him from behind, he looks like a bullet with a shirt on. I spent half my life trying to please the son of a bitch, but he was never pleased, or if he was, he sure never told me about it.

It's hard to imagine a Polish guy my father's generation not drinking, but he didn't, not even a beer. He'd been a real lush when Linda and I were little, but then he quit, and he never fell off the wagon that I know of. My strongest memory of him—you know, on festive occasions—is of him sitting back out of the way, kind of watching everything go by, with a 7UP in his hand.

He worked his whole life for Raysburg Steel. He was a heater, which is just about as high up as you can get before you pass from union into management. He liked being a heater, he said, because you have to think all the time. He used to brag that he'd started at the bottom and on his way up he'd worked every job in the mill, and twice they offered him promotions to turn foreman, and twice he turned them down. He told me that when everything goes right for a change—

that's once in a blue moon—making steel can be real satisfying. Starting when I was about four years old he said to me at least once a week, "Listen to me, Jimmy. If you end up working in a steel mill, I'll kick your ass from here to Ohio."

Whatever shift the old man was on, the rest of us had to fit in around it. He'd come home dog tired and all covered with red dust, and the last thing he wanted was any shit from you. When he wasn't working, he was always fixing things around the house. Like it'd never cross his mind to call in a plumber or a carpenter or an electrician. Paying somebody else to do what you could do yourself was just a waste of money. Looking back on it, I'd have to say I learned a lot from him, but I had a hell of a time trying to talk to him. I don't want to give you the impression he was mean or anything like that, but he was the kind of guy that—well, let's just say he was a man of strong opinions and after he expressed them, he didn't leave you a lot of room.

He threatened us plenty. He had this story he just loved to tell about *his* old man, how he had this goddamn whip hanging on the wall, you know, like a cat-o'-nine-tails, and if any of the kids got out of line, he'd tan their hides but good, and if we didn't straighten up, he was going to send over to the old country and get one of those damn things. Poor Linda believed him, but I figured out pretty quick it was all hot air, and it's true, he never laid a hand on us—although I could see a few times he was sorely tempted. Mom was another story. She had a short fuse, and she'd just haul off and belt you one, but she couldn't stay mad longer than ten minutes, and she never held a grudge. Old Bullet Head could stay mad for years, and he never forgot anything— Well, that's not quite right. Some things he forgot and some things he didn't.

When I ran forty-five yards and scored a winning touchdown against the Academy, he forgot that in about a week, but for years he just loved telling the stories of my various little escapades. Like, "Hey, Jimmy, remember that night when you were in high school and you and—I don't know who all—was it Georgie Mondrowski and Bobby Burdalski? And you stole a couple fifths from the PAC and got shitfaced and got arrested for knocking over a parking meter while doing a U-turn on a one-way street in Barton, Ohio, at four in the morning?"

So anyhow, there we are at dinner, and he can't get me for missing half a day's work, but he has to get me for something, so he starts in about Dave Lemish's boy, how he got out of the service and figured he'd take advantage of the GI Bill, so he's down at Morgantown getting himself a degree.

"Come on, Dad," I say, "I already had a run at that one, and if you recall, I didn't exactly distinguish myself. Besides, you got me that damn job with Vick."

"Well, you're not exactly going anywhere fast on that one, are you?" he says just like I've been working for Vick for ten years.

You remember the generation gap? Everybody was talking about it back in those days. So here's the generation gap opening up at our kitchen table. My father wants to know what exactly is it I want out of life anyway. What are my plans? And I'm saying, hey, I just got out of the service. Plans? The biggest plan I got is getting up in the morning, and so he's got to tell me yet again that when he was growing up, it was the height of the Depression and he didn't even finish high school—let alone play football or go to proms or any of that other good shit—and then it was the war, and when *he* got out of the service, he already had a kid—me, to be exact—and all he could do was grab the first job he could find and hang on to it for dear life, and he sure as hell didn't have the luxury to let his hair grow halfway down to his asshole and sit around staring at his navel, and so, of course, Linda and Mom have got to defend me and talk about how times have changed, and all the kids are wearing their hair long now—it's just a style—and how I've just got to find myself, and how I'll be surprising him one of these days. "Oh, yeah?" he says. "I already got more surprises out of him than one man can handle."

"Give him a break, Dad," Linda says, *"jeszcze się taki nie urodził, co by wszystkim dogodził."*

My sister is the only person I know our age who would suddenly break out in Polish like that, and it's just one of those old sayings that's almost exactly like what we'd say in English, "Nobody can please everybody," but Linda thinks— I don't know what she thinks. Maybe if she says it in Polish, it'll come out all covered with ancient peasant wisdom like dirt on a potato she's just dug up. My parents give her that look they always give her when she does that. They respect her in a weird kind of way for her lifelong attachment to the Polish language, but they also think she's totally nuts.

"Yeah," Old Bullet Head says, "that may be. But let me tell you a little secret, Lindusia"—that's what he calls her when she's been talking Polish at him and he wants to tease her about it—"you got to please *some* of the people *some* of the time."

It's true, I wasn't pleasing anybody very much, and least of all was I pleasing myself. All I really did that spring was drive around in Vick's panel truck. The last few months I'd been down at Eglin, I'd been like a convict doing hard time, but then when I got home, I kept thinking, hey, I got out for *this?* Everything bugged me or made me sad. There I was in the Ohio Valley where I'd sworn I'd never live again, and I just couldn't get used to the idea that Ron Jacobson was dead.

I'd go out on a call to someplace—like Bridgeport—and I'd be gone two hours because once I got in the truck, I just had to keep driving. How Vick put up with me, I'll never know. And everything looked so damn familiar because that's where I'd grown up, and everything looked— I don't know, just ugly as all hell because I didn't want to be there. The river defines everything—you're either going up the river or down the river or away from the river. You're either on the West Virginia side or the Ohio side. And all along the river on both sides there's steel mills with their stacks sticking up, pouring crap into the sky. The hills in the summer look like lumpy green sponges, and there's a million little roads twisting around them, and they keep slapping up more highways so you can drive faster from one end of the valley to the other, going nowhere.

Neither one of my grandfathers was planning on staying here. I don't remember Dziadzio Koprowski, my dad's dad. He died when I was a little kid, but I grew up hearing all these stories about him. He was a steady, quiet man— my dad always said that about him—and like a lot of guys back in the old country in those days, he was wandering around all over the damn place looking to make a few bucks. That's back when Poland was partitioned, and he was desperate for work, so it didn't seem like a big deal to try America, where they said a strong man could always get a job and every day you ate meat like you were a landowner.

Now Dziadzio Wojtkiewicz, my mom's dad, I remember him real clear and I always will. He was a *góral*—that means a guy from the mountains—and he was real proud of it. "Yeah, I'm a Polak hillbilly," he'd say with his big laugh. He liked to drink vodka, and if he got enough in him, he'd sing you those Polak hillbilly songs with that old-country wobble in his voice. The guys from the mountains—well, hell, they were the best damn men in the world. They could sing, and they could dance, and they could work, and they could fight, and they could screw better than anybody—that's what he told me—and when he came over here, he was going to make the big bucks and then he was going to go back and buy himself a nice little place up there in the Tatra Mountains.

Both my grandfathers got hired as common laborers at Raysburg Steel, and neither one of them made it back to the old country. And those guys and their wives—all that first generation—settled down in South Raysburg close to that blast furnace in Millwood, and they worked their asses off.

God knows how they did it, but they built St. Stanislaus Church, and they brought in a young Polish priest straight out of the seminary in Detroit to minister to their spiritual needs—that was Father Joe Stawecki—and they built a little school and brought in the Felician Nuns to teach at it so their kids could get a good Catholic education. They had Polish baseball teams and basketball teams and football teams, and Polish Boy Scouts, and half a dozen different Polish political organizations, and a Polish choir, and for a while there even Polish dancers. They kept up the customs they remembered from the old country, and they stuck together and minded their own business, and they made it through that big ugly strike in 1919, and they made it through the Depression, and they helped build the USWA in the valley, and they hung on to their little bits of property any way they could and kept up their houses real nice, and they sent their sons off to the war—the big one—and if you want to read the names of the ones that didn't come back, they're on a bronze plaque at the back of the church. And they did all that so assholes like me could have a better life. And I didn't give a shit about any of it.

I didn't give a shit about much of anything. I didn't want to see any more of that polluted river. I didn't want to see any more steel mills. Any day now I was going to Austin, Texas, but in the meantime I was just driving around, killing time. Christ, I kept thinking, nothing makes any sense.

They'd just slapped up a little mall on the Ohio side out near St. Stevens. By modern standards, it wasn't much of a mall, but it was the first one anywhere around here, and it was already pulling in lots of people. I had no call whatsoever to go out there, but it was spring, and I liked sitting on a bench watching the honeys go by.

So I see this girl, right? In my head I called her "the Mommy" because she had a little kid with her. I don't remember much about the kid except it was a boy. I didn't exactly have kids on my mind in those days.

I figured she was about my age. She had on an outfit that made everybody stare at her. It was pink and looked like a jumper you'd put on a four-year-old— you know, with a real short skirt and the straps that go over the shoulders and those little-kid shoes the girls wore back then—and she had an extremely well developed figure, much too well developed for that outfit. She was wearing mirror sunglasses, and she had dark brown hair and a Beatle haircut with bangs that came right down to the top of the sunglasses, and she didn't look like anything you'd expect to see in the Ohio Valley.

I followed her into the record store and pretended to be looking for something. I got close enough to her to smell her perfume. She looked well kept, and of course she was wearing a wedding ring. What I thought I liked in the girl department was those Texas skinny-ass blue-jean babies, and the Mommy wasn't like that at all. I don't know if I've got the point through to you or not, but she was *exceptionally* well endowed, I mean centerfold stuff. "Hey, honey, you're looking good," I said to her.

She didn't seem surprised. "Don't call me honey," she said. She sounded bored, like I was some fool she'd known for years.

"Okay, honey," I said, and she didn't move away. I told her some lies about how I'd just got back from Nam and she was the prettiest thing I'd seen since I got stateside.

She had a way of standing with her ass stuck out that I found extremely interesting, so I told her what I'd like to do to her. Exactly. Like a bull humps a cow, is what I said. Then I went on and described it to her in graphic detail. She didn't look like she was paying any attention to me, but she didn't walk away either. The kid was over on the other side of the store, so I just kept on talking my trash to her.

It wasn't the first time I'd said something like that to a girl, but it was the first time I'd done it sober. Usually what happened was nothing, and the best that ever happened was the girl laughed and said, "Shut up and buy me a drink, you asshole"—that was in Fort Worth and it says something about Texas girls—and the worst that ever happened was I got a frozen daiquiri thrown in my face. It'd never crossed my mind that a girl might be offended, like deep-down offended. It was just a dumb thing you did if you were in the service.

She turned to me, and where her eyes should have been, all I could see was myself looking back in those dead-eye sunglasses. In the same kind of voice you'd say "nice weather" she said, "Follow me, but don't be obvious about it."

She took the kid into the pinball gallery. When I came along behind them, she was talking to the man in there, and he kept shaking his head no, but she laid a bill on him, and it must have been one of those higher denominations because all of a sudden there was no problem, and he went and found a chair for the kid to stand on. She asked me if I had any change—so much for not being obvious about it—and I gave her all the change I had, and we left the kid there and walked out into the sunshine.

"Where do you want to do it?" she said.

"I've got a panel truck," I said. She followed me. We climbed in, and I moved the toolboxes out of the way and shut the doors. I tried to kiss her, but she pulled away. "That isn't what you said you wanted to do," she told me.

I needed to see her eyes, but she didn't take the sunglasses off, and I knew somehow I shouldn't reach out and take them off her. She didn't say another word, but she pushed back from me, kind of like, come on, you jerk, give me some room, and sat down cross-legged and took her shoes off. She hiked her skirt up and pulled off her pantyhose and her panties and tossed them over on top of her shoes. She turned over onto her knees and lay facedown and shoved her ass up. She just waited like that, absolutely still, with her bare ass sticking up under that little pink skirt.

For a minute all I could do was stare at her, and I remember thinking, hey, what if I can't get it up? Because it was like she was daring me to do exactly what I'd said I wanted to do. But then, all of a sudden, the old lust kicks in and I've got no problem—just like I'd said, I'm a bull on a cow. Humping away. Not a thought in my head. I can hear her trying not to make any noise, but she can't help it. A kind of whistling, moaning sound's coming out of her, and I just love that sound, and then it's over in nothing flat, and she stays where she is like she's turned to stone.

I wanted to say something but I didn't know what. I mean, what the hell could you say? We're both of us covered with sweat because it's real close in there with the doors shut. Eventually she sits up. She puts her pantyhose in her purse and her panties back on and her shoes on over her bare feet. She still doesn't say a damn thing. She points to the doors. I open them up, let her get out first. The fresh air feels wonderful. We couldn't have been in the truck ten minutes, if that long.

"Don't follow me," she says and walks away.

I got the Jack Daniel's out and had my first drink of the day. I didn't give a shit who saw me. I had that wonderful satisfied feeling you get like you're on top of the world. At the same time, I felt kind of sad, and— Well, you know that feeling you get sometimes that something terrible is going to happen but you can't imagine why or what it could possibly be? I leaned back against the truck and looked up into the sky. I've thought about this plenty, but still I couldn't tell you exactly what was going on in my head. I remember I was faced away from the sun and the sky was so bright it was like looking at nothing.

TWO

You'd think I'd be feeling pretty good about myself, right? Scoring like that? But I didn't feel all that good, even right afterward, and eventually that crazy girl I'd tapped at the mall turned out to be just something else to get depressed about. But I couldn't stop thinking about her.

Half the time I couldn't believe it'd been real, and it would have made a terrific story to tell the guys at the PAC, but somehow I never got around to telling it. I had a strong feeling for that girl—which was weird considering I didn't even know her name—really protective of her or something. Like, hey, you dumb broad, you should be more careful. You shouldn't be screwing strange guys in the back of panel trucks, like the next strange guy might not be a nice guy like me, why, Christ, he might be *anybody*, and how could you do something like that *with your kid with you?* And I kept doing reruns in my mind— seeing her laying on the floor of Vick's truck with her bare ass sticking up—until I began to get sick of it. It made me feel itchy and jumpy, you know what I mean?

Well, a couple weeks went by, and then Vick was telling me that some girl's been coming into the shop looking for me. "What girl?" I said, playing dumb, but I knew who it was. She must have memorized Vick's address from the side of the truck. "She's got more on her mind than her picture tube," Vick said.

I took to hanging around the shop in the afternoons, and she finally turned up late in the day. "When do you get off work?" she said. "I need to talk to you." No hi, hello or any damn thing. Shit, I thought, she's pregnant.

The minute she walked into the shop, my heart practically jumped out of my throat, because, my God, I hadn't just been making her better in my mind.

She really did have a figure that would stop traffic. "I can take off now," I said. "You want to go somewhere and have a drink?"

She shook her head. "Let's go for a walk."

Well, you can walk around in Center Raysburg, but it isn't exactly a place where you *go for a walk*, so I took her down to the river. There's a spot where it's all overgrown and nobody can see you from the street, as I well know because I used to go there with the boys back in high school before we had our draft cards. We'd always be able to find somebody's uncle who'd slip us a case out the back of the bar—"Huh, huh, huh, I'm glad this is for your grandmother"—and we needed a place to drink it. I hadn't been down there for years, and it felt strange taking the Mommy there.

She wasn't wearing her little-kid outfit that day, but she was wearing a miniskirt—with white socks and perfectly clean little white tennis shoes—and for some crazy reason I thought that was sexy. And then on top of everything else, I was wondering what the hell I was going to do if she was carrying my kid. I might have been a shitty Catholic, but there was no way in hell I was going to have anything to do with an abortion.

She wasn't talking, and I kept searching my mind for something to say. It was right after Neil Armstrong had been walking around on the moon, and I remember saying some dumb thing like, "Hey, pretty big step for mankind, huh?" and she looked at me like I had two heads.

She was wearing her dead-eye sunglasses just like the last time. We're standing there on the riverbank, and I light a cigarette, and she's staring across at the Ohio side, and she says, "I'm a married woman."

"I did manage to notice the ring," I say, "not to mention the kid."

"I've got another one. A little girl. She's just turned four."

We're standing side by side looking at the river. The sun's still high, and it's hotter than hell, and I'm waiting for her to drop the bomb on me.

"My husband's a doctor at the St. Stevens Medical Center," she said. "He's highly respected. We have a good marriage. We're very happy." She said it like she was back in the second grade, reciting in front of the class.

"I don't even know your name," she said. I told her, but she didn't tell me hers.

"Listen, Jim, I don't want you to think I do that sort of thing all the time."

I didn't say anything. I didn't want to make any more of a fool of myself than I already had.

"I've never done anything like that in my entire life. I was shocked at myself afterward. It was, I don't know, just some kind of crazy stunt—"

"Right. Yeah, I figured that's what it was. Just some kind of crazy stunt."

I could see she was suffering, and I just wished the hell she'd get to the point. "Look," I said, "don't think twice. Everybody has their crazy moments. Why don't we go somewhere and have a drink?"

"No, I've got to get home. I left my kids with the girl next door, and my husband will get home, and he'll wonder where I am. I'm always home when he gets home. You do understand, Jim, I can't see you again."

"Sure, I understand that."

She didn't make a move to go, and we stood there for so long it was starting to get ridiculous. "Honey," I said, "are you pregnant?"

She looked like I'd hit her, and then she laughed. "Oh, God, no. I'm on the pill."

Then, even though the sun was beating down like hell, she took off her sunglasses and put them in her purse. She turned and looked at me, and she had great big brown puppy-dog eyes, and I thought, oh, Christ, that's all I need—because she was just absolutely drop-dead gorgeous. She looked straight into my eyes, and I saw how she was looking at me, and finally I got it.

I bent down and kissed her, and she started kissing me back like I was her long-lost love she hadn't seen in years. I pushed her up against a tree. She was like a big doll—didn't move or anything—let me push her anywhere I wanted her to go. I reached up under her skirt and pulled her panties down. She helped me do it and stepped out of them. I felt like I was in a trance—hey, this can't be happening. Anybody on the river could have seen us, but I didn't give a shit. When I came into her, she screamed bloody murder. That stopped me, and I said, "What's the matter? Did I hurt you?"

"No," she said and grabbed my ass with both hands and pulled me into her, and then, just like the last time, it was over in about two minutes flat.

She pushed me away and picked up her panties off the ground and started to cry. I mean really hard. Sobbing.

She started walking along the riverbank, crying, and whenever I'd get too close to her, she'd motion me to go away, but I'd be damned if I was going to go away. We must have done that for the better part of an hour. I kept trying to say dumb things to her, like, "Come on, honey, what's the matter?" but she wouldn't say anything, so finally I just shut up and followed her, keeping a few feet back. I offered her a smoke, and she took it and puffed on it like somebody who doesn't smoke. It was ridiculous, but she was still carrying her panties in her hand. The first thing she said was, "We can't do this again."

"No, of course we can't," I said. "Let's go somewhere and get a drink."

"I can't have a drink with you," she said.

"Why's that?"

"Because I'm a married woman."

I began to wonder if she had all her smarts. "Sure you can," I said. "We'll go someplace really quiet. Someplace where you can be sure nobody knows you. Okay? You pick it, okay?"

Eventually she said, "Oh, hell, anyplace will do. We never come down here."

So we started back up to the street, and she still hadn't put her panties back on, and I made a motion like, hey, aren't you forgetting something? and she said, "I stepped all over them. They're all muddy," and she put them in her purse.

There was a Greek place near Vick's shop where I used to go for lunch and I knew they'd sell me a shot. I took her into the back room. It was still early, so we had it to ourselves. I told the Greek I wanted a double. She said, "Can I have a gin and tonic, please?" and the Greek and I just looked at her.

"This is West Virginia, honey," I said.

"Oh. That's right. I'm sorry."

The Greek asked her if she wanted a shot of gin. "Yes, please," she said, and the Greek brought us our shots. I knocked mine straight back, and she watched me do it, and then she knocked her gin straight back, and the Greek grabbed the glasses and shoved them in the pocket of his apron. I ordered a pitcher and a couple cheeseburgers. She said, "I can't have an affair."

"Okay."

"I mean it. This is the last time I'm going to see you."

"Any way you want it to be is how it's going to be," I told her, and I believed it.

Her name was Constance Bradshaw. She's got to be kidding, I thought. Nobody is named Constance Bradshaw. But that really was her name—Connie to her friends. She and her husband were from Baltimore, and they both came from prominent families there. That's exactly what she said—prominent families—and she even told me her maiden name just like it might mean something to me. I was tempted to tell her that the Koprowskis were fairly prominent in South Raysburg too, but I didn't. I'd got my rocks off, and I had that double shot in me, and there was a beautiful cold pitcher of beer sitting on the table, and I honest-to-God thought I'd never see her again, so I was being just as nice as pie. Somehow it was important to me to act like a nice guy and not like an asshole. I still thought I was in control of things.

She told me that she and her husband had been in the valley only a couple years and she still wasn't used to the place and wasn't sure she ever would be. Some days she just plain hated it. "I don't know why I'm telling you any of this," she said.

She asked me what it was like in Vietnam. "Honey, I lied to you," I told her. "I was in the service, but I wasn't in Vietnam."

She looked disappointed, so I thought I'd better tell her some war stories. "You heard of Rolling Thunder? Going to bomb them back into the stone age? Well, I was part of that. I was stationed on Guam. I was one of the guys that maintained the aircraft."

She asked me about being in the service, and everything she asked me, I answered her honestly. I think I even told her about Jacobson getting killed. I asked her what her life was like, and she said, "I have a good life. I love my husband, and I love my kids. We have a wonderful home. I just wish we could have stayed in Baltimore, but it's okay. We're not going to be here forever."

We sat there for maybe an hour, and she started to get fidgety, so I delivered the little speech I'd worked out—"You're really a beautiful woman, Connie, and I really like you. I'm glad we got together in this crazy way we did. And I just want to wish you all the best, okay?"

"Thank you," she said. "You're a nice man, Jim."

When we stepped out onto the street, it was twilight—that blue-gray time of night that's so pretty it hurts. She said, "I'll tell him I went shopping in Raysburg and I'm going to a movie. It's kind of weird, but he'll believe me. I've never done anything like that before, so he'll believe me."

She went in a phone booth and called her husband, and I guess that's what she told him. "The funny thing," she said to me, "is we have a perfectly good sex life."

I walked her to her car. It was parked kitty-corner to Vick's shop. It was a red Mustang, brand-new. She didn't make any move to get into it. "Has your boss gone home?" she said.

I took her into the shop and screwed her on the floor in front of Vick's workbench. This time we weren't in any hurry. I'd never in my life had sex with a girl that was so damn easy. Usually there's a lot of fumbling around until you get used to each other, you know what I mean? But with Connie everything was perfect right from the start—like maybe we'd gone through the preliminaries in some other life. Afterward, she just totally stank of sex, and I said, "I'm sorry we haven't got a shower in here, but there's a little sink in the back where you can wash up."

"Oh, no, it's all right," she said. "I'm okay." I thought, oh, come on, your husband hasn't got a nose? But I didn't say it.

I walked her to her car, and she said, "Don't you ever dare call me at home. I really mean it. I can get away next Tuesday afternoon. Is that okay for you? Can you take time off in the daytime?"

"Sure," I said, "so long as you don't mind the back of the truck."

"I don't mind the back of the truck. You know the wharf parking lot?"

"Yeah."

"Two o'clock, okay? Go to the level just below the roof and park. If there's anybody in there, anybody at all, just wait until they go away. And then I'll get in the back. Okay?"

She kissed me and got into her Mustang. She rolled the window down and said, "If you ever tell anybody about this, I'll never see you again."

I knew there was something more, so I waited to hear it. "If you ever tell anybody about this," she said, "I don't know what— Look, Jim, I really want to impress this on you. You can't tell anybody. Not your best friend. Not *anybody*."

"Okay."

"You could wreck my whole life. You've got to promise me."

"Okay, I promise."

"I want you to swear to it."

"Okay, Connie. Sure. I swear to God, I won't tell a soul."

She drove away up the river. It was after eleven by then, and I wondered what she was going to say to her husband the highly respected doctor when she got home.

I was true to my word. I didn't tell anybody about Connie. But the person we both forgot about was Vick Dobranski. I go into work the next morning, and he says, "So, did you replace her picture tube?"

If I'd seen it coming, maybe I could have dreamed up some lie he would have believed, but he took me completely by surprise, so I go, "What the hell you talking about, Vick?"

"The girl in the miniskirt."

"Oh. Her. Yeah, I replaced her picture tube all right," and I gave him a big grin hoping that would be the end of it, but of course it wasn't.

Okay, so now we're into the Jim and Connie Show, Phase One. About once a week—sometimes twice when she can get away—Connie and I are doing our spy routine. I go sailing into the wharf parking lot, wait till the coast's clear, open the door to the back of Vick's truck, and she jumps in. I drive over to the south end of the Island, park somewhere, usually down by the Downs, and we fuck our brains out. At the longest, it doesn't take much more than an hour, and the only talking we do is to arrange for the next time. And every time I'm thinking, oh, my God, sex doesn't get any better than that, and then the next time it gets better than that.

You'd think this would be the perfect arrangement for a hot-blooded young guy twenty-five years old, right? You've got a fantastic-looking girl who loves doing everything you love doing, and you've got responsibility zero. You don't even have to talk to her. It's like the best jerk-off fantasy you could ever dream up, so what could possibly be wrong with this picture? Well, right from the start I knew there was something wrong with it, but I just didn't want to think about it.

I'll never forget when it all came together in my head. I'd got stoned with Georgie Mondrowski and we ran into Dorothy Pliszka right in front of Czaplicki's grocery store. You know how when you're stoned, your mind makes all these weird connections? So anyhow, Dorothy was the first girl— But wait a minute. I'm getting ahead of the story here.

You see, Georgie got out of the service that summer too—well, no, to be exact, he'd gotten out in the spring sometime, but he'd been in the VA hospital, and then, finally, he turned up in Raysburg—I guess it must have been sometime in July—and he'd already been home for a few days before I even knew about it, and I thought, hey, why didn't you call me, you son of a bitch?

Like me, Georgie has a little sister, and his little sister was talking to my little sister, and Georgie's family was worried sick about him. Except for going to the can, he hadn't set foot out of his bedroom since the day he'd come home. They had to bring his food to him in there, and he wouldn't even talk on the telephone. So Darlene asked Linda to ask me if I'd come over to see him, maybe cheer him up or something, and I felt really shitty because I should have *already* gone over to see him—like the minute I'd heard he was back. But the problem was, he hadn't been an up-in-the-air junior birdman like me, he'd been one of those sorry bastards down in the jungle, and I was afraid he'd hold it against me.

Of course it wasn't as clear in my mind as I've just made it sound. All I knew was I was really reluctant to go see him, and the longer it went on, the more reluctant I got. Until one night Old Bullet Head's yelling at me, "Jesus, Jimmy, this guy's been your best friend your whole damn life. Why don't you at least pretend you give a shit?"

Okay, so I just couldn't put it off any longer, and one Sunday afternoon I go over there. The way George's mom and dad were, you would have thought *I* was their long-lost son. "Oh, Jimmy, it's just wonderful to see you, just wonderful. Georgie is going to be *so* glad to see you." And they keep glancing upstairs to where his room is like they think he can hear us through the floorboards. "I got to apologize about his room," his mom tells me, kind of half whispering. "He won't let me touch anything. He won't even let me make the bed," and I follow her upstairs, and she bangs on his door and sings out in a big cheery voice, "Hey, Georgie, honey, look who's here to see you."

I'm not sure what I'm walking into. All the blinds are down so it's really dark and the room just reeks of cigarette smoke and dirty underwear. He's sitting in the corner with his back to the wall, wearing an old pair of gray sweatpants and a sweatshirt with a hood just like something left over from track practice in high school, and after my eyes adjust, I get a good look at him, and it's shocking how thin he's got. His cheekbones are like big knobs on his face, and he's all hollow around the eyes. He must not have had a shave or a haircut since the day he got out. "Hi, Gee-O," I say.

"Hey, Jimmy."

I'd been afraid he wouldn't be able to talk, but there's no problem with that—he's going a mile a minute. But something's happened to his voice—it's quiet and hoarse—and I've got to get practically on top of him to hear what he's saying. He's sitting right next to his stereo, and he's telling me about his record collection. What with us both being in the service, I haven't seen him for a couple years, but, yeah, that's how he starts the conversation. Do I like Janis Joplin? How about the Grateful Dead, Country Joe? Hey, isn't that Gracie Slick something else? Have I ever heard this group called Love? They're really far out.

So he cranks up the stereo full tilt. He must have listened to those records a million times because he's got the songs memorized. His lips are moving along with the words. He keeps trying to tell me about things in the music—anyhow, I think that's what he's trying to tell me, but I can't hear a damn thing he's saying, so I yell at him, "Hey, you dumb fuck, let's get out of here."

I thought he was going to give me a big argument, but he says, "Okay, sure." Then it takes him like an hour to figure out what to wear, and finally I've got to say, "Just put some jeans on, asshole."

We go downstairs and everybody is totally blown away that George is going *out*, but they're all trying to pretend it's perfectly normal—"You boys have a good time now!"

"Wow, it's a nice day," George says, like it's a great discovery. It is a nice day. The air's clear and it's not too hot.

"So how the hell you been?" I say, and he just smiles at me.

He's walking fast like he's in a hurry to get somewhere, but we're not going anywhere that I know about. "Central going to have any kind of team this year?" he says.

"I don't know. I haven't heard a damn thing about it."

"I haven't seen a high school game in years."

"Yeah, me neither."

"How the hell you been?" he says. "I should be able to answer a simple question like that, huh? I should be able to say, Oh, I've been shitty—or great— or so-so—or something, right?" and he laughs, so I laugh too. "Hey," he says, "let's go to St. Stans."

So we walk over to the church, and I follow him inside. Like automatic, we both genuflect and cross ourselves, and then he stands there staring down the aisle at the altar. I haven't been in St. Stans for a couple years, but nothing's changed. You've probably been in a Catholic church, right? There's that heavy quiet feeling you've always got—the smell of incense, candles burning, and a couple old ladies saying their rosaries. But it's more than that. This isn't just any Catholic church, it's *our* church.

I always loved the two angels standing on either side of the altar. They've got wings taller than they are, rising up behind their heads, and they're holding lamp stands—three bulbs with crystal shades coming out like petals of a flower—and I always thought of them as girl angels, although with angels, I guess, you never know for sure. Then there's the two sections off to the front where you light votive candles. On the right, Christ has his side—you know, the Sacred Heart—and the Blessed Virgin has her side on the left, with the Holy Mother of Częstochowa and her sad, mysterious eyes. When I was a kid, I was afraid to pray to her because she had to worry about all the Polish people in the world and I didn't want to bother her with my little problems. "You been to Mass lately?" George says.

"No."

"Yeah, me neither."

I don't know what he's thinking about, but left to my own devices I'm pretty sure I wouldn't have gone into St. Stans. It's making me sad, maybe because I grew up there and it's all so much a part of me—and maybe because I don't believe in much of it anymore. I think Georgie might want to pray or light a candle, but no, he turns and walks right back out onto the street. "We had some good times, didn't we?" he says. "Remember the atom pearls?"

Oh, yeah, sure I remember the atom pearls. You know what those things are, don't you? They're about the size and shape of BBs. You drop them on the floor and somebody steps on them, they go off, BANG. We scared the shit out of the nuns with those atom pearls—until they caught us, and then that was another story.

When people ask me what it was like going to school with the nuns, I always tell them this old joke. Stop me if you've heard it. There was this bad-ass kid, and he'd been bounced out of public school, bounced out of about a dozen private schools, and his parents were just about at their wits' end with him. They weren't Catholic, but they decided to send him to school with the nuns because they'd run through all their options and that was the last resort. So he goes there a week, and then two weeks, and then a month, and his parents keep waiting for the bomb to drop, but no, nothing. His old man's amazed, and he calls the kid in and says, "Hey, what's going on? Usually by now you would have been expelled. How come you're not in trouble yet?"

The kid says, "Well, Dad, I walked in the first day, and I looked up and saw how they had that guy up there hanging on a cross, and I thought, hey, these nuns are *serious*."

That's absolutely true. The nuns were *serious*.

But not all of them were mean. "You remember Sister Regina?" I say.

"Oh, yeah," he says, "she was something else." Sister Regina was big on apparitions. Any time the Blessed Virgin ever appeared to anybody since the year zero, she knew all about it, and she made sure we knew all about it too. We thought apparitions happened to people all the time. "Yeah," I say, "she had me believing that any day now I was going to be walking home from school and there'd be the Blessed Virgin waiting for me right in the middle of Pulaski Park." I really wanted to see the Blessed Virgin waiting for me in Pulaski Park. Other people had seen her. Why shouldn't I?

Naturally, Georgie and I were choirboys. Our priest was old Father Joe Stawecki. He was a little guy with a face like a bulldog, and he used to brag that he could say Mass faster than any priest in the Ohio Valley, and he wasn't kidding—in and out of there in twenty minutes flat. He'd get cranked up, he'd be going faster than a hillbilly auctioneer, all in Latin—getting rid of the Latin was the dumbest thing the Church ever did, if you ask me—and if you slow him down, your ass is grass. You're supposed to have all that Latin memorized, right? And there were cards you could look at if you forgot. But you don't sweat the small stuff, so you're just mumbling along lickety-split. Like, "*Confiteor Deo* a mumble, a mumble a mumble, *sanctis et omnibus*, mumble a mumble, *pecavi* a mumble, *mea culpa, mea culpa, mea maxima culpa,* mumble a mumble a mumble a mumble, *Dominum Dominum Dominum*."

You go make your confession to him, same thing—in and out of there, bingo, five minutes tops. "Bless me, Father, for I have sinned—I've, ah—you know, committed impure acts—"

"Oh, yeah? Who with? Somebody else or by yourself?"

"By myself, Father."

"What's the matter with you, Jimmy? Can't you find a nice girl to go out with?" and I'm sitting there in the confession box, and I think, hey, what did he just say to me? I'm supposed to go find a nice girl to make it with instead of jacking off? And naturally he knows exactly what I'm thinking. "You find a nice girl, you got a reason to keep yourself pure. Okay, one Act of Contrition, three Hail Marys," and that's it, I'm gone. He preached short and sweet too, all in Polish, and he'd get real personal sometimes. "Hey, I heard Stas Rzeszuski's been stepping out on his wife again. He better stop that." No parish priest today could get away with that shit.

"Too bad about old Father Joe," Georgie says.

"Yeah." Father Joe always said he'd never die until the last of the first generation had died, and he almost made it.

"What's this new priest like?"

"I don't know. Linda likes him."

I'm just following along wherever George wants to go, and now it looks like we're headed down to the river. "I saw some asshole at the VA," he says, "and he says I've got a sleep disorder. It's not that unusual. You know, for combat veterans. It's supposed to go away on its own. You want to do a J?"

When it comes to grass, I'm a real juicehead. Doren and Jacobson did their best to turn me on, but they never succeeded. "Hey, Jimmy," they'd say, "juice is just a dumb body high," and I'd say, "Well, shit, I got a pretty dumb body, and Jack Daniel's is about as high as it wants to get." Oh, I gave grass a good run a couple times, but all it ever did was make me gloomy and paranoid, so I got to the point where I just stayed away from it, but there's no way in hell I can say no to George, so we cross the tracks and walk on down to the riverbank, and he hasn't just got some dope and papers, he's got a pocket full of joints all rolled up and ready to go. He fires one up and hands it to me to take the first toke. "When'd you get out?" he says.

"June."

"You were right, Jimmy. I should have gone in the air force with you."

We'd talked about joining up together, and he had considered it, but he was working at Raysburg Steel back then and hoping he'd move up the ladder there, and he figured it'd keep him out of the service. Well, maybe it would have. Steel manufacturing is vital to the war effort, you know, even if all you're doing is sweeping cinders off railroad tracks. But then they did some heavy-duty layoffs and you've got your FIFO rule—first in, first out—so there he was unemployed. And before he could do anything about it—things were tight in the valley even then—he got the greetings from Uncle Sugar.

So we sat there watching the river go by, and we did the J, and I was thinking it was lousy dope, catnip maybe, because I wasn't feeling a thing, and I'm thinking, Okay, what do I say now? *How was Vietnam?* Yep, that's a good conversation opener, all right.

So I start telling him about being on Guam. "It was like you weren't really in the war, but you were. People getting killed every day, but chances are, you weren't going to be one of them. You're maintaining the aircraft, and the aircraft are dropping bombs, but you never see the bombs drop," and everything I say, he just smiles at me—"Yeah, yeah. Right."

"Nothing to do on Guam but drink."

"Yeah," he says.

"We're just bombing the hell out of Vietnam, probably killing civilians right, left, and center, but we're on Guam, and we don't give a shit, right? And you know what I feel really bad about? What I feel really bad about is I don't feel bad about it." That one gets a laugh out of him.

"I just heard, like just last week," I tell him, "three guys from my shop got killed in Da Nang. One of them I was real tight with."

"Yeah," he says.

I don't have a clue what he's thinking—is he thinking, what the hell's Jimmy talking about? Some guy getting killed? What's *he* know about guys getting killed?

"Yeah," he says, "nothing worse. I been there, man. That's really the pits."

I look right at him, and he's got the saddest, kindest expression in his eyes I've ever seen on a human being in my life, and then, WHAM, I finally get it—I'm whacked totally out of my skull. That dope was the strongest shit I've ever smoked, and I'm just *ruined*. I can't even talk. "Hey, Jimmy," he says, "hey, hey, hey," and he takes my arm and hauls me onto my feet and leads me back up to Main Street.

We get up to Czaplicki's, and wouldn't you know it, there's Dorothy Pliszka out for a walk with her little kid. I haven't seen her in years, and I'm so stoned all I can think about is what we must look like to her—these two weirdos standing there grinning at her who can't find a good word to say—and I'm seeing Georgie through her eyes. There's no stoned hairy freaks in Raysburg yet, so he's probably the first one she's ever seen, and I can see her looking at him, like, oh, my God, get me out of here! But she's got to stand there and make conversation with us because she's known us her whole life.

Of course she's not Dorothy Pliszka anymore, she's Dorothy Green, married to that asshole Jack Green—his grandfather's name was Grondzki, for Christ's sake—and Dorothy's saying, "Jimmy, I haven't seen you forever. How have you been?"

"Just great, Dorothy, just terrific, how about you?"

When we were little kids, Mom made sure we never missed our Mass obligation. It wasn't like today when all you worry about is getting your kids' *bodies* into church, never mind what they've got on them. Back then boys had to have at least a clean shirt and pressed pants and their hair combed, and little girls had to be super neat. If they had the kind of moms who went nuts over that stuff, you'd see little girls that were just too good to be true—you know, with hats and snow-white gloves and patent-leather shoes and snow-white socks—and I remember the high point of Mass for me was Dorothy. She was the perfect picture of what everybody's mom thought a little girl ought to look like at Mass, and I'd sit there and stare at her across the aisle like I was hypnotized. I just couldn't imagine anything in the world as cute as Dorothy Pliszka.

You know what they're teaching now, that little kids can't commit mortal sin? I think that's probably right—I just wish somebody had told us that when we were little kids—and I know I wasn't having any impure thoughts about Dorothy Pliszka, not at seven I wasn't.

Later on, yeah, I had an impure thought or two. She was the first girl I ever kissed—it must have been in the eighth grade—and in high school she broke my heart. I can remember being dead drunk, sixteen or seventeen, stumbling into St. Stans at one in the morning, praying to the Blessed Virgin, "Oh, please let me be worthy of Dorothy."

So there I am, stuck on the street with Dorothy, stoned up to my eyeballs, and she's saying all these dumb polite things, and they all sound totally ridiculous—I can't believe she can't hear how ridiculous everything sounds—and it really hurts me to see her, and I'm thinking, my God, what is this? Have I still got a thing for her after all these years?

And then, straight out of left field, George goes, "I love little children. They're so clear."

Dorothy stops what she's saying and turns and looks at him. Dorothy's little girl—she's about two—is hiding behind her mom's legs. "See, she's afraid of me," he says, "and she doesn't have to pretend she isn't," and if Dorothy's got any smarts at all, she's just got to know he means, I know *you're* afraid of me, Dorothy.

You know how it is with dope, how it makes everything feel like it's connected to everything else—yeah, and so what can it all *mean?* So why did I run into Dorothy *right then?* And why does it remind me of picking up Connie in the St. Stevens Mall? Oh, because they both had their kids with them. And what could *that* mean? And then it hits me. It's clear as a bell. Hey, Koprowski, you dumb shit, you shouldn't be screwing around with a married woman.

All of a sudden George squats down on the sidewalk in front of Dorothy and starts talking to the little girl hiding behind her mom's legs. "You don't have to be afraid of me, honey," he says in that strange, quiet, hoarse voice he's brought back from Vietnam. "I'm your uncle Georgie. Yeah, that's right. That's exactly who I am. Your mommy and I went to school together. Yeah, we went to school down here at St. Stans with the nuns, and then we went up to Central with another bunch of nuns. Your mommy always got straight A's, but your uncle Georgie didn't. No, sir, he sure didn't."

Dorothy's wearing shorts and George is hunkered down right smack in front of her crotch, but he isn't paying any attention to her crotch, he's talking to her little girl. He holds out his hand, offering the kid his index finger. Dorothy and I are staring at him, and then she looks at me, and her eyes are saying, help, Jimmy, what do I do now? and I'll be damned if I know.

George keeps on talking, and then, very slowly, the little girl comes out from behind her mother's legs, and very slowly she reaches out and takes ahold of Georgie's index finger with her little hand, and she and Georgie just look into each other's eyes, and they're smiling at each other, and all of a sudden I'm all choked up, and I know if I try to say a word, I'm going to start bawling like an idiot right there in front of Czaplicki's grocery store, and I think, oh, God, what's wrong with me?

George stands up and says to Dorothy, "What a little sweetie you've got there," and then it's over—thank God—and we're walking away.

"You still like her, don't you?" he says.

Ordinarily I would have denied it, but I was so stoned I couldn't bother. "Yeah, sure."

"She's a nice girl, but she's too straight for me. I always liked the crazy ones."

I was so gloomy I couldn't find a thing to say. George kept walking me around the neighborhood, and I was thinking, never again. Grass is really a bummer. The pits. And I was having all those dark, hairy thoughts that come with grass—about Ron Jacobson, and about Foley and Hewitt—Doren hadn't told me how they'd bought it, and I wished he had—and about that horrible flight to Goose Bay, Labrador, with Ron Jacobson, and now he's dead, and about all the death George must have seen, and about how we're all going to die, so if we are, shouldn't we be trying to make something of our lives, do something that really matters? Yeah, but what really matters? Let's get specific here, Koprowski, but I'll be damned if I know what really matters. And I want to tell George what I'm thinking, but I can't get the words to come out.

"There's a lot of nice girls like Dorothy," he says, and I'm thinking, yeah, I suppose there are. Then something else goes click in my head. It's like the next logical step. I might be having the greatest sex of my life, but there's one thing I don't have, and that's a girlfriend.

We walk around some more, and he says, "I wanted to stay in the VA hospital. I told them, 'You guys can't send me home. I'm nuts.' And you know what that asshole doctor says to me? 'Don't worry about it, son. It's normal. You're bound to encounter difficulties reintegrating yourself back into civilian life,'" and he laughs his ass off.

So I finally got home and all I wanted to do was lay down and go to sleep for a while, but I had to eat Mom's Sunday dinner, and the first bite I took, I realized I was so hungry I could've scarfed up everything on the table all by myself, so I'm sitting there silent as a stone just shoveling in the food, and Linda's already talked to George's sister, and she says, "That was really nice of you, Jimmy. Getting him out of the house. You really cheered him up."

I found out later it was Thai-stick we'd been smoking, or some shit like that, anyhow about a hundred times stronger than your ordinary dope, and that's why I'd got so fucked up. I couldn't believe some of the things that'd been going through my head. Seeing Dorothy Pliszka had been like a rerun of high school, and I don't know what it was about Dorothy anyway. I'm not sure I even liked Dorothy. She was cute as a button but nothing special, just your ordinary standard-issue nice Polish girl.

I'll never forget how we started going together. It was the fall of my sophomore year, and I'd been out with the boys on Saturday night, and the next morning my mother hauled my ass out of bed and I'd just made it through Mass with a horrendous hangover, and all I could think about was drinking about a gallon of something cold and fizzy. I step out of the church and dip my fingers in the holy water and cross myself—to this day I can remember the feeling of that little drop of water on my forehead—and I look up and there's Dorothy looking straight into my eyes and she's got a smile like a sunrise. She must have thought she could see my halo shining or some damn thing, and that was probably the best I ever looked to her the whole time she went out with me.

I always thought it was mean of her to wait until after the senior prom to break up with me. I guess she wanted to be sure she had a date. "I'm sorry, Jimmy," she said, "I'm just not ready to settle down." What she meant was, she wasn't ready to settle down *with me*, and I can't say as I blame her. When a nice Polish girl is just dating, maybe it matters to her if you're a hot-shit football player or if your old man has a nice big blue Chrysler you can drive her around in or if you're lots of fun and everybody likes you, but when she's getting serious, all she wants to know is, will you straighten out and get a good job and marry her and give her babies? And any girl with half a brain could see that's not where Jimmy Koprowski was headed.

When I was growing up, we had two religions at my house—the Catholic Church and the USWA. Old Bullet Head worked his whole life for Raysburg Steel, and he always said to me, "Jimmy, make something out of yourself. Stay in school. Or learn a trade. Get some ambition. Because if you don't, you know what's going to happen to you? You're going to piss away your whole life in a steel mill *just like me*."

Dziadzio Wojtkiewicz—my mom's dad—you'd give him a drink of vodka and he'd go into these rants, half in English, half in Polish. "You kids don't know nozzing," he'd say to me. "You don't know how good you got it."

"That's right," my father would say, "you kids just take it all for granted—just like everything else you didn't have to work for."

"Back in them days," Dziadzio would say, "they meke Polaks work the hard dirty job, and they don't pay for shit."

Polish guys never moved up. It didn't matter how many years they'd been working in the mill, they stayed unskilled labor forever. Any American guy could be there six months, and he'd be bossing the Polish guys around. Dziadzio worked twelve-hour days, six days a week, and he made just enough to support himself, forget about a family. When he got married, Babcia had to work in the bakery; later on she took in boarders. And every other week he's on the long turn, twenty-four hours straight. "Drag yourself like old dog," he says, "like dead man."

Gases from the furnaces could kill you in minutes. Sometimes you'd get a hang or some damn thing and the furnace blows—guys blinded, burned horribly. "Lotta Polaks killed in them days. Company say sorry, pay the widow fifty bucks funeral expense, go away don't bodder us. Hey, you know what I seen, Jimmy? The tap hole. They didn't pack her right. Steel come down in the pit, kill fourteen, fifteen guys. You know what they do? Melt 'em back in the steel."

"That's no lie, Jimmy," my father says. "That's what they did in the old days. Can you imagine that? Jesus. 'I'm sorry, Mrs. So-and-so, your old man got killed last night. Yep, buried alive in molten steel. Too bad about him, but anyhow we got the steel. You want to pay your last respects, we'll show you which ingot he's in.'"

"Company don't give a damn, do what it want," Dziadzio says. "No union to protect you."

"That's right," my father says. "You pay attention, Jimmy."

They always say the same thing. I've heard it a million times. My grandpa always goes back to this terrible strike they had right after the First World War when the company totally creamed the union. They brought in the scabs and the Pinkertons—"nozzing but a bunch of tugs and murderers," Dziadzio says. They beat up union organizers, ran them out of town, broke their arms, and threw them in the river. They made Dziadzio kiss the American flag—he's always stomping up and down and banging his fist on the table when he tells this one—"I good American. I love this country. I work hard. I don't meke trouble for nobody. 'You kiss the flag, you goddamn Hunky,' they say. *Niech ich szlak trafi!*"

On and on they go, and eventually we get to the Great Depression. Dziadzio lost even the little bit he had, everything he'd worked for all those years. "'You no work today,' foreman say. 'You go home. Maybe work next week. Maybe work next munt.'" Not enough money to feed his kids. His boys had to go on the bum. His beautiful daughter, she had the voice of an angel. She had to go sing in the bars for the gangsters. Every cent she made, she brought home to keep the family together.

"Then FDR, he meke a law. Thet law say we got the right to organize. John L. Lewis, good man. He talk to boss at U.S. Steel, and they got the union jist like thet"—Dziadzio snaps his fingers—"but Old Man Eberhardt, he say, 'Screw your law. Screw U.S. Steel. No union here!'"

My father remembers this too. It's when he was growing up, and he was a red-hot union guy right off the bat, so now he's chiming in with all the shit he went through. Listening to them is like listening to the nuns tell the stories of the saints—how you've got to suffer to get anywhere, but no matter how horrible it gets, you know it's going to turn out all right because you've got God the Father, God the Son, and God the Holy Ghost, not to mention the Blessed Virgin and the whole Communion of Saints, waiting for you at the end of the line.

"You don't gotta teach Polaks union," Dziadzio says. "Polaks stick togedder. We just keep going like this, one step and then anozzer step and then anozzer step"—Dziadzio takes his first two fingers and marches them across the table in these slow careful little steps—"and we beat the old man good. We got the union, *dzięki Bogu*. Everyting we got, we owe to the union, and thet's the trut."

"You pay attention to your grandfather, Jimmy," my father says. "He's giving it to you straight."

When I was growing up, the mills were going twenty-four hours a day. All you had to do was look south toward Millwood where the old man worked and you'd see that fire in the sky. Yeah, and they still ran open hearths in those days, and all up and down the river there they'd be, looking exactly like hell—fire and sparks and smoke and little black figures moving around in the fire like the souls of the damned. My sister told me that when she was little, she thought it *was* hell. I remember being afraid I'd never be grown-up enough, or a man enough, to work inside that fire the way my dad did.

I don't know why Georgie and I were such fuckups. We were the third generation so what we were supposed to do was go out and make something of ourselves, and a lot of the guys, that's exactly what they did. Jack Green who married Dorothy Pliszka was one of them. Good grades, scholarship to Carnegie Tech. A few years older than us so getting married young and staying in school and having a kid meant he had no problem with the draft. Got into the engineering department at Raysburg Steel and did real well there. Long before Raysburg Steel went down the tube, he'd already got himself a better job out west somewhere, and it was good-bye Ohio Valley. You've probably known guys like that, right?

So what was it with George and me? I don't know, maybe it was the sixties. See, if you think long enough, you can always find something to blame it on. But anyhow, after we got out of Central, we went down to Morgantown where we lasted about a year and a half. I was going to study accounting and he was going to study engineering. Anyway, that's what we told everybody.

We tried out for football. Neither one of us was big enough or mean enough for college ball, and halfway though the tryout, we looked at each other and said, "Fuck this shit, man. You want to go get a beer?" We were roommates in the men's dorm along with a whole bunch of other animals, and there you are for the first time in your life with no parents around, and, naturally, it's, "Hey, party time!" and we made a point of distinguishing ourselves in that particular area.

The university is a land grant institution, so they've got to take any sorry son of a bitch from the state of West Virginia who's managed to graduate from high school, and that's a lot more students than they can handle, so they've got to flunk out as many as they can, and I don't know how it is these days but back then, believe me, they got right down to it. The freshmen had these gigantic required courses with like three hundred students crammed into a lecture hall, and there's some boring old fart droning on about a million miles away down in the front, and you've got a TA who doesn't give a shit, and you get pick-a-winner exams graded on the bell curve, and half your class is gone by Christmas, so it was a minor miracle we made it through the year. Naturally we ended up on probation.

I remember one night Georgie was over at our house, and Old Bullet Head went on at us for hours. "Stay in school," he said. Every argument we came up with, he had a better one—the good old 2-S deferment for starters.

"Shit," he said, "if you guys ever worked a day in your life, you'd know what I'm talking about." We thought that was pretty unfair because we'd both of us worked—summers, after school, any chance we got.

"Worked?" he says. "Jesus, that's a laugh. Listen, I don't mean a frigging paper route or mowing lawns. I don't mean hauling trash out of somebody's garage. I don't mean helping Bob Pankiewicz paint houses. I don't mean unloading boxcars for a couple days so you can brag to the girls about how you busted your ass. I mean *working for a living.*" Yeah, yeah, yeah, we say. Big deal, we say. We can always get a job. "You guys just don't get it," he says.

"Stay in school," he says. We can't get away from him. He's pursuing us all around the goddamn house. It's the most worked up I've ever seen him in my life. "Stay in school!" he's yelling at us, "stay in school, stay in school, stay in school!"

Well, by the end of what should have been our sophomore year, Georgie's got himself some shit job up at the Staubsville Mill and I'm a pre-racker in the Sylvania plant. What the pre-racker does is, the light bulbs come along on an assembly line, and he puts a little doohickey on the light bulb so the racker can put the next little doohickey on over the top of the first little doohickey. Well, God did not design a human being to spend eight hours putting little doohickeys on light bulbs, and my back and neck would go into knots hard as concrete, and my brains would turn to mush, and every Friday night, Georgie and I would get together in some bar and bitch about our jobs, and we didn't give a rat's ass about anything except drinking ourselves shitfaced.

God knows why, but I stuck with Sylvania for over a year. And one day I'm working away putting little doohickeys on light bulbs and I found out it's true, you really can tell yourself a joke you've never heard before, and I'm laughing like a hyena, and the foreman comes by and says, "Are all Polacks nuts or is it only you?" The next day I enlisted in the air force.

It occurred to me later that maybe I should have asked Old Bullet Head about it. "What difference does it make?" he said. "You've already done it."

"I just want to know your opinion," I said.

If I'd thought about it, I could have predicted exactly what he'd say. My whole life I'd heard him telling me what his old man told him, and if you want that ancient peasant wisdom straight from Poland, I guess this is it—"You don't work just to live." That means it isn't enough just to support yourself; you've always got to be a few bucks ahead, socking it away, improving your lot in life. So of course what my old man said to me was, "Okay, Jimmy, being in the service is like anything else. You can use it to get somewhere, or it can just be another four years of your life."

It was just another four years of my life.

THREE

Near the end of the summer, the Jim and Connie Show entered Phase Two. "Why don't you pick me up at the mall?" she said. That didn't make any sense to me. If you live in St. Stevens, wouldn't you think that the St. Stevens mall would be the last place in the world where you'd want to get picked up? "We haven't made a lot of friends here," she said, "and I never see anybody I know. Besides, I can be talking to a TV repairman, can't I? There's nothing wrong with that, is there?"

Okay, Connie, I thought, it's your ass, so I started picking her up at the mall—which may have saved *her* time but sure as hell didn't save me any, and it turned out that now she had plenty of time anyways because she'd hired a lady to come in every afternoon to look after her kids.

I got to be an expert on the secondary roads of eastern Ohio. "What is it you're supposed to be doing?" I said.

"What do you mean?"

"You know, going out in the afternoon. What does your husband think you're doing?"

"I'm not sure he even thinks about it. I told him I needed some time to myself." Hey, I thought, a very understanding husband—a lot more understanding than I would have been under the same circumstances.

So I started filling up the picnic cooler with beer and bringing along some Jack Daniel's and some gin, and after we got our rocks off, we'd sit around and shoot the shit, and what used to take an hour was taking all afternoon. She was great at asking questions, and she got pretty much my whole life story, but trying to get anything out of her was like pulling nails out of a board. The things I found out about her, I got in bits and pieces.

She wasn't, like I'd thought, the same age as me; she was four years older than me. She was damn near thirty. She was scared to death of turning thirty. "I got married too young," she said. "I wasn't ready."

"I don't know about that," I told her. "You know what everybody says? Have your kids young, get it over with."

"But who says I had to have had kids?"

She had an honors degree in philosophy. She told me there's a kind of philosophy that's like mathematics, and that's what she'd been interested in. She'd liked it because it was hard and she had to work her ass off at it, and she'd thought for a while she was going to go on and get her Ph.D. and teach—which is what some of her girlfriends did—but she got married instead, and she kept thinking she'd made the wrong choice.

She always called her husband "he" or "him." It was like he didn't have a name. "This doesn't have anything to do with *him*," she'd say. "He's a perfectly fine man. I have no complaints about him at all. This has to do with *me*."

And then other times she'd say, "Oh, God, he doesn't deserve this. I'm such a bitch."

Before she'd got married she'd been wild—that's the word she used. "But I vowed I'd be good. And I have been. At least most of the time. Up until now."

"Do you have any idea," she said, "what it's like being cooped up with a six-year-old and a four-year-old in a big house in a quiet neighborhood in a town you hate where you don't know a soul and don't *want* to know a soul with a husband who works twelve to fourteen hours a day?" Nope, I said, I didn't have a clue.

One of her favorite things was complaining about the double standard and she couldn't see why women—and, by God, I should never call them *girls*—so why shouldn't women be as sexually active as men? And I'd say, "Gee, Connie, I don't know. Why the hell shouldn't they?" I wasn't exactly checked out on women's lib in those days, and all this stuff was news to me.

Then one night I'm crashed out in the living room watching TV with Old Bullet Head. He's reading the paper, and Mom and Linda are out in the kitchen cleaning up so they can't hear us. The old man's eyes have been perfectly fine his whole life, but practically overnight he needs reading glasses—it's funny, but the same damn thing's just happened to me—and so he gives me the icy blue stare over the top of his glasses, and he says, "Okay, so who's the woman?"

"What woman?"

"The married woman you been screwing in the back of Vick's truck."

"Jesus, Dad, I don't know what the hell you're talking about."

"Don't give me that shit. Somebody's been doing *something* in the back of that truck. She left her unmentionables—"

"Her *what?*"

"Her frigging underpants. Come on, Jimmy, don't play dumb with me or I'll bounce your ass right out of here. Who the hell you think you're fooling? You drive away for a single call at noon and you haven't made it back to the shop by closing time, what the hell you think Vick's going to think? He figured it was the girl in the miniskirt—you know, the one *with the wedding ring on her left hand*. You following any of this, or am I way over your head?"

"I'm following you."

"Yeah, I thought you were. Okay, there's just two things I got to say about this. One is, what you do on your own time is nobody's business but yours, but Vick's just trying to make a living like the rest of us. Is what you're doing fair to him?"

"No."

"Okay, and here's number two. I'll let you in on a little secret, bright boy. Getting involved with a married woman is just about the dumbest thing you'll ever do in your life." And that's that. He picks up the paper and starts reading it like he hasn't said a word.

I was so steamed I walked out, went straight down to the PAC, had a couple shots to calm down, said to Bobby, "Hey, put the word out, will you? I'm looking for a place to live. Someplace cheap. A fixer-upper maybe."

The next morning I said to Vick, "You know, sometimes when I'm off with the truck, I'm not working for you. It's kind of obvious, right? Okay, suppose when I do that, I put the time back later?"

A big grin spread across his face, and he said, "Okay, Jimmy, that's okay with me."

All that was left was Connie. "Okay, Miss I've-got-a-degree-in-philosophy," I said, "what are you doing leaving your panties in the back of Vick's truck?"

It was like I'd dumped cold water on her, and then, just for a second, she looked like a little kid when you catch her pulling the cat's tail. She couldn't meet my eyes. "Oh," and she gives me this little hee, hee kind of phony laugh, "is that where they went?" And I'm feeling a buzz, like, hey, this doesn't add up.

Looking back on it, I suppose I could say it was the distant early warning of better things to come.

It must have been the Jim and Connie Show that kept me stuck in Raysburg those first few months. I don't know what else it could have been—and yeah, I've got to admit that I took a certain interest in our little escapades. Of course it couldn't last forever. But we did make it till damn near September before we blew up, or imploded, or whatever the hell it was we did. The excuse for the fight we had was Vietnam, of all damn things.

Connie was more than a dove; she wanted the Viet Cong to win, and I just couldn't go there. Georgie Mondrowski used to say, "Don't tell me Charlie's a nice guy. Charlie is *not* a nice guy," and that's exactly the way I felt too, and I haven't changed my mind any over the years.

I don't want to give you the impression that everybody and their dog talked constantly about the war back in those days. A lot of the time you just tried to forget it. But it was always there, like—I don't know, some kind of dull roar in the background. A kind of muddy dirty feeling about it. You'd turn on the news, and there'd be the latest installment of death and destruction, and then some asshole from the government would be lying to you about it, and then there'd be some protest going on somewhere.

I had nothing against protests. At least when they were starting out I didn't. When I was in the service—well, even in my alcoholic stupor, I did manage to notice that the times they were a-changing. Martin Luther King got killed and Bobby Kennedy got killed, and there was all that shit going down at the Chicago convention, and Johnson threw in the towel, and Nixon got elected saying he had some plan to end the war, but the war was still going full tilt. Then by the time I got home you'd start seeing these protests where the kids weren't just chanting and singing songs, they were trashing the campus, and I couldn't buy that.

It's funny how something you see on the tube can stick in your mind for years. There was some protest somewhere, and there's this guy about my age, right? And he's got hair down to his asshole and these John Lennon glasses, and just looking at him you know he's never worked a day in his life. And he's got this big, smug, self-satisfied grin on his face. He's playing for the camera, right? And he takes his draft card and he *eats* it. I wanted to jump right through the tube and strangle the son of a bitch with my bare hands.

But on the other hand there was Gene McCarthy, and lots of ordinary people were coming out against the war, and I don't know, I think most people were just plain getting sick of it. The guys my father's generation had been in the big one, so they had a knee-jerk reaction, you know, my country right or wrong, and we got to go stop the Commies—especially if they had any feelings for Poland they thought that—but not too many of them was exactly saying, "Well, son, it's your patriotic duty to go get your ass shot off." I mean, my old man talked a good game, but the feeling you got from him was more like that World War II thing I heard him say a million times—"That's all well and good, Jimmy, but don't volunteer for anything." You know what's funny? He cared more about my hair than what I thought about the war.

And the guys I went to school with— The best I can tell, most of us felt— Well, it was like what the hell can you do about it anyway? Nothing. So if you had to go, you went, and if you could get out of it, you got out of it, and it was kind of the luck of the draw whichever it was, and all you could do was try to survive the best way you could.

The closest I'd come to the war had been seeing the bodies unloaded on Guam. There they were, in uniform, and they just looked like ordinary guys, except they were dead. And then there was Hewitt, Foley, and Jacobson. And if you want to know the truth— Well, okay, this is not one of those well-informed, well thought out, highly reasoned opinions we're all supposed to have in order to function at our very best in a democracy—this is your hairy, no-bullshit, four-in-the-morning take on things. What I *really* thought about Vietnam was that the whole goddamned country was not worth the life of a single one of those guys.

Connie told me that thinking like that made me a racist. "I'm sorry, honey," I said, "but I don't have a lot of sympathy for the Viet Cong, and I don't have a lot of sympathy for whatever bunch of clowns we're propping up in Saigon this week either."

We're in the back of the truck out on a dirt road where I'd pulled off by some cornfields. I've got the doors open to try to get a breeze, but there's no breeze, and Connie and I are sitting there stark naked, drinking beer out of the picnic cooler, and she's telling me how I'm wrong about Vietnam.

I've got just enough beer in me to hit that point where you say, piss on it— like getting back to the shop before Vick goes home, like getting Connie back before her husband gets home, like driving somewhere and getting something to eat so maybe we won't get totally shitfaced, like doing anything the least bit sensible—just piss on it.

To celebrate my arrival in the Land of Piss-on-It, I got the Jack Daniel's out of the toolbox and took a hit, and then, as a joke, I offered it to Connie. She didn't drink out of the bottle, but that day she did. "You're terrible, Jim," she says, "the things you make me do."

If you're a real drinker, there's a point when the rush starts, and you can't beat that. For a real drinker, nothing can beat that, and I'm feeling totally satisfied and pleased with myself, and the sex is over for the day so I'm off duty and we can settle down to some serious drinking, and I'm feeling that wild burst of happiness—that crazy drinker's rush—and I remember thinking, this is it, Jimmy boy. Life doesn't get any better than this.

I get it into my head that I'll tell her a story that will make it clear to her what I thought about Vietnam. "So I've only been on Guam a few weeks," I say, "and I'm checking out a system because the commander of the ship reported a malfunction—the power supply to the fuel-quantity gages. It's one of the systems can ground an aircraft. And the commander—the captain or major or whatever the hell he is—wants to know if I can get the system corrected in time for the takeoff. They're about to make a bomb run, you see.

"Well, there's nothing wrong with the system. Where I'm working puts me right behind the copilot, so he can't see me, but the captain's looking straight at me, and I say, 'Can't find a thing wrong with it, sir.'

"'Listen,' he says, 'I'm not going to take up an aircraft that's unsafe.'

"And then something happens. He doesn't wink or smile or anything, just keeps looking at me, but all of a sudden I know he doesn't want to fly. There's two currents going into that system, an AC and a DC, so—right there with him watching me do it—I jump the AC into the DC and torch the thing out. Sparks, puff of smoke, while it burns its little heart out. And I say, 'Yeah, you were right, Captain. It's malfunctioning.' And he gives me a big shit-eating grin. 'I said I wouldn't fly an unsafe aircraft.'"

"I don't get it," Connie says.

That stops me because I thought it was obvious. "He didn't want to fly," I say.

"Right. He didn't want to fly. Why?"

"That's the way it was—like, you know, just the way it was." I don't know what else to say to make her see it.

"You mean, nobody wanted to fly?" she says.

"Of course there were guys who wanted to fly. There were lots of these gung-ho—"

"You mean, he was sympathetic to the Viet Cong?"

"Oh, for Christ's sake, no, he wasn't sympathetic to the Viet Cong. *Nobody*

Connie's breakdown

was sympathetic to the Viet Cong. Jesus, Connie, what do you think? He just didn't want to fly. It's like, honey, when you don't give a shit—"

"What are you trying to tell me, Jim? I really don't get it." She's staring me right in my eyes, and she looks real puzzled. "Oh," she says, "*you* don't give a shit? Is that what you're trying to tell me? Everything's a joke with you?"

That was the first time with Connie when I felt—I don't know how to describe it. Something like a tilt, and then the world starts to drop away from under your feet. But I thought, hell, she's a smart girl and what I'm saying's real simple so if I start over again and tell her the story all over again, she'll see how simple it is, so that's what I did.

Everything I said was wrong. "You're being patronizing," she said. "Just who do you think I am? You do know what it means to patronize somebody, don't you, Jim?"

Well, that really pissed me off—that she'd think I'd never heard the word "patronize." We're chugalugging that bottle of Jack Daniel's like soda pop, and she's started giving me a lecture on American foreign policy—I mean a *lecture*. She starts with George Washington and works her way forward. I sit there and listen as long as I can, and then I say, "Hey, wait a minute, honey. Now who's being patronizing?"

She stops talking and looks at me like she'd never seen me before. She looks like somebody when you yank them up straight out of a sound sleep. Then she starts screaming. "Who the hell are you? Jesus Christ, just who the hell *are* you?"

I reach out to touch her, and she bats my hand away. "Who do you think *I* am? Some little slut? Jesus, what am I doing here?" And before I know what's happening, bang, she's out of the truck and running.

It's so quick I just sit there and watch her go—this girl, completely bare-ass naked, running off into some farmer's field, screaming her head off. It's late in the season and the corn's ready to harvest, and she's crashing the stocks and knocking them over, and stumbling and falling down, and scrambling up and running and crashing into more stocks. Screaming the whole way—no words that I can make out, just this horrible wailing, loud, and I keep watching it like a movie, and I'm thinking, Christ, I wonder where the farmer is.

Eventually some sense of self-preservation must have got me moving. I didn't know how drunk I was until I pulled my pants and boots on and jumped out of the truck, and then, hey, wow, I can hardly stand up, and then there we are—me and Connie—and we're both of us totally shitfaced in the middle of the afternoon, running around in somebody's cornfield, and she's buck naked. I catch up to her, and she bites my arm—I mean, *bites* it like a dog.

I let go of her, and she's crouched down on all fours, screaming, "Don't hit me. Don't you ever hit me."

It hadn't occurred to me to hit her. I spread my hands open and say, "Connie, this is ridiculous. Get in the truck, okay?"

Well, she stayed where she was, screaming and crying, and I thought maybe I *would* have to hit her to get her in the truck. But finally when I reached out for her, she didn't do anything, so I got her over my shoulder and started carrying her back, and she threw up all over me.

I got her clothes back on her. She didn't help at all. She kept crying and talking, but nothing she said made any sense, and I was so drunk myself, it took everything I had just to function on the most basic kind of level—like one cut above a chimpanzee. She kept saying, "I'm a slut, a real slut, a real little slut." It's ninety-some degrees, and not a breath of air, and the whole world smells like whiskey and vomit. "Oh, God, I'm such a slut," she says.

"Jesus, Connie," I say, "give me a break."

I drove into some dumb little town and made her drink a milkshake and some coffee, and I thought she was getting herself back together. "Oh, God," she said, "I feel awful. I don't know what happened to me." Then I drove her back to the mall where she'd left her car. "Do you expect me to go home like this?" she said.

"Honey," I said, "if there's someplace else you want to go, you tell me about it and I'll take you there."

She looked at me for a long time like she was getting ready to say something, and I kept waiting, but nothing. Then, all of a sudden, she jumped out of the truck and went storming over to her Mustang. She was obviously really pissed off at me, and I didn't know why. I hadn't held her nose and poured the Jack Daniel's down her throat.

I walked over to her car and leaned down to look in the window at her. "Hey, can you drive?" Thinking, you know, that maybe I could drive her home and she could say the Mustang broke down or something.

"Of course I can drive," she says. Her voice is like somebody else's. I mean it. She doesn't sound like herself. She doesn't even sound real. She sounds like she's in a bad movie. "I can see, Jim," she says, "that you have a lot to learn about relationships."

"Oh, to hell with you, Connie," I say.

"Fuck you, you goddamn pig," she says. I'd been leaning on the Mustang, and she pulled out so fast if I hadn't jumped back as quick as I did, she could have run over my foot or some damn thing.

———

I didn't know whether I'd ever see Mrs. Constance Bradshaw again, and to tell you the truth I didn't give a shit. A couple days later, Vick says, "Some girl called up here asking for your home number. I think it was that girl in the miniskirt."

"Oh, yeah? Did you give it to her?"

"Hell, no. I figured if you wanted her to have your home number, she'd already have it."

"That's right, Vick," I said, "that's exactly right."

The next week I ran into my uncle Stas in the PAC, and he said, "Hey, bill collectors after you or something?"

"Not that I know of. Why?"

"Some broad called up asking for you. I told her I never heard of any Jimmy Koprowski."

I thought that was really funny. Connie must have figured out how to spell my name right—that it's a W, not a V. There's only three Koprowskis in the phone book, and I knew I'd be hearing from her eventually.

We were right in the middle of dinner. My mom handed me the phone with her eyebrows raised.

I pretended I didn't know who it was. "This is *Constance*," she says. It was the first time I'd ever heard her call herself that. "I'm sorry to call you at home. Is it all right?"

"It's all right this once, but don't make a habit of it."

"I should have called you sooner, but I was too ashamed of myself. I'm just so sorry, Jim. Can you get away?"

"I don't know. When?"

"About ten."

"What? You mean tonight?"

Yes, she did mean tonight. She'd meet me down by the river—"*Remember our spot?*" It didn't make any sense. Where the hell were her husband and kids? But I wasn't about to ask her that, and eventually I said okay. A perfect example of a guy letting his prick do his thinking for him.

So I changed my clothes and drove up to Center Raysburg and parked by Vick's shop and walked down to the river. Got there a little before ten.

By ten-thirty I'm getting fidgety, pacing up and down, staring at the lights on the Ohio side, smoking cigarettes. Oh, she's changed her mind, right? Or she's jerking me around. But I'll give her a few more minutes. Then I hear foot-steps, and I see this girl walking toward me. Honest to God, I didn't know it was Connie until she was practically on top of me. I looked at my watch, and she was forty minutes late.

A miniskirt was like a uniform for her, and I didn't even know for sure if she owned a pair of pants, but she's wearing skintight blue jeans, the old-fashioned kind that fit tight all the way down, and a short leather jacket and high heels—I mean those real high spikes girls hadn't worn since I'd been in high school—and she looked exactly like one of those chicks who'd be climbing onto the back of a Harley in some sleazy old biker movie. I don't know what the hell I said, but she didn't pay any attention. She kissed me, stuck her tongue halfway down my throat, and I could taste the gin. "Take me somewhere and buy me a drink."

That's a hard one. Do I want anybody to see us together? The nearest bar is Wallach's, but it's Polish and I'll know everybody in there. "You want to drive somewhere?" I say, and she shakes her head.

So I walk her two blocks up to J. P.'s because it's not Polish. She grabs ahold of my arm and hangs on to me. It takes us forever. She's not doing too well in her high heels, or maybe she's just not doing too well *period*. I'm trying to figure out how drunk she is. With Connie, it's hard to tell.

We step inside J. P.'s, and luck's not with me. The first person I see is Larry Dombrowczyk's old man. He's standing at the bar with a couple of his buddies. They've still got their work clothes on and their lunch buckets are sitting at their feet, so they must have just got off shift. Larry's old man sees me, and he takes a good, long slow look at Connie and gives me a big wink.

I get us a booth and a couple beers. She takes off her leather jacket, and she's wearing a thin white blouse under it, one of these semitransparent numbers, and she hasn't got a bra on. Every guy in the place is staring at her, and I'm thinking, oh, terrific. One of these clowns is going to make a move on her, and I'm going to have to duke it out with him, and I want to do that about as much as I want to swim to Ohio.

She's wearing gobs of makeup and she's not wearing her wedding ring. I'm trying to make conversation, but she doesn't say much, just gives me this weird glittery smile, and I'm feeling *tilt* like just before she ran screaming into the cornfield, and eventually it crosses my mind that there's lots of things I'd rather be doing than sitting around J. P.'s with this crazy woman.

I couldn't believe what she starts doing. She's sliding the pointy toes of those high heels up under my pants legs, and I'm thinking, hey, what is this?

Have we gone through a time warp, or what? All I want to do is get it over with—like any idea of fun has pretty well gone down the drain—and I figure the place to do it is the floor of the shop, so I haul her back up onto her feet and back out onto the street, and now I know how drunk she is. If she hadn't been hanging all over me, a couple times she would have gone flat on her face.

It's a relief to get her into Vick's with the door shut. The minute we're inside, she's down on her knees unzipping my pants. She obviously doesn't give a shit if people on the street can see us through the window, or maybe she's too drunk to notice. I can't stop thinking about the fact that we're right smack in front of the window, and it *is* Vick's shop, you know what I mean? And I work there. A couple times I try to push her head away, but, no, she won't budge, and I think, oh, what the hell.

I get done, and I pull my pants up, and she just stays there on her knees. I hold out my hand to her, like, here let me help you up, but she doesn't pay any attention to it. She says in her ordinary, everyday voice, "You could say thank you."

"Thank you, Connie."

Then she just falls over on the floor. She says something else, but I can't get it, so I kneel down on the floor next to her and say, "What?" and she gives me a little kiss on the cheek and says, "I'm sorry, hon. I'm afraid I have to sleep for a little while," and she's passed out cold.

So what do I do now? Well, what could I do? I had a fifth in the car with a few shots left in it, and I got that, and we're in a TV repair shop, right? So I pick the set with the biggest, brightest picture, and I fire it up and sit there and watch it. She's out for—oh, I don't know, over an hour. Long enough for me to kill the bottle anyway. Then I hear this little shaky voice going, "Jim? Are you in here?"

She's a mess. Stumbling around half crying, telling me how sorry she is. "Oh, God, I don't know how I drove down here. Oh, God, it's a wonder I didn't kill myself. Oh, God, I'm poisoned. I wish I could throw up."

"Go in the can back there and stick your finger down your throat," and by God, she does it. I hear about a gallon of liquid pouring out of her.

She comes out and flops down on the floor with her back to the wall. "Oh, God," she says, "I should be institutionalized."

Vick had an old electric kettle, so I made her some coffee, put in a ton of sugar and coffee whitener, and she told me again how sorry she was. "Don't worry about it, honey," I said. "There's no problem that I can see."

I'll never forget this. I hadn't turned on any lights because anybody on the street could see us even where we were in the back. She was sitting on the floor drinking her coffee, and she was just a shadow. In this absolutely flat dead voice she says, "He thinks I'm having an affair."

"Oh, yeah?" I say. "Whatever gave him that idea?"

"I'm not sure, Jim, but perhaps coming home dead drunk might have contributed to it. Why'd you let me go home like that? It was crazy, just crazy."

"Christ, Connie, what was I supposed to do with you?"

"You could have talked some sense into me. I was counting on you. I should have called him, told him I was going to a movie—or something. I don't know. *Anything.* We should have gone to a hotel, and I could have had a shower. Oh, hell, I don't know. I don't know what I'm talking about. There was nothing you could have done, really."

"So what happened?"

"Oh, not much of anything. He was very nice to me. He put me to bed. He took care of the kids. He waited a whole damned day, and then when we were going to bed the next night, he said, 'Okay, Constance, tell me about the man.'

"I denied it, of course. I told him I was so bored I went into a bar in Bridgeport and got drunk all by myself. We've been fighting ever since. He took some time off. He never takes time off, but he took some time off. He took the kids and went back to his parents'. 'You want to be alone, Constance?' he said, 'so be alone.'"

This story did not fill me with joy. Naturally I was thinking, okay, Koprowski, you dumb shit, it's time to bail out of this one.

"I never wanted to get married in the first place," she said. "I told him that. I said, 'We had a perfectly good relationship until we got married. Now you think you own me.' I said, 'You knew what I was like, and you married me anyway. The question is, can I be married to you and have my own life or not?' He kept asking me who the man was. He asked me a million times. I started yelling at him. 'You've got sex on the brain, asshole. Who the hell am I supposed to be having an affair with? I don't *know* anybody in this goddamn miserable shitty-ass town to *have* an affair with.'

"The kids are all upset. They're very perceptive. They always know when something's wrong. Bonnie's been crying herself to sleep every night. I feel terrible. He doesn't deserve this. The kids don't deserve this. Even you don't deserve it. I don't know what the hell's wrong with me. I think maybe I need to see somebody—a psychiatrist or somebody. Oh, God, I'm so fucked up."

I didn't know what to say to her. I told her I was sorry.

"You don't have anything to feel sorry about," she said. "*I'm* the one who started this whole crazy mess. Do you think I've never had guys coming on to me before? Guys were coming on to me when I was twelve, for Christ's sake. I don't know what I was thinking. You were a big, good-looking guy, and I thought, oh, he wants to fuck me. Well, why shouldn't he? No big deal, right? Isn't that sick?

"What was I thinking? Just what in God's name was I thinking? And then I couldn't just leave it at that, could I? Oh, no, that would be too sensible for wacko Connie. I had to go and track you down—and it took some effort, believe me. Oh, God, I should be locked up."

We talked— No, that's not right. She talked and I listened until two in the morning. She kept saying what a nice man her husband was and how, if she wanted to be married, he'd be the perfect guy to be married to, but she just didn't want to be married, and I kept thinking, Christ, do I ever need another drink. I offered to drive her home, but she said she could drive. I offered to follow her to make sure she got there okay, and she kept saying no, but I could tell she didn't really mean it, so she drove away in her Mustang, and I followed her in my Chevy.

I don't know whether it was having me behind her or not, but she drove like somebody's grandmother—in a dead straight line and not much over forty the whole way. I knew I should have been thinking about the mess she was in, and maybe the mess I was in right along with her, but the only thing I could think about was where I could get a drink at that hour. We got into St. Stevens and she pulled over. She rolled down her window and motioned me to stop.

I got out and walked over to her car. "We're just a couple of blocks away," she said. "I'm okay now. I don't want the neighbors to see you. Not that any of them would still be up. Oh, hell, this is crazy. Look, Jim, I'm just so sick of the back of that goddamned truck. Can you get us a hotel room for tomorrow night? Not too sleazy, okay? I'll pay for it, if that's a problem."

"Sure," I said.

"He said he'd call around five," she said, "and I'll need to talk to the kids, so okay, I'll meet you down by the river. The same place, around eight?"

"That's fine," I said.

"Oh, God, do I ever feel awful," she said, and she just sat there with the engine off, looking at me. I didn't know what she was waiting for.

Then, of all the crazy things for her to do, she reached out the window and shook my hand. "Thanks for being so understanding, Jim," she said.

I burned out of there and went sailing into Bridgeport because I was pretty sure I knew a place where if I scratched at the back door, they'd let me in, and I was right. I had a couple boilermakers and thought things through. Any fool could plainly see that Mrs. Constance Bradshaw was bad news, and I sure as hell didn't want to be the one making her little girl cry herself to sleep every night. Right, so what I was going to do was call her up tomorrow and tell her to forget the whole thing.

The only hotel in Raysburg that's not too sleazy is the McClain, but it's not exactly cheap either, not to mention that it's right smack downtown, so I booked Connie and me into the new Holiday Inn out on Route 70 as Mr. and Mrs. Johnson. Did I have a credit card? What, are you kidding? So I had to drive out there and leave them a twenty-buck deposit. I threw my toothbrush and a change of clothes and a couple fifths into my flight bag. Then, just in case she turned up early, I made sure I was down on the riverbank waiting for her by seven-thirty.

By nine I was starting to get steamed, but I kept reminding myself that she'd been late the night before. I'd been planning on staying halfway sober so when we hit the sack I might be able to put on a halfway decent show, but eventually I said piss on it, went trotting up to Wallach's, had a couple shots, and bought a six-pack to keep me company. I was pretty damn quick about it because I didn't want her to turn up and not find me waiting for her. By my watch, I'd been gone less than half an hour.

By eleven I was through the six-pack, but my flight bag was in the trunk of my Chevy, so I started in on the Jack Daniel's. I was calling her every name in the book, but then I'd think, no, wait a minute. Maybe it's not her fault. What if she'd showed up while I was gone? Well, that would have meant she couldn't wait even a lousy half an hour—and besides, she would have seen my Chevy. So what was going on? Had her husband come back from Baltimore? Had she got herself so drunk she couldn't drive? Was she jerking me around intentionally? I gave her till midnight. The thing that really got to me—like the last straw—was that twenty-buck deposit.

Needless to say, I was fairly well plastered by then, but I was in one of those I'll-show-you-bitch moods, so I started making the rounds. There's lots of bars in Raysburg. How the rest of the night went I couldn't tell you because I had—well, I won't say it was the first, but it was the first *big* blackout. A whole chunk of my memory gone just like somebody took a pair of scissors to a videotape.

I'm laying on the floor in the piss and cigarette butts in some can somewhere with my arms wrapped around the base of the commode. It's broad daylight, and Lazarus waking up in the tomb couldn't have felt any worse than I do.

I go lurching out to try to figure out where the hell I am, and lo and behold, I'm in the back room at the PAC, and I'm locked in there. Just about the time I'm thinking about trying to crawl through a window, Bobby Burdalski turns up. "How you doing, numbnuts? I figured you might be conscious by now."

He told me what'd happened. I'd gone sneaking up behind the bar and grabbed a fifth of Seagram's. "You were giggling to yourself," he said, "and you were crawling along on all fours pretending you were invisible." He said I wouldn't give the fifth back, and I wouldn't pay for it, and I kept yelling that I'd fight anybody in the goddamn place who tried to take it away from me. I can't imagine myself doing that, but what the hell do I know about it?

Eventually I passed out on a table, but if anybody came too close, I'd jump up and take a swing at them. "You weren't landing anything," he said, "but it wasn't because you weren't trying."

There were two schools of opinion on what to do with me—and I'm telling you the story exactly the way he told it to me. One school advocated punching me out and the other advocated locking me in the back room and leaving me there. The two schools contended until the wee small hours of the morning, but eventually the second school prevailed because they pointed out that once I was punched out, they would have to deliver my body somewhere, to my home most likely, and the thought of waking up Władysław Koprowski at four-thirty in the morning was too horrible to contemplate.

"What you need," Bobby said, "is Burdalski's world-famous award-winning ancient Polak hangover cure." That turned out to be two shot glasses. In the first was a raw egg with a jolt of bitters; in the second was chilled vodka. "The trick," he said, "is to get to the vodka before your mind has a chance to dwell upon the egg. *Na zdrowie.*"

FOUR

I slept all day and when I woke up, I felt all right. My mind was clear. I lay there staring up at those *Playboy* bunnies plastered all over my ceiling, and it occurred to me that I'd seen way too much of those damn bunnies and I wouldn't mind a bit if I never saw any of them again. And it occurred to me that being stood up by Mrs. Constance Bradshaw might be just about the best thing that ever happened to me.

At that time in my life I was certainly not what anybody would call a practicing Catholic, but I still knew right from wrong, and screwing a married woman was not something I could justify. How would I feel in her husband's place? Here he is, working his ass off trying to make a good life for his family, and meanwhile she's off fucking some idiotic goof in the back of a panel truck. And it occurred to me—believe it or not, this was the first time it had occurred to me—that maybe I was drinking too much.

I do not have to stay here, I thought. I do not have to repair ancient television sets for pissass money for Vick Dobranski. I do not have to live with Old Bullet Head who watches every move I make so he can be the first to point it out to me when I fuck up. As a matter of fact, I do not have to go through the rest of my life in this sorry valley. I've got a reasonably good-running Chevy and a few bucks in the bank, and not only that, I am a trained and certified government-issue instrument technician with an honorable discharge, and the skies of America are filled with aircraft, and you know what? When those aircraft come down, somebody's got to maintain them.

All they've got in Austin is a dumb-ass little airport—kind of surprising for the capital of the state—but at least an airline or two operating out of there and openings did come up from time to time—anyhow that's what I'd been told. And if that didn't pan out, I could always work for Doren's old man. He ran a service station, and he didn't pay a whole hell of a lot, but hell, Austin's a cheap place to live. The last time we were there, he told me, "Anytime, Jimmy. If you need a place to stay, a job, anything at all," and I could tell he meant it. Right, so how about leaving tomorrow?

I was feeling almost cheery, and I thought, well, shit, if I'm serious about this, I've got to get a set of new tires and a tune-up and a brake job. And I've got to give Vick some notice; it's only fair. And maybe I should call up Doren's old man and tell him I'm coming. And I was feeling really pleased with myself, you know, because I was being so sensible and responsible—even though the reality of it was that I hadn't managed to get out of bed yet.

It was quiet in the house. All I could hear was my sister playing the piano, some pretty classical piece, the notes far away, drifting up the stairs, maybe Chopin, and then I remembered—oh, Christ, Jacobson's dead. I'd forgot it there for a minute.

I got up, pulled on some clothes, and went downstairs. My sister was flipping through some music books. "Where's Mom and Dad?" I said.

"Dinner and a movie. You know, big night out."

I went in the kitchen and opened the icebox. I'd been planning on an ice-cold Iron City, but I thought I should have something in my stomach first, so I poured myself a glass of milk.

Then something stopped me, and I don't know what. Maybe it was thinking about Jacobson—you know how it takes forever to get used to the idea that somebody's dead—but anyhow it was so quiet in the house I could hear the ice-box humming. It was late in the day, and the sun was low, pouring in the windows around the front door, and the sunlight came all the way down the hall and into the kitchen, and I could see the little, you know, the dust motes floating in it. For some reason I just got stuck there, taking it all in. It was like I could stand there forever. I was listening so hard I could hear my sister breathing all the way out in the dining room.

Then, just like everything was planned to go with everything else, Linda started to play something. Lots of Polish tunes have real pretty melodies, and this was one of them. It's a tune I've heard a million times since then, and they've turned it into a polka, but she was playing it slower than that and she started to sing the words. *"Zakochał się młodzieniec w dziewczynie i chciał się z nią ożenić—"* In English, that means, "A young guy fell in love with a girl and wanted to marry her."

Linda's sung in the church choir since she was in high school, and everybody's always said she has a great voice for a choir, not a big voice, or a voice that knocks you dead, but a clear easy voice that blends in. Singing by herself, she sounds like a little girl. I could tell she wasn't singing for me. She'd forgot all about me. And I was kind of surprised that I remembered enough Polish to follow the story, but I did.

Well, the families weren't big on the kids getting married. The fathers said, "No way, buddy," and the brothers said, "Forget it." What I'm giving you here is, you know, what they call a free translation. So anyhow, they told the boy to go out in the world and make something of himself. And he does that. And when he comes back, naturally he wants to see his sweetheart. He goes up to her house, and he peers through the window, and he sees that her mom is real sad, and his heart's going a mile a minute. So he says, *"Powiedz mi, moja mamusiu droga, gdzie twoja córeczka jest?"* That means, "Please tell me, my dear Mother, where's your little daughter?"

And the girl's mom says that the girl died just a week ago yesterday and the sheets are still warm on her bed. She says the girl's in the cemetery, three graves over from the monument, right near the three roses. So the boy goes to the cemetery to find her, and the three roses bow to him and show him the way to her grave. And how the words go in Polish— It's hard for me to explain this. Okay, in an English song, you'd expect it to pause, you know, take a break every once in a while, but the Polish words just keep tumbling along. It's always reminded me of water running over stones.

"Powstań, moje lube serce," the boy says, *"powstań. Przemów słóweczko do mnie.* Rise up, my beloved heart, and say a little word to me," and the girl says, *"Luby, jak mam powstać i z tobą rozmawiać kiedy ja już twardo śpię?* Oh, my love, how can I rise up and speak to you when I'm sleeping so hard?"

Linda got to the end of the song, and I walked into the dining room. "That's just about the saddest song I ever heard in my life," I said, and she turned around on the piano bench and looked at me.

"Yeah, it is, isn't it?" She had that sad sad look in her eyes she used to get when she was a little kid right after Babcia Koprowski died.

It was Saturday and I said, "Haven't you got a date?" and she shook her head, and I said, "Yeah, you do. With me. I'm taking you out to dinner."

"You're kidding."

"No, I'm not."

"Don't *you* have a date?"

"Not tonight, I don't. Come on, Linny, anywhere you want. The Pines, the Far East, Tomerellis', that new place over on the Island, you name it."

She lit up like a light bulb. She's so transparent it breaks your heart sometimes. "Oh, Jimmy, that's so sweet of you. Let me get changed. You know where I want to go? Franky Rzeszutko's," and I had to laugh because that's where we used to go with Mom and Dad when we were kids.

Neither of us had been in Franky's place for years, but except for a coat of paint, not much had changed. There was the bar for the guys in the front— Franky had put in a color TV since we'd been in there—and in the back was a big room with tables for families. On a good night in the old days you'd see everybody in that back room all the way from babies on up to Grandma and Grandpa, and if you felt like dancing to the jukebox, you'd push the tables back and go to it. Franky told us once that he'd had to have the floor reinforced. Some of those old guys doing the *oberek*, stomping their heels down, he was afraid they'd end up in the basement.

The minute we're sitting at a table, Franky comes over and starts in with, "Hey, it's great to see you kids. How've you been?" and we've got to do that number for a while—all about my wonderful years in the service and Linda's wonderful years getting her B.Mus. She says how sorry she is about Franky's mom, and of course I didn't even know his mom had died. She did the cooking in the old days, good home cooking, so you could get *pierogi* or *gołąbki* or whatever, but when Linda and I were kids, we didn't want any part of that stuff— that was just what we'd get at home—so we'd have cheeseburgers and French fries and Cokes. The cheeseburgers were real thick and came with a big slice of raw onion on them.

"Ethel Warsinski comes in now on the weekends," Franky says. Everybody knows Mrs. Warsinski. She used to keep house for Old Man Cotter back when he'd been the head honcho at Raysburg Steel, and she'd been the number-one cook at the church for years.

So Linda says, "Oh, it must be good then. You tell her whatever she recommends, that's what we'll have."

I know Linda will only drink a glass or two of beer, but I've got a hell of a thirst, probably from sleeping all day, so I order us a pitcher. Franky keeps his pitchers in the freezer, and they come out all covered with frost, and I'm just happy as all hell to be drinking cold beer and shooting the shit with my sister. Naturally we've got to reminisce about our childhood.

When we were little, we'd go out for dinner usually about once a week—it was like family night—and we'd always go to Franky's. My mom would put on a nice dress and lipstick and her high heels and she'd look like a million bucks and the other moms were always saying to her, "It's just not fair, Mary Koprowski. How can you have a figure like that after two kids?"

"I always thought Mom was the last word in glamour," Linda says. "I thought I could never be as glamorous as Mom."

Damn near everything on the jukebox in those days was Polish. Linda and I would shove our quarters in and punch the numbers at random. I don't know who those bands would have been back in the fifties. Linda could give you a better guess than me. I know Walt Solek was on that jukebox because I remember playing "Who Stole the Kishka?" and there must have been some of the big Eastern bands because that was their heyday, and for all I know Li'l Wally was on there, but whoever those bands were, that music sure sounded good.

It wasn't every night that people danced, but on those nights when they did, everybody danced. I mean, everybody danced with everybody. I danced with Mom and my aunts and my cousins and any girls from St. Stans who were there with their families—it was just whoever came in any particular night—and I danced with Linda until I got to the age where dancing with your little sister was definitely not cool. Then later on, when I got to be a teenager, even going out to dinner with your family was definitely not cool—that's when me and the boys thought we were a gang and wore cheap phony leather jackets and called ourselves "the South Raysburg Rats"—so that left Linda to go out with Mom and Dad.

"You know, Jimmy," she said, "those nights were magical."

I don't know if I'd go that far, but they were fun. It's nice to see your parents having a good time. Mom liked her beer, and she'd get silly and flirt with the old man, and he'd grin back at her and drink nothing but 7UP. He never made a big deal out of not drinking, but he was serious about it—he wouldn't even drink a beer—but he could get pretty damn happy sober, and he was one of those guys Franky must have been worried about stomping through the floor. "I loved dancing the *oberek* with Dad," Linda says. "He'd spin me around and around and around until I thought my head was going to pop."

So anyhow, after we do the childhood nostalgia number, we move up to the present. Now if I'd been paying the least bit of attention to Linda before that, I could have guessed that some asshole had broken her heart. He was a grad student down at the university, and he must have talked a good line because he had her convinced he was going to marry her. As she's telling me about it, two great big tears come rolling out from under her glasses. "Naive?" she says, "I should get some kind of major award. Well, that's what I get for spending my life glued to a piano stool. Oh, well, it's probably for the best. He wasn't even Catholic."

"Aw, Linny. Boy, would you have been in deep shit."

"Yeah, I know. Mom would have killed me. But it's left me feeling— I really thought he loved me. I don't know if I've got any love left in me for anybody else. I don't know if I can trust anybody again."

So I've got to come up with all the usual dumb things—of course you'll fall in love again, just give yourself time, and so on. It's like a rerun of the conversations we used to have in high school. You see, Linda's one of these girls who's totally convinced she's not pretty even though she is.

She got the old man's coloring, and on her, it looks good—dark ash-blond hair and clear blue-gray eyes and pale skin with those naturally pink cheeks that make her look like she's just come in out of the cold. But she didn't get his big nose, thank God. *I* got it. Linda got Mom's features. I was going to say they're Slavic, but what the hell's that mean anyhow? Okay, there's a look some Polish girls have that you know in two seconds they're Polish, but I'll be damned if I can describe it. It's sort of like they have faces like little cats. So anyhow I always thought Linda was a very pretty girl, but no matter how much I told her, it didn't do any good.

The way she dressed didn't help any—and it wasn't Mom's fault. Mom used to yell at her, "Linda, for God's sake, do you mean to tell me you *paid money* to look like that?" Maybe it was because she spent her whole life at the piano, but she was completely out of it when it came to clothes. Whatever was in—like go-go boots or bell-bottoms—she wouldn't wear it until she was totally convinced it was safe, and by then, of course, it'd be out. Even back then, when skirts were just about as short as they were ever going to get, just above her knees was the most Linda would allow herself.

So I did my best to cheer her up, and I got her to tell me about getting her B.Mus.—that's one thing she's really proud of—and finally I asked her, "Hey, so what's with the trumpet?"

"I'm starting a polka band."

"Oh, yeah? Who else is going to be in it?"

"Well, so far, there's just me and Mary Jo Duda."

I had to laugh at that one. Mary Jo Duda was a real character, an old gal who called herself "the Polka Lady." She was our parents' age, maybe older. She'd been playing in bars when Linda and I were still kids. Any bar you'd walk into where you'd hear an accordion in the back room, chances are it'd be Mary Jo, and any polka you'd ever heard in your life, you'd call out the name of it, and she'd sit there and think about it for a few seconds and then she'd belt it out for you. She played weddings and lawn fetes too, and she'd been the accordion player in three or four different bands. She was a big lady, bleached her hair out into that real brassy hooker's blond, and she wore gobs of blue eye shadow, and she was married, had grown kids—even had grandchildren—and what old Gene Duda thought about his wife sitting around in bars every night playing her accordion and getting loaded I really couldn't tell you.

I don't mean to say there was anything disreputable about Mary Jo. She'd been a mainstay in the sodality at the church for years, but if you mentioned her name to anybody, they'd usually laugh, and the thought of my little sister—my shy, conservative, straight-A little sister who'd busted her ass to learn to play Chopin—the thought of her playing *anything* with Mary Jo Duda just seemed to me absolutely ridiculous.

"Okay, Linda," I said, "let me see if I've got this right. You went to West Virginia University for four years and got yourself a degree in music so you could play polkas with Mary Jo Duda?"

Linda was laughing, but she was annoyed at me too. "So what are you going to do," I said, "accordion and trumpet duets?"

That's how I got the Polka Lecture. There was absolutely no way I could get out of it. We had to go home right after dinner, and I had to sit on the end of Linda's bed while she paced up and down yacking at me and played me a million polkas on her stereo. Because Mom and Dad were out, she played them really loud.

Okay, so here's Linda's story, the best I remember it. When she was about ten, she went to the Pączki Ball at the parish hall, and there wasn't anything unusual about that—she'd been going to things at the church with Mom and Dad her whole life—but it was the one and only time that Li'l Wally Jagiello ever played in South Raysburg, and it was also the first time they'd had a real good, red-hot, pure Polish polka band playing at St. Stans since before the war. I have no memory of this whatsoever. I don't know where I was—probably off with the boys somewhere pretending I was a South Raysburg Rat—but anyhow I missed it. Linda sure didn't. If she had to list the most important events of her life, it'd be right up there, not far below her first Communion and getting married and having kids.

Li'l Wally was this little guy in checked pants. He played the drums, and he was absolutely nuts. He was banging away on the drums and belting out all these songs in Polish and yelling in that way musicians do to get the dancers going—*Hop, hop, hop, hopla!*—and just yelling period, high-pitched yips and yelps. Now Linda had been playing the piano since she was six and she was already up to some high level at it, and whenever there was any kind of concert anywhere in Raysburg, Mom always took her to it. So Linda was used to seeing guys read music, but with Li'l Wally's band, there was not a piece of music to be seen, and that really impressed her. She thought it was amazing that the guys had all those tunes in their heads. They had a trumpet and a clarinet and I don't know what all—a concertina probably—and they were just wailing away like crazy, sweat pouring down their faces, and the people in the hall were going berserk.

The place was packed and the word had gone out, so there were people piled up outside trying to get in, and they threw open all the doors even though it was a cold night because they just had to get some air through there. People dancing like total fools. Old folks jumping up and dancing who hadn't danced in years. Young kids dancing on the tables. A couple Raysburg cops showed up thinking there was a riot going on, and they ended up sticking around and dancing their asses off, and they weren't even Polish. The beer was flowing by the gallon, and the people in the back were eating up a million *pączki*, and even Father Stawecki was grinning ear to ear—and it took a lot to get him grinning, believe me.

Just like me, Linda had grown up hearing polka music, but she'd never heard anything as wonderful as that. She said the music burned straight through to her soul. Everybody loved everybody, people were hugging each other, people were weeping for joy, and when Linda saw that, she started crying too, and she was standing there with the tears running down her face, and Old Bullet Head leans down and whispers in her ear, "Hey, Lindusia, I'll tell you a secret. This is *the real thing*." She said she'd never in her life been so proud of being Polish.

So what Linda learned the night Li'l Wally played the parish hall was that there was a kind of Polish music that was unbelievably wonderful, and the minute Polish people heard it, they knew what it was, and that was what her father had told her it was—*the real thing*.

———

Now we jump ahead a few years, and Linda's down at Morgantown getting her B.Mus. and she takes a course called "Ethnomusicology." What they do is, they get tape recorders and they drive out into the hills of West Virginia and find old crocks who know a tune or two from the old days, and they record them and go back and write the tunes down and compare them to all the other tunes people have yanked out of the hills. The professor who taught the course was writing a history of old-time music in West Virginia, and Linda liked the course so much she took the next one, "Advanced Ethnomusicology," so she would get to do some fieldwork of her own. She asked the professor if she could do her work on Polish music in America, and he said he didn't know what she meant, so she started explaining it to him, and he got a funny look on his face and said, "Oh. You don't mean *polkas*, do you?"

This really pissed her off, so she said to herself, I'm going to show him, because she knew that there was *the real thing* out there somewhere and all she had to do was find it. So the first thing she did was interview everybody in the Ohio Valley who'd ever played a polka.

Well, it turns out that back before the war, the valley had been a real hotbed of polka music, and Linda found lots of musicians who played the real thing. For starters, there was Mary Jo Duda—you know, the polka lady—and Linda asked her where she'd learned all the tunes she knew, and Mary Jo said the first ones she'd learned went straight back to Poland because an old guy named Pete Ostrowski, now deceased, had taught her when she was a kid. He played the old Chemnitzer button box. And Mary Jo played for Linda the first tune she'd learned from him, "The Krakowiak," and it wasn't exactly a polka, but you could hear that it was like maybe the grandfather of the polka.

Later on, Mary Jo said, she just learned the tunes off records. Linda was very impressed because she is, as she says, "a paper musician," and anything she has to write down from a record, it takes her a million years, and she thinks that people who can play by ear are specially blessed by God.

So Mary Jo gave Linda the names and phone numbers of every polka musician she knew—and she knew them all—and Linda went and interviewed them. A lot of them were out in Ohio, like in Mercersville and Crestview and out that way because there's a big Polish community there, but some of them were in South Raysburg too, and everybody loved Linda to pieces and talked her ear off. She interviewed the old guys who used to play in Joe Marchewka's Warsaw Orchestra back before the war, and the Andrzejewski brothers who everybody said had the best band going these days, and Ray Pahucki and Ray's mom who'd taught her kids all the tunes she knew from Poland—and I don't know who all else she interviewed. She has a whole list of them if you want to ask her.

She loved hearing about the old days. All those musicians had regular jobs—like Joe Marchewka worked his whole life for Raysburg Steel, and the Andrzejewski brothers worked in the rolling mill in Crestview, and they'd work their last shift on Friday, then they'd play the whole weekend. Get maybe an hour's sleep and be back on the job Monday morning. You played for a Polish wedding back in those days, you didn't take a break like the kids do today. They wanted you playing nonstop for four or five hours at a clip—and those weddings went on for three days.

Well, it was, Linda said, like everything was leading her right back to where she'd started because everybody she talked to mentioned Li'l Wally Jagiello and said what a big influence he was. Before Li'l Wally, they'd all played Eastern style—you know, real fast—and Li'l Wally had been the one who'd introduced that slower Chicago style, that down and dirty style played from the heart that we call honky. So Linda figured she wasn't finished with her research unless she went to Chicago.

The person she should be talking to, our mom told her, was her own Ciocia Jean—Mom's big sister—who'd lived in Chicago for years and had probably sung every Polish tune there ever was. "It was amazing," Linda said. "Everything I needed was right in front of my nose."

Jean had always been our favorite aunt. When we were little, she came to visit about once a year. Sometimes she'd bring Uncle Johnny with her, and a kid or two, and sometimes she'd come by herself, and it was always a big occasion. She liked Linda and me, and she'd yell, "Come on, kids, hop in the car," and she'd take us for a drive, and she'd always stop somewhere and buy us banana splits. She drank Miller's Highlife for lunch, and she had a huge laugh that started down in her toes, and Mom said, "Jean's always been lots of fun."

Of course we knew that Auntie Jean had been a singer. It's the family legend that Auntie Jean has been singing since she'd learned to talk. Dziadzio Wojtkiewicz would stand her up in the center of the table and she'd sing *"Pockaj, pockaj, powiem Mamie"* in her little-kid voice—four years old and perfectly in tune—and by the time she was a teenager, she'd learned every Polish tune anybody knew, and when the Depression hit, she started singing in bars because people would always throw her some change. She didn't sing American music until she got hired by a band playing in a gangster joint up in Staubsville, and she did so well there she went out to Chicago and got in with a famous jazz band. "The only reason I got to finish high school was because of that money she sent home to us," Mom said. "God bless her."

So Linda called up Auntie Jean, and she said, "You hop the hound, honey, and get your pretty little butt out here," and my shy little sister went sailing off to Chicago with her tape recorder.

There's so many Polish people in Chicago, Linda says, you wonder if they've got any left back in Poland, and everywhere she went, Linda kept running into *the real thing*. She met Eddie Blazonczyk, a nice young guy who'd started a polka band, and oh, boy, was that a hot band. And Linda didn't get to meet L'il Wally because he'd moved to Florida, but she met Marion Lush and heard that two-trumpet style of his, and she sure liked that too. And she met a lot of the old-timers who told her all about the music in the good old days, including a nice old guy who ran the Polish music store, and he had every Polish-American record ever recorded going all the way back to the year zero, and he let Linda tape a lot of them, so she stayed there a month and came back with a million tapes she'd recorded, and a million records, and she thought she'd been to heaven.

She wrote her paper on Polish-American music and got an A+ on it. Her professor said, "Thank you, Miss Koprowski. I didn't know anything at all about this music before," and he said if she wanted to go on and get her Ph.D. in ethnomusicology, he'd be happy to recommend her. She thought about that. But her scholarship was for piano, and if she went on for another degree, she'd have to get some help from Old Bullet Head, and she had a hard time imagining herself explaining to him what ethnomusicology was and how it might be useful to her in later life. And then it dawned on her that she didn't really want to study Polish-American music anyway, she wanted to play it, so she said to Mary Jo, "Let's start a polka band."

"You sound like you're in a Judy Garland movie," Mary Jo said. "Sure. What are you going to play?"

Well, Linda had fallen in love with that bright brassy trumpet sound, and any good Polish polka band has got to have a trumpet or two in it, so she went to Kaltenbach's—you know, there at the end of the Suspension Bridge—and bought herself a trumpet on the installment plan.

"A lot of people wouldn't do that," I said.

"What?"

"Just decide to pick up another instrument like that."

"Oh. Well, practicing is something I understand. You practice a couple hours a day, eventually you can play anything."

Okay, so here comes the Polka Lecture. Don't worry, I'm not going to give you the whole shooting match; this is more like the *Reader's Digest* condensed version. When I heard it, I was sitting on the end of Linda's bed sipping a little sour mash so I didn't even mind when she played me a few hours' worth of her million tapes and records.

She started out with a band straight from Poland in the old days. She said they had a different scale from us, but let me tell you, that's not the only thing that was different. They were all playing fiddles, and these were peasants, right? So they didn't go buy their fiddles at the music store, they made them out of trees, and they came in all sizes from tiny little ones to great big huge ones, and they get to sawing away on these damn things, and some guy's yelling his head off in Polish over the top of all that racket, and they might as well have recorded some godforsaken tribe in Borneo for all it sounds like music to me.

Now I should tell you something about me and the polka. Since then, I've been polkasized but good. I wouldn't claim to know as much as Linda does, but I know a hell of a lot. So let's say you put on an American polka, I could tell you in about two seconds flat if it's Czech-Texas or Southwest Tex-Mex or Midwest Dutchman or Slovenian out of Cleveland like Frankie Yankovic played—or if it's Polish. And if it's Polish, I could tell you if it's Eastern or Chicago style—that's easy; that takes only about half a second—and probably I could tell you who the band is, and maybe even the names of all the guys playing and, give or take a year, when it was recorded.

But back in those days, I was into the Grateful Dead and Country Joe and Gracie Slick and all that other doped-out California rock. I've always liked dancing, and to me, polka music was just something you danced to. You didn't take it seriously, you know what I mean? Polka music was just that dumb stuff my parents liked—and Linda liked for some crazy reason—and I couldn't imagine any music more straight and square and corny and stupid. If you've heard one polka, you've heard them all, right? They all go one, two.

But I'm humoring my sister because I can see how much all this means to her. She keeps slapping on the records, telling me to listen for this or that. So you've got weird peasant music from Poland, and it mixes up with American popular music and you start to get something brand-new, something that's not like anything they've got back in Poland—the Polish-American polka.

Chicago's one of the main crossroads where it all comes together. Jazz guys—you know, like Louis Armstrong—coming up from New Orleans, play-

THE CLARINET POLKA · 63

ing hot, blowing the doors off the clubs. Polish guys learning to play jazz—the most famous one's Gene Krupa—and they're just trying to make a buck, right? Some of them, like Auntie Jean, one weekend they're playing jazz, the next they're playing polkas. Okay, so you can't swing a polka—if you do, it stops being a polka and you won't be able to dance to it—but you can sure play it *hot*, and you can make up your parts right there on the spot just like in jazz, and that's the beginnings of that hot Chicago style.

I'm sitting there sipping my drink, going, "Oh, yeah? Uh-huh. Is that right? Oh, yeah, that's interesting," and eventually Linda figures out that I'm not really getting it. "Okay, Jimmy," she says, "listen to this," and she puts on a tape.

It must have been recorded back when there were still dinosaurs. Heavy-duty hiss and crackle, and then, very faint, there's this dumb old tune I've known my whole life.

"It's the first Polish tune that Columbia ever recorded," Linda said. "In the old days they called it *'Dziadunio,'* but now we just call it 'The Clarinet Polka.'"

Then she put on a record. It was that great Eddie B. version of the same tune with Lenny Gomulka on clarinet, but I sure didn't hear how great it was that first time. I was tired of listening to polkas, and I couldn't hear all those neat twists and turns and curlicues that Lenny was putting on the melody. All I could hear was "The Clarinet Polka" done by a modern band. Linda was looking at me, waiting for me to get it—whatever it was I was supposed to get. "Yeah, so?" I said.

"That was just recorded last year. Well, it's sixty-some years later, and that tune's still around, still being played."

"Yeah?"

"It goes straight back to Poland."

"Yeah, okay."

"And people are still playing it, putting their own feelings into it, their own styling to it—don't you see what I mean? The music's alive, it matters, it's *the real thing*. It's great popular dance music. It's as good as early jazz. It's still going strong after all these years, changing, developing, absorbing other styles—"

"Yeah, so?"

She was so frustrated with me she was getting tears in her eyes. "Don't you see, Jimmy? *It's ours.*"

Yeah, Linda's always been big on being Polish. Hardly anybody else our age gave a shit, but she was years ahead of her time—into it long before anybody thought of making red-and-white T-shirts with "Kiss me, I'm Polish" on them. "The new ethnicity," they're calling it now. You've got to have a name for everything, right? And by the time you get around to talking about the *new* ethnicity, you can be damn sure that the *old* ethnicity is just about dead as a post.

Like when you get down to the kids in the fourth generation—whether they want to be Polish or not is something they've got to decide for themselves. Except maybe for having a last name that nobody ever pronounces right. But if you're like Dorothy Pliszka's father-in-law and you'd rather be Green than Grondzki, you can always change your name. And most of the kids today think it's all just a matter of polkas and *pierogi* anyhow. "Pierogies" they'd say. Well, some of them know better.

So anyhow, when Linda and I were going to Saturday school, they were always telling us, "Be proud you're Polish," and most of the kids would go, "Yeah, yeah, yeah," but Linda was always real serious, and she took it to heart. She used to follow me around and say, "Hey, Jimmy, did you know Stan Musial was Polish?"

"Yeah, I knew that."

"How about Carl Yastrzemski?"

"Yeah, I knew that too."

Oh. Well, how about Madame Curie, Gloria Swanson, Wanda Landowska, Stella Walsh?—and on and on and on, and she'd tell me about every two-bit movie star who was ever Polish, and every scientist or statesman or scholar who was ever Polish, and naturally we knew that Chopin was Polish because she played him on the piano day and night. Now she's really got the last laugh on everybody—you know what's coming, don't you?—the *Pope's* Polish.

And Linda's always been attached to the Polish language—and that's putting it mildly. When she was little, she just flat-out refused to learn English. Can you believe that? It went on for a long time after Babcia Koprowski died. If you said anything to Linda in English, she'd put her hands over her ears and run away. Usually it was the other way around—kids refusing to learn Polish—and nobody had ever seen anything like it. Mom and Dad were real worried about her, but we went on speaking Polish at home because if we didn't, Linda would just cry. And Old Bullet Head would say, "She'll get over it. She was real close to Mother, and when she gets over that, she'll learn English."

Well, Linda didn't get over it. They let her finish the first grade, but she still didn't know hardly any English. She didn't have any friends to play with because the other kids just thought she was weird, and even the nuns couldn't do much with her, and they usually were fairly persuasive, if you know what I mean. So finally Mom got Father Stawecki to come over to the house.

Old Father Joe could be real brutal sometimes. He squatted down on the floor so his eyes were right level with Linda's, and he took her hands, and he talked to her in Polish. He said, "Listen to me, little Linda. We do not live in Poland. We live in the United States of America, and the people here speak English. If you don't learn to speak English, we'll have to send you back to Poland, and you won't like it over there because you'll miss your mom and dad and your brother, and the people over there are Communists and they don't believe in Jesus or in his Holy Mother. You got that?"

Then he stood up and said, "And while you're at it, why don't you get her eyes checked? The sisters tell me she's blind as a bat."

So Linda got her first pair of glasses and went around just amazed at how sharp and clear the world looked, and when she decided to speak English, she was speaking it perfectly good in about a week.

Babcia Koprowski was the one who took care of us when we were kids. She lived with us. Guys my father's generation don't like their wives working, but Mom had worked all during the war when he'd been overseas, and they took over the house after Dziadzio Koprowski died, so Mom got a job up at Krogers to help pay off the mortgage, and we got left with Babcia Koprowski. She was, I guess you could say, your standard-issue old Polish peasant lady.

I remember in her bedroom she had a picture of the Holy Mother of Częstochowa with a candle in front of it, and she just loved plants, had potted plants all over the place. She even tried to grow things out on the edge of our little bit of yard, but she didn't have much luck, what with all the red dust coming down.

She did that old-time cooking that takes all day long, the kind that nobody does anymore, and believe me, there's nothing like it. She made all these wonderful soups with these little *uszka*, you know, dumplings, and she'd bake that dark bread that each loaf weighs about fifty pounds. She'd put a cabbage leaf under the bread so it wouldn't stick to the pan, and for years I thought that's what everybody did when they baked bread. There was always a big meat dish except on Fridays, but that didn't mean you didn't eat on Fridays. It's heart-attack city, that cooking—everything you saw had sour cream in it—but to this day I'd rather eat *kapuśniak* than steak.

I was older than Linda, so I'd go out and play with the kids in the neighborhood, and then of course I was going to school, but Linda just stuck to Babcia like a little burr. And I used to look forward to coming home after school because there'd always be a nice snack—Babcia had learned how to bake American-style cookies—and sometimes if the weather was lousy, I'd hang around because I liked the old lady too. And whether it was just Linda or the both of us, Babcia talked nonstop all day long. She'd never been to school—I don't think she could even read and write—but she had wonderful stories, I guess they must have been folk tales. I can't remember much of what they were about, but I can remember the feeling I had as a kid, you know, hanging on every word—and she didn't speak much English. Well, that doesn't quite get it. You'd say anything at all to her in English, she'd say, "Very good, thenk you," and that was it. So we were a Polish-speaking household. I picked up English when I started in school, but like I told you, Linda didn't.

And Babcia taught us our prayers. Every night before we went to sleep we were supposed to say the Hail Mary, and the Our Father, and the Confession, and she made sure we did it. You know, it's funny. To this day, I can rattle off those prayers in Polish ten times before I could even start to remember how they go in English.

So anyhow the year I was nine and Linda was five, Babcia got a real bad case of the flu, and it turned into pneumonia, and they put her in the hospital and she died. It hit everybody hard, but it hit Linda especially hard because she was so little and I guess because Babcia had been the person she'd been closest to, and poor Linda wandered around like a little ghost for months after that and refused to learn English. And Mom had to quit her job to take care of us. And that's when Old Bullet Head got heavy into the sauce. It's a damn good thing he quit drinking when he did because he made our life miserable for about a year.

We'd get the distant early warning that something was up when he didn't come home for dinner. Mom would wait and wait for him, and then she'd just give up and feed us, and she'd get so steamed, she'd be talking to herself and banging pots around, and I'd see Linda start to shiver, and I'd pray to the Holy Mother, "Please send Dad home soon," but some nights the Holy Mother wasn't much help, and he wouldn't come home till one or two in the morning. He'd be so loaded he could barely stand up, and Mom would start screaming at him, and it'd go on for hours.

Sometimes I'd sneak down to listen to them. A couple times Mom hauled off and belted him one. I mean, WHAM, right across the face. He's a big man, and he could have snapped her like a matchstick, but he'd just stand there look-ing sad and amazed, and that would drive her absolutely nuts.

So anyhow, what always happened if it went on long enough, is that Linda would wake up and come looking for me. If I'm in bed, BANG, she'd jump right onto my bed. She'd shake all over like a dog, and she was so scared she couldn't even cry. I'd take her by the hand and lead her back to her own bed and tuck her in just like Mom did, and I'd get her to say her prayers for me just the way Babcia used to do, and I'd sit there and tell her stories until she fell asleep.

I was scared too. I wanted somebody to tuck me in and tell me stories and make me feel better, and taking care of my five-year-old sister did make me feel grown-up—a big boy—but I would have passed on it if I'd had the chance. I'd hear them yelling, and I'd pray, "Oh, please, Holy Mother, don't let Linda wake up," but she'd always wake up, and there I'd be again, stuck with her. I don't know what stories I could have told her. It was probably all the fairy tales Bab-cia ever told us mixed up together.

Oh, I just remembered this. Babcia had a little song she used to sing to put Linda to bed. It goes like this, *"Ta Dorotka, ta maluśka, ta maluśka—tańcowała, do koluśka, do koluśka—"* It's about a little girl named Dorothy, and she dances around and around in a circle. She's dancing in the morning dew and stamping her little bare foot. And then she's dancing in the middle of the day when the sun's laying by the well. And then she's dancing in the evening when the sun's setting behind the hills. And now she's sleeping in her little bed on her little pink pillow as the sandman walks beside the fence. *"Cicho bo tam śpi Dorotka, śpi Dorotka,"* it says. "Be quiet because little Dorothy is sleeping, little Dorothy is sleeping."

It had a dance that went with it, and Linda just loved doing that dance, so we'd sing Babcia's song, and I'd let her do the dance a couple times, and then I'd tuck her into bed. And I'd sing the song for her again, and I'd change Dorothy into Linda, and I'd hope that when I got to the part where little Linda is sleep-ing—*"śpi Lindusia, śpi Lindusia"*—she would be, and if I was lucky, she was.

Looking back on it, I'm really glad I did it, that I never let her down—that when I was nine I had enough backbone, or whatever you want to call it, to take care of my little sister—because it was the right thing to do, and I knew it. I only wish things stayed as clear for me for the rest of my life as they'd been when I was nine.

FIVE

Fall's the nicest time in the Ohio Valley. The heat lets up, the leaves are turning, you start to get that bite in the air that makes you think, hey, football season, and I can remember waking up in the morning feeling halfway decent for a change. Georgie and I would get together in the PAC and ask each other, "Well, you got yourself reintegrated back into civilian life yet?" and have a laugh over it, but the truth of the matter is we were both making an effort.

Georgie surprised everybody by buying himself an old junker VW bug and fixing it up and taking off in it to that big demonstration they had in Washington. He was gone a couple weeks, hanging out with a bunch of crazy Vietnam vets he met there, and when he came home, he'd turned into a one man antiwar movement. His position was real simple—peace now. People would ask him how on earth we were ever going to get out of Vietnam, he'd say, "We get out exactly the same way we got in—by aircraft."

Like me, he was feeling kind of optimistic. "Things are bound to get better, Jimmy," he'd say. "They sure as hell can't get much worse." Of course the only time he wasn't stoned was when he was asleep.

That big demonstration really impressed him. He couldn't get over how many plain ordinary people there'd been. "Sure, there was weirdos, you know, but there was all kinds of people too—moms, housewives, guys with jobs, you name it." He wandered around talking to everybody, and he went off on a side demonstration where the Weathermen tried to smash through the door of the Justice Department with a battering ram, and he got himself gassed.

He was really proud of that one. "Okay, so you want a crowd to disperse, right? So you give them some place to disperse to, right? So what do they do?

They block off all the side streets and then they just gas the living bejesus out of everybody. Disperse? That's a joke. It was, 'Oh, you want to demonstrate, do you? Okay, assholes, here's what you get.'" They'd used CS gas, which is against the Geneva Convention, and he'd brought back a canister to prove it. He passed it around at the PAC.

After Connie stood me up, I figured any promise I'd made to her about keeping things secret was pretty well off, so I told the whole story to Georgie, and he thought it was just about the funniest thing he'd ever heard in his life. "Yeah, that woman's really sane," he said. "Some big hairy swinging dick drops down out of the rafters, starts talking dirty to her in the St. Stevens Mall, and she goes, 'Hey, I can dig it, dude, lead me to the nearest panel truck. Oh, and by the way, I got to park my kid somewhere.'"

When I got to the part about her running naked through the cornfield, he was laughing so hard he was practically hysterical. "Yeah, she's *perfectly* sane. Listen, asshole, it's got nothing to do with you. It's all about her and her old man. So do you want to wander out into the middle of that one?" And of course he was right.

I was almost enjoying working for that old bastard Vick Dobranski, if you can believe that. I kept coming up with all these schemes on how he could expand his business, get into retail in a big way, and not just TVs but home stereos, car stereos, pretty much anything electronic, and how maybe he could run some radio ads, or newspaper ads, you know, or anything to get beyond servicing the same old customers he'd had for the last thirty years. And he'd always say, "If I was a younger man just starting out in business, that'd make a lot of sense."

One afternoon we've completely run out of work. Vick's drinking coffee and smoking cigarettes and reading the paper, and there's nothing I hate worse than having nothing to do, so I start fixing up his front window. Before I came along, most of the sets he took in trade just went into the Dumpster, but I'd started rebuilding them—anyhow the ones that didn't need a picture tube—so I'm shoving them in the window with amazing prices on them, you know, like fifteen bucks for an old RCA twenty-one incher that works perfectly well, and I'm humming away to myself and Windexing the window, and Vick's peering at me over the top of his glasses, and he says, "You know, Koprowski, I never would have guessed it, but you got a lot of ambition."

The funny thing about me is that I've always liked working—if the work, you know, has a little more to it than putting doohickeys on light bulbs—but back in those days I'd never admit it. "Not me, Vick," I say. "I just get bored easy."

He sits there watching me for a while, and then he says, "I'd love to get out of this sorry business, spend some time with my grandchildren. Why don't you think about buying me out? I'd give you a fair price."

I just laughed at him. I couldn't imagine ever being in the position where I could buy him out—although the idea did stick in my head. Yeah, I thought, I could run a little business like Vick's. As a matter of fact, I could do a hell of a lot better job than he was.

Another thing that made me feel halfway decent that fall was moving out of the house. Bobby Burdalski had put out the word for me—"a fixer-upper," I'd said, and that's how I got the trailer. It was sitting on a pad on Bow Street. You know, down behind Raysburg Hill when you're going in town the back way. Dirt cheap because it needed a lot of work.

I slapped on a coat of paint and got the fridge and stove working. I picked up some nice furniture cheap from the Sally Ann, and I salvaged a bunch of components and built a pretty good stereo, and there was a little TV that Vick was going to throw away, and I got that working just fine. I even put curtains on the windows. I'll tell you a secret. To make curtains, you don't have to know how to sew. You've just got to be able to operate a staple gun.

So I've got my own place, and immediately I'm getting along great with Old Bullet Head. I'm still eating dinner at home five nights out of seven, and every time I get a paycheck, I slip Mom a few bucks. I know she's going to take it and she knows she's going to take it, but we always have the same conversation. "You sure you're okay, now, Jimmy? You don't need anything?"

"No, Mom, I'm just fine."

"You sure now?"

"Yeah, Mom, everything's fine," and the money instantly vanishes into her pocket.

After dinner, Mom and Linda are washing up in the kitchen and I'm sitting in the living room in front of the tube with the old man, and he passes me part of the paper, and sometimes we even have something like a conversation. I'm there, but I don't have to be, and we both know it, and of course he knows about the money I'm slipping Mom, and so I'm A-okay in his book, and life just kind of falls into a routine. And you know what? That's not a bad thing.

———

Somehow or other that fall I got to be the godfather to Linda's polka band. She kept talking to me about it, and I kept offering my opinions, and the next thing you know she was talking to me like it's my band too—which in a funny kind of way it was.

Now the first big problem was that Linda and Mary Jo Duda were at cross purposes right off the top. Linda didn't want some slick, high-power outfit that'd be stealing work from the Andrzejewski brothers; she just wanted a nice friendly little band playing old-time Polish tunes, preferably with all the musicians from St. Stanislaus Parish. But for years Mary Jo had been trying to form an all-girl polka band, and I guess because Linda was a girl, Mary Jo took it as a sign from God.

Mary Jo wasn't thinking that much about the music. She figured with her playing the accordion, the music would pretty much take care of itself. A polka's a polka, right? What she wanted was a bunch of young pretty girls dressed up in cute outfits so they could play all over the tri-state area at every Polish, Slovak, Slovenian, Serbian, Croatian, Hungarian, Czech, Bohemian, or German event where people liked polkas and pretty girls, and make lots of bucks.

"I don't know where she thinks all these girls are going to come from," Linda said, but she thought the best thing to do was humor her, because Mary Jo just naturally believed, what with her many years of experience and all, that whatever band there was, she was going to be the leader of it.

Well, the way South Raysburg was in those days, all you've got to do is say, "Hey, my sister's starting a polka band," and the next thing you know everybody and their dog is giving you free advice. So I'm talking to Burdalski in the PAC, and I'm saying, "Well, if there was any *girl* musicians, you know—" and he says, "How about Patty Pajaczkowski?" Her name kept coming up, but I didn't pay much attention because the word was that Patty was crazier than a shithouse rat.

Finally I'm even hearing about her from Linda. "Hey, Jimmy, what do you know about Patty Pajaczkowski? Everybody says she's a fantastic drummer, and Darlene Mondrowski told me she's playing with an all-girl country-western band."

So what did we know about Patty? Nothing really. It was all myth and legend. She went to Central for a while, and Georgie took her out a couple times when he was a senior and she was a freshman. "Hooo, Patty," he says, "she was weird even back then." Patty dropped out of school and turned into one of those teenage runaways. She went out west and lived in a hippie commune, somebody says. No, she lived with the Indians, somebody else says. It was the Hopis. No, I heard it was the Navajos. She got in some kind of trouble out there—wasn't she busted for possession? And somebody else heard she was down in Nashville making records. Or maybe it was San Francisco. But wherever it was, she's the drummer on three records. Or maybe it's four. Can she play? Everybody agrees on the answer to that one. You bet she can play. She's a regular Gene Krupa.

It turned out that Patty Pajaczkowski really was in an all-girl country band and they were playing in the Sugar Shack over in Bridgeport, which is how Linda and I ended up in there one Saturday night.

"Oh, God," Linda says when we walk through the door. The place is wall to wall shit-kickers, so you've got your young bucks on the make with a hundred and forty-seven empty beer glasses on their tables, and your honeys with their spray-painted blue jeans, and your bartender that looks like a fat gorilla with the hair shaved off, and everybody's having themselves one hell of a good time. We cram ourselves into the edge of a table up front so Linda can check out the band.

I forget what they called themselves, but they were your classic bar band— lead guitar, rhythm guitar, bass, and drums—and they would've been a major hit with that crowd before they even played a note, you know, what with their pink cowboy hats and sequin vests, white cowgirl boots and super-short pink miniskirts. Doing old classic numbers like "D-I-V-O-R-C-E" and some fifties rock 'n' roll countrified and covering whatever was on the country charts in those days. The rhythm guitar was the lead singer; she wasn't half-bad, and she knew how to work the crowd, and they were going over just fine. Patty Pajaczkowski on drums. "How is she?" I asked Linda.

"She's just keeping time. I don't know. I don't think she's trying very hard."

When the first set was over, I invited Patty to come over and have a drink with us. She sort of knew us, just like we sort of knew her, just like everybody in South Raysburg sort of knows everybody. "What are you guys doing in here?" she says.

"We came to hear you," Linda says.

"Oh, yeah," Patty says and stares off into space and starts tapping on the tabletop. Linda and I order a couple more beers, and Patty orders two Cokes—

Patty

no ice, huh?—and when they come, she downs them both in ten seconds flat.

Patty was one of the most downright peculiar-looking girls I ever saw in my life. You could start with the lizard tattooed on her shoulder, and that was years before girls were getting themselves tattooed. Washed-out, I guess you could call her, but that doesn't even come close. Her skin looked like she'd once been pink like a normal white person but then she'd had some kind of solvent dumped on her that got most of the color off and left just a few pink spots here and there. Dead straight hippie hair halfway down her back—that stupid kind of blond that's like no color at all—and just about the palest eyes you could imagine, not even dark enough so you could call them gray. But the thing that was really creepy about her is that she was sexy as all hell—if you like your girls skinny as drawn wire. She had to scrape six guys off her just to get to our table.

I'm feeling sorry for my sister. There she is in her powder blue pantsuit, and she's doing her best. "We're really enjoying your music."

"Oh, yeah. Shit. Glad somebody's enjoying it."

I see Linda get a hurt look on her face, so I jump in with, "Georgie Mondrowski says hi."

"Oh, yeah. Georgie, huh. Tell him I'm glad he didn't get killed."

Patty never once looks at you and she never once smiles. Now she starts gnawing on the ends of her fingers. She's really going at it. The ends of all her fingers are red and chewed. "Heard you were down in Nashville," I say.

"Yeah. About a year."

Long silence. "So what brings you back to the valley?" Linda says in a cheery little voice.

"Temporary insanity."

Linda gives me a look that says she's ready to leave, and I give her a look back that says, let's stick with it a little bit longer, so Linda and I are both trying to think of more stupid things to say while Patty's sitting there twitching and staring into space and gnawing on her fingers and tapping on the tabletop. Then the bass player comes over and introduces herself, "Hi, I'm Bev Wright. You friends of Patty's? Mind if I sit down?"

Bev has no problem talking. In about a minute and a half we know everything there is to know about her. She's from Barnsville, Ohio. Her brother gave her that Fender bass she's playing; it's a honey. Her brother's on the Jamboree all the time, plays with the Mountain Men. Maybe we've heard him? Jumping Jack Wright? When she was a little kid she used to follow him around going, "I want to play, I want to play, I want to play," so he taught her guitar out of self-defense. Too many rhythm guitar players in the world already, so she switched to bass.

Bev's cute as a button, a friendly freckle-faced country kid with a big mop of curly brown hair, and while she's talking our ears off, Patty out of nowhere says to me, "Georgie got any smoke?"

I go, "Huh?"

"Mondrowski. I heard he's got some pretty good smoke."

"Could be," I say.

"Smoke in this fucking town's shit," Patty says. "Bummer. Might as well be tea leaves. He still in the same place?" I tell her that he is.

Their break's about over and we still haven't got down to business, so I say to Bev, "My sister's trying to get an all-girl polka band together."

"Oh, wow," Bev says, "that's really neat. I love playing with all girls. I love polkas. I used to listen to that show on Saturday mornings," and she's going on about how much she loves polkas—real happy music, she says—so Linda starts telling her about how the music from the old country crashed into pop music and jazz and made the Polish-American polka and about Eastern and Western styles and so on, and Bev's going, "Hey, wow, is that ever neat," and Patty staring into space says, "My parents were into all that polka shit."

We stop to give her room to say something more, but there isn't anything more, so Linda starts telling Bev about how great it'd be to have a friendly little polka band in the valley playing old-time Polish music, and again Patty comes sailing in out of left field, "You know that tune that goes, 'Hey—'?"

"Hey?" Linda says.

"My old man used to sing it to me when I was a little kid. It was his favorite tune. He'd sing it to me when I was going to bed. It goes, 'Hey—'" and she kind of shrugs, and she hums a little bit of the melody. She makes a face like, oh, God, sorry, I can't sing for shit, and she tries it again. "It's that Polak hillbilly tune," she says.

I see the light bulb go on in Linda's head. "Oh!" she says. My sister amazes me sometimes. As shy as she is, she starts singing in her choir-girl voice right there in that country-western bar. She doesn't seem the least bit embarrassed. She's singing:

> "Hej, góral ja ci góral,
> Hej, z pod samiuśkich Tater,
> Hej, descyk mnie wykąpał,
> Hej, wykołysał wiater—"

That means like— Well, it's kind of tricky to translate. The first "hey," is like if you'd say, "Hey, I'm a mountain man." The next "hey" says, "right from the honest-to-God Tatras," like from where the mountains are the highest. The next two "heys" are easy. They say, "Hey, the rain has washed me. Hey, the wind has rocked me," you know, like a baby in a cradle.

"That's it," Patty says. "God, I haven't heard that tune in years."

"Wow," Bev goes, "what is that language? Is that Polish?"

"Martian," Patty says.

"Oh, I wish I was anything but a dumb-ass WASP," Bev says.

And all of a sudden—slam, bang, pow—Patty's playing the table. She's beating away on the top with both hands and she's kicking the leg with one of her cowgirl boots. "That's the polka," she says like she's daring us to say it isn't, and, by God, it is. She's got that polka beat nailed. You could dance to it.

The break's over and the girls are getting ready to go back up on stage. Patty grabs a Sugar Shack matchbook and borrows a pencil from a waitress and writes her number on it. "You get a gig," she says to Linda, "you call me."

"Me too!" Bev yells.

So there was Linda's rhythm section if she wanted it, but she wasn't exactly what you'd call ecstatic about it. We talked it over, and we both concluded that "you get a gig, you call me" didn't translate into "sure, we'd be glad to rehearse with you once a week and then sit around afterward for a few hours and talk about the evolution of Polish music in America." And cheery little Bev Wright wasn't even Polish. Did it matter? "I don't know," Linda said. "I guess not. All she has to do is play root five on the beat."

Linda told Mary Jo about Patty and Bev, and the first thing Mary Jo wants to know is not how they played but if they were cute. Well, cute was certainly the right word for Bev Wright, but Patty Pajaczkowski? Well, maybe if you took "cute" and stretched it around the block a few times. And Mary Jo just loved it to pieces that they were playing in an all-girl country band and she wanted to hear what they were wearing right down to the finest detail, and once she heard that, she knew the girls were perfect. "We'll call ourselves Mary Jo and the Polka Dolls." You can imagine how much Linda liked the idea of being a Polka Doll.

"Mary Jo sees herself as Mom surrounded by all these pretty little chickies," Linda told me. Like Mary Jo was going on about some Polish dance group she saw somewhere, how cute their costumes were, and so she figured she'd dress the girls something like that, only with bouncy little white skirts with red polka dots—*polka* dots, get it?—real short, you know, like majorette skirts, but they could have matching panties under them so they wouldn't look immodest, or maybe the panties could be red with white polka dots, and flower wreathes in their hair, probably get good quality artificial flowers because real ones you have to replace every time, and that's an expense, and white boots up to the knee, you know, like peasant girls. "Right," Linda says, "I'll bet you could find thousands of peasant girls in Poland who wear white boots up to the knee on a daily basis."

I thought all this was pretty funny, but Linda didn't. "If I ever get a real band together," she said, "we'll outnumber her."

"Okay," I said, "but let's just say for the sake of argument that Bev and Patty worked out. Who else do you need?"

"Another trumpet or a clarinet."

Girl trumpet players don't exactly grow on trees, but a clarinet player? Well, that turned out to be nowhere near as hard as it seemed. I pop into Czaplicki's to buy a pack of smokes, and Mrs. Czaplicki corners me so we've got to do the how's-your-family routine, and just for something to say, I go, "My sister's starting a polka band, and she's looking for a girl clarinet player. You wouldn't happen to know one, would you?"

Mrs. Czaplicki goes, "Yeah, as a matter of fact I do. You know the Dłuwieckis?"

Naturally I know the Dłuwieckis. Everybody does. They're, I guess you could say, notorious. And it turns out that Mrs. Czaplicki's niece Sandy is best friends with the Dłuwieckis' youngest kid—they play in the band together at Central—and the Dłuwieckis' kid plays the clarinet, and everybody says she's incredible, maybe a musical genius. "Mr. Webb—you know, the music teacher—says she's the best student he's ever had in his life," Mrs. Czaplicki tells me.

Linda doesn't think it's too likely a high school kid is going to have the kind of chops she's looking for, but you never can tell, so there we are with the Czaplickis at the Central band recital.

We're sitting on those damn hard bleachers in the gym, and all I have to do is walk through the doors and smell that sorry place to remember how much I hated it, and the band sounds just the way you'd expect the Raysburg Central Catholic band to sound, and wouldn't you know it, the Dłuwieckis' kid's solo is the next to the last number in the whole program.

"The things I do for you, Linda," I say. "I can't believe it sometimes."

"Well, I've got to admit," she says, "they're not exactly giving us fresh new insights into the masterworks of band literature."

To amuse myself, I'm trying to guess which one of the girls playing the clarinet is Janice Dłuwiecki. Her father's a tall skinny guy with dark curly hair, so I pick a girl I think looks like him, but I'm wrong. When solo time comes, this little kid stands up. She's blond as butter, and she's wearing her hair in pigtails. She looks about twelve.

The number they did was some famous Dixieland tune—I forget which one—and, boy, did that little kid ever make the Central band sound crappy. It was like they were in one universe and she was in another. It was like, I don't know—well, imagine Benny Goodman sitting in with the Fairmont, West Virginia, Salvation Army Band. Notes were coming out of her clarinet about a million to the minute, and she made it sound easy. She played it so hot and fast, whenever the band came in with her, they were like a pile of mud. She got finished and made a little curtsy, and naturally the audience went nuts. It was the first real music we'd heard since we'd walked in there. I said, "Well, Linny, is she good enough for you?"

Yep, Janice Dłuwiecki was plenty good enough, so all Linda had to do was figure out a way to get her. The Dłuwieckis were straight from the old country, and everybody knew what snobs they were, and probably the last thing in the world they'd want was their darling daughter playing in a polka band. But Mr. Dłuwiecki had a soft spot for Linda, and she planned to run into him accidentally somewhere and approach the subject sideways. You see, Linda had been his best student in advanced Polish.

When the Felician Nuns started teaching in Raysburg—that's back when our parents were little—it'd been all Polish, but eventually it dawned on them that it wasn't the world's greatest idea to be sending kids to high school who'd been taught no English whatsoever, so they switched to half a day in Polish, half a day in English. Well, that would have been okay for me and Linda, but by the time we hit St. Stans, the majority of the kids didn't speak Polish at home anymore, and you don't want your kids after their first day of school telling you, "Hey, guess what? Up till lunchtime the nuns talked funny, and I couldn't understand a word they were saying." So by the time I got into grade school, they'd switched to all English, and Polish was just one of the subjects they taught.

Then one of the organizations—Polish people love political organizations, and I never could keep track of them all—began to worry that the Polish language in America might be lost forever, so they started a school on Saturdays—you know, for the kids who'd left St. Stans and gone on to Central. So for a few years—up until it died from its own sheer stupidity—we had Polish school on Saturdays. Anybody who knew more Polish than the kids was fair game to teach in it, and so you'd go over there and you'd have to put up with somebody's mom.

If you survived long enough, eventually you were supposed to get to Mr. Dłuwiecki who taught *advanced* Polish. But what most of us tried to do—I'm talking me and Georgie and Bobby and Larry, *the boys*, right?—we tried to be such total and complete assholes that we wouldn't have to go back there ever again, and we succeeded very quickly. The girls, being girls, hung on longer, and then they started dropping off, and not too many kids made it all the way up to Mr. Dłuwiecki, but naturally Linda did. In fact, she got so far she was the only one left, and every Saturday it was just her and Mr. Dłuwiecki shooting the shit in Polish in one of the side rooms in the church, and naturally he'd always thought she was just about as nice as a South Raysburg girl can be.

A few days after the band recital, Linda gets her chance. She's doing some shopping uptown, and she sees Mr. Dłuwiecki walking into Eberhardt's, so she follows him and accidentally runs into him in front of the men's shirts. They stop and have a chat—mostly in Polish, of course—and she tells him about hearing Janice play in the band recital and how wonderful she was.

Well, he's the kind of guy if you want to tell him his daughter's wonderful, he'll stand and talk to you all day and on into the night. Yes, he's amazed at her musical ability. He's only sorry that she started on a band instrument. He's been trying to get her to switch to the oboe, but so far he hasn't had much success with that. She can be very stubborn. But he'd like to see her go on with it, perhaps get a degree in music. "You have a degree in music, don't you?" he says.

The conversation's going exactly right. Linda gets to tell him about ethnomusicology and writing her paper on Polish music, and then she lets drop that she's trying to put together a Polish musical group.

"Hey, wait a minute," I say. "Did you tell him it was a polka band?"

"Well, not exactly. I think I just said *zespół*."

"Is that a polka band?"

"It's a broad term. You could use it for a polka band."

Mr. Dłuwiecki took her bait—hook, line, and sinker—and allowed as how it would be a wonderful thing for his little Janice to be playing authentic Polish music, so next Sunday after Mass, Linda invited Janice to dinner. "You did *what?*" Mom said.

Linda has only lived here her whole life, and you'd think that she would have figured out how things are by now, but no. Linda lives in her own world, and she keeps doing this—making dumb mistakes about things that should be absolutely obvious—and then Mom goes berserk. She used to get so mad at Linda she'd chase her across the room pinching her—it looked like a big bird pecking at a little bird—and Linda would wrap her arms around herself and just keep backing up with tears running down her face because she could never understand what was going on. Linda's too old to pinch now, but Mom can still yell at her. "Holy Mother of God, why do you do these things to me?"

And Linda says what she always says—"What? What did I do?"

The big problem here is that Mom can never really tell Linda what she did because these things are so obvious to Mom she couldn't put them into words if she tried. But I know how she thinks, and it goes like this. Step one is that people don't come as separate units, they come as parts of families, and you can't invite somebody else's kid over to the house, you've got to invite the whole family. Step two is that it's your relatives you invite over to the house, not other families. If you want to socialize with other people, that's why God gave you the church, but if you invite another family over to dinner, they'll think, oh, shit, *what do they want?* And if they come, then they'll have to invite you to their house, and you'll have to invite them back again, and there you'll be, stuck inviting each other back and forth with no way to get out of it for the rest of your lives.

And the last straw for Mom is exactly who this particular family is. "The Dłuwieckis! Oh, my God, Linda, how could you do this to me?"

If I expect you to follow much more of this, I guess I've got to tell you about what my father called "that old-country crap." Okay, so if you take your Eastern European immigrants, we're the largest group in the valley, but you've also got enough Slovaks so they had their own community hall down in Millwood, and some Czechs and some Hungarians and some Slovenes and Croats and a few little pockets of various other Slavs. And a lot of these folks went to St. Stans even though everything was in Polish.

So if you look at it right, we're all sort of like cousins, or at least like distant relatives, but that first wave of immigrants that came over, they didn't see things that way. Back in those days, there wasn't any Poland, and the Polish people were divided up into three chunks. Mom's family was from the Austrian chunk, and so they figured they had real culture, but people from the Russian chunk, like Dad's family, were just ignorant peasants. And Dad's family didn't much care for Mom's family because they were from the mountains, and everybody knows those *górale* are a wild and crazy bunch, and they drink too much and get in fights and like that. So when Mom and Dad first started going together, they got treated a little bit like Romeo and Juliet.

And of course all the Poles got to look down on the Slovaks because back in the old country the Slovaks were shit on even worse than the Poles, and what the Slovaks said about the Poles was that Poles are naturally arrogant and suspicious and you couldn't ever really trust them. And so on, and so on. People not liking each other because of a bunch of crap that went on in the old country. But the Americans—that's what we called the people who spoke English and ran everything—but the Americans couldn't tell a Pole from a Pomeranian, and no matter where you came from back in the old country, they called you a Hunky.

Well, most of that old-country crap died with the first generation, and my father hated all that stuff, wouldn't put up with it for half a second. Just about the worst chewing-out he ever gave me was when I called a guy I was playing football with—Joey Dubik, his name was, and I called him a "dumb Slovak." Now I didn't mean anything by it. It was just something to say. If anything, I probably thought it was us Slavs against the world. But Old Bullet Head just about murdered me. He's banging on the table with his fist. He's yelling, "I won't have any of that old-country crap in this house, you hear me, Jimmy?"

You see, when they talked about the *brotherhood* of steelworkers, he took it serious—he believed in that—and he was just about the least prejudiced guy I ever knew. He probably could have gone up the ladder in the union if he'd wanted to, and he did get elected to this or that little position over the years, but he was a rank-and-filer his whole life. From his point of view too many damn decisions got made in Pittsburgh anyway, and the guys who went up in the union got way too cozy with the company way too fast, so the only guys he trusted were the guys he worked with, and he really did try to treat them all like brothers no matter who they were. It's something I always respected him for.

Anyhow, the first generation got old and the second generation started taking over, and most of that old-country crap faded away, but then right after the war you've got your displaced persons coming over so you've got a whole new wave of old-country crap. There weren't a lot of DPs in Raysburg, maybe four or five families, but absolutely nobody liked them—I mean when I was growing up, DP was practically a swearword—and of all the DPs that turned up, the Dłuwieckis pissed people off the most.

When they first got here, you never saw anything more pathetic in your life than the Dłuwieckis. That's what my mother said anyway. They'd been living in some refugee camp, and they had ragged old patched-up clothes that didn't fit, and they were so thin it hurt to look at them, and they had a tiny little boy so hungry he couldn't even cry. So why should people like that piss people off? Well, I'll tell you.

Czesław Dłuwiecki—yeah, it's Czesław he calls himself, and don't you ever try to call him Chuck—doesn't take the job they got for him at Old Reliable. He speaks good English— Well, that's not quite it. He studied English in Poland back before the war, read Shakespeare and all that other good shit, and he may have a thick accent, but he speaks this high-flown fancy English, and he's an absolute whiz with numbers, so he gets a job keeping the books at the Benbow Lumberyard, and the next thing you know he goes to night school and gets himself a CPA ticket and goes into business for himself. In a year or two there's not a tax loophole he doesn't know by its first name, and he's got more clients than he can handle, so what does he do? He moves out of South Raysburg, buys himself a big house out in Edgewood, and sends his boys to the Raysburg Military Academy along with all the rich out-the-pike WASP kids. You can see how people got pissed off, right? But you still haven't got the whole story.

Father Stawecki used to put out a newsletter at St. Stans whenever he got around to it, a couple times a year maybe, and the first newsletter Mr. Dłuwiecki gets, he's over at the church waving it in the priest's face. The newsletter's in Polish, right? And Czesław has gone through it with his red pen and marked all the errors. He is, he says, absolutely appalled at the lousy Polish that is written and spoken in South Raysburg. It is a disgrace to the fatherland.

This is how Father Joe dealt with complaints—anything you came to him complaining about, the next thing you know, you're in charge of it, so that's how Czesław Dłuwiecki got to be the editor of the St. Stans newsletter for the next ten years—up until it switched into English—and you better believe the Polish in there was perfection itself. And so was the Polish that came out of Mr. Dłuwiecki's mouth, and that's what he wanted to hear coming out of your mouth, so if you tried to have a conversation with him in Polish, you'd get about three sentences out and he'd be correcting your grammar.

Okay, so the Polish spoken in South Raysburg was peasant Polish to start with, and then it got kind of blurry over the years, what with bumping into English and picking up a lot of English words, and it may not be the world's greatest Polish, but hell, it's *our* Polish, and we're not delighted to have some asshole straight off the boat from the refugee camps of wartorn Europe telling us we don't talk right, so Mom's yelling at Linda about how we brought those *gów-niarze* over here, and they didn't have a pot to piss in, and we clothed them and we fed them and we opened our homes to them and we helped them get on their feet, and how do they repay us? They go around looking down their noses at us. We're not good enough for them, oh no, we're just a bunch of ignorant peasants, them and their big house out in Edgewood.

When Mom's really mad, she turns into a pressure cooker. Her voice drops down to a hiss, and you can almost see the steam coming out of her ears. Linda's just standing there staring at her. "We don't speak good Polish, huh? Well, screw him, that *sukinsyn*. His *dupa* may be in the Ohio Valley but his mind never left Poland. Maybe he should go straight back there!"

So now, of course, we're all set to have a wonderful time at dinner.

Babcia Wojtkiewicz—that's Mom's mom—always comes over for dinner on Sundays, and she always brings something with her, usually a big pot of soup. That Sunday she'd made *barszcz*—that's just fine with me—but Mom's worried is it okay to serve with roast chicken to *the Dłuwieckis' kid*. "Of course it is," Linda says.

Then right when the kid's supposed to show up, she shows up—like to the minute. She's so on time she must have been standing outside counting off the seconds on her watch. Mom's hissing, "Linda, Linda, Linda, there she is," so Linda runs out to let her in—"Oh, Janice, how nice that you could come." Janice has got her clarinet case with her. When she first walks through the door, I think she's wearing her school uniform, but no, that's not it. Even though she's off duty, she's wearing an outfit that's exactly *like* her school uniform—you know, the blazer and the pleated skirt and the kneesocks. She's still wearing her hair in pigtails. They're really long, like practically down to her waist.

So Janice perches on the edge of a chair with her knees together, and, oh, my God, we've got *the Dłuwieckis' kid* in our living room. I know other people don't think this about us, but Poles are the politest people in the entire universe, and we're all doing our best. Ordinarily when Babcia was there we'd be speaking mainly Polish, but now we're sticking with English, and we sound like bad actors on television. Mom pops in, wiping her hands on her apron, and says, "Well, Janice, it's so nice to see you. How are your parents?" This, of course, is to remind everybody that Mom hasn't forgotten for half a second that Janice is the Dłuwieckis' kid.

"Fine," Janice says.

I'm watching all this go down, and—well, maybe it's because I was away four years and it's given me a different perspective on things, but I feel like the Polak from another planet. Okay, so Babcia's English isn't too bad for an old lady born in the old country, but she's not exactly what you'd call at home in it. And if you gave the matter some thought—like much longer than about eight seconds—you'd expect Mr. Dłuwiecki's kid to speak Polish, wouldn't you? So why are we speaking nothing but English? Well, where do we live? The United States of America. What language is spoken in this fair land? Yep, you guessed her. And if we were to speak Polish, we'd be up to our eyeballs in that old-country crap.

"I bet she'd like a Coke," Mom says to me. "Jimmy, why don't you get Janice a Coke?" Nobody has ever drunk a Coke before Sunday dinner in the entire history of the Koprowski household, but I say, "Sure, Mom," and while I'm getting Janice a Coke, I get myself a beer, and Mom gives me a look that would peel the paint off the wall, but she can't say a thing because the Dłuwieckis' kid might hear her.

Old Bullet Head is peering at Janice over the top of his reading glasses. He's speaking in slow motion. "So. Janice. Tell me. What grade. Are you in?"

"I'm a sophomore, sir," she says.

"Oh? You don't look. That old."

"Everybody always thinks I'm younger than I am."

Now I don't know what Mom told Babcia about Janice—she must have told her something—but you can see that Babcia's having a hard time figuring out what this little girl is doing at our house, but whatever it is, Babcia's going to do her bit to make her feel welcome. "You go to Central?" she says.

"That's right," Janice says, and she nods about six times. She's just as uptight as the rest of us. "I go to Central."

"Good, good," Babcia says with this big smile like it's the greatest thing in the world to go to Central.

Janice has got to be fifteen, but she still looks about twelve to me. She's taller than she looked on the stage at Raysburg High—it's kind of surprising; she's a little bit taller than Linda—but she hasn't got any figure that you could notice. She looks like— Okay, for a while the Communist government in Poland used to put out a magazine, and God knows why, but we used to get it at the PAC, and sometimes if you were bored, you'd pick it up and flip through it for a laugh. It was straight propaganda, all about how wonderful everything was in Poland, and they had these real crude color pictures, you know, where all the colors are too bright, and there'd be a picture of a peasant on a big, brand-new, shiny red tractor, and he's happy happy happy. And there'd be another picture of peasants on a collective farm, and they're happy happy happy. And there'd always be a picture of peasants doing their peasant dances in their peasant costumes, and you better believe they're happy happy happy. And they'd always find the most beautiful little peasant girl in all of Poland to put in that magazine, and there she'd be in her peasant costume—you know, with the wreath of flowers in her hair—and she'd have eyes as blue as the sky and hair as blond as a haystack, and that's exactly what Janice Dłuwiecki looks like.

So we go in and sit down around the dining room table, and Old Bullet Head is still trying to get something started that might have a chance of turning into a conversation. "So. Janice. Linda tells me. You're quite the musician. You play the clarinet?"

"Yes, sir."

"I'll tell you a secret, Janice. You don't have to call me sir. I work for my money." That's supposed to be a joke, right? But we've all heard it a thousand times, and nobody cracks a smile.

So we're all sitting at the table now—with the Dłuwieckis' kid—and Mom says, "Walt, why don't you say grace?" Except for big-deal occasions like Christmas Eve, the last time we said grace before dinner was probably back around 1958 when we had Father Stawecki over.

My dad folds his hands and sits there a minute, and then he kicks into probably the only grace he knows—*"Pobłogosław Panie Boże nas i te dary, które z Twojej świętej łaskawości będziemy spożywać. Przez Chrystusa, Pana Naszego. Amen,"* and we all go, "Amen."

Babcia liked hearing the grace in Polish, so she says, *"Jak przyjemnie usłyszeć modlitwę po polsku,"* and Janice says to Babcia, *"Ale proszę Pani, oczywiście modlitwa musi być po polsku,"* and Babcia stares in total shock at this little kid in pigtails sitting next to her and says, *"Hey, she's talking Polish!"* and Janice says, *"Bo ja jestem Polka,"* and then, bing, like somebody pushed a button on one of those headsets they've got at the United Nations, everybody's speaking Polish—well, all except for yours truly.

The minute Polish starts to come out of her mouth, Janice lights up like a Christmas tree. You wouldn't believe it was the same little girl. She's giggling, she's waving her hands in the air, she's talking a mile a minute in that educated Polish that always sounds to me like somebody chewing up crisp lettuce leaves.

I should tell you something about me and the Polish language. It was the first language I spoke, and I went on speaking it for years when I had to, and I even got A's in it from the nuns, probably because most of the other kids at St.

Stans didn't speak Polish at home, and that gave me an unfair advantage. But I
never paid any attention to the grammar; whatever people around here said,
that's what I said, and I never read anything in it besides the boring crap they
gave us in school, and I'm not like Linda—I never went out of my way to hang
on to the language, and you use it or lose it, right? So I could follow everything
that was going down, but as for saying something back, well, just forget it. By
the time I'd thought of something I could say, the conversation was already a
mile and a half down the road.

Well, Babcia said something to the effect of, "She talks just like the upper
crust," and we all had a good laugh, and that pretty well broke the ice. So we
started shoveling in the food, and eventually we switched back to English,
except whenever Janice said anything to my grandmother, she said it in Polish.
Mom asked Janice how she'd learned such good Polish, and she said her father
didn't give her much choice in the matter—which we could have guessed.

Mom and Dad pumped her about her family. Of course we sort of knew
them—they went to our church—but we didn't know all that much about them
because they didn't live down here, and like I said, they weren't exactly popular
in the parish. I vaguely remembered her oldest brother, John. He went to St.
Stans for a few years before they moved out to Edgewood. Well, now he was out
at Ohio State getting himself an advanced degree in something or other. He'd
got his B.A. from Ohio State and had a good job in Columbus, but then he
decided that what he really wanted to do was further his education. That's the
kind of story Old Bullet Head just loves hearing, and he gives me what you'd
call the significant look. Her brother Mark was in his senior year out at the
Academy. He was applying to a whole bunch of schools, but he was hoping to
get a scholarship to Yale, and Old Bullet Head was just as impressed as all hell.
"I kept telling this one to stay in school"—he jerks his thumb at me—"but he
wouldn't pay any attention to me." Of course he doesn't say a word about
Linda's B.Mus. because that's good for absolutely nothing.

So by the end of dinner everybody decided that Janice was a really nice lit-
tle girl—everybody except me. I thought she was a pain in the ass. And then
Linda sat Janice down in front of the piano and delivered her the Polka Lecture.
I figured if I heard it one more time, I could deliver it myself.

Linda got out some music and put it on the piano. Janice looked at it a
minute and said, "I wish Dad would quit bragging about me all the time. It's
embarrassing. I'm not really that good."

"You don't have to be modest, Janice. I heard you in the band concert. You
were wonderful."

"Thanks." Janice shrugged like it was nothing.

"Why don't we try this?" Linda said.

"I'm sorry," Janice said, "I don't read very well."

"Oh, that's all right. We'll go slow."

Janice got a look on her face like she was going to take her medicine even if it killed her. "I'm sorry. I don't read very well at all. I know I shouldn't have done it, but I've been fooling everybody for years. I'm really sorry."

Linda was having a hard time with that one. "How do you play in the band?"

"Oh, as soon as I hear the other kids play something, then I can play it."

"You take lessons, don't you?"

"Oh, yes. With Mr. Webb."

"How do you do that?"

"When he gives me a new piece, I always get him to play it for me first, and then when I play it, I pretend I'm reading it. After a few times, I can even sort of read it."

"And he's never caught on?"

"Well, sort of. But he doesn't really know how bad I am."

"Well, good grief, Janice, how'd you learn that solo you played with the band?"

"Mr. Webb lent me the record."

"You learned it *off a record?* What record?"

"I should know, shouldn't I? It was somebody or other's New Orleans band. The clarinet player was a guy named Sidney Arodin. I guess he's famous, huh? It was really hard. It took me forever."

"Oh, I bet it did. How long did it take you?"

"Oh, I guess it took me a whole weekend."

Linda sat there forever without saying a word. Then she said, "If I play something on the piano, can you play it back to me?"

"Oh, sure."

Linda played the beginning of "The Clarinet Polka." Janice picked up her clarinet case. "I've got to pull out," she said. "Your piano's a little bit flat." She started putting her clarinet together.

"What do you mean it's flat?" Linda said.

Janice looked at Linda like she was plain nuts. "You know, *flat.*"

"Oh," Linda said, "you mean it's out of tune with itself."

"Well, yeah, it is, but the whole thing's a little bit flat too." Janice blew a few notes and stopped.

I want to make sure you're getting this. After hearing Linda play, Janice never once checked her clarinet against the piano. She fiddled with the top end of her clarinet, pulled it out just a tiny bit more, and she blew a few more notes and that seemed to satisfy her, so she played the beginning of "The Clarinet Polka" just the way Linda had played it. Then she just sat there looking like a little kid waiting for the next part of her lesson.

Linda reached over and hit a note on the piano and it was perfectly in tune with the last note Janice had played. Linda stared at Janice like she'd just seen the stigmata break out on her. "Oh, my God," she said, "you've got perfect pitch."

SIX

I'm not sure why Janice Dłuwiecki bugged the hell out of me, but for a while there, it was like nails on a blackboard every time I laid eyes on her. Oh, I could list all kinds of things that annoyed me. For starters, those long blond braids and her Central uniform that made her look like this perfect Catholic schoolgirl, and then the way she sucked up to grown-ups, like talking Polish to my grandmother, and the sound of it—that soft, hissy snappy Polish with zero defects—and the way she always said *pan* or *pani* no matter who she was talking to, like that's how you talk to a priest or how little kids are supposed to talk to their parents, like calling my father "sir" in English, which she always did. And something else about her that was just, I don't know, queer and old-fashioned, maybe from being second generation and so close to the old country—you know, that she could speak Polish at all—and my mother saying all the time, "What a nice little girl," but Janice seemed to me just way *too* nice, you know what I mean? Like a little girl designed by the Legion of Mary. Yeah, and then there was that perfect pitch Linda kept talking about—what a rare gift, possessed by only a tiny percent of the population, and on and on and on—so I started calling Janice "Perfect."

Linda was rehearsing with Mary Jo and Janice Dłuwiecki every Tuesday, and everything in South Raysburg gets connected up to St. Stans eventually, so Father Obinski let them use one of the rooms at the church. Janice would come down to our house straight from school and stay for dinner—which was a lot for Mom to handle, but she could always blame it on my crazy sister who never did anything right, and she liked Janice. Everybody liked her but me.

Well, my sister did have a driver's license, but back in those days she didn't own a car for the simple reason that, just like all the other Koprowskis, she was too cheap to spend her money. And Central is only about four blocks from Vick's shop, so Linda says, "If Janice walked over there after band practice, could she get a ride home with you?"

"Sure," I say, "no problem," and about half the time Perfect turns up at the shop the way she's supposed to, but the other half, band practice runs late so I've got to go over to Central and get her. Then I bring Perfect home with me, she eats dinner with us, she and Linda go off and rehearse, and then they come back, and pretty soon it's, "Oh, Jimmy, would you mind running Janice home?" The bus service in South Raysburg on weekday evenings is kind of shitty. I guess the company figures there's nobody down there but a bunch of Polaks and they don't go out after dinner much anyway, but anyhow if Janice takes the bus, she's got to transfer, and it takes her an hour and a half, and somebody can drive her home in ten minutes, and that somebody of course is me, so pretty soon I'm providing Perfect with a free taxi service every Tuesday night.

Well, sure, Linda, it's always been my greatest ambition in life to drive somebody else's kid around. I'll just drop whatever I'm doing at nine-thirty so I can drive Perfect back to the big house in Edgewood her father bought so he wouldn't have to live down here with the rest of us where his daughter wouldn't have any trouble getting from point A to point B because she could damn well walk.

But I really don't know what I was bitching about. At nine-thirty on a Tuesday night about the only thing I'd be doing would be watching the tube with Old Bullet Head or sitting in a bar somewhere with Georgie Mondrowski, and after a while I kind of got used to having Perfect around once a week. Well, no, that's not right. I don't know why I said that. I never got used to having her around.

Sometime that fall I got a postcard. It had a picture of the Dallas Cowboys Cheerleaders on it, and all it said was, "I'm in the Soap Creek Saloon and your act is not playing." He didn't even sign it, but of course it was from Jeff Doren, so he'd got out of the service.

I bought a postcard with a cartoon hillbilly on it—big hairy barefoot guy holding a jug of moonshine in one hand and a shotgun in the other—that said, "Welcome to West Virginia," and I wrote Doren a note telling him I was working on reintegrating myself back into civilian life and I wasn't doing half bad. I was still coming to Austin, I said, but the way things were looking, probably not before spring.

I felt like I owed it to Jacobson to go back to Austin just the way he and Doren and I used to talk about all those times on Guam, and I never let that idea go. That first year after he died, I kept dreaming about good old Ron Jacobson. One dream I remember clear as anything. He's sitting on the end of my bed. I open my eyes and there he is, absolutely real, and he says, "Jimmy, I thought you were never going to wake up." It's funny how dreams can stick with you.

I don't know if I've told you much about Jacobson. He was just about the best damn bullshit artist I ever saw. His stories always started out perfectly believable, and he told them in this quiet apologetic voice. He'd get this sad, worried look on his face, and he never cracked a smile. He could haul people in about ten miles before it dawned on them they were being had.

Like one night in a bar in Fort Worth he was telling a bunch of honeys how he'd been stationed for a while in the old Kingdom of Seram. The U.S. had just a tiny little base there so most people didn't know much about Seram—that's what he said—but it was a fascinating place. And he made up all these details about the Kingdom of Seram that were, you know, just totally convincing. He even had me sort of half believing it was true. Then, after about an hour of this shit, he tells us that the people who live there are called "Seramics" and they live in huge golden castles made out of pottery.

After basic, the first place I got stationed was out at Carswell, and if you're a young single guy, you can have a lot of fun there. I used to think that all the shit you hear about Texas can't be real—just something in the movies—but it's real all right. They've got real cowboys, and naturally, if you want to have real cowboys, you've got to have real cows. I never saw so much beef on the hoof in my life. And Carswell's where Doren and Jacobson and I got to be tight. Jeff was from Austin, and he was like our tour guide to Texas. He kept telling us that Fort Worth was nothing but a two-bit cow town and Austin was where it was happening, and he was right.

We went to Austin every chance we got, and it never let us down. It's hard to think of anyplace in Texas as mellow, but Austin was mellow. To give you an idea, let's say a gay guy walked into a bar in Fort Worth, he'd live, oh, maybe fourteen and a half seconds. Gay guys walking around Austin, nobody gives a shit. The first super-short miniskirts I ever saw were in Austin. And the first real hippies. Hanging out in a place called Hippie Hollow. And chicks walking around topless, people drifting up to you, offering to sell you grass. And you've got your coffeehouse scene with folksingers. And you've got some of the best damn country music you'd ever want to hear, twanging away in those good-time saloons, and you've got these great Mexican hole-in-the-wall joints where you can go at two in the morning and wolf down flaming-hot chili or a whacking-big spread of tortillas for a couple bucks. And then there were the Texas honeys— Well, that was the height of the peace and love scene, and the Texas honeys were a real treat.

I've had people tell me I should have seen San Francisco back in the sixties, and maybe I should have, but Austin's where it was happening for me—my idea of paradise. Golden sunshine and sweet girls and just floating along, going with the flow—yeah, we really did talk like that. "Good vibes," we said, and "making the scene," and all that other sixties bullshit that was, I swear to God, really real and meant something for a while. Well, it never occurred to me it could change. In my head, it was always there waiting for me exactly the way I remembered it.

Sometime in October I got a call from Mrs. Constance Bradshaw. Just like that other time she'd called me, it was right smack in the middle of dinner. My mom grabs the phone, hands it to me. "It's a young lady," she says, and I'd got Connie so totally out of my head, I'm thinking, young lady? What young lady? And this little voice says, "Jim? It's me, Constance."

It wasn't anything I thought about. It was more like a reflex. I was almost ready to say something, but I just couldn't do it. Very quietly I hung the phone up. Mom's looking at me, and I go, "Wrong number."

Then about a week later I'm in the shop, and it's like two minutes to five, and the phone rings. I'm the closest one to it, so I grab it. I never could answer the phone straight, so I do one of my goofy lines, "Dobranski's world-famous TV repairs, all your electronic problems taken care of," and I hear, "Jim? This is Constance." She's being firm this time. No nonsense.

Vick's looking at me, wondering who it is, if he should take it. "Jim, I really think we need to talk," Connie's saying, and it hit me, you know, that I wanted no part of her. It was really clear to me.

We were always getting calls for the florist's, so I say, "Oh, no, no. We're *the TV repair*. Try six seven *four*."

"Don't do this to me, goddamn you!" Connie yells in my ear.

"No problem," I say and hang up. I was really hoping that time she'd get the message.

———

What else can I tell you about that fall? I wasn't feeling half bad, and— Oh, yeah, there was a period of, I don't know, maybe a month when my sister took to hanging around with me and Georgie. Linda still hadn't patched her heart back together from Mr. Graduate School Asshole in Morgantown, and one of the results of Georgie's head being twisted in Vietnam was that he was afraid to get involved with girls, so the two of them made a pretty good pair.

But Mom was nervous as all hell about it. She liked Georgie—everybody liked Georgie—but since he'd turned into South Raysburg's original whacked-out weirdo hairy freak, he'd sunk a few notches below zero in the potential son-in-law department. "What's with Linda and George Mondrowski?" she asks me.

"Absolutely nothing, Mom."

She couldn't believe it. Georgie had been the heartbreaker of Raysburg Central. "What do you mean, absolutely nothing?" Mom says.

"Nothing means nothing," I told her. "Look, Mom, he gourded out in the war effort. He's not ready for—you know, something normal with a girl. He just wants somebody to hang out with."

"Hang out with?" She just looks at me with her eyebrows raised like she can't believe anybody could possibly be as dumb as me. From her point of view, if you leave any healthy boy and girl in their twenties alone together for longer than about ten minutes, they naturally start screwing like rabbits. I never could convince her it was totally harmless.

But Georgie and Linda and I would go out for dinner sometimes, or go to a movie, or sit in the PAC and have a beer. One night we just walked along the railroad track throwing stones in the river. Only once I remember that George said anything about Vietnam. He said that when he first got there, he thought it was like football.

"You know that crap you get from the coach? 'You can't hold back, boys. That's when you get hurt. You go in there, give her your best shot, you'll never get hurt.' And you know, it sort of works. Okay, so it's my first time in country, and I'm stone-cold cherry. We're humping a million clicks through this god-awful terrain. Thorns? You never saw thorns like that. Every damn plant that grows in that goddamn country has thorns on it. No sign of Charlie, right? I'm starting to think Charlie doesn't exist, like it's all a bad joke.

"So finally we make contact, and who's Charlie? Charlie is a bunch of little gooks running away like the track team. And I'm firing at anything I can see, having a great time. John Wayne, right? Not holding back a thing, because, shit, that's when you get hurt. And damned if we don't come out of that one smelling like roses, and I think, hey, it's just like football—only a little more exciting. I'm going to do just fine over here.

"Well, about a week later, we're humping the boonies, and we're back to zero Charlie. Not a sign of the little bastards. And then, ka-BOOM—trip wire rigged to a Claymore, and all hell breaks loose. We're pinned down. We've got gooks everywhere. We've got incoming mortar fire, for Christ's sake. You don't know which way anything's coming from, you don't know what to shoot at, you don't know nothing.

"Well, ol' John Wayne here, he's hit the dirt, making like a worm. Three-quarters of the guys bought it, and I got out without a scratch on me—well, except for the thorns. And it was nothing I did. Just the luck of the draw, that's all. Nothing you can prepare for. Nothing you can make go away by—you know, by having the right attitude. And I'd thought it was like football? Well, shit."

"Was it really bad over there?" Linda asks him.

He just looks at her a minute, and then he says, "Linda, honey, I know you're trying to be nice, but, you know, I'd just as leave not talk about it anymore."

"I'm sorry," she says.

"Oh, don't be sorry for asking," he says. "I'm kind of glad you asked. You'd be surprised at the people who never mention it. They just pretend Nam doesn't exist—like maybe you were away on a nice vacation somewhere. But here's what's happening—I got all these pictures in my head, and they're not lots of fun. And I don't see any reason why you should have those pictures in your head, you know what I mean?"

I've met a lot of guys who came back from Vietnam angry, but somehow Georgie didn't. Well, that's not exactly right. He could get plenty angry sometimes. I think if he ever walked into a bar and saw McNamara sitting in it, he'd murder him with his bare hands. But the main feeling you got from him about Vietnam was—I guess you could say, it made him really sad.

And meanwhile, the band was getting off to a good start. Janice took it dead serious. Every Tuesday Linda would lend her some more records and tell her which songs to work on, and Janice would come back with the clarinet parts memorized note for note. "Nothing seems too hard for her," Linda said.

Naturally Mary Jo thought Perfect was the greatest thing since the invention of *pierogi*, and she kept asking Linda when they were going to get together with Patty and Bev. Mary Jo figured they should be getting some gigs. "No point in us just sitting around playing for each other," she said. She was just dying to go into the fabric department at Eberhardt's and start looking for some nice white satin with red polka dots, you know, for the miniskirts.

Perfect, of course, being the little goody-two-shoes she was, would play anything they told her to, but Linda and Mary Jo kept getting into arguments about what they should be doing. Mary Jo wanted to do a bunch of the good old tunes that everybody knows, like "The Pennsylvania Polka," and "Just Because," and "The Blue Skirt Waltz," but Linda said, "No way. We're not doing pop polkas. We're doing Polish polkas," and just in case Mary Jo wasn't up on Polish polkas, Linda had, oh, maybe fifty records she could lend her.

Well, hell, Mary Jo said, she knew plenty of Polish polkas. She'd been playing Polish polkas when Linda hadn't even been born yet, and if we're talking records, she had maybe two hundred she could lend Linda. But if you sing in nothing but Polish, you cut yourself off from the younger generation. Tough, Linda said, that's the younger generation's problem, and besides, do you think the younger generation wants to hear "The Pennsylvania Polka"?

"Fine and dandy," Mary Jo said, or words to that effect, but if she didn't see this band turning into something real, she was going to take her accordion and go play it in somebody's bar for a few bucks just the way she'd been doing for the last thirty years, and Linda and Janice could play trumpet and clarinet duets with each other in the basement of the church to their hearts' content.

I gave Janice Dłuwiecki a pretty rough time. I remember thinking, hell, everybody in the world thinks Perfect's perfect, but that doesn't mean I have to. She kept trying to engage me in conversation, and I'd answer her in monosyllables or maybe grunt at her like, you know, your basic Neanderthal. Pretty soon she got the picture, and we'd just ride along in my car in dead silence with me staring through the windshield like I'm lost in some deep and profound thought. Yeah, I was a real asshole.

So one Tuesday night I pull up in front of her fancy-ass house out in Edgewood, and she said, "Would you like to come in?" She usually asked me that, and I said what I always said, "No, I don't think so. Thanks anyway."

But this time she goes, "Dad doesn't think you're very polite. You drive me home every Tuesday and you don't come in. Dad says if you were a polite boy and you'd been brought up right, you'd come in and say hi. I just thought I'd better tell you that."

My first thought was that her dad could take his polite and shove it, but then I had a second thought, which was that I owed it to my sister to make sure the Dłuwieckis stayed cool with the polka band, so I said, "Oh, yeah? I guess I better come in then."

I swear to God, her dad must have been waiting to pounce on me the minute I stepped through the door. "*A, witam cię,* Jimmy," he says, and he takes my coat and steers me into the living room. Perfect follows along behind us.

If her mom and brother were in there somewhere, they must have wrapped themselves up in cotton balls or hung themselves in the closet or some damn thing. It was the quietest house I was ever in. Perfect and I plunk down on either end of the couch, and her father sits down in a big chair opposite us. The room looks like something out of a magazine. All the furniture is this modern squared-off stuff, and there's about six lamps going and they're all aimed off in screwy, useless directions, you know, shining on the wall or on the ceiling or off into a corner. I'd never seen indirect lighting before, and even after I knew what it was, it never impressed me much. All I could think was, what a waste of lights; you couldn't read by any damn one of them. A big gray cat comes in, quiet as nothing, and jumps into my lap. I hate cats, and they always know it and come straight for me.

There's a real oil painting over the mantel, a pretty scene with some hills and clouds and a cow, and there's family pictures in frames sitting around all over the place, and I have a weird moment because I'm just glancing around and I see a picture of Dorothy Pliszka dressed like for her first Communion, and I go, hey, that doesn't make any sense. Why the hell should the Dłuwieckis have a picture of Dorothy Pliszka in their living room? And then I take another look, and of course it's not Dorothy, it's Janice. And I think, what's the matter with me? Am I an idiot or what?

There's a painting of Marshal Piłsudski, and I don't even know enough to know that's who it is. There's a Polish newspaper on the coffee table and about three or four issues of the *National Geographic*, and I'm thinking, yeah, Czesław Dłuwiecki is exactly the sort of guy you'd expect to subscribe to the *National Geographic.* He's tall and skinny with bushy eyebrows—did I tell you that? I mean really wonderful, steel gray, industrial-grade eyebrows with hairs sticking out everywhere in forty-seven different directions. He's wearing a sports jacket, and he's still got his tie on. He smokes a pipe. We're having this absolutely wacko conversation.

"*Bardzo miło że Janice tak często bywa u was na kolacji,*" he says.

"Oh, no problem. We enjoy having her."

"*A jak rodzice?*"

"Oh, they're fine. We're all fine. Pretty much, you know, the same as usual."

We go a few more rounds like that, with him speaking Polish and me answering him in English, and then he says, "You don't enjoy speaking Polish?" It was obvious, you know, that I was getting pretty much everything he was saying to me.

"With all due respect, Mr. Dłuwiecki," I said, "if I was to speak to you in Polish, you'd be spending all your time correcting my grammar, and we wouldn't have much of a conversation."

That must have been the funniest thing he'd heard in a year or two. When he quit chuckling about it, he asked me if I wanted a drink. A drink, huh? Well, maybe if you jerked my arm up behind my back and twisted it hard a couple times.

He didn't say a word to Perfect, but being perfect as she was, she got up and brought a silver tray with a crystal decanter and two tiny silver glasses about the size of thimbles. He poured us each a snort and it's *na zdrowie!* I don't know what it was, vodka or schnapps or some damn thing, but it must have been 140 proof—God knows, maybe 200—and my mood improved considerably. We shot the shit for a while—he'd switched over to English—and he offered me another one, and I just couldn't say no. He and Perfect walked me to the door, and he thanked me for stopping in and I thanked him for having me, and I staggered down the stairs and I was—well, I think the word you usually hear for this state is "reeling." But the funny thing about that firewater he drank is that an hour or so later I'd be perfectly fine.

So I took to stopping in to see good old Czesław Dłuwiecki on Tuesday nights, and the craziest damn thing happened—I got to like him. He'd always ask how my family was doing, and I'd say they were doing fine, and I'd ask him about his family, and they were always doing pretty good too, and then once we got that out of the way, we'd move on to the real important stuff like the conduct of the Vietnam War, the gutless nature of the administration in Washington, the sorry state of affairs in Europe, and the way the wind was blowing in the Vatican these days. Well, gee, Mr. Dłuwiecki, I'm not really up on the Pope's latest pronouncement; perhaps you could enlighten me? And while you're at it, sir, no, I wouldn't mind at all another thimbleful of kerosene. Yep, you just keep talking, sir, I'm all ears.

And so he'd tell me his opinion of where the Church was going, or the U.S. government, or the younger generation—pretty much all straight down the tube—and Perfect is sitting there watching us, not saying a word. She could have been the cat for all the attention he paid to her.

Poles love to argue. Somebody who's not Polish listening to them would think they were just about to jump up and start duking it out any minute, but no, they're just enjoying themselves. It's like that old joke—you put ten Polish guys in a room and get them talking politics, an hour later you'll have ten different political parties. So I'd give him all the stuff Georgie Mondrowski was saying, how we're never going to win the war and it's not worth another American life and we never should have gone over there in the first place and who gives a damn if Vietnam goes Commie anyway? And he'd say that godless Communism was the greatest evil ever to appear on earth—well, the Nazis were worse, but not by much—and it was our moral imperative to stop Communism wherever it reared its ugly head.

You talk about your old-country crap, well, Czesław was so deep in it he couldn't see daylight. It was a toss-up who he hated more, the Germans or the Russians, and there wasn't any bullshit about, oh, it's not the people, it's the governments—he hated Germans and Russians personally, right down to the last man, woman, or child. And there wasn't any forgive and forget now that the war's over—not only would he never consider buying a Volkswagen, he wouldn't even *ride* in one, and if a German person turned up anywhere he was, he walked out. He thought the carpet bombing of Dresden was delightful—it was just too bad they hadn't done more of it—and one of his main regrets about WW II was that it hadn't lasted long enough so the Americans could nuke out a few German cities.

Don't get me wrong here, I'm not putting him down. It's just that he did have, I guess you could say, real strong opinions. But I learned a lot from him. There's all these things you think you know something about but you don't, not really, and he filled in some of those blanks for me—like about the Warsaw Uprising and the Katyn Massacre and how FDR and Churchill, those *zdrajcy*, had sold out Poland at Yalta. Yeah, they'd just laid down and let Stalin wipe his shitty boots on them. And he also told me things I'd never heard about—like how the Polish Resistance had been the first to get the word out to the Allies about what the Germans were doing to the Jews—the greatest crime in the history of the world, he called it—and they even told them exactly where the railroad lines were, you know, running into the death camps, but the Allies couldn't be bothered to bomb them. He wasn't too pleased with the Allies, and he wasn't too pleased with the Vatican, and when you came right down to it, he wasn't too pleased with anybody.

The funny thing about listening to him talk was that when it came to the war, he'd only go so far and then he'd stop. He never said one word about what *he* was doing in the war, or about what the war did to his family, and if I asked him anything about it, he'd slip off onto some other topic.

He did tell me about his hometown before the war, Krajne Podlaski, and he made it sound like paradise. Nice and friendly, and everybody knew everybody. Big quiet river running by there; in the summer they fished in it, in the winter they skated on it. You'd go out in the country, and there'd be peasant cottages and those wonderful, dignified big white storks making their nests on the thatched roofs. I asked him if it was mainly a farm community, and he said, oh, no, there was lots of trade, even a certain amount of industry. They had a big town hall and a good library. Krajne Podlaski, he said, was maybe half the size of Raysburg. By West Virginia standards, that's a reasonable-sized town, and I guess it is by Polish standards too.

He was, he said, a rough-and-tumble little boy, always in trouble. He loved to go to the market where everybody was haggling over everything, trying to make a deal, with horses, cows, chickens, and geese running around—people laughing and talking a mile a minute in Polish and Yiddish. The market was mainly run by the Jews. They'd lived there for hundreds of years and had their own separate community, but they got along okay with the Poles, anyhow up until the Endeks—that's the Polish right wingers—started making trouble.

There were only a few doctors in Krajne Podlaski, and his father was one of them—the best one, he said—so they were pretty well off, but his wife's family, the Markowskis, were what's usually called "gentry" in English, but Czesław said that wasn't a good word for them because it makes you think of England, and Poland was nothing like England. The Markowskis had lived on their land forever, and they didn't have a lot of money but they had a lot of pride. His wife's father lived in town and engaged in business—he ran the distillery—so he was looked down on by the other Markowskis. Most of them lived out of town on their estates. They were the kind of folks that the girls were spoiled and beautiful and a little bit nuts, and the men went off and hunted wild boar in the huge dark forests of Poland—primeval forests, Czesław called them. He said there were still a few Polish partisans hiding out in those forests fighting the Soviets all the way into the 1950s.

He went to the Józef Piłsudski University. That's in Warsaw. Then the Germans came in and closed all the schools because the Poles were supposed to be slave labor for the Reich, and slaves don't need an education. He'd been studying modern languages. English was his favorite, and he'd memorized a whole bunch of speeches from Shakespeare. He recited a couple of them for me, "To be or not to be," and like that. He said if the war hadn't come along, he might have been a university professor.

When it came to the U.S. of A., Czesław was playing somewhere way out in right field, and he was always talking about the American *Republic*, and how, even though our freedoms were being rapidly eroded on all sides, it was still the greatest nation on earth. Where else could someone like himself accomplish everything he'd accomplished in such a short time? "The problem with these long-hair hippies or yippies," he'd say, "or whatever the hell they're calling themselves, is they don't want to work. There's no excuse for them. It's a matter of *character*. If a man is willing to work in America, there's nothing he can't accomplish."

Well, yeah, and it helps if you come from a well-off family back in Poland like he did, instead of, you know, being a peasant, and it helps if you've got a good education and speak good English. I figured if work is what we're talking about—like busting your sorry ass eighty-some hours a week at Raysburg Steel for chickenshit money and every day running the risk of getting turned into an ingot—then both my grandfathers could have taught him a thing or two. They'd had plenty of *character* all right, and where had that got them? But I kept my mouth shut. As much as he liked to argue, I didn't think he'd enjoy arguing that particular point with me.

So I slipped on through the fall in my little routine, and things weren't too bad, and the winter was starting to sneak in on us, and then something happened that flipped me around about Janice Dłuwiecki. One Tuesday night it was raining to beat hell—one of those icy, driving rains that blows damn near sideways—and she and Linda came back from the church looking like two drowned rats, and I figured I'd better get Perfect home before she melted.

Well, I'm driving up Highlight Road, and the rain's hammering the car like sixty-five fire hoses, and I'm creeping along at about thirty because I can't see dickshit and I've got Czesław Dłuwiecki's kid in my car. She says to me, "Are you scared?"

That pissed me off—almost everything she did pissed me off—so I kind of snapped at her, "No, honey, I'm not."

She says, "I can't see anything. Can you see anything?"

"Probably more than you can. The windshield wipers on your side are kind of shot," but then I'm thinking, hey, Koprowski, she's just a kid, and she doesn't know you very well. Maybe she's thinks she's riding that thin edge of death.

"Look, Janice," I said, "I've driven this road a thousand times, and we're going at a snail's pace, and if anybody's coming down, I'll see his headlights. Don't worry about a thing, okay?"

"Okay." Then after a minute, she says, "What scares you? What are you afraid of?"

Oh, God, I think, she's such a little kid. "I don't know," I say. "Dying before my time, I guess."

It was just a dumb thing we used to say in the service. Somebody would say, "Anything bothering you, Jimmy?" and you'd say, "Not a damn thing except dying before my time." And then it hit me that the guy who used to say that all the time was Ron Jacobson. Yeah, it was Jacobson's line.

"You don't have to be like that," she says. "I was just trying to get you to talk to me. You could be serious, you know."

All of a sudden I'm so mad at her I feel like squashing her like a bug. "Yeah?" I say. "Well, I am serious. The guy who used to say that all the time got killed in Vietnam."

Of course that stopped her. But after a minute she says, "I'm sorry. What happened to him?"

Well, the last thing in the world I want to do is tell her what happened to Jacobson. I should say something, but I'm so mad I can't think of a thing. We're up the hill by then, and I turn onto Edgewood.

"Oh, I give up," she says. "I know you don't like me. I don't know what I did, but I must have done something."

"You didn't do anything." And I'm thinking, oh, for Christ's sake, now I've hurt her feelings. Now I've got to try to fix things. I don't need this shit.

I was all set to tell her a whole bunch of lies—not big lies, just the little piss-ass lies you tell to somebody to make them feel better—like, oh, it's not that I don't like you, Janice, it's just that I've been kind of preoccupied, got a million things on my mind, or whatever the hell I was going to say. I don't know what I was going to say, but I turned and looked at her and I couldn't say any of it.

She had a way of looking straight at you that felt— It was, I guess, an honest way of looking at you. All of a sudden, I didn't want to be driving. I pulled over. "Aw, hell," I said, "I was pissed off because of you asking about Jacobson. I don't feel right talking about him."

It was still raining like crazy. I rolled the window down and lit a cigarette. It's funny, but saying that it didn't feel right talking about Jacobson, somehow that made it okay. So I told her about the night raid in Da Nang, about him and the other guys getting killed. Guys I'd been stationed with at Carswell. Jacobson getting his arm blown off, and part of his face, and hanging on till the next day.

I don't know why I told her any of that. I didn't really care what she thought about it. I wasn't looking for sympathy. I didn't expect anything from her. I didn't like her much, but I knew somehow she wasn't the kind of kid who'd say something stupid that would make me feel worse.

"How did you find out about it?" she asked me. That seemed like a pretty strange question, but I told her about getting the letter from Jeff Doren. "Yeah," I said, "he wrote me as soon as it happened. He knew I'd want to know what happened as soon as it happened."

"Was he right? Did you want to know how it happened?"

I didn't have a clue what she was getting at. "Well, sure. Of course I did."

"Why did you want to know?"

"Well, hell, Janice, what? You think ignorance is bliss? You've got to know. Don't you understand that? It wouldn't be right if you didn't know."

"It's not morbid to want to know?"

"Oh, Christ, no. Where do you get that morbid business? What the hell are you talking about?" I was getting mad at her all over again.

"My grandfather," she said, "my father's father—was tortured and killed by the Gestapo."

Now that's not a line you expect to hear dropped into casual conversation, you know what I mean? And it pretty well stopped me.

"I've asked my father a million times to tell me what happened," she said. "I wanted to know what my grandfather was doing, how he got caught. I wanted to know what they did to him—how he died. He won't tell me. He says, 'Janice, you're being morbid. You don't want to know these things.' Do you think I'm being morbid?"

"Oh, hell no."

"I don't want to think about it like it's some dumb old movie, you know, like 'Ve haff vays of making you talk.' I know it wasn't like that. But he won't tell me what it was really like."

That cold rain was really hammering my Chevy, blowing in my open window. We were parked at the end of her block. Big houses on big lots, and trees all up and down the street, bending in wind, most of their leaves gone, and I remember how dark the sky was and how cheery the lights in the houses looked against that sky, and us out on the street in my car in the dark. I don't think we would've had that conversation if it'd been a nice sunny afternoon, you know what I mean?

She must have wanted to talk about this with somebody for a long time. The words were just pouring out of her. "As long as I can remember, my dad's always said to me, 'Thank God, Janice, you'll never know what it was like. You'll never have to see what we saw. You'll never have to do what we did.' And then other times, it's not 'thank God,' it's like he's angry with me—furious with me—because I got out of it. Because I didn't have to live through it.

"He was in the Home Army," she said, "and Mom was in a labor camp. We've always known that, but they won't tell us anything about it. We have relatives in Poland, but he won't even tell us their names. He gets letters from Poland, but we're not allowed to see them. We get letters from England too, and sometimes we even get letters from Israel. Why on earth would we be getting letters from Israel? It's got to be something to do with the war, but he gets mad if you even ask him about it. 'Janice,' he says, 'thank God you'll never know what it was like.' Over and over and over he says that. But I *want* to know what it was like. Don't I have a right to know?

"'Janice,' he says, 'you're an ordinary American girl.' Well, that's just crazy. How on earth does he think I could possibly be an ordinary American girl? He made us all learn Polish. We had to study it just like we were in school. We read to each other in Polish every Sunday night. Mark and I used to play Polish Resistance and pretend we were hiding from the Germans. That's an ordinary American childhood? 'Be happy,' my dad says. 'You have all the advantages. You have everything we didn't have.'

"You know what my older brother said? Johnny. He was born in a DP camp in Germany. The last time he came home, he kept trying to get Dad to tell him about the war, and Dad just kept getting madder and madder until they were yelling at each other. John said, 'This house has too many damn secrets in it,' and he just stormed out and drove back down to Columbus. He hasn't been back since."

So Janice and I sat there and talked for—oh, I guess it must have been over an hour. It was really intense. There's nobody in the world more intense than a fifteen-year-old girl. Well, one thing led to another, and I ended up telling her about the Red Alert when I was stationed down at Carswell. I hadn't told that story to anybody before. I don't know why I'd never told it to anybody before.

"I'm driving onto base," I say, "and they're just shoving those B-52s up as fast as they can get them airborne—faWOOM, faWOOM, faWOOM—and I say, 'Hey, what's going on?' and it's a Red Alert, and that's nuclear war."

The way they'd run tests before went like this. The klaxon sounded, and they told you, "Now you're on alert," and then they'd time you—like how quick you could report to the aircraft—but when they were running those tests, they never even fired up the aircraft. I was part of what they called "Leapfrog Mobility," and the tests were to check out our response time in case of nuclear war. But this time it was different. There was no klaxon. Nobody said it was a test. We jumped on board the aircraft, and they fired it up and away we went. We thought it was for real.

"So the first thing you've got is this crazy euphoria, like, hey, wow, we did it. Because we'd got off the ground ahead of the incoming missiles. And then it starts to sink in. Oh. Christ. Where are the nukes coming down? I knew the Russians would hit the valley, you know, because of the steel mills."

"Mother of God," she says, whispering it.

"So anyhow, they sent us to Goose Bay, Labrador. The next thing we're worrying about is what we're going to find on the ground when we get there. Like is anybody going to be there to meet us, or has it been nuked out? Will we even be able to land? Well, we get to Goose Bay, and they say, 'Surprise, it was all a test. You guys did real good.'"

"Oh, you must have been so scared," she says.

"Well, yeah, what do you think?" And then it dawned on me that I'd just answered the question she'd asked me driving up the hill. I'd forgot all about it.

"I'm really afraid," she said. "You know Our Lady of Fatima? The Third Secret. I'm really afraid of what it could be."

"What? You think it's nuclear war?"

She just nodded.

"Yeah," I said, "it gets kind of depressing if you think about it too much.

Sitting there on that flight to Goose Bay— You try to imagine what the world's going to be like. And you know that your life, whatever happens, the most you can hope for— Well, whatever happens, you know it's going to be fairly grim. It's not something you can come back from. Do you understand what I'm telling you? You're just not the same person after that."

We probably could have kept on talking for a couple more hours, but then suddenly it hits me, hey, we're late. I'm looking at my watch, going, "Oh, my God, we've got to get you home."

Czesław jumps on us the minute we walk through the door. He looks mad enough to spit carpet tacks. "Where have you been?" he yells at Janice in Polish. Her mom's right behind him, and she's going, "Oh, we've been worried sick."

It was the first time I met her mother and her brother Mark—I mean other than just seeing them, you know, at Mass. Janice's parents are falling all over us, and Mark's kind of standing there in the background trying to keep them calmed down. They'd imagined us going off the road in the rain and laying dead at the bottom of Highlight Road somewhere. Janice flips instantly into Polish, telling them that we've been sitting in my car talking about my experiences in the war effort, which I guess we have.

"If you want to talk," Czesław yells at Janice, "you come home and talk. Never, never, never do something like this again." And of course she's going, "I'm sorry, I'm sorry, I'm sorry. I didn't know how late it was."

Well, you would've thought we'd been standing out in the rain all that time, not sitting in a car. We've got to huddle up by the fire, and I get to knock back a couple shots of paint thinner, and I'm doing my best to blend right into the woodwork—you know, sitting there watching it all go down.

Janice's brother Mark looks just like his dad, only smaller and younger. Tall and thin, dark curly hair cut real short because he goes to the Academy. Big Adam's apple sticking out, black-framed glasses—yeah, he looks like somebody who gets straight A's. But Janice's mom was the one that really got me. She was a lot more dressed up than you'd expect for somebody just staying home on a Tuesday night. She had a skirt and sweater on, dark colors, and high heels. Not the tacky kind, the expensive kind. I'd seen her in church lots of times and wondered who she was, because—well, the point I'm trying to make here is, she didn't look like somebody's mom.

She was a paler blond than Janice, and she had these wide-spaced, light blue eyes. She wasn't tall, but for a minute you thought she was, because she stood straight as a plumb bob. Even when she sat down, her back was perfectly straight. She had to be in her forties, but— Well, it wasn't like she looked a lot younger than that; she was the kind of woman, it's hard to guess her age. She was the kind of woman you'd turn around and stare at on the street as she goes sailing by not giving you a glance. When she was a girl back in Poland, she must have knocked all the boys dead within a radius of about ten miles.

Looking at her parents, I can see how their genes went together to make Janice. She got the best of both of them. Janice was a head taller than her mom and skinny as a peeled stick, so she'd got that from her dad—and his dark blue eyes. From her mom she'd got the blond hair and something else. I don't quite know how to—Well, let's say you were in a room with one of them, and they weren't saying anything or even doing much of anything, you'd still always know they were there.

I was nervous as all hell because I was the one, you know, who'd screwed up and didn't get Janice home on time, and my Polish sure wasn't good enough to jump into their conversation, and then it's like Mrs. Dłuwiecki was reading my mind because she switches into English and says, "Oh, how impolite of us. You must feel terribly excluded."

I'd been thinking that maybe they'd been speaking Polish because her English wasn't too good, but I gave up that idea pretty quick. "No, problem," I say. "I can pretty well follow everything."

So she launches in, saying all these polite things to make me feel like a welcome visitor in their home and not some totally irresponsible jerk—like how nice of us to have Janice over on Tuesday nights and how kind of me to drive her home and apologizing for all the fuss they made when we came in. "You must think we're terribly strict with Janusia," she says, "but we just want to know she's safe. Every time you open the paper, you read about such terrible things that can happen to people."

SEVEN

You ever do a 180-degree flip on somebody you didn't like and end up liking them a lot? Well, that's what happened with Janice. After that night in the car, I stopped thinking of her as Perfect, and we got to be pretty relaxed with each other, and I looked forward to our little bit of time alone together on Tuesdays. Sometimes I'd turn onto Edgewood and park in the spot where we'd been that night in the rain, and we'd sit there for a few minutes more and try to wrap up our conversation, but I was always careful to get her home on time. After a while we got so we were doing, I guess you could say, a once-a-week debriefing on each other's life. It was nice. It was like having another little sister.

Most of what I'd thought about her turned out to be dead wrong. She may have looked like a little goody-two-shoes, but she wasn't like that at all. I'd figured her for an honors student, but she was kind of mediocre in school. She did as little as she could get away with, so if her little bit got her an A, like it did in English, that was okay, but if her little bit only got her a C+, like it did in math, that was okay too. She liked playing her clarinet and hanging out with her girlfriends and sitting alone in her room reading books that had nothing at all to do with her schoolwork. She felt like she was attached to St. Stanislaus Parish, but she didn't feel very attached to Raysburg Central Catholic. Most of what went on at Central she thought was totally ridiculous.

Naturally she talked a lot about her family. She was real fond of her older brother, John. The year he left home and went off to Columbus, she was going into the fourth grade, and she cried for days. She thought she was a lot like him. "We both know our own minds," she said, "and we're both stubborn like our dad." John always treated her with respect even when she'd been a tiny little girl, and she never forgot it. "It's probably because of John," she said, "that I feel so comfortable with older boys."

Her brother Mark she got along with okay, but she didn't have too much in common with him. He was top of his class at the Academy, sang in the glee club, collected stamps, studied books on chess moves, and basically did a bunch of uncool stuff like that, and he hung out with the other uncool guys in his class, and he brought them home for dinner. Janice's mom kept telling her she should go out with them—because they were Academy boys, you know, from out the pike—but Janice thought they were all hopeless. "I'm a big disappointment to Mom," she said.

To Mrs. Dłuwiecki, everything that was good and true and beautiful was Poland before the war. She went on and on about the beautiful china and crystal and silver her family used to have, and all the oil paintings that'd been in the family for generations. She remembered all the fancy outfits she'd ever worn, and she described them to Janice down to the finest detail. She even remembered things like her white veil and her little white shoes from her first Communion that she'd saved in a special wooden box, and the little silver scissors her mother had used to cut the roses—and all that beautiful stuff was gone, lost, plundered by the Germans. She didn't even have any photographs from those days. She said she'd lost her precious heritage and all she had left was memory.

The main person Janice talked about was her dad. He was a strict old-fashioned papa straight from the old country, a real tyrant. All the time they were growing up, the kids had Polish lessons with the old man, and if they didn't get their work done, all hell broke loose. On Sunday nights they read out loud to each other from the great works of Polish literature, and if they mispronounced anything, old Czesław was on them like a shot. But he cut Janice a lot of slack because she was a girl—his darling daughter—and she could usually get him laughing. Her brothers he rode day and night.

Her dad liked things real quiet—well, saying that doesn't give you the full horror of it. He was totally looney tunes, whacked out of his skull, bananas about noise, and the minute he walked through the door, unearthly silence descended. He took the phone off the hook. Nobody could play the radio or the TV. Everybody tiptoed around the house in their stocking feet and talked in whispers.

You couldn't wash dishes after he got home because the sound of the plates banging together in the sink bothered him. If you were going to sneeze, you ran into the bathroom to do it. If you were doing your homework, you had to make sure your bedroom door was shut because the sound of a pencil scratching on paper bothered him. Flies buzzing bothered him. The locusts in the trees bothered him. The cat walking across the carpet bothered him. Her parents' bedroom had double-pane glass on the windows and like forty-seven layers of drapes, and still her dad would wake up in the middle of the night if a dog barked six blocks away.

Now you'd think a man like that, the last thing in the world he'd want would be for his kids to play musical instruments, right? Wrong. Good old Czesław was determined that there was going to be music in his house, and by music he meant Mozart and Beethoven and Chopin and all that other good shit. He was big on culture, and he had a huge stereo in the living room, and he was the only one who was allowed to play it, and somehow the sound of that didn't bother him at all, and he'd sit there with a big smile on his face with the damn thing cranked up to the last notch. "If I never hear *Eine Kleine Nachtmusik* again," Janice said, "it'll be too soon."

Both the boys had violin lessons. To this day her brothers would rather drink carbolic acid than listen to classical music on the violin. Janice came along, and she was supposed to play the violin too. She was in the fifth grade at St. Stans, and Sister Angelica told her dad she was gifted, so he figured he better get her a fiddle and get her started.

"Dad," she said, "please let me play the clarinet so when I go to high school I can get into the band and just for once be like all the other kids." He thought that over and said okay, and she about dropped dead of surprise. He took her down to Kaltenbach's and bought her the best clarinet in the store, and the minute she got her hands on it, you couldn't pry it loose from her.

"I don't know why I loved it so much," she said. She loved everything about it—the shiny keys, the black wood, the way it felt when she held it, and after she stopped squawking, she even started to like the sounds she made. "I don't want to sound conceited or anything, but I knew I was going to be good. I knew it was something I could do better than the other kids."

She took lessons with the old lady at Kaltenbach's, and Janice would always say, "Could you play it over for me, please, so I can get the hang of it?" and the old lady would play it a few times on the piano, and Janice would memorize it right there on the spot and come back the next week and pretend she was reading the music. The old lady kept giving her harder and harder pieces. Sometimes Janice wouldn't remember exactly how it went, and she'd make it up, and the old lady would sigh and say, "That's very pretty, Janice, but that's not what's written here."

Janice got bored with the pieces from the old lady and spent all her time playing along with whatever was on the radio. "That's how I learned a lot of new keys," she said.

Eventually the old lady said, "I don't know what to do with you, Janice. You'll be going up to Central, won't you? I think you'd better take some lessons from Mr. Webb."

Well, Mr. Webb didn't know what to do with her either, so he started lending her jazz records. "That was wonderful," she said. "I could play them over as many times as I wanted." She memorized a whole bunch of jazz tunes. That's when she was in the eighth grade.

Her freshman year at Central, Mr. Webb put her right into the senior band. The band music was really easy, "baby stuff," she said, and she could play any of it just so long as she got to hear it first. Halfway through the year, Mr. Webb called her into his office. "He started out trying to be calm," she said, "but he got all worked up. He got so mad at me he broke a pencil."

She was misusing her God-given talents, he said. He'd been teaching music for twenty years, and he'd never seen anybody with the gift she had. "Janice," he yelled at her, "you can't go on like this. *You've got to learn to read music!*"

It was a year later and she still couldn't read music. "I keep trying," she said, "and I still feel guilty. But it's just so boring."

So how do you practice the clarinet in Czesław Dłuwiecki's house of silence? Well, most nights he worked late. After he got home, Janice would carry her clarinet and her little record player down into the storage room back of the furnace in the basement. She'd shut every door there was. He could still hear her, but he'd put up with it for as long as he could because she was his little musical genius, so if she was lucky, she could play a couple hours before her dad would send her brother down to tell her please to stop because that faint bit of music was coming up through the floorboards and driving him nuts.

Janice had a good sense of humor about her father. She could do his voice in both Polish and English, and she had him down to a T—the way he waved his hands in the air, the way his eyes bugged out when he got pissed off.

"What's he going to do when he finds out you're playing in a polka band?" I said.

"Oh, he's not going to like it one little bit. I know exactly what he's going to say. 'Those people'—he means everybody in South Raysburg—'Those people don't have a real culture. It's a degenerate peasant culture.'"

I had to laugh at that. "Degenerate, huh?"

"That's right. *Zdegenerowana*. Well, I don't care what he says, it's *my* music."

The first thing Linda gave Janice to learn was "The Clarinet Polka." Linda lent her about a dozen different versions of that tune—a whole bunch of records and even some tapes so Janice could hear the way they'd played it back in the Second Ice Age—and by the time Janice listened to all those versions about a million times and learned to play it her way, she was hooked but good on polka music. It wasn't just something fun to play like New Orleans jazz, it was *her* music. "Maybe it's in my blood, I don't know. I thought, oh, now I know why I've been playing the clarinet. I was born to play this stuff."

The way I was going, I could have drifted along for God knows how long, thinking, hey, this may not be great but it's not that bad either. If I'd had a girlfriend, maybe I could have gone along like that for years, you know what I mean? Working for Vick, going home for dinner most nights, talking to Linda about her polka band, driving Janice around and having our little talks, knocking back a few with Georgie in the PAC. It was a strange time. I wasn't drinking much more than what seemed reasonable, and whatever was bothering me, I'd got real good at putting it out of my mind. I was sitting in deep neutral, and when I came out of it, I could have gone a lot of different directions. I still kept thinking, okay, Koprowski, one of these days, you're going to Austin.

Then—well, it was sometime in December. I remember I was worrying about my Christmas shopping. It was one of those nights when the Ohio Valley looks like shit. Bitterly cold, lots of air pollution, muddy gray sky, dirty old snow frozen onto the sidewalks, everybody saying, "Jesus, if it snows tonight, the road's going to be a nightmare." It was a Wednesday night. You'll see in a minute why I remember that.

I did the usual when I got off work, popped into the Greek's for a quick one. I forget what was going on at home; maybe Mom was doing something with the sodality, I don't know, but anyhow dinner wasn't happening, so I ordered lamb souvlaki to go. The funny thing is that I was feeling pretty good. I was looking forward to getting out of the cold and curling up in my little bed in my trailer and sipping at a fifth and eating my Greek dinner and watching TV and basically just dialing out on the world. You don't expect somebody to be in your car, right? You just open the door and get in, right? Connie was sitting in the passenger seat.

I jumped back out of the car like somebody had shot me. She was just sitting there reading a book. "Yeah, it's me," she said, "the bad penny."

I could still feel the adrenaline. I yelled at her, "Get the hell out of my car."

She got out, and we stood there looking at each other. "Scare the bat piss out of me, why don't you?" I said, or something like that, and she said she was sorry. She was all in black leather—black coat and black boots up to her knees and black gloves and even a black leather beret. She looked like an ad for something.

"I'm sorry I broke our date," she said.

"Well, shit, honey, that's all right. No problem. It's only been three or four months since then, but what's a little time between friends?"

"Don't give me that, Jim. I called you. I called you *twice*. You hung up on me. You were terrible."

"Yeah, I guess I was. It's true."

"If you want me to go away, just say so."

It's totally ridiculous sometimes why you do what you do. I'd paid five bucks for the souvlaki dinner, and I was standing there with the bag in my hand, and it was getting cold. "Look," I said, "I got a trailer over back of Raysburg Hill."

She got her car and followed me. I parked where I always did, and she parked across the road. It was starting to snow, but not much. I watched her walk across the road. She looked good in black. We went in my trailer. She took her coat off, and she was wearing a black leather minidress. Quality leather, that soft, ungodly expensive stuff that feels almost, you know, buttery. "Is there any heat in here?" she said. "I'm half frozen."

"You want some Greek food?" I said. Turned out—surprise—all she wanted was a drink. I poured her a shot of Jack Daniel's and she downed it. "You mind if I eat?" I said.

"Oh, heavens no. Go ahead."

I had a good heater in there. Little forced-air oil furnace. I fired it up, but she still couldn't get warm. She kept her gloves on. Dress gloves. The real tight kind. "I've turned thirty," she said, "so I guess you can't trust me anymore."

A lot of things I could have said to that, but I didn't. I looked at her, and I thought, hell, kid, if a man was into leather, he'd be creaming his jeans by now. I won't lie to you and try to say I wasn't enjoying the show, but at the same time something didn't feel right about Connie being in my trailer. Other than me and the landlord, the only people who'd set foot in my trailer were George and my sister, and I'd just as soon have kept it that way. I didn't like it that Connie even knew where I was living.

"I owe you an explanation," she said. "Do you want to hear it?"

Of course I wanted to hear it. Wouldn't you?

"Well, you remember what a mess I was?" she said. "I'd been drinking since about two in the afternoon. And you remember how late I got home? All

I wanted to do was sleep. I wanted to sleep all day. At eight in the morning the phone started ringing, and it wouldn't stop. It rang over twenty times. I finally picked it up. He was calling me from Baltimore. He'd had a nice long chat with Tommy, man to man, and—well, Daddy explained to Tommy that when Mommy talked about keeping secrets, she hadn't meant keeping secrets *from Daddy*. So Tommy told Daddy all about the funny man that Mommy had met in the record store and about how he'd got to play the games in the penny arcade."

You can imagine my delight at hearing that. She was talking in her I-could-care-less voice, and every once in a while she'd give me her weird creepy little smile—like, get the joke? Now if you give me half a chance, usually I can get the joke, but I sure wasn't getting this one.

"I threw some things in a suitcase," she said, "and I caught the next plane to Baltimore. We left the kids with his mother and checked into a hotel. I was terrified. I was sure my whole world was going to come crashing down around my ears. We talked for two days nonstop. I agreed to everything.

"I told him about you," she said, "but not really you. I wouldn't tell him your name. That's the only thing I wouldn't give in on. That was not negotiable. I told him you were an insurance salesman—married, in serious trouble with your marriage. I told him you had two kids. I told him we mainly sat around together and drank and I listened to your sad tale of woe. I knew he'd never believe I hadn't been to bed with you, so I told him we'd done it once—a quickie in a cheap hotel room. I said we'd both been so nervous it hadn't been very good. I said I hadn't felt much of anything. I said I felt sorry for you.

"He told me that if we were headed for the divorce court, he had no intention of being nice about it. He said I could be as free as I wanted just so long as I didn't sleep with other men. That was *his* non-negotiable demand, and he had no intention of budging on it. But anything else was okay.

"So I agreed to give our marriage another try, to really work at it this time. I said I'd never see you again. I said I'd never sleep with another man again. He said he'd cut back his hours and spend more time with the family. He agreed that as soon as he could, he'd try to open a practice in Baltimore so we could get out of this godforsaken hole. He said I'd been drinking too much, that he was worried about me, so I agreed to cut back.

"As part of my new life, I'm taking a night course at Raysburg College. It's on Wednesday nights. That's where I am right now. He didn't want me to go out tonight, but I said I'd be careful. I said I'd come home at the first snowflake.

"Because I slept with another man once, I seem to be damaged goods. Or tainted. Or something. At any rate, he seems to be having some difficulty touch-

ing me. I'm to give him time so he can get over the deep hurt I've done to him
and trust me again. So I'm currently living in a state of celibacy—"

"Chastity," I said. I don't know what made me say it.

"What?"

"Celibacy's when you can't marry. Like a priest or a nun. Chastity's when
you're not getting any." See what a Catholic education can do for you?

"You're right, Jim," she said, "you're absolutely right. Yes, chastity is certainly the correct word for it."

Okay, and while we're considering the correct words for things, I guess the
word you often hear used for this kind of shit is "inevitable." We're laying there
afterward, and I'm smoking a cigarette, and she's pretending to smoke a cigarette, and she says, "Where's your phone?"

"Phone?" I go. "What phone? Who needs a phone?"

"*We* need a phone. Get one, okay?"

"Yes, boss."

"I mean it."

"I know you mean it."

"You do want to see me again, don't you, Jim?"

Now what the hell do you think I said to that? Well, she couldn't see me
again till after Christmas. She only had one more class before the end of the
term, and she figured she'd better go to it, but she'd call me in the new year.
Was that okay? Oh, you bet, honey.

For the longest damn time, the way I told this story to myself was that I was
doing just fine till Connie came along and screwed my life up, but that's just
bullshit, right? You look back years later, and most of what you did, honest to
God, you can't imagine doing much different because you were just stumbling
along from one thing to another and doing the best you could and you didn't
know shit from Shinola. But there's bound to be a few times when things were
clear, and that night in December 1969 was one of them. As a matter of fact, it
couldn't have been any clearer if somebody had slapped up a road sign. You
want to know the truth of the matter? Okay, I'll tell you the truth of the matter.
I knew that getting involved with Connie again was the wrong thing to do, and
I went ahead and did it anyway.

On Christmas Eve we have a special supper with no meat. It's called *Wigilia*,
and for the older generation it's more important than anything on Christmas
Day. We've always had the same relatives over for as long as I can remember. A

few times when we were little kids, Auntie Jean came from Chicago with her family, and that was a big deal, but usually it was my dad's brother Stas and his wife, Eva, and Mom's two older sisters, Aunt Helen and Aunt Stella, and their husbands, and we always had their kids, our cousins, and then when they started having kids, we had a whole bunch of little kids for a while. And Babcia Wojtkiewicz was there, so we had four generations at one table.

But over the years our cousins started moving out of town. It was a matter of going where you could find work, and there wasn't much in the valley unless you wanted to try to get on at Raysburg Steel or Sylvania or one of the chemical plants—and jobs were always tight even when there were jobs. And the last of our cousins had moved away just that past summer, out to California. So you see, the exodus was well under way by then, and when the steel industry went belly-up in the eighties, that really put the old quietus to it. Linda and I've got cousins scattered all over the States, so there's a whole fourth generation of kids who won't have any memory at all of what the old Polish community in South Raysburg was like.

Well, that night—Christmas '69—was the first time anybody could remember when there weren't any kids at *Wigilia*, and everybody thought that was strange and sad. The men had taken over the living room, and my uncles were having themselves a snort of vodka and yanking my father's chain about him not drinking the way they always did, and he was saying what he always said, "You guys have one for me." The damn dentist Linda worked for had let her off early, but she'd just got home, and she and I didn't have anywhere to fit, so we're kind of in the way—just hovering around the kitchen door smelling all that great food—and our kitchen is not exactly spacious, and there's Babcia and Mom and our aunts in there trying to get things ready, and they just want us out of their hair.

"Go watch for the star," Babcia says to us. That's a joke, right? Back in Poland you couldn't eat dinner until you'd seen the first star, but we'd never observed that custom for the simple reason that if you're waiting to see a star on Christmas Eve in Raysburg, West Virginia, you might end up standing there till April.

So Linda and I go outside just like we're kids again. It's one of those pissy nowhere days you get in the valley around Christmas—not cold enough to snow but not warm enough to be pleasant either. When we were little, we'd always get sent out to look for the star, and most of the time we'd never see one, but we'd always pretend we did. It's getting dark, and there's nothing to see in the sky but a big gray glop.

I've got a pint in my coat pocket, so I take a snort, offer her one. She shakes her head. She's been fasting all day just like we were living back in the old country in the olden days. "Linny," I say, "you're crazier than a bedbug, you know that."

We keep pacing up and down in front of the house, peering up into the sky just like we might really see a star. I know perfectly well we won't. "How are you doing, Jimmy?" she asks me. "I mean, really. Are you doing okay?"

"Aw, hell, I don't know. I'm not half bad. Yeah, I'm all right."

"You were so miserable when you first came home."

I don't know what to say to that. "Yeah, I guess I was."

I may not have been fasting like my nutty sister, but that doesn't mean I'm not hungry. I'm about ready to eat the paint off the walls. So I have another snort. "You're drinking too much," my sister says.

My first reaction is to get pissed off, but then I think, what the hell, it's Linda. "You know, kid," I say, "the same thought has passed through my mind on more than one occasion."

"I'm not sure there's enough for you here," she says. She means the valley.

I'm not sure about that one either, but I do know that if we continue exploring these topics much further, we're going to end up plunged into the deep gloom, which is where you don't want to be on Christmas Eve. Then all of a sudden Linda says, "Oh, Jimmy, look!"

A bit of that gray glop's torn apart, and right in the hole is a little star. Of course a star would come out for Linda. So we go running into the house like a couple little kids, yelling, "Hey, we saw a star. Honest to God, for real. Let's eat."

With all our aunts and uncles there, there's a lot of Polish being spoken. Babcia says that back in the old country, we'd all kneel down and pray now, but nobody takes her up on it; Old Bullet Head saying his little grace is the most she's going to get. She says the same things she says every year. Back in the old country, we'd have straw under the tablecloth to remind us of the manger where the Christ child was laid, and we'd have thirteen different courses, and we'd be doing this, and we'd be doing that, and we'd be doing the other. *"Co kraj, to obyczaj,"* Uncle Stas says, and that's the Polish version of "When in Rome—"

Well, we may be in Rome, but we've set an extra plate for the stranger that might turn up at our door, and we've got an odd number of dishes and an even number of people, because, by God, that's the way it's got to be, and when we sit down, all of us check to make sure we can see our shadows because if you can't see your shadow when you're seated at the table on Christmas Eve, you'll get real sick or even die during the year.

Now the big deal at *Wigilia* is the breaking of the *opłatek* with the members of your family. *Opłatki* are wafers, sort of like Communion wafers but rectangular, about the size of business envelopes, with a Nativity scene on them, and here Babcia is going to have her way. "Władysław," she says, "you break the *opłatek* with your son. Jimmy, you break it with your father." You see, in order to break the wafer with anybody, you have to forgive them whatever bad they've done to you in the last year, and Babcia had managed to notice a certain tension between me and the old man—although we have been getting along pretty good lately. So I break the wafer with my father, and I say the thing you're supposed to say, *"Wszystkiego najlepszego."*

He says, "Aw, Jimmy, you're not a bad kid." From Old Bullet Head, that's as good as it gets.

It was a pretty jolly dinner once we got into it. *Wigilia* is your classic time for *pierogi*. If all you know about *pierogi* is that crap you get frozen in the supermarket, then forget it. Real *pierogi* are rolled out by hand by Polish ladies and stuffed with anything you can think of that's not meat—try the sauerkraut, that's my favorite. Yeah, throw a little butter on, a little sour cream, but lay off the salt, they're salty enough to start with. And naturally you've got your fish— pickled herring and something cooked. Mom always liked halibut. And you've got your *barszcz* and your dumplings and your stewed prunes, and you always finish up with a big poppy-seed cake.

Our aunts kept teasing me and Linda about how we should be supplying the next round of kids. When they're talking to us, they switch into English. "What's the matter with the two of you?" Aunt Stella says. "You're not even married yet."

"I don't know about Jimmy," Linda says, "but I've joined the Holy Virgins of Mary."

"Holy Virgins, my ass," Aunt Stella says.

"I heard she was dating that Mondrowski kid," Aunt Helen says.

"Who?" Aunt Stella says. "Frank Mondrowski's kid? The one that was in the service? What's with him anyways? He forget where the barber shop is?"

"There's nothing going on with me and Georgie Mondrowski," Linda says.

"Yeah, that's right," my mother says. "They're not dating. That's what they tell me anyway. They're just hanging out."

"Hanging out?" Aunt Stella says.

"What's the matter with you, Stell?" my mother says. "Aren't you with it? Kids don't date anymore. They hang out. You know, like two T-shirts on a clothesline."

"Oh, Mom!" Linda says.

While all this has been going on, Old Bullet Head and my uncles have been having their own conversation, muttering along about how shitty the economy is in the valley these days or some damn thing, but now my father says, "What the hell are you girls talking about?"

"These two," Aunt Stella says, "the next generation."

So our aunts start coming up with suggestions on who Linda and me can go out with. Most of their ideas are totally ridiculous, and for some reason it's annoying the hell out of me and I just wish they'd shut up.

Uncle Stas decides to put his two cents in. "Aw, let them alone," he says. "She's just a baby, and he's just got out of the service. He wants to batch it a while yet."

"Yeah, goina be a while before that one's husband material," Old Bullet Head says, jerking his thumb at me.

"To hell with that," Aunt Helen says. "A guy's got to settle down some-time."

"It ain't just guys," Aunt Eva says, giving Linda the look.

They just wouldn't let the topic alone, and I was getting fairly pissed off—like I had no sense of humor about it at all. I hated to admit it, but it was true—no girl with half a brain would take me for husband material. Which was kind of a bummer because sometimes the only thing I thought I really wanted was to be married—you know, to some nice girl like Dorothy Pliszka—and just be living an ordinary life with the rest of the fools.

At some point, one of our aunts translates the gist of the conversation for Babcia, and she gets a good laugh out of it. "I'd like to see some more great-grandchildren," she says in Polish.

"There you go, kids," Aunt Helen yells at us. "You heard what your grandma said. Go forth and multiply!"

Ordinarily after dinner we'd light the Christmas tree and open our pres-ents, but seeing as there's no little kids this year, we haven't got a tree, and we've decided to do the presents tomorrow when we turn back into Americans and have our turkey dinner. But you always go to midnight Mass on Christmas Eve—that's what we call *pasterka*—and if you're at all close to the church, you walk there. Even old folks like Babcia. The old people always walked every-where as long as they could, which is probably one of the reasons they lived as long as they did.

Linda's gone on ahead of us because she's in the choir, and the rest of us go outside and make this procession down the street, and everywhere you look there's everybody else on their way to the church. It's like the whole world's turned out, and the closer you get to the church, there's more people, wishing each other a Merry Christmas, waving, stopping to chat. I always loved this part of Christmas Eve when I was a kid—seeing everybody, all the neighbors walking to St. Stans—and I think, hey, this is nice, this is really nice.

We intersect the Mondrowskis walking down from Jacob Street, and Georgie gives me a big bear hug, lifts me right off the ground, and I see Old Bullet Head checking out all Georgie's hair, and I can read his mind. He's thinking, well, I guess he's allowed to be nuts; he was in Vietnam. And then from the other direction here comes Dorothy Pliszka with her husband and her kid and her parents and her in-laws. Of course I'd have to see her, and I get hit with the same little pang in the pit of my stomach I always get. She's wearing one of those Jackie Kennedy outfits, and she looks like a million bucks. She gives me this dumb wave like you'd give your uncle Bob from Buffalo, and I'm thinking the same thing I always think—am I going to go through the rest of my life feeling like shit every time I run into Dorothy? We're right in front of St. Stans by then, and the church bell rings twice, and that means we've got fifteen minutes till Mass.

Czesław Dłuwiecki pulls up in his big blue Buick. Everything that everybody holds against him, they're still holding against him—he thinks he's better than us, is what it boils down to. And so everybody has got to be just as polite to him as possible. His wife gets out of the car, and then Mark, and then Janice. She's wearing her hair down. I can see why she wears it in pigtails most of the time because it's so long she could almost sit on it, this big curtain of blond hair hanging down over her coat.

We get into the church and the people clump up at the end of the aisles—genuflecting and crossing themselves—and I'm standing there waiting with Mom and Old Bullet Head to get into the pew, and Janice is right in front of us. She gives us a nice warm smile. She's taken her coat off, and she's wearing a velvet dress, a blue that's so dark it's almost black, and— Well, okay, so the thing for the teenyboppers back in those days was trying to look like little kids—even a lot of grown-up women tried it, and they usually looked totally ridiculous if you ask me—but with a girl like Janice, it just— Okay, so Janice has on this beautiful velvet dress, and the skirt's about a foot above her knees, and white tights and little-girl shoes—you know, black patent leather—and the only figure she's got is two faint bumps under her dress, and she doesn't look like Twiggy or somebody like that, she looks like she really *is* a little kid. And she's cute and all, but she's not ten, she's fifteen, and it kind of bothers me, you know what I mean? Shouldn't she be dressing a little older? What boy is going to want to take her out?

The Dłuwieckis sat in the pew right in front of us, and I kept looking at Janice's hair. When you keep long hair braided in pigtails, it makes these tight tiny waves all the way down. It didn't look real. It looked like something made out of gold. "She looks just like a little angel, doesn't she?" my mother said. Of course my mother would say that, but it was true. Janice did look like one of the angels they had down in front of the altar.

The church was packed, and I knew everybody—maybe not all their names, but I knew all their faces. I hadn't been to Mass at St. Stans for a couple years— not since I'd been home on leave when I was stationed down at Carswell—and I was wondering if Father Obinski was going to be okay. He'd been there three years, but everybody was still calling him "the new priest." Well, he was just fine. He did half his sermon in English, half in Polish, to try to make it meaningful for everybody, Linda said. She was a real fan of his and always defended him because the old folks in the parish thought it was a crime that there was any English at all. "This is a national parish," they said. "If you want to hear English, you can go to St. Mary's."

Father Obinski spoke that educated Polish, but he went slow and kept it simple so everybody who knew any Polish at all could follow him. They'd got together a big choir, and we sang the old Polish hymns I've known my whole life like *"Dzisiaj w Betlejem."* I'd been worried about taking Communion because I hadn't been to confession—I had no intention of going to confession—but I didn't want to make a spectacle of myself by not taking Communion, you know what I mean? I'd talked it over with Linda, and she'd said, "Look, Jimmy, there's a confession in the Mass." It's that part of the Mass you call in Latin the *Confiteor.* "You don't need to make your confession to a priest."

Well, I was pretty sure that old Father Joe wouldn't have looked at it quite like that, but if anybody knew the way the winds were blowing at the Vatican, Linda would, so I took her word for it.

I don't know when it hit me, but at some point during the Mass I started thinking about the Christmas I'd spent on Guam with Doren and Jacobson. We gave each other presents and got shitfaced and talked about our Christmas customs back home, and remembering that, I thought, hey, here I am with my family, and Doren's there in Austin with his family, but Ron Jacobson's not with his family, and he's never going to be with his family again. It really got to me and I couldn't get it out of my head.

When I said the confession, I thought, what the hell have I been doing?

One of my best friends is dead, and what's it mean to me? Have I tried to do anything right? No. Just goofing off, drifting along day to day. And then there I was involved again with Mrs. Constance Bradshaw.

I took Communion, and I walked back down the aisle with the wafer in my mouth—that funny papery taste—and I thought about how if Christ was real, and the Church was real, then I'd been forgiven. I don't know how to say this, but it was—I don't know. I don't want to try to pass myself off as somebody who's super-religious. I'm not any more religious than the next guy, but it was just too much, and I was, I guess you could say, kind of choked up.

We sang a hymn and finished up the Mass and Father Obinski dismissed us. I still remember that from the Latin Mass—*"Ite missa est"*—even though he said it in Polish, and everybody started getting it together, putting on their coats and all that, and I didn't want to talk to anybody for a minute, so the first chance I got I pushed my way through the people in the aisle and went on ahead of my family.

There were knots of people leaving, and I dipped my fingers in the holy water and crossed myself, and I remember looking back and seeing my mom and dad, and my aunts and uncles, and Babcia Wojtkiewicz way back there still talking to everybody, and I looked around for Linda. She should have been coming down out of the choir loft, but I didn't see her. Czesław Dłuwiecki and his wife and kids were right in front of me, and just before we were going to step outside, he stopped to help Janice on with her coat, so I stopped too. He kept on going, and she started to button her coat up, and then all of a sudden she turned around like looking for something behind her—I don't know what she could have been looking for—and I was right behind her.

We both of us stopped dead. God knows why. She looked right into my eyes and I felt— This is going to sound crazy, but it's true. I felt something like a huge power surge, a million volts, and it was in slow motion and just rolled right over me, big as a river rolling over me, and for maybe a second or two I was, I guess you could say, honest-to-God terrified. I didn't know what was happening. I wanted to flinch away from her eyes, like when you're in a dark room and you walk outside and the sun's too bright.

I thought, hey, what is this? This is just too weird. How do I get out of it? So I said, "Merry Christmas, Janice."

She didn't smile or anything. She said, *"Daj ci Boże szczęście, Jimmy."* Then she turned and walked through the door with her family.

By the time I got down to the street I was telling myself it was ridiculous, nothing strange had happened at all. It was all just some kind of weird blip in my mind. I stood there on the sidewalk with my family and the Mondrowskis and chatted awhile and waited for Linda to come out, and we all wished each other a Merry Christmas.

Then I walked home with Linda and my family, and I felt worse and worse, and I kept thinking about Janice. I thought, well, it's too bad. That little girl just thinks I'm a nice guy she likes to talk to on Tuesday nights, Linda's big brother.

It didn't feel right to me to be driving away. I wanted to crawl though my little doghouse door and spend Christmas Eve in my old room where I'd grown up, and it wouldn't have been a problem. All I would've had to do was open my mouth and I could have stayed there, but then I would have missed out on the brand-new fifth of Jack Daniel's I had waiting for me.

By the time I got back to my trailer, boy, did I feel shitty. I cracked open the whiskey and turned on the tube. Christmas Eve, right? So what's going to be on the tube? You guessed it. Same thing on the radio, so I got out my records and started playing—well, not whole albums but just the songs I liked, the ones that went with the mood I was in—which was, okay, Koprowski, go wallow in self-pity right up to your eyeballs. I played "Crimson and Clover" about a dozen times, and "The Boxer" about two dozen times, and some of the songs from that group Love that Georgie had turned me on to, and whiny old Sweet Baby James. If I hear any of those songs on the radio today, I can't move quick enough to change the station.

It's funny how some of the times when you were totally miserable stick in your mind and seem real important years later. I remember one night I was drinking with some of the boys in Wallach's back room. We didn't have our draft cards yet, but if you hit the right place at the right time, sometimes they'd forget to ask, so we were seeing how much we could pour down before closing time, and I got super bummed out. I was with Georgie and Bobby and Larry and I don't know who all, and I was going on and on and on about Dorothy Pliszka, and they just got sick of listening to me. Looking back on it, I can't blame them a bit. Larry Dombrowczyk said, "Come on, Jimmy, what do you think? She's an angel from heaven? Hell, she's just a girl," and I got up and walked out.

Somebody must have had a car, and I could have waited and got a ride, but no, I was offended and I just had to get out of there, and I walked along the railroad tracks from 25th Street all the way down to South Raysburg, and I can remember how walking alone in the night worrying about my problems felt good in a strange kind of way, and I went into St. Stans to pray. I did that a lot. Try that with a Catholic church today, you'll find it locked up tighter than a drum, and that's a crime, if you ask me. Sure, I know that times have changed, but a church has got to be a place where some asshole can stumble in dead drunk in the middle of the night to pray to the Holy Mother.

So anyhow, that Christmas Eve was turning into one of those miserable nights that's going to stick in your mind forever. The biggest problem was I didn't know what was bothering me. I knew I was feeling bad about Jacobson, and I knew I was feeling bad about the useless kind of life I'd been living, and I knew I was feeling bad about Dorothy Pliszka—surprise, surprise. I kept thinking that my life would have been totally different if I'd married her—which it would have—and other useless thoughts like that.

And I was feeling bad about getting involved with Connie again. So just how the hell had that one happened? You're probably getting a good laugh out of this—at my expense, right? But it didn't feel like anything I had any control over. I couldn't figure it out. It felt like a magic trick or some damn thing.

And then there was being alone in a trailer out back of Raysburg Hill on Christmas Eve, but the festivities were over for the night and everybody else in the world but me was already asleep. I'd said maybe I'd go to church with my family in the morning, but now I knew I wasn't going to make it. I'd had enough of church.

I'd bought nice presents for Mom and Dad and Linda and Babcia, and silly little presents for my aunts and uncles, and I'd even got something for Georgie, and now I was worried they weren't right—weren't big enough or thoughtful enough or something enough, and I was wondering if maybe I shouldn't have got something for Janice, although, God knows, you weren't expected to give presents outside your family and close friends. And the longer I sat there and drank, the lower I sunk, and it finally hit me how sad it was that there hadn't been any little kids at dinner so Babcia could tell them how on Christmas Eve back in Poland you could go out and talk to the cows and the sheep and they'd talk back to you. You see, they'd been granted the gift of speech on that night because they'd welcomed the baby Jesus into the world. And I kept thinking about Janice Dłuwiecki. Even when I hadn't liked her, I'd never thought of her as a strange little girl, but that's how I thought of her now. Honest to God, the hair on my arms and the back of my neck had stood up when she'd looked at me like that. Why had she said, "God bless you," to me in Polish?

EIGHT

Whatever weird thing happened between me and Janice on Christmas Eve, she never mentioned it, so maybe to her nothing happened. I wasn't going to bring it up. I began thinking maybe it was just my problem—some malfunction in my mind, you know, like a scratch on a record. I was still driving her home on Tuesday nights, chatting with her in my car, stopping in to have a drink of Clorox with her dad. I was still working for Vick and eating dinners at home and getting loaded with Georgie at the PAC and, you know, still doing pretty much everything I'd been doing before Christmas. There was only one difference, and that was The Italian Renaissance. That's the course Connie was supposed to be taking.

We had more time together than back in the summer, but not that much more. We hated looking at our watches every five seconds, but that's probably what saved us. She had to get home between eleven and midnight, and she had to get there reasonably sober. She counted her drinks—I mean she literally ticked them off in her mind—and I saved my serious drinking until after she left.

"What about The Italian Renaissance?" I said. "Aren't you going to fail it?"

"It's not for credit."

Well, The Italian Renaissance had only been playing for a couple weeks when Connie says, "It'd be nice to be able to go out somewhere, wouldn't it? Charming as it is, the inside of your trailer does get a little claustrophobic," so I asked her if any of the folks she and her husband hung out with—the hot-shit young doctors and their wives—would ever have any reason to go up to Staubsville.

Just about the only thing that's happening up there is the Staubsville Mill, and it's your standard-issue milltown—you know, the mill itself takes up damn near the whole town, stacks sticking up, trains rolling in and out of it night and day, and then you've got a bunch of dumb, cheap-ass little houses, a supermarket and a hardware store, maybe eight churches, and four hundred million, sixty-three thousand, nine hundred and forty-seven bars. It's kind of heavy in the smoke department and nobody's seen a blue sky in recent memory. The streets have that funny kind of shiny, evil, metallic look to them, and, yeah, there's lots of that good old red dust, and when you get a slip in a furnace, tons of black crap gets blown out and comes pouring down all over everything. "No," Connie said, "I can't imagine anybody I know going up there for any reason whatsoever."

In Staubsville they've got this famous club called the Night Owl, and that's where Auntie Jean used to sing for the gangsters back in the thirties, and when I started telling Connie that story, I saw her eyes glaze over. She never showed much interest in a lot of the things I tried to tell her, so eventually I quit trying to tell her anything. "It's an old-time Italian place," I said. "Been there forever, and the food's terrific."

"Oh, they make good pasta?"

"Screw your pasta, baby, I mean a goddamned plate of spaghetti."

It wouldn't have mattered what they served; the minute Connie saw the place, she loved it to pieces. There's a huge parking lot wrapped around two sides of the building, and not a light in it, maybe because the kind of clientele they had back in the old days liked their parking lots a little on the dim side. Out front there's a neon owl with a top hat and a walking stick. I remember him from when I was in high school. When all the neon was working right, the owl was supposed to wink at you, but by the time Connie and I got there, a lot of his tubes had burned out and he'd developed a short so all he did was crackle every few seconds.

The restaurant inside was damn near as dark as the parking lot. Walls lined with booths, little pissy lights in them, like a quarter of a watt. A bunch of tables. A few candles in those glass things scattered around. A dance floor and a bandstand. On the weekends they still had live music—country bands, mostly—but if you wanted music on Wednesday nights, you played the jukebox. We'd stop just inside the door because you've got to let your eyes adjust, and then eventually we'd be able to make out this shadow that turns out to be Joanne, the waitress. She floats over like she's just dropped her fourth Quaalude, which probably she has. She's got your classic hoopie accent, and after she gets to know you, she says things like, "Youins goina have yourself a real ball tonight, huh?" Her skirts are so short her panties show, but it doesn't matter a whole hell of a lot in the—what was it Connie called it?—oh, yeah, the stygian gloom.

Whatever Connie ordered to drink, even Scotch on the rocks, it always came with a little pink umbrella in it because it was, you know, for the lady. The spaghetti was always terrific. We'd sit in a booth, and we'd sit side by side so we could play with each other under the table because our main purpose in going to the Night Owl was to get each other as hot as a couple shithouse rats.

Yeah, it was sex that got us together in the first place, but now we pretty much stopped pretending we were interested in anything else. I knew she still had a husband because she called him up from my damn telephone, and I assumed she still had a couple kids, but she never mentioned them. She sure didn't want to hear about anything I was doing in real life.

"All men have fetishes," she says. "What are yours?"

We're talking a guy who taped up *Playboy* centerfolds all over his ceiling when he was in high school, so my fetishes are fairly standard issue, but when you've got a girl with a figure like Connie's, it doesn't take a whole hell of a lot to get me going. I say the first thing that pops into my head, "Well, that black leather minidress you had on—you know, when you were waiting for me in my car? Well, that was pretty hot." The next Wednesday she turns up wearing it, and when we're in our booth at the Night Owl having our first round of drinks, she says, "Guess what I'm wearing under this dress?" and I say, "Gee, Connie, I couldn't tell you," and she says, "Nothing." That information, of course, has the desired effect, and I guess you could say, it established a precedent.

Somewhere in the middle of the sixties some sorry asshole invented pantyhose, and like a lot of guys my age, I always thought that was one of the great tragedies of Western civilization. I expressed this opinion to Connie, and— Okay, here's what's happening most Wednesday nights. Connie likes to have a bite of dinner with a couple of the girls from The Italian Renaissance—that's what she tells her husband—so the lady she's hired to take care of her kids and do her housework for her stays late and makes dinner. Connie takes off about four, and I leave work early, and we meet at my trailer. If she gets there ahead of me, she has a key so she can let herself in, but she always waits till I show up to do her little show. Then, with me sitting there watching her, she takes all her clothes off. She lays her bra and panties and pantyhose very neatly on my table. She puts on stockings and a garter belt and gets dressed all over again in whatever she'd been wearing, and I don't mind this one little bit.

We hop in my car and drive up to the Night Owl. We have a couple drinks and eat dinner. We talk dirty to each other and play games under the table. We stumble out to my car and go sailing back down to Raysburg—it's amazing how fast you can drive if you put your mind to it—and go leaping into my bed. No matter how hard we try to make it last, it's usually over pretty quick, which is a good thing because there's only enough time for one more drink. She puts her underwear back on and gets dressed again. She calls her husband on that phone I'd had put in for her—and paid for—and she tells him she's so sorry how late it's got but it was a wonderful class and she had a great dinner with the girls and she just stopped for a quick drink with one of them but she's leaving right now and she'll be home in twenty minutes. I walk out to her Mustang with her, give her a kiss, and ZAP, she's gone. I walk back into my trailer and get loaded.

Even after we'd just had it, sex was pretty much all we talked about. She was big on sexual fantasies, and she wanted to hear all about mine, but I was a washout in that department because my fantasies are usually just about me screwing somebody. She had some dandies. Some, she said, were fun to act out, but others should just stay fantasies. Like the German shepherd. "You don't want a real dog," she said. "No, a real dog slobbers all over you and barks and has fleas and might give you anthrax. The dog you want is the dog in the mind."

That got to be a joke with us. I'd say, "I know what you want, baby. It's the dog in the mind."

Connie subscribed to about a million radical newspapers, and whatever was going in the women's lib department, she was for it, and one thing that all the women's libbers agreed on was that marriage was the pits and the family was fucked. Marriage had been invented by men and was run by men for the benefit of men, and women were just bought and sold like cattle. And another big problem was that a man's sexuality is totally different from a woman's. A man comes once—squirt—and it's all over, but a woman, if she's allowed to, will go at it until she drops from exhaustion, so women should have multiple sexual partners. In an ideal society, there'd be no marriage. The women would screw lots of guys, and it wouldn't make any difference who a kid's father was—most of the time you wouldn't even know—and the kids would be raised by trained professionals who liked that sort of thing.

This stuff was all news to me, and I listened to it go by, and it was like— Well, let's say you're stationed on Guam where there's not a damn thing to do—as I'm sure I must have told you before, seeing as that's the main thing there is to say about Guam. First thing you see when you get there is a big sign that says GUAM IS GOOD. The joker who put that sign up should be beaten to death with baseball bats and his body left for the crows. But anyhow, let's say you're stationed on Guam, and you've just come off duty, and you've cracked open a brand-new fifth and sat down and started to work on it, and some guy says to you, "Hey, Jimmy, I just read in the *National Geographic* how over in Siam they've got cats with two heads," and you say, "Oh, yeah, is that right? That's really *interesting*." That's how I was with Connie. She used to accuse me of not taking her seriously, and she was right. If I had taken her seriously, I would've said, "Connie, honey, all that stuff you're spouting is the biggest pile of horseshit I ever heard in my life," and where would that have got me?

If you're talking party time, the biggest Polish event of the year is the Pączki Ball. It used to go on for three nights in the old days, but by then it'd shrunk down to just one night—Shrove Tuesday—and in case you're not up on your liturgical calendar, Shrove Tuesday is the day before Ash Wednesday and the start of Lent. Well, Easter came early that year so Lent came early, and the Pączki Ball was in the middle of February. I kind of cringe now when I remember it, because, boy, did I ever distinguish myself that night.

Pączki is the Polish word for "doughnuts," and that's what you eat at the Pączki Ball. Now the Polish doughnut hasn't got a hole in it; it's just a round blob, sometimes with jelly inside, deep fried, and it's a fairly heavy-duty little hunk of starch. Yep, you can sure soak up a lot of beer with a *pączek* or two. The Pączki Ball's in the parish hall, and it's a fund-raiser for the church, so you don't mind spending your money, and they always try to get in a good hot band for it—the best they can find—and if you're inclined to dance the polka, that's the night you're going to do it, and you always make sure to get good and loaded so when you're at eight o'clock Mass the next morning and the priest marks your forehead with ashes and tells you that *you* are nothing but ashes, you're in the proper state of mind to believe him.

My mother always said, "If you don't have fun at the Pączki Ball, it's your own fault." So I guess that year it was my fault.

Janice wanted to go—she wouldn't have missed it for the world—but her family wasn't going because the Pączki Ball was a perfect example of what her father called our "degenerate peasant culture," so she came over to our house after school and changed into a party dress, and she and Linda and I walked over to the church. The girls were in a good mood. I wasn't.

What I needed was to loosen up. That's what I told myself anyway. They'll sell you beer or setups, and if you want something hard you bring it yourself, so I've got a fifth of ol' Jack in a brown paper bag. I pour myself a good jolt into a plastic cup, down it, chase it with an Iron City so I can get the evening started off right.

Janice and Linda have connected up with Mary Jo Duda, and they've nailed down a table up close to the band where they can check it all out, because the Pączki Ball is exactly the kind of event they want to play at, and they want to see what kind of competition they're going to get.

The best polka band in the valley in those days was the Andrzejewski brothers—the Jolly Gentlemen, they were calling themselves—and they were the first band around here to play that Marion Lush two-trumpet style. And the second-best band was probably Norm Kolak's boys. But what we had at the Pączki Ball that night was neither one of those bands because they'd both been asked, but they'd both been booked elsewhere, so we had the third choice.

"This here's what's left of Ray Pahucki's old Polak orchestra from out in Mercersville," Mary Jo tells me. "You should have heard them thirty years ago—whew, they were hotter than chili powder."

It was a weird outfit, like if you took the top off an old-time Polish polka band and the bottom off a country bar band and tried to get them to fit together. So you've got your old crocks on accordion, clarinet, saxophone, and fiddle and your younger guys on rhythm guitar, bass guitar, and drums, and they don't quite merge. The guy on rhythm guitar seemed to be their main singer, and he was singing in English. They were big on your standard country tunes, polkasized. Linda wasn't impressed. She said they were just a step away from being a Slovenian band.

I guess I've got to tell you something about Slovenian polka music. That's a style that started out in Cleveland, and the guy you usually think of who plays it is Frankie Yankovic, and what he was trying to do was get rid of anything the least bit wild that might have snuck in from the old country—you know, just basically smooth out and Americanize the sound so he could slide into the pop mainstream. And it worked because he sold a zillion records right after the war. Nobody in a Cleveland-style polka band has been known to sing a word of Slovenian recently—no, they always sing in English—and Slovenian polka music blends right in with country music so you'll get these polka bands that the only difference from a country bar band is that they've got an accordion in them. They'll use a lot of country tunes and turn them into polkas. So you get this smoothed-out, laid-back, countrified kind of polka that's real popular in the valley.

Well, Linda is not real big on Slovenian polka music, and I've got to admit I'm not that big on it either. But I don't want you to get the wrong impression here. It has its avid fans. Yep, there are sure those who love it. And this is a big country, so they're welcome to it. But I'll tell you what Slovenian polka music has always sounded like to me.

Let's say your wife has just left you. For the third time. But this time she left the kids with you. And you're a couple months behind in your rent. And you've just come off shift at the Staubsville Mill, and it's been a really shitty shift. Even shittier than usual. And you're walking because you can't afford the insurance on your car. And you duck into the first bar you see. Well, along about the time you're drinking your fourteenth beer, what you're going to want to hear is Slovenian polka music.

But that band we had playing that night hadn't got totally Slovenianized yet. They still had a bunch of good old Polaks on top. "The old guy on the fiddle," Mary Jo says, "that's Ray Pahucki. The nice-looking fellow playing guitar, that's his son. The kid on the drums, that's his grandson."

"Yeah, it's always been a family affair," Linda says. She'd interviewed most of those guys when she was writing her paper. "It's a crime that nobody ever recorded them. What did they sound like in the old days?" she asks Mary Jo. "Were they good?"

"Oh, yeah, the best. When Ray Pahucki and the boys started to play, you'd jump right to your feet. It's sad. A lot of the guys from that old orchestra must be dead by now—or in the old folks' home."

Naturally Linda liked the leftover old guys; she especially liked the way Ray Pahucki played the fiddle. It was that authentic Polish folk style with no vibrato, she said. But she didn't care for the younger guys making up the rhythm section, and Mary Jo agreed with her. The kid on drums was kind of crude. The guitar and the accordion kept getting in each other's way. "We've got to be better than that if we want to get anywhere," Linda says.

"We've got to get *those other two girls* if we want to get anywhere," Mary Jo says with acid dripping off her voice.

Linda's been hearing this from Mary Jo for a while now, and she says what she always says, "They're professionals. They want to get paid."

"Yeah? Don't we all."

Do I hear the guitar getting in the way of the accordion? Do I hear the drummer being kind of crude? Oh, hell, no. They've kicked into an instrumental—"Money Money," I think it was—and what I hear is a good hot polka, and that boilermaker's started knocking at the base of my skull. It's the Pączki Ball, isn't it? Well, you don't stand around and talk about the damn band. You dance. I grab Janice and yank her right out onto the dance floor.

She didn't see me coming, and she lets out a huge squeal. I'm leading her right smack down the floor in front of the band, and when I do the polka, I like to step right along. Once Janice gets over her shock, she's a pretty dancer, light and airy. A kid, you know, so she's got energy out her ears. White tights and her little shiny shoes, her short skirt flipping around, she looks all legs, and we go by the band, Ray Pahucki starts egging us on—*"Hop, hop, hop, hopla!"*—and Janice is laughing, her pigtails flying behind her.

We go sailing around the edge of the dance floor and Larry Dombrowczyk gives us a big cheer. He grabs Arlene Orlicki and comes chasing along behind us. He's got a goofy way of dancing, taking these great big stupid steps—like imagine Abe Lincoln doing the polka—and people are cracking up. We're coming back around to where we started, and I see that Gene Duda's managed to get his ancient ass out of a folding chair, and he and Mary Jo are doing that old one, two, three polka step we all learned as kids, staying in one spot and barely moving their feet. And Mondrowski's dancing with Linda. He's a smooth dancer, turns the polka into something like a jitterbug. Well, it's like my mom always said, "If you're having a good time, there's no wrong way to do the polka."

We're galloping by the band again, and they just love us to pieces. *"Do tańca!"* that old fiddle player yells at us.

"To grajcie!" Janice yells back at him, and he cracks up. It gives you a real kick to see somebody happy like she is, her eyes sparkling. A cowbell's clanging away somewhere—probably my Aunt Helen, she loves to do that—and I think, yeah, I'm going to have a good time, what the hell.

You don't want a polka to last too long; otherwise some of the older folks might start dropping dead on you. So this one's run out and we've slid to a halt, and I'm standing there gasping for breath, and Janice says, "Jimmy, you're a wonderful dancer," which makes me feel good, like I can still crank it up, you know, even though I'm regretting every cigarette I've ever smoked in my life.

"You ain't no slouch yourself, kid," I say. She's not even breathing hard.

The Pączki Ball brings out the whole parish. You've got the young moms passing their babies to each other, and the little bitty girls being whirled around by their daddies, and grade school kids from St. Stans running around all over the place, and the girls Janice's age dancing with each other because most of the boys haven't showed up yet. They'll turn up later, after ten, pretending to be drunker than they are, and if Father Obinski's anything like old Father Joe, he'll greet them at the door just so they'll remember where they are. And your parents and your relatives are there, and it used to be that everybody you went to school with would be there, but looking around that night it really hit me how bad our ranks had been thinned out—you know, what with the Sylvania plant shutting down and Raysburg Steel doing all those layoffs.

But the old ladies sure were still there, like Babcia Wojtkiewicz working in the kitchen to make sure there's always plenty of *pączki* and later on, after you've worked up a real appetite, some *pierogi*. The festivities stop dead at midnight because that's the start of Lent, and before it's all over, those old ladies are going to be out on the dance floor for a polka or an *oberek*, and if you don't watch out, it's you they're going to grab. The oldest person is Mrs. Polzin who's something like ninety-four, sitting there in her wheelchair sipping a little beer and smiling at everybody as they go by.

The band finally decides to do one in Polish, a tune everybody knows. The fiddle player sings, *"Jakie czasy już nastały, że się baby powściekały"*—in English that means something like, "What's happening these days when the old ladies are going bananas?"—and then he goes, *"Oj, dana dana, oj dana,"* and everybody in the hall gets to yell back at him, *"OJ, DA NA!"* You don't even have to know any Polish to be able to do that.

Mondrowski grabs Janice, and Larry grabs Linda, and I grab Arlene Orlicki, and away we go. Arlene was a majorette back in high school and she dances what I guess you could call a majorette-style polka—showing off her legs—and she gets a few whistles, which is exactly what she wants. That tune's got just about everybody up on their feet, and I see Mom and Old Bullet Head stepping along in fine form, and then, coming right behind them, Dorothy Pliszka and her husband—yeah, she really is Dorothy Green now—and I get the same damn miserable feeling I always get. Shit, I think, it's been seven years. This is ridiculous. I figure I better dance with her once before the night's over just to take the jinx off—if that makes any sense. Well, I never did get to dance with Dorothy.

After that last polka I'm sweating out of every pore, and what I need's a cold one. I walk over to where they're selling the beer. Boilermaker number one went down so nice I figure what's called for is number two, so I dig up my fifth and pour out a good jolt into a cup, and lo and behold there's Linda looking right at me. "Come on, Jimmy," she says, "why don't you take it easy tonight?"

I'm super pissed off for some reason, thinking, hey, it's going to be a cold day in hell when my little sister starts telling me what to do, but I say, "Oh, yeah, sure," and give her a little smile.

Then I go wandering off talking to people, and I wait till Linda's not looking at me, and I pour another good glug into my cup and down the whole works. Real mature, huh? And I buy two beers so I don't have to keep standing in line, and I'm looking around for somebody to dance with, and then—whoa back there, boys!—the world's starting to go a little bizarre on me so I figure I better eat a *pączek*. And just as quick as I'd got mad at my sister, I'm feeling bad about it, and I'm thinking, oh, hell, she didn't mean anything by it. She was just trying to keep me out of trouble—fat chance of that because I've already drunk maybe a quarter of a fifth of Jack Daniel's and four beers on an empty stomach in little over an hour.

I ate a couple *pączki*. The band kicked into a waltz, and you want to dance a waltz with your girlfriend if you've got one, but I didn't have one, so I went and propped up a wall.

A waltz gives you a break from all the polkas so you've got a chance to breathe, and it gives you a chance to talk to the person you're dancing with, and if you're inclined to say something heartfelt and soppy to her, it gives you a good excuse because the waltzes they play at Polish dances are really soppy. Whether they're in English or in Polish, they've always got sweet pretty tunes—haunting, I guess you could say—and they're about falling in love, or having a broken heart because the one you love doesn't love you, or loving somebody who's an asshole, or missing your wonderful old mother now that she's gone, or missing your kids because you had to leave them, or missing the beautiful mountains of Poland that you haven't laid eyes on for three generations, or saying how strange life is, over in a flash, and in a year, in a day, in a moment, we'll be together no more—anyhow, the whole point of a waltz is to take your heart-strings and give them a real good yank.

Little kids don't like waltzes for the simple reason that little kids aren't sentimental. No, they go, "Hiss, boo," and go off and have a Coke or something. Everybody else wades in up to their eyeballs. There's not that many waltzes played in the course of an evening, but each one they play is soppier than the last one—or maybe it just seems that way because you're getting loaded—so by the time you get to the last waltz, everybody in the hall's practically drowning in soppiness. That's when the old folks are remembering what it was like when they first fell in love a million years ago, and the young marrieds are thinking, hey, all that shit—you know, the baby crying and working night shift and never having enough money—well, it's all worth it because we love each other, and the unmarried kids are saying things that will embarrass the hell out of them the next day. Like the last waltz at the Pączki Ball my junior year in high school when I said to Dorothy Pliszka, "Dorothy, I'll love you forever," and she said to me in that pissy little voice she could get sometimes that always drove me right up the wall, "Don't say it, Jimmy, if you don't mean it." She made me so mad at her, I promised myself I'd never say I love you to a girl unless I really meant it, and I never have.

So I'm standing there not waltzing with anybody. And it's not like there's no girls there, you know what I mean? There's lots of girls, and I've known every single one of them my whole life. There's Shirley Zembrzuski, there's Arlene Orlicki, there's Georgie's little sister and Bob Winnicki's little sister, there's those crazy Wierzcholek girls—well, you get the picture, right? I could have found somebody to waltz with, but why the hell bother? South Raysburg felt like it had shrunk down to the size of a pea, and all the time I'd been at Central I'd been telling myself, I've got to get out of this damn valley, so why am I still here? Why am I screwing somebody else's wife every Wednesday night regular as a cuckoo clock? Why am I drunk at the Pączki Ball? Why am I not in Austin, Texas?

Right in the middle of this excursion into the Land of Gloom, Janice Dłuwiecki comes over to me and says, "Ladies' choice."

"Who says?" I ask her.

"Me," she says, and who can argue with that?

So I'm waltzing with Janice, this weird little kid, and I don't know what to say to her, and she isn't saying a damn thing to me. Dancing with her reminds me of dancing with Linda when Linda was that age—you're holding this skinny sweaty little girl and she's easy to lead—but Linda was always heartbroken over some guy who wasn't paying any attention to her, so if he was a friend of mine, after the waltz I'd go say, "Hey, would you mind dancing with my sister?" Sometimes they wouldn't mind at all. Linda could have had a lot more active social life if she hadn't been so shy, or so conservative, or so something—but anyhow, I don't know what I'm thinking about, too damn drunk way too early, and if Janice Dłuwiecki is heartbroken over some jerk, she sure isn't telling me about it. She isn't telling me anything. Why did she ask me to dance in the first place?

We danced the whole waltz, and all she said to me the entire time was—we were right in front of the band, and she said, "I want to be up there playing so bad I can taste it," and I said, "Well, I guess you will be one of these days." We got to the end, and she said, "Dziękuję," and gave me a cute little curtsy like she did after playing her solo with the Central band. And for some reason I gave her a little formal bow the way you see the old guys do sometimes, and—Well, if I tried ahead of time to say it, I never could have done it—and maybe because I was drunk, I don't know—but someplace deep in the back of my brain kicked in, and I heard myself saying, *"Cała przyjemność po mojej stronie."* That's like what you'd say to a princess if she'd just thanked you for a dance.

She looked kind of startled, and then we both laughed, and that was that. Except I had that soppy waltz feeling hanging on to me—not to mention being plastered out of my mind and it wasn't even nine o'clock yet—feeling gloomy and sad and thinking, shit, forget about having a good time. No, I'm not going to dance with Dorothy. It'll just make me feel even worse to dance with Dorothy, and it was really crappy in high school, going around crazy dumb-ass in love with her like some stupid poisoned pup, but at least I was in love *with somebody*—aw, what the hell, the only thing to do is have another drink, and a polka kicked in, and it sounded like good music to be drinking to.

It wasn't as bad as the night Connie stood me up. I didn't lose every single damn memory. Nope, there were a bunch of them clear as little snapshots left in my head the next day to haunt me. But a lot of it was gone.

I don't remember telling old Mrs. Bognar how horrible it was on Guam—although Linda tells me I did—and why I should have picked Mrs. Bognar, I don't know. She's a nice old lady, and Linda says she kept smiling and nodding at me, but she doesn't speak hardly any English at all. I don't remember passing out in the men's can, and when Georgie and Larry picked me up and carried me into one of the Sunday school rooms, I don't remember that either.

I remember waking up and thinking, shit, how did I get in here? And I go lurching back into the parish hall to find my fifth, and it's empty, and I'm going, goddamn, son of a bitch, who drank my whiskey? And of course it was me who drank my whiskey. And I remember buying six beers and lining them up and starting to drink them one after the other. And I remember laying on the floor between a couple folding chairs with my head propped up against the wall at a weird angle and the whole world was one big polka pounding in my ears and I couldn't quite get it together to move my head and Janice Dłuwiecki was looking down at me and laughing, saying, "Oh, Jimmy, you're soooo drunk. Just don't move. Just stay there till I get your sister."

And, God help me, I remember throwing up on the sidewalk in front of the church. Yeah, you're supposed to have a good time at the Pączki Ball, but you're not supposed to get so drunk you're obnoxious, and you're not supposed to pass out cold as a mackerel in the men's can so your uncle, or your father, or your father's friends, or *maybe even the priest* has got to step over you to take a leak, and you're not supposed to fall down in the parish hall and then just lay there staring at everybody like a demented fool, and you're not supposed throw up on the sidewalk right smack in front of the church as people are driving by leaving, shining their headlights on you.

I don't remember Georgie and Larry dumping me into the back of my car. I do remember them getting me out of it and me going, "What the hell's happening? Come on, you guys, I need a drink," and they're going, "Shut up, numbnuts, or we'll deck you."

They hauled me in and dumped me on my bed. I'm going, "Hey. Shit. I need a drink. I really need a drink."

They kept shoving me in bed and I kept jumping out again. I sort of remember that, but not real clear. And finally the only way to get me to stay in bed was to find the other fifth I had stashed away and give it to me.

Well, as you could probably guess, I did not have a delightful night's sleep. You could probably also guess that I did not make it in to work the next day. About noon I'm sitting in the laundromat watching my sheets and pillows and blanket go round because there was no way in hell I was going to take that disgusting stuff home to wash it. You know, if you want to make a man with a terminal hangover feel right on top of the world, there's nothing beats mopping puke out of a trailer.

So I got everything looking good again, and I curled up on my bed and fell sound asleep. The next thing I know, there's Mrs. Constance Bradshaw letting herself in. I'm so far down, it takes me a few seconds to figure out who she is and who I am and where the hell I am and what's going on. "God," she says, "it positively reeks of Lysol in here. What's this, cleaning day?"

Well, my desire to drive up to the Night Owl was a little below zero, so I said, "Let's just stay in tonight, okay?" and I told her I'd got monumentally loaded the night before and was just beginning to scrape myself back together.

I could see she was disappointed, but she was doing her best to be sympathetic. "Do you want me to go and get us a pizza?" she said.

Oh, yeah, a pizza. That's all I need. "I've got some soup. You want some soup?"

She didn't want any soup. She took her clothes off and got in bed with me—both of us, you know, crammed into that narrow little space—and that was the first time ever that sex was, I guess you'd have to call it, lousy. She seemed shy just being there naked with me, and my body felt like it was something made out of old parts from Wolchak's junkyard. I wasn't turned on at all, but it seemed easier to go through with it than have to face all the bullshit talking we'd have to do if I didn't.

We're laying there afterward, and I'm trying to smoke a cigarette although it's making my head worse, and I don't know why I said it, but I said, "It's Ash Wednesday. You know, the first day of Lent."

"Oh," she says, "does that mean something to you?"

"I guess not. I didn't go to Mass."

There's a long silence, and she was probably thinking, oh, God, what do I say now? So she comes out with a really stupid line. She says, "I've never known any Catholics."

If I hadn't been feeling so shitty, I probably would have just laughed at her, but what I said was, "Oh, I bet you have. We don't all wear St. Christopher's medals around our necks, you know. So you can't always tell. Yeah, Connie, you're surrounded by secret Catholics on all sides."

"Boy, are you in a rotten mood!" she says and hops out of bed in a huff and starts getting dressed.

I didn't have the energy to try to come up with something to save the situation, so I just lay there and watched her. She didn't say another word. She just went banging out, leaving the door to my trailer open. I could hear her across the road laying rubber with her goddamn Mustang. I don't know where she was going. It wasn't late enough for her to go home. The Italian Renaissance wasn't over yet.

When I'd been out, I'd bought some hangover food, so I made a can of mushroom soup on my little stove. I'd bought a fifth of vodka because it's, you know, pure and easier on your system than sour mash whiskey, so I mixed a couple shots with chocolate milk and downed it, and I was thinking, shit, Koprowski, a man would have to be a fool to live like this.

NINE

After my splendid performance at the Pączki Ball, everybody and their dog was telling me I was drinking too much. Naturally I got the good word from Old Bullet Head. "Let me tell you a little secret, birdbrain. You'll never be able to drink it faster than they make it." And from Mom. "How could you do this to me, Jimmy? Everybody's talking." You see, that was the worst thing that could possibly happen to her—all the other moms going yatta ta yatta ta yatta, oh, poor Mary Koprowski, what a jerk she has for a son. Yep, at that moment among the good folks of South Raysburg I was about as popular as head lice. Even Linda was giving me shit. "Oh, Jimmy, when are you ever going to grow up!"

Then Vick Dobranski, that son of a bitch, put me on by the hour. "You're a good worker when you show up," he told me. "I got no quarrel with that. But there ain't no money tree growing in here, and I got no intention of paying you for not working." Boy, did that piss me off. I'd just got out of the service, hadn't I? It'd only been—what? Nine or ten months since I'd got out of the service? So of course I deserved to get paid for not working.

Well, you want to know a simple truth of life? If damn near everybody in the world is telling you you're drinking too much, you probably are. Of course Connie wasn't telling me I was drinking too much. No, she was right in there with me up to her eyeballs and things were getting—

Well, I've told you how dark it was in that parking lot at the Night Owl— well, it was a damn good thing. One night we walked out to the car, and I opened the door, and Connie went down on me right on the spot. She got me cranked right up to the stratosphere and then she stopped and said, "That's just to keep you interested."

I thought, okay, honey, so that's how you want to play it, huh? So the next time we're up there, when we're leaving, I push her over so she's laying across the hood of my car, and I come into her from behind. "Oh, God, no," she says. That's what she always said. You know that campaign they had a few years back to stop date rape or something, and the slogan was "No means no." Well, somebody should have told Connie that. For her, no meant she was so turned on she was about ready to die. When she really meant no, what she said was, "Stop it, Jim," but she hardly ever said that.

So anyhow, there she is facedown on the hood with me pumping away, and a couple guys come out and head for their car. Connie's going, "Oh, God, no, no, no," and I don't even slow down. The guys look over at us and then look away. They get in their car and drive off. I stand her up, pull her skirt down, and shove her into the passenger seat. I go, "That's just to keep you interested, honey."

So we got into these games of— It was like, let's see how hard we can pull the tiger's tail before he turns around and claws us. All it requires is getting so loaded you don't give a shit. We did it in the Wharf parking lot. We did it in the Kroger's parking lot. We did it on somebody's lawn out the pike. I'm a fairly big guy, and screwing in cars has never been my strong suit, but if you've got a girl wearing a miniskirt and no underwear and you sit in the backseat and get her to sit on your lap with her back to you, and if you lift her up until she's folded across the seat into the front, you can ease on into her and you've almost got enough room. We did that parked in front of the main entrance to the Staubsville Mill. I knew we had a good hour before shift change, but Connie didn't.

Meanwhile, back at the polka band, Mary Jo was getting more and more antsy. The Pączki Ball had really got her going. The church shouldn't have to bring Ray Pahucki and his boys in from Mercersville, she kept saying. There should be a good hot polka band right here in St. Stans parish.

Right, Linda said, that was the whole idea. So what about those other two girls? Mary Jo said. What are we waiting for, Christmas? So Linda worked up her courage and called the number on the Sugar Shack matchbook that Patty Pajaczkowski had given her, and some guy on the other end goes, "Patty *who?* Oh, you mean Patty the drummer. No, she split. No, I couldn't really tell you."

Mary Jo was not pleased. "We should have grabbed her while she was in town."

"We'll find some other people," Linda said.

"Yeah? Where?" It had been awhile since Mary Jo had been talking about polka-dot miniskirts, and Linda was hoping that maybe now Mary Jo would let go of the idea of the all-girl band and just let her round up some of the loose polka guys she knew about.

But one thing that kept them going on Tuesday nights was they discovered that Janice Dłuwiecki didn't just play the clarinet, she could sing too. Up till then, they'd been a little thin in the vocal department. Mary Jo could honk out the words to a polka when she had to, but she'd been smoking her vocal cords with Kool cigarettes for the last thirty years, and she had a deep, raspy voice— you know, the kind that whenever you hear it, you keep clearing your throat— and nobody in their right mind would ever take her for a singer. And Linda had her little-girl choir voice, and that was okay for a soppy waltz at the end of the evening, but not great for a polka. So at some point it occurred to them to ask Janice if she could sing.

"Sure," Janice said. When she'd been little, her mom used to sing to her all the time, and she'd learned all her mom's songs and they used to sing them together, so she knew lots of old Polish songs—the real sad sentimental ones her mother liked. "But I don't have a very pretty voice," she said.

No, it wasn't a pretty voice, Linda told me, but that's exactly what was great about it. "It's really close to Polish folk vocal production."

"Oh, yeah," I said, "so how do Polish folk produce their vocals?"

So of course I got to hear Linda's lecture on vocal production. When Janice was trying to sing pretty, she was using her head voice and she sounded real thin—kind of like an asthmatic chipmunk—but the minute you asked her to forget that crap and just sing naturally, she dropped down and used her chest voice, and then she had a lot of power and sounded like somebody had just found her milking a cow in Prokowo.

Linda and Mary Jo are egging her on—"Hey, that's terrific, that's wonderful!" and Janice is going, "Come on. You're kidding me. You want me to sing like *that?*" Yeah, they said, exactly like that—and while you're at it, you might even be a bit more like that, and Linda lent Janice some tapes of the old-time singers from the Tatra Mountains so she'd really get the idea.

Naturally, being perfect as she was, Janice got the hang of what they wanted lickety-split, and pretty soon she knew about twenty good hot polka tunes.

"She's a real ham," Linda said. I had trouble believing that. "Oh, you ought to hear her."

"Sure," I said, "how about next Tuesday?" I was, you know, getting real curious to hear what they sounded like.

Linda goes into a panic. "Oh, no, no, no. I didn't mean now. We're not ready yet!" Which gave me a pretty good idea how annoyed Mary Jo must have been getting with her.

Oh, and while we're on the subject of Janice Dłuwiecki, I should tell you about her sixteenth birthday party. They sent us an invitation to it, I mean an invitation like out of Emily Post. It was addressed to the Koprowski Family, and it was one of those "Mr. and Mrs. Czesław Dłuwiecki request the pleasure of your presence—" Mom really appreciated the bars through the *l*'s.

"What's wrong with that?" Linda says. "That's the proper Polish spelling."

Mom just rolls her eyes. "Where's he get off sending these things anyway? Who the hell does he think he is—Paderewski?"

"I think it's sweet," Linda says.

"Yeah, you would," my mother says. "Well, I think we're going to have a prior engagement."

"Aw, come on, Mary," Old Bullet Head says, "that kid's been here so much she's practically a part of the family. The least we can do is show up and give her some kind of present."

So what kind of present? It can't be clothes, Mom says, that's too personal. So how about a book then? Well, no, a book's not personal enough. Okay, so she's musical, isn't she? How about a record? "No," Mom says, "not just a record. That's not big enough. It's got to be one of those boxed sets. You know what she likes, Linda. You pick something." So Linda comes back with a boxed set of Benny Goodman, and everybody's satisfied with that.

We figure with that kind of invitation, it's got to be a dress-up affair, and that means I've got to go into a barber shop for the first time in months and convince deaf old Adam Cieliczka that all I want's a little bit off the sides—"That's a haircut?" my father says—and my dad and I have got to wear ties, so we dig out our funeral suits, and Mom and Linda go over to Zarobski's House of Beauty, "appointments not always necessary," and come back looking like two poodles. "Why are we doing this?" Mom says. "That arrogant bastard is going to talk Polish at us, and if we say anything back to him, he'll be looking down his big nose at us because we talk like peasants." Well, turns out she didn't have to worry about that.

We drive up in my dad's car, and it's one of those perfectly good blue Chryslers he buys every few years, but all up and down Edgewood there's all these Buicks and Cadillacs and Lincolns, and I'm thinking, what the hell? We go in, and there's Czesław speaking English, "How good of you to come," and there's his wife looking like she stepped off the society page, saying all these nice things about how she's eternally in our debt for all we've done for Janice, and it's all in English.

They lead us into the living room, and there's these stuffed shirts and their dressed-up wives. Who the hell are these people? Well, it's the guys old Czesław works for, and he's an accountant, right? So you've got your businessmen and your doctors and your lawyers and people like that—you know, anybody who's making the big bucks and needs a wizard with numbers to come in and cook their books for them.

I've never seen my parents so uncomfortable in my life. I can see them adding up the money like they've got cash registers behind their eyes—ding, ding, ding—and, my God, you should have seen some of those women, the clothes they had. There's a pink punch for the ladies, and a table with hard stuff for the men, and there's every kind of booze you've ever seen in your life. About ten different kinds of Scotch, the ones that cost your left nut. I sampled most of them. And big silver trays with little twirly sandwiches and shrimp and meat-balls that you're supposed to eat with toothpicks and dumb things on crackers with an olive on top. Is there a nice plate of *pierogi* anywhere to be seen? Are you kidding?

Are there any South Raysburg Polaks in the room? Yes, four of them. Their names are Walt, Mary, James, and Linda. I was really pissed off at old Czesław. Would it have killed him to invite Mary Jo and old Gene Duda? Janice had been playing music with Mary Jo every Tuesday night for months. Would it have killed him to invite *anybody* from St. Stans? Why did he even bother tak-ing his family to St. Stans? They should have gone to St. Joseph's with all the other out-the-pike micks who'd ever made a buck. And why the hell did the Koprowskis rate, peasants that we are? Because we'd been feeding his daughter once a week? What he should have done was invited us to dinner.

Mom's giving me a look that says this is just too damn much—although not any worse than she'd expected—and we're sure as hell going to hear her opin-ion about it later. Old Bullet Head has checked it all out, and he starts to sweat.

I mean right there before our very eyes little beads keep popping up on his forehead, and he keeps patting them away with a napkin. Here he is, a good union guy, and he knows who these people are. He's surrounded by the enemy.

Janice's older brother had come back for the occasion, and the two boys were helping out, walking around making sure that everybody was happy and had plenty of booze in their glasses. I was glad to see that Johnny Dłuwiecki had lots of hair—even more than I did—and I figured it must have given his poor old dad a fit or two.

Linda and I were propping up a wall, and John came over to have a little chat with us. "Boy, have you guys ever made a big impression on Janice," he says. "She never stops talking about you." We all sort of vaguely remembered each other from when the Dłuwieckis were still living in South Raysburg and he was going to St. Stans. He was the only kid other than Shirley Zembrzuski and us who could speak Polish. And of course, I remembered him from football— you know, when I was playing for Central and he was playing for the Academy. He wasn't very big, but he was a tough little bastard, and once at the Island Stadium he hit me with one of those tackles where you lay there on the field for a few seconds afterward and contemplate Eternity.

So anyhow John asks us if we want to see the birthday girl, and sure we do, so he takes us down into the basement where his dad has built himself a rec room with the wood paneling and the recessed lighting and the leather-covered bar, the whole bit. And you know what's funny? Czesław's still got posters from the Goldwater campaign plastered up on the walls.

Well, the party was divided up by age, so you've got all your teenyboppers down in the rec room, and your chips and chip dip and your stereo playing Donovan, and we walk in, and I check out this one girl, and I'm going, wow, far out, who's the cute little chickie with the long legs? And then I do a kind of, hey, whoa there, buddy, because the cute little chickie with the long legs is Janice.

I honest to God didn't recognize her for a second. She was wearing one of those Twiggy dresses, real short, and I guess I must have told you by now she's a tall girl, so the first thing you see are these legs that go on forever and then these— She always wore little-kid shoes—you know, with the strap—but that pair had quite a heel on them, and that made her even taller. Well, having a birthday didn't all of a sudden give her a figure, but somehow that didn't matter anymore.

Her hair's down, some kind of doodad holding it back, and she's got a couple long strings of beads around her neck, and she's got makeup on. First time I ever saw her with makeup on, and she didn't go overboard on it—it's mostly around her eyes—but it did change her. On Christmas Eve I'd been thinking, hey, Janice, you should dress a little older, and there she was dressed a little older, and to tell you the truth, it made me uncomfortable.

"Sweet sixteen, huh?" I said. "You look terrific."

"Yeah," she said, "I'm polished up like an apple." You probably had to be there, but the way she said it, she really cracked me up.

She seemed very calm for somebody on her big sixteenth birthday. Sometimes Janice was, I guess you could say, real self-possessed. Little hint of a smile, and you don't know what she's thinking. Naturally her good buddies were there—that pack of St. Stans girls—and a bunch of other kids from Central. Linda and I knew all the Polish kids, so we're going, "Oh, hi, Sandy— Hi, Maureen— How's your family?" and like that. And one of the boys—a dark kid, not Polish, good-looking, well, a little bit too good-looking, if you know what I mean. He was so gone on Janice it was kind of pathetic. The way he was looking at her, it made me feel protective of her, like, hey, kid, watch yourself.

All of a sudden she says, "Oh, Jimmy, let me show you where I practice," so I had to follow her out of the rec room and across the basement and around the side of the furnace to this tiny room in the back. There's nothing in there but a kitchen chair and a wooden bench with her clarinet on it, and a record player, and some of Linda's polka records, and a neat stack of paper with the words to some polka tunes written out in Polish. It did have a window, one of those little low things at ground level.

"Hear how quiet it is," she says and shuts the door.

You couldn't hear much of the party in the rec room, and you couldn't hear the party upstairs at all. "Yeah," I said, "it's real quiet," and I'm thinking, hmmmm, I wonder why she didn't ask Linda to come along and see her little room where she practices.

We're just standing there looking at each other. She wasn't kidding about being polished up like an apple. She'd even got her nails done. I'm going, "Yeah, well, Janice, it is kind of neat down here. Not too bad at all. You had me thinking it was more like a broom closet or something."

"If it wasn't for the window, I'd probably go nuts."

"Yeah," I said, "I can see that." I really wanted to get the hell out of that little room.

So I'm going, "Janice, I hope you have the greatest sixteenth year any girl ever had," and dumb stuff like that.

She says, "Thanks, Jimmy, I appreciate it," and I can't think of anything more to say, so we just look at each other. Her eyes are that real dark, real intense blue the sky gets sometimes after the sun's been down for a while, and they looked really huge that day. All of a sudden I'm remembering Christmas Eve, and I feel this little shiver inside, and— Yeah, she really is beautiful. When I first met her, it just, you know, annoyed the hell out of me how beautiful she was. And I'm thinking, what's going on inside your head, you weird little kid? Then she turns and walks out and I follow her back to the party.

You can call me a liar if you want, but it was the first time I ever thought of her as anything but—I don't know, something like a little sister. I stood there sipping her dad's expensive Scotch and watched her with her friends—and watched that dark pretty boy watching her—and it made me feel kind of sour and old.

The next Tuesday Janice was back to looking like her normal Catholic school-girl self. It turned out that she didn't like her party much more than we did, and she's telling me all about it. "I asked them not to do that," she says. "I didn't want all Dad's dumb clients there. I just wanted a few of my friends, you know, and some hot dogs and a cake or something, but I guess he had to make a big deal out of it because of his business."

The Dłuwieckis threw two big parties every year, she said, one around Christmas and one in the summer, and her dad always invited his clients. "He thinks they're his friends," she said, "but they're not his friends. I see how they treat him. They look down on him something awful. They can't even be bothered to learn to pronounce our name right. The men all kid around with Mom because she's so beautiful, but Dad—they think he's just a funny old guy with an accent. They're so obvious about it, it's embarrassing. But they have to show up, you know, because it's *business*.

"At Christmas they give him bottles of expensive liquor, and when they come back in the summer, they drink it, and they just stand around and talk to each other. They never invite us to their homes. And he still thinks they're his friends, but— You know the only person who ever comes into our house and sits down and talks to him? That's you."

"You're kidding."

"No, I'm not kidding. He likes you. He thinks you're real smart—'a diamond in the rough,' he says. He thinks he can educate you."

I had to laugh at that. "Well, it's been tried before."

I was just turning off Highlight Road. "Don't take me home yet," she says.

"Where do you want me to take you?"

"I don't care. Just stop somewhere." So I parked on Edgewood.

"I hate coming home sometimes," she says. "I don't want to live out here. I want to live in South Raysburg. I want to live so close to St. Stans I can walk to Mass. I want an ordinary family like yours."

All I can do is laugh. "No, I mean it," she says, "like yours or Sandy's or Maureen's. They have nice families. I mean they're not perfect. Nobody's perfect. But they're nice. Ordinary. They laugh and talk to each other. They don't have to have complete silence when Dad comes home. They don't have deep dark secrets nobody can talk about."

"Oh, I bet they do."

"But not like ours. It's like there's this wall. You can only get so far, and then, bang, you're up against this wall."

We sat there as long as I thought we could get away with, talking about her family and this and that, and I kept glancing at my watch because the last thing in the world I wanted was to have her parents on my ass.

She told me about how her mom had wanted them to join the country club. That was after her dad had started making the big bucks and they'd moved out to Edgewood. And the goddamn Raysburg Country Club was the same as it's always been, one hundred percent WASP, and that means no Jews and no Hunkies, and our friends and neighbors of the African-American persuasion aren't even on the radar. But Janice's mom figured that the Dłuwieckis were an entirely different class of people from us peasants down in South Raysburg, so there'd be no problem, right? Unfortunately the folks at the country club didn't understand the real important differences between various kinds of Polaks.

That was pretty hard for Janice's mom to take, but she swallowed her disappointment and thought, hmmmm, well, maybe we can't be members of the country club, but that doesn't mean Janice can't go to country club dances. You see, most of those country club boys went to the Academy with Janice's brother Mark, so that turned into Mrs. Dłuwiecki's major campaign, to get Janice to date some of those boys, but Janice just kept saying no, no, no.

"The Ohio Valley is not Poland before the war," Janice said, "and the Raysburg Country Club is not the Hotel Europejski in Warsaw, and I am not my mother— But I could never in a million years say that to her."

Well, I wanted to lighten things up, you know what I mean? So I started teasing her. "You don't like those Academy boys, huh? They too stuck-up for you?"

"No, it's not that. They're just—jerks. The ones that Mark knows anyways."

"But that pretty boy at your party? Now he's a different story, right?"

She kind of laughed. "Who do you mean? Tony? Yeah, he liked me right from the first day I walked into Central. I don't know why. He's Italian. I think maybe he just likes blondes. We're, you know, exotic."

"How about you? You think he's cute?"

"Oh, sure he's cute. A lot of girls think he's really cute, but—"

"Yeah? But he's not your type, huh?"

"Oh, it's not that. It's— Well, boys my own age just seem so immature."

One night in the spring when The Italian Renaissance had pretty well run itself out, Connie and I are sitting in our booth at the Night Owl. She's wearing a tight white sweater with a big round hole built into the middle of it—some Italian designer she said it was, but it looked more like Frederick's of Hollywood to me. I was probably telling her how much I admired the way she filled out that sweater. I really don't remember what I was telling her. But she looks up—you know, out into the stygian gloom—and goes into shock. I mean for real. Like she's been flash frozen.

"Oh, my God," and she grabs my hand and starts squeezing it. "Don't look," she says. "Just look at me," and she scrunches back in the booth like hiding behind me.

Well, I've got to sneak a look. I just can't help it. And there's this couple in a hurry, walking away from us. I'd heard the girl's heels on the floor and hadn't paid any attention, but they must have been right smack in front of our booth, and now he's hustling her out of there. He's a thin little guy with a mustache, thirty-something, wearing fancy bell-bottoms—an older guy pretending he's a hip young dude—and she's a little bleach blond honey who's trying to look like Linda McCartney.

"They gone?" Connie says.

"Yeah."

"Are you sure?"

"Yeah, I saw them go out the door. Hey, take it easy," and I pry her loose from that death grip she's got on my hand.

"Oh, God," she says, "Jesus, Jesus, Jesus. Oh, God, I think I'm having a heart attack."

She's fanning herself. Whatever it was she was drinking that night, she downs it. "Let's get out of here."

So we go burning down the river road back to Raysburg. We couldn't get there fast enough to suit her. "That was Dr. Andy Hamilton," she says. "From New York City, hot damn. Family practice. He's supposed to be first rate. Married to a really sweet girl. She has a bit of a weight problem. They have the most beautiful little baby boy—well, not a baby anymore. About eighteen months. The trashy little slut who was with him is one of the nurses—Jayelle or Rayelle or some damned Elle. I don't care what her name is."

"You sure they saw you?"

"Of course they saw me. He looked straight at me, and then he did a double take and looked again just to make sure."

"He going to tell on you?"

She thought about that for a while. "No. There's nothing in it for him. If he told on me, I could tell on him, and then where would we be? Two wrecked marriages. No, it's not him I'm worried about, it's that little white-trash slut. Oh, God, I hate it that she has something on me."

"Well, you've got something on her."

"Big deal. What's she got to lose?"

"Well, her job for starters."

"I hadn't thought of that. Yes, she could very well lose her job, if it all came out."

So we've got to go over every possible angle of who's got something on who and trying to guess the motivations of everybody involved, like, you know, trying to work out the plot of a spy movie, and the more we talked about it, the clearer it was getting that nobody had any room to maneuver and if anybody opened their mouth, the whole scene would be blown wide open and they'd all lose. "See," I said, "you're safe."

"Safe? Oh, Christ, is that ever funny."

We get back to my trailer, and she says, "I was going to go home, but that would be stupid, wouldn't it? What was I thinking? That would be really really stupid. I should go home at exactly the same time I always go home."

She couldn't sit still. She kept pacing up and down. She was shaking all over. Even her teeth were chattering. "Turn on the goddamn heat in here, will you?" she said. It wasn't that cold a night.

I thought she was just scared, but that wasn't what it was. She asked me for a drink so I poured her a shot. She held it in her hand and looked at it. Then she dumped it down the sink. It drove me crazy the way she could waste things like that.

"I don't want to drink," she said. "Just for once, for Christ's sake, don't you drink either," and she took the glass out of my hand and set it on the counter. I almost said, "Screw you, Connie," but then I took a good look at her and I kept my mouth shut.

It's hard to describe what she was like. Energy was crackling off her like to the tune of about four million volts. If you could have figured how to plug her in, you could have run the whole Ohio Valley off her for a year or two.

"I have to figure things out," she said. I thought she meant the whole spy movie thing, and we'd already been over it, but that's not what she meant.

"Is it worth it?" she said.

"I don't know, Connie, you tell me."

"Are we hurting anybody?"

"I don't know, Connie, are we?"

"Fuck you, Jim. Don't do that to me. I asked you a question. Are we hurting anybody?"

I told her the truth. "Shit, honey, we're probably hurting lots of people."

"But it shouldn't be like that, should it? It shouldn't make any difference what we do, should it?"

There's not a lot of room to walk up and down in a trailer. She goes pace pace pace to one end, turns around, goes pace pace pace to the other end.

"I don't want to wake up one morning with no husband and no kids," she said, and she laughed. "You know why? Because what would I do then? I wouldn't have anybody to blame but myself."

I tried to say something, and she told me to shut up. "Just wait a minute," she kept saying. "I've got to figure this out." She wasn't talking to *me*. She was talking to herself inside her head, and every once in a while she'd fill me in on the latest thing she'd just said to herself.

She was real hard to follow. A lot of it I don't remember, but one of her things was what she called "the hollow landscape." That's when you realize that nothing's real, that everything you're looking at is hollow like a movie set and all the people around you aren't people at all, they're robots. Then the next step is you realize that you're a robot too—just a beautifully designed machine.

Sometimes she'd stop to stare at me—I mean stare right into my eyes—and then she'd go back to her animal-in-a-cage routine. Talking all the time. Nonstop. It was not a lot of fun to watch her go through this shit, and I really needed a drink. "Connie," I said. "Hey. Come back to earth. You're acting crazier than a bedbug."

"Am I?"

"Yeah, you are."

I kept telling her that, and eventually it had an effect. "You're right, Jim.

Yes, you're right," and she opened up her purse and pulled out a pill bottle and popped a pill.

"What's that?" I said.

"Just something I take. I'll have that drink now, please."

We each had a drink, and very slowly she started to come down. "When I'm with you, Jim," she said, "life is always interesting. Life is not very interesting most of the time. Don't you find that to be the case?"

She must not have been coming down fast enough to suit her, so she popped another pill. "Do you know what you're doing?" I asked her.

"Oh, yes. Don't you know that about me yet? I always know exactly what I'm doing."

I could see her energy draining away right before my eyes. She plunked herself down on the chair. She was going, "Pain or nothing, pain or nothing, pain or nothing," almost like she was praying, and other stuff I couldn't make out.

"Connie, for Christ's sake, make sense, all right? You want somebody to lock you up over at the RGH?"

"No, no, it wouldn't be the RGH. They'd keep me right there in the St. Stevens Clinic. They'd just lock me in an examination room and throw away the key. But my little dilemma, my little dilemma— Oh, I've always felt free with you, Jim. You have always made me feel as though I could do anything I wanted."

I watched her run right down. She was melting into that chair. She yawned a couple times. "I'm sorry," she said. "It was quite a shock seeing that asshole Hamilton. I really am quite sorry. I suppose I should go home now. Is it late enough for me to go home? Will you help me up, please? If you don't, I'll just sit here forever, and I'm sure you wouldn't like that very much, now would you?"

I helped her up. She started taking her clothes off—you know, so she could put her underwear back on—and she looked at me and said, "Oh, poor Jim. We didn't get to do anything tonight. There's still a few minutes if you want to."

"It's okay, Connie," I said.

"No, really. We have at least another fifteen minutes."

"It's okay."

"Would you like me to give you a blow job? It's no trouble, really."

"Connie, honey, I'm not exactly in the mood."

"Oh, I thought you were always in the mood. Oh well, next time."

I asked her if she was okay to drive and she kept telling me she was. I walked her out to her car. "I'm worried about you," I said.

"Don't be," she said. "I have a husband to worry about me. He worries about me and doesn't fuck me. You don't worry about me and you do. You see, it's the perfect division of labor."

That one left a bad taste in my mouth, so one night I'm having a few with Georgie Mondrowski—well, to tell you the truth, he's having a few and I'm having lots. I say, "Hey, Mondrowski, you know I'm seeing that doctor's wife again, don't you?"

He just smiles and nods. Something goes click in my head and I say, "Does everybody know I'm seeing her again?"

His smile gets wider and he nods again. I say, "Am I making an asshole out of myself?"

He's grinning ear to ear. There's a beer glass and a shot glass sitting in front of me. The beer glass is half full and the shot glass is empty. He reaches over and goes *ping* on the shot glass. "Let me ask you something," he says. "When's the last time you went a whole day without a drink?"

"You're a great one to talk, asshole. When's the last time you went a whole day without a smoke?"

"Grass is different," he says. "Booze is an evil drug. Doesn't do a damn thing for your head, man. Just wrecks you. Besides which, we're talking about *you* right now. I know I got problems. You want to talk about my problems, we'll talk about my problems later. Just let me ask you again, when's the last time you went a whole day without a drink?"

That was, like they say, one of those damn good questions. "I don't know," I say, "back at Carswell, I guess."

"So how long's that?"

"Three years—maybe close to four. What, you think I'm drinking too much?"

"No, man, that's not the point. It's not that you're drinking too much. It's that you're hooked. You got to get off that shit. A lot of the fucking up you been doing's directly related to that shit. Like the Pączki Ball. Let's just put things in perspective here. Why'd you start seeing that doctor's wife again?"

I was really pissed off at him. "Because she's a good fuck," I said. "Come on, asshole, do you mean to tell me you'd pass up a good fuck?"

"Hey, Jimmy, did you forget who you're talking to? It's me, your ol' pal, Georgie Mondrowski."

"Oh, hell, man, I don't know why I started seeing her again. She's crazy. I mean really crazy. She scares the bat piss out of me, if you want to know the truth. Yeah, I'm in way over my head. The sex we're having is—I don't know, it's getting kind of over the edge. Screwing in parking lots and that kind of shit. I mean it's great sex—but hell. I don't know what I'm doing. I'm not even sure I like her." I didn't know I thought any of that until I heard myself saying it.

"I've been worried about my drinking for a while now," I said, "but I can't seem to do a damn thing about it. My whole life feels like it's pointless. Like there's no purpose. Shit, I might as well have stayed in the air force. You know, Mondrowski, what's the saddest thing? I can't even think of anything I want— you know, like seriously *want*. I used to want to go to Austin, but I'm not even sure about that anymore. If it wasn't for going to work for that asshole Vick, I wouldn't have any reason to get out of bed in the morning."

"I know exactly what you mean," he says.

And we talked about his problems a bit. His insomnia and all that, and jumping ten feet every time he heard a car backfire, and once he gets to sleep, waking up about an hour later, pawing around in the bed for his weapon that's not there, and other cheery little difficulties he was having trying to reintegrate himself back into civilian life. And we did what we've always done all the way back to high school—gave each other a good pep talk and said we'd get together and do something. "They've got some beautiful new equipment in at the Y," he says. "Let's go hit it. Let's pretend we're getting in shape for football season."

"Yeah," I said, "great idea," but even when I was saying it, I knew I wasn't going to do it.

Comes the next Wednesday of The Italian Renaissance and Connie doesn't show up. I've got back from the shop, and I've had time to shower and change my clothes, and still there's no sign of her. Then the phone rings. I did not get a whole hell of a lot of calls on that phone.

She was cranked, talking a mile a minute. I gathered that the shit had hit the fan. "What?" I said. "That doctor tell on you?"

"Oh, no. But it's almost as bad. He found out I haven't been going to The Italian Renaissance."

"Oh, great."

So they'd been locked into one of their marathon, two-person encounter groups ever since, and she'd told him some lie and ducked out to call me. And she's going, "I won't be able to see you for a while, but I'll call as soon as I can. When's the best time to get you? Maybe we can arrange something so you'll be there at a certain time every day, and if I can get out, I'll call. He's bound to go back to Baltimore sometime. He always does. Oh, Jim, I'm so sorry," and on and on she goes.

Something in me snapped, and I said, "Connie, let's just forget it."

She goes, "What?"

I said, "Look, honey, you just pull this one out of your ass the best you can, and let's just forget it."

There's a long pause, and then she says, "I'm calling you from a phone booth."

"Connie—we ran it right to the edge and peered over. What more do you want?"

I'm sitting on the end of my bed listening to the funny little distant sounds on the telephone line. And I hear a car drive by wherever she is. And I've just had it with her, you know what I mean?

"I think you better shit or get off the pot," I told her. "Either quit fucking around on that guy or leave him." Then I heard the click when she hung up on me.

TEN

That spring I was sinking lower and lower into the pit. I kept trying to do something about my drinking, and it wasn't just that I couldn't get started, it was even worse than that. Every time I'd come up with some plan—like okay, today nothing but beer, or you don't drink till you get off work, or whatever it was—something about even *making* a plan would kick me off into oblivion. Hell, I was drinking more trying to cut back than I'd been when I hadn't even been thinking about it at all. And then eventually I'd crawl back to consciousness and I'd think, oh, you weak gutless son of a bitch, what's the matter with you?

I knew it'd been the right thing to tell Connie to get lost, but I had to admit I missed The Italian Renaissance. It'd been fairly entertaining while it lasted—or like Connie used to say, "not without a certain charm"—but now there was really nothing holding me to Raysburg, and I kept telling myself I had to get my ass to Austin. I could have left anytime I wanted to. It was only a three-day drive. I even had money in the bank. But I just couldn't do it—any more than I could cut back on my drinking. I was stuck good, and I couldn't figure out why.

The lowest I sunk—anyhow, the lowest I sunk that time around—got kicked off on Holy Thursday. That's the Thursday before Easter, and for me it's the biggest bummer in the liturgical calendar. That's just my own personal take on it, you know. Most people think Good Friday's heavier, but I don't. If I'd had half a brain in my head I never would have let myself be dragged to that depressing Mass.

Lent's been going on, right? Of course that doesn't mean a damn thing to me, but it does to Linda. She's been singing the Bitter Lamentations at church and doing the Stations of the Cross and all that other cheery stuff you're supposed to do for Lent. And she's got a real sweet tooth, so she's given up sugar and pastries and ice cream and like that. It'd never occur to her to give up something like playing her trumpet. And ever since I've come home, Linda in her own quiet way has been trying to save my immortal soul, so she keeps trying to get me to go to one Mass or another, and I keep going, "Come on, Linny, I'll make it for Easter, okay? Isn't that good enough?"

I'm back at the house for dinner on Thursday night, and Janice is there because she and Linda are going to Mass. In spite of the age difference between them, they'd got to be real tight, and one of the things they've got in common is they're both religious girls, and so they're double-teaming me, going, "Come on, Jimmy," and finally I say, "Okay, okay, okay," more just to shut them up than anything else. I figure it's a short Mass, I can put up with that.

Now I should tell you something about me and Catholicism. When I was a kid, I had my own crazy ideas which I didn't bother to check out with anybody for the simple reason that little boys don't go around discussing religion. Well, maybe if you're the kind of little boy who's going to grow up and be a priest you do, but I sure didn't. And when the nuns were talking to us, usually I'd dial them out—like, oh, yeah, right, I've heard it all before. So some things I had in my head were not exactly your standard-issue Catholic doctrine, you know what I mean? And for years I believed that after Christ died on the cross, he went to Hell and suffered right along with the damned down there.

Where could I have got something like that? It's easy. We said it every time we went to Mass. It's right there in the Creed. You know how it goes. "I believe in God, the Father Almighty, Creator of heaven and earth, and in Jesus Christ, His only Son, Our Lord." And it goes on with what happened to Jesus until he was crucified, died, and was buried. And then you know what? We did not say it the way we're saying it today—"He descended to the dead." Nope, that's sure not what we said when I was a kid. In the Mass we said it in Latin, which naturally I don't remember, but we learned to recite it in both English and Polish, and in English it says, "He descended into *Hell*." In Polish it's— Well, it says, "*Zstąpił do piekieł*," and that means something like "he stepped down into Hell," so when I was a kid, I used to imagine Christ stepping off into space and just dropping straight down into Hell—you know, like somebody in a Bugs Bunny cartoon—but any way you cut it, Hell was the place where he was headed.

Okay, so Christ gets betrayed. And they flog him and mock him and put a crown of thorns on him. And then he's got to carry his own cross, and it's so heavy, he falls down three times. And he's got to see his mother watching it all and see how heartbroken she is. And then they crucify him, which is not a barrel of laughs, and then God the Father doesn't give him any help, so it's not just the physical pain he feels—anyhow, that's the way it's always seemed to me—and he cries out, "My God, my God, why have you forsaken me?" Then he dies just like we all have to, and they take him down and lay him in the tomb. That's where his body is, right? But where's his spirit? Well, the Creed said it plain as anything. For three days, he's in Hell. And when I was a kid, that was just about the worst thing I could imagine.

On Holy Thursday we remember a number of things. It's when Christ gave us Holy Communion at the Last Supper, and it's when he said, "Thy will be done," and gave himself up to suffering and death, and it's when that little community of his got scattered every which way and Peter denied him three times. But the reason why the Holy Thursday Mass has always seemed to me just about the heaviest, gloomiest, saddest Mass in the liturgical year is that's when we remember the anguish Christ suffered in the Garden of Gethsemane when he was begging God the Father to let him off the hook.

The first time anything religious really got to me—I mean, you grow up hearing all this stuff, and it kind of seeps in through your pores, but that doesn't necessarily mean it gets to you in any kind of a real way. So I'm just a kid, and I'm listening to Father Joe's homily, and it's about Jesus in the Garden of Gethsemane. Jesus falls down flat on his face on the ground and prays. He's feeling heavy as death, and the sweat rolls off him like big drops of blood. He prays, "Father, if it's possible, take this cup from me." Because he knows what's coming—betrayal and suffering and death and having to go to Hell, *and he's completely alone.*

I've heard it all before, but that time I really *heard* it, and it gets to me. I'm about ten years old, right? I swear I felt a horrible chill, and I got tears in my eyes, and I thought, hey, he really didn't want to have to go through all that shit *all alone.*

Well, every time I go to a Holy Thursday Mass, I remember that, and then they go out of their way to make things just as gloomy for you as possible, because at the end there's this procession around the church, and they strip everything off the main altar and carry it over to the side altar, and then they drape all the statues with purple cloth. It's to symbolize what it's like in the world with Christ gone, so they don't leave you a thing.

I remember it being a chilly night with a little bit of rain and the sky burning bloodred down in Millwood from the blast furnace—just perfect for Holy Thursday—and the girls aren't saying much because they're already getting themselves in a nice miserable mood for Mass. Except for the old ladies, there's not a lot of people in the church, because most people, if their main purpose is to get themselves good and bummed out, they'll come on Good Friday.

Well, Father Obinski delivered some kind of homily, but I don't remember much about it except it was gloomy. And I took Holy Communion just the way I did at Christmas Eve, but I didn't feel good about it. Even if there is a confession in the Mass, I knew perfectly well what old Father Joe would say about that if he was around to say it, and I knew perfectly well I wasn't in a state of grace. So if the Church was real and Christ was real, I hadn't been forgiven for a damned thing. And if the Church was *not* real and Christ was *not* real, then what was I doing there? Any way you cut it, I felt like a hypocrite. And we do the procession around the church, and they strip the altar and cover everything up, and I'm thinking, thank God, it's over—I'm dying for a smoke—but I forgot all about the prayers afterward.

You see, after the Holy Thursday Mass, a few people stick around to keep vigil, and in the old days, there were always people praying in the church all night long because what you're remembering is when Christ said, "Watch and pray." And then his disciples fell asleep on him and left him completely alone, and so *you* don't want to fall asleep on him, right? And of course Janice and Linda are going to want to stay there awhile and pray, and so what am I supposed to do? I can't really say, "Sorry, girls, I know we're supposed to stick with Christ in his hour of darkness, but I got to take a leak and get a smoke in, so if you'll please excuse me, I'm going to duck out to the PAC and get loaded."

There's no candles burning, and they've dimmed the lights in the church down to this depressing brown murk, and a lot of people have gone home, but we haven't gone home. Oh, no. The three of us are kneeling there, and the girls have got their rosaries out, and they're praying away, and when you look up at the altar, everything's gone because Christ is gone. There's no crucifix and no statues because they're all covered up. They've even carried away the little angels. And the altar table's bare. There's no altar cloth, no hangings, no host, no chalice, no purificator, no paten, no chalice veil, no candlesticks—no nothing. And then some weird thing in my mind takes it one more step, and I think, *no people.*

The closest I ever got to Hell was on that flight to Goose Bay, Labrador. Kneeling there in the church, I kind of relived it. I always kept a carton of smokes and a fifth of Jack Daniel's in my flight bag for emergencies, and we're airborne, and I'm congratulating myself, like, good going, Koprowski. For once in your life you thought ahead. You talk about stupid, right? And we go through this kind of giddy few minutes where we're yelling, "Hey, hot shit, we made it," and like that—you know, getting out ahead of the missiles. They announced that we had orders for Goose Bay, and then, bang, it sort of hits everybody at once. Shit, nuclear war. When we get to Goose Bay, will we be able to land or will it be nuked out? All of a sudden nobody's saying a word.

It had only been a few years before when the Kennedy brothers and Nikita Khrushchev had been going eyeball to eyeball over the missiles in Cuba, and that little peek into the nuclear abyss was still clear in everybody's heads, and the way that drill was going, there was nothing to give us a hint it wasn't real. Do you understand what I'm telling you here?

If I'd thought of doing it, I probably wouldn't have done it, but automatic, I cross myself. And I look up and Ron Jacobson's looking right at me. His eyes are just glued to mine. And for half a second I'm really pissed off at him because he's from Wisconsin and I can't think of anything out in Wisconsin the Russians would want to bomb, but then I realize what a piss-ass rotten thing that is to think. And we're all in the same boat anyhow. And I'm trying to remember where Linda is, if she's in Raysburg or back down at WVU, and then I think, oh, what the hell good would that do? It won't take long for the fallout to drift down to Morgantown. We're in SAC, you know, so we're not exactly uninformed about nuclear war—like what happens at the epicenter and so many miles from the epicenter, and the effects of radiation burns and radiation sickness, and, you know, the whole rotten works. And of course we all know about that good old *assured mutual destruction*.

If they launched the nukes, they're already coming down, and there's steel mills all up and down the river, so maybe already there's no people. My mom and dad and grandma and all the girls I went to school with and any of my buddies who're still in town and all the old folks in St. Stanislaus Parish and all the kids at Raysburg Central Catholic and just, you know, everybody. For a minute or two you're trying to think of everybody. And all the time I'm thinking this, I'm looking at Ron Jacobson, and he's looking at me, and I know he's thinking the same thing. And we're still alive, but for what? What's our lives going to look like? Who the hell wants to be alive?

Up until then I'd always had some kind of crazy little optimism about life, like—I don't know, like a little robin in spring that followed me around or some dumb thing like that, but by the time we got back from Goose Bay, it was gone, and I'd never had it again. So I'd got out of the service, and I'd decided not to think about any of this shit anymore. I mean, what good does it do you? But just because I wasn't thinking about it didn't mean it wasn't still going on. Right at that moment while I was kneeling there in the church, there were B-52s over my head carrying nuclear payloads, and there were missiles all over the world all aimed and ready to go, and the whole thing was just, you know, poised and hanging on a thread.

And Jacobson, the guy I went through all that shit with, he's gone through his own crucifixion and death, just the way we're all going to have to. But why'd he have to hang on so long, suffering like he did? Where is he now? If there's no life after death, then he's just gone. The nicest guy I ever knew in my life is just gone. And if there is life after death, where is he? Joined the Communion of Saints? In Purgatory? In Hell? The nuns told us that Protestants went to Hell. Did I believe that? No way I believed that. He told me, but I can't remember what kind of Protestant he was, but if he's in Hell, that's where I'm going too. And if there's nothing afterward, then we're all just like Connie said when she was so weirded out, nothing but a bunch of robots, and nothing means nothing means nothing.

I don't know why it came down on me so heavy right then—well, I guess there was all kinds of things leading me to it—and I don't know if I can tell you what I was feeling. It was like I was an old car or some other piece of worthless junk, and I was just being hit over and over with a sledgehammer and reduced down to shit. I'm there in the church with these two good Catholic girls, and they're both saying their rosaries, and so I just grab the first prayer that comes into my head, and I say it like maybe a dozen times. *"Zdrowaś Maryjo, łaskiś pełna, Pan z Tobą, błogosławionaś Ty między niewiastami i błogosławion owoc żywota Twojego, Jezus. Święta Maryjo, Matko Boża, módl się za nami grzesznymi teraz i w godzinę śmierci naszej. Amen."*

I don't know how long we were in the church. We walked outside, and I was thinking, oh, God, do I ever need a drink, and the girls hugged each other. They just threw their arms around each other and for a minute or two they hung on to each other for dear life, and where my head was at, that didn't seem the least bit strange to me. Then I drove Janice home, and nobody said a word. Then I drove Linda home. I pulled up in front of our house, and she said, "You coming to the service tomorrow?"

"Good Friday? Come on, Linny, I'm bummed out enough for the week." I was trying to make a joke, right? But she didn't even smile.

"You're coming to the Resurrection Mass." She wasn't asking me.

"I am?"

"Yeah, you are."

She got out of the car, and I had most of a fifth of Jack Daniel's in the glove compartment. I went down to the riverbank and I drank it.

The start of that little binge I remember real clear. I didn't feel like going in a bar. I didn't feel like talking to anybody. As drunk as I was, I had enough sense to ooze along at about twenty driving back to my trailer. I turned on the TV, but I wasn't really watching it. I had a gallon of Paisano Red in there, and I started in on that. After I got a ways down in the bottle, I found a half a fifth of gin Connie had left there from The Italian Renaissance, and I poured that in the wine jug—you know, to up the octane. I had some beer in the fridge too, so I figured I was set for a while.

I don't remember much of Good Friday. I got some more wine and some Jack Daniel's from somewhere. The state stores were closed, so I probably got it from Burdalski at the PAC. I must not have made an asshole of myself in public because nobody said anything to me about it afterward, but the next time I had a coherent thought was Saturday morning. I'm laying on the riverbank, and I'm chilled right down to the bone marrow. I've got my Levi jacket on, and it's wet, and everything's wet—from the dew, you know—and the sun's just come up. Well, sort of up; it's a murky morning. I don't even know where I am or how I got there, and I've puked all over the place.

I must have carried the fifth and that gallon jug down there, and the only thing that stopped me from starting in again was that both bottles were empty. I crawled up the riverbank, and lo and behold, I'm just down on the other side of the railroad tracks from the church, and there's my car waiting for me, and I'm pawing around in the glove compartment and in the trunk and under the seats looking for another bottle, but there's nothing. I drive back to my trailer and crank up the heat in there to the last notch, and then I go through every inch of my trailer looking for another bottle, but everything there was to drink, I'd drunk it.

I figured I had to pull myself together enough so I could make it to the State Store, but I couldn't even do that. I was just too sick. I crawled into bed and fell asleep for a few hours, and that's what broke the binge. I woke up, and you can imagine what I felt like. I knew if I kept on with that kind of drinking, I was on the one-way road to nowhere.

Everybody's got their things they do for a hangover, and I did mine, and I ended up wrapped in a blanket watching TV. When the pain starts to back off—well, it's not like you're happy or anything, but there is a kind of peace that sets in. I was so beat to shit I fell asleep about midnight. The next thing I know it's the middle of the night—still pitch-black—and somebody's banging on my trailer door.

Tried to ignore it, but it wouldn't go away. Just bang, bang, bang, over and over. Some girl yelling, "Jimmy, Jimmy, get up." The only girl I can think of it could possibly be is Connie, and I'm thinking, boy, is she ever going to get it.

I go lurching over to the door, and it's Linda—the one person in the world I can't just start yelling at. She shoves a takeout coffee at me. "You've got plenty of time," she says. "You need a shave." And it dawns on me. Oh, yeah, Easter. Oh, yeah, the Resurrection Mass. That's *at dawn*.

I'm going, "Aw, Linny, give me a break. I don't think I can make this one. I've had kind of a hard time. I don't feel so hot."

She isn't buying a word of it. "I'll bet our Lord didn't feel so hot hanging up on the cross either."

I'm really pissed off at her. Like here we go again—my little sister trying to run my life for me. And then I look at her, and she's really dressed up for Easter. I mean dressed to the nines. She's even got a nice new pair of little white shoes, and she looks terrific. And the only way she could have got out to my trailer was by borrowing Old Bullet Head's car. Hell, I think, she must have got up hours ago, and she's out here on Bow Street, and our house is only two blocks from the church. And what's wrong with her running my life every once in a while? It's not like I was doing such a terrific job with it on my own.

So I scraped my act together, and I even put a tie on, and I went to the Resurrection Mass. Even as hung over as I was, I was glad to be there. It was just what you'd expect at Easter, right? There was the procession, and everybody was wearing their best—the moms had got all their little boys with ties on and their little girls in their cute little white dresses the way they always do—and we processed in and sang all the old hymns in Polish that you always hear at Easter, and candles were burning and everything was restored because Christ had risen.

I don't remember what Father Obinski talked about. I do remember the Gospel he was referring to—it was the resurrection story in John. It's always seemed to me you don't really have to add anything to that story, so that's probably why I don't remember Father Obinski's homily. You know that story in John, right?

Mary Magdalene goes to the sepulchre where Christ's body was laid, and she sees that somebody's taken the big stone away from the entrance. Well, she runs and tells Simon Peter what's happened, and he and another disciple go running back, and they see the grave clothes laying there, so it's kind of obvious that somebody's taken the body.

Well, Peter and the other guy go home, but Mary sticks around. She's weeping. She looks into the sepulchre, and there's two angels in there, and they ask her why she's weeping. "Because they've taken away my Lord," she says, "and I don't know where they've laid him."

She turns around, and a man's standing there, and she thinks he's the gardener. And he asks her why she's weeping. "Who are you looking for?" he says.

"Sir," she says, "if you're the one who's moved him, tell me where you've laid him, and I'll take him away."

But it's not the gardener, it's Jesus. And he says to her, "Mary."

You always hope you'll have a nice sunny day for Easter, and that year we sure had us one. I dipped my fingers in the holy water and crossed myself and stepped outside, and the sun was wonderful. I'll never forget this. People standing on the sidewalk, standing on the street, hanging around in little clumps, you know, because you don't get up in the middle of the night to come to the Resurrection Mass just to go rushing home afterward. No, you want to take a few minutes to say hi to everybody—all those other crazy Polaks who managed to get up so early—and wish everybody a happy Easter, especially if you've got a real pretty morning with a big fat bright sun pouring down on you.

So there's this buzz of voices, people laughing, and I remember talking to Mondrowski and Burdalski and their families, and I was with Mom and Dad, of course, and my aunts and uncles and my grandma, and I remember seeing Dombrowczyk and Arlene Orlicki, and Bill Winnicki and I don't know who all. Well, everybody, that's all—the people you've known your whole life—and I remember feeling this little lift, like, yeah, maybe— Yeah, maybe there is a way for me after all. And I thought, well, if Easter's not about getting another chance, what is it about?

Janice was there with her family. They'd been on the other side of the church, and I hadn't had much of a chance to— It was crowded, you know, but you couldn't miss her wonderful hair with all those tiny waves—it was like spun gold—and Mom and Dad stopped to say a few words to Janice's mom and dad, real polite and awkward the way they always were with each other, and Linda had caught up with us. You always had to wait a minute or two for her because she had to go hang up her choir robe.

"You going to come home with us?" Linda asked Janice. She'd promised Janice she'd show her our Easter eggs, and Janice said to Linda and me, *"Wesołego jajka."* That's an Easter greeting that means in English something like, "Happy egg." We all laughed, and Linda wished her the same back, *"Nawzajem."*

Janice looked at her mom, and her mom said, "Oh, Janusiu, you shouldn't have told the Koprowskis you'd go to their house. You should be home on Easter."

"I am going to be home on Easter," Janice said. The Dłuwieckis were having a big fancy Easter dinner, but that wasn't until five, and Janice kept saying she'd be home in plenty of time to help her mom with it. "Come on, Mom," her brother Mark said, "let her go."

"We don't want to disturb your plans," my mom said, trying to keep the peace.

"Of course she can go," Janice's dad said, "for a short time," and his wife gave him a dirty look. "Be home by two," she said. "Promise me."

"Oh, I promise," Janice said.

So we walked back to our house. That dress Janice had on— It wasn't white. It was one of those natural colors like wheat, only more pale, and you couldn't imagine anything more simple. The skirt came down almost to her knees, and it had a short little jacket with it, and it wasn't tight. It flowed with her when she moved, and it made her seem so tall and lean and willowy, the most grown-up she'd ever looked to me.

We got home, and I excused myself and went shooting up to my room and got the Jack Daniel's down from my emergency stash I'd hid in my closet and had a good snort. That eased the pain considerably. I rinsed my mouth out with toothpaste so I wouldn't smell like a distillery, and when I got back downstairs, Mom and Linda and Janice and my aunt Eva and my grandma were laying the food out—a real nice breakfast spread—and seeing as Lent was over, Linda was going to get to eat all the sweet things she loved, so there's doughnuts and sweet rolls and like that, and scrambled eggs and fried *kiełbasa* naturally, and Linda's going, "Oh, yum."

Whenever my parents or my aunt and uncle drifted off into Polish—talking to Babcia Wojtkiewicz—Janice drifted right along with them. Stas and Eva had never really talked with Janice before, and naturally they were amazed at her just like everybody always was. Instead of getting annoyed the way I used to, I thought it was nice that Janice could speak Polish. I even thought, hell,

Koprowski, if you put some effort into it, maybe you could croak out a word or two yourself.

So we had a nice breakfast, and Janice admired our Easter eggs. Have you ever seen Polish Easter eggs? *Pisanki* we call them. The ladies do these wonderful, complicated traditional designs. You put the wax on the egg where you don't want the dye to take, and then you build it up, layer after layer, and the colors get real rich and deep, and if you want to keep them, you use blown eggs. It's a real art, and we've got a terrific collection going all the way back to when Mom was a little girl. Every Easter she takes them out so we can see them again.

Janice looked so grown-up and— Well, she didn't have much more figure than a boy, but that little jacket kind of disguised it, and dressed up the way she was, she looked a lot older than she usually did, and Aunt Eva whispered in my ear, "You better grab that one, Jimmy, before somebody else does," and I'm going, "Come on, Auntie Eva, she's just a kid."

It was such a pretty morning. Janice and Linda and I went out on the back porch to drink our coffee. Naturally Mom's cleaned every square inch of everything for Easter, but she's got to run out and wipe down the glider one more time to make sure Janice won't be getting any red dust on her pretty dress. "Oh, this dress," Janice says, "it's more trouble than it's worth."

She told us that for Easter she was one hundred percent designed by Mom—Mrs. Dłuwiecki had made that dress from a pattern, and she'd bought Janice shoes to match. They were definitely not little-kid shoes, and they made her feet look real dainty like— I don't know, like the tiny hooves on a deer. And her hipbones—well, when you're used to seeing somebody in little pleated skirts like the Central Catholic uniform, you don't really notice her hipbones, but in that dress, her hipbones were these two sharp points.

"It's nice out here," Janice said, and I laughed and said, "It is?" You go out onto the back porch at *her* house, you see hills and grass and trees. On our porch you're looking across the alley into the back of the Lewickis' house.

For some reason I told her about how when I was a kid, me and the boys would hop the trains—if they were going slow enough—and we'd ride up to the top of 30th Street and jump off onto the big sand piles they had at the cement plant. Lots of trains in those days—they were still running big-time back then— and if they were long enough, we could get four or five jumps off one train.

Janice kept asking us questions about what the neighborhood was like when we were growing up and what we remembered about our grandparents, where they'd come from and all. "Babcia Wojtkiewicz is right there in the living room," Linda said. "You should ask her. She'd love to tell you about being a little girl in the old country."

"Maybe I will," Janice said.

And so we just sat there and chatted and drank our coffee, and I heard myself saying, "You know, this was a great place to grow up." It surprised me that I'd say that, but you know what? It *was* a great place to grow up. It's not like we enjoyed living a few blocks away from a blast furnace—that's not what I meant. It's the old Polish community I was talking about.

Well, it was a wonderful Easter morning, the sun shining down on us, and I could feel some of my old optimism coming back. If I'd had half a brain in my head, I would've known what was happening, right? But I'm the king of denial. You give me anything the least bit heavy, I'll deny it, right, left, and center. About all I'd admit to is that I couldn't think of anything in the whole world anywhere near as pretty as Janice Dłuwiecki's hipbones.

ELEVEN

Easter changed something for me. It's like I'd sunk right through the soggy bottom of the Dixie cup and there was no place to go but up. And somehow I'd got some of my old hope back, and somehow that hope had something to do with Janice, but I couldn't tell you exactly how. It's not like I thought anything could happen between us. I was still thinking of her as a little kid, just obviously way too young for me, and— Hell, I wasn't thinking real clear about it, but it was— Okay, let me try it this way. You know how you want to do your best for your little sister? Because she's looking up to you and admiring you and respecting you? Well, somehow I wanted to do my best for Janice. I wanted to be the person she thought I was. Does that make any sense?

So I made a plan and stuck to it—for a while, anyway. I talked to Georgie, and I said, "I want to do something about my drinking. Can you give me a little help with it?" and he said no problem, what could he do?

I explained to him how the worst time for me was right after I got off work. Tuesdays were cool because I was driving Janice around and I had to stay reasonably sober for that, but every other weekday, I'd head straight over to the Greek's and knock back a boilermaker or two. Then going home for dinner was just a minor pause in the festivities, like as soon as I've got the food shoved down, I'm in the PAC having a couple shots—you know, to aid my digestion— and it's straight down the tube from there. So I told Georgie, "Right at five, you pick me up, and like you said, let's hit the Y."

First time, I go sailing through all the fancy new exercise machines they've got, and I'm pumping out twenty reps here and forty reps there, and moving the weight up, and saying, "Hey, you know, Mondrowski, I'm not in as bad shape as I thought." The next morning I wake up and I can't move. Hobble around like I'm ninety years old. So after that I started easing into it gradual.

But the plan was working. Every day right on the dot, there's Georgie. He never missed once. We're in the gym for a couple hours, have us a good long shower, and then we go catch the leftovers at his house or my house, and by then I'm so bagged the last thing I want is to perch upright on a bar stool at the PAC and inhale everybody else's cigarette smoke. I won't say I wasn't drinking at all. Oh, hell no, stopping completely would have been way too radical for me. I'd end up back in my trailer watching the telly and sipping a couple shots so I could sleep. But I'd cut way back and I was feeling pretty good about it.

So I'm in bed one night watching the eleven o'clock news, and I'm about half asleep, and the phone rings. That first time, I was reaching for it, like automatic. The phone rings, you answer it, right? But I caught myself. Georgie's over on the Island getting stoned, and Mom and Linda and Old Bullet Head are in bed by now, so who could it be? Yeah, I know who it is. Twenty rings. Stops. Starts over. Twenty more rings. Then the next night, same thing. The night after that, same thing.

Then it starts ringing at one in the morning. And if it's not one in the morning, it's four or five in the morning. When I go to bed, I take it off the hook. Then one day I get up to go to work, and I put the damn thing back on the hook, and the minute I hang it up, it starts ringing. I jumped about a foot. Well, that day I called the phone company and had that sucker yanked right out of there.

Georgie had taken to hanging out with a bunch of potheads over on the Island—this motley crew of Vietnam vets and their chicks and assorted other freaks and whoever else fell by who liked a bit of smoke—so one night we're pumping iron and he says to me, "Patty wants to know when she's going to get to play some polkas."

"You're putting me on," I say. But, no. Seems like Patty Pajaczkowski was part of that bunch he was hanging out with. The all-girl country band had broken up. The lead guitarist had been married to the manager, but he ran off with the rhythm guitarist, and everybody went their separate ways, and Patty had nothing to do with herself except complain about life and smoke a lot of weed. She was looking to play music with somebody. "She was waiting for your sister to call her," George says. "She loves playing polkas."

"She does?" Linda said when I told her. She couldn't believe it.

It took about a dozen tries, but Linda finally got Patty on the horn and

Patty said far out. They arranged to meet at Patty's place on Sunday afternoon. "When?" Linda said. "After Mass?"

Now I wasn't the one talking to Patty, and I couldn't claim to know her all that well, but I was pretty sure a girl like Patty Pajaczkowski would not want three-quarters of a polka band turning up on her doorstep right after Mass. "What did she say exactly?" I asked Linda.

"I don't know, Jimmy. I think she said, 'Come over sometime in the afternoon.'"

"Yeah, right. So just cool out. Read the paper or something."

Linda was too nervous to read the paper or something. She went in her room and started blatting up and down a bunch of scales on her trumpet. I was sitting in the living room with Janice and Old Bullet Head. He looked at me over the top of his glasses and said, "It could be worse. It could be a trombone."

"It could even be a tuba," Janice said. She had a real knack for saying things you didn't expect her to say, and it was just starting to dawn on me that she had a sense of humor.

Then Mary Jo showed up, and my mother was required by the ancient rules of Polish hospitality going back to somewhere around the time of Casimir the Great to make a gigantic lunch for everybody, and by the same rules we were required to eat it. By that time Linda was a basket case. "Come *on*, Jimmy! It's going to be *one o'clock* before we get over there. We've got to get *going*."

So we all pile into my Chevy and I drive over to the Island. The address Patty gave my sister is an old beat-to-shit house on the south end down by the Downs. The lawn didn't get cut much last summer, and then it got rained on and snowed on all winter so it has this mud-brown, crapped-out, halfhearted jungly look to it, and then there's an old Chevy Impala up on blocks, rusting away. And a three-quarter-ton pickup truck painted with red primer, looks like about a '48, but at least it's running. You can tell that from the tire tracks through the grass. A bunch of spare car parts are thrown around here and there for decoration. The house is one of these things divided up into two apartments. I try the front one first.

I press the doorbell and don't hear a thing so I knock. Nothing happens. No curtains on the windows, so I peer inside, and what I see is the front room stacked from one end to the other with cartons. Cartons of what, I couldn't tell you. A big fat white bulldog—you know, one of those things with the ugly pushed-in face and the bow legs—comes waddling over, lurches up, plants his front paws on the windowsill, and looks me straight in the eye. You could see him thinking about it, and he's going, oh well, what the hell, I am the bulldog, aren't I? And so he just gives me one big woof. I decide to try the rear apartment.

Linda can't stand waiting in the car anymore, so she jumps out and follows me, and then Mary Jo and Janice jump out and follow her. Linda keeps going, "Jimmy? Are you sure this is the right place?" The house looks like if you gave it a good swift kick at foundation level, the whole thing would come down. I knock on the back door. I don't expect much to happen, and nothing much does. I look through the window right into the kitchen. I know it's the kitchen because the folks who live there, every takeout food known to Western civilization, they've taken it out, and all the boxes and bags and cartons are all over the place. I give the door another good swat, and from somewhere deep within the recesses of the house, I hear a thump.

You've got to see this picture, right? Mary Jo, Linda, and Janice are all wearing what they wore to Mass, and that grown-up dress Janice had on at Easter was just for the occasion, so she's back to normal. So you've got Janice in her pigtails and kneesocks, and she looks like they've just let her out of the convent school, and you've got a fat lady in her sixties with bleached blond hair and bloodred lipstick, and she's wearing a white pantsuit, and you've got my conservative little sister with her glasses and her real earnest look, and she's wearing a blue pantsuit. And they're all holding their instrument cases and standing lined up staring at the back door of this rat's-ass little house.

The door finally swings open, and there's Patty Pajaczkowski. Her hair's all in her face, and her eyes are like two thin red gashes. She's got an old, stained, gray blanket wrapped around her shoulders, holding it shut over her chest, and all she seems to be wearing is a pair of pink panties. Bikini cut. With a little pink bow in the front.

"Shit," Patty says and just turns and walks away. Inside we hear her yelling, "Hey, Don! Get up."

"Come on, ladies," I say. "I think we're supposed to go in."

I lead everybody through the kitchen and on into the living room. There's nothing in there but a little table and a bunch of old chairs with their stuffing coming out and Patty's drum set. It's a pretty big drum set, and I bet the neighbors just adore her. There's a couple ashtrays on the table and enough roaches in them to stone out the whole Island for a day or two. And just at the point we're walking in from the kitchen, there's a guy walking in from the hallway. I got to know him years later when he was working with Georgie in his Vietnam vets' trash removal service, and his name was Don Henderson, and he was a hell of a nice guy, but right then we don't know who he is or that he's a hell of a nice guy. All we see is an enormous black man with no shirt on. He gives us a little apologetic smile and says, "Hey, uh, just make yourself at home. Patty'll be with you in a minute." That doesn't seem very likely because Patty has thrown herself down on the couch and wrapped herself in her blanket, and it looks like she's just died.

I don't know what Janice is thinking. Her eyes are big as saucers. But Linda and Mary Jo are exchanging the meaningful glances, and I know perfectly well what they're thinking. They've just stumbled into one of those hippie dens of iniquity you read about. You know, one of those places where the Ten Commandments and every other rule or regulation ever devised by God or man to assist us all in living together in peaceful accord are broken routinely on an hourly basis.

"Come on, babe," Don says. "Get it together. You got guests."

Patty reaches one hand out of the blanket and sticks it up into the air. Don grabs ahold of her hand and yanks her up onto her feet. He wraps his arm around her and guides her out of the room.

"I don't think we should be here," Linda whispers.

"We're here, ain't we?" Mary Jo says and plops her big bottom down in a chair.

We all look at each other for a minute, and then—bang—like the curtain going up for the next act, here's Bev Wright kicking through the back door. She's like a little whirlwind. Mop of brown hair, nonstop smile like one of those happy-face drawings. Got her Fender bass in its case and a big box of doughnuts. Yelling, "Patty Cakes, where the hell are you?" Running around shaking everybody's hand, "Hi, I'm Bev. I'm the bass player. I love playing polkas. It's such happy music. Hey, guys, give me a hand with my amp, will you?"

So Don and I haul in the amp and this speaker box that's not quite as big as the wall. Bev whips out her bass, plugs in, goes caBUNG, BUNG, BUNG-BUNG-BUNG. She's got it so loud the whole house shakes. In between notes, she's telling everybody about her famous brother, Jumping Jack Wright, and about how sad it is the all-girl country band broke up, and about how she loves playing with all girls, and how she's bored out of her skull living back at home in Barnsville, Ohio, a fate worse than death.

Patty stumbles in. She's put on cutoffs and a T-shirt. Her eyes are all glittery, and she's going sniff, sniff, sniff, like she's got a bad cold, and shaking her head and going, "Wheww, wow," and Bev takes one look at her and yells, "Hey, Don, you got any more of that shit?"

"Sure, babe," he yells, and Bev's gone like a shot.

Patty sits down at her drum set and goes caBANGA caBANGA BLAM, caBANGAcaBANGAcaBANGA BLAM. Bev pops back in and now *she's* going, sniff, sniff, sniff, "Wheww, wow, far out." Don's managed to make a pot of coffee, and he's passing out mugs of it. Then he and Bev and Patty are slurping back the coffee and scarfing up the doughnuts like it's the last food on earth. The rest of us are still trying to digest Mom's scrambled eggs and fried potatoes and *kiełbasa*, so we're going, "No, thank you. We just had lunch." Linda's perched on the very edge of her chair like any minute she'll break into a thousand pieces.

Well, you've got your sugar, and you've got your caffeine, and you've got your toot, so the rhythm section is higher than a couple jet-propelled bats. Off they go in this weird drum-and-bass duet. It lasts, swear to God, damn near half an hour. Super-colossal quadruple-time, lickety-split, power-charged, rocket-assisted, full goddamn tilt. Bev's all up and down her fingerboard. Patty's trying out all of her drums and cymbals and toys. They're both getting in every tricky maneuver they ever learned in their lives. The windowpanes are rattling in their frames. The walls are shaking right down to the bowels of the earth. They achieve this avalanche of sound like, you know, your basic earthquake maybe twelve notches above the end of the Richter scale, and then bring it down to a halt like a B-52 has just crashed and burned. They're going, "Hey, wow, too much, far out, yeah, man, out of sight," and other similar original comments.

"Hey, stud," Patty yells at me, "you got another one of those cancer sticks?" So I throw her a cigarette.

"Who plays the box?" Bev says, pointing at the accordion case.

"I do," Mary Jo says. Real grim.

"Hey, wow, that's great. Get it out. Let me tune to you. Hey, I didn't catch your name."

"That's Mary Jo, the polka lady," Patty says. "I heard you play a million times when I was a kid," she says to Mary Jo. It's the first good word she's had to say since we showed up.

"Yeah, you probably did," Mary Jo says. "Yeah, I know you too, Patty. I went to school with your mom's dad."

"Oh, did you?"

"Yeah, I did. He was a few grades ahead of me. I played at your parents' wedding."

Patty had started out friendly enough—well, friendly enough for Patty—

but now they're giving each other the evil eye. Mary Jo's look says, how can you live like this, a girl from a nice Polish family like you? And Patty's look says, piss off and die, old lady.

Bev isn't catching any of this. "Come on," she says, "let's play something."

So they get out their instruments and tune to the accordion. I've got nothing to do but sit there with Don and smoke cigarettes and watch the action. Patty's still cranked to the eyeballs—she's twitching and tapping on her drums and gnawing away on her fingers—and she's not happy. Mary Jo's usually laughing and talking, but now she's silent as a stone, and she looks like she's been gargling with vinegar. My poor sister's so nervous she's sweating buckets. She keeps wiping her hands on her pants. The only one who seems completely unfazed is Janice.

"Okay, polka lady," Patty says, "squeeze out a good one."

Mary Jo kicks into that old standard, *"na około czarny las."* Only somebody who's been playing their whole life could play like Mary Jo. She doesn't have to think about a thing. It's just down in her bones, you know, like she owns the damn tune. Like she's always owned the damn tune.

The first one to join in is Janice. She slides in over the accordion like honey, and you can see Patty light up a little when she hears the sweet sound Janice gets out of her clarinet. And then Patty slips in underneath, nailing it down. A lot quieter now so she won't drown anybody out—nobody's amplified but Bev—and she's really inside that polka beat. I mean, she's *there*. Bev's turned her Fender way down, and there's a couple bongs till she finds the key, and then she's putting her boom, boom right where it ought to be. You can hear them listening to each other and pulling it tight. They haven't been playing together longer than a minute or two, and already they sound like a perfectly respectable polka band. Then Linda tries to come in.

Maybe she waited too long. Maybe she was hearing how good Mary Jo and Janice sounded with a good solid rhythm section under them and figured she couldn't possibly come up to that. Maybe she was just nervous as all hell. But she sounds terrible. I mean, she sounds even worse than that. Out of tune. Fluffing her notes. When she does manage to squirt out a note, it's like the horn on a forties Buick. I can see the sweat just pouring down her face in buckets, and I'm kind of, you know, wincing inside on her behalf, thinking, oh, you poor kid, come on, you can do it.

They get to the end of the tune, and Linda's going, "Oh, sorry, sorry. I don't know what's wrong with me," and you can see how embarrassed everybody is. Patty is just sitting there with her mouth shut, but everybody else is going, "Don't worry. Take it easy. Happens to the best of us," and like that. Linda gives me this horrible look—*help!*—and says, "Jimmy, can you get me a glass of water, please?" so I get her a glass of water.

Maybe Patty's coming down off her coke high, I don't know, but it's like there's this big cloud of gloom settling over her. You can almost see it pressing her down. "At the end of a polka," she says to Bev, "you don't leave nothing hanging out. It just ends, whoom," and she makes a chopping gesture to show how sudden it ends.

"How am I doing?" Bev says.

"You're doing just fine. It's not too different from country. The beat's got to bounce. Like, you gotta dance to it, you know. But you don't have to be so bare. You can fill it in, like at the ends," and then Patty turns to look at Mary Jo— Okay, what next?

"Sing something," Linda says to Janice.

"I will. But not yet. Let's just wait a minute."

Mary Jo has a disgusted look on her face like she's thinking, come on, what are you guys farting around for? and she just starts belting away on "The Clarinet Polka," so there's nothing for Janice to do but jump in with her clarinet. It's a show-off piece for Janice, but there's a trumpet part in it—they told me that later—and Linda doesn't even try it. She just takes her trumpet mouthpiece and walks away and stands looking out a window, going buzz, buzz, buzz.

Patty and Bev are real pros—you can hear it. They're making a nice solid polka groove for Janice to ride on, and Mary Jo's doing the bellows shake, filling in the middle and pushing the tune along, and Janice blows through the melody as easy as whip cream, and then she blows through it again, taking it apart and putting it back together in a different way. Some of those runs, she starts down with the lowest note she's got, and then she shoots it right up into the ozone layer. It's really something to hear. Patty doesn't smile much, but Janice has got her smiling. "Do it again, sweetheart," she says.

Janice has another go at that old tune. This time she really flips it around backward, upside down, inside out, every which way. You keep wondering if she's going to come out right, and she always does. It's really fun. Bev's laughing at her. They wind it up and Patty says, "Hey, doll baby, you're far out on that stick. How the hell old are you anyways?"

"Sixteen." Janice has got a real offended look like a cat you've just tossed water on.

"No shit? A lot of people wouldn't believe that." Patty turns to Mary Jo. "How you gonna play in bars with her?"

"We're not gonna be a bar band."

"Oh, yeah. Is that right? Where you gonna play?"

"Well, for one, the church."

"The church, huh? Does the church pay?"

"You bet. The church pays good." And Mary Jo goes through her thing about lawn fetes and street fairs and county fairs and Polish days and anywhere people like polkas. "Weddings," she says, "you get the real big bucks."

Patty sits there behind her drums thinking it all over. Or thinking something over. The gloom is pressing on her good now. Linda comes back with her trumpet and takes a deep breath and says, "Let's do Eddie Zima's."

So they play through that one, and Linda manages to get most of her notes, and she manages to stay in tune most of the time, but she's working hard at it, and that's exactly what she sounds like. I've heard her playing a million times better just standing in her bedroom with the door shut. They finish that one up, and Patty says, "Okay, you got an *oberek*?"

"Sure," Mary Jo says, "we got lots of them."

"You going to play for dances, you need a couple *obereks*."

"You don't need to tell me that, Patty. I been playing Polish dances for forty years."

How much Patty and Mary Jo hate each other's guts is showing all over them. "I never got no awards for diplomacy," Mary Jo says. "Whatever I'm thinking, I just speak my mind."

"Well, far fucking out."

"Yeah. Right. That's some mouth you got on you, Patty. I'm sure your mom and dad would be happy to hear the stuff coming out of your mouth. But that's neither here nor there. Let me ask you something. Is this the kind of music you want to play?"

"You saying I'm not playing it right?"

"No, I'm not saying that. You're a good drummer. You're a real good drummer. But I just don't know why the hell you'd want to play polka music."

"Look, polka lady, I don't give a shit what you think of me. And maybe I don't want to play polka music. I don't know. I'm just seeing if I can get behind it, you know what I mean? But let me tell *you* something. I grew up on this music. My dad had a stack of records a mile high. Old 78s. That's all he played. I don't know the names of the tunes, and I don't know the names of the bands, but it's all in here," and she pats her heart, looking at Mary Jo like she's daring her to say it's not true.

"Come on, Patty," Bev says, "be nice. Don't fight. Come on. Let's just play."

Linda kind of takes a step forward with her trumpet and says, "How about 'The Iron Casket'?"

I don't know what Patty was thinking, maybe just that she was sick of Linda not playing very well, and standing there sweating and gulping water and going, "Sorry, sorry, sorry," and I think Patty was trying to be kind in her weird way, but what she said was the wrong thing—or maybe the right thing, depending on how you look at it. "Mellow out, sweetie," Patty says, "this ain't Carnegie Hall."

Linda goes white. I mean for real, the color just goes whoosh right out of her face, and I see something go flash in her eyes. If you think my sister can't get mad, you don't know her.

"An *oberek*'s in a weird kind of three," Patty says to Bev.

"Yeah," Linda says to Bev, "that weird kind of three's called three-eight. The bass should take it in two."

They kick into that *oberek*, and Linda's so pissed off it's improved her playing about a thousand percent. She's still kind of stiff, you know, but she's getting it all in, and there's even a kind of punch to it. They sound like they could go play the Pączki Ball that night if they had to. They finish up, and Patty says, "So what do you think, Beverly? You like this Hunky music?"

"Oh, yeah," Bev says. "I like it just fine."

"How about you, Don?" Patty says. "What do you think? Us Polaks got soul or what?"

Don's an agreeable guy. "Sure, babe," he says, "you got lots of soul." He fires up a couple smokes and hands her one of them. I don't envy him, if he's trying to have something like you'd call a relationship with Patty Pajaczkowski.

Nobody knows what to do next. Patty looks at Bev, but Bev's run out of the good word. Then she looks at Mary Jo. Then she looks at Janice and Linda. They're all looking at her. "You got enough tunes for a set?" she says.

"Sure," Mary Jo says, "we got enough for two sets."

"You got any waltzes?"

"Sure, we got lots of waltzes. Some real pretty ones." Now you'd think Mary Jo would play a waltz, wouldn't you? But she doesn't. Patty finishes her smoke. The gloom is hanging heavy on her.

"Don't any of those tunes have words?" Bev says.

Instantly, like answering Bev's question, Janice starts to sing. It's a good old polka tune going back to the year zero. Being perfect, she doesn't need anybody to give her a note; she's got the note in her head.

She's clapping and stomping down on the beat. There's no sound but what's coming out of her mouth and her hands slapping together and one of her little-kid shoes banging down on the floor, but she's laying out that beat so strong she's a polka band all by herself. She's singing with a real strong rhythm like this—

"POD MOS-
tem NA MOŚ-
cie stoją róże dwie czerwone.
POD MOS-
tem NA MOŚ-
cie stoją róże dwie."

What that means in English is, "Under the bridge, on the bridge, there's two red roses." In a lot of those old Polish songs, a rose isn't really a rose, you know what I mean? They just say it that way to be poetic. These two roses are a couple kids—young half-baked teenagers they always seemed to me—like Dorothy Pliszka and me back in high school. And what they're doing on the bridge, or under it, is having exactly the kind of dumb fight you'd expect a couple kids to be having—he's trying to get somewhere, and she's saying no.

So I'm sitting there listening to this incredible voice singing this old song, and it's like my brain cells got hit with a power surge and shorted right out. It was the first time I ever heard Janice sing, and— Well, you'd think I'd know what to say about it, wouldn't you? I just wish you could have heard her.

You ever hear little girls yelling at each other when they're playing a game and they don't know you're paying any attention to them? Yelling something like, "Hey, it's my turn!" Well, she was singing like that, kind of like yelling in tune.

No, but that's not right. It was more— I don't know. It was more than just a little girl yelling. It was beautiful and, well, I guess you'd have to say, beautiful and wild.

There's some polka singers got a sweet, easy voice you can listen to all night long—like Marion Lush or Happy Louie. Then there's others—like Eddie Blazonczyk or Scrubby Seweryniak on their best tunes, or Walt Solek on damn near anything—and they've got a voice that goes straight through you like a laser, and you just can't get enough of it. It's like you've been waiting your whole life to hear that voice. Janice had a voice like that. What was Poland like in the old days? Do you know? I sure don't. But the feeling was that she'd just shot us right back there.

Don has been sprawled back on the couch, totally mellowed out, but he sits up so fast you'd think something stung him. And I swear to God, the hair's standing straight up on the back of my neck. Janice is singing

"Obiecała buzi dać,
 ale nie dała, psia mać!"

That means something like, "She promised to give him a kiss, but now she's changed her mind—damn it!"

"Oh, *yeah!*" Patty yells and comes blasting in with her drums. My sister, like instantly, is right there with her, and she's taking those big trumpet notes and shoving them in our faces.

"Nie dam ci,
 nie dam ci,
 bo by było znać."

That's "I won't give it, I won't give it, because it'd leave a mark." It's not like the girl in the song really thinks a kiss is going to leave a mark on her. It's more like she's afraid everybody's going to be talking about her.

And they've blown free of the vocal and blasted off into the drive. Mary Jo and Bev come in together like they'd rehearsed it a million times.

Janice and Linda are facing each other, the trumpet and clarinet locked so tight they might have been welded. Both of them sweating like pigs. Doing bent notes, you know—that old-country sound—right bang together. Then Janice sings the next part. That's where the girl says, "If you kiss me, I won't forgive you. Have you lost you mind, or what?"

"Boś nie małe dziecię," she says. "You're not a little kid, so there's not going to be any kissing for you, buddy."

The boy's pretty pissed off. "I'll never believe in a girl again," he says. "You promised, but then you didn't deliver. You'll answer for this in hell, you bad-news girl!"

Then they hit the drive again and don't hold back nothing, and Mary Jo's big foghorn voice comes ripping up out of her, and she's going, *"Hop, hop, hop, HOPLA!"* You could almost see a whole hall full of dancers going crazy.

They slide into home, whoom, and it's over. Stopped dead. And we're all completely blown away. Everybody kind of lets out a breath, like, wheww. For a few minutes there, they weren't just a good polka band, they were the best polka band anybody had ever heard in the history of the world.

We're all just thinking our own thoughts. Then Patty stands up like somebody coming to attention, and she faces Janice, and she presses the palms of her hands together, and she bows to her. Just once. Then she sits down. Janice doesn't know what to do with that.

"We need someplace people can hear us," Patty says. "No point in just playing for each other."

"You know Franky Rzeszutko's place?" Linda says.

"Yeah. Sure. We used to eat there when I was a kid."

"I'll bet he'd let us play in there some Saturday night."

"Oh, sure he would," Mary Jo says. "He'd be glad to do that. He used to have musicians in there all the time in the old days. We could pass the hat. Come out with a few bucks."

They're packing up their instruments. Nobody said, "Let's stop now," but when it's over, it's over. "We need a PA system," Patty says.

"You can rent one at Kaltenbach's," Bev says.

"Jimmy," Linda says, "you can do that, can't you?"

"Sure," I say.

"Wow," Patty says, "is my dad ever going to shit when he hears this. We got a name?"

"Mary Jo thought we should be the Polka Dolls," Linda says. Kind of doubtful.

"Naw," Mary Jo says, "that doesn't feel right anymore."

"How about 'Three Hunkies and a Hick,'" Patty says and gets a laugh.

"Well, Mary Jo is the Polka Lady, right?" Bev says. "Why don't we be the Polka Ladies?"

Patty groans. "No way. Nobody's going to make a lady out of me."

"How about the Polka Dots?" Mary Jo says.

"Isn't there a band already called that?" Linda says.

"It's too cute anyway," Patty says.

So they're tossing ideas back and forth. They try out the Raysburg Polka Girls. No, that's just dumb. Besides, Bev's not from Raysburg. Well, does that matter? They try out the Tri-state— the Nail City— the Friendly City— the Steel City— Polka Girls. "Isn't the Steel City Pittsburgh?" somebody says. And do they want to be Polka Girls anyway? They try out the Polkatones, the Polkateers, the Polkarettes."

"Come on," Patty says, "nothing that ends in 'ette.'"

"But the name's gotta say we're all girls," Bev says, "even if it hasn't got Girls in it."

"Look," Linda says, "we're not going to solve this today."

"Patty," Mary Jo says, "you'll clean up a little bit, won't you?"

"Aw, come on, Mary Jo, I got common sense. When you're playing for people, you're playing for people. You gotta make the folks happy."

We wandered out of the living room and through the kitchen and out to my car. There was a funny kind of feeling. It wasn't till hours later it dawned on me what it was. It was the same feeling you get walking out of Mass.

I dropped Mary Jo at her place, and then I shot up to Edgewood to drop Janice. I was still trying to get my head wrapped around what had just gone down.

Once when I was in the eighth grade, we were having football practice on that little field in Pulaski Park, and practice was over—the coach was blowing his whistle and waving us to head back to the school—and somebody flips the ball up in the air, and easy as pie Georgie Mondrowski catches it and takes off running. And like instantly, the name of the game is get Mondrowski. We were all of us trying to get Mondrowski—kids all over that field trying to tackle him. But none of us got Mondrowski. It was the sweetest little bit of broken field running from a kid my own age I ever saw—all the way across to the other side of the park. Well, he slammed the ball down like he'd made a touchdown, and he came back laughing, and we walked back to the school, and I remember looking at him and thinking, Mondrowski, you're wonderful.

So it was the same feeling. I kept looking over at her riding in my car and thinking, Janice, you're wonderful. We got to her house, and I asked her, "You have a good time?" She hadn't been saying much of anything.

"Oh, yeah." And then she just stood there a minute with the car door open. You know what she said? "I'm just so thankful."

Then I'm driving back down to South Raysburg, and there's this dead silence, so just to get the air vibrating I say to my sister, "Pretty good start for your band, huh? That Patty Pajaczkowski's something else."

Linda goes, "I hate her, I hate her, I hate her, I hate her."

"Yeah, but she's a good drummer, isn't she?"

And Linda just explodes crying. I pull over, and I'm going, "Come on, Linny. Hey, come on, it's okay." I don't think I ever heard anybody cry so hard in my life.

She's howling, you know what I mean? She's pounding her fists on her legs. She going, "I've got a *degree* in music. All those damn years— I sacrificed. I could have been— So what did I get out of it? I can read anything—on the piano. I can play Chopin. I can play Bach. It doesn't matter a damn. I was terrible. I was pathetic. I was shitty. I've never been so mortified in my life."

She finally gets so she can talk. "Do you know what's funny? It was my idea in the first place. Isn't that funny? I don't want anything to do with it now. It's all ruined for me now. They'll have to find somebody else. They even sound okay with just the clarinet."

"Come on, kid."

"I mean it. *I just can't do it.*"

"Yes, you can."

She starts crying again. "Do you know what I had to go through to get that degree? Dad gave me shit the whole time. He never let up, not once."

"Oh, yeah? I thought you were his darling baby girl who could do no wrong."

"Not that time, I wasn't. All I heard was, 'Aw, Linny, where's it going to get you? Why don't you switch into education?' Oh, God, Jimmy, why did I ever think I could learn to play the trumpet!"

"Come on, kid, cut yourself some slack. How long you been playing the damn thing?"

"A year and a half—no, a little bit longer. Almost two years."

"So what do you expect? In two years you're going to be Louis Armstrong?"

So I start giving her my pep talk. I sound just like the Central Catholic football coach. I'm telling her how much she improved when she got relaxed, and how good the band sounded at the end, and like that. How she's just got to give herself some time. "Listen to me, Linny," I say, "you may not be the best player in that group, but you're the heart of it. Without you, there's no band."

We sit there and look at each other. She's cleaning her glasses. She's cried herself out, and now she's just quiet and sad. "It's nothing like I expected," she says.

She thinks about it awhile longer, and then she says, "I guess I'd better call up Mr. Webb and take some lessons. How the hell did I think I could learn to play the trumpet without ever taking a single lesson?"

TWELVE

Summer was right around the corner and I wasn't feeling half bad. I'd even catch myself sometimes and I'd be almost cheery. You can't be working out four days a week and not be feeling at least a little bit better about yourself, you know what I mean? And I had my drinking turned back into what I thought was normal. That means I only got falling-down dead drunk on the weekends. So comes this one Sunday morning—it was early in May, the best I remember—and I've got my usual end-of-the-world hangover, and somebody's knocking on my trailer door.

Guess what? It's my long-lost buddy, Mrs. Constance Bradshaw. She's got a tracksuit on— No, wait a minute, let me get it right because she was kind of spectacular.

She'd had her hair cut real short but still with the long bangs, you know, kind of Twiggy style. And she had on top-of-the-line running shoes, like right out of the box, not a mark on them, and this little track top and shorts. Pink. I mean, except for her shoes, everything was pink. Even her socks were pink. Her goddamn fingernails were pink. She was wearing a lot of makeup, and she looked like if the Dallas Cowboys Cheerleaders decided to have a track team, she was on it.

What she wasn't wearing was her wedding ring. She used to take it off when we went up to the Night Owl, but other than that, she always wore it. She didn't say a word about not seeing me since The Italian Renaissance, and if she was pissed off at me for not answering my phone all those times, she didn't mention it. She was acting like the last time we'd seen each other had been a couple days ago, and she was cheery as all hell, laughing at the sorry state I was in.

I put some coffee on and had a shower. That gave me a minute or two to scrape myself together and try to get my head wrapped around what was going down. Was this just a friendly little visit from an old girlfriend, or did she have something more serious on her mind?

Now I hadn't been thinking too much about Mrs. Constance Bradshaw lately. In fact she'd practically slipped right out of my mind. Who I'd been thinking about was Janice Dłuwiecki—which is probably not going to come as any surprise to you, right? But I'm a little on the slow side sometimes, and I was still having a hard time admitting to it, but— Well, to make a long story short, Janice was starting to get to me.

It had started off totally innocent because to me Janice was just a little kid, and then after I got to like her, she was just a second little sister. So we'd had all this time together, all those Tuesday nights, to get to know each other, talking about anything at all. But then— I don't know when it started exactly, maybe it was her birthday, maybe it was Easter, maybe it was hearing her sing over at Patty's place, but I'd crossed some kind of line and there was just no way I could see her as a little kid anymore, and— Oh, hell. After I first noticed her hipbones, I couldn't *stop* noticing them, you know what I mean?

I liked the way she looked, and I liked the way her mind worked, and I liked the person she was turning out to be, and I just plain liked *her*—and I liked her a whole hell of a lot—and there was absolutely no way any of this was leading anywhere because of the simple fact she was sixteen years old. I wanted to do the right thing by her, and I'd been asking myself over and over what that right thing was, and I always came up with the same answer. The right thing for me to do about Janice Dłuwiecki was absolutely nothing.

I never said a word to her that was the least bit suggestive, and I was always real careful not to touch her. When we walked anywhere together, I even left plenty of space so our shoulders wouldn't bump. And it was kind of obvious she had a little kid's crush on me, but whenever she alluded to it, like making remarks about how she'd always liked older boys, I'd just ignore it, but anyhow—

I've probably told you how the nuns were always yammering away at us about impure thoughts. Well, when you're a little kid, you don't have a clue what they're talking about. I remember thinking, hey, I got real mad at Mom yesterday. Is that an impure thought? That's how out of it you are at six. But then the years go rolling by and all of a sudden, yeah, you know what an impure thought is, all right. And I'd been having an impure thought or two about Janice. And it just bothered the hell out of me. And the whole thing was, I guess you could say, starting to put a certain amount of strain on the old peace of mind.

So there I am in my little phone-booth-sized shower, and I'm contemplating the fact that Mrs. Constance Bradshaw has just turned up looking pretty damn fine. It's amazing the excuses you'll give yourself, but I thought, hell, Connie may be crazy as six loons, but we sure had some wild times together, and here's the clincher. Okay, Koprowski, maybe what you need in your life right now is some of that *adult* companionship.

I came out of the shower and told Connie I was glad to see her—especially looking just lovely the way she was at the moment—and I got a big bright smile for that. She told me she had a surprise for me. "Oh, yeah?" I said, "am I going to like it?"

"You're going to love it."

What she wanted me to do was get in her Mustang and go somewhere with her. "Honey," I said, "there's a basic rule with me. I don't go anywhere unless it's under my own steam."

She'd been laughing a lot ever since she showed up, and she laughed at that. "Oh, you're so paranoid. What do you think I'm going to do, kidnap you? Okay, take your own car then. Follow me."

So I followed her on out to St. Stevens. Ended up on this quiet, picture-postcard street—you know, with your shady old trees and big front porches and lawn sprinklers going. I park behind her, and we both get out, and I follow her around to the back of this house and up the steps, and she unlocks the door and pushes me inside. "Ta-DUM," she says, "it's mine."

It was a pretty sunny little apartment, everything in it neat and clean as a pin. "We're separated," she said. She told me that she and her husband were doing one of those trial separation things. He was still in the house with the kids not too far from there, so she could see them anytime she wanted.

She's going, "This is mine, mine, mine! What do you think, Jim? Isn't it fabulous?"

I looked around, pretending I was admiring everything, but I didn't know what I thought. Her furniture looked brand-new. She had pictures of her kids all over the place, but none of her husband. I'd never seen pictures of her kids before, and it gave me a jolt. They were beautiful kids. I didn't like seeing their little faces looking at me.

After she and her husband had the big fight when he'd found out she hadn't been going to The Italian Renaissance, everything had worked out just fine, much to her amazement. Of course it took days of bitter slogging to get there, but now they were seeing a marriage counselor, and they'd decided it was a good idea to keep the kids in their familiar environment, so they'd hired Mrs. So-and-so to look after them full-time. That meant Connie could come and go as she pleased. Her husband had even agreed to an open marriage. He was hoping it wouldn't always be like that, but he could live with it for the time being.

Up until then I'd always felt sorry for Connie's husband, but now I was thinking, okay, let me see if I've got this one right. She moves out, leaves the kids with him, gets him to agree that she can screw other guys, and he's still paying for everything? That guy must be the biggest damn fool who ever walked the earth.

Ever since she'd showed up, she'd been working hard to show me how happy happy happy she was, so naturally I was starting to wonder if she was really as happy as all that, and yeah, there was something phony about it. Like the way she was talking didn't sound like herself. Like she couldn't quite meet my eyes. Like that little tinkly laugh was just pathetic. Like I could see her hands shaking.

She showed me this book called *Aerobics* she'd been reading and told me how it'd changed her life. She'd been jogging every day. "I'm almost up to a mile. Isn't that wonderful? And I've always been just about the least athletic person you could imagine. Oh, I'm going to be so fit."

She takes me in her bedroom and shows me all these clothes she's bought. During the worst of it, she said, she'd gone home for a few days—when she said "home" she always meant Baltimore—and she'd treated herself to a few new things. I swear, a dozen of these minidresses and miniskirts in that ungodly expensive melt-in-your-mouth leather she liked. All colors. White and pink and red and blue and yellow. She's going, "Oh, I just adore leather. Don't you, Jim? It's just so sexy. I'd wear leather panties if I could find someone who would make them for me."

"Honey," I say, "clothes hanging on a hanger don't do much for me. I like to see them with a woman inside."

She gives me a good ha-ha over that one.

"Do you like athletic girls?" she says. Standing there in her pink tracksuit. The drapes drawn on the bedroom window. I hadn't been laid since The Italian Renaissance, so what do you think I did?

Well, it started out okay. I'd drive out there late in the morning on Sundays, and Connie would cook one of those brunch things—you know, the eggs and the orange juice—and then we'd retire to the bedroom. It didn't have the high-octane kick we used to get back when we'd been riding that thin edge, but it was nice. We'd snooze a bit after we got done, and then we'd lay there and have a couple beers and, you know, chat about nothing in particular. We were having what she called "a Mature Relationship." I guess that means you get to screw somebody once a week and not have any responsibilities.

Then afterward I'd say, "Well, I got to go home for dinner. Big family thing on Sundays, you know," and that seemed okay with her. But she'd always want to know exactly when I was coming back. "We haven't got a lot of room for spontaneity," she said.

She made me swear on everything sacred that I'd never just turn up unannounced. "He can sort of handle it when it's all in the abstract," she said, "but if he actually saw a real human being, I don't know what he'd do."

Well, I didn't want to run into her husband any more than she wanted me to, so I played by the rules. I could call her any time I wanted, but if she said, "Oh, hi, Barbara," then I was supposed to get the message that her husband was there. But I didn't call her too often. To tell you the truth, I didn't think about her all that much when I wasn't with her.

Meanwhile Linda started taking trumpet lessons with Mr. Webb, and she called up Franky Rzeszutko and he told her, "Sure, kid, any Saturday night you want to bring your band in here, that's fine with me. It'd be great to have live music again. How about *this* Saturday?"

No, no, no, that was way too quick for Linda. She decided they should wait till school was out. "It's only fair to Janice," she said. Well, Janice didn't care, so the person Linda was being fair to was herself because she wanted to cram a million hours of practice in before she had to stand up and play that horn in front of God and everybody.

Seeing as Bev and Patty were professionals and knew everything there was to know about the music business—that was how they saw it anyway—they had a serious talk with Linda. Told her there were a number of heavy-duty things the band had to do if it was going to be for real. Number one on the list was they needed a manager. "Jimmy?" Linda says.

"No problem," I say. "Since about the age of four, it's always been my burning ambition to be the manager of a polka band." So I go up to Kaltenbach's and check out the PA systems they got for rent and pick one that'll do the job at Franky's place just fine.

Nobody could figure out what the band's name was, but they all kept trying. Mary Jo came up with the Red-Hot Polka Girls.

"Aw, come on," Linda said, "it sounds like we're the residents of a polka dancers' whorehouse."

Janice suggested, *"Wesoła Polka."* You see, in Polish "polka" means a Polish woman, so that meant "the happy Polish woman."

Mary Jo said, "That's cute. But if you don't speak Polish, you wouldn't get it."

Even Patty had a shot at it. Phone rings in the middle of dinner, Mom answers it, says it's Patty Pajaczkowski.

Linda hisses at me, "You get it, Jimmy. I don't want to talk to her."

So I pick up the phone, and I'm hearing in the background Janis Joplin wailing away and a bunch of whacked-out people speed-rapping—that goofy laugh has got to be Mondrowski—and Patty goes, "We got it."

"Got what?"

"The name. We're going to be the Polestars, okay? And then when we start making albums, they're going to be, 'Heavenly Bodies,' 'Polka Heaven,' and 'Lead Me On.'"

I convey this to Linda, and she raises her eyebrows, so I say to Patty, "We'll take it under advisement."

"Oh, God," Linda says, "maybe we should be Poles Apart."

"Hey," I say, "that's pretty good."

But that got her thinking, and the next day she decided—for real—the band should be the Magnetic Poles, and their albums would be "Opposites Attract," "From Pole to Pole," and "Push and Pull."

"Everybody's working too hard," Mary Jo said. "All we need is a nice simple name people can remember—like 'Mary Jo and the Polka Girls.'"

Nobody said anything to that.

"Hey," Bev said, "you heard of Crosby, Stills, Nash and Young—?"

"No," Linda said, "there's no way we're going to be Duda, Koprowski, Dłuwiecki, Pajaczkowski and Wright."

On the first Sunday in May we had the procession to the church the way we always do. The cops come down and rope the street off, and the procession goes from St. Stans school around a couple blocks and ends up at the church. Everybody in the parish turns out for it.

The sodality elects a May Queen and her court. The May Queen's a girl out of high school who's not married yet, and she's supposed to be pretty, but when they're picking her, they also take into account how active she's been in the sodality and like that. The May Princesses are usually her girlfriends, and they're all dressed up in these old-fashioned ball gowns. In the old days the May Queen had a long train on her dress, and a couple little boys had to carry it so it wouldn't drag on the ground. When I was a little boy, I always went way far out of my way to make sure I wouldn't get picked to do that.

The different grades at St. Stans school have different costumes they wear, and the kids really look cute. I was in it for years, and if you're a little kid, of course you're not thinking you look cute, you're thinking you look ridiculous and you hope nobody laughs at you. Like I remember wearing a robe and a cape and a hat trimmed with white fur, that fake stuff. The littlest girls are dressed all in white like First Communion dresses, and the bigger girls wear long dresses, and the eighth-grade girls carry a statue of the Blessed Virgin. The procession ends up in the church, and the May Queen crowns the Blessed Virgin with flowers, and then you have Mass. It's a nice happy springtime event, and you look forward to it every year.

But from Czesław Długwiecki's point of view it was yet another example of our degenerate peasant culture. Janice had got sick of hearing him say that, and she told him it wasn't fair, so he took that opportunity to explain a few things to her once again.

The peasants in different parts of Poland, he said, have lots of different customs, but the only thing that even resembles a queen is in that harvest festival called *Dożynki*. The peasants pick a pretty young girl and crown her with a wreath made out of grain and decorated with ribbons and flowers and berries and like that. She's not really a queen, but if you wanted to stretch it a bit, you could maybe call her a harvest queen. And there's festivals in honor of the Blessed Virgin all over Poland, he says, and the crown of the Blessed Virgin is an important symbol in Polish Catholicism, but May Queens? There's not a real May Queen to be seen in all of Poland.

So where did this weird ceremony at St. Stanislaus come from? Well, her dad's going to give Janice the straight scoop on that. The people who first settled here—that's our grandparents he's talking about, right?—were poor peasants with no education whatsoever. You could hardly even call the language they spoke Polish, it was so crude. Poland was partitioned in those days, so they had no sense of a common nationality. The economic conditions were truly terrible, and a lot of them had already been displaced from the land and were just wandering around loose, and then they ended up in America. And the long and the short of it is that these poor folks were basically so ignorant they couldn't tell a *dupa* from a teacup.

So they settle in Raysburg, and they've got some dim recollections of their peasant past back in Poland, and dim recollections of Polish history, and somebody thinks they ought to have a celebration on the 3rd of May to commemorate the signing of Poland's constitution. And somebody else thinks having a May Queen is a good idea—even though the May Queen is a *British* folk tradition not a Polish one—and then they decide to make it a little bit like an American beauty pageant, and then the Church jumps in the way it always does to make sure the whole thing's Catholic, and there you've got it. *Degenerate.* When Czesław uses that word, he says, that's exactly what he means, and that's exactly what it is.

This didn't go down too well with Janice. She'd gone to school with the nuns at St. Stans just like the rest of us, and she'd been in the May procession for eight years just like the rest of us, and she thought it was beautiful. "It's such an important part of the life of the parish," she said, "how can he object to it? Oh, he's so self-righteous. He thinks he knows everything."

Well, she wasn't about to let it go, and she asked him something I'd been wondering about myself. "If you feel that way, why are we even members of St. Stanislaus Parish?"

"It's a Polish parish," he said like it's obvious. "Don't get me wrong, Janusiu. Those people are good people. Good Catholics. Sincere, honest, shrewd, hardworking. The salt of the earth. They were very good to me and your mother when we first came here, and we will always be in their debt."

"Yeah, except they're ignorant and degenerate," she said. "Oh, he just drives me right up the wall!"

Janice did a lot of complaining about her parents. When you're sixteen, it kind of goes with the territory, and that spring they were really getting to her. Like her dad wanted Janice to stay a little girl forever, but her mom kept remembering when *she'd* been sixteen back in Poland before the war, so she wanted Janice to look like what she called "sophisticated," which meant these weird grown-up clothes Janice wouldn't wear on a bet. And her mom liked to see Janice with makeup on, but if her dad caught her with anything more than just a little lipstick, he'd make her go wash her face.

Then there's the pigtails. Now what do I know about pigtails? I figure a pigtail's a pigtail, right? Well, that just goes to show you how ignorant I am. Janice hadn't had her hair cut since she'd been like four or five, and her mom was the one who'd put her in pigtails in the first place because it's cute on a little girl—

you know, the braids hanging down her back—and Janice still did her hair that way when she was in school because the nuns liked it. But when she was out of school, she did what all her girlfriends did—the braids in the front, Indian style, so her hair covered her ears. And the little-girl pigtails her mom thought were pathetic on a sixteen-year-old, but the Indian braids drove her absolutely berserk because they made Janice look like a hippie. Which is exactly why Janice and her pals did it, right? Meanwhile Czesław didn't really give a damn whether they were braided in the front or in the back. He just thought braids on young girls were very becoming, and if Janice ever got her hair cut, it'd be a major tragedy.

But her mom wanted Janice's hair cut so bad she was freaking right out about it. Janice just kept going no, no, no, and in the last year it'd reached fever pitch. Her mom kept saying, "One of these nights when you're asleep, I'm going to sneak in with a pair of scissors and cut those damned braids off."

Janice didn't really believe her mom would ever do that, but she started locking her bedroom door when she went to bed. "I swear, Jimmy," Janice said, "if they don't let me alone, I'm going to become one of those teenage runaways."

Well, the tension kept building up in the Dłuwiecki household, and Janice and her dad finally had themselves just a dandy brawl—over Vietnam, if you can believe that. You see, the war just kept ticking along in the background, and you couldn't really ignore it for very long because every once in a while it'd jump up on your television screen and bite you again. That spring the good old U.S. of A. invaded Cambodia.

An incursion is what they called it. That scumbag Nixon came on the tube and did his song and dance about how he'd rather be a one-term president than have America turn into a second-rate power, and America shouldn't be acting like a helpless giant, and we've got to go hit the Commies hard to defend freedom in the world, and, you know, basically ranted on. It was kind of scary.

I remember talking to some of the young guys in the PAC—guys who'd just got their draft cards—and they were saying, "What the hell's he talking about? I thought he was winding the sucker down. What's this—the war that goes on forever?"

You remember that silent majority Nixon thought he had behind him? Well, I don't know how behind him it was at that point. If the silent majority meant people like Old Bullet Head, I'll tell you what he said about our little incursion into Cambodia. "Hell, Jimmy, Nixon's got no plan to end the war and he never had one. We're going to be bogged down in Southeast Asia for the next twenty years."

I think most Americans were fed up with the war by then and just wanted us to find some way to get out of it that wasn't too messy. But there was one issue where Nixon really did have the silent majority behind him—and that's when it came to the protesters. After Nixon's speech, the college campuses went up like a bunch of firecrackers, and that student protest stuff was starting to really grate on people's nerves. I was feeling kind of that way myself. Lately we'd been seeing kids seizing buildings on their campuses, and trashing offices, and generally acting like assholes, and people thought—

Well, again let me give you Old Bullet Head on the topic. From his point of view, you send your kids to school so they can get a good education and have a better life than you did, and it costs a bundle, and it's a big sacrifice. To him those campus radicals were just a bunch of ungrateful spoiled brats. "The girls should be sent home and have their asses paddled," he said, "and the boys should get drafted so fast their heads would swim."

And then when you're remembering all the players from those days, you can't forget your Weathermen from SDS—yeah, banana city. They'd been out rioting and busting windows in Chicago, and a few of them had been holed up in New York somewhere making bombs, and they'd slipped up and blown themselves to shit. But God knows, maybe there were some others hiding out somewhere who were a little bit less clumsy, you know what I mean? So that was something else you had to worry about.

Yeah, it was a real cheery time all round. Nixon makes his speech, and we're seeing all these protests on television, and over at Kent State in Ohio, the kids burn down the ROTC building, and the governor of the state sends in the National Guard, and most people—including me—are saying, "Yeah, well, that's exactly what he should do."

It was kind of amazing when you think about it. Why Kent State of all places? It's not that far from Raysburg. It's right smack out in the center of middle America. You'd think it would be the quietest, most conservative little school you could possibly imagine. But the Ohio National Guard occupied the campus, and the students had some kind of protest, and the guard fired into those students and killed four of them.

I was having a beer with Mondrowski in the PAC, and I made this automatic knee-jerk statement, just something that was real easy to say in those days. I said something to the tune of how it's about time some of those damn protesters got a chance to see what war is really like.

Georgie went ballistic on me, like in half a second. "What the hell you talking about?" he's yelling at me. "You think it's a good idea to start shooting protesters?"

I'd forgot for a minute there he was South Raysburg's one-man antiwar movement, that he was, you know, in that vets' organization and read their newsletters like the Bible—he kept giving those dumb things to me and I'd throw them away—and any idiot should have known he was bound to have some fairly strong feelings on the topic. For a few seconds there, I thought he was going to pound me one. Of course that didn't shut me up.

"What the hell we doing over there anyway?" he's yelling at me. "We're supposed to be fighting for democracy, right? That's a joke. What we're fighting for is the right for some goddamn gook to make money off the black market. We're fighting for the right of twelve-year-old girls to sell their asses to a bunch of horny GIs. We've ruined that country, is what we've done. Everybody hates our guts over there. Even the people who are supposed to be our friends hate our guts. But it's supposed to be for democracy, right? So you shoot anybody who's against it, right? Is that democracy?"

I'm going, "Wait a minute, wait a minute. That's not what I meant."

"We still got a Constitution?" he's yelling at me. "The goddamn Constitution still mean anything?"

Georgie is leaning over, staring me right in the face. He's slamming his fist down on the bar. "The right of peaceful assembly—remember that? It's one of the reasons we fought the goddamn American Revolution."

"Those kids weren't exactly peaceful," I'm yelling back. "They burned down the ROTC building. That's goddamn peaceful assembly?"

Old Joe Nigbor's sitting at that same table playing cards with the same guys he always plays with every night in the PAC. He pushes himself up and walks over to us and says, "Tell you what, boys. You want to fight the Vietnam War, why don't you try fighting it in Vietnam?"

Georgie didn't bother to tell old Joe that he'd already done that. We took us a little walk. Down to the riverbank. Georgie smoked a joint and mellowed out, and I had a second thought or two and allowed as how he had a point.

"But you can understand those guys in the guard," I said. "Here you are, and you're just a kid from some dumb little town in Ohio. And the reason you joined the guard in the first place is so you wouldn't have to go to Vietnam and get your ass shot off, and that tends to make you kind of super-patriotic. And so they send you onto this campus to impose some peace, and you're scared shitless. And here are all these long-haired hippie weirdos, and they've all got 2-S deferments, and there's no way in hell your family could afford to send you to college in the first place. And those long-haired hippie weirdos are taunting you and calling you names and maybe throwing rocks or something, and you just lose it."

"Sure, I can understand that guy," Georgie says. "That's why you don't send the National Guard onto a college campus."

"But they were burning down the ROTC building!"

"What? They haven't got cops in Ohio? And even if you bring in the guard, there's just no way in hell you use full firepower on unarmed people."

"Listen," I say, "this is stupid—us arguing like this. There's nothing we disagree about. No, they shouldn't have shot those kids. No way in hell they should have shot those kids. But there are still guys dying every day in Nam—"

"You think I don't know that? Jesus, Jimmy."

"Okay, okay, okay. But all those guys that are still over there. Don't they deserve something?"

"Yeah, they do. They deserve to come home in one piece."

He was right, of course, but it was real hard back in those days to think anything through in any kind of calm way. It's like everybody had an opinion and didn't want to get confused with facts.

So I'm sitting in the Dłuwieckis' living room having myself a thimbleful of embalming fluid with good old Czesław, and, boy, does he have some opinions. He's fairly pissed off because they've closed down Ohio State, where his oldest boy's in grad school, and he thinks all the protesting students from coast to coast are part of one big conspiracy. So shooting four of those radical punks at Kent State was a good start, he says, but they stopped too soon. They should have shot forty more of them.

"You know, Jimmy, they get their marching orders straight from Havana. Don't laugh, the Cubans have been financing most of these radical groups. And that Weatherman outfit—the ones with the bombs—they're infiltrating high schools now. Can you believe that? Self-avowed Communists, and that's their next target. *High schools!* We've got to stop it right now before it goes any farther. The governor of Ohio was right—they're worse than the brownshirts."

Now ordinarily when her dad and me had our little chats, Janice would just sit there on the end of the couch not saying a word. That day she says, "Why are they like the brownshirts?"

Her dad goes, "Pardon? What did you say?"

"Why do you think they're like the brownshirts? Why aren't they like the gallant students of Prague you used to talk about?"

So all of a sudden you've got your world-famous generation gap opening up between Czesław and his daughter right there at our feet, and it's about the size of the Grand Canyon. Janice has got a take on Kent State that's just as clear as her dad's.

After Nixon widened the war by invading a neutral country—which he didn't have any legal right to do, she says—the students at Kent State naturally were upset, and they were demonstrating for peace, and then their own government murdered four of them in cold blood. It's the first time I ever heard Janice express a political opinion, and it kind of surprised me. She didn't have any doubts about what she thought.

"She thinks those dead punks are martyrs," he says, pointing at his daughter like she's Exhibit A. "She's got that girl's picture taped up on her wall." It was that famous picture, you know, of that girl kneeling by one of the dead students, and she's waving her arms in the air and she's got an expression on her face that's like, oh, God, no!

"It's my room," Janice says, "and I can put anything I want to on my wall. And they *are* martyrs. And we've got to stop the killing."

"See what high ideals she has," he says to me. "She means well, but American children are so naive."

"Stop talking about me in the third person," she says to him. "I'm right here, and I'm not a child."

Now I'm checked out on sixteen-year-old girls. Linda turned sixteen when I was still working at the Sylvania plant, and she and Old Bullet Head used to get into it, and she'd get so mad at him, she'd burst into tears and go running out of the kitchen and up into her bedroom and slam the door like a pistol shot. He'd be left sitting there looking at Mom going, "Hell. What did I say this time?"

So I'm expecting Janice to do pretty much the same thing. Her face turns bright red, and her eyes are filling up, and she's shaking all over, and she's so mad that when she tries to say anything, she's got to half choke herself so she's not yelling at him. But damn it, she's not going to let herself cry. And she's not going to run away. She's going to sit right there and argue with her old man, by God. It's the first time I realized how much alike they are—both of them stubborn as bulldogs.

So he's going on about how he got to know the Nazis and Commies—you know, up close and personal—and if she'd seen what he'd seen, she wouldn't be saying any of those ridiculous things. And when he was in university in Warsaw, the Endeks were trying to destroy it just like these campus radicals today—that's the Polish right-wingers he's talking about—and they'd beat up students on the street and come right into the classrooms to beat people up, sometimes even the professors, and he and his pals fought them off with fists and clubs and stones. And when he says that, he looks like if you gave him half a chance, he'd jump up and start fighting them all over again right now—so you don't have to tell him about campus radicals. He knows all there is to know about campus radicals.

And Janice is telling him his mind's stuck in Poland, and the United States is not Poland, and he's got everything twisted around backward. It was the students who were trying to defend the traditional freedoms of the university, and the Ohio National Guard was worse than the Endeks. They were like the Gestapo.

"The Gestapo," he's yelling at her, his eyes bugging out. "What would you know about the Gestapo? You don't know anything about the Gestapo."

"That's right, I don't," she yells right back at him, *"because you won't tell me."*

He looks like he's just on the edge of totally losing it, but then he yanks himself up short, and he takes a deep breath and says, "Janusiu, you forget yourself."

"I'm sorry, *Tatusiu*," she says, "I guess I did."

So then they both back off a notch or two, but they won't shut up. Oh, no, not by a long shot. She's going on about how stupid American foreign policy is—we'd just inherited a big mess from the French—and Vietnam was no threat to American security whatsoever, and the war was wrecking America, and we've got to stop it right now. I was surprised how well informed she was. And every argument she's got, he's coming right back at her with his side of things.

As you can imagine, I kept my mouth shut. There was no way I was going to get caught in between those two. And every once in a while, this really weird thing goes down. Czesław looks over at me, and he's got a little half smile on his face and he does this little nod, like he's saying, see, Jimmy, what a terrific kid she is, and then he turns back to Janice, and he's all grim again. It's like— Well, never in a million years would he have admitted that anything she was saying had even a grain of truth to it, but he sure admired her for the way she could stand up to him.

After about a half hour of this, I figured the best place for me to be was anywhere else. Janice walked me out to the car. She was shaking all over. "Oh," she said, "he makes me soooooo mad."

Here's something else I almost forgot. It's just a dumb little thing, but maybe it'll give you a feeling for the time. After Kent State, a lot of demonstrators came to Washington, and one night that asshole Nixon wandered out of the White House and ended up trying to talk to some of them at the Lincoln Memorial. He rambled on incoherently and the demonstrators didn't know what to think. Mondrowski says to me, "Hey, the sucker's losing it," and I go, "Yeah, it looks like he is." That's the president of the United States we're talking about, right? The guy with his finger on the button.

Kent State, yeah. You know, it was even worse than it seemed at the time. It's like everything else—what first hits the papers and the TV is never even close to the whole story. Yeah, the truth always comes out later when nobody gives a shit anymore. Well, maybe a few people still give a shit. God knows why, but I'm one of them. You want to know what really happened, I'll tell you a little bit of it.

That demonstration where the kids got shot was a peaceful demonstration, and it was really stupid to try to break it up. Most of the students who got injured were over two hundred feet from the guard, so when the shooting went down, the guardsmen weren't in any danger at all. The guardsmen turned and fired like they'd planned to do it. None of the kids who got killed had anything to do with burning down the ROTC building, and one of them was even in ROTC. He threw himself down on the ground and they shot him in the back. One of the girls who got killed wasn't the least bit political, and she hadn't been in any of the demonstrations. She'd just been walking to class.

THIRTEEN

The band was just a few days away from making its premiere performance at Franky Rzeszutko's when it finally occurred to Linda to ask Janice if she'd ever let her dad in on the little secret that they were playing polka music. Nope, Janice said, she hadn't quite got around to it yet. "Oh, my God," Linda said, "when are you going to tell him?"

"Don't worry," Janice said. "It'll be okay."

It's fairly useless to say, "Don't worry," to Linda. Anything you want worried about, she's your girl.

"Janice *has* to tell him," Linda said. "She can't just let him walk into Franky's expecting to hear some—I don't know what—some ancient folk songs from the *Kolberg Collection*, and all of a sudden everybody's dancing the polka."

What Janice always said was, "Nobody's going to stop me from playing this music. It's *my* music," but Linda was pretty sure that if Mr. Dłuwiecki really put his mind to it, he could probably do a pretty good job of stopping her, and seeing as Janice was turning out to be the star of the polka band—even Mary Jo had managed to figure that one out—that might put the old quietus to the whole works. Comes the big night and Linda says, "So, is everything okay with your father?" and Janice says, "Oh, it will be."

"What do you mean, it *will* be? You *still* haven't told him?"

"Well, no. But don't worry, Linda. He's my father, and I know him really well. We're members of St. Stanislaus Parish, and he's not going to do anything in public to embarrass me—or embarrass himself. Believe me, everything's going to be fine." And then she said to me—but not to Linda—"And if he gets upset about it, it serves him right."

So of course Linda was worried sick about Mr. Dłuwiecki. That on top of worrying about playing her trumpet—and a million other things that absolutely had to be worried about. I'd rented the sound system at Kaltenbach's, and I'd hauled it over and set it up, and the band had gone through a sound check. Janice had been real fascinated by the mike—holding it up close to her mouth, whispering in it, holding it a foot away and yelling into it, just generally seeing all the tricks she could do with it, but Linda was convinced that when the time came for them to play for real, Janice would screw it up.

Then when everything was set up and ready to go, Bev said, "I'm going uptown and meet my brother. What time we supposed to be back here?" and so naturally Linda has to worry about Bev not getting back on time—or at all. The last straw was that the band didn't even have a name yet, and Linda figured it was her responsibility to come up with the perfect one before they started playing.

Linda was in a state where she was just annoying everybody. Georgie comes up to her and starts stroking her back. She jumps about a foot. "Stop that!" she yells at him.

"I'm just trying to get your fur to lie down," he says. Which the rest of us thought was pretty funny, but she didn't.

"Come on, kid," he says to her, "we're taking a walk."

"Walk? What? Where?"

"Shhh," he says and wraps his arm around her and starts leading her to the door.

Linda's wailing, "Where are we going? There's all these things I've got to do!"

Georgie puts his hand over her mouth like he's kidnapping her. "There's nothing you've got to do," he says and gives us all a big grin and they're out the door. All of a sudden it's real calm in there. I don't know where he's taking her. I just hope it ain't down to the riverbank to get her stoned for the first time in her life.

It was a warm night in early summer. Not hot yet, but pleasant. Not quite dinnertime, but getting there. Some of Franky's regular customers were coming in, saying, "Oh, there's going to be music? Great."

The band had a table over on the wall next to Patty Pajaczkowski's drum set. I'm sitting there drinking a beer, and on one side of me there's Mary Jo and old Gene Duda and on the other side Patty and Janice, and I'm just enjoying the hell out of the show.

Mary Jo and Gene are talking about Gene's colon. He's had some problems with it lately. They're mainly talking in Polish, but every once in a while they swing over into English. A lot of the older folks from the second generation are like that—you can't figure out why they pick one language or the other. Maybe it's like whenever they have a thought, whatever language pops into their head with it, that's what comes out of their mouths. But when they're speaking English, there's always a little Polish tossed in, and when they're speaking Polish, sometimes half the words are English words with Polish endings crammed on them. Like Gene's talking about the *barium enemaia* he had, which he didn't enjoy much and whether or not the *palisa*, you know, the *helt insiurns*, is going to pay for it. It's the kind of Raysburg Polish that gives Janice's old man the fits.

Red and white are the colors of the Polish flag, so Janice is wearing a red jumper with white kneesocks and a white blouse, and little-kid shoes like she always does, only this pair's red, and she's got a silver Polish eagle pinned on her blouse. That night she's wearing her pigtails little-girl style, and she looks like she's going to be in the eighth-grade recital on Pulaski Day. Patty's got cleaned up for the occasion too. She's dug up a top and a pair of pants that she last wore maybe back around 1958. The top is one of those things that doesn't have any sleeves in it, so you can see the lizard tattooed on her shoulder clear as anything.

Patty is perched on the edge of her chair twitching away, tapping out a little drumbeat on the table. Janice is asking Patty if she knows any Polish. Patty says, "Oh, yeah. Sure. You want to hear my Polish? *Daj mi piwo, dziękuję, na zdrowie, pocałuj mnie w dupę*—That's all the Polish I've got." That's, "Give me a beer, thank you, here's to ya, kiss my ass," and naturally Janice cracks right up.

Gene's talking Polish, and he's saying that all he needs is a lot of cabbage. Especially red cabbage. No, Mary Jo says, that gives you gas. "To hell wit that," Gene says in English. Back in the old country, he says in Polish, they ate a lot of cabbage, and they never had problems with their colons. You want to bet? Mary Jo says in English. Her friend so-and-so's mother ate cabbage every day of her life, and she died of colon cancer. "The doctor says it ain't cancer," Gene says.

"You eat too much cabbage it will be," Mary Jo says.

"Does your mom make you dress like that?" Patty's asking Janice.

"Oh, no. She wants me to get my hair cut and wear dumb little dresses and high heels."

"What? You're saying, to hell with you, Mom. I'm never going to grow up?"

Janice looks startled. She's not used to people talking to her the way Patty Pajaczkowski does. Nothing's too personal for Patty, even if she's only known you five minutes. "Of course I want to grow up," Janice says, "but I'm going to do it my way."

Mary Jo's very patiently explaining to Gene what the doctor told him. His colon's got these things sticking out of it that are like pockets in a pair of pants. Shit gets trapped in there and causes pain. *"Masz rozum?"* he says, "You think I don't know that?"

Patty wants to know if Janice would do a braid for her. "Sure," Janice says, but then nobody's got a comb. I didn't think Mary Jo was paying any attention to the girls, but she reaches in her purse and hands Janice a comb, and Janice starts combing Patty's hair. "I love people touching my hair," Patty says. "It puts me right to sleep."

Janice runs her fingertips over Patty's lizard, like tracing the outline of it. "Why'd you get a lizard?" she says.

"Because he's my ally. He's a sacred lizard."

"A sacred *lizard?*"

"Yeah. He's older than time. He crawls down in the cracks in the earth and brings us back messages from the ancient entities that live down there."

"You're kidding."

"No, I'm not kidding. Just when you've forgot all about him, he crawls up on your shoulder and whispers in your ear."

Now Janice is sure Patty is putting her on, but she's decided, I guess, to humor her. "What's he say?"

"Well, one time he said to me, 'Patty Pajaczkowski, you are wasting your life.'"

"Oh, come on."

"No shit, sweetheart. I thought I was doing just fine. I was on a couple records, and I was getting a lot of work—and I was doing some of that heavy-duty partying. Just enjoying the hell out of myself. But the lizard climbed up on my shoulder and told me I was wasting my life. And I *was* wasting my life."

"So what did you do?"

"I went out into the desert and I found a sacred place and I stayed there till my life came back to me."

Mary Jo says, "Patty Pajaczkowski, you are nuttier than a fruitcake. What are you telling that poor little girl?"

"Me?" Patty says. She's laying back in the chair with her eyes shut. "You must have heard wrong. I ain't saying a thing."

Everybody in the band had friends and relatives that turned up that night at Franky Rzeszutko's for dinner. Mom and Old Bullet Head got there early to get a good table, and then all our aunts and uncles started coming in, and Babcia Wojtkiewicz showed up with a couple other old ladies. Patty Pajaczkowski's parents came, and we found out that her dad and Old Bullet Head had worked together at the mill for years. And Patty's big sister with her husband and kids— two little boys going, "Hi, Aunt Patty. You gonna play your drums, Aunt Patty?" And then Patty's grandma, and of course she turned out to be tight with our grandma. And some of Mary Jo and Gene Duda's kids, and their kids. And that rat pack of Polish girls Janice hung around with, and they'd brought their families with them. And the Mondrowskis, and some of Linda's friends from high school.

Franky was almost out of tables when Janice's mom and dad came in with her brothers. Old Czesław and his boys were the only guys in the place with suits and ties on. I was a little surprised that John Dłuwiecki would have driven all the way from Columbus just to see his little sister playing in a polka band, but he said, "I wouldn't miss it for anything," so I gave him top scores in the big-brother department.

Speaking of big brothers, Bev Wright came back in plenty of time, and she brought her famous brother with her—introduced him to everybody and never once mentioned he played on the Jamboree. I guess we were all supposed to know it. And Georgie finally brought Linda back. I wouldn't say she was as calm as a still lake in August, but she was in a hell of a lot better shape than when she left. "I took her to the church," he said, "and we sat there awhile and contemplated the eternal verities."

Of course there were all Franky's regular customers too. He hadn't had so many people on a Saturday night for years, and he was grinning like Christmas had come early. Yeah, it was old-home week all right—frosted pitchers of beer arriving by the dozen and people walking around to each other's tables, doing the well-how-the-hell-are-you? number.

My father and Patty's dad are bitching about something or other at the mill, another one of those grievances that went nowhere. About how they have all these levels a grievance has to go through now, and it takes forever, and then when they finally decide on it, there's a guy from Pittsburgh representing the union, and he doesn't give a shit about the local problems, so he just makes another Judas deal with the company and the grievance goes zip down the old *dziura*. "Yeah, right, terrible," they're saying. "In the old days the union meant something."

A pair of scissors or a razor blade still haven't come nowhere near Georgie Mondrowski's head, and he's taken to wearing his hair in a ponytail—which got it out of the way—but there wasn't much he could do about his beard. Just a great big ball of blond fuzz starting below his nose. So he might as well be wearing a sign that says, "Hi, I'm your friendly neighborhood fucked-up Vietnam vet," and everybody's going out of their way to be nice to him.

Old Bullet Head reaches out and shakes his hand. "How you keeping, Georgie?"

"No problem but the rent," Georgie says, "and the rent's paid."

My father doesn't find that funny. He's not checked out on GI talk so of course he's going to take it straight, and he's probably thinking, what the hell's the rent he's talking about? Georgie Mondrowski's still living at home the last I heard.

Right in the middle of all this cheery pandemonium, Bill Winnicki and his girlfriend come popping in to see what's going on, and they check out the band setup, and he yells at me, "Hey, Koprowski, who's playing in here tonight?"

I yell back, "My sister's polka band."

Patty says, "That's it. That's our name."

Linda's going, "What, what?"

"Our *name*," Patty says. "When it's just handed to you like that, you gotta take it. *My Sister's Polka Band.*"

"Hey, neat," Janice says. "Well, maybe," Linda says. "It's better than nothing," I say.

And naturally we're all checking out Janice's dad—kind of out of the corners of our eyes, you know—and he's sitting there at his table with a glass of beer he's not drinking, and he's staring at the full drum set and the mike and the monitor and the two big columns and the electric bass and the bass amp and the humungo bass speaker. Well, it doesn't take a musical genius to figure out that they aren't about to be playing any ancient Polish folk music, and Mr. Dłuwiecki clamps his mouth shut and gets this expression like he's just bit off something real nasty. Janice says, "Wow, Jimmy, look at my dad. Maybe I should have said something to him."

"It's a little late now, kid."

At the last possible minute the priest comes in. There's no tables left, and even the bar's packed, and Franky's been turning away people at the door, but it's Father Obinski, right, and he's got to sit somewhere, so we make a space for him at the band table, and all of a sudden a plate of *kiełbasa* and a pitcher of beer arrive in front of him, and he didn't order either one of them. "It's really nice of you to come, Father," Linda says.

Father Obinski winks. It's like he's sharing a big secret with you. It's one of the first things people noticed about him—"Hey, you know the new priest? He's kind of weird. He winks a lot." And he says, "I wouldn't miss it for the world. The whole parish is buzzing about it."

Well, Mary Jo figured they should get a few polkas in before people got down to serious eating because it's kind of hard, you know, to dance the polka with your stomach crammed full of *pierogi*, and she's bugging Linda, so Linda's bugging me. "Jimmy, Jimmy, say something. Get it started."

Why me? I don't know. Maybe because I'm the manager. So I jump up and run around behind the mike and turn it on, and I do my Barnum & Bailey voice, yelling out, "Okay, folks, this is the moment you've all been waiting for. Here they are, live and off color—My Sister's Polka Band."

Then Mary Jo gets up and says, "Hi, folks. You all know me. I'm Mary Jo, the polka lady. Well, awhile back I got together this bunch of pretty girls, and— I don't think I need to introduce anybody, do I? Everybody knows everybody? Oh, that's Beverly Wright. She's a nice kid from Barnsville, Ohio, and she's so good on that electric bass we made her an honorary Polak." And she's gassing on about how they've been practicing real hard, and they've got some real good old tunes from the old country, and like that. You give Mary Jo a microphone and you can't shut her up.

Janice is standing next to me, holding her clarinet, and we're both sneaking looks at her dad. The word "polka" has been spoken aloud a few times by now, and he is definitely not pleased. His mouth's all turned down, and he's sitting there still as a stone. "Linda was right," Janice is whispering. "Oh, boy, is he ever going to kill me!"

I figured it wasn't the right time to say, "Well, you should have paid some attention to my sister when she brought up that topic—like a couple months ago." What I told her was, "Listen, kid, you just play the hell out of that clarinet. That's the only thing that's going to get you out of this one."

She gives me a look like, yeah, that's right. Mary Jo finally shuts up and sits down and picks up her accordion, and Janice and Linda walk up in front of the band. Janice has got this little sickly half smile. She takes a deep breath and looks over at Patty and Bev, giving them the tempo—you know, beating it out for them with her hand—and they come in bang together, Mary Jo squeezing out the melody.

You'd think it wouldn't be too hard to play a good polka beat, right? You're just laying it down in two, right? But it's a lot harder than you'd think. It's got to have a lot of energy to it, but it's also got to sound totally relaxed—a nice, easygoing, bouncy groove but still with plenty of zing to get people up and on their feet. And that's exactly what they're laying down. It's just about the sweetest little polka groove you ever heard, and you can feel this sort of ooooh from everybody—like, hey, they're all right.

They opened up with "The Clarinet Polka"—that's the one that Janice had started calling "*my* polka," I guess because she was the clarinet player—and she always played it like she owned it, really showing off her chops. As worried as she was that night, you sure couldn't hear it. The notes were just pouring out of her clarinet like sunlight, and the minute people heard that sweet sound, you could see them start to relax, smiling at each other, because anybody who could play like that sure must have it all taken care of. And people were jumping up and starting to dance, because—well, that's the point of a polka band, right?

Czesław and his family—it's kind of funny. It's like he's the king in one of those historical movies, and his wife and boys are his flunkies, and they're staring at him waiting to get their cue so they'll know what to do. And the band's going through the tune again, and Janice is flipping it around upside down and backward, playing four million notes to the minute, and the thing that really gets to you is how much she loves playing—like you can hear the joy in it. And she's Czesław's darling daughter, right? And he'd have to have a heart of stone not to be getting off on it at least a little bit. So finally he does crack a smile, and he nods like, well, yes, she certainly can play, can't she? And his wife and kids all nod back at him and smile, like, yes, indeed, you're right on that one, Pops.

I'd been concentrating so hard on Janice, I hadn't been paying much attention to Linda, and then it dawns on me—hey, she's doing okay. I mean, the clarinet's the main thing happening in that tune, but there is a trumpet part, and she'd been holding her own. I was real pleased for her.

So they get to the end, and they get a big round of applause, and right away they kick into the next polka. Again it's Janice who counts them in, and she steps up to the mike, and we know she's going to sing, but nobody else does. Mary Jo lays out the melody once, and here it comes again, and this time Janice comes belting in with that old-country voice she's got—"*Zosia, Zosia, Zosia kuchnię zamiatała, i Ma— i Ma— i Macieja zawołała—*"

I told you how the first time I heard Janice sing, it totally blew me away. Well, that's how it hit just about everybody. They can't believe it. Especially they can't believe that wild voice is coming out of a little kid in pigtails wearing red patent-leather shoes. So there's like a few seconds' delay while it's sinking in, and then people let out this kind of whoop, and damn near everybody in the place jumps up and onto the dance floor.

Naturally I'd been watching Czesław. Well, the minute Janice starts to sing, he looks like somebody ran across the room and drove a broom handle into his solar plexus. I'm not kidding you here. He lets out this kind of oooofff, and he bends forward, and his mouth's even hanging open. And Janice is soaring up into the high part of the tune—

"Zosia kuchnię
zamiatała
i Macieja
zawołała—"

It's one of the great old polkas. It's about this girl Zosia, and she's sweeping the kitchen. And she calls to Maciej. The song doesn't say what she calls to him, but it's probably along the lines of, "Hey, Maciej, get your ass in here." And it's got a pause built into it, like when the singer goes, *"Zosia,"* you're supposed to yell back, *"ZOSIA!"*

So Janice is into the second verse, and people are starting to yell back at her in the right places—

"Matka— MATKA!
matka— MATKA!
matka lampę zaświeciła,
i Ma— I MA!
i Ma— I MA!
i Macieja zobaczyła—"

That's Zosia's mom, and she lights the lamp and she's checking out Maciej, giving him the hairy eyeball, you know, to see what he's doing with Zosia there in the kitchen. And after that verse, the band kicks into the drive. Patty boots it real good, and Linda's playing the melody with Janice riding on top, and Mary Jo's doing the bellows shake to push it along, and the band's cooking like you wouldn't believe. Patty's yelling, "Yeah, yeah, yeah, yeah!"

Well, when you've got a polka band that hot, it's impossible to sit still, and the dance floor's jammed. I hadn't been planning on dancing—I'd thought I'd just give them a good careful listen, make sure their sound was balanced and like that—but I just can't help it. I grab Georgie's little sister, Darlene, and away we go.

As I go swinging by with Darlene, I take another look at Janice's dad, and he's just stunned. Sitting there with his wife and two boys, staring at his daughter.

Patty drops down, SWOOSH, leaving a nice space for Janice to come in on the last verse. *"Wy, Ma— Wy, Ma— Wy, Macieju, co robicie? Że tak, że tak, że tak Zosię całujecie?"*

Linda had told me that Janice was a real clown, but I'd never seen it before. This is where Mom asks Maciej just what the hell he's doing. And the grammar's not right. It's what a peasant would say. And when she hits that part, for a couple seconds Janice turns right into that old peasant lady. Her eyes are popping out and she looks absolutely incensed, and she says, *"Co robicie?* What are you *doing?"* and her dad cracks completely up.

It's amazing, but Czesław's laughing his ass off, and he looks around at his wife and boys, so they start laughing too, and he slaps the tabletop, like, can you believe that? Yeah, she's something else, isn't she? But they're still not dancing.

Janice is singing, *"Wy, Macieju, co robicie? Że tak Zosię całujecie?* Hey, you, Maciej, what are you doing, to be kissing Zosia so hard?"

Well, after that, they can't go wrong. All the friends and loved ones there, of course they're going to like the band—they would've liked it even if they'd been playing cigar boxes with rubber bands on them—but everybody was amazed, saying, "Hey, you know, they're really *good.* They're damn near as good as the Andrzejewski brothers."

Next they played about four instrumentals in a row, "Eddie Zima's Polka" and like that, and Janice got to show off some more on the clarinet, and Linda's playing was exactly how she described it to me later—perfectly respectable. And then Linda sang a waltz in her sweet little-girl choir voice—"The Linden Tree." It has one of the prettiest melodies you'll ever hear, and she did a real good job with it. They ended with Janice singing, *"Pockaj, pockaj, powiem Mamie."* Everybody knows that one. It's a cute polka, perfect for a girl to be singing, and I think that's why they picked it to end on. It's the one that says, "You tried to kiss me, you bad boy, and I'm going to tell Mommy on you!"

I think everybody in the place danced at least once except for the Dłuwieckis. But all the old folks danced, and they were fanning themselves, going, "Wow, was that ever a workout! One of these days I'm gonna drop dead, and it'll be the polka that killed me," and everybody's ordering more beer, and the combination dinner, making Franky Rzeszutko just as happy as a clam. And everybody was congratulating the band, telling Mary Jo she'd really put together a hot group that time—and they're all so pretty!—and they were going over to the Dłuwieckis' table, saying, "Oh, you must be so proud! How'd your little girl ever learn to sing like that? And she plays that clarinet like an angel."

Janice came over and whispered to me, "I think it's okay. I made him laugh."

Right when they'd stopped playing, Patty Pajaczkowski's dad ran straight over to her and lifted her about three feet in the air and gave her a great big hug, and Bev's famous brother said they had polka bands on the Jamboree every once in a while, and maybe he could arrange something. Did they know any tunes in English? Franky passed the hat; Mary Jo counted it later, and it turned out to be $87.75—which everybody thought was just fine—and naturally all the band members got a free dinner, including me.

We were all feeling pretty good, but then I saw that Janice's dad had taken her off in a corner, and he was telling her something or other, and she was looking up at him real serious. Well, he's an early-to-bed-early-to-rise kind of guy, so he gathers up his wife and his boys and goes home.

Linda's going, "What did he say? What did he say? Was he mad?"

"Oh, yeah," Janice says, "but he couldn't really blow up at me here in front of everybody."

"Well, what did he *say?*"

"He congratulated me and all, but he was real stiff. He said I looked like I was born to be on the stage. He said I had an enormous God-given talent, but— Oh, I could tell there was a whole lot more he wanted to say."

"How mad do you think he is?" Linda wanted to know, and Janice just shook her head.

Meanwhile, Father Obinski was talking to Mary Jo. He was asking her if she thought the band might be interested in playing at the annual street fair in August. Well, when Linda catches the drift of that one, she jumps in between Mary Jo and the priest and says, "Excuse me, Father, but you should talk to our manager." That's yours truly. Mary Jo didn't care for that much, but she kept her mouth shut.

"We were trying to get the Andrzejewski brothers," Father Obinski says to me, "but they're booked somewhere up in Pennsylvania that weekend."

"Yeah," I say, "they're a terrific band. They're getting to be too popular."

Well, then there's Norm Kolak's band or Ray Pahucki's band, Father Obinski says. He hadn't talked to them yet, but he really did want to have our band because it was a local group from the parish. But maybe in addition to another band. The street fair goes on for a while, and that's a lot of polkas.

So I step off to one side with the good father—where we can, you know, go at it man to man—and I launch into this thing about how he's heard only a fraction of our material and we've got enough tunes for three or four sets, and of course I'm making all this up. I don't know how many tunes the girls have got.

Finally, we get around to the price. He mentions a figure, and it sounds okay to me, but I'm the manager, so what the hell?

I go, "Excuse me for asking, Father, but is that what you'd pay the Andrzejewski brothers?" I see him hesitate a second, and I go, "I know it's a fundraiser for the church, and we're just starting out, so we're not trying to drive any kind of hard bargain here—"

And he's going, "Well, you're right, Jimmy, fair's fair at the street fair, if you don't mind the pun," so I go no no no, and he goes yes yes yes, and lo and behold I've just bumped the money up by fifty bucks.

He gives me a wink, and we shake on it, so the band's booked. I go back to Linda and Janice and tell them what I've done, and Linda goes, "Oh, my God! How many sets?"

Janice says, "We can do it."

"Sure we can," Mary Jo says.

The evening was winding down. Georgie helped me lug the sound system out, and Bev Wright left with her famous brother to go hear some country music, and Mary Jo and Gene Duda were getting loaded with some of the other old crocks, and Patty Pajaczkowski and her father, you know, hadn't had anything resembling a conversation in years so they just couldn't stop talking to each other. But Linda and Janice were still worrying about Czesław. "I thought I'd get away with it, but I don't think I did," Janice said. "Boy, am I ever going to get it when I get home."

We were kind of holding our breath to hear what happened with Janice and her dad, but for the next few days there wasn't a peep out of her. Central was out for the summer, but rehearsing on Tuesday nights had become a kind of tradition so they were just going to keep on with it. Then Janice calls up and says she can't make that next Tuesday's rehearsal. Naturally Linda wants to know what's going down, but Janice tells her, "I can't really talk right now. I'll tell you when I can."

Linda hangs up the phone and gives me this gloomy look. "That sure doesn't sound very good," she says. "Oh, the little nitwit, why didn't she pay any attention to me?"

Well, I usually went home on Saturdays. Like at one or two in the afternoon when my hangover was starting to let up, I'd drift on down to the house and fix myself a sandwich and slip Mom a few bucks and maybe put in a load of laundry, and just hang out until I felt a little better and figured out what I was going to do that night. Saturday was Linda's piano students day, and I'd always come in through the back door so I wouldn't disturb her. There'd be these tiny girls all dressed up by their moms, real serious with their music books in their hands—one sitting at the piano getting her lesson and one or two more waiting in the living room, kicking their feet against the couch, till three or four in the afternoon.

I'll never forget this. That day Old Bullet Head was out front washing his car. He always drove a blue Chrysler. Every few years he traded it in and got another one, and he always kept them immaculate—you know, for the resale value—and he says to me, "Why don't you clean up that piece of crap you're driving around?" and I say, "Come on, Dad, the dirt's the only thing holding it together," but I thought, why not? What else have I got to do?

So Old Bullet Head and I are washing our cars and joking around—the best way to get along with my father is to do something with him—and I look up, and here comes Janice walking along the sidewalk. It's a hot day, and she's wearing old tennis shoes and what looks like gym shorts and a wrinkled gray T-shirt that must've belonged to one of her brothers. I'm surprised because usually she's neat as a pin.

She goes, "Hi, Jimmy. Hi, Mr. Koprowski," and Old Bullet Head goes, "Oh, hi there, Janice. How's your mom and dad?"

"Oh, they're fine." And she says to me, "What's Linda doing?" and I say, "It's piano students day."

"Oh," she says, and she looks up and down the street—like maybe there's somewhere else she could go that's suddenly going to jump up and wave its arms at her. Then she says, "You want some help with your car?"

"Sure," I say. I hadn't been planning on putting any wax on it. I mean, what's the point? But she picked up the can of wax and started in on the hood.

Well, you never saw anybody more miserable in your life. She was just radiating it. I say, "What's the matter?" and she says, "Oh, nothing."

So we wax my dumb-ass Chevy, and she's not saying a word, and I go, "So what's happening? Your dad tell you you couldn't play any more polkas?"

"No, he didn't say that. It's up to me if I want to play in the band or not."

"But he did say something, huh?"

"Oh, yeah. He said plenty."

I keep waiting for the rest of the story, but another ten minutes goes by without a word out of her, and we've got my silly green-and-white car looking just about as good as it's ever going to get—it looks ridiculous if you want to know the truth—and she's starting to drive me nuts, so I say, "Okay, Janice, just go ahead and sink under your misery and drown if you don't want to talk about it."

She sighs. Then she says, "Take me somewhere."

I thought she meant someplace specific—like back home or out to the mall to buy something—so I say, "Sure. Where you want to go?"

"I don't care."

We stand there and look at each other a minute, and then I say, "Okay, kid, get in the car."

Now I've got this silent miserable girl in my car, so what am I going to do with her? Well, what I did was drive out to Waverly Park. A beautiful day like that, it seemed like a good idea.

I parked by the pool and bought us a couple Cokes. A cold beer would have tasted good, but—well, I may be a fool, but I'm not that big a fool. At least that day I wasn't. She said, "I've got a cousin in Poland exactly my age. Her name's Paulina. I've got her address. I can write to her if I want."

"That ought to make you happy," I said. "You wanted to know about your relatives in Poland."

"Yeah, I'm glad I found out about her," she said in this absolutely dead voice. "I know about a lot of other things too."

The park was packed with people, and we walked away from the pool, up onto a hill where we could be alone—sort of alone—and sat down under a tree. "I can't stop crying," she said. "Oh, I don't mean like now. I'm not going to start crying right here in front of you. You don't have to worry about that. I mean at night. When I get in bed."

"So what are you crying about?" I said, and she told me the whole story.

Last Saturday night when we'd dropped her off, it'd been close to midnight. She'd been steeling herself for whatever her dad was going to dump on her—but still hoping, you know, that maybe he'd just be asleep. So she walked into the house and smelled his pipe smoke and thought, oh, rats, he's still up—he's going to pounce on me.

She peeked into the living room and saw him sitting there in the dark. She figured he was having a few jolts of the old furniture stripper—which he did on a regular basis when he had trouble sleeping. She knew he must have heard her come in, and she waited a minute for him to say something, but he didn't, so she went out into the kitchen and had herself a glass of milk. She came back and started for the stairs and bumped right into him in the hallway. She hadn't heard him coming, and he just scared the living daylights out of her. *"Dobranoc, Tatusiu,"* she said.

What he said back to her was, "You are a very clever girl." The thing that really got to her was that they always spoke Polish at home, but he said it in English. And it was his tone of voice too—hard as nails.

"I couldn't move," she told me. "My blood ran cold."

"You lied to me," he said.

"No, I didn't. I never lied to you."

"Don't quibble about definitions. You lied by omission."

"Okay, I did," she said. "I'm sorry."

Then he switched into Polish, and he said, "The day the Germans invaded Poland, they weren't playing polkas on Polish radio. They were playing Chopin."

There was absolutely nothing she could say to that, so she just looked at him.

"What you were playing tonight," he said, "it's a disgrace to Polish culture. Polish folk melodies turned into cheap, vulgar American songs. They might have Polish lyrics, but they're not really Polish."

Without even stopping to think, she said back to him something she'd heard from Linda—"That's like saying Louis Armstrong isn't really African."

She could see him making a real effort not to blow his cork. They were standing in the hallway with no light but just that one little lamp they always kept on for a night-light, and the house was quiet quiet quiet. It was kind of creepy, she told me.

"You may certainly play whatever music you like," he said, "but never lie to me again."

"I won't, *Tatusiu.* I promise."

"You didn't have to lie to me. Please, *Janusiu,* just listen to me. You could be playing serious music. You could be playing the oboe. You could be playing chamber music, symphonies. You could— I didn't know you could sing. I was amazed. God has blessed you with enormous talent. Can't you respect that talent? You could take voice lessons. You could sing lieder, even opera. You could go to Juilliard."

She didn't think it was the right time to point out to him that they don't let you into Juilliard unless you can read music. She kept searching her mind to find something to say, but she couldn't find a thing.

Then it was like he was disgusted with her for just standing there silent as a stone, so he made this motion like, oh, get the hell out of here and go to bed, and he said, *"Dobranoc,"* and she said, *"Dobranoc,"* and she was thinking, wheww, that was awful, thank God that's over, and she ran up the stairs, and just about the time she gets to the top, he's yelling at her, *"Janusiu!"* So she's got to take a deep breath and walk all the way back down again.

Well, he started off fairly calm. He said, "When you stand up in public and sing in Polish, you have a certain responsibility. You're representing the Polish people. Do you know what that means?"

She shook her head. She really didn't know what he meant by that. So he starts in with this stuff she's heard her whole life. About Poland in the old days, a land without stakes—you know, where no one was ever burnt for heresy— and about the religious dissenters coming to Poland from all over Europe, and Poland the bulwark of Western civilization against the Asiatic barbarians, and the Old Republic where the aristocracy was a fraternity of equals, where even the peasants were proud. None of this stuff is exactly news to her, right?

And he's going on about Poland of Mickiewicz and Słowacki, Poland who sent her sons to die for freedom all over the world, Poland of Kościuszko and Pułaski. Poland lost and partitioned. Poland rising again like a phoenix. Piłsudski's dream—a free and democratic Poland where Poles and Ukrainians and Lithuanians and Jews could all live together in peace and harmony. He says, "You do understand what I'm saying, don't you?"

Well, she wasn't just playing dumb. She really wasn't getting it. "You taught us Polish history, *Tatusiu,*" she says.

He makes this exasperated gesture like, oh, for Christ's sake. "When Hitler invaded Poland," he says, "what did our gallant allies do? There were a hundred and ten French and British divisions massed on the border with Germany. Did they come to Poland's aid? No. When the Luftwaffe bombed Warsaw into rubble, did the British bomb Germany? No. Did anyone lift a finger to honor their commitments to Poland? No."

They had a rule in their house that if anybody was in bed, you had to talk in whispers and just float around quiet as a ghost, but that rule had pretty well gone down the drain by then. He got more and more cranked up until he was yelling his head off. She just stood there and watched him lose it. "Do you understand Hitler's plan for us? While the war's on, we're slave labor for the Reich. After the war's won, we'll be exterminated like our Jewish brethren. Did you know that?"

She shakes her head because she didn't know that. He'd never told her that. And he's going at her full tilt, yelling right in her face. She said it was like being hit by a volcano.

"The Nazis butchered us. Three million Polish Christians dead. Three million Polish Jews dead. Bodies hanging from lamp posts. People shot in front of walls day after day. And the death factories— We too died at Auschwitz, at Treblinka. Death squads. Mass graves. And the Russians deported half a million of us. They starved us and worked us to death. Polish babies stolen from their mothers and sent off to be raised as Germans. Polish girls used as experiments—as *experiments*—by the Nazi doctors. Unspeakable tortures. My father, your grandfather— Did they spare a single one of your grandparents? No, not a single one was spared.

"The Jews in the Warsaw Ghetto slaughtered— The Soviet Army at the Vistula—sent the message, 'Rise up, rise up. Now is the time.' So Warsaw rose, and the Soviets stood by and watched while we were crushed utterly. Yes, they let the Nazis do their dirty work for them—the bastards—and then they marched into the city. Girls fought, did you know that? Girls as young as you. Girls younger than you. Dying, slaughtered. Raped, tortured. Poland betrayed again, sold out at Yalta. Crushed under the boot heels of the Soviets. My comrades-in-arms, my brothers and sisters, the flower of my generation— We who fought the Nazis. We who suffered and bled. The Soviets called us fascists. We were shot, deported, put on public trial. And to this day Polish children are told lies, lies, lies. Do you understand? Poland betrayed. Poland crucified. Poland the Christ of nations. *And you think being Polish is playing in a polka band?*"

She felt like he'd rolled right over her and squashed her down to nothing. Her eyes filled up with tears, and they ran down her face, and she just stood there like she was frozen.

Her dad had got himself so worked up he was panting. He pressed his hand against his chest and kept taking these big breaths until he pulled himself back together. It was like he'd gone somewhere else, but when he came back so he could really see her again, he got this terrible look on his face. Very gently he wiped her tears away with his fingertips.

"I'm sorry, *Janusiu*," he says. "It's my fault."

He reaches out for her. They weren't a very huggy family, you know what I mean? But he puts his arms around her. She says, "Oh, Daddy," and just starts bawling. He keeps stroking her head, and he says, "My darling, I'm so sorry. Please forgive me."

Nobody had a good night. Janice went to bed and cried awhile, and drifted off, and then maybe two in the morning she heard her parents talking in their bedroom, and she never really got back to sleep after that. Every time she'd get about half asleep, she'd wake right up again with this awful feeling in the pit of her stomach. Then about four, she heard footsteps—real slow and deliberate—and she looked out her window and her dad was pacing up and down the sidewalk. He'd walk down to the end of the block and then turn around and walk back. Over and over. Smoking his pipe. And she thought, oh, it's all my fault.

The whole family went to Mass as usual, and her dad didn't have a good word to say. They came home, and he announced, "I think I'm going to go back down to the church and see the priest." He didn't say about what.

Well, you don't just pop down on Sunday afternoon and see the priest. If he's one of these new-style priests like Father Obinski, you better make an appointment a week in advance. So Janice and her brothers figured the old man would be right back, but he didn't come back for a couple hours. Then he walked into the house and took his wife off into the bedroom. When they came out, he announced that they had something to say.

The whole family went into the living room and sat down. It wasn't unusual for Czesław to call a family meeting like that; it was something he'd done on a regular basis their whole lives. He said he'd been wrestling with himself all night long, and then he'd had a good talk with Father Obinski and now he saw things in a new light. He and his wife—"your dear mother"—had only been trying to do what they'd thought best. They'd wanted their children to be happy, to enjoy the benefits and advantages of America. They'd wanted their children to grow up to be ordinary Americans.

"We did not want to cast a shadow over your childhood," their mother said.

"You have asked us to tell you about the war," he said. "Each of you has asked—many times—but we have never told you. We were wrong. We understand that now. John, you have left us already, and you, Mark, and Janice will be leaving us soon, and there are things you need to know. Now we will tell you everything that you need to know."

FOURTEEN

Janice and her brothers grew up on stories of Krajne Podlaski in Poland. I guess you could say they were just shoved into that place up to their eyeballs. "It was a real town to us," she told me. "In some ways it was more real to me than Raysburg—but it was real like a fairy tale." When she was little, it was all kind of blurred together in her mind, so she didn't know the difference between her parents' lives and the stories in those picture books her mom read to her.

The woods where Little Red Riding Hood had to walk to her grandmother's house, and where Hansel and Gretel got lost—well, those were the dark scary woods outside of Krajne Podlaski, and she knew that her daddy had escaped into those same dark woods and lived there like Robin Hood and fought against the bad Germans. There were some mines not too far from Krajne Podlaski, and that's where the Seven Dwarfs worked, and that's also where some of the partisans hid out near the end of the war. One of the Markowskis—some distant guy in her mom's family—was called Prince Markowski, and so naturally he was the prince in Rapunzel or Cinderella. And you know how many princesses they've got in fairy tales? Well, her mother, Marysia Markowska, and her mother's beautiful cousin, Krystyna Markowska, had to be real princesses because all they ever thought about was fancy balls and what they were going to wear to them, and going to Warsaw—which Janice was sure had to be a magical place with castles in it—and the clincher was Janice's mom used to say, "Krystyna really could feel the pea under all the mattresses—poor Krystyna."

There's a river running right by Krajne Podlaski, and in the summer the river's like glass, and you could walk from the church right down to the river, so Janice thought it was the Ohio because she thought "like glass" only meant you could see your reflection in it, and you could walk from St. Stans down to the river, and it flooded sometimes in both Krajne Podlaski and South Raysburg, so of course it had to be the same river. If you went from Edgewood to South Rays-burg—"That's a huge trip if you're five years old," Janice said—you were going to a place where only the old people spoke Polish, but if you kept on going, you'd come to Krajne Podlaski in Poland where everyone spoke Polish. She used to say to her parents, "Let's go to Poland," and they'd laugh and say, "Maybe someday, Janusiu." She thought that when she was old enough to go to school with the nuns, they could go on down the river to Poland.

Every Sunday night their family read Polish poems and stories to each other, and some things they'd read over and over—like this long poem called *Pan Tadeusz*—and when Janice was little, it was just a bunch of big words flow-ing along that'd put her straight to sleep, and she'd always wake up in her bed and not know how she got there. But every year she looked forward to those same stories coming around again. All those people in those stories were like her old friends.

She got older, and she started sorting out what was real from what was just stories—although she said she wasn't sure she ever got it really straight—but Poland still had that strange sad feeling, "like an enchanted kingdom," she said, but she knew it wasn't a place she could ever go visit because everything about it had changed, been destroyed by the war. That's what her parents kept saying. And all that was left was memory. But her whole life Janice dreamed of Krajne Podlaski in Poland.

"Even in the dream, I'll think, oh, I've come back again." She dreamed the busy market and the town square and the peasant houses with their thatched roofs and the old Jewish quarter where the streets were narrow, just dirt, and buildings were packed in tight together. She never told her parents about these dreams because she was afraid they'd say, "No, it wasn't like that," and she wanted it to be like that.

Janice's mom was Marysia Markowska and her grandad was Pan Piotr Markowski who owned the distillery. He also did a lot of heavy-duty business deals, so he went to Warsaw a lot, and some of Marysia's happiest memories were of getting to go to Warsaw with him. Janice's dad's dad was Dr. Dłuwiecki, and he had a little clinic—a *przychodnia*—and Czesław grew up sneaking in to look through the medical books, trying to figure out, he said, "the secrets of human reproduction." He played cowboys and Indians, can you believe that? It's true. There were books in Polish for little boys all about that wild place called America, and Czesław read them by the dozen. He and a bunch of the other tough little boys would run off into the forest and pretend they were Iroquois Indians.

Janice and her brothers had a million details about Krajne Podlaski in their heads. When their dad was little, it was a really big deal to have indoor plumbing, and most people had outhouses. They had keys to them, and if you made the midnight dash on a winter's night and you'd forgot the key, boy, were you mad. Your water came from the water carrier. He showed up in a horse-drawn wagon and brought the water to you from barrels hanging on each end of a yoke over his shoulders. And the ice man brought you ice cut from the river in the winter, and you'd put it in the basement and cover it with sawdust, and that's how you preserved your food in the summer. And only the fancy section of town had sidewalks and streetlamps, and the lamps were still gas right up to the war. Janice used to imagine Lili Marlene, or anyhow some Polish girl like her—you know, in a trench coat—standing under one of those gas lamps.

So Janice and her brothers could have told you lots of things about Krajne Podlaski, this town in Poland they'd never seen and never would see—not the way it used to be—but all they knew about the war was that their father had been a partisan in the Home Army and that the Germans had put their mother into a labor camp. Just that much, and a few other little bits they'd overheard, and then it'd been, "Thank God you weren't there."

But that day their father was asking them what they wanted to know. And what they wanted to know was *everything*. There was this long silence. They didn't even know the right questions to ask.

Her brother Mark, Janice said, has a very logical mind—always wanting to see things go from A to B to C in a straight line. "Start at the beginning," he said. "Start when the war started." So their parents started with the invasion of Poland and the bombing of Warsaw and like that, and the boys wanted to hear all about the *blitzkrieg* and the fighting, but Janice didn't.

"It was just like when we were growing up," she told me. When they'd been reading all that Polish stuff to each other on Sunday nights, her brothers would get all excited in the parts about hunting or fighting, but Janice was mainly interested in the girls—what they were wearing and who was in love with who, and "in the little details of life," she said. So Janice kept stopping them because she wanted to hear all those little details. "Where were you when you heard about it?" she asked them. "What did you see?" She wanted them to make it really real for her.

When the war started, Czesław said, he and his father had been driving back to Krajne Podlaski from Warsaw. The road was jammed with people going in both directions—fleeing to wherever they thought was safe, but the problem was, nowhere was safe. German planes flew in low and strafed the road. If Czesław and his dad hadn't run away from their car and jumped into a ditch, they would've been killed. They saw peasants in carts killed. They saw dead horses all along the road. They saw an entire family killed, even the children. A plane chased the children running and caught them with machine-gun bullets, even a little girl not more than six or seven.

Janice's mother was at the Markowski estate where her cousin Krystyna lived. The girls were out riding. "I was just your age, Janusiu," her mother said. The girls heard a strange droning in the sky and so they reined in their horses and looked up. There was a formation of German planes going over, and the girls didn't even know enough to be afraid but just stared up like they were looking at a comet or an eclipse. "We watched the planes move across the blue bowl of the sky," her mom said, and Janice loved the way her mom had said that—"the blue bowl of the sky"—and even when they couldn't see the planes anymore, they could still hear their engines, and then they heard the dark low thunder when the bombs began to fall.

The Germans occupied Krajne Podlaski for two weeks. The soldiers went from house to house and took anything they liked. From Janice's mom's house they took the silver and the paintings off the walls; from the clinic, they took surgical instruments and drugs. They burned down the new synagogue in the Jewish quarter, and they rounded up a few hundred Jews and carried them off in trucks, and nobody ever saw them again. Then the Germans went back across to their side of the line, and the Russians took over.

Czesław said to his kids again something they'd heard him say a million times before. Like the liturgy in the Mass, Janice said, the words never changed. I knew just what she was talking about because I'd heard him say it too. "Hitler and Stalin, those two devils, signed a pact, as one devil to another, and only God can decide which was more evil." And those two devils divided up Poland between them.

It was a lot easier, Janice said, getting the little details of life out of her mom than out of her dad. Unless you pushed on him—you know, asked him a lot of direct questions—he just gave you a bunch of facts. Like the Russians occupied Krajne Podlaski for twenty-one months. There were approximately two thousand Jews in Krajne Podlaski, and they made up slightly over ten percent of the population. The Jews first began coming to Great Poland after Bolesław the

Pious welcomed them about seven hundred years ago, and they'd been in Kraj-ne Podlaski for at least five hundred years.

When the Red Army arrived in Krajne Podlaski in 1939, a bunch of people greeted them with flowers and songs and banners that said, "Long Live the Peo-ple's Revolution," and to Czesław those folks were traitors to Poland. There weren't a whole hell of a lot of Polish Communists in Krajne Podlaski—not more than a dozen—and naturally all those nutcases turned out. But some of those traitors to Poland out there waving red banners were Jewish.

Czesław knew most of the Jewish people who welcomed the Red Army, and some of them, the Kestin kids to be exact, he'd thought were friends of his. Their father, Jakob Kestin, was in the lumber business and he was a fairly rich guy. There was a small segment of the Jewish community that was up-do-date and not very religious—you know, that pretty much fit in with the Polish com-munity—and the Kestins were part of that. Heniek Kestin had been one of those tough little boys Czesław had played Iroquois Indians with, and he'd been the first Jewish boy ever to go to the Polish high school, and Czesław had been for dinner at the Kestins' house lots of times, and Heniek had been to his house lots of times. So when he saw Heniek and Icchak and Rachela Kestin waving red banners at Russians in tanks, he felt personally hurt and betrayed. The Poles and the Russians had been enemies forever.

Over the years Czesław had mellowed out enough to try to be fair about things, and here's what he had to say, trying to be fair. Jakob Kestin was in the Bund—that's the Jewish Socialist party—and the Communist ideals of equality for all probably looked pretty good to the Kestin kids. And nobody in Krajne Podlaski had seen yet how those ideals had absolutely nothing to do with Stalin's brand of Communism—although they were about to see it, all right. But there was something else that was really the clincher. From the Jewish point of view, the main thing the Russians had going for them was that they weren't Germans.

The Russians were crazy—both Czesław and his wife said that. The Russians loved wristwatches and if you were wearing one, they'd rip it right off you. Some of those guys had three or four watches on each arm. You had to be care-ful because sometimes one of those Asiatic barbarians would get so drunk he'd chase you right into your house and stick you with his bayonet. All around Krajne Podlaski they put up pictures of Hitler and Stalin embracing, and they renamed everything—like all of a sudden there was a Stalin Street and an

October Revolution Street and a Lenin Street—and the people who lived in Krajne Podlaski weren't Polish anymore, they were Byelorussians. They shut down all the religious institutions—the Catholic Church, and the little Ortho- dox church with its onion-shaped domes, and the synagogues—and put up signs in Russian on them that said God didn't exist and all religions were lies and superstitions.

Janice's mom and dad got to be friends in the Lenin Communist Youth Union of Byelorussia—all the youth in Krajne Podlaski joined up if they knew what was good for them—and they laughed at how weird that was. Of course they'd known each other their whole lives, because everybody in Krajne Pod- laski knew everybody, but before that, Czesław had just seen Marysia as a pretty little girl—the stuck-up daughter of Piotr Markowski—and now all of a sudden she was sixteen, a beautiful young woman he kept running into at those boring youth meetings and maybe could even talk to if he got his courage up.

What were the Russians like? Their parents were kind of at a loss trying to figure out what to say about that. The Russians weren't all drunken assholes with five watches on each arm. The guys who ran things—the guys in the party and the NKVD—were like cats, they said, complicated and strange. In a million years you could never guess what they were thinking. They had spies, and spies spying on the spies, and even more spies spying on them. The old folks said it was worse than the time of the Czar.

The Russians had real clear memories of the Polish-Soviet War—which they'd lost—and they didn't trust the Poles much. So when they took over the administration of Krajne Podlaski and appointed new officials, lots of those new officials were Jewish. Czesław and his dad were in a small group of Poles who got along okay with the Russians. Most of the well-off Polish people were get- ting deported, but they needed Dr. Dłuwiecki to help them run their People's Health Collective, or whatever they called it. Czesław spoke pretty good Rus- sian, and he'd been in some leftist organization in university, so he knew all the right things to say to the comrades. So for the time being, the Dłuwieckis were considered to be "progressive elements."

The kids hadn't heard about the deportations, and they asked a lot of ques- tions about that. The first people the Russians deported were the handful of Polish Communists. Does that make any sense to you? You'd think they'd wel- come fellow Commies with open arms, but no. Stalin had dissolved the Polish Communist Party in 1938, so those guys went straight to Siberia. After that, they mainly deported Poles, and sometimes you could see why they picked who they did, but other times it didn't make any sense at all. They deported some Jews too, and sometimes they even deported each other.

The entire twenty-one months the Russians were in Krajne Podlaski, Czesław said, was like holding your breath. Why wasn't he deported? Or why wasn't he drafted into the Soviet Army? Was it because he was useful—he was doing his best, you know, to look useful—or were they just biding their time?

The Russians were sloppy and inefficient, and people had to eat. Even the Russians had to eat. And you could bribe the Russians—or maybe they just wanted it to seem that way—and the black market was going big time. The Kestin boys were what's called in Yiddish *machers*—they made things happen—and Heniek Kestin, Czesław's friend from high school, turned out to be a real friend after all and pulled Czesław into their operation. Czesław was useful to them because of his Polish connections. You want something illegal picked up here and delivered there, and maybe make a little profit on it, then the right person has to be paid off and a few words said to some official—and you've got to remember you owe him—and some other Russian gets a case of vodka. If you kept track of all these threads, then maybe you could make it through one more day.

Unless they were stupid, the Russians had to know exactly what was going on, and sometimes Czesław thought they really were that stupid, and other times he thought, no, they're waiting like cats—you know, with those blank evil eyes cats get when they're trying to give the mouse the impression they don't care if he tries to run or not. And to make things even more interesting, Czesław joined up with the Polish underground resistance that was starting up in Krajne Podlaski. "Do whatever the Russians say," they told him, "just keep us informed." Sometimes he'd lie in bed at night and think about what he'd been doing that day, and what he was going to be doing tomorrow, and he'd shake like a leaf.

Janice was fascinated by that Jewish family, the Kestins. She'd never heard about them before, and she kept asking about them. "Heniek was a little guy," Czesław said, "wiry and tough as nails. He was a real survivor." Right off the top, Heniek knew which way the wind was blowing. "Those Soviet bastards are a lot more Russian than they are Communist," he said.

"Well, it was you out there waving red banners at them, not me," Czesław said.

Heniek said to him the same thing he'd always said when they'd been friends back in high school—"You've read too much Romantic literature, Czesław. We've got to be realistic."

Even then they were talking about running away into the forest. They'd got to know the forest really well when they'd been playing Iroquois Indians. In the summers when they were teenagers they used to take off into the forest for days at a time—and give their parents the fits—so Heniek was saying, "You know, if we had any sense, we'd cache some supplies out there just in case we might ever need them." And that's exactly what they did.

Czesław had grown up hearing his father say, "Poland wouldn't be Poland without the Jews." But Marysia's father didn't subscribe to that point of view. Remember those Endeks that Czesław used to duke it out with at the university? Well, Piotr Markowski was in their party, the *Narodowa Demokracja*. Polish politics doesn't really translate into anything outside Poland, Czesław said, and, yes, the Endeks were real right-wingers, but they weren't anything like the Nazis. No, they were real strong anti-German, and they didn't like the Russians either; what they believed in was Poland for the Poles. And they thought it might be better for all concerned if the Jews in Poland went to live somewhere else—like Palestine, for instance, which the Zionist Jews kept talking about.

Marysia told her kids that her head had been stuffed full of even more of that Romantic stuff than Czesław's was—like she could get all teary-eyed about the ancient warriors and priests and prophets and martyrs who'd fought for Poland's freedom for hundreds of years, but when it came to the political parties in her own day and age, she couldn't tell one from the other. Her father used to talk about the Jewish problem, and she didn't have the faintest idea what he was talking about because to her there *was* no Jewish problem. You see, Rachela Kestin was in Marysia's class at the high school, and they'd got to be real good friends.

"She was so beautiful," Marysia said. "She had auburn hair and sea blue eyes, and you should have seen how she dressed. She was so stylish!"

Marysia and Rachela got the highest marks in Polish in their class, and they used to walk along by the river and read Polish poetry to each other. Janice wanted to know exactly what poems they'd read, and it turned out they were a lot of the same poems that Janice and her family used to read to each other when she'd been growing up; she loved hearing about that, and she kept asking her mom about that Jewish girl.

Well, it was like they had their own generation gap back there in Poland. Rachela thought that her people were still living in the Middle Ages. Her father was an enlightened man, but when her brother Heniek had refused to keep on going to the Jewish school where all the boys went—you know, to study their religion—her father had nearly disowned him, and most of the Jews in Krajne Podlaski didn't consider Rachela and her brothers even to be Jewish anymore. But Marysia's dad, even though he was a kind, decent man—well, he never forgot that the Kestin kids were Jewish, and he wasn't real pleased that Marysia was hanging around so much with that Jewish girl.

"Wait a minute," Janice said, "you always told us that the Poles and the Jews in Krajne Podlaski got along okay."

"Well, they did," both their parents said, "at least most of the time." But the Jews pretty much stuck to themselves. A lot of the older generation didn't even speak any Polish. They just wanted to live together and practice their religion in peace—which is why the Jews had come to Poland in the first place, because Poland had always been one of the few places in Europe where they could do that—and the relationship between the Poles and the Jews had never been what you could call intimate, but it'd always been, like Czesław said, livable. Back in the old days under Piłsudski, the left-wing Jews and the left-wing Poles even used to have parties together sometimes. But then in the years leading up to the war, things had got kind of rough because of the Endeks, and especially their extreme right wing that had been doing anti-Jewish agitation, so there was a lot of tension building up.

Marysia and Rachela didn't care what other people thought. They figured—well, it's like the buck stops here. Any bad feelings, or prejudice, or whatever between the Poles and the Jews was going to end with them. Yep, the girls were going to fix it all, just between the two of them, and be an example to the whole world, and in the next generation everything would be different. "You should understand how idealistic we were, Janusiu," Janice's mom said. "You're exactly the same way."

It was Rachela and her brother Heniek who got Czesław and Marysia together. Because even though they saw each other in that Communist youth group, Czesław was too shy to even speak to Marysia. She was gentry, and she was as beautiful as an angel, and all he could do was admire her from afar, so Rachela and Heniek had to do their matchmaking thing—"Hey, she really likes you. Make your move, buddy," and like that.

There was a short time when things seemed, you know, not half bad in Krajne Podlaski under the Russians. They got some education classes up and going—for the ordinary folks—and they were having musical concerts and plays and dances in the People's Square. And remembering all that, Janice's

222 · KEITH MAILLARD

parents were shaking their heads over what a sweet girl Rachela was, a real dreamer, always looking on the bright side of things, and how sad that was— what with the way everything turned out. Rachela kept saying that when the war was over, the Russians would go home, and the progressive Jews and Poles would build a new life in Krajne Podlaski, and everyone would be educated, and the dark age of fear and prejudice and ignorance would vanish forever.

They remembered one of those dances, and that night was like a soap bubble, Janice's mom said, beautiful and fragile. "What do you remember?" Janice asked them. Well, the sky was full of stars and they looked so close you could maybe reach up and take a handful home with you, and the square was lit with paper lanterns, and it was like time had stopped. The best Polish and Jewish musicians were in the orchestra, and music never sounded better, and it'd never sound that sweet again.

Everybody danced with everybody—the Polish kids danced with the Jewish kids, and Czesław danced with Rachela and she danced with Czesław's little brother Jan, and Marysia danced with Heniek and Icchak Kestin, and every few dances, Czesław and Marysia found each other so they could dance together again because they were so in love. It was strange, they said, how you could remember a single night thirty years later and it would seem so sad and beautiful. The kids were standing around at the edge of the dance floor, and Rachela made a big gesture that included everyone there—all the young people in Krajne Podlaski were at that dance that night—and she said, "You see," and she used a phrase in Yiddish. It means, "We're wound together and knotted."

Then just a few weeks later most of the Markowskis got deported. They left Marysia's father alone, and he didn't know why—maybe the Russians figured that the one thing they really didn't want to screw up was the distillery—but all the other Markowskis were deported that spring, three whole families of them.

The way you get deported goes like this. The NKVD comes knocking on your door in the wee small hours of the morning just before dawn. And it's not like you're being arrested or charged with anything, and even if you're stupid enough to ask, nobody's going to tell you what you did. Because it doesn't matter what you did, or even if maybe you didn't do it, because if you weren't guilty, your name wouldn't be on the list. Usually they're not real mean about it, but they do want you to hurry up or you'll miss your train, and they can't allow that to happen. Food? Oh, don't worry, that's all taken care of. Clothes? Don't worry about that either. Where are you going? Well, you're going to work on a farm for a while, and everything you need will be supplied in due course.

They give you maybe twenty minutes to pack, and then they truck you to the railroad station and shove you in a freight car. Not a whole hell of a lot of food or water, and if you want to relieve yourself—well, there's a hole cut in the floor for that, or maybe a bucket. And away you go, the trains roaring along as fast as they can get them cranked up. If some old folks or some babies die, well, tough, but the train's got to keep on rolling. Maybe half a million Poles got to take the big train ride.

The Markowskis went to Kazakhstan. Nobody in their right mind would want to go to Kazakhstan. There's not an awful lot to eat there, and nobody lives there but the Kazakhs, and they're not real happy to see a bunch of strange Polaks showing up—you know, more mouths to feed. The train finally stops, and they open the doors, and everybody climbs out of the freight car and stands by the tracks looking at this weird empty land under an endless sky. It looks like it goes on forever, and it's true, it does go on forever. Nobody's going to walk out of Kazakhstan. Hi, comrades, welcome to your new home. You think this is bad, just be glad it's not Siberia.

No message ever came back to Krajne Podlaski from Kazakhstan. If you asked the Russians, they said, "They all arrived safely. They're working on a collective farm. They're well and happy and send their regards." Marysia knew better than to believe that. She felt bad for all the Markowskis but especially for Krystyna, who was her favorite cousin. Krystyna had always been pampered and spoiled, and getting deported to Kazakhstan was probably hell on earth for her, and for days afterward Marysia cried whenever she thought of poor Krystyna.

But meanwhile, life in Krajne Podlaski kept rolling right along in its own crazy way. On the surface everything seemed just dandy. Czesław was teaching some peasants the basic principles of bookkeeping. He hadn't known a damn thing about bookkeeping before, but when Comrade So-and-so asks you to teach something, you're sure not going to tell him that you're not checked out on it. And Czesław was still doing his black-market number with the Kestin boys and doing his secret stuff with the Polish resistance. But he was thinking real hard about Siberia. If they deport you to Siberia, they give you some good honest work to do—like digging tunnels through mountains with your fingertips in a place that's slightly colder than the planet Pluto while you get to see how long you can live on a little watery soup—and Czesław knew if the NKVD picked him up, Siberia was where he was headed.

He and Marysia vowed that they would love each other forever—in this life and on into the next one. "Only God knows what's going to happen," Czesław told her, "but whatever happens, if we get separated, I swear on everything sacred—if I'm alive, I'll find you."

Then Hitler turned on his great friend Stalin—one devil betraying another the way devils always do—and invaded the Soviet Union. The Red Army retreated. By the time they got done, they'd retreated all the way to Moscow. The first anyone in Krajne Podlaski knew about it was when they heard artillery firing in the night. And so the Germans came back to Krajne Podlaski.

Well, Janice's parents didn't much enjoy telling their kids what the Germans did, and Janice didn't much enjoy telling it to me, and I'm not going to much enjoy telling it to you. Pretty soon after they started talking about the Germans coming back, Janice didn't want to hear all the little details of life anymore and she stopped asking. She kept getting this awful nauseous feeling, and she'd think, I've got to get out of here, I can't listen to any more of this. But she stayed and listened because she had to—because she'd always wanted to know, and because she thought it was her duty to know.

The German occupation, Czesław said, was like being ruled by the Antichrist—you were rewarded for doing evil and punished for doing good. The Russians left you a little room to maneuver—until you ran out of room— but the Germans didn't leave you anything at all.

The Germans put up a loudspeaker in the town square, and they drove around town with loudspeakers mounted on trucks, and they announced in both German and Polish that Poles caught assisting the Jews in any way would be killed along with their entire families. It was something I hadn't known—and Janice hadn't known it either—but Poland was the only country where the Germans were that harsh. The Nazi occupation of Poland made what they did in places like France or Denmark look like a Sunday school picnic.

Well, Rachela's dad had a pretty good idea what was coming down, so the whole Kestin family slipped away at the last possible minute and hid out with some nice peasants outside of town. They were staying in a barn, and the Kestin boys figured that their parents would have a better chance if there weren't quite so many of them crammed in there, so what they ought to do was take off into the woods and try to make contact with the Home Army, or anyhow with some partisan group—you know, some friendly dudes with guns. They begged Rachela to come with them, but she wouldn't leave their parents.

Meanwhile, Czesław and his brother Jan had run off just as soon as the coast was clear. It was one of those times, Czesław said, when if you hesitated even half a second, you'd be dead. They hid out with some peasants for a while, and then, when they were sure the Red Army was long gone, they escaped into the forest where he and Heniek Kestin had stashed their supplies. And guess what? They ran right smack into the Kestin boys, who were doing the same thing, and they teamed up together and went off looking for the Home Army, and eventually they found it. So the story of what happened in Krajne Podlaski after that, Janice and her brothers heard from their mother.

Several hundred Jews fled, but most of them stayed where they were because they didn't know what else to do. The Germans made a ghetto in part of the Jewish quarter and forced all the Jews into it, put up a fence around it and patrolled it with dogs, and no one was allowed in or out. Then they rounded up anyone who'd ever served in any official way under the Russians—Jews and Poles—and shot them.

There were a few Poles—those slime called *szmalcowniki*—who collaborated with the Germans, and the Polish resistance executed them whenever they got a chance. "We got a lot of them by the end," Czesław said, "but some of them slipped through our fingers and are probably still alive to this very day." And in a few places the local Poles turned against the Jews and got into killing and looting and all that. And then there were even a few Jews who helped Germans catch other Jews, if you can believe that—the Germans told them they'd protect them and their families, but like Czesław said, the devil always lies.

The Germans were royally pissed off at all the Jews who'd got away, and the Germans were, you know, real efficient. They went through public records to account for everybody, so they pretty much knew the exact number of Jews that were missing, and they began to search for them.

When the Gestapo found out that Dr. Dłuwiecki had two sons who'd run away, they figured that the boys had probably joined the Polish partisans—which was true—so they tortured Czesław's father for a few days to find out what he knew. They kept him in a cell filled with water up to his waist so if he fell asleep, he'd drown. Every night they'd take him out and beat the crap out of him, and then they'd throw him back in there. Well, eventually he must have told them something—everybody always told them *something*—but Czesław figured that it probably had just a few true things here and there to make it sound good, and most of it must have been lies, because the Germans never found any of the partisans. Then the Germans hanged Dr. Dłuwiecki in front of his own clinic, and nobody was allowed to take his body down for twenty-four hours because they wanted to make an example of him.

Well, Rachela and her parents were doing okay living in that peasant family's barn, but some bastard ratted on them. When they heard the Germans coming, Rachela's father whispered to her, "Run," and she ran. She got into the forest and hid there. She kept trying to find her brothers, but she wasn't checked out on the forest, and it just scared her. The Germans took her parents to the compound where they were keeping the Jews they'd caught. The peasant family that had been hiding them got shot—every single one of them right down to the little kids.

It's the middle of the night, and Marysia hears a tap on her window. Her heart jumps right into her mouth. She raises the drapes like an inch and peeks out and it's Rachela.

Rachela was like a sleepwalker. She didn't cry. She didn't show any emotion at all. She was, their mom said, in some kind of deep shock. "I didn't know where else to go," she said. "I can go back into the forest if you want."

Marysia said, "We're wound together and knotted. Shut up and get in here."

Marysia woke her father, and he thought about what to do. Well, his political position was that Poland would be better off if the Jews lived somewhere else, but all of a sudden here was this Jewish girl in his house. Just by being there, she was putting the life of his whole family in danger. "But my father was a Christian and a Pole," Marysia said, "and he knew what he had to do."

"You are Krystyna Markowska," he told Rachela. "You escaped from the Russian transport at the last minute, and we've been hiding you ever since."

When the Germans thought they'd caught all the Jews they were going to catch—about three hundred of them—they marched them off into the woods. They'd brought in some Ukrainians, and some Poles from a slave labor camp, and they made them dig a deep wide pit. Several of these Polish men survived the war, so there were witnesses.

The whole area was surrounded by the SS, but the Germans that did the dirty work were from one of those special units they brought in. The Jews had to take all their clothes off, and then the Poles had to separate the clothes into different piles—you know, shoes here and coats there and like that. They had to be real careful to get all the rings and jewelry.

The Jews were marched up in a single line—naked, you know—and they had to kneel down along the edge of the pit, and the special-unit guys shot them in the back of the head at point-blank range. Blood and brains were getting splattered everywhere, and the special-unit guys weren't having a real good time. One of them had to walk away for a few minutes, but he threw up and pulled himself together and came back and got on with his work.

Some Poles had to come along behind the Germans and push the bodies into the pit. There were other Poles in the pit who had to look in the dead Jews' mouths for gold teeth and pull them out with pliers, and then they had to arrange the bodies real neat so they could cram in as many as possible.

Some of the Jews were screaming and crying. A few of them tried to run— just, you know, in a blind panic—and the SS shot them down. Some of them were crawling at the feet of the Germans and begging for their lives. Others just stood there and waited for their turn. One of the women was begging for the life of her baby, and a German soldier ripped the baby out of her arms, threw it on the ground, and stomped on it.

There were only six Germans from that special unit, and it takes six men a long time to kill three hundred people. Rachela's parents died there in that forest. When all the Jews were dead, the Poles and Ukrainians had to shovel in dirt and cover them up, and then the Poles and Ukrainians were loaded onto trucks and transported back to the labor camp.

Well, the Jews that were left in the ghetto, the Germans kept them locked up in there with hardly any food. Then in the summer of 1942 the Germans got their Final Solution up and running, so they took all the Jews out of the ghetto and loaded them into trucks and transported them to the railroad station and loaded them into freight cars and took them to Treblinka where they gassed every one of them. Then the Germans put up signs that said Krajne Podlaski was Jew-free.

Marysia and her mom worked like crazy to turn Rachela into Krystyna. They taught her all the prayers she'd know as a good Catholic girl, and how to cross herself, and they went over the Mass with her step by step. They threw Markowskis at her night and day until she'd memorized how she was related to all of them. And Marysia would ask her things like, "Do you remember the first time we went to the Hotel Europejski in Warsaw?" and Rachela would say, "No, I don't quite remember that. Remind me."

But a day or two later, Rachela would say, "Oh, of course I remember. How could I ever forget it? We were with your father, and he indulged our every whim. He even allowed us to wear lipstick. Do you remember the little silver bowls of ice cream?"

The real Krystyna was somewhere in Kazakhstan doing God knows what, but her baptism was on record at the church, and her papers were registered at the municipal hall, and all Rachela needed was whatever papers Krystyna would've had if she'd got away from the Russians. The Polish resistance was getting into full swing by then, and the papers arrived under the straw in a basket of eggs. Whoever did them was real good.

Mass was celebrated in the church for the first time since the Russians left. Afterward the priest said to Rachela, "I'm so glad to see you, Krystyna," and she said, "Thank you, Father," and so the word went around on the grapevine. When the girls finally dared to go out, friends of Krystyna's would come up to chat and ask Rachela if she'd heard anything from her family in Kazakhstan, and peasants would say, "Good day, Panno Krystyno."

Now you'd think that in that whole town there'd be somebody who'd give her away, right? That's what Janice and her brothers thought. "It's because of who we were," Janice's mom said. "That's how much respect there was for us. The Markowskis. We were the only ones who could have got away with something like that."

One night when the girls were going to bed, Rachela asked Marysia, "What do you suppose the Germans did with my horses?"

Marysia was taken by surprise, and she thought, I must never again think of her as Rachela. If I do, I'll give her away. From that moment on she always thought of her as Krystyna.

Eventually the Germans came to visit. There were two SS officers—the one in charge and a short fat man who seemed to be some kind of assistant—and a dozen soldiers. The way the Germans were, they never asked, they just stomped on in and started shouting. The soldiers searched the house. Marysia's mother inquired politely if the officers would care for a drink, and the officer in charge all of a sudden got just as polite as she was and introduced himself and the other man. Krystyna and Marysia served them some little cakes and the Markowskis' best orange-flavored vodka.

The short officer was a German from central Poland, so he spoke Polish. He asked to see Krystyna's papers, and then he started asking her questions in Polish. At first she answered him real polite, but after a few minutes something snapped and she just lost it.

Krystyna's eyes were flashing, and she was speaking a mile a minute in her high-flown Polish, and she traced her lineage on both sides going all the way back to the Old Republic, and she told him exactly how she was related to Prince Markowski, and about everybody else the Markowskis were related to— the Tarnowskis and the Radziwills and all those other blue bloods. She told him

THE CLARINET POLKA · 229

about how the Russians, those barbarian pigs, had looted her home, and about how she'd slipped away from them, those idiots, and she asked him to tell her, if he would be so kind, what they had done with her horses.

The fat guy's jaw kind of drops open. He looks at the other SS officer and he kind of shrugs like he's saying, yes, she really is Krystyna Markowska. There's nobody else in the world she could possibly be.

The officer in charge stands up and clicks his heels. He kisses Pani Markowska's hand. "It is my fondest hope, dear lady," he says in German, "that we might meet again in happier times," and then he goes, "Heil, Hitler!" and they're gone.

Well, happier times weren't exactly in the works. A few weeks after that, another one of those special units came to town. The folks in Krajne Podlaski must have really pissed off the Germans. Maybe it was that too many Jews had escaped or too many of the boys had run off and joined the partisans, but anyhow the Germans were going to teach them a good lesson—with what they called a "special pacification act." That means cleaning out the Polish intellectuals, and they did a real thorough job of it. They got anybody they thought might show any sign of resistance or turn out to be any kind of leader.

The Gestapo had their lists already made up, so the SS starts rounding these people up, and if they had families, then the whole lot of them right down to the babies. Schoolteachers. Librarians. Lawyers. The priest and the nuns. Anybody who had a university degree. Anybody who'd ever been in anybody's army, even old guys in their eighties. Anybody who'd ever been active in any of the leftist political parties. Anybody who'd ever managed anything of any size— like a distillery.

They were herded into a compound, and then the Germans selected the young able-bodied ones—like between the ages of fourteen and forty, Marysia said, but they didn't ask your age, just picked you out by eye. Krystyna and Marysia and Marysia's mother got picked, and Czesław's sister Helena got picked, but grief had aged Czesław's mom, and she didn't make the cut. The young and able-bodied were divided into men and women and transported off to work in slave labor camps. Everybody else was executed.

They did it just the way they'd done it to the Jews—the pit in the forest, the bullet in the back of the head. Czesław's mother and Marysia's father died there in the forest. The Germans murdered nearly a hundred people there.

The women who got picked were shipped to Germany where they worked in a munitions factory. They shaved them all over—Marysia said it was one of the most humiliating experiences of her life—and then they made them take a shower, and that was the only bath of any kind they got as long as they were there. They slept on little wooden platforms that looked like shelves on a wall, and their only clothes were what they had on when they were picked up in Poland. They had to wear the letter P so that everybody would know they were Polish and treat them like they were a notch or two below human—which is what the Germans said the Poles were.

They marched you into the factory at dawn and worked you till late at night, and if you didn't work fast enough, they cut your rations, and if you got onto that slippery slope and stayed on it too long, that was the end of you. All they gave you to eat was soup and a little bread, and the soup usually had maggots in it. Krystyna turned out to have a lot of courage and fortitude, and she was always saying things to try to help the other women keep going. "Be sure to eat the maggots," she said. "They're dead and they won't hurt you, and they've got good food value."

There were so many fleas it looked like a jumping carpet everywhere you went, and all the women were infested with lice. There weren't enough latrines, and they were never cleaned, and the floors in the latrines were smeared with shit. Typhus is carried by lice, and maybe a quarter of the women died of it. The women never received any medical care. Typhus raged in that work camp until it burned itself out, and then a new shipment of women would come in—they were starting to get Ukrainian and Russian girls—and the typhus would have a go at them. Marysia's mother died of typhus.

While the women were working in the munitions factory, Czesław was off in the forest with the Home Army—the *Armia Krajowa*. Czesław told them the name of his unit and his rank and his *nom de guerre* and the exact years he'd been in the AK. He said they generally operated in the forests in the region of Krajne Podlaski, but they moved around a lot. They had to if they wanted to survive.

"What did you do?" John asks him.

"The main thing we did," Czesław says with this thin little smile, "was try not to get killed."

They disrupted communications. Sabotaged roads and rail lines. Once they burned a bridge. They executed collaborators. They fought with other partisan groups. They tried to maintain order, but that was impossible. "By the end, there were God knows how many other groups in the forest. Some were legitimate, but many were simply bandits—riffraff with no moral or political convictions of any kind."

"But the Germans," Mark asks him, "didn't you fight the Germans?"

The Germans had a policy of one hundred to one, Czesław tells them. They'd kill one hundred Poles for every German killed, so the AK had to be careful not to cause reprisals. A lot of times the Germans did it even better than one hundred to one. A little village called Biebrz near Krajne Podlaski—someone fired from that village. Just a couple shots, hit nobody. The Germans burnt the village to the ground and shot anyone who tried to escape from it.

When they got caught off guard, the AK fought skirmishes with the Germans, Czesław said, but they didn't stick around to see how things turned out. Near the end of the war when the Red Army was rolling over everything, his unit finally did get a chance to get their licks in. The Germans had been running out of men, and a lot of the soldiers were mere boys. The AK ambushed a bunch of them, and they surrendered without putting up any fight at all. "They fell on their knees begging for their lives," Czesław says. "They were crying like babies." He kind of shrugs. "It was too bad."

Janice said that she felt all the blood rush out of her head—or maybe it wasn't doing that, but it felt like it was. She could hear her own heartbeat in her ears.

Czesław sees how his kids are looking at him. "You don't understand how it was," he says, hard and angry. "I knew you wouldn't understand. It's foolish to try to tell you. But we couldn't take prisoners. You'd have to feed them and watch them all the time, and they'd slow you down. It would have been suicide to take prisoners."

That sets him off remembering another German. This one he stalked for hours through the forest. "He was part of a unit that had been sent out to look for us. He became separated from his comrades. He was lost and badly frightened—and I knew the moss on every tree. Well, he got tired. He sat down under a tree to try to collect himself. He laid his rifle down, poor fellow." He kind of stares off into space for a minute. "I was glad to get that rifle. He had a damned good pair of boots too."

"Did you feel bad about it?" Mark asks his father.

Czesław looks kind of startled. "What? About that German? Why should I feel bad? He was a soldier."

"Well, how about the young Germans—the ones who were crying like babies?"

"Well, of course I felt bad about them. But you did what you had to. I have no regrets about any German."

He sits there for a while staring off into space, and then he says, "You ask me if I felt bad. It's a question you could ask—you weren't there. I'll tell you what I did feel bad about. Living. So many good people died, and I was spared, and I kept asking why. You could fool yourself. I think sometimes that you *had* to fool yourself. You could say it's because you were young and tough and smart—that's what kept you alive. Or maybe God spared you. And it helped to tell yourself things like that. But all it came down to in the end was luck."

For a while Czesław was sunk in the old deep gloom and nobody was saying anything. The kids figured the story was pretty much over, but it wasn't. Finally their mother starts to talk.

One day a group of men came to the munitions factory, and the women had to walk by them one at a time. Marysia was in the group that was picked to walk by them again, but this time they had to take all their clothes off. Whatever they were looking for, she had it, because she was one of about fifty girls who were taken away in trucks. They were each given a bowl of good soup and a piece of bread that wasn't moldy. They were each issued a sliver of soap, and they had a shower. Then they were examined by this German doctor. He looked into their eyes. He studied their ears. He had this metal gadget, and he measured their skulls with it.

Marysia was one of about twenty girls who passed all the tests. The girls were all in their late teens or early twenties. They were all blond and blue-eyed. They didn't look like much because they'd been starving and they were covered with insect bites and open sores and like that, but you could tell that they'd all been pretty once. They didn't know what was going to happen to them, and as you can imagine, they were scared shitless.

The doctor came and gave them a little talk in German. They should be very happy, he said, because his exhaustive tests—the most scientific and accurate tests possible—had demonstrated that they all had pure Aryan blood—pure Aryan blood that had, up until now, been lost to the Reich. But that blood would be restored to the Reich. He was also testing fine young men of our victorious Wehrmacht, and only those with pure Aryan blood would be selected, and together with those fine young men, all of the girls would be privileged to make pure Aryan babies.

There's a little pause, and then Czesław comes in, catching them up with his part of the story. Near the end of the war, he says, the fighting in the forest just got stupid and crazy. The peasants suffered the most. Everyone was hitting them up for food. The Soviet partisans were being supplied by the Red Army, and pretty soon they were the heaviest dudes going. They offered amnesty to the Polish partisans. To Czesław, the Soviets were foreign invaders just like the Germans, and he was ready to die before he gave up to them, but nearly half his unit—including the Kestin boys—decided to throw in their lot with those bastards.

Heniek Kestin came sneaking back secretly—and he really hung his ass out on a limb to do it—just so he could tell Czesław, "You were right. They accepted us—all the Jews. But they shot the Poles. I'm sorry."

What was left of that AK unit disbanded, and Czesław headed west. The underground had kept them informed of everything that had been going down in Krajne Podlaski, so he knew he had to get to Germany somehow if he wanted to find Marysia. Crossing Poland, he said, was like crossing hell. The Soviets were going after anybody who'd fought in the Polish resistance, shooting them or sending them to camps in the Soviet Union or calling them fascists and putting them through these big public trials—you know, for the propaganda.

The underground slipped Czesław onto a convoy of French prisoners from a German prison camp. His French wasn't that hot, but it must have done the trick, and he crossed the border into the part of Czechoslovakia occupied by the Allies.

Czesław served with the American army as an interpreter, and the Americans helped him find Marysia. He found his little sister Helena first. The women in the munitions factory had been liberated by the Americans, and she was in a DP camp. "Don't go back to Poland," he told her. "The Polish soil is soaked in blood, and the Russians are everywhere."

Rachela Kestin was in that DP camp too. She told Czesław that she'd been Krystyna for so long that when the Americans liberated them, Rachela hardly existed anymore—all that was left of her was just this tiny spark deep inside. She kept hearing the names of the American officers, and one of them gave her a strange feeling. He was called Major Rosenbloom. She couldn't stop thinking about him. She saw him talking to some other Americans, and she walked up to him. She couldn't help herself. She began speaking to him in Polish. Of course he didn't speak Polish, but he smiled at her. He had, she said, the kindest eyes.

She didn't know a word of English. She was so stupid, she said. She stood there and thought, no, I must not speak to him in German, or in Russian either.

Oh, maybe he speaks French. She still remembered a little French. But then she finally realized that there was a language that maybe they both knew, and she was right. She started to cry, and she said to him in Yiddish, "I'm a Jew."

"Rachela lives in New York now," Czesław said. "She has four children and two grandchildren."

Then Czesław and Marysia started telling their kids what'd happened to all those other people. Like some of the Markowskis who'd been deported to Kazakhstan died, and some joined the Polish army and went to Iran—of all crazy places—and ended up in England. And Czesław's brother got killed in some dumb skirmish, and his sister ended up married to a Polish soldier and was living in England, and some of the Markowskis got back to Poland—like Krystyna who's still living in Krajne Podlaski and has a daughter the same age as Janice. And Janice and her brothers are going, "Wait a minute, wait a minute. We'll never remember all these people," and their parents said they'd write it all down for them.

But the story's still not over yet. It took Czesław months to find Marysia. When Czesław found her, she was in a British DP camp with her baby.

"Imagine our joy when we saw each other again," Czesław said, "alive after all those years." They were married right away.

What baby? Janice and Mark are looking at their brother John. Everybody had always said he was the spitting image of his mom, and he didn't look a thing like their dad. They all got the message at pretty much the same time, but they didn't dare open their mouths. Janice's mom said, "He wasn't a bad man. He never hurt me."

"His name was Wolfgang Heiber," Czesław said. "He was from Aschersleben. We never knew what happened to him."

It seemed like nobody was ever going to say it—you know, straight out in so many words. Then John just started yelling. "I don't give a damn what happened to him. Why the hell do you think I'd care what happened to him?" And he said to Czesław, *"Ty jesteś moim ojcem."* That means in English, "You're my father."

That really got to Czesław, and for a couple seconds he looked like he was going to break down. Janice and her mother had been crying off and on all afternoon, but Czesław and the boys had been holding it all in. Janice thought it was incredible that John and her father didn't hug each other. That's what she wanted them to do, but it didn't seem to occur to either one of them. After a minute Czesław got up and went in the other room, and their mother followed him.

John jumped up and started pacing up and down. He looked like he wanted to murder somebody. "I don't give a damn what his name was," he yelled at Janice and Mark. "Wolfgang Heiber—what a goddamn ridiculous name. I don't care where he was from. Why the hell would I care where he was from? It was the Nazis who believed in blood and all that racial bullshit. It doesn't mean a goddamn thing. I'm still me." Janice had never seen him that angry, and she just felt sick and scared.

FIFTEEN

Janice didn't tell me her parents' story straight through like I've just told it to you. There was lots of it she had trouble getting out, and sometimes she just had to stop. The first time she did that, it kind of took me by surprise. We're sitting on top of the hill with our backs against the same tree, and I've got sucked into what she's telling me, and I want to hear what's coming next, but she stops dead, right in the middle of a sentence.

I'm waiting for her to go on, but she doesn't. I look over at her, and she's staring down the hill like she's frozen. The park's packed with people. Families with little kids running around, teenagers—the boys flirting with the girls—and other people just strolling, taking it easy, having a beer, laying on towels, catching a few rays, doing exactly what you'd expect for a Saturday afternoon on a beautiful day like that.

Janice takes a breath. Real deep. And then she exhales real slow. And then she takes another breath. And I'm just watching her breathe. I see her throat move a couple times like she's swallowing. I don't know why it was so important to her not to cry in front of me, but it was. Hell, I figured she had the right to cry as much as she wanted to, but she never did. So what do you say? Nothing is what you say. I reached over and took her hand and held it and waited for her to get to where she could talk again.

After her parents left the room, she was afraid her brother John was going to break something he was so mad. He yelled at Mark and Janice—all about how it didn't matter a damn and why the hell hadn't they told him about it before—and then he jumped in his car and drove away. They didn't know if he was going back to Columbus or just around the block.

Her parents were, I guess you could say, shattered. They couldn't do much of anything, so Mark and Janice finished making the dinner their mom had started, but when they tried to eat it, none of them had much luck. John came back around midnight a little worse for a few gallons of beer—I could sympathize with the guy—and he wanted to start in again, you know, and hash everything out to the bitter end, but their parents said they just couldn't hack it anymore that night. They'd be glad to try tomorrow.

The next morning they get up—all of them awake at some horrible hour like five-thirty because they'd had a rough night—and John must have had the worst night of all because he'd packed his things and taken off for Columbus. He left them a little note saying he'd come back after he had a chance to digest everything. Since then, they hadn't heard from him.

Janice went down to St. Stans that day and did the Stations of the Cross, and while she was doing that, it hit her that she had to learn everything there was to know about Poland in the Second World War—like somehow it was her religious duty to do that—so when she got home, she looked at all her dad's books and picked out one called *Hitlerowski terror na wsi polskiej*. After she'd been reading it for a few minutes, she had to go back and get the big Polish-English dictionary because her Polish wasn't quite as good as she'd thought it was. And she'd been slogging away at that damn book ever since. She could only read a little bit at a time, and that wasn't just because she was having trouble with the Polish.

"I don't know, kid," I said. "I don't know if that's the best thing for you to be doing right now."

We'd been sitting there holding hands for—oh, I don't know, over an hour, and that whole time it'd never crossed my mind what we might look like to somebody else. But then I thought, hey, that's all we'd need—to have somebody from South Raysburg see us. So I gave her hand a little squeeze and let it go, and she turned and looked right into my eyes with those absolutely huge blue eyes of hers. "What do we do now?" she said.

Good question. We walked around the park. She told me she'd been to see the priest. Yep, Father Obinski sure earned his money that week. The first thing he told her was that she should quit blaming herself. Because she was still thinking that it was all her fault. She'd been pushing her dad to tell her all that stuff, and seeing her in the polka band had given him the last push over the edge. But she thought maybe it would have been better if things had just gone on the way they were before, with nobody knowing the whole story.

Father Obinski told her that the truth had to come out. If you keep secrets, they turn poisonous on you. She said, well then, maybe her father should have told them years ago. He said, yes, he probably should have, but can you blame him? Can you imagine how hard it was to take that baby and raise it as his own? And what a perfect example of Christian love. Yes, she said, she'd thought of that.

She asked him how people could do such terrible things to each other as what went on, you know, on a regular basis in the war. Well, he's a priest, right? So what do you expect him to say? He said human nature was naturally sinful, and people will do evil things like that when they turn their backs on God and on his Church. And she should remember that her mother and father never lost their faith, and that's what brought them through.

She asked him why the Holy Father had sat there in the Vatican and not done much of anything. That's not quite the way Czesław had put it. What he always said was, "sat there on his *dupa* in the Vatican twiddling his thumbs," but she didn't think that Father Obinski would want to hear it put that way.

He said, "Those were terrible times, Janice. Just thank God that we'll never have to make the decisions the Holy Father had to make."

She didn't like that answer much, but she didn't say so.

She said she felt terrible for her brother. Knowing that he was only her half brother and that he was half German didn't change anything for her, but she was afraid it'd change something for him. She didn't know what she was going to say to him when she saw him again. And Father Obinski quoted to her from the Bible where it says, "There is neither Jew nor Greek, there is neither bond nor free, there is neither male nor female: for ye are all one in Christ Jesus."

She knew that verse, and she'd always liked it, but now she thought something else that she didn't say to Father Obinski. What about those millions of dead Jews who were not in Christ Jesus?

"God didn't care that they weren't Christians," I said. "If God was with all the Poles who got killed, he was with all the Jews too." I had a pretty good idea that might not be standard-issue Catholic doctrine, but to tell you the truth, I didn't really care. It was kind of obvious to me.

Well, we walked around the park talking for maybe another hour, and it was getting close to dinnertime, and I figured maybe she ought to go home. "I can't stand to be at home," she said. "I walk in the door, and it's like walking into a funeral."

It was driving her brother Mark nuts too, she said. He was spending all his time with his girlfriend. Their parents hadn't said a word about anything serious since their big talk. They had to be thinking about John, but they never mentioned him. They kept trying to act like everything was normal—you know, the stiff upper lip that Poles are so good at—except nothing was normal, and there was this huge, ugly, dark cloud hanging over the house.

"After everything they went through," she said, "I keep telling myself I shouldn't get mad at them, but I still get mad at them. I keep tiptoeing around them like they're—I don't know, something fragile. Made out of glass. I can't stand it— And I don't know if I can ever play in the polka band again. I don't know if I'd ever feel right about it."

Oh, Linda's going to just love hearing that, I thought.

So anyhow, Janice called home and said she was going to my house for dinner, and that was cool with them. She said her mom even sounded relieved she wasn't coming home. So we went back to our place. Saturday nights, you know, Mom and Old Bullet Head usually go out, but Linda was there, and naturally she knew something was up, but I gave her the significant look so she didn't ask any questions. The three of us made ourselves this homey little dinner out of some leftovers and toast and scrambled eggs. It was fun in a quiet sad kind of way. And then we just sat around watching the tube. Janice seemed real tired by then. Hell, I guess she had every right to be.

When I drove her home that night, she said in this absolutely couldn't-careless voice, "You doing anything after Mass tomorrow?"

Now that was an odd question from a number of different angles. First off, I hadn't been to Mass since Easter, and so she wasn't exactly used to seeing me there. As to what I was doing tomorrow— Well, okay, here's my usual Sundays. I crawl out of the sack at whatever point the pain in my skull forces me to, and I scrape myself together. Then I stop by Carlotti's newsstand to pick up *The New York Times* for Mrs. Constance Bradshaw, and I drive out to St. Stevens and we have us a nice little brunch, and it's usually got some dog hair in it—your champagne and orange juice in the chilled glasses—and then we have us our Mature Relationship and end up snoozing in her big bed. Yeah, just lazing around, laying there reading the paper. And that's the way Sundays go, and it puts me back in South Raysburg feeling halfway human just in time for Mom's dinner. It was a nice way to spend Sundays.

I looked into Janice's big sad blue eyes, and I said, "I don't usually make it to Mass these days, but I don't really have anything happening tomorrow."

"You want to do something?"

"Sure," I said.

It wasn't like I was planning to see Janice Dłuwiecki damn near every day after that, but that's pretty much how it turned out. She practically moved into our house. With my mom, you never have to guess what she's thinking, and what she said was, "That poor little girl's having a rough time." Naturally, I told the whole story to Linda, and she felt real bad for Janice and her family, but she also felt real bad for the polka band. "I know it's selfish of me," she said, "but I just can't help it. We put so much time and effort and love into it, and she's just so *good*. We couldn't ever replace her." And she went off and had a good cry about it.

I kept saying, "Oh, she'll come back to the music," but I wasn't sure she would.

Well, Janice had a ten o'clock curfew on weeknights and midnight on weekends—which even back in those ancient days was fairly harsh to lay on a sixteen-year-old in the summer, but I guess her parents were still operating on old-country rules. But she could stay out later if she was with Linda and me. Why that should be, I'm not really sure. I guess they figured we were safe or something. So lots of nights Linda would be yawning by nine-thirty or ten, and then, as far as she knew, I was taking Janice home. And I'd drop Janice off around midnight, and her parents would be in bed, but as far as they knew, it was me and Linda dropping her off. So what did Janice and I do alone together for a couple hours? It's not what you might think. All we did was talk.

We'd sit on the riverbank, or sometimes I'd take her up to various points high above the city where we could get that famous panoramic view, or sometimes we'd just drive around. We never got tired of talking to each other. She'd fill me in on how things were at home and how she was doing with WW II. By the time she'd plowed through that first heavy book, she figured she'd done her duty to the Polish language, so she switched to books in English. She was reading *The Rise and Fall of the Third Reich* and *The Diary of Anne Frank* and other cheery things like that.

I don't suppose there was anything about myself I didn't tell her—lots of childhood stuff like about Babcia Koprowski and Linda refusing to speak English, and playing football in high school, and how I fell madly in love with Dorothy Pliszka, and going off to Morgantown with Mondrowski, and my war stories about the air force, and just you know, the whole shot. Well, Mrs. Constance Bradshaw I didn't mention, but that was about the only thing. So Janice and I got real close, and I kept reminding myself she was just another little sister.

She went back to see the priest a couple more times. He told her that what she was wrestling with was something that had worried people in the Church forever. There was even a name for it—"the problem of evil"—and it went like this. If God is infinitely good, how come he allows evil in the world? Yeah, Janice said, that pretty well got to the heart of it.

Father Obinski told her it had to do with free will. God's given man free will to be able to choose good or evil, and it's a real choice. Evil comes from man making the wrong choice. And that sounded pretty good to Janice except that— Well, you know how something can fall into place in your head where it all makes sense and you go, oh, yeah, right? Well, just talking about it in general, what Father Obinski was telling her sounded okay, but when she thought about God allowing the Nazis to run those death camps, or allowing the Russians to deport all those people into those horrible places where lots of them died, then Janice just couldn't quite hit that point of going, oh, yeah, right.

The last time Janice saw Father Obinski, he asked her if she thought she had a vocation. I guess he hadn't seen too many sixteen-year-old girls trotting into his office wanting to talk about the problem of evil. "You could have knocked me over with a feather," Janice said. She told him—in a nice way, you know, but she made it real clear—that her desire to be a nun was a little less than zero.

I don't want to give you the impression that Janice was always heavy into the gloom that summer. When she'd had enough of peering into the pit, then this silly goofball side to her would come out. It was like she was saying, okay, enough of this, now I'm going to be normal. And when she was with her girlfriends, boy, was she ever normal. You see, if Janice and I wanted to do something together on the weekends, we had to find other people to do it with so it wouldn't look like we were going out together. It wasn't something we had to discuss—we both knew it. And Linda wasn't always available. So once, and only once, I took Janice and a couple of her girlfriends swimming out at the park.

There were, I don't know, maybe four or five Polish girls in that rat pack Janice hung out with, and they all dressed alike with that kiddy look that was cool back then. Her two best girlfriends were Maureen Wierzcholek, the youngest of those crazy Wierzcholek girls, and Sandy Czaplicki. Sandy's dad's not the one who owned the grocery store, that's her uncle. Her dad's the one who worked for the phone company— Hell, you don't need to know that. But anyhow, when Janice was with her girlfriends, she acted just like them, so what

I've got on my hands are three shrieking, giggling, gum-chewing, standard-issue teenage idiots.

Now I'm not saying they weren't cute. If you're the kind of guy who gets off on teenage idiots, you would've thought they were real cute. They're in my car, and they're yacking away to each other and passing around this little brush to do their eyelashes with, and I'm going, "Come on, girls, one of you's going to put her eyes out," but they don't pay any attention to me whatsoever. Maureen's got a new lipstick, and they're passing that around too, and they're doing the teenybopper talk—funky, heavy, far out, bummer, and like that. And naturally the main topic of conversation is who's cute in the boy department. Oh, there's so and so, he's sooooo cute, giggle, giggle, giggle—yeah, groovy, wow, out of sight. And I'm feeling slightly older than a trilobite.

We get into the pool, and wouldn't you know it, there's Larry Dombrow-czyk and Arlene Orlicki. Larry says, "What're you doing, Koprowski? Starting a harem?"

"Aren't they a little young for you?" Arlene says. "Seems to me they were all in diapers about a year ago."

Yeah, right, ha ha ha. "I'm your friendly neighborhood chauffeur service," I say. "I should have my head examined." I'm hoping that took care of it, but anybody but a total fool should have known perfectly well it didn't.

So I lay down on my towel next to Larry and Arlene, and we're chatting about this and that, and I'm doing my best to give them the impression that, oh, boy, is it ever a relief to see them there because now I've got somebody to talk to. And I'm laying on my face in the sun and wishing I had a drink, and eventually I drift off about half asleep, and which one of the teenage idiots do you suppose thinks it would be real funny to run a Popsicle up the center of my back?

Of course, then there was my Mature Relationship. The first Sunday I canceled out on Connie, I could hear how pissed off she was, but she was working real hard to be cool with it. Things come up, right? That's life, right? When I canceled out the next Sunday, she wasn't the least bit cool. "Do you want to stop seeing me? Is that what this means?"

"No, no. Of course not. Of course I want to see you. It's just, you know, stuff I can't get out of. Family stuff—"

"How about Wednesday night then? Why don't you come right out from work and have dinner? You could spend the night."

What could I possibly say to that? So I drove out there the next Wednesday night. The minute I walked through the door, she said, "Who's your other girl? She must be really hot." I just laughed at her.

Connie was a good cook, and that night she really did it up right—these little pancake things rolled up with creamy crab stuff inside, and lots of them—and she had candles on the table and a bottle of French wine, and she was wearing one of her leather outfits with nothing under it, so we followed nature down that old inevitable course, and then we settled down to some serious drinking.

Things got ugly fairly fast. Why didn't I get a phone again? So we could keep a little closer contact? She was starting to feel, she said, just a teensy bit neglected, and I'm going sure, sure, right, no problem—although I had no intention whatsoever of getting another phone. I liked it that people had to expend a little effort to find me.

And she was onto me about my "other girl." She wasn't jealous, she said. Just curious. Of course I had the right to live my own life. So did she, for that matter. But she thought it was important that we be open and honest with each other.

So I told her for the hundred millionth time that there wasn't any other girl, and she told me that she was disappointed because I obviously didn't trust her.

"Honey," I said, "if I start fucking somebody else, you'll be the first to know."

That pissed her right off and we yelled at each other for a while. I thought maybe I should leave, but she's going no no no, don't leave, and we had us another drink to contemplate my not leaving, and it's about one in the morning by then, and we decide to hit the sack. Wednesday, right? So I'm obviously working the next day—that's the theory anyway—and I've got to get up early enough to drive from St. Stevens into Center Raysburg and get there by nine.

That's the first and last time we ever tried to sleep in the same bed. I'm fairly loaded, so I'm drifting right off, and she says, "I guess if I get too horny, I can always call the plumber." I'm going, what, what are you talking about?

"I'll call the plumber," she says, "and then I'll put on something *really* slutty and wait for him to get here," and she goes off into one of her tinkly little laughs that means it's a joke.

"Honey, give me a break."

"You think I'm kidding?" she says. "I fucked the TV repair man, why shouldn't I fuck the plumber?"

"Nice, Connie. Real nice."

"Oh, I forgot. You don't like to be teased."

244 · KEITH MAILLARD

Now I'm wide awake. I'm laying there next to her in the dark. She's got real thick drapes, and it's black as the inside of a coal mine in there, and I'm just fuming. She's passed out and she's even snoring. Well, what I can do is either lay there for hours staring into the dark, or I can get up and have another drink.

In about ten minutes she's padding out of the bedroom in her bathrobe. "What's the matter, honey? Can't you sleep?"

Nothing that another drink won't cure, I tell her. "But what's the matter with you, honey?" I say. "You were out like a light."

"I can't sleep because you left."

"Connie, that doesn't make a lot of sense to me. What do you do on the million and one nights I'm not here?"

So there we go. Right in the middle of another screaming match. About what, I really couldn't tell you.

We're knocking back the booze, and we're stumbling around yelling at each other, and she's banging her fists on the kitchen table to make her point, and I'm kicking the walls to make mine, and we're pouring drinks just as fast as we can get the bottles tipped over, and I'm smoking cigarettes by the pack, and she's grabbing my cigarettes and puffing on them, and we're bouncing off the walls and just having ourselves a ball. Naturally I'd seen her loaded before, but not quite that loaded. I mean your classic staggering, slobbering, slurring, falling-down, totally hopeless, stupid dumb-ass dead drunk. Eventually she passed out, and I picked her up and dumped her into bed. By then, it was damn near five in the morning. I slept on the couch. If you could call it sleep.

Of course I didn't make it into work the next day, and of course she was sorry as all hell about that, and of course I told her not to worry. Vick wasn't paying me that much anyway, and what the hell, it's only money, right? And I drove away from there, and you know what? I was honest-to-God wishing she'd get back together with her husband. He had a lot more practice dealing with her than I did, and he was probably a damn sight better at it.

One night—it must've still been in June sometime—Linda dialed out early so it wasn't even ten yet, and Janice and I walked down through Pulaski Park to the river. You cross the railroad tracks and head south toward Millwood and you hit this little stretch that's pretty well hidden from the road. It's one of those places where we used to go back in high school if we'd managed to score a case of beer.

It's pretty dark, and the first I know there's somebody else down there is I smell the dope. Nothing else smells like that. I stop like automatic, but Janice is a couple steps ahead of me and she keeps right on going, and I hear this voice saying, "Hey, Goldilocks."

"Oh, hi," Janice says, kind of startled.

There's two dark shapes sitting there on the riverbank. One of them's Patty Pajaczkowski and the other one's Georgie Mondrowski. I'm thinking, oh, shit, but they've already seen us, and there's not a whole hell of a lot we can do about it. We plunk down next to them, and Georgie offers me the joint they're smoking. I shake my head, so he offers it to Janice. "Are you going to turn me on?" she says.

You know how when you're stoned, something can strike you as hysterically funny? Well, Patty and Georgie are howling like two hyenas.

Now I would've thought Janice would've been deeply offended, but she says, "Come on, you guys. I can't help it if I'm not as old and cool as you are."

Janice takes the joint sort of gingerly like it might explode, and she looks at me like, hey, should I do it? I can't begin to tell you how much I did *not* want her to smoke that joint, but at the same time I didn't want to come on like your friendly neighborhood nark, so I kind of shrugged, like suit yourself. She takes a puff on it and about coughs her head off.

"No, honey," Georgie says, just as helpful as can be, "you do it like this," and he shows her how to take a tiny bit of smoke and then WHOMPF, inhale and hold it. It takes her a few tries, but she finally gets the hang of it. "There you go," he says. I am feeling, I guess you could say, real apprehensive.

She offers the joint to me. "He doesn't like smoke," Georgie tells her. "He's your classic juicehead."

"Smoke makes me gloomy and paranoid," I say, hoping she'll get the message and stop. But she doesn't. Every time the joint comes around, she takes a hit on it. Then after a couple passes I start smoking the damn thing. I don't know why I did that. Maybe I wanted to keep her company.

"So how's your summer going, Rapunzel?" Patty says.

"I don't mind you teasing me," Janice says, "but please don't call me by a German name."

"Oh, okay," Patty says, real serious. "I didn't even know it was a German name. I'll remember that."

"She's been reading up on the Nazis," I say. I don't know why I felt I had to explain Janice to those two goofs, but I did.

"Nazis?" Georgie says, "that's some heavy shit."

"Why are you doing that?" Patty says.

Dope affects different people in different ways. Me it's always made silent as a stone, but some people get real talkative, and Janice was one of them. She started out telling them about her parents and the war. I guess Georgie and Patty must have decided to be nice to her, or maybe they were real interested in WW II, or maybe it was just that thing that when you're smoking dope, anything can be interesting. But, anyhow, they keep asking her questions, and pretty soon she's giving them big chunks of the story. She's talking faster and faster.

There's something strange happening to her. Of course she's getting stoned; that's not what I mean. What's strange is how it affects her. She's speaking English the way she speaks Polish, and I've never heard her do that before— It's kind of hard to describe. She's using the same voice she uses when she speaks Polish—kind of high and breathy—and the same gestures. It's weird. Or maybe she's not doing that and it only seems that way because *I'm* getting stoned.

She stops in the middle of a sentence and goes, "Am I supposed to feel something? I don't feel anything." Which is ridiculous because she's obviously whacked out of her gourd.

"Well, shit," Georgie says, "we better fire up another one then."

"Maybe they were right all along," Janice says. "Maybe they shouldn't have told us. There's all these things I wish I didn't know. I can't get them out of my mind. They keep going around in my mind."

"Yeah, I know that one," Georgie says. "That's a hard one."

"All those poor people kneeling on the edge of the pit, getting shot in the back of the head. I keep wondering what you'd think about while you're waiting to get shot in the back of the head. I guess I'd pray— And the Germans hanging my grandfather in front of his clinic. I can almost see it— And my father killing those German boys, and that soldier sitting under a tree. I don't know why that bothers me so much. The Germans were awful. I don't have any sympathy for the Germans. But I keep thinking, my *dad*? My dad *did that?*"

"People do things in war that—" Georgie doesn't know quite how to get at it. "You know, war's like a different— It changes you. You know what I mean?"

"No, I guess I don't." He passes her the new joint, and she takes a hit on it. She's been imitating the way Patty and Georgie smoke dope, so she's got to where she can hold the smoke in real good. She passes the joint to Patty, and she's still holding the smoke in. Finally she exhales. "I keep trying to imagine it," she says, "but I know I can't—like really really imagine it. When you— When you first got to Vietnam, was it a big shock for you?"

For a minute I didn't think he was going to answer her. Whatever it was

Georgie had that night—Well, it wasn't as strong as the Thai-stick we'd smoked that other time when I'd got stoned with him like a stupid idiot, but it was real intense, and I could feel like this little vibration that went through him and the way his mind was moving with it. Up till then he didn't know for sure that she knew he'd been in Vietnam, and I could feel him dealing with it. He says, "Yeah, I guess it was a shock. They try to prepare you for it, but they can't. Not really."

"You know what I can't understand?" Janice says. "Down deep, I just can't understand how people can kill each other."

We sit there for the longest damn time and then Georgie says, "You want to know the sorry truth, honey? It's as easy as pie."

Patty hasn't said much for a while. I figured she'd been on the nod. But now she says, "That's the reason you came down here. So he could tell you that."

Janice goes, "What?"

"We all of us had a reason to come down here tonight. That's yours."

"What's your reason?" Georgie asks her.

"It hasn't figured me out yet. When it does, I'll let you know."

Then we fall into one of those pockets of silence you get with dope—you know, where you get lost inside your head and you can't really focus on anything and you're afraid of where you might be going. And I'm thinking, come on, somebody say something—because I sure can't. "Easy as pie?" Janice says. "Is it really like that? As easy as that? Oooh, that's sickening."

"You want to know what's really sickening?" Georgie says. "You come back and you can't forget how easy it is. It makes things kind of harsh."

"Yeah," I say, "reintegrating yourself back into civilian life," and we both get a laugh out of that one, and I'm congratulating myself because I managed to choke some words out, and I'm hoping that now the conversation can maybe drift off in some direction that's not so heavy, but no such luck.

"The Indians out where I was," Patty says. "If someone's been in battle, and if he's killed anybody, they make him take the cure for insanity before they let him come back."

"Hey, I like that," Georgie says.

The joint's coming around again, and I realize I've had enough, like more than enough, and I say that. "No thanks. That's enough of this shit," trying to send Janice a message, you know. Georgie and Patty are somewhere out beyond the asteroid belt by now, and pretty soon Janice is going to be joining them.

It's dark down on the riverbank, and we can't really see each other, but I can sense how she's looking at me. "I don't feel anything," she says and takes another hit.

"Sometimes I wish I could go back to the way I was when I was little," Janice says, and she starts telling them about how she thought Krajne Podlaski was just down the river a ways, and how she dreamed of it, and it was a fairy tale place for her.

"Yeah," Patty says. "Yeah, I can dig it."

And then Janice just launches into this speed rap. "Every Sunday night we read to each other in Polish," she says, "and my parents would correct our pronunciation. I can recite parts of *Pan Tadeusz* from memory—'Litwo! Ojczyzno moja! ty jesteś jak zdrowie—' Oh, and we read 'Śmierć pułkownika.' That's about the Virgin Maid of Lithuania. She fought the Russians. And the prophet Wernyhora. He told the Poles and the Jews and the Ukrainians to love each other for we're all children of the same mother, and it was— What am I saying? I'm kind of losing track— Oh, it's that scary— In fairy tales when you don't want to hear the bad part, the scary part. I didn't want to hear what the witch was going to do to Hansel and Gretel— Why are children in fairy tales always *German*? There must be Polish fairy tales. Oh, right, I remember. When I was little I didn't want to hear the scary part, but everything they told me was the scary part, and I wish sometimes I could go back. You know what? I don't like how I feel sometimes, how much I hate the Germans and the Russians. Maybe it is easy to kill. I can find— Sometimes I have this feeling, that, yes, I could kill somebody. There were girls in the Resistance. Girls fought the SS. That's incredible. Isn't that incredible? Girls got killed all the time, and killed people. The Virgin Maid— But see, that was a story. It's not a story anymore. I almost wish they hadn't told me. I don't know if I could kill somebody or not. How could you put somebody in a cell full of water and torture them every day? How could you take millions of people and gas them and burn them? Where was God? You could pray and pray— I keep wondering if I'd lose my faith. I read where the Nazis— This poor girl— Did you ever read about the rabbit girls? The Polish girls? What they did to them? Oh. God. Help— I feel— So awful— Oh, God, please— What's happening to me?"

She takes a deep breath and goes, "Am I dying?"

"Not any faster than you were before," Georgie says.

"Don't mind-trip her, Mondrowski," Patty says. "She's out there on that thin ice."

Patty puts her hand on the back of Janice's neck and rocks her back and forth a little, very gentle. "Come here," she says. "Come on." Janice scoots over in front of Patty, and Patty starts massaging the back of her neck. "Oh, boy, are you tense," Patty says.

Now I'm sunk deep in the paranoid gloom. I keep thinking of things I should say, but by the time I go through this whole thing in my head about whether I should say them—am I going to make things worse?—the time when I should have said them is long gone. Why do I do this? I should know by now that grass doesn't agree with me. What am I, some kind of moron?

"Look out there," Patty says, pointing at the river. "There's Poland."

Janice goes, "What?"

"You see the city in the river?" It's the reflection she's talking about—the reflection of the lights on the Ohio side. "When I was a little girl, I'd come down here, and I'd want to go into that city so bad. You know what I learned from that? How close some other world is."

Patty starts unbraiding Janice's hair. "We all love you," Patty says. "We're not going to let you fall."

Even in the dim light, Janice's hair is like this torrent of gold. Patty runs her fingers through it, like combing it out, and then she starts massaging Janice's scalp. "Oh, that feels good," Janice says.

"You're on a spirit quest," Patty tells her. "That's something the Indians do. When a boy gets to be a certain age, he's got to go off by himself until he finds his spirit guide—his ally. Until *it* finds *him*. But you don't have to go off into the woods. Or the desert. You can do it right here. Anything can be a message. You can get a message from me or Georgie or Jimmy—or even from looking at the river. And anything you do, and anything you say, and anything you think—it changes that other world. See it out there?" She points at the river. "Well, it's real dangerous, it's true. But you can come back, you know? To where the river's a river again."

"Did you come back?" Janice says.

"Yeah, I did."

"Is it okay?"

"Yeah, sure. I came back so you could tell me things."

"What things? What am I supposed to tell you?"

"You already told me. Poland's in the river. And we can stand up right now and walk over to it. You want to go?"

Patty takes Janice's hand and they both stand up kind of poised, and for a second there I think they're going to take off and walk right into the river. Then Mondrowski stands up, and I stand up, and he goes, "Whoa, Patty, are you ever a trip."

Janice looks around for me. She reaches out her hand for me, and I take it. "Are you all right?" she says.

"Yeah, sure. Are *you* all right?"

"Yeah, I think so. This is so weird. Do people do this for fun?"

"Well, *you* don't do it for fun, that's pretty clear," Patty says.

"I got the munchies," Georgie says. "Is there someplace we can get some ice cream?"

I look at my watch and it's a quarter of twelve. "Naw, everything's closed." And I say to Janice, "I should get you home. Your dad's going to kill me."

We walk up the hill and into Pulaski Park. We can see each other again, and it's like back to reality—instead of, you know, just being these strange voices in the dark. "There's air to breathe and dirt under our feet and nobody's shooting at us," Georgie says, "so we must be doing fine." The sky to the south is burning bloodred from the blast furnace.

Janice is holding my hand—it's like she doesn't even think about how it must look to them—and her hair's still down, this wonderful golden curtain. It swings when she walks. "You feel okay, Rapunzel?" Patty says. "Oops, sorry. I'm not supposed to call you that."

"It's okay. You let down my long hair, so you can call me that. I'm okay. I guess I am. How long's it take before it goes away?"

"Just go to bed. You'll be fine in the morning."

We stop by the swings. "I'm going to run her up to Edgewood," I say. "What are you guys doing? You want to have a beer?"

"Yeah, sure. You want to meet us somewhere? The PAC?"

"I wouldn't go in there on a bet," Patty says. "Probably run into my old man in there."

There's this kind of pause where we're all just trying to pull ourselves back together enough to function. "Listen, you guys," Janice says. "I'm sorry, okay?"

"You've got nothing to feel sorry for," Georgie says. "Does Franky Rzeszutko stay open this late? I wouldn't mind a sandwich or something."

"There's a place on the Island," Patty says. "I think they're open till one. Or we could go out the pike."

"Lots of places in Center Raysburg open," I say.

I think I've told you how stubborn Janice is. She's just not going to let it go.

"But I do feel sorry," she says to Georgie. "You were there. You were in Vietnam. What right have I got to—to be so—?"

"Aw, hell, honey, come on. There's no problem that I can see."

"No, I mean it. Everything I've read about it—it must be such an awful war. And it must have been so hard for you to come back home. I don't know, that's what I read anyway."

He's looking at her with this kind of puzzled expression. It's obvious she's real sincere and all that. "Yeah, well, it had its harsh moments I got to admit," he says. "Yeah, and coming back home was kind of weird."

He looks over at me like maybe I'm going to bail him out of this one. "Most of the guys will tell you that," he says. "But what the hell did we expect? They were going to meet us with marching bands and majorettes? Yeah, I could have used a majorette or two— But seriously— Yeah, maybe a little bit more than what we got. Yeah, that would have been nice."

"Like what?" Janice asks him. "What would have been nice?"

He makes a face like, hey, doesn't this little girl ever know when to quit? He stands there for the longest damn time. Then he says, "Well, somebody could have said thank you."

SIXTEEN

When she considered her close encounter with the weed, Janice thought it had been interesting and all that, but she said, "Whew, it was like being in a freaky movie. I never never never want to do that again."

She remembered it all in that super-heavy, high-reverb way you do when you're stoned, and she'd turned into a one-girl Patty Pajaczkowski fan club. "She was so sweet to me," she kept saying. "I never would have guessed she could be so sweet." And she took to heart all that weird stuff Patty had been saying to her, but being a good Catholic girl, she put her own spin on it. Going off into the desert and talking to lizards was not something she could relate to, so she decided she wasn't on a *spirit* quest, like Patty said, but she was on a *spiritual* quest. And for the next part of her quest she had to go see her brother.

They hadn't heard a good word out of him since he'd gone back to Columbus, so eventually Czesław called him up, and the whole family's waiting around with bated breath to hear what he has to say, and Czesław gets off the phone and says, "Everything's fine," you know, kind of stony-faced, so of course they knew that nothing was fine. "You wouldn't want to drive me to Columbus, would you?" Janice asked me.

"Oh, sure. Your old man would just love that."

"I'd get his permission."

"Are you kidding? He's not that crazy. Come on, kid, where's your head? And on top of that, there's this wonderful piece of legislation called the Mann Act." I told her it was easy to get to Columbus. You take the bus.

"Dad would never let me."

But she asked him, and to her total amazement, he said yes. Both her parents thought it was a good idea for her to go see her brother. She had to call them the minute she got there, and John had to promise to meet her at the bus station, and she had to call home every night. Janice goes, yes, yes, yes, she'd do all that. She was really excited. It was the first time in her life she'd ever gone anywhere by herself.

She was gone five days, and I spent most of that time brooding. We'd got to the point where we were practically living in each other's pockets, and it was getting harder and harder for me to run the oh-she's-just-my-little-sister num-ber. I was starting to notice a lot more than just her hipbones, you know what I mean? She'd got me to the point where I thought kneesocks were sexy, and believe me, that's a real accomplishment.

"I can see why you like her," Mondrowski said. "She's beautiful, and she's real smart, and she's mature—"

"Well, sometimes she is."

"And she's just nuts about you. That's kind of plain to see. And she looks like Dorothy Pliszka."

"Come on, man, that's ridiculous. She doesn't look a thing like Dorothy."

"Sure she does. They're exactly the same type. Blond, blue eyes, nice legs, little Polak faces. That kiddy look Dorothy had back in high school."

And I'm going, no way, man. Just no way I was going to admit to that one. But I'm thinking, shit, he's got a point. How come I never saw it before?

"But I just want to offer you a word of caution, Koprowski. Her old man was in the Polish Resistance, right?"

"Yeah, he was."

"Any chance he's kept some of his old hardware? You know, like maybe he's got a forty-five laying around, or one of those WW II rifles with the long bayonet?"

I'm laughing, but it's not that funny. "I've never laid a hand on her."

"Yeah. Right."

Well, Janice went to Columbus hoping to make her brother feel better and maybe get him talking to their parents again, but it mainly turned out to be her next big bummer. Janice said she'd never felt closer to John, but— Well, it wasn't that she wished she hadn't gone. No, it'd been a great trip. They'd had some wonderful times, but— "Oh, he's so angry," she said.

Finding out that Czesław wasn't his real father was the least of his prob-lems—or anyway that's what he told Janice. He and his girlfriend had just moved into a little apartment, and Janice helped them unpack and put things away. Of course Janice knew that some young people lived together before they got married, but she hadn't thought her brother would do that, and she was kind of shocked. All the time she was there she had to keep pretending she was cool with all kinds of things that shocked her right down to her toenails.

Her brother was one of those dangerous student radicals her father ranted about. John had met his girlfriend back when they were undergrads and they'd both been in the Catholic antiwar movement—I didn't even know there *was* a Catholic antiwar movement, which tells you how well informed I was—and they'd been dangerous radicals together ever since. If Janice had come to Columbus only a week or two before, she would have found them living in a commune—a real commune where they had these heavy-duty meetings and planned political actions and like that.

The main thing John and his girlfriend were talking about was what they called "the fragmentation of the left." They'd been in that dangerous radical organization SDS, and it had split into two big groups—one of them was those crazy Weathermen—but John and his girlfriend hadn't been in favor of either one of those big groups. They'd been in some tiny little splinter that nobody else agreed with because it wasn't radical enough. And everyone in the commune had agreed that John and Anna weren't radical enough. Real radicals, you know, were into smashing things—like they were going to smash the state, and smash racism, and smash imperialism, and one thing they were going to smash real good was monogamy. So everybody was supposed to sleep with everybody else, but John and Anna didn't want to sleep with anybody but each other, so they were considered just hopeless. That's why they'd moved out of the commune and got their own apartment.

"In the history of the American left," John said, "1970 is going to go down as the Year of the Big Mouth." Like every word you said, you had to sound like you were the meanest mother on the block. The real heavy radicals were talking armed revolution and underground cells and all that crap, and John and Anna just couldn't relate to it. They said the Weathermen were the worst. "They're completely out of touch with reality," they said. "They're living in some sick violent dreamworld."

That spring there'd been some real serious rioting going down at Ohio State. It'd already been going on for a week when they heard about the kids getting killed at Kent State, and that just freaked out the whole campus even more. They brought in the National Guard at Ohio State too, and everybody was paranoid that those guys would start shooting and then they'd have their own blood in Columbus to deal with. The university finally got closed down. It was open again now, but with high security. "Now it really is a police state," John said, and he and Anna were sick at heart over everything.

There was nothing left for them to belong to. They told Janice that when they'd first joined up with SDS, one of its main goals was to make a world where love is more possible—she really liked that—but nobody was mentioning that lately. Now people were talking about Mao and Fidel and Uncle Ho, and sometimes they even had nice things to say about that pig Stalin, and some of the girls were going off into these women's lib groups where they considered all men to be scum, and John and Anna didn't want to be part of any of it. Meanwhile the war was still going on and people were being killed in it every day, and the student movement, they said, was "rushing off into irrelevance and committing suicide." So you could see how finding out you were half German wasn't exactly high on John's list of things to worry about. That's what he told his sister anyway.

Then he got around to talking about their family. It was pathogenic, he said. That word really got to Janice; she kept saying it. "Pathogenic. Pathogenic? *Pathogenic!*" That meant it drove people nuts. Like John would have been driven totally nuts if he hadn't gotten away from their parents and gone off and lived his own life, and Mark was already totally nuts, and it was just too bad Janice was still stuck in high school because the way things were going, she was going to get driven totally nuts pretty soon herself.

The way the kids got driven nuts, John said, was from getting all these double messages. Like, "You're Polish, you're American," and "Think for yourself, don't contradict me," and "You're nothing without the family, get out of here and make something of yourself." The minute Janice heard about the double messages, the light bulb went on in her head because she knew exactly what he was talking about, and she started laughing and coming up with her own, like, "The people in South Raysburg are ignorant peasants, they're the salt of the earth," and "You're a little girl, you're a sophisticated young woman." Yeah, John told her, she'd got the idea, and it was easy enough to laugh at it now, but when you're a little kid, it just warps out your mind for you.

He did feel sorry for his parents, John said. He'd always felt sorry for them, and after hearing their story, he really felt sorry for them. And he did love them—just so long as he could keep a few hundred miles between them and him—but he'd figured out early on that they couldn't handle anything real, so all he ever told them about himself was, like he said, "the official lie." No, he hadn't gone back to grad school to better his lot in life, climb up higher and faster on the ladder of success. He'd gone back to school to stay out of Vietnam.

He didn't even know for sure what he was doing in grad school. He was registered in the Ph.D. program in political science, but he was getting nowhere fast with it. Maybe he'd get a Master's. Maybe he'd drop out. Who the hell cares?

And as to being half German, well, that was meaningless. But the question Janice should ask herself was why her father had kept his mouth shut for years and then picked that particular time to tell them all about it. "He was getting even with you," he said, "for going against his wishes and playing in a polka band."

"Oh, no," she said. "No, no, he wouldn't do that."

"Oh, yes he would. I'm not saying it was a conscious decision on his part, but just look at it, okay? That's exactly how petty and vindictive he can be."

But the craziest thing of all, John said, was Polish. "They've produced three kids who are fluent in a useless and totally irrelevant foreign language spoken only in a backward, third-rate, Soviet-bloc country somewhere to the east of Europe." The Poland they'd grown up hearing about had never existed. That nice little town with its tough little boys playing Indians in the forest, beautiful aristocratic girls riding horses, wise peasants tilling their fields, quaint old Jews studying the Torah, and everybody getting along with everybody, was just a romantic dream. That great man Piłsudski was really just a clumsy thug who'd ruled Poland as a dictator. And all those martyrs and saints and patriots were just a pile of horseshit. Just think about how crazy it was, he said, all of them sitting around on Sunday nights reading Mickiewicz and Władisław Reymont and those other heavy-duty Polish writers to each other. It'd be like if you had an American family somewhere in Poland, surrounded by people who didn't speak a word of English, and they were supposed to learn to be Americans by reading *Huckleberry Finn* and *The Leaves of Grass*.

"I'll tell you what," he said to Janice. "Let's make a date for ten years from now. You and me and Mark. We'll get together and see if any of us speaks a word of Polish."

So Janice came back to Raysburg, and she was in fairly horrible shape. "I don't know what I think anymore," she said. "I don't even know who I am anymore."

I tried to help her the best I could. I listened to her. I said dumb things like, "Look, you can't just take what your brother says as gospel. You've got to form your own opinions." I kept wishing I could find exactly the right thing to say—like when she was stoned and Patty said exactly the right thing while I'd just sat there. But nothing I was saying seemed to be much help.

Janice kept coming up with these nasty mind games she'd run on herself. "Suppose I found out I was adopted and my real parents were *Swedish*. Would I still be Polish?"

"I don't know. Would you?"

"Of course I would. It's what I feel—I'm Polish right down to my bone marrow. A lot of times I even *think* in Polish. So that means it's language, not blood. So what does that make you? Are you Polish?"

"Oh, for Christ's sake, we're all Americans."

"Yeah, I know we are, but is that just a nationality? Or is it something more?"

And so on and on she goes, around in circles. Does blood mean anything, and if you think it does, doesn't that make you just like the Nazis? But if you don't think it does, how can somebody who doesn't speak a word of Polish think of themselves as Polish? Like her friends Sandy and Maureen, like most of the younger people in South Raysburg? And how can you ever know who you are anyway?

Well, I've had a problem or two in my life, but wondering who I was has never been one of them. It's always been real obvious—I'm a South Raysburg Polak, and my old man's Walt Koprowski who works at Raysburg Steel, and my mom was one of the Wojtkiewicz girls, and everybody knows them, and everybody knows *me*. "But you see," Janice said, "I can't say that. I'm not anything. I'm not really Polish."

"Oh, come on, you just said you were Polish. You're as Polish as Paderewski."

"Yeah, I feel that way, but do you think my cousin Paulina in Krajne Podlaski would think I'm Polish? But I'm not an ordinary American girl either. Sometimes I feel like we don't belong anywhere—like we've never stopped being refugees."

Of course all the time this is going on, I've got Linda asking me if Janice has said anything about the band, and I've got to say, "Well, no. Right at the moment that doesn't seem to be a topic that's real high on her list."

"What are we going to do?" Linda says. "Oh, Jimmy, this is terrible! We're supposed to play at the street fair in August. Should I call Father Obinski and tell him he's got to find another band?"

"No," I said, "not yet. There's still time. Maybe she'll come back around to the music." But I wasn't sure she would.

Nope, Janice wasn't saying a word about music. She was still worrying about the Nazis and the problem of evil, and then she decided to throw Vietnam in on top of everything else. It wasn't just enough to say we ought to end the war, what could we do to bring real peace to the world? Why couldn't we just love each other the way Christ taught us? And shouldn't she join an antiwar group?— Yeah, right, I said, just pick one of the four thousand real active antiwar groups they got in Raysburg— And John had told her that the war was being fought by working-class boys. How many South Raysburg boys were in the war?— Aw, hell, I don't know, I said. Not as many as you'd think— And what if her brother was right, and her family really was pathogenic and she was being driven nuts?

I'm only giving you a fraction of what was going on in her head. It was like every time she turned around, she ran right into another big hairy question. She was wearing me out. "Come on, Janice," I said. "It's not your family that's driving you nuts. You're driving *yourself* nuts."

Janice had never announced it when she'd decided she was going to start seeing me every day, and she didn't announce it either when she decided she was going to stop. It was like all of a sudden she just wasn't there anymore.

Now I could understand it, right? She'd had enough of that heavy shit and she was taking a break, you know, and making a stab at being normal. Sandy Czaplicki had just got her driver's license, so I'd be driving somewhere and Sandy's car would pull up next to me and go beep beep, and I'd look over and there'd be Janice and some of the other girls from the rat pack, and they'd all wave at me, and I'd wave back, and I'd think, well, good for you, kid—you're probably better off impersonating a teenage idiot than hanging around with me and driving yourself nuts. But understanding something only gets you so far, right? And guess what? I was hurt. I was real surprised at how hurt I was.

I kept telling myself I had no right to feel like that—she was just acting her age for a change—and I felt like a fool. Because I'd got to the point where I was kind of depending on her, you know. And what she was doing was probably good for her, but it wasn't all that good for me. And all of a sudden I've got lots of spare time on my hands—like four million hours of it—and you remember Mrs. Constance Bradshaw, don't you?

I didn't have any reason not to, so I started seeing a lot more of Connie. I even spent the night a few times. I didn't try to sleep in the same bed with her though; I slept on the couch. When I wasn't there, she'd have her husband over. She didn't tell me that, but it was obvious. For one thing, she was still paranoid that I'd just turn up unannounced, and she kept reminding me never to do that.

And then there was a couple other things. She was real fanatical about washrags—which I wasn't supposed to call them because that was low rent. She corrected me a million times. "They're wash*cloths*, Jim." But whatever you call them, if I touched hers, I was dead meat. She had her towel rack and I had mine, and she stood in the bathroom and banged it into my head. "This side's girls, women, female, *mine*. See, they're pink. That side's boys, men, male, *yours*. See, they're green. Got it?"

So one morning I'm shaving and I grab the green washrag, and it smells funny. I use Old Spice, and I always have. It goes back to whatever age I was—thirteen, fourteen—and I come home from school and guess what's waiting for me on the dinner table right in front of my plate? A razor, a mug of soap with a brush in it, and a bottle of Old Spice. And Old Bullet Head says, "Welcome to the club, fuzzface." So I take a good sniff of the green washrag, and it ain't Old Spice. It's one of those real fruity things—you know, with a name like *Eau de Homme*—and I think, hmmm, well, Dr. Bradshaw doesn't mind paying the big bucks for his aftershave.

And the other tipoff was the leftovers. Whenever I dropped in, there'd be the remains of some wonderful gourmet dinner in the fridge. I'd look forward to it. You know, those pasta dishes with the cream sauce and the red and green peppers, a block of Parmesan so you could grate it fresh right onto your plate. Chicken cooked in wine with potatoes and carrots and little pearl onions. Once there was roast pork with applesauce. And I thought maybe that was Connie's way of trying to get back together with her old man—invite him over, throw a good feed into him, and nature does the rest, right?

And you know what I thought? It's kind of weird what I thought. I'm standing there in her bathroom smelling that green washrag, and it feels kind of right that her husband should be there—a hell of a lot more right than me being there, you know what I mean? And maybe Connie and her husband were getting back together again, and that'd be a good thing. They've got two kids. So what did that make me? The home wrecker, that's what.

So what the hell was I doing there? Well, I was there shaving in Connie's bathroom because I'd spent the night and had my Mature Relationship—and the mature adult way to look at things is that nothing means nothing because you're old enough to know better and everything's a joke, and if it's not a joke, then you do your best to turn it into one, and if you're having trouble doing that, well, you can always get loaded. And I thought about Janice and how she was a million light-years away from all that.

That terrific intensity—you know, when things matter, when it matters what you believe, when you're still asking yourself how to live your life so it counts for something. When you can still say something like "Why can't we just love each other the way Christ taught us?" and you don't feel stupid and uncool and embarrassed for saying something like that— I don't know if you're getting what I'm trying to tell you here. That's how intense Janice was, and that's how intense I felt about her. And it hit me that I'd been using Connie and Janice like a seesaw—one end goes down, the other goes up—and I really hated myself for doing that. And you know the thing that really got me? With neither one of them was I the right guy in the right place.

One night I'm floating around town with Mondrowski, and as per usual he's stoned to the eyeballs, and he's suddenly seized by the desire for ice cream— and not just any old ice cream, he's got to have the triple-mondo sundae at Tommy's. He can, you know, visualize it—the three scoops of different flavors, the three different syrups, the whipped cream, the nuts, the cherry—so I'm laughing at him. "Okay, you sorry asshole," and I go shooting out the National Road to Tommy's. What I'd forgot is that place is teenybopper city.

We get there, and I say, "You want to eat in the car?" and he says, "Oh, hell, no. Let's go in and check out the honeys," so we step through the door, and the first thing I see is Janice sitting in a booth with Maureen Wierzcholek and Sandy Czaplicki. I feel this bang in the pit of the stomach that's got real familiar over the years because it's what I always feel when I run into Dorothy Pliszka. I'm going, hey, what is this?

Walking into that place is like walking into a spiderweb. There's kids from Central, kids from Raysburg High and Canden High, young studs from the Academy, and they're all connected up to each other by these strands of the web—like super-aware of each other even though they're too cool to show it— and if you're not in high school, you'll never understand all those connections, not in a million years. I can remember being in that web, and you probably can too, right? It's real exciting and it can be real scary. "Well, hi, girls," Georgie's saying. "What's the good word?"

"Come on, sit down. There's plenty of room," Maureen says.

"Oh, no," Georgie says. "You're doing your thing. You don't want a couple old farts like us falling into your space."

"Yes, we do," Maureen says. "Come oooon, Georgie Porgie." She knows him pretty well because he used to go out with one of her sisters. Donna, I think it was.

I keep trying to find some dumb funny thing to say, but nothing is coming out of my mouth. Janice is sitting on one side of the table and Sandy and Maureen on the other, so Janice stands up to go over with them and let Georgie and me have her side. I step back to give her room, and she pauses right in front of me and says, "Hi."

"Hi," I say. "How are you doing?"

"Oh, I'm okay. I guess. How about you?"

"Oh, I'm okay. Just fine."

Those three girls were dressed so alike they must have planned it—I mean, it was practically a uniform—and then they must have spent hours getting themselves together because they've achieved teenybopper perfection. They're wearing their hair down, held back with those band things. And they've done their eyes the same way—you know, like Twiggy—and they've got the same pink lipstick, and these little blouses and miniskirts. It was the look all the girls were going for in those days—like half-sexy, half-grade school.

I'll never forget this. The skirt Janice had on was so short it was higher than the tabletop. I'm not kidding you. It had little buttons up the front, and you could see how flat her stomach was. And white kneesocks the same as always, except this pair went right up over her knees. And little-kid shoes, black and white, but with a real high heel, and where there's usually a strap, they're tied with ribbons. Then she sat down on the other side and slid her long legs under the table. I looked over to catch her eye or something, but she was looking down at the tabletop.

Well, the girls had scored big-time getting a couple older guys like us at their table—yeah, lots of points in the teen scene—and Maureen starts flirting with Mondrowski like you wouldn't believe. He knows it's harmless, she knows it's harmless, everybody knows it's harmless. She's probably always wanted to do that ever since she was nine and he was coming over to take out her big sister. And he's throwing the one-liners back at her, and every time he says something, she and Sandy go off in this explosion of giggles. But what he was saying, I really couldn't tell you. All I'm hearing is this kind of distant yatta, yatta, yatta because I'm in another world. I'm just waiting for Janice to look up at me.

Janice must not have been hearing them either. She's just sitting there looking down. No expression on her face at all. Finally she looks up. And her eyes lock onto mine, and she gives me this deep blue look from her deep blue eyes. She's got big eyes to start with, but with all that black stuff on her eyelashes, they look as big as two headlights. She's got real pale skin, did I tell you that? It's almost white. And I see the color rise up into her face. Right there in front of me she just turns pink. Then she looks away, and my mouth's gone so dry it feels like it's stuffed full of sand.

I wanted to say something to her, but what the hell could I say? I'd been planning on eating something, a cheeseburger or something, but all of a sudden I couldn't have eaten anything if you'd held a gun to my head.

Georgie had his ice cream, and I drank about three glasses of water, and if you can believe it, Janice and I did not say a single word to each other. I wanted to get out of there as quick as I could, and I wanted to sit there and look at her forever—if that makes any sense.

The problem with Mondrowski is he knows me too well, the son of a bitch. When we were leaving, he gives me this sly smile, and he says, "So Jimmy, how do you like being back in high school?"

A few nights later I'm in bed dead to the world and somebody's banging on my door. I look at my alarm clock, and it's after one. I jerk the door open and it's my sister. "Is Janice here?" she says.

"Linny," I say, "do you think I'm completely and totally insane?"

It seems like Janice had run away—or some damn thing. Mom and Dad and Linda had all been asleep when the phone rang. It was a good thing Mom got it instead of the old man. It was Czesław Dłuwiecki—apologetic as all hell—asking for me or Linda. "He was just beside himself," Linda says. "He kept switching from English to Polish, and I don't think he even knew he was doing it."

They'd had a big fight with Janice—an unpleasantness, Czesław called it—and she'd just walked out and they hadn't seen her since. After eleven they started to get worried. After midnight they got real worried.

"Hell," I said, "it's not that late—not if you're sixteen. She's off somewhere with Maureen and Sandy. Sandy's got her driver's license, you know. One of Maureen's sisters probably bought them a case of beer."

No. Czesław had already thought of that. He'd called the Wierzcholeks' and the Czaplickis'. Sandy and Maureen were both home in bed. Neither one of them had seen Janice that night.

Czesław was right on the edge of calling the police, but Linda said, no, no, no, don't do that. Not yet. I'll check around and see if I can find anything out and I'll get back to you. And she'd jumped in the old man's car and driven right up here, praying the whole way that Janice wasn't with me.

I looked Linda right in the eyes, and I said, "Linny, do you think I'd do anything with that little girl?" She shook her head.

Well, it took me all of about thirty seconds to figure out where Janice had to be. I told Linda to go home and call Mr. Dłuwiecki and tell him I was on the case, that I'd either bring Janice home or call him. And then I drove over to the Island, fuming the whole way, going, oh, you dumb little girl, what do you think you're doing?

I didn't knock, just went storming into Patty Pajaczkowski's, and there's that whole sorry crew slouched around her kitchen table. Patty and Bev Wright, that black guy Don, some other Vietnam vet whose name I don't remember, and Georgie Mondrowski—I could have murdered him—and big as life, pigtails and all, Miss Dłuwiecki herself. The dope in the air's so thick you could have sliced it and made a sandwich out of it. Patty says, "Well, hey, look who's here. It's Sunshine Superman." I'm so mad I've got steam coming out my ears.

"Come on," I say to Janice, "I'm taking you home."

She goes, "No, you're not," and all the potheads yuck their asses off.

"Okay, then, call your dad. He's real worried about you."

"No," she says, just like that—flat, bang. And that one's really the joke of the century. Everybody's practically pissing themselves laughing at me. I feel like a total idiot.

"Sounds like one of those Mexican standoffs to me," Georgie says, and I give him a look like, okay, buddy, one more word out of you and your head's going through that wall.

"Then *I'm* going to call your dad," I say to Janice. There's a phone on a shelf in the corner of the kitchen. I walk over to it, pick it up, and start dialing. Janice follows me and slams her hand down on the bar—you know, breaking the connection—and we're standing there glaring at each other. Before that, I never could have imagined her mad at me. Or me mad at her. I could feel this high-energy charge coming off her. Her eyes were like blue fire.

"Hey, you guys," Mondrowski says, "mellow out."

I suppose I could have physically removed her hand from the phone, but something told me it wasn't a good idea. "Janice," I said, "this is ridiculous. You going to make me drive over to that phone booth on Huron Street?"

She just walks away and out the door, and everybody's laughing at me again. I go running after her. I was thinking she'd just take off and I'd have to chase her. Looking back on that horrible moment, it gave me, like they say, some insight into what it must be like to have teenage kids who won't do what you tell them. At what point do you just pound them one? And if you're like me and you could never in a million years just pound them one, then what do you do?

But she didn't make me chase her. She just got into my car. I started driving back, and we didn't say anything for the longest damn time. Then I asked her if she was stoned.

"No, I am *not* stoned. I told you I didn't want to do that again. Did you think I would lie to you?"

Big silence. "You don't have any right to even ask me that," she says. "Who do you think you are?"

Another big silence. I know she hadn't meant it like a real question, but I was thinking about it anyways. I wasn't her boyfriend, and I wasn't her father, so who the hell *did* I think I was? Maybe I should have just left her in Patty Pajaczkowski's kitchen with that bunch of stoners. But I didn't like that one either.

We get to her house, and I pull up, and she says, "I'm not a child. Stop treating me like one," and jumps out and BANG, slams the car door.

I felt—I don't know, just sick and miserable. I watched her go stomping up the steps and into her house. I should have driven away, but I was like paralyzed. I was calling myself every kind of name—fool, moron, idiot, shit-for-brains—because all Janice was doing was acting like she was sixteen, which is what she was, which I should have expected. If I'd built things up in my mind into something a lot bigger than it was, then that was my problem, not hers. What the hell was wrong with me?

Well, I sat there too long. I'm just starting to pull away when here comes Mr. Dłuwiecki running down the steps and waving his arms in the air. His hair sticking out in all directions. Scared the shit out of me. I thought maybe he was going to smash me one in the mouth right through the window of my car, but he shoves his hand through the window. I take it, and he pumps it up and down and goes, "Thank you, Jimmy, thank you."

We had us this weird little chat. "She says she was with this person Patty Pajączkowska. Who is this person Patty Pajączkowska?"

Well, that was the sixty-four-thousand-dollar question, wasn't it? I gave him the short answer—that Patty was the drummer. "Oh, the drummer," he says, "that strange girl with the—"

"The tattoo."

"Yes. The tattoo. Is she a bad influence?"

I told him that Patty was pretty much harmless. He's running his hands through his hair and shaking his head. "American children!" he says. "When I was a boy, we kissed our father's hands—like this," and he holds out his hand like there's an invisible kid standing there ready to kiss it. "She never gave us any trouble before. What is it, Jimmy? American children. Having things too easy? We always gave her everything she wanted."

I told him the ways of American children pretty much beat the hell out of me too but I sympathized with him—which I did—and he says, "Thank you, thank you," again, and he pumps my hand again, and that's that.

I went back to my trailer and got really loaded and didn't make it into the shop the next day till noon. Naturally I gave Mondrowski shit when I saw him. "Man," I said, "you don't have the brains of a carrot."

"I don't know what you got so upset about, Jimmy," he says. "She was perfectly safe. She was with us." The ridiculous thing was, he meant it.

All right, so here comes that horrible moment of truth you hear so much about. I'm sitting on the riverbank and I'm trying to get loaded, but I don't really feel like getting loaded—if you can believe that. I have a couple drinks, and then I'm just staring at the water. And I'm thinking, hell, what's the matter with me? It felt real familiar. It was like Dorothy Pliszka revisited.

I thought maybe I'd never see Janice again—oh, I might see her, but things might never be the same again—and it was like somebody had died. I had a rough few days—you know, where the only thing that gets you out of bed in the morning is you've got to go to work. I couldn't sleep much. I couldn't even eat—and believe me, when I can't eat, I'm in fairly horrible shape. Connie called me up right in the middle of this, and I put her off with something or other. Right then I couldn't have touched Connie with a barge pole. I kept thinking, hey, this can't be happening. It's so stupid. And it's just not right.

If it'd gone on much longer, I'm pretty sure I would've just got up one morning and said piss on it and tossed a few things in my car and driven to Austin. It wasn't one of those numbers where you're conning yourself, like—oh, hell, one of these days I'm going to Austin. I was right on the edge of really doing it.

When you feel that bad, you just got to keep going through the motions, right? What else can you do? So comes Friday, and Mondrowski and I hit the weight room, and I bust my ass—one of those workouts where you finish it up and you're shaking all over. And we sit in the steam room for a while, and we have us a nice long shower, and I've reduced myself down to Silly Putty. Then we're walking through the lobby of the Y, and the main thing on my mind is an iced pitcher of beer, and who's sitting in one of those chairs they got lined up along the wall but Janice.

This time it wasn't just the little tap in the pit of the stomach. It was like somebody hit me in the chest with a tire iron. And Mondrowski laughs and raises his eyebrows at me and keeps on walking. "Hi," she says.

"Hi," I say. "What're you doing here?"

"I'm waiting for you. What else would I be doing here?"

So I plunk down in the chair next to her, and we sit there and look at each other for a while. I keep telling myself that the main thing I've got to do is keep my cool—giving myself a pep talk, you know, exactly like I'm back in high school.

"I guess I should apologize," she says, "for being such a brat."

What do you say to that? I had enough sense to know what I shouldn't say—"Yeah, you were pretty much of a brat, all right." She was dressed up like for some big occasion—maybe even a date—so I figured she was going to make her little apology and then be on her way. "No problem," I say. "Is everything all right?"

"Yeah. Well, sort of. No, not really."

"Yeah? So what's happening?"

She shrugs. "I guess I blew it."

There's a couple of the fat old guys you usually see hanging around in the Y, and young studs coming in for their workout—the real fitness nuts, you know, or the losers who've got nothing better to do at seven o'clock on a Friday night—and it seemed kind of a ridiculous place to be having that conversation. Also I was dying of thirst. I kissed good-bye to that pitcher of beer in my head and bought myself a Coke from the machine. "Let's get out of here," I said.

We walked to my car. She had her hair in a different way. It was still braided but wound up on her head in this, I don't know, real complicated style. I didn't know whether I liked it or not. "Can I drop you somewhere?" I said.

She didn't answer me. She had her full-tilt teenybopper makeup on—I remember that shiny lipstick—and she was wearing a dress. That's why I thought she must have a date or something. It was weird, what she had on. This short dress and over the top of it this other thing, kind of like an apron—you know, with straps going over the shoulders—but a skirt that goes almost all the way around to the back. Like from the front it's two skirts, one over the other. And white stockings and little black kiddy shoes, flat as pancakes. She sure looked cute, and it just annoyed the hell out of me.

We got to my car, and she said, "I'm still mad at you, you know."

I was pretty mad at her too. "You want to go for a ride or what?"

She got in and I went tearing out of there. "What are you mad about?" I said.

"The way you came into Patty's like that. The way you treated me."

"Yeah. Well. What did you expect?"

If you drive up Pike Street—you know, in North Raysburg—there's this turnoff to this strange place where somebody was building a house once and just gave up. It's been there as long as I can remember. Like they poured the foundation and started some walls and that's it. You get a wonderful view of the city from up there, and the whole curve of the river from the Top Mill practically down to where we live. I'd taken Janice up there before. We walked to the edge and looked out at this, I guess you could say, spectacular panorama. We got a great view of the air pollution.

"Did Linda really get you out of bed?" she asked me. "That's what she told my father."

"Yeah, she did." That was Linda covering for me. If Czesław was any kind of suspicious guy, he might have thought Janice had been out with me the whole time.

"I'm sorry," she said.

She told me she'd got in a huge fight with her parents, mainly about her brother John. She'd been "playing little Miss Fix-It," she said, kind of bitter, and she'd been trying to get them to see just a hint of John's side of things, and they went ballistic. So she walked out on them and caught the bus into town and walked across the bridge to Patty's. She didn't feel the least bit bad about walking out on them, but she should have called home. That was really stupid of her—and wrong. "I hate admitting I'm wrong," she said.

"Oh, yeah? You must have a great time in confession."

"That's different."

She said her parents were going to have me and Linda over to the house some night when things calmed down and they felt like entertaining again. "Dad says you're a real friend of the family. And I'm supposed to thank you for rescuing me—from whatever it is you rescued me from."

"I rescued you from your father calling the cops, okay? And them maybe coming into Patty's and busting you and that whole sorry crew for possession, okay? My God, Janice, where's your head?"

"You still didn't have to treat me like that."

I just looked at her.

"I know you must think of me as a little kid," she said, "but you never treated me like that before."

It was a kind of ridiculous thing for her to say, dressed the way she was. But I told her the truth. "I don't think of you as a little kid."

A kind of flicker goes over her face. If I hadn't been looking at her so close, I might have missed it. "I always thought we were—I guess, like equals," she says.

I couldn't tell you what was in my head. I didn't have a clue what anything meant. But all of a sudden I could see her point. I hadn't treated her like an equal.

"Look," I said, "maybe I was wrong too. Maybe I should have gone in there and sat down and had a few laughs with everybody and then said something like, 'Hey, Janice, can I talk to you a minute?'"

"If you'd done that, everything would have been fine."

"But I didn't do that. I'm sorry."

She goes, "Whew. That's what I wanted you to say."

"What?"

"'I'm sorry.' Thanks for saying it. I always thought we could—you know, work things out. I always thought we weren't like other people."

And that was the perfect time for me to say, "Janice, just what the hell are we doing?" But I didn't. I was afraid to hear how she'd answer that one.

So we looked at the view. "How's everything at home?" I said.

"Not too good. If we were still in Poland before the war, I wouldn't be sitting down for a week. But seeing as we're in America, they're just going to make me feel as guilty as possible. I never thought they'd just come out and say it, but they did. They said, 'How can you treat us like this after everything we've done for you?'"

"Oh, yeah. That's a rough one."

So we talked about how she was doing with her parents. Yeah, that was a safe topic. But what we were *not* talking about was just hanging over our heads, making us both uncomfortable. I was smoking lots of cigarettes. "So where you going tonight?" I said.

"Nowhere."

Oh, is that right? That meant she'd got all dressed up to go have a fight with me—using her, you know, feminine wiles. Before that, I wouldn't have thought Janice even had any feminine wiles. "You want to do something?" I said.

"Yeah. Sure. I just have to call home every once in a while to let them know where I am. They always have to know where I am."

I was kind of at a loss—just, you know, trying to figure out exactly what was going on—and she goes, "Did you miss me?"

For a couple seconds I was just furious. It was exactly like the crap I used to get from Dorothy. But then I looked right into her eyes and something went click in my head. It's true—she did look a little bit like Dorothy, but she wasn't Dorothy. She wasn't a thing like Dorothy. If Dorothy had said that, she would've been jerking me around, but there was just no way Janice was doing that. All she was doing was asking me if I liked her. "Yeah," I said. "I missed you."

"I missed you too."

I remember staring down at the river like I was totally fascinated by the view and feeling this enormous sense of relief—and at the same time thinking about what a bind we were in, how hopeless it all was.

"I figured you'd got to the point where you couldn't take any more of that heavy stuff," I told her, "and you just wanted to go off with your girlfriends and cool out."

"Oh, I knew you'd understand. You know me really well, don't you? You know me better than *anybody*."

I hadn't understood how scared she was until she stopped being scared. I saw her start to relax—like she'd been hanging on to this huge monster spring and now she was letting it go. "I thought it'd help," she said, "to hang out with Sandy and Maureen. And it did help. For a while it did."

And she's telling me how all Sandy and Maureen want to do is spend forty-seven years getting dressed and then go somewhere the boys can see them, and if they're not doing that, then they're talking about the boys they're going out with, or the boys they wish they were going out with, and so on and so on. It sounds like nothing's changed since I was in high school.

The sun was starting to set, turning the sky red, and I remember the light coming straight at us. I remember the golden braids wound up on her head, and how we had to squint looking into the sun. Then she turned to look at me and the light fell on the side of her face and her eyes were just sparkling—this intense blue—and her skin was just glowing, you know, like I could see right through it, like I could see the little blue veins in her temple. And that weird outfit with the two skirts didn't look dopey to me anymore, and the light even made her legs glow, and I could see the pink of her long legs shining through those white stockings. Yeah, that light was something else, all blue and gold, and she was so radiant, she looked so alive, she looked so beautiful I can't begin to tell you.

She was saying how there were all these things she couldn't get out of her head—all that shit her parents went through, and her brother telling her that Poland was just a backward third-rate country somewhere to the east of Europe, and her dad saying, "the Polish soil is soaked in blood," and she was tired of thinking about all that stuff, but she couldn't stop thinking about it, and she wished it could all be different.

"Sometimes I wish I could be a child again," she said, and she looked right at me. "Oh, isn't that funny? For me to say that? After giving you hell for treating me like a child."

Our eyes locked together for a few seconds, and then she took her turn staring down at the river and getting totally fascinated by the view. "It's like I was in a cocoon," she said, "but now I've got to come out and face the real world—and maybe I'm just not ready for it.

"Jimmy?" she says. "You know what's so hard? I've lost my dream." And she's telling me again about that dream of Poland—Krajne Podlaski with its river like glass that she'd thought was the Ohio—and all that romantic Polish poetry, all that stuff that meant so much to her when she was growing up. And I'm thinking, oh, for Christ's sake, Janice, don't just keep talking about Poland.

But then I flip that one over—why shouldn't she be talking about Poland? And her lost dream and all that? Because it's weighing heavy on her mind. And there's something else too. If she wasn't talking about Poland, what else would she be talking about?

The bind we were in— It wasn't just stupid or ridiculous or funny or any of that shit. It was painful. I could feel it in my chest. Like I was really hurting. And that's probably why I blew up at her. I mean it was good-natured and all, but I just let her have it.

"Come on, Janice," I said. "Wasn't it a good dream? Wasn't it just a dandy dream? Your mom and her cousin riding around on their horses, and your dad running through the woods with his pals, and that nice little town where everybody got along with everybody? And the old prophet guy, what's-his-name, saying everybody should love everybody because we're all children of the same mother. And people fighting for Poland's freedom like that virgin maid, whoever the hell she was. Who could ask for a better dream than that? I think it's terrific your folks gave you that dream. It's probably what got them through. And if I was you, I'd hang on to that dream for dear life."

SEVENTEEN

In the Ohio Valley, you always get a spell in the summer when it's even worse than usual—the temperature shoots up way over ninety and it's so humid you think you can wring out the air like a sponge, and you walk around with your tongue hanging out, and the smoke from the mills gets trapped and doesn't go nowhere, and the mosquitoes come out at twilight and have a field day on you, and everything kind of stinks of sweat and misery. You always forget from one year to the next how awful it can be, and then, BINGO, there you are again, stuck in it for however long it lasts. That summer it hit the first week in August.

So there's this one day that really takes the cake in the misery department— I mean it's just sickening—and we're real busy at the shop. I guess when people are too hot to move, they watch a lot of TV. And good old Constance Bradshaw calls me up and says, "Why don't you come out for dinner? I'll make something nice—and you can spend the night if you want." She sounded kind of pathetic. It wasn't anything she said, but there was this kind of whiny tone in her voice.

Now I hadn't been seeing much of Connie. Well, to get specific here, I'd have to say I hadn't laid eyes on Connie since that night when Janice ran away from home. If I told you I had a plan all worked out in my head, I'd be lying, but what I was doing in my half-assed way was letting the Jim and Connie Show die a natural death.

I was seeing a lot of Janice again. It was like she'd decided on a compromise—sometimes she'd hang around with her girlfriends and sometimes she'd hang around with me—but I was never sure when I was going to see her, because if we made all these arrangements, that's called *dating*, and we both knew we shouldn't be doing that. So sometimes when I'd come home from work, she'd be there—pretending she'd come to see Linda—and sometimes she wouldn't, and I knew perfectly well I shouldn't ever get to where I was depending on her, but it really pissed me off that I couldn't depend on her. And then I got pissed off that I was pissed off, you know what I mean? Because she wasn't my girlfriend so I had no right to get pissed off. Oh, yeah, I was having just a dandy time.

That conversation we'd had up there on the hill at the end of Pike Street kept going around and around in my head, and there'd been a whole hell of a lot of things we hadn't said—you know, straight out in so many words—but one thing seemed pretty clear. The mess we were in wasn't just *my* problem. Yeah, she liked me too—although for the life of me, I couldn't figure out why. In my own mind I was just this total loser, going nowhere fast, and I thought she was nuts for liking me—or maybe it was just a schoolgirl crush that didn't mean anything—but anyhow, I was real pleased she liked me. But I just didn't have a clue what to do about it.

So I'm standing there in the shop, listening to Connie whining away on the phone, and— I don't want to make excuses for myself, but I was in, I guess you could say, your classic state of hopeless confusion. Nothing seemed right to me. It didn't seem right to see Connie feeling the way I did about Janice and knowing that Janice felt something for me too—but on the other hand, how can you betray somebody who isn't your girlfriend? And maybe I wasn't doing Janice any favors by encouraging her. And maybe this, and maybe that, and maybe the other.

But you know what tipped me over the edge? This is something I'd just as leave not tell you because it makes me sound like a total pig, but I'm trying to be honest here, right? You see, earlier in the summer, Connie had gone out and bought herself an air-conditioning unit. Seeing as money's never a problem with her, she'd got the super humungo heavy-duty model, and they'd delivered that sucker and it'd sat in the middle of her bedroom floor until I'd gone out and installed it for her. We'd cranked it up, and, lo and behold, that thing sure kicked out the cold air. Her apartment was on the small side so that unit didn't just take care of the bedroom, it pretty well chilled out the whole damn place.

Well, to make a long story short, I got off work and drove out to St. Stevens. Mrs. Constance Bradshaw meets me at the door, and it's kind of a shock. When we'd been having our Mature Relationship on Sundays, we'd been real heavy into the good taste. Like brunch wasn't just eggs and toast, it was your eggs Florentine or Benedictine or Augustine or some damn thing, and we ate them off the family china. We hit the sack in good taste too—nice shower first, with the round soap that smells like gardenias, and then you've got your one hundred percent cotton sheets ironed all crisp, and Connie's sweet little bod all clean and shaved and scented and powdered and naked, or maybe with just a wisp of white lace.

So she opens the door for me, and I note right away that good taste seems to have gone down the drain for the night. She's got your whorehouse makeup and your biker's girlfriend heels and God knows where she got it, but she's stuffed herself into one of these tacky plastic minidresses—fire engine red—a couple sizes too small so she's spilling right out of it. She's drunk, naturally. Not really slobbering yet, but definitely off to a good start. "I'll bet you can guess what I want to do," she says. Well, gee, Connie, I'm not exactly sure. Let me search my mind.

Yep, it was cool in there, a real relief, and I can do a Pavlov's dog number on your low, crude, tasteless sex appeal as good as the next guy, and I'm thinking, yeah, it was a good idea to come out here. This is probably just what I need. So we get right down to business. Afterward she brings me a cold beer and jumps into the shower. I'm hungry as a horse, so I chug the beer and it goes straight to my head. I pull my jeans on and go have a peek in the kitchen.

Well, at least Connie had the dinner planned. There's all the stuff to make it laying out there on the counter—some raw vegetables, and a head of lettuce, and a whole bunch of lamb chops—but she hadn't got any further than that, and I'm thinking, Koprowski, you dumb shit, you should've grabbed a sandwich before you drove out here instead of trying to save yourself a couple bucks.

She comes out in her bathrobe, her hair wet and her makeup all scrubbed off, and pours herself a gin and me a Jack Daniel's, and after a drink or two, I'm thinking, aw, what the hell, I guess I don't need to eat right away, because it's sure nice and cool in there and we're sailing out on that first rush, you know what I mean? Come on, folks, give us a break here, it's happy hour. Bunch of raw chops laying out in the kitchen, nobody paying any attention to them. Oh, no, that sweet first hour when you're getting loaded is too good to miss for anything as stupid as cooking dinner.

I've seen the show before, plenty, and I should know how it goes, so why does it always take me by surprise? We start off having something you could call a conversation—yeah, yucking it up and enjoying each other's company just like normal drunks, but eventually we shift into Phase Two. Then what's supposed to happen is Connie gets to talk and I get to listen. That's when I start hearing, "Shut up. You're interrupting my train of thought."

So she's telling me that the only thing she ever learned about sex is that it's totally its own thing. "Sex is supposed to be related to all these other things. Love. Friendship. Respect. Well, that's hogwash. The only thing sex is related to is sex."

Then for her next act she turns into Connie the Dictator of the Universe, and she's telling me how she'd fix things if she had a chance. You take marriage, for instance. It's one of the stupidest institutions in the world. You're supposed to get everything rolled into one person, but that's just ridiculous. If things were run right, you'd have one guy to hang out with, one guy to screw, trained professionals to raise your kids—and on and on she goes.

Just like always, I'm getting sick of listening to her, and I've heard it all before anyway, and I'm seriously shitfaced by then and thinking how it might not be such a bad idea to get started on the goddamn dinner. So I stumble out into the kitchen to see what I can do with the chops. It shouldn't be too hard. Piece of meat, right? You aim some heat at it for a while and then you get to eat it. She stumbles out behind me, and she's yelling at me because I just walked out on some brilliant point she was about to make.

"What do you do with these things?" I say. "Fry them?"

"Christ, all you think about is your goddamned stomach."

You're goddamn right. I'd walked in there hungry, and I'd guzzled down a couple beers and a good whack of Jack Daniel's, and my requirements in the nutrient department were getting to be kind of urgent. All that raw meat I just couldn't contemplate, so I started going through her fridge.

"What the hell are you doing?" she's yelling at me.

"What the hell's it look like I'm doing?"

She goes crashing over to the sink, jerks open the door under it, hauls out the garbage can, and starts throwing the chops into it. One chop at a time. She misses with a couple and they go skidding across that clean shiny linoleum floor. "Great, Connie," I say, "there goes ten bucks' worth of meat."

She starts screaming at me. I mean full tilt. Like, okay, folks, let's just blow every circuit right out of the system. Some of those old guys that worked at the mill with my old man had pretty foul mouths, but they had nothing on Connie when she got cranked up.

"Hey, honey," I say, "this is an apartment you're living in here. You do have neighbors, you know."

There's one of those casserole things way in the back of the fridge, and I pull it out and open the lid and I've hit the jackpot. Leftovers from one of those terrific dinners she made for her husband. Scalloped potatoes and half of one of those little mini-hams. "Get out, get out, get out," she's yelling at me.

"Sure, honey," I say. "Right." I'm banging through her drawers looking for a carving knife.

All of a sudden she turns the volume down on herself. She says in this quiet reasonable voice, "Jim, you're in my space."

I couldn't argue with that. I was there all right. "Will you please leave now?" she says.

"Sure," I say, "in a minute." I've finally located a knife, so I start slicing up the ham. "You know, Connie, you should eat something. You're not looking too good."

"Didn't you understand what I said? I want you to leave right now."

"Well, maybe there's something you don't understand, honey. I'm kind of fucked up. Same as you are. And I've had a lot of practice driving drunk, but there's a thin edge you don't want to cross over. You understand what I'm telling you here?"

"Fuck you," she yells at me. She's jumping up and down and banging her fists on the counter she's so mad. Then she runs at me and starts banging her fists on my chest. I grab her wrists and hold them. She's thrashing around trying to get free, and of course she can't. She looks real surprised. I've got my eye on her in case she decides to kick me, but that doesn't seem to occur to her.

"Connie," I say, "you be a good girl now." I let go of her and she jumps back. "Honey," I say, "we're down to basics, okay? Food. Sleep. Rest and recuperation. Like that. Just calm down. Eat something. Watch the telly or something. I'm getting out of here just as fast as I can. So don't worry about that. And then you'll have your space back all to yourself. So you just cool out now, okay?"

She stands there staring at me a minute. Like maybe I'd just materialized from some alien planet. Then she walks out.

Well, I ate all the scalloped potatoes and most of the ham and a couple slices of bread. I had a big glass of milk. And then it's like somebody hit me over the head with a shovel. I go lurching back into the living room, and I don't make it any farther than the couch.

I wake up and it's pushing one in the morning, and I've got just about the sweetest little hangover you ever saw. What I want is a gallon of water, and I can't even force myself up to get it. Then I remember that Connie has a few cans of pop in the fridge, and when you've got one of those terminal hangovers, wow, those bubbles sure taste good.

So I stumble out into the kitchen and chug down a can, and I'm eyeing these two pathetic chops laying on the floor, and I'm thinking, hmmm, I wonder what happened to Connie. Boy, is she ever going to be one sorry girl when she wakes up in the morning.

To this day I don't know why I decided to check on her. Where I expected her to be was in bed, and that's where she was, but she hadn't got into it. The light on her table was still on, and she was laying on top of the covers. She didn't look real comfortable. Like she'd just fallen over—plunk—and the way she'd landed, that's the way she'd stayed. One of her legs was sticking off the bed—like if she rolled over even a little bit she was going to end up on the floor—so I picked up her feet and swung her over so she was in the center of the bed, and there was something weird about the way her body felt. Like so much dead weight. And then I took a good look at her, and I swear to God I thought she was dead.

What got to me was I couldn't see her breathing. And then I see the pill bottle laying on its side with a few pills spilling out of it, and I'm going, oh, Christ, no, this can't be happening. And there's her glass. Nothing left in it but some mostly melted ice cubes. I'm slapping her face, yelling, "Connie, Connie, Connie," and nothing. As gentle as I can, I pull back one of her eyelids, and there's nothing but white. I kneel down and put my ear right in her face, and what I hear is nothing.

So I try to find her pulse. It looks so easy when some doctor does it to you— you ever tried to find somebody's pulse? That's when I really thought she was dead. I'm pawing up and down her wrists and I can't feel a damn thing. I pull that bathrobe about half off her and just glue my ear to her chest—right over where I thought her heart ought to be. And there it is. I've got to work to hear it, and it sounds kind of slow, but what do I know about heartbeats? At least she's got one.

She makes this cough noise—no, it's more like a snort—and if I put my hand right under her neck, I can feel the breath going in and out. Very slowly. It's funny what your mind will do at moments like that. My mind's going, "Zdrowaś Maryjo, łaskiś pełna, Pan z Tobą—" you know, the Hail Mary.

Then I come back to myself and I'm panting like a dog. I'm telling myself the same thing I used to tell myself in the air force—don't panic, asshole, take it one step at a time. I grab the pill bottle. If you've never contemplated the side of a pill bottle, you'd be amazed at how much is written there. It says, "BRAD-SHAW, CONSTANCE." It says, "SECONAL" and however many milligrams it was. It says, "Take one at bedtime. Do not exceed recommended dosage. Do not use with alcohol." There's her doctor's name, "Dr. Andrew R. Hamilton," and the date. It says there's thirty capsules in there.

The date's just four days ago. I count eight pills left. That means there could be eighteen or nineteen pills in her. She was drunk when I got there, and she'd been hitting it pretty hard ever since, so there's a fuck of a lot of gin in her too. I'm thinking, Christ, what do I do? Call her husband? Call her doctor? Hell, no, asshole. She could be dying right in front of your eyes. Call Emergency.

They asked me a bunch of questions, and then they said, "Don't try to move her. Don't touch her. We'll be right there."

Now comes one of the biggest chickenshit moments of my life, and I'm not real proud of it. I got her wallet out of her purse and opened it up to her driver's license and put it right in front of her so they'd know who she was, and then I made my break. I left the door wide open. I went shooting across the back alley—her apartment faced the back—and I found myself a big black shadow and I stood in it. I was already hearing the sirens. St. Stevens is a nice little Ohio town, and those boys were quick. If it'd been South Raysburg, it might have taken them a week or two.

I watched them go running into the apartment, and I watched them come running back out with Connie on one of those stretcher things. I waited till they went roaring away with their sirens going, and then I hit it on down the road for the great state of West Virginia.

By the time I got back to South Raysburg, I was calmed down, so I went in the PAC to use the phone. I called the St. Stevens Medical Center, and yes, she'd been admitted. And she was in stable condition, but unless I was a member of the family, they couldn't tell me anything more than that. The next day I called again, and it turned out that she'd come up a notch and was in good condition. And she had a telephone in her room. She sounded—well, I was going to say flat, but it was flatter than that. She sounded like she'd been *squashed* flat. "I owe you one," she said.

She didn't know when they were going to let her out. Maybe not for a while. "They think it was a suicide attempt." Well, gee, Connie, how could anybody ever come up with a totally insane idea like that?

"Don't come here," she said. "It's not a good idea." Right. I'd never wanted to meet her husband, and the way things were at the moment, I *really* didn't want to meet him.

The next day when I talked to her, she sounded a little bit perkier. "It's hard to kill yourself with pills and booze," she said. "Did you know that? I didn't know that. They tell me it's a very popular way to try it, but it hardly ever works. Oh, God, Jim, imagine the worst hangover you ever had in your life and then multiply it by a thousand. Death would have been preferable, believe me." And she tells me again that it wasn't a suicide attempt, just a stupid mistake. But how you could take eighteen or nineteen sleeping pills by mistake was something I could never figure out. "I've been seeing the shrink," she says.

I called the fourth day, and she'd been discharged. I called her apartment and she was there. I was a little surprised. I'd thought her husband would have brought her home with him—at least that's what I would've done if my wife had just tried to knock herself off, no matter how estranged I was from her. "I thought you'd be at home," I said.

"I am at home," she said.

When I got off work, I drove out there. She opened the door for me and gave me a little kiss on the cheek and said, "Thanks." She was wearing pajamas—I mean the baggy flannel kind. I never would've figured Connie for a baggy-pajamas girl.

The shrink thought she needed extensive long-term psychotherapy—his exact words if I remember them right. She'd signed up to see him three times a week. The shrink had told her to lay off the sauce, and she was doing okay with that. She hadn't had a single drink. Instead, she was taking these little beige pills he'd prescribed for her. "They make me *feel* beige," she said.

She kept telling me how it wasn't a suicide attempt. "Christ, everybody must think I'm a moron. If I'd been trying to kill myself, I would have taken the whole bottle, wouldn't I?"

She told me I could have a drink if I wanted, it didn't bother her. She said she was sorry she didn't want to make love, but she just didn't feel up to it. In her beige state, she probably wouldn't be a lot of fun to make love to anyway. I had a drink and said I was cool with not making love and with her being in a beige state. Then these big fat tears started rolling down her face. In her baggy pajamas, she looked absolutely pathetic. "Oh, Jim," she said, "I know you're going to leave me someday, but please, don't leave me yet."

———

For a while I was shooting out to St. Stevens like once a day to check up on her. It was a hell of a time. I was bouncing back and forth between Raysburg and St. Stevens like a Ping-Pong ball, and there was no way I could fit everything in. When you've got to sacrifice something out of your life, it says something about you—what you decide can get sacrificed and what can't. I could miss some work—even though that meant money—and I could miss hitting the weights with Mondrowski, but I wasn't going to miss seeing Janice. If I left the shop in the middle of the afternoon, and if everything went okay with Connie, I could be back in time to catch up with Janice in the evening, and— Hey, this is funny. You know what? I was spending so much time driving back and forth, most nights I didn't even have enough time to get good and loaded.

The beige pills reduced Connie down to your basic pulp. She slept eight or nine hours a night, and then getting out of bed and having breakfast was a real big effort so she needed a nap around eleven. Taking a shower in the afternoon was like running the marathon, so she had to have a little bit of a snooze after that. If she needed anything—like milk—I had to go get it for her. She said, "Just take some money out of my purse."

I did her laundry for her, which wasn't hard—all she was wearing was pajamas. I'm not much of a cook, but I'd slap together something or other—hot dogs, scrambled eggs—and we'd eat it and watch television for a while, and then I'd get antsy and want to get my ass back into town. She didn't give a damn what she ate or what was on the tube. She didn't give a damn about anything. It was like the speed knob on her had been turned down to low. I don't think she bothered to eat when I wasn't there.

She never made a phone call—which surprised me—but she got a few. The first time her husband called, she's going, "I told you not to call me. I said I'd call you. Yes, I'm fine. Yes, I'm taking my medication," and she puts her hand over the mouthpiece and says, "Jim, honey, would you mind taking a little walk?" Me mind? Oh, hell no.

She called it "Connie's Beige Period," and I kept thinking, hmm, I can't quite recall when I signed on for this gig. But it just didn't seem fair to run out on her when she was having such a rough time—and when her husband obviously didn't give two shits. So I figured I was stuck with her until she was on her feet again.

Connie's Beige Period didn't last too long, thank God. There's this one Sunday when I spent the whole day with Janice, and right on into the evening too, and I just couldn't quite get my ass out to St. Stevens. So I was feeling a little bit guilty about my old drugged pal who hadn't attempted suicide, and the first of the week rolls around and I take off from work early—like about two—and go shooting out there to see how she's doing.

Lo and behold, the door to Connie's apartment is standing wide open. The air conditioner's turned off, and the windows are open. She's airing the place out. "It smelled like death in here," she says.

You know the kind of dress that the plainer it is, the more it costs? Well, she's wearing one of them. Navy blue. And just the right makeup to go with it, and pantyhose, and navy blue shoes—the tasteful kind with the not-too-high heels—and I swear to God a string of pearls. She looks like she's going to go have tea on a nice autumn afternoon in one of those nice little mansions they've got out by the country club and maybe get her picture on the society page. But it's not a nice autumn afternoon. It's August and hotter than hell. "Wow," I say, "you're looking good. Where you headed?"

"Fuck you, Jim," she says.

Oh, well, gee, sorry for inquiring. She's not going anywhere, she says—as should be perfectly obvious. She's set up her ironing board in the middle of the living room, and she's ironing her sheets— Oops, that's not what I'm supposed to call them. Her goddamn *linens*.

She's got Bob Dylan going on the stereo. I was never big on him. He always sounded to me like somebody's grandfather. But Connie thought he was a prophet or some damn thing, and she owned every record he ever made, and she's got all of them stacked up on her turntable—like hours and hours of Bob Dylan. She isn't playing him loud. Just this scratchy old man's voice droning away in the background.

I fire up a cigarette, and she says, "Please don't smoke in here." Oh, okay. She never minded before, but I'm an agreeable guy, right?

I look around and there's not an ashtray in sight. I trot into the can to dump my smoke, and she's got the toilet so immaculate it's a shame to use it, and everywhere I go in that apartment I'm smelling the Dutch Cleanser and the Windex. Now Polish ladies are big on clean, right? My mother's really big on clean, right? So I'm checked out on clean. But this is just nuts—I mean, this is clean out of *Star Trek*.

I stroll back into the living room and it finally sinks in that every damn thing you see is lined up perfectly—like maybe Connie had some land surveyors come in to help her get it right. You can sight down the chairs. The pictures of her kids are arranged in order of size and are perfectly equidistant from each other.

Connie's radical newspapers are stacked perfectly in the center of the end table—like she probably found the exact location by the use of a T-square and a triangle.

Her damp linens are in a heap in a big basket, and she yanks them out, slaps them on the board, and irons away at them madly like she's trying to press those suckers to death. When she's done, they're perfectly flat and folded and wrinkle-free. They look like big sheets of typewriter paper. She's got little beads of sweat breaking out on her upper lip, and every time she reaches for another of her linens, I see that her armpits are like they've got faucets in them. The sides of that expensive dress are just soaked.

You want to know what's going down? It's day two without the beige pills. She got up on Sunday morning and realized she'd rather be dead than go on with the beige pills, so she chucked them in the garbage. Then comes Monday morning, she goes to her appointment with her shrink and tells him about it, and he says she absolutely has to take the beige pills or there's nothing he can do for her. She tells him to take his beige pills and shove them. "You know what those damn pills were designed to do?" she says. "They were designed to take a perfectly normal fucked-up adult woman and turn her into a mental patient."

So she's not taking the beige pills, and she's not taking her good old pills either—you know, the Valium for her anxiety attacks, and the Seconol for not attempting to kill herself with—and she's quit drinking too she tells me. "No more better living through chemistry," she says. It's the first time I've ever seen Connie on absolutely nothing. Connie on absolutely nothing is pretty damn scary.

You remember how she'd always talk about her husband without ever saying his name—just calling him "he" and "him"? Now she's going on about "they" and "them," and I couldn't quite put my finger on exactly who *they* were. At first, I thought she meant her husband and the other doctors. She's going, "They just want to shut me up. Connie's an embarrassment. Connie's a pain in the ass. Connie's not playing by the rules. Well, what they should have done was give me a lobotomy when they had their chance. Yeah, that would have taken care of everything."

Every cell in her body is angry. She's just sizzling with it. "I've had my share of humiliating experiences, believe me," she says, going BANG, SLAM with the iron. "Growing up was one constant humiliation. But that one took the cake. Every goddamn doctor in the medical center I know socially. And I arrive in a goddamn coma. They pumped my stomach. Said it was probably a little late for it, but they did it anyway. Just to cover their tracks. Bullshit. Just to humiliate me is more like it. It's too bad I don't remember a goddamn thing about it. I'm sure they'd prefer that I remembered something. It'd be far more humiliating if I remembered something. But I was in a goddamn *coma*, for Christ's sake. They probably checked for semen while they were at it. They could have done anything. Oh, I bet they just loved having an unconscious woman on their hands."

On and on she goes about all the bad things *they* kept saying about her. "Connie's a liar. A filthy-minded little bitch. Nobody's going to believe a filthy-minded lying little bitch. Let's really humiliate her this time. Let's do it in public. Yeah, that'll fix her little red wagon. Well, they better watch out because Connie knows what *they're* up to now. Connie can see through *them* like a windowpane." And the gist of it is that Connie's taken far too much crap from *them*, and she's been taking crap from *them* her whole life, and by God, she's not going to take it anymore, and *they* better watch out because the worm has turned.

"What are you laughing at?" she yells at me. Maybe I'd been trying for a weak smile, but laughing was something I hadn't achieved yet. She's glaring at me like she's trying to burn holes in me with her eyeballs. "Do you think this is funny?"

Yikes! Seems to me I've got an appointment in downstate West Virginia—way downstate, if you know what I mean. Yeah, it slipped my mind up till a couple seconds ago, but I'm already late for it.

"Go ahead and run out on me, you prick," she says. "Everybody else always does."

So how do you figure what you owe somebody? There's what you owe from just one human being to another, and then there's what you owe because you're responsible somehow—and yeah, I did think I was responsible somehow, even if I couldn't have split hairs like a Jesuit and told you exactly how. But by then I was figuring I'd pretty well paid it off.

EIGHTEEN

Meanwhile, life in South Raysburg had been rolling right along. A couple days after Connie had gotten out of the hospital, I went home for dinner one night, and Janice was there, and my sister of course, and guess who shows up? Patty Pajaczkowski. Wearing old ratty cutoffs and one of those muscle shirts—you know, to show off her lizard. Linda goes to the door, and she leads Patty back into the kitchen, and she sends me a look like, oh my God, what is she doing here?

"Oh, hi, Patty," Mom says like she's used to seeing her dropping in on a regular basis. "Get a chair for her, Jimmy. Sit down, Patty. Can I get you something?"

Now a lot of people if they turn up right smack in the middle of dinner and you offer them something will say, "Oh, no, no. I already ate, thank you," but not Patty. "Sure," she says, and she starts digging in like she hasn't seen food in a week. You'd be amazed at how much that skinny girl could pack in. I practically had to arm wrestle her for the last couple *gołąbki*.

Old Bullet Head is asking how her dad is, and she's going, "Oh, fine, fine, fine, no problem," and she's got this funny little smile on her face like the cat that ate the canary—and that's a fairly un-Patty-like expression. She looks at me and Linda and Janice, and she says, "It's a sign, finding all three of you here at the same time."

She has something to show us, she says. She wouldn't say what. But there's something about Patty that you've just got to take on faith, so we finish dinner and stand up and follow her out the door and over to her parents' house.

We didn't get the whole story till later, but the way it'd started out was like this. Patty and her dad had got themselves reconciled. You see, they hadn't had a good word to say to each other for years. Patty's big sister had done everything right—finished high school, married a nice guy, settled down, had a couple kids—but Patty didn't exactly follow in her footsteps. Nope, Patty took up the drums at any early age, dropped out of school, ran away from home, ingested every known drug and a few unknown ones, screwed around with guys of assorted races and an occasional other girl if you want to know the truth, lived with the Indians, got tattooed, and committed a number of other good whole-some acts along those lines, so, for an old-time working stiff like Bob Pajaczkowski, his little Patricia was pretty much the daughter from hell. Then he sees her playing in a polka band at Franky Rzeszutko's, and it's the first time she's done anything right since maybe her tenth birthday, and when he gave her that big hug after their set was over, it was a fairly heavy-duty moment for him—and for her too, I guess.

So they're standing around afterward trying to talk to each other in an embarrassed kind of way, and Patty says, "Hey, Dad. You know those polka records you were always playing when I was a kid? You still got any of them?"

"Yeah," he says, "I've got every single one of them."

Well, Patty doesn't think about it much but it keeps ticking around in the back of her head, and then finally she goes home for the first time in years and sits around shooting the shit with her parents, just, you know, pretending she's a normal human being, and she remembers the records. So her dad takes her down in the basement and shows her all these cartons, and there's 78s going back to when he was still in high school—and that's the thirties, for Christ's sake—and then there's 45s and LPs, just carton after carton of those damn records. "Are they all polkas?" Patty says.

"Yeah, well, there's some Christmas tunes and like that, but they're pretty much all polkas."

She starts pulling out these old 78s and blowing the dust off them, and of course there's L'il Wally and Johnny Bomba and Eddie Zima, but there's also Ed Krolikowski's Radio Orchestra and Gene Wisniewski's Harmony Bells Orchestra and Frank Wojnarowski's Orchestra and all these other ancient orchestras, and this is all the stuff she grew up listening to, and things kind of fall into place for her—you know, like why she'd come back to Raysburg in the first place and why she was playing in a polka band.

So we walk over to the Pajaczkowskis' and in the front door, and there's her parents sitting in front of the tube and they're kind of startled to see us. "I just want to show them your records," Patty says to her dad, and we follow her down into the basement.

Linda starts looking through the cartons, and she goes, "Oh, my God, this is priceless! We've got to archive it."

Patty says, "Archive away to your heart's content, sweetheart. I just want to hear it all again." And she looks at Janice with that little pussycat smile and says, "What do you think, Rapunzel?"

Well, Janice doesn't know what to think. It's been awhile since she's said a word about the band, and the last I heard, she'd been saying she wasn't sure she could ever play a polka again. There's a rat's-ass hi-fi from the fifties down there, and Patty has it plugged into a light socket. She takes one of those old records and puts it on the turntable and drops the needle on it, and behind all this hiss and rumble, what we hear is Walt Solek. Now he speaks English just as good as you or me, but he's got this dumb-shit immigrant voice he uses sometimes when he's performing—you know, to be funny—and we hear him saying in this thick Polish accent, "All right? Are you ready? Once more polka. *Raz Dwa!*" And BANG, there's "The Marching Trumpets Polka."

It's a real manic polka. And Walt Solek's got your classic old-country voice, and he just belts it out good, and if you're inclined to like Polish music but you've never heard him before, he's going to blow you right through the wall. And we're all of us standing around that old hi-fi listening to him singing away in Polish. And then the band kicks into the drive with the trumpets blazing, and he's yelping his head off—egging on the dancers—and Janice has got this smile like the sun coming up in the morning.

If you didn't know Janice, you would have thought all that heavy stuff she'd been worrying about had slipped completely out of her mind, because all of a sudden she was instantly back into the music. She hated practicing. She never practiced. But every morning she got up and hopped on her bike and rode it down to South Raysburg and went into the Pajaczkowskis' basement all by herself and played along with those old records for a couple hours. You see, that wasn't practicing—that was just having fun. Patty's mom said she liked having Janice around—hell, everybody liked having Janice around—so she could spend as much time down there as she wanted.

Janice had a girl's four-speed her dad had bought for her twelfth birthday, and it had just been sitting in the garage getting rusty, and at some point it dawned on her that Edgewood to South Raysburg is downhill practically every inch of the way—like she didn't hardly have to pedal and she'd still make it down there damn near quick as a car. Well, I cleaned up that bike and oiled it for her and raised the seat and made sure she had good brakes, and then I tried not to think about her sailing down Highlight Road at thirty or forty miles an hour. I knew perfectly well that's what she did. "You be careful," I said to her about a million times, and she'd always go, "Oh, sure. I'm always careful."

It would have taken her maybe four hours to pedal back up, so I'd throw the bike in my trunk and deliver it—and her—back to her house. It gave us a perfect excuse for me to be driving her home every night.

Once she was down the hill, she could ride her bike anywhere she wanted. You don't really need a bike to get around South Raysburg, but if you've got one, you can be anywhere in about thirty seconds flat. So she could go see her girlfriends, or pop into the church to pray—which she did from time to time, being a serious Catholic girl who was still on a spiritual quest. And then in some magical way she'd always run into me. And then after Connie's Beige Period was over and I wasn't going out to St. Stevens anymore, I had lots of time to make sure I was available to be run into.

The one place Janice couldn't stand to be for very long was at home, and she kept getting into fights with her parents about it. "It's the summer," she kept telling them. "You can't expect me to sit around the house in the summer."

In that hot weather Janice wore nothing but swimsuits. She had two of them; one was red, white, and blue stripes, and the other was all blue, and if you were wondering what her figure looked like, you didn't have to wonder too long when she was wearing one of those things. She shoved her feet into tennis shoes and didn't bother with socks. She had a schoolbag she strapped onto the back of her bike, and she'd put her clarinet in there, and a few bucks in case she wanted a Coke or something, and a little bag with her makeup—I couldn't believe how much makeup she carried around with her—and a pair of shorts in case she needed to look a little more modest later on in the evening. And then she was all set to ramble around all day and go where she pleased.

It's true, she really didn't have much of a figure. I mean she was definitely a girl but that was about it. Her mom was always onto her to wear a bra and she'd say, "Mom, what would be the point?" That gives you some idea how far we'd gone in the direction of being able to tell each other anything—that she could tell me something like that.

One afternoon Janice went to see my grandmother—you know, Babcia Wojtkiewicz—and they sat around drinking tea and talking in Polish for a couple hours. Babcia told my mom she'd been pleased as punch to have that little girl visit her. "You didn't tell me you were going to do that," I said to Janice.

"I don't have to tell you everything I'm doing, do I?"

They talked about the old country, and then Janice got to hear about the early years in Raysburg, how they built St. Stans and how hard it was for the steelworkers to get the union organized. "Wow, that strike in 1919 was really ugly," Janice said.

"Oh, you bet."

She'd started picking up some of my expressions. It was kind of weird hearing me coming back at me out of her mouth. "The Depression wasn't exactly a barrel of laughs either," she said.

It's funny, but I can close my eyes and still see her sailing along on that blue bike, looking the way she did that summer she was sixteen. She didn't make any effort to get a tan, but just being outside she turned a beautiful golden color that matched her hair.

Well, I put a new belt on Bob Pajaczkowski's old turntable, and I replaced the needles, and jacked in a little amp I salvaged, and wired up a couple good-sized speakers, and lo and behold, we've got enough power to rattle the basement windows. And then I slapped in a tape deck so the girls could record any of the tunes they liked well enough to want to learn to play.

Mary Jo said she had better things to do with her time than sit around in somebody's basement listening to old polka records—the girls didn't want her around anyway—and Bev was home in Barnsville being bored, so we were down to your hard core. That's Patty and Linda and Janice, and when I could fit it in, yours truly. And we'd get together in Bob Pajaczkowski's basement. It was always nice and cool down there, and it was a good place to be in that heat wave we were having. Linda wrote all the information about the records into a big notebook, but Patty and Janice were looking for tunes they could perform.

For years Bob Pajaczkowski had pretty much bought every polka record he ever saw, so there was lots of Chicago stuff, but he'd also bought about a million Eastern-style records. My sister had a prejudice against Eastern-style, so Janice hadn't heard too much of it before and she just loved some of those bands, and so, lickety-split, she's learned to sing about a dozen new polkas. And you know what? Linda and Patty Pajaczkowski got to be pretty good friends. None of us could quite believe it. But I think it changed something for Linda to see that Patty had parents like the rest of us—that she hadn't been, you know, just beamed down from some little violet-colored spaceship in the middle of a bad night. And so my sister's going through the cartons, writing everything down, and there's a polka blaring away, and Janice is singing along with it, and Patty's slapping out a drumbeat on an old tabletop, and one Saturday afternoon Bob Pajaczkowski comes down to see how we're doing, and somehow he can't manage to leave. "Hey, you kids want a beer?"

Well, sure, maybe we could choke down a beer or two. He comes back with a case of Iron City, and we're all listening to polkas. The next thing you know, there's Patty's mom. "You can't fight 'em, join 'em," she says, and Patty's mom and dad are dancing the polka around the basement, and we're clapping our hands and yelling, "Go, go, go." Then, eventually, Patty's mom invites us upstairs to dinner, and while we're eating, Patty says, "Hey, Dad, would you mind if we rehearsed down there?"

And he says, "Oh, hell no. I'd love it." So Bev comes in from Barnsville and crashes with Patty over on the Island, and we pry Mary Jo off her ass, and the band starts rehearsing in Bob Pajaczkowski's basement—because, you know, we're getting real close to St. Stans street-fair time.

I remember one night when Patty's mom and dad came down to listen to the band, and Patty says, "Hey, let's do 'The Mountaineer Polka' for my parents." Her grandpa had died just a few years ago, and he'd come from the mountains just like my Dziadzio Wojtkiewicz. She says, "Remember this one, Dad? You used to sing it to me when I was going to bed."

When Janice starts to sing, *"Hej, góral ja ci góral,"* Bob Pajaczkowski gets all misty-eyed. "I wish your Dziadzio was still around to hear you kids," he says to Patty. "You kids are really something special."

Being as stubborn as she was, Janice never let go of the idea of getting her brother and her father talking to each other again—you know, getting her family all reconciled—so she'd been on the horn to Columbus half a dozen times trying to convince John to come home for the street fair. Finally he agreed to do it, but he was going to bring his girlfriend, he said. Anna had always wanted to see that crazy place he came from, and it was probably about time she met his family anyhow because he and Anna had decided to get married.

But he wasn't going to come, he said, unless he and Anna could sleep in the same bed. If they didn't sleep in the same bed, it'd be sheer hypocrisy. "You know perfectly well that Mom and Dad would never let you sleep in the same bed," Janice said.

Well, they'd stay in a motel then. "You're not going to stay in any motel," she said. "They'd take that as a real insult. Don't be so childish. Why are you doing this? You guys have been living together for a year. It's not going to kill you to sleep in separate beds for a few nights."

Then her parents were saying they weren't sure they were up to having both John and this strange girl they'd never met before. "Yes, you are," Janice said. "You should be pleased he wants to bring her home. Make an effort." Janice said that sometimes she felt like she was the only grown-up in her family.

Things were a little better at home but not a whole hell of a lot. Her parents had gone back to sweeping it all under the rug—just soldiering on—and it was like nobody had ever said a word about World War II. But it was still hanging in the air all the damn time, and Janice felt this terrific strain whenever she walked into the house. Was she going to do the right thing, say the right thing? Was it all her fault in the first place? She said sometimes she felt like running away for real—instead of, you know, just that one night when all she'd been doing was being a brat. She said sometimes she wished she really *was* an ordinary American girl from an ordinary American family so she could be a brat without the world caving in on her.

I hadn't seen or talked to Mrs. Constance Bradshaw since the day of the Great Clean, but the week before the street fair she calls me at work just before quitting time. "Do you have a minute?" she says.

"I'm on my way out the door, honey."

"Can you call me back?"

"Well, not right away." I know she thought I was giving her the brush-off, but I wasn't. We'd had a good rain and it'd broke the heat wave and I was trying to get back into working out. Mondrowski was already standing there waiting for me. "I'm on my way to the Y," I said.

"Okay, so call me when you get finished."

Janice and I hadn't planned anything—we never planned anything—but I had a pretty good idea I was going to run into her later on. "I'm going home for dinner," I said, "and I really can't call you from there— How you feeling?"

I heard her sigh. "A lot better. I'm sorry about the last time you saw me. I was pretty much at my worst. When *can* you call me?"

"It might be kind of late."

"Oh, for Christ's sake. Okay, call me when you can."

"It might be after midnight—"

"Jim, I don't give a flying fuck what time it is. Just call me *tonight*, all right?"

What I should have done was tell Georgie to wait and let Vick go home and then had that conversation she wanted to have right when she wanted to have it. Because I spent the whole evening worrying about it.

Well, I didn't get around to calling her until I ended up at the PAC at about a quarter of one in the morning. She answered on the first ring, and I could tell instantly she was back to better living through chemistry. It wasn't the beige pills. With those suckers, she wouldn't have even been conscious at that hour. It sounded more like her old pal Gilby's gin, and a whole lot of it. She was slurring pretty bad, and her voice had this sad whiny sound to it, and she was going around in circles, saying the same things over and over.

Right off the top she's onto me about how sad it makes her that I don't trust her. Just like I'm supposed to, I ask her why she thinks I don't trust her. Because I won't tell her about my girlfriend—and I've obviously got one. "Connie," I say, "let's not get into that one, okay? That topic's not going to take us anywhere at all."

She wanted to tell me how much she appreciated all I'd done for her—she kept coming back to that one—and she especially wanted to tell me that because we were obviously at the end of the road. We were like two people who'd met at a crossroad one sad dark night, and we'd shared some precious time together, and now we were going off on our separate directions. She wished me well, and she wanted me to know that she appreciated all the help and support I'd given her, and she wanted to apologize for the last time I'd seen her. She'd been having one of her terrible anxiety attacks, but it passed. They always do. Just like everything else. Oh, yes, and she wanted to say that without me she might not even be around anymore, and she's well aware of that one too, but I wasn't to think that I was responsible for her. No, nobody's responsible for anybody. We're born alone and we die alone—that's the sad sorry truth about human life—and in that tragically brief time between those two infinite icy black states of nothingness we snatch at whatever little scraps of happiness we can get, and she wished me well, snatching at whatever little scraps I might have coming my way.

"Connie," I said, "I think maybe you better catch a few Z's. Things are kind of hectic around here right now. I'll call you in a week or so." Or maybe never, I thought.

The day of the street fair was perfect. Blue sky, big fat clouds, sunny but not too hot. The Wozniak boys over at Interstate had got them to loan us a flatbed truck to put the band on, and I rented the damn best sound system they had in Kaltenbach's—a real big mother with lots of watts. It cost a lot more than the girls thought it did, but I threw some of my own money in and didn't tell them. They were going to be out in the open air, you know, and I wanted them to have a good clean sound and volume that just wouldn't quit.

There's a huge amount of work goes into an event like that, and it's a fundraiser for the church, so almost everything's volunteer. Like the dads are bringing their barbecues and firing up the charcoal briquettes in plenty of time to start cooking the *kiełbasa* and *kiszka* and chicken, and the moms and old ladies have been making their *pierogi* and *gołąbki* all week, and the guys from the PAC are filling up those good old Raysburg Steel garbage cans with ice and beer. And you've got people setting up the over-and-under game and the roulette wheel and, in the parish hall, all the tables for bingo. And then there's things for sale—like sacred pictures, and peasant straw art that somebody imported from Poland, and pastries and embroidery the old ladies have made, and even some slightly used polka records you can pick up for fifty cents apiece.

Naturally everybody you know turns out, and you've also got lots of people coming down for it from outside the parish. You don't have to be Polish to enjoy drinking a beer and eating some *pierogi* and dancing a polka or two. Back in those days when St. Stans Parish was still going strong, we could put on a real good event, and you'd get just a huge number of people passing through before it was all over.

Well, Janice's brother did come home for the street fair, and he brought his girlfriend with him, and they slept in separate beds, and everybody went around not saying what they were thinking, but at least nobody had blown up at anybody yet. Janice stuck pretty close to home in case she was needed, you know, to pour a little oil on the old troubled waters. Then the day of the street fair she turns up at our house, and she's jumpy as fourteen cats.

Mary Jo had been pushing for them to have like a band uniform, and the girls thought that was okay, but then they'd had these endless arguments over it, and they never did agree on anything—which was typical of them. The only thing they ever agreed on was how to play a tune. And finally all they'd been able to come up with was that they should wear something white with something red. So maybe half an hour before they're supposed to start playing, Janice gets dropped off at our house, and she walks in the door and she doesn't say a word—not hi or anything. She looks at my sister. And Linda, being Linda, is wearing this real simple outfit—just a red-and-white blouse and white shorts and tennis shoes—and Janice says, "I knew I was going to look ridiculous."

She's wearing exactly what she'd had on the night they'd played at Franky Rzeszutko's—the white blouse with the red jumper and the red little-kid shoes. "What's wrong with that?" Linda says. "you look fine."

"It's too formal for the street fair," Janice says, "and besides, I look like I'm about twelve. And I'm *already* too hot."

She's carrying a couple bags with her. She goes zipping into Linda's bedroom and comes out in a red miniskirt. I think I told you she wore her skirts real short, didn't I? Linda's trying to be tactful. "Mary Jo will like that," she says.

"Yeah, but will anybody else?"

You see, a girl singer in a polka band is supposed to be cute, but she's not supposed to be sexy. She's supposed to look like a girl you might see kneeling next to you in Mass the next morning, so there's a fine line you don't want to cross over—and everybody knows that except for maybe Mary Jo.

I'm going, "Come on girls, we're running out of time."

"Jimmy," she says, "please don't bug me," and off she goes back into the bedroom.

Linda's whispering to me, "What on earth's the matter with her? She's being a real pill."

So Janice just kept trying on this or that, and she finally got it down to a white blouse and shorts with her red shoes and a red scarf. Then it was the scarf that was giving her the fits. She tried it on her head, you know, tied in the back, but she didn't like that because whenever she looked even slightly like a peasant, she got hell from her mother. "She's says it's an insult to real peasants. Does that make any sense to you? Where are the real peasants who are ever going to see me?"

Then she tried it tied around her neck, but she didn't like that one either. "I look like I'm in the Polish Girl Scouts."

Naturally I'd set the sound system up that morning, and I'd checked it out the best I could, but to get everything right I needed to do a sound check with the whole band, so I'm tapping my watch and going, "Hey, come on, kid. Get serious here." Janice just wads the scarf up and throws it across the room and grabs her clarinet case and walks out the door.

Linda and I exchange a look, and then we go running after her, and we get about half a block up the street, and Janice says, "The only red I've got is my shoes, and they look ridiculous with shorts."

"Oh, come on," I say. "The old ladies will love your red shoes."

Linda's doing her best. "Red shoes are big in Poland. There's even a polka called 'The Red Shoes.'"

"Yeah," Janice says, "but we don't play it."

Already the street's filling up with people, and of course we've got to run right into that rat pack of girls Janice hangs around with, and they kind of surround her, all of them talking at once, and I'm going, "Oh, for God's sake." Even before we left the house, we were late.

"Have you seen my family?" Janice is asking everybody, and nobody has.

Linda and I keep pushing her along until we get to the flatbed. The rest of the band's already set up and ready to go. Mary Jo's plunked down in a folding chair, talking to some other old ladies standing there at the side—Mrs. Lewicki and Mrs. Bognar and I don't know who all—and you'd think somebody as big as Mary Jo would know better than to wear a white blouse with red polka dots, wouldn't you?

Patty and Bev have got themselves flaming red T-shirts, and they're slurping back the coffee and bouncing around like a couple Ping-Pong balls and, you know, getting their adrenaline levels kicked right up into the ozone layer. Bev keeps yelling at everybody about what a beautiful day it is, and Patty yells back, "Yeah, it sure beats playing the tablas in the Black Hole of Calcutta."

Janice gets up on the flatbed, and she's still asking, "Hey, has anybody seen my family?" Everybody else is getting ready to play, and she's just standing there staring out over the crowd. She hasn't even got her clarinet out yet. "Come *on*, Janice," Linda hisses at her.

Father Obinski comes floating up to my side. "Is everything okay here, Jimmy?"

"Absolutely, Father, you bet." And I'm yelling, "Hey, sound check!"

Mary Jo squeezes out a few bars of "The Helena Polka," and she's coming through real strong and clear, and Patty and Bev go BANGA-BANGA-BANG, BONG BONG, and my sister blows that Marion Lush riff—do, mi, so, tada yata yata ya—and everything's just dandy. Janice opens up her clarinet case and takes out this folded-up piece of paper. I figured it was a set list or the words for some polka she hadn't memorized yet or something like that. I didn't think too much about it, to tell you the truth—but she just stands there staring up the street, slapping that piece of paper against her leg. "Hey, sing something," I yell at her. She just looks at me. I'm going, "Come on, kid, I gotta check your mike."

She walks up to the mike and goes, "Test, one, two, three, four," and Linda just glares at her. Janice puts that piece of paper back in her clarinet case and gets her clarinet out and puts it together, and meanwhile everybody else is waiting, you know, and fidgeting around. They were supposed to open up with "Zosia," but Janice says, "I don't feel like singing yet. Let's do Eddie Zima's."

My sister's usually a fairly patient person, but she just loses it. "Oh, for God's sake, Janice," she's screaming, "don't be such a prima donna!"

"I *said* I didn't want to sing yet."

Well, that screws up the order of songs they had worked out, and they're all looking at Mary Jo—like she's the oldest and wisest member of the band and she should fix everything. Mary Jo just shrugs. She could care less. "Sure we'll do Zima's," she says, and she steps up to the mike and makes the same dumb little speech she always makes, and then she counts off the tune. Linda's so mad she fluffs a few notes.

Nobody was planning on opening with that polka, and you could hear the band having to work to pull themselves together. But Janice was soaring along like she didn't have a care in the world, which was kind of surprising, you know, as weird and uptight as she was. I think with her clarinet playing she could always just put it on automatic pilot.

A few people started dancing, and a whole bunch of Central kids came up and planted themselves right in front of the flatbed—Janice's rat pack, naturally, but a whole lot of other kids too. That Italian kid Tony was one of them. He stands there with his dark eyes shining up at Janice—looking at her like she's the Blessed Virgin—and it's crazy, but all of a sudden I'm so jealous it's like somebody's turned an acetylene torch on me, and I'm thinking, whoa there, Koprowski, get a grip.

Lots of people are coming up to the flatbed—drawn to the music—and here comes Janice's younger brother, Mark, with his out-the-pike girlfriend. The band finishes off the tune, and Janice hunkers down to talk to Mark, and I drift over in case I should need to get my two cents in, and Janice is going, "Where on earth *are* they?"

Mark kind of shrugs. "They're just sitting out in the backyard drinking tea."

Janice just can't believe it. *"Drinking tea?"*

Meanwhile, Linda's hissing at her, "Janice, Janice!" because she wants to get their next tune going.

You can see that Mark's not real pleased to have to break the news. "Yeah, Jan," he says, "you know how they are. The lunch that goes on forever, and they decide to have some tea, and— Well, they're all just sitting out there, and Dad said it was so pretty in the backyard he didn't feel like moving. He said to tell you they'd come down later. You do play again later, don't you?"

"*Matko Boża!*" Janice says. I'd never heard her do that before. She *never* dropped Polish into her English like that, and it really startled me.

She stands up and she goes, "Oh, I am sooooooo mad!"

Linda's about having a bird. "Come *on*, Janice!" And Janice turns around and gives her *the look*. Then she marches over to the mike and she takes it out of the stand just like some rock singer on television. She doesn't give the band a hint what she's going to do. She walks over right to the edge of the flatbed so she's looking down at all her classmates from Central, and she just starts belting out a tune she learned off one of those records in Bob Pajaczkowski's basement—"*A nasza kompania tam w okopach stoi, tam w okopach stoi, tam w okopach stoi. I pisze do Cara że się go nie boi, że się go nie boi, hopaj siup!*"

Those words go back to the good old days when we were always making trouble for the Russians—like, "Our company stands there in the trenches and writes to the Czar that we're not afraid of him, hey, hey!" And, yeah, I'd got them a good clean sound system all right—and loud. They probably heard Janice all the way down in Millwood.

I don't think they'd rehearsed that polka more than a couple times, but what's the band going to do but come in with her? They hit the chorus, and BANG, they're all of them right there, and you know what? They've never sounded better. "Yeah!" Patty yells. And then everybody's singing the chorus—I mean everybody in the band and half the people on the street, because it's one of the great old polkas and everybody knows it—"*Hopaj siupaj hopaj siupaj hopaj siupaj, dana—*"

You talk about your right tune at the right time, hell—all of a sudden everybody's dancing the polka all up and down the street for two blocks, and Father Obinski gives me a big grin because all you've got to do is hear Janice's voice come belting through the PA system and you just know that everybody's going to have a real good time at the street fair.

The girls played a long set—over an hour—and everybody and their dog was saying to me, "Hey, what a great band."

They finished up, and immediately Janice was mobbed by those Central kids and they whisked her off somewhere. I mean she was a real celebrity, and naturally she'd go off with her friends—that's what high school kids do, right?—and I'm left standing there by the flatbed with my sister. Linda wants to hear over and over that she played okay and the band played okay and everything was okay. "What's with Janice?" she says, "God, she was a pain. You forget sometimes she's a teenager, and then all of a sudden she's just so awful."

"Yeah, but she's always great on stage."

"Oh, yeah. She's always great on stage." I could see that Linda had a lot more she wanted to say on the topic of Janice but she was restraining herself. "You want to go to Mass?" she said.

There was a five-thirty Mass, and for anybody who had a suspicion they might be feeling a little rocky the next morning and maybe would want to stay in bed, it was a good way to get their Mass obligation out of the way. Well, my Mass obligation was totally out of hand by then, so I said, "I think I'll pass on it."

We strolled around to see who was there—and everybody was there. I had a *kiełbasa* sandwich. With all that great food they had that day, I'd sort of eaten my way though the afternoon. And all of a sudden, here's Janice. She walked straight up to me and said, "Come to Mass with me."

"I just love the way she orders you around," Linda says.

"Sure," I say to Janice.

"Boy, have you ever got the magic touch," Linda says to Janice.

"Hey, girls, let's all of us just take a little break here," I say, and we start walking over to the church.

For somebody who'd just been playing all that happy music, Janice seemed kind of down—or kind of something, I wasn't sure what. "Are you okay?" I asked her.

"Oh, yeah. Sure."

"You guys sounded great."

"Yeah, I thought we did okay."

We got into the church, and everybody else seemed to have the same idea. Naturally there was all the old ladies because most of them will—you know, like automatic—go to every Mass there is. And then a lot of that crowd from the street fair must have decided on the spur of the moment, so the church was really packed for a Mass at that time of day. My aunts and uncles were there, and Mom and Dad, and I saw Mondrowski come ducking into a pew at the back. And then, lo and behold, here comes the whole rest of the polka band following us. I never in a million years would have thought I'd see Patty Pajaczkowski at Mass, and she probably thought the same thing about me—and we exchanged these looks, like, hey, man, can you believe this?

It was peaceful in there, and it was nice to get out of the sun. Janice wasn't paying any attention to anybody. As soon as we got into a pew, she knelt down, and clasped her hands, and pressed her forehead into them. I mean she's praying, right? And I'm just watching her breath go in and out and looking at the nape of her neck—how beautiful it is, you know, with the tendons and all the little blond hairs. That's how far gone I am by then—that I think the nape of her neck is beautiful.

You get no homily with your five-thirty Mass, so it's a pretty quick service, and Janice and I have this funny moment when we're leaving. Like she's already looking through the doors, maybe to see if her family's out there somewhere, and I'm looking at her face, and our hands hit the holy water at the same time and, you know, collide. It's kind of startling, and there's this little pause, and we cross ourselves at exactly the same time, and then we both laugh. "Let's do it again to music," she says, and we step out into the last of that hot sunshine—early evening in August—and wouldn't you know it, there's her whole family waiting for her outside the church.

The first thing that hit me was— Well, I hadn't seen Janice's dad for a while, and you know how people can age overnight? All that heavy stuff that'd been going down over the summer must have really got to him, because he was looking kind of chewed—tired and gray, with the big bags under the eyes and all the lines in his face just dug in there. He seemed real glad to see me, pumping my hand and asking me how I've been.

He was glad to see Linda too, his best student in Advanced Polish—well, his only student—and they had to exchange a few good words in Polish, but then he switched back to English right away on account of John's girlfriend, Anna. Naturally Linda and I got introduced to her, and Maureen and Sandy and some other of Janice's pals got introduced to her, and she couldn't possibly remember who's who, but she was trying her best, just smiling her face off, poor kid—working real hard to show John's parents that she was great daughter-in-law material. A dark, pretty girl, wearing sandals and one of those long skirts imported from India. Got her hair in Indian braids, and I thought that was kind of funny, you know, because it sure wasn't going to be earning her too many Brownie points with Mrs. Dłuwiecki.

While we were at Mass, the streets had really filled up—practically wall to wall—and that's the way it was going to be for the next few hours, and you could see a lot of those people were getting itchy to dance the polka. I checked my watch and said to Janice, "We better get started." She just nodded at me. The minute she'd laid eyes on her family, she'd got silent as a stone.

We finally made it back to the flatbed, and Janice's parents and her broth-

ers and their girlfriends lined themselves up right in front of it like they were
going to be listening to a concert. Janice gave me this real long look, and I didn't
have a clue what she was thinking. I was waiting for her to say something, but
she just climbed up onto the truck.

I checked the sound system, and the girls were doing their little good-luck
things they always did before they played. Patty's banging away on all her toys,
and Bev's checking her volume, and my sister's going buzz buzz, and Mary Jo's
the only one who never does anything, maybe because she's always been ready
to play for the last forty years. Janice usually blows like this whole bunch of
notes—zippity zip up and down a scale. But she doesn't do that. She takes that
piece of paper out of her clarinet case.

Meanwhile Czesław's saying to me, "Don't be a stranger, Jimmy," and
telling me how he's missed our little talks and I'm going to have to come up and
visit him one of these days. And it dawns on me that he isn't just being polite—
he really does like me—and it wouldn't have hurt me to go up and see him over
the summer. Yeah, he'd been dealing with some heavy shit, the old soldier, and
my heart, you know, kind of went out to him.

People can see that the band's about to play, so there's a kind of pileup in
front of the flatbed. You look up the street and you see this absolute mob of
people. Mary Jo steps up to the mike and her big voice comes booming out
through that high-power system. "Is everybody having a good time?" Some
cheers and whistles and like that, telling her they're having a good time.

"This is My Sister's Polka Band," she says. She didn't like their name much,
but she was doing her best with it. "Everybody up here is *somebody's* sister,
right? And yeah, folks, it's polka time again, and we're going to kick things off
for you with the good old 'Clarinet Polka.'" And she steps back from the mike,
big smile on her face, and Janice whispers something in her ear. She looks surprised. She goes back to the mike and says, "But first Janice wants to say a few
words."

Janice is taller than Mary Jo, so she adjusts the mike, raises it up to her level.
And then she says in Polish, "Ladies and gentlemen—" Well, in Polish it's
"Szanowni państwo," and that's like "Honorable ladies and gentlemen." And
she says in Polish, "I know everyone wants to dance, and I won't take too much
time, but I have a few things I want to say."

Speaking Polish, she's talking to only a fraction of that crowd. She's talking
to the old folks, and to a lot of people my parents' generation, but she's not talking to anybody younger than that. Of the people my generation, there's proba-

bly only me and Linda and Shirley Zembrzuski that can understand her. And of course her parents and her brothers can understand her.

Well, it's really startling to have a kid with pigtails talking Polish at you. People who don't know her are whispering, "Who *is* that little girl? Why's she speaking Polish? Is she from Poland?" And other people are whispering back, "That's Czesław Dłuwiecki's daughter." They're so amazed she can speak Polish at all that they aren't paying much attention to what she's saying. So she's got to do her "honorable ladies and gentlemen" a couple times before she's starting to get everybody's attention. It's pretty clear she's not going to go on until people are listening to her. I told you she's stubborn, didn't I?

Just like everybody else, she really took me by surprise, and I'm scared for her—like I don't have a clue what she's doing, but whatever it is, I just hope she doesn't blow it—so I walk right to the edge of the flatbed, like giving her moral support. From where I'm standing I can see her legs shaking.

She glances down at her piece of paper, but she doesn't really need it. She's got what she wants to say in her head.

She says that when Polish people came to America, they brought their traditions with them just like they brought their faith, and they didn't lose either one of them. And some of the most important things to Polish people are their songs and music and dances, but in a new country those things were bound to change, and they did change. They became part Polish and part American, and that was wonderful because that way they got the best of both the old world and the new world.

"So we're going to play some of that Polish-American music for you," she says, "and we're really proud of it, and we hope we play it right, and we hope you enjoy yourselves."

I'm watching Janice, but I've also got my eye on her father to see how he's taking it. He was just as surprised as anybody else, but now he's paying real close attention, sort of nodding, like, well, yeah, I guess that makes sense. Or maybe he's just thinking, good going, kid, you haven't made any mistakes in your grammar yet.

And then Janice stops talking. She looks out over those hundreds of people. And it gradually gets real quiet. The people who have been chatting or whispering just shut up—I guess because they're afraid she's forgot her next line. There's this tension building up—like, come on, little girl, you can do it.

She starts to talk again, and you can hear this little quiver in her voice. That really shuts people up. "It was really hard back in the old country," she says.

She's keeping her Polish real simple. "And it was really hard in the new one too. It took a lot of sacrifices to start a new life, and to build this beautiful church here, and to carry on our traditions, and to hand them down to a new generation. It took many many people making sacrifices so we could have this music to play here today. It took—" and her voice breaks. She looks up to the sky, like, oh, please, don't let me cry.

It's so quiet you can hear the locusts in the trees. "It took many many people making sacrifices so we could even be *alive* here today to play this beautiful music. And I just want to say—to all of you—thank you."

There's this kind of sigh moves over the crowd. The old people have been following Janice pretty close, and now I see my grandma and Shirley Zembrzuski's grandma and Mrs. Bognar and some of the other old ladies are all dabbing at their eyes. Then Janice says in this firm, clear voice, *"Jeszcze Polska nie zginęła póki my żyjemy."*

You don't have to think about it. If you speak Polish, you just react to that. So there's this huge yell goes up, and everybody who doesn't speak Polish is going, "What's that? What'd she say?"

Janice's father looks like he's been hurt. He kind of caves in on himself and presses his hand against his chest.

What she said means in English, "Poland is not lost for as long as we are alive." If you're looking out at a street full of Polish Americans when you say that, you're bound to get to them—anyhow to the ones who can understand you. And a lot of them can understand you because it also just happens to be the first two lines of the Polish national anthem.

Janice yells, *"Raz Dwa!"*—counting in the band, and she steps back from the mike and puts her clarinet in her mouth, and they kick into "The Clarinet Polka," and all of a sudden for two whole blocks people are dancing. Oh, boy, does that music sound good.

Janice's brothers are both kind of stunned, and then they look at their girlfriends, like, hey, let's do it, and off they go, dancing. Janice's father is just standing there. He's hunched forward and he's just looking down at his feet. His wife is standing next to him, looking real worried.

I couldn't imagine what he could be doing just standing there looking down like that. Then he raises his head. And he looks around. And all around him are all these people dancing.

He looks at his wife, and he's like somebody who's just woke up from a long sleep. And he smiles. And he bows to his wife, and she does a little curtsy for him, and he opens his arms for her, and she steps into his arms, and it's just too much, you know what I mean? Czesław Dłuwiecki is dancing the polka. He's got that smooth, old, gracious European style, but he's stepping right along. He's dancing all the way down to the end of 46th Street, and he makes a big loop through all those crazy Polaks and he comes dancing back again with his wife in his arms, and he spins her around and around. I never saw anybody dance such a beautiful polka.

NINETEEN

All of a sudden it's September and whoosh, it's like somebody let the air out of the balloon. Summer's over and everything's getting back to normal.

The street fair was over so the band wasn't having those frantic rehearsals damn near every day, and I wasn't seeing Connie anymore so I didn't have to worry about her not killing herself. And Georgie Mondrowski got himself a full-time job with the city. Truck comes roaring up, slams to a stop by your place, the guy who jumps off and grabs your garbage can is him. He said he liked getting up early and all the exercise, but he was just bagged by the end of his shift, so I lost my training partner and I just couldn't motivate my ass into the Y on my own.

Janice was back in school, and I was only seeing her a couple days a week. The band was rehearsing on Tuesday nights again, and I was picking her up from Central, and I'd usually watch the rehearsal, and then I'd drive her home just like last year. I couldn't take her out on Friday nights because that's called a date, but most Saturdays we'd run into each other, you know, accidentally. And then on Saturday nights maybe she and Linda and I would go do something, but I wasn't sure how much longer we could go on running that one—because if people keep seeing you hanging around with a sixteen-year-old, naturally they're going to think you're going out together, but if they keep seeing you hanging around with a sixteen-year-old *and your little sister*, they're going to think you're just plain weird. I don't think we were fooling anybody anyway.

I'd been doing pretty good—I kept telling myself that. From Easter right on through the summer it'd been like I had my life under control, and I'd bitched and moaned to Mondrowski about how I hadn't had two seconds to myself, but at least I'd never got bored. Then comes September and it's boredom city. Well, it's amazing how fast you can slip back into the sauce—like there's no slack and you're just *there*—and I was drinking as hard as I ever had in my life.

On Tuesday nights I'm stopping in again at the Dłuwieckis' to have a couple shots of creosote with Czesław, and you would've thought he'd never had a harsh word to say about polka music. "You know, Jimmy," he says, "many serious musicians play popular dance music on the side."

"Oh, is that right?" I say.

"Yes, it's quite common," he says. "It's good practice for them, and they can make some extra money that way too. Sometimes very good money. Why, you'd be surprised at the number of musicians in symphony orchestras who financed their higher education by playing in dance bands."

Then at one point when Janice is off in the kitchen talking to her mom, he leans over to me—giving me the straight scoop man to man—and he says, "You know, Jimmy, girls can be a problem in their teen years. So it's a good thing if they have serious outside interests—like music. It keeps them out of harm's way."

"Oh, right," I say. "My mom's always said that."

Yeah, Czesław was pretty much back to his old self. He'd lost that chewed look he'd had in the summer, and he was all full of piss and vinegar again, smoking his pipe and holding forth like he was king of the world. He was doing what Polish people are real good at—getting on with life. It's something we've had lots of practice at.

He didn't know that I knew about all the heavy shit that had been going down, so he didn't talk to me about it, but naturally Janice did, and she said it was like a big wind had blown through the house and cleaned out the gloom. She never would take much credit for turning things around, but it was kind of obvious to me that the speech she'd made at the street fair had hit her dad pretty hard.

Then, for their next act, Czesław and John had got themselves reconciled. You see, John had been stewing over what he could say to Czesław to fix things up, and he came up with something, and he tried it out on Janice, and she said, "Yeah, that's it—that's perfect." So the day after the street fair, he laid it on the old man. "You know, Dad, if the Germans had won the war, they would have taken this half-Polish kid and raised him as a German. But you won the war, and you really got even with them. You took this half-German kid and raised him as a Pole."

Czesław laughed and laughed. And then they sat out in the back yard alone together and talked for a couple hours, and after that you never would have guessed they'd ever had a problem with each other. Of course John still had a problem or two, but he was keeping that to himself.

So Mark went off to New Haven, and Czesław could brag that he had a kid at Yale, and John decided he was going to get himself a Ph.D., after all, and that was pretty good bragging material too, and both Czesław and Marysia had decided they liked John's girlfriend—she was sweet and pretty and sensible and *Catholic*—and they took a little trip to Toledo to meet Anna's folks, and the two families hit it off, and so there was this nice big wedding in the spring to look forward to.

And guess what? Janice was back to normal too. For a while there it'd looked to her folks like she might be turning into a weird hippie brat who was going to defy them on a regular basis and have to be dragged home from dens of iniquity by an old friend of the family, but no, she's a good kid after all—playing in a polka band to make some extra money while she gets on with her serious music and stays out of harm's way.

A lot of Saturday nights, Linda would dial out, and so Janice and I would go somewhere and talk. Those heavy topics like World War II and the Nazis and what it means to be Polish did arise from time to time, but generally speaking, the name of the game was getting back to normal, and when things are back to normal, what people usually talk about is just, you know, their lives. So I get to hear all about who's going out with who in the eleventh grade at Raysburg Central Catholic. And what she's got for homework. And how the band's doing, and Mr. Webb telling her he doesn't care how much of a virtuoso she's turned into, she'll never make first chair until she learns to read music. And all about clarinet reeds—and that's a lot more complicated topic than you'd think and I'm not going to bore you with it.

And one of the great burning issues of Western civilization is the length of Janice's skirts. You see, Janice and the girls in the rat pack, their main object in life was to wear their skirts as short as humanly possible. And the nuns wanted to see their girls looking like nice, modest, decent Catholic girls, which is why they've put them in a uniform in the first place. So the girls are saying, "Oh, Sister, I'm sorry. I didn't realize—I guess I must have *grown* over the summer!"

Well, if you're sixteen, you don't grow over the summer, and even Sister Mary Rose of the Immaculate Conception has got to know that. So the girls have to go in the office and kneel down, and their skirts have to touch the backs of their legs. Before they take that little test, they pull their skirts down till they're practically falling off them, and then when they're still too short, they move into the good old delaying tactic—"Oh, I'm so sorry, Sister, my mom hasn't got around to it yet"—so they can go one more day showing off their underwear to all the horny young studs at Central. *I* even thought Janice's skirts were too short, but who gave me the right to have an opinion?

Of course I got to talk about my normal life too—mainly bitching about working for Vick Dobranski. And Janice goes, "Why don't you look for another job?" Good question, right? I can see that now, but at the time all it did was piss me off. And sometimes she'd tear out the ads in the paper for electronics technicians and things like that and she'd give them to me. And I'm thinking, okay, Koprowski, this is truly wonderful. Now you've got a sixteen-year-old in pigtails trying to run your life for you.

Oh, there's something I almost forgot to tell you—and I've got to admit I really did want to forget it just about damn near quick as it happened. Back in August, John and Anna had stuck around in Raysburg for a few days after the street fair, and one night they took Linda and me and Janice out to Tomerelli's for dinner. It was nice. And we drove up to the park afterward just to enjoy the evening. We're just strolling around, and John's a sometimes smoker, and he says, "Can I bum one of those?"

So I give him a smoke, and I fire up one for myself, and the girls are walking on ahead of us, and John says kind of under his breath, "You know, Jimmy, my sister's deceptive."

I'm going, whoops, here it comes. "Oh, yeah?" I say. "How's that?"

"Well, she's always been a serious girl. Maybe too serious for her own good. And sometimes she can seem—well, really mature for her age. But she's still very young—and still very vulnerable."

I'd never thought of Janice as particularly vulnerable. I'd always thought of her as one tough little cookie. But hell, what did I know? "I'd hate to see her get hurt," he says.

For about half a second there I saw him in a Nazi uniform. I mean, he really did have those looks—the ice blond hair and the eyes so blue they kind of snap—but then I thought, come on, Koprowski, give the guy a break.

He's going on about one thing or another, still approaching things sideways, talking about what he calls "the counterculture," and saying how the winds of change are blowing through the land as any fool can plainly see, and he'd be the last person in the world to want to put limits on somebody else's personal choices, especially in terms of their lifestyle—and he just keeps laying these good words on me right, left, and center. It was kind of obvious what he was getting at, and I didn't see any reason to keep pussyfooting around it. "Don't worry, John," I said. "We're just friends."

"Oh?" he said. "That's not what she thinks."

Okay, so what was stopping me from saying to Janice, or her saying to me, "What are we going to do about this bind we're in?" Nothing that I could see—except maybe sheer terror. That day on the top of the hill at the end of Pike Street, we'd gone sidling up to the topic, but then we'd both jumped back from it like pulling your hand away from a hot stove. But it was getting real clear we couldn't run from it too much longer.

Janice was pretty much the only thing I gave a damn about. I admired and respected her too much ever to lay a hand on her, but when I was with her, I'd look at her sometimes and I'd get this—well, you know, your basic horrible ache, and I'd think, oh, God, it's all so hopeless. Then pretty soon the only sobriety I had left was when I was with her. I won't say I didn't drink at all around Janice, but it was important to me that she'd never see me drunk, and her parents would never see me drunk, and they never did. Everybody else did.

I'd been building up a little bank account, but now it was getting eroded for the simple fact that I was having a hard time getting my ass into work. One day I stagger into the shop around noon, thinking, hell, I've got to make a few bucks for a change, and Vick says, "Koprowski, what the hell do you think you're doing? Don't come in here drunk."

So I go staggering back out again, half pissed off and half relieved because I hadn't felt much like working anyway. And it couldn't have been more than a few days later, I went home for dinner, and Old Bullet Head was where he always was—kicked back in the living room with his nose in the paper—and we had us like an eight-word conversation. Any idiot could see the state I was in, and of course he'd been talking to Vick so he was all prepared for me.

He puts down his paper, walks over to me, grabs me by the hand, and yanks me to my feet. Then he says to me in this absolutely dead quiet voice, "Never, never, never walk into this house drunk. You got that?"

What could I say? "Yeah, sure, sorry," is what I said.

Then he grabs me by the arm and waltzes me down the hall and shoves me right out the front door. "You ever want any help, Jimmy," he says, "all you got to do is ask for it," and he closes the door in my face.

I was getting to the point where I had to have a good stiff jolt first thing in the morning just so I could get my ass out of bed. And I was drifting into that binge drinking where you lose a couple days at a time and you can't quite recall where they went. It was getting so bad I even admitted to Janice I was worried about it—although I didn't tell her it was anywhere near as bad as it was. She goes, "Why don't you get some help?"

That's one of those things people say that you don't know whether to laugh or cry because you know perfectly well there isn't any help. "Yeah? Where?" I say.

"I don't know. How on earth would I know? Talk to Father Obinski."

Of course I thought that was totally ridiculous—although I didn't tell her that because I didn't want to hurt her feelings. But looking back on it, I'd have to say she was right. Any parish priest worth his salt can at least aim you in the right direction. But that was way too simple for me. The last thing in the world I would have done at that time in my life was go to a priest with my problems.

So I went drifting on into the fall trying to convince myself that things weren't really as bad as I knew perfectly well they were, and I was getting through life the same way I'd got through the service, but when you're in the service, you can always blame it on being in the service. You can say, okay, once I get out, things are going to be different. But you know what? Now I didn't have anything to get out of.

Well, if you're a junior in high school and you're pretty, boys are going to start asking you out. They had a big school dance sometime that fall, and Janice told me she wasn't going to it. "Why not?" I said.

"Oh, I don't feel like it."

Then when the dance was only a few days away, she started having regrets. All her friends were going. She felt left out. "You could still go," I said. Well, no she couldn't. A boy had asked her and she'd turned him down. She'd told him she had to do something with her family—one of those things that's booked months in advance, you know—and in the meantime he'd asked somebody else, and she couldn't just turn up at the dance by herself.

"What's the matter with the boy?" I said. "He got two heads?"

"Oh, no. He's nice enough. You probably met him. Remember Tony? He was at my birthday party. He's got kind of a thing for me."

"Yeah? Why didn't you want to go with him?"

"I don't know. I just didn't feel right about it."

I looked her in the eyes, and she looked back at me with that honest look she's got, and I'm thinking, oh, you poor kid, boy, am I ever screwing up your life for you. So I said—I mean, it just popped out—"Look, you can't just sit at home feeling bad. I'll take you somewhere."

And she goes, "Oh, would you? That'd be really nice," lighting up like a Christmas tree. Yeah, me and my big mouth. Because I'd meant that maybe we'd do what we usually did—go sit on a hill somewhere, or drive around, or go to a movie with Linda—but that's not how she took it. Damn fool that I was, I'd just asked her out on a date.

"I'll get Sandy and Eddie to drop me off," she says. Sandy Czaplicki had started going out with Larry Dombrowczyk's little brother Eddie. "Is that okay with you? I always wanted to see where you live so I can imagine you there."

Well, sure, kid, anything you say, although we're obviously going to be putting one over on your parents, which neither of us wants to mention.

So where the hell was I going to take her? I searched my mind, and all I could come up with was this Japanese restaurant out in Bethel Grove. It'd just opened up in the past year, and it was the first one in the valley and still, you know, kind of exotic. The waitresses dressed up in Japanese outfits, and they had these little booths where the doors slide shut, and I couldn't think of anyplace any more private than that, so I called up and made a reservation.

That Saturday I spent the whole day cleaning my trailer. It was *Better Homes and Gardens* by the time I got done, and you would've thought *I* was in high school—that's how nervous I was—and right on time Sandy Czaplicki's dad's Chevy pulls up with Eddie Dombrowczyk driving it because he's the boy, right? And Janice gets out of the backseat. She waves at them, and Eddie beeps the horn, and off they go. "They'll pick me up here at a quarter of twelve," Janice says. "So I can be home by midnight. Is that all right?"

"Sure. No problem." I take one look at her and my heart sinks because she's dressed up like she's going to the school dance, and I know that's what she's told her parents. I usher her into my trailer. She'd said she'd always wanted to see it so she could imagine me in there, and I was just hoping she wasn't imagining me drooling all over myself dead drunk passed out in front of the TV at four in the morning.

She goes, "Oh, it's like a little self-contained world."

"Yep. Right. A little self-contained world. That's what trailers are like."

There's only one chair in the whole damn place, and she perches right on the edge of it, and, hell, she's just as nervous as I am. That night she was—well, there's nothing else to say except spectacular. If I'd been a junior at Central, I would've dropped dead at her feet. A blue dress, that real intense color I guess you call electric blue, and her hair down. She had a silver butterfly holding it back. And I wondered how she'd got by her dad wearing that much makeup. She even had perfume on. It smelled kind of silvery, if that makes any sense. Not being a total fool, I'd put on a suit and tie.

"Show me where everything is," she said, so I had to show her my little TV and the stereo and the mini-fridge and the little cupboard where I kept my soup. "I love it," she said. "It's like a dollhouse."

I gave her a Coke, and she was just chattering in that lickety-split kind of harebrained way girls do when they're nervous, which she hardly ever did with me. And for some reason she started talking about her mother. It wasn't anything I hadn't heard before—how when her mother turned fourteen she got to go into Warsaw with her dad, and sometimes her cousin Krystyna got to go too. "Her parents were just the opposite of my parents," Janice said. "It was her *dad* who let her wear makeup," and she's telling me how all these years later her mom remembers every little detail of the Hotel Europejski, and every little detail of the clothes she wore, and even the color of the lipstick she wore, and how all the men flirted with her—grown men, friends of her father's. "And it was all perfectly innocent," she said. "I guess that's what girls did in Poland before the war. I guess it's how they grew up. It must have been a totally different world— but she told me she never really kissed a boy until she kissed my father."

I guess she must not have been planning to say that—one of those things that just pops out—and she turned bright pink. That's a problem you've got if you're as fair as Janice—every little blush shows—and being, you know, this wise older man, I should've found something to say to make her feel better, right? But my mouth had gone dry as a desert, and I swear I felt like I wasn't a day older than she was.

She jumps up and starts walking around, pretending to look at everything again. "Don't you get lonely?" she says. "I'd get lonely."

"No, I don't get lonely. I like being able to come in here and, you know, shut the world out."

"If I lived here, I'd put up pictures," she says. "You don't have a single pic-ture. I wish you could see my room. Oh, I'd like you to see it—so you could imagine me there. But they'd never let you. Boys don't ever go into a girl's bed-room, and that's just one of those rules you can't even question, but— Oh, I've got pictures everywhere. All over the place. Every inch."

"What kind of pictures?"

"Well, there's sacred pictures, just exactly what you'd expect, and there's things out of magazines. Anything I like, I tape it up. Clothes I like. Boys I think are cute. I've got a poster of Donovan. And a poster of Alice in Wonderland standing in front of the caterpillar."

"What else you got?"

"All my dolls from when I was little."

"I never figured you for a girl who played with dolls."

"Oh, really? Well, I did. I played with dolls a lot."

I know she wasn't thinking anything at all about it, but she'd sat down on the edge of my bed and the skirt on that electric blue dress was just as short as any of her other skirts—and those long long legs, you know, with those silvery stockings—and all of a sudden I'm checking my watch, going, "Hey, we've got reservations. We've got to get rolling here."

So we go shooting out the pike, and the minute I'm behind the wheel, I start to feel reasonably okay again. We get out to the Japanese restaurant, and I'm just praying that there's not forty-seven Polaks in there, and we're in luck, we don't know a soul. The waitress—in her little geisha outfit—shows us to our booth. You know these places, right? You've got to sit down on the edge and take your shoes off, and then inside there's a hole in the floor where you put your feet. Janice had never seen anything like it. "Wow, is this ever neat."

I didn't want to fool around with the menu, so I told our geisha just to bring us the full spread. She slides the doors shut and closes us in there, and Janice goes, "Oh, Jimmy, this is magical. Thanks for bringing me here. This is perfect."

Yeah, I guess it was perfect—private but not *too* private, you know what I mean? And we got relaxed with each other again, just the way we usually were, talking about one thing or another, and she says, "Let me get this out of the way before I forget it."

She was carrying a purse—this delicate little thing with a chain—and she opens it up and tells me how she went to see Father Obinski and they had them-selves a little talk about alcoholism.

Instantly I'm so mad I'm practically seeing shooting stars, but I'm trying to keep it to myself because I don't want to hurt her feelings. "So what the hell did you say to him? You've got a friend who drinks too much?"

"Sure. That's exactly what I said." And Father Obinski told her that alcoholism's a disease and your body gets dependent on the chemical so willpower doesn't really have much to do with it, and most people find it real hard to quit on their own. And the only way most people could stop was through AA, and it was an excellent organization and there was nothing in AA that was incompatible with the Catholic faith. In fact some people in AA ended up being even better Catholics. And she hands me this brochure she's been carrying around in her purse. It's a list of every AA meeting in the Ohio Valley.

I took the damn thing, and I just couldn't believe it. Alcoholics Anonymous? That's for the real losers—the guys you see slurping soup down at the Sally Ann or the assholes the cops sweep up off the street with dustpans. Was that where she thought I was headed?

"What's the matter?" she said. "You aren't mad at me, are you? You *asked me*. Did you think I wouldn't take it seriously? I was just trying to help you the way you've always helped me."

"No, no, I'm not mad at you. It's just kind of— Well, it's one of those things that, you know, throws you for a nine-yard loss." I took that brochure and I put it in my pocket. I was starting to calm down, and I had to admit it was sweet of her to go to all that trouble—even if it was, you know, like wasted effort. But it was a nice thing to do. Well, she was a nice girl.

We both went jumping away from that topic pretty quick, but I'd ordered *sake*, and I sat there wondering if I should drink it. What the hell, I thought, it's not any stronger than wine. And the Japanese food started coming—you know, in these little bowls and trays they use. It's kind of touching to take somebody to a Japanese restaurant for the first time in her life and see how she finds it all so amazing.

I don't remember what else we talked about, but we'd been there about an hour and she said right out of the blue, "Oh, I wish I could talk to you in Polish."

"Go ahead," I said. "If you don't go too fast, I'll follow most of what you say."

So she started speaking Polish to me. The English language and the Polish language were so different, she said, that the whole world seems different depending on which one you're speaking, and sometimes she felt like there were two of her—the English Janice and the Polish Janice—and the Polish Janice was the person she really was, down deep in her heart. The Polish Janice was that little kid with the dream of Poland just down the river—that little kid going to sleep at night, drifting off when the sound she heard in her mind was Polish. For years when she was alone, she thought in Polish, she daydreamed in Polish. But now it was getting smaller and smaller—that Polish world inside her—and she caught herself most of the time now thinking in English, and she was afraid that Polish world inside her would get totally snuffed out by English. She was afraid that what her brother had told her was true, that in ten years they wouldn't speak a word of Polish anymore. And then she would have lost something very precious. And it felt like her very heart.

She said she was trying to fight back. She read the Polish newspaper from Chicago now, and she was trying to read books in Polish, and she'd started keeping a diary in Polish. She wrote down in Polish everything her parents told her about the war. And she wished that I spoke Polish, because if she spoke to me in Polish, I would be seeing the real true heart of her. And if she'd tried to say any of that in English, she couldn't have got out more than a sentence or two before she died of embarrassment.

It was damn near one of the most touching things I'd ever heard in my life, and God knows how, but I managed to croak out some Polish back at her. I told her that I'd understood pretty much everything she'd said, and I thanked her for telling me all that.

Well, we sat there in our little booth with the doors shut as long as we could. I had everything timed down practically to the last second because I didn't want to be alone with her back at my place any longer than I had to be. So I drove back in town, and Sandy and Eddie pulled in just a couple minutes behind us, and we got out of my car, and I walked her over to their car, and we just looked at each other, and she said, "Oh, thank you so much. Everything was so wonderful. I'll see you on Tuesday," and she got into their car and they drove away. I stood there outside my trailer for the longest damn time.

In some crazy way I'd never been happier in my life, but still I felt like— You know the feeling you get sometimes that something terrible is going to happen? I knew what we'd done was wrong. I mean, I'd just taken her out on a date. The only thing missing was the good-night kiss. And we'd been putting one over on her parents—on her dad who thought of me as a friend of the family. The thing that really got to me was that Czesław trusted me—he'd always trusted me, the damn fool—and I felt like a real piece of shit.

A few days later I'm coming home for dinner, right? And you know how some-times you can feel there's something wrong the minute you walk in the door? Old Bullet Head's reading the paper, and he doesn't even look up to see if I'm sober enough to let in the house. But I am sober—well, reasonably sober any-ways—and I keep on going out into the kitchen, and Mom and Linda are deep in conversation. They whip around and stare at me. Mom's in one of her pressure-cooker moods—steam coming out her ears—and she hisses at me, "Jimmy Koprowski, I need to talk to you." I look at Linda, and she casts her eyes up to the heavens like, sorry, Jimmy, I can't help you on this one.

"I don't want your father to hear this," my mom says, and she shoves me out the back door and pulls it shut behind her, and there we are standing on our back porch looking out across the alley at the back of the Lewickis' house. "What the hell do you think you're doing with that little Dłuwiecki girl?" she says.

My heart kind of misses a beat, and I go, "Aw, come on, Mom. What do you mean? I'm not doing a damn thing with her."

"Don't give me that crap, Jimmy. I wasn't born yesterday."

"Who you been talking to?"

"It doesn't matter who I been talking to."

"Sure it does. We always got the right to know who's accusing us. I think that's in the Constitution somewhere." I'm trying to get a laugh out of her, but fat chance of that.

The doctor hadn't scared my mother into quitting smoking yet, so she's pawing around for her cigarettes, which is ridiculous because when she's cook-ing, they always end up on a shelf by the stove. I take out my pack and offer her one, and then we both just stand there blowing smoke at each other. "Betty Czaplicki," my mother says.

Well, that figures, right? Sandy's mom. And there's not a Polish girl from here to Crakow can keep her mouth shut longer than about four and a half sec-onds. "What'd she say?"

Instead of answering me, my mother just launches in. "You think you got troubles now, buster, try a wife and a kid. Hell, Jimmy, you can barely wipe your own ass. How far you think what Vick Dobranski's paying you is going to go to supporting three people? And you think you're going to get any help from her family? You think they're going to thank you for her dropping out of high school? I know they've got plans for that girl—college and all—so how you think they're going to take it? And she'll be bitter and resentful, so how good a mother's she going to be? Not even out of high school. All her friends still in high school. Married to a part-time TV repairman who spends half his life in the PAC—"

I'm going, "Hey, Mom, slow down. Wait a minute here. There's nothing happening with me and Janice."

She doesn't even take a breath. "Holy Mother of God, Jimmy, where's your brains? You've always been crazy, but I at least thought you had good sense. And that poor little girl— Religious girls, God help them. They just don't know what hits them. What they got between their legs might as well be a flowerpot for all they know about it—"

"Mom! Hold on a minute. Give me a break here—"

But she's not going to give me a break here. I've just got to stand there listening to her until she runs out of steam. "Come on, *Mamusiu*," I say.

"Don't give me that *Mamusiu* crap, you jerk." She's softening up just a touch, I can tell. After all, she is my mom.

"Give me a chance," I say. "Just listen to me a minute, okay? She's like a little sister. I never laid a hand on her. You can go get the Bible and I'll swear on it. You can ask Linda."

I was hoping she could ask Linda. I didn't have a clue what Linda was thinking on the topic these days.

"So I took her out to dinner," I say. "Big deal." I was hoping that's all Sandy had told her mom.

"You've been doing more than that."

"Yeah? What have I been doing? You want to tell me? Come on, *Mamusiu*, tell me what people are saying."

She just makes a face at me. "Mrs. Dłuwiecki's not active in the church," she says, "but she does go to Mass. How long you think it's going to be before somebody says something to her?"

I didn't have a good answer to that one. "Tell me what people are saying," I asked her again.

"It doesn't matter a damn what people are saying, it's plain as the nose on your face. All you have to do is look at the two of you— You kids are so in love with each other it's like something out of a movie."

That one really got to me, and I guess she could see it. "Aw, hell, Jimmy," she says.

"Mom, I swear on everything holy, I never touched her."

We stand there looking at each other for a while, and then she says, "I got to finish my dinner."

It was getting close to Halloween, I remember that, and we were having this last little burst of Indian summer—still hot in the afternoons—and it's a Saturday and it seems like Janice's parents have invited me over to the house. Kind of a picnic thing, you know, for late in the afternoon.

I turn up and Czesław gives me the glad hand—*"Witam cię, Jimmy"*—and ushers me out onto the back lawn. This was back in the days before people were getting into decks or patios, so they'd set up some card tables out there. "Your sister can't be with us tonight?" Czesław says, and I think, hey, Janice, you really did a number on me, didn't you? And I go, "Oh, Linda sends her regrets. She had a date or something," and I'm looking around to catch Janice's eye, but she's off helping her mom.

Needless to say the crystal decanter came out, and I had a couple snorts of Lysol with Janice's dad, and we had a nice dinner out there on the lawn—everything friendly and relaxed. Mrs. Dłuwiecki told me that Janice had insisted they cook a real Polish dinner. She kept apologizing about it, making it absolutely clear that she usually cooked American but she was only doing this for her nutty daughter. So anyhow we had this soup, *szczawiowa zupa,* that's so damn Polish I don't even know if there's a name for it in English. And then we had this beef dish, *zrazy,* that you cook slow for a million years so it melts in your mouth, and it makes a terrific gravy to go with the *kasza*—which is, well, you know, kasha. Is that an English word? Hell, I don't know. But it's like this grain stuff, and I hadn't eaten it since Babcia Koprowski was alive.

Whenever Janice's mom and dad would drift into Polish, they'd catch themselves and switch back into English—I guess on my behalf—and Janice said, in Polish, "Don't worry. He can understand you. And I'm going to get him speaking Polish yet," and they all thought that was pretty funny.

Her mom was teasing Janice about all her newfound domestic urges—that's how she put it—like I guess Janice had all of a sudden decided she'd better learn how to cook when she hadn't shown the slightest interest in it before. And then Mrs. Dłuwiecki got to reminiscing about her mom, like she hadn't been much of a cook because they'd always had a peasant lady who did their cooking for them. And that gets Czesław reminiscing about his mom, and it seems she'd been one hell of a cook. Like he's mentioning this dish and that dish she used to make, and damn but they were good—he could still taste them.

Naturally they didn't know that I knew anything about it, but it gave me a funny feeling hearing them talking about Janice's two grandmothers like that—because I couldn't help thinking about how one of them had died of typhus in a German slave labor camp and the other one had been shot in the back of the head and buried in a common grave in the forest outside Krajne Podlaski.

I'll never forget this. The sun was starting to go down and it was getting chilly, but we were still sitting out there because the view was so nice. All those streets in Edgewood are built along the ridges of hills, and from their backyard you were looking down over all these rolling hills—a real West Virginia scene—and the trees had changed color so there's these flaming oranges and reds and yellows, and we were getting that gorgeous slanting golden light you get late in the day in the fall sometimes, and it was, I guess you could say, just pretty damn wonderful.

I'd never seen Czesław in a better mood. Big smile on his face, looking out over his back lawn like a king over his kingdom. And I thought, well, it's probably a relief to him—all those secrets he'd been keeping all those years, and now they're out in the open, and everything's worked out fine.

Janice went in the house to get a sweater for her mom, and then she started carrying plates and things inside. Her mom said, "Wait awhile. We don't have to do that yet," and Janice said, "You sit still, and let me do it," and I got up to help her, and she said, "That means you too, Jimmy Koprowski. Sit down and relax."

She carried a load of plates into the house, and when she came back, she put her hand on her dad's shoulder and said, "Isn't it beautiful, *Tatusiu*?" and he said, "Yes, it's beautiful," and then he said, "God has blessed us." He looked up at Janice with this absolutely wonderful smile, and he said, *"Mój aniołek,"* and all of a sudden I was all choked up.

After everything they'd gone through, he could say, "God has blessed us." It really got to me. And I thought about how it had always been in Poland, where maybe you'd want to pray, "Oh, God, please give me a little time where I can have something like a normal life"—you know, in between wars.

All of a sudden I was remembering Ron Jacobson. You know that strong clear sense of a person you can get sometimes so if you turned around and they were standing right there, you wouldn't be surprised? Well, that's what it was like, and I felt bad because it'd been months since I'd thought of him at all. I mean, he'd just slipped completely out of my mind, and I thought how sad it was that somebody could be so important to you, and then they die and after a while you quit thinking about them.

You don't imagine Protestants having big families—anyway I don't—but he had two sisters and a brother. His kid brother, he used to say, really looked up to him. It kept him honest because sometimes he'd think, well, I'd better do this one right because Kevin's looking up to me. And I thought about that hole he must have left in their family, that emptiness that was never going to be filled up.

And it hit me that I wanted to have a family. I'd sort of played with the idea, but I'd never felt it that strong before—like something I really believed in—that it'd be good, you know, just to have a decent job and a family, so in the end you could think how it'd all been worth it. And how it'd be great to have kids, to have a daughter as wonderful as Janice so you could say to her, "My little angel." And I thought about how far away I was from anything like that.

I don't know how she knew it, but it was like Janice could feel I was sad or something because she came over and stood by my chair, and she put her hand on my shoulder just the way she'd put it on her dad's shoulder, and she left it there.

Except for holding her hand sometimes, we'd never touched each other. I'd been real careful about that. And I sat there just like everything was perfectly ordinary, and I felt her hand on my shoulder. It was probably only a few seconds, but it seemed like an eternity. Then she took her hand away and left this tingle on my shoulder.

I don't know if you like twilight as much as I do—that little bit of time when the sky seems kind of smoky and everything starts to go blue on you. Her dad said, "Maybe Jimmy would like another drink," and Janice filled up a couple of those tiny crystal glasses for us, and Czesław and I toasted each other— *Na zdrowie!*

Janice and her mom carried everything into the kitchen, and Czesław and I folded up the card tables and carried them into the house. Janice said to me under her breath, "They're too polite to tell you, but now's the time for you to leave."

So I thanked them for the wonderful dinner and wished them good-night, and Janice walked me out to my car. "Now that I'm here, I can't go out again," and she made a face about that. It was still real early. "I'll see you on Tuesday," she said.

I said, *"Dobranoc, Janusiu,"* teasing her, you know, by speaking Polish. Or anyhow that's what I thought I was doing.

We were standing there by my car. I hadn't opened the door yet. Her parents were in the house, and we were outside in that smoky blue-gray twilight with about a foot of space between us. She just stepped across that little bit of space and kissed me.

Listen. I honest to God don't know what to say about that kiss. Well, I guess I'd have to say it was a sacred moment for me, so I wouldn't feel right talking about it too much. But I don't want you to get the idea it was a little kid's kiss. No, it wasn't. By the rules the nuns taught us at St. Stans, it was definitely in the mortal sin department. And it went on for quite a while. Like neither one of us wanted to stop. It was the most intense feeling I'd ever had for a girl in my life.

We were probably both remembering her parents inside the house and wondering how long it'd be before they noticed she was gone. So we stopped. I looked straight into her huge blue eyes, and I thought, okay, Koprowski, what do you do now? Shoot yourself? "I'm sorry, Jimmy," she said. "I got tired of waiting."

The only thing I could possibly have said back to her was, "I love you," and I didn't say it. Not because I wouldn't have meant it, but I didn't say it—well, for all the reasons I couldn't say it. Instead I put my arms around her, and I gave her a good hug. Then I got in my car and drove away.

TWENTY

I got about halfway down the hill and I started to cry. I hadn't seen it coming, and I couldn't stop it. It was as bad as that day when I'd got the letter telling me that Jacobson was dead. Hell, it was worse. The first chance I got, I pulled off Highlight Road, and I just sat there in my car and bawled like a baby.

When I got myself straightened up, I drove down to the PAC, and I sat by myself and drank boilermakers. I kept trying to find any way at all that Janice and I could go on, and I just couldn't find it. And I kept thinking about Jacobson and all the shit we'd gone through together, and I guess I'd hit the point where I knew he was honest-to-God dead. And as dead as he was, that's how dead I was going to be someday.

I kept going over my whole life, and it seemed totally pointless, you know what I mean? A total waste. Well, I sat there till closing time and then I slipped Bobby Burdalski a couple bills and he slipped me a fifth of Four Roses, and I took it down to the riverbank and drank it. The inside of my head was like mud.

I killed that whole damn fifth. You can imagine the shape I was in. But somehow or other I decided that the only thing to do was go to the church, and I managed to stagger over there. I went creeping in and knelt down in a pew at the back, real quiet, you know, because I didn't want to bother anybody. Fat chance of that at three in the morning or whatever time it was by then.

I was glad to be in the church. It was all so familiar. The smell of the incense, and the little angels down by the altar, and the Sacred Heart of Jesus on one side, the Blessed Virgin on the other—with that picture of Our Lady of Częstochowa. I think I said the Hail Mary. I'm pretty sure I said the Hail Mary. And I prayed for Janice. And I passed right out.

I woke up and I was just a mess. I was drooling all over myself. Still kneeling, kind of fallen over onto the pew in front of me, and I hauled out my handkerchief and wiped my face with it, and I thought, hey, what am I doing here? And then it starts to come back to me. And it was the strangest thing—I wasn't at the back of the church where I'd started out. I was down at the front.

I was kneeling in front of the picture of Our Lady of Częstochowa. Now it's obvious how I got there, right? I must have got up and walked, right? But I didn't have any memory of doing it, and it felt like somebody had just picked me up and carried me. I don't know if you've ever seen a picture of Our Lady of Częstochowa, but, believe me, she's powerful. When I was little, I was afraid to pray to her.

The original picture's back in Poland in the Church of the Assumption of the Blessed Virgin Mary in Częstochowa. It's been there since sometime or other back in the Middle Ages, and later on one of the Polish kings proclaimed her Queen of Poland. She's dark with age, almost black. At some point some heavy-duty barbarians invaded, and one of them struck her twice with his sword. You can still see the slash marks on her cheek. He tried to hit her the third time, but then he dropped dead.

The first thing you see is her eyes. Anyhow, that's what's always got to me. She'd been there, you know, watching the crucifixion of Our Lord, and she's seen every evil thing that anybody ever did to anybody ever since, and her eyes aren't just sad—they're way beyond sad—it's like after seeing all that evil and suffering in the world, she's just completely blown away.

I had no plan whatsoever of doing this, but I said, "Holy Mother, I commend to you the spirit of my friend, Ron Jacobson. He used to say, 'My strength is the strength of ten because my heart is pure,' and he meant it as a joke, but his heart was pure. He was the nicest guy I ever knew. He got killed in Vietnam. And he wasn't Polish, and he wasn't even Catholic, but, please, Holy Mother, take him into your care and watch over him."

Well, I must have passed out after that—or anyhow something happened—and I woke up again and everything felt real quiet. I'd thought that Our Lady of Częstochowa had been looking away from me, maybe looking off into eternity, but I was wrong, she was looking straight into me. I felt like this enormous power coming from her, and I knew she could see right down into my soul.

Well, a picture's just a picture, right? Even if it's old and holy and there's been lots of miracles happened because of it. But it's not the picture, it's what's behind the picture, you know what I mean? And what was behind that picture was Mary, the Blessed Virgin, the mother of our Lord, Christ Jesus. And I felt her there, and I wanted to pray for myself, but I didn't feel worthy. I felt like a total piece of shit, if you want to know the truth. So finally I prayed the only prayer I could, which was just, "Help."

I knew after that I should go home, so I got up and went stumbling out of the church and went home.

The key to the house was still on my key ring with my car keys, so I unlocked the front door and just kept right on going, I guess on automatic pilot—trying to be quiet, you know, so I wouldn't wake Old Bullet Head—and I had a piss and climbed on up to my little room in the attic just the way I'd done a zillion times before—coming home dead drunk in high school. My bed was all made up for whatever guest might turn up, and I just crawled into it and passed out. It never crossed my mind that I lived in a trailer out on Bow Street.

About dawn I woke up and somebody was sitting there watching me sleep. Really scared me. I sat up and it was my sister.

"Aw, Linny," I said, "I'm so fucked up."

"It's okay, Jimmy," she said. "Just go to sleep now. Just go to sleep."

I slept all day and when I woke up, I felt pretty rocky but my mind was clear. I lay there staring up at those *Playboy* bunnies plastered all over my ceiling, and I thought, hell, man, you graduated from high school in 1962. What are those damn things still doing up there?

It was real quiet. Naturally I felt like an asshole. Even as drunk as I'd been, how could I have forgotten I didn't live at home anymore? I could hear my sister playing the piano, some pretty classical piece, the notes far away, drifting up the stairs, maybe Chopin, and I was going over all of it in my head—you know, Janice kissing me, and getting loaded and stumbling into the church and praying for Jacobson and all that, and it took me awhile to reassemble all those bits and pieces, and I thought, oh, Christ, everything's a mess.

I got up, pulled on some clothes, and went downstairs. My sister was flipping through some music books. "Mom and Dad gone out?" I said.

She nodded. "They're over at Uncle Stas's."

I went in the kitchen and opened the icebox and poured myself a glass of milk, and then something stopped me. I don't know what. I looked out into the hallway, and I could see the sun coming in the windows around the front door—shining, you know, down the hall and into the kitchen—and it was so damn quiet I could hear my sister breathing all the way out in the dining room.

I got that eerie feeling you can get sometimes— Well, it's not just that everything's familiar, it's that you've been there before.

I walked into the dining room, and Linda looked up at me, and I said, "Hey, you remember that night you gave me the polka lecture?"

"Oh, sure," she said. "That was another time when you came home drunk and slept it off the whole next day."

"Yeah, that's right," I said. "Yeah, that's exactly right. Hey, play something for me."

She gave me a little smile, and then she just started playing—something she'd memorized, you know. And I don't think I ever in my life listened to somebody playing the piano the way I listened to her that day. It was a real serious piece, and I couldn't begin to describe it to you, but believe me, it was complicated. And I swear I heard every damn complicated thing in it.

"That's Bach," she said. "On the pianoforte, that's as good as it gets— Okay, Jimmy, tonight's my turn," and she took me out to dinner at Franky Rzeszutko's. Of course that's where she'd want to go—back to where the nights were magical when we were growing up.

It was nice being with my sister, drinking an iced pitcher of beer and eating the combination dinner. "What did Mom and Dad say?" I asked her. "There I am stumbling into the house last night— God, I feel like such an idiot."

"Mom was really mad at you, but Dad said, 'What do you want him to do? I figure it's better he comes home when he's drunk instead of driving around and killing himself.'"

I had to laugh at that. "Well, that's big of him."

Sitting there with Linda, I couldn't shake this feeling—I don't know how to describe it. Like things coming around full circle, or something like that. And I had these real clear memories of her as a kid—sitting at a table there at Franky's with her glasses and her bangs and her patent-leather shoes and her coloring book. She was such a serious little girl. I used to clown around a lot just to see if I could get a smile out of her. And it hit me I'd been neglecting her for months—like I couldn't remember the last time we'd had a real conversation.

Well, I told her about going into the church and praying to the Holy Mother, and a little bit about having dinner at the Długieckis', but I didn't tell her about Janice kissing me. Maybe I should have. Yeah, I probably would have felt better if I'd told her—or told somebody—and Linda was just about the only person I could tell, you know what I mean? I don't know why I didn't tell her.

So we're talking about one thing or another, and Linda says, "Janice called for you. Around two."

"Oh, yeah? So what'd you say? He got dead drunk last night and he's upstairs sleeping it off?"

"Oh, sure. Of course. That's exactly what I said— She said to tell you she's got a lot of homework. You're welcome to stop by there later on if you want." She kind of shrugged when she said that.

I looked at my sister, and I could feel where she was headed, and it was bothering the hell out of me anyway, so I said, "Oh, God, Linny, I don't know what to do."

I thought for a minute she wasn't going to take me up on that one, but then she said, "The funny thing is, Jimmy, she's not too young for you. But you're sure as hell too old for her."

"Yeah, that makes sense in a weird kind of way."

We just looked at each other for a minute. "She's a wonderful girl," Linda said. "I can see why you love her. But she's in high school."

"Tell me about it."

"Yeah, well— Okay, I *will* tell you about it. You know, everybody's talking."

"I figured they were. I got the big-time lecture from Mom."

"Oh, I know. She's worried sick. She thinks Janice is going to be pregnant by spring."

"Yeah, that's what she said."

"I know you wouldn't do that, Jimmy, but— It's just that you're not a kid anymore, and Janice is. You're a grown man with a grown man's needs. Doesn't she deserve the chance to be a kid for a few more years?"

"Linny, you're not saying anything I haven't thought myself. I'd rather die than hurt her. But what am I supposed to do?"

The Holy Mother, you know, doesn't have a body down here in the world. So when she wants to act directly in the world, she usually uses a human being to do it for her. Linda opened up her purse and got out her checkbook and wrote me a check for five hundred dollars. "What's this?" I said.

"You know that buddy of yours from the air force? The one who lives in Austin?"

"Yeah. Jeff Doren."

"Well, he must be out of the service by now."

"Yeah, he's been out for about a year."

"Okay," she said, "what are you waiting for?"

When we got home, I called Jeff and I said, "Well, I'm a little late, but I'm on my way."

He said, "You're never late, Koprowski. Whenever you show up, you're right on time."

He was working for Braniff. That was an airline they had in those days, operating out of Texas. It went belly-up in the early eighties, so maybe you've never heard of it, but it used to be one of the major carriers in the States. "You think I could get on there?" I asked him.

"You know, I think you might have a pretty good chance. My supervisor was just bitching to me about how short we are. How fast can you get out here?"

So after pissing around in Raysburg for a year and a half, I got everything done in a day and a half. I don't know why it seemed so important to me to do it, but I cleaned out my old room up there in the attic. I hauled all those ridiculous clothes from high school off to the Sally Ann, and I packed up that picture of me and Dorothy Pliszka at the senior prom, and my yearbooks, and my football trophies, and, you know, all that nostalgia stuff, and I crammed it into a couple cartons and shoved them into the back of the basement—*way* back, if you know what I mean. And I ripped down all those damn *Playboy* bunnies. And then I took Linda up there and said, "Now isn't this a nice place for you to practice your trumpet?"

"Oh, Jimmy, it's so sad!"

"No, it's not. Everybody's got to leave home sometime. Just keep the bed there for when I come back to visit."

I closed my bank account and bought some whiskey and beer so I wouldn't get thirsty driving to Texas. Gave notice on my trailer, slapped new tires on my car and tuned the sucker, broke the news to Vick Dobranski, told him I was sorry I didn't give him at least a couple weeks' notice. "Aw, hell," he said, "I don't care about that. Good luck to you, Jimmy. You're a good worker when you're halfway sober."

I had a few drinks with Georgie Mondrowski and said good-bye to him. "Hey, I'm really going to miss you, buddy," he said, which kind of surprised me. Well, he was my best friend, and I was going to miss him too. I said good-bye to Mom and Dad and Linda. Got some road maps and worked out my route. I wasn't going to bust my ass driving. The first day I figured would put me in Nashville, the second day somewhere between Little Rock and Dallas, and the third day in Austin.

THE CLARINET POLKA · 325

So what about Janice? On the list of shitty things I've done in my life, this one sits pretty high, but I just couldn't face her. I was afraid if I looked into those big blue eyes of hers and tried to tell her I was leaving town, I'd end up not going anywhere— Well, no, it was even worse than that.

When it came to the topic of Janice, I kind of switched back and forth between total panic and deep denial. Like half the time I couldn't even admit to myself how serious it was. But what if I'd decided to talk to her about it? I mean, I couldn't imagine doing that, but just suppose I did. Well, she might be real surprised and say, "Oh, I thought we were just friends," but somehow I was pretty sure that's not what she'd say. And then what? Knowing the kind of kid she was, she'd— I don't know, she'd be writing me a letter every ten minutes, and I don't know what all, and even though I was in Texas, I'd still be screwing up her life.

So I told Linda to say good-bye for me—to tell Janice I had to leave real sudden because there was a job opening for me, and that I'd write to her. Which I fully intended to do.

Did I need to say good-bye to Mrs. Constance Bradshaw? Hell, I must have thought I did—maybe that I owed it to her or something. I can't quite recall what I was thinking about her at that point. The sensible thing to do would have been just to hit it on down the road and not give Connie a second thought, right? But sometimes the sensible thing ain't what's happening. So anyhow I called her up. "Great to hear from you," she says. "I thought you'd written me off."

I'm going, "Aw, come on, honey—just been up to my eyeballs, you know what I mean? So what are you doing tomorrow afternoon? Thought I'd pop out and see you." Terrific, she says, it'd be nice to catch up. Why didn't I come out for dinner?

So I drove out to St. Stevens on whatever day it was. I'd given my TV to Mondrowski—hell, I could always salvage a TV—but I had my stereo and my tools, and all that junk you accumulate that seems absolutely essential to the maintenance of human life. Took up the trunk and most of the backseat. I figured I'd crash at Connie's, and if that didn't work out, I'd just drive west until I crapped out and grab a cheap motel out in Ohio somewhere.

She met me at the door and gave me a little kiss, and she was wearing one of her leather outfits and— Well, it's not like she was all tarted up or anything, but she had made an effort—you know, her hair and makeup all nice—and I felt that ZAP between us just like in the old days. She got me a beer. She'd been cutting back on the sauce, she said, so she was drinking white wine.

Well, if you're a total pig, you go to bed first and tell her later, but I couldn't do that, so I broke the news to her straight out. I don't know what I expected. Like I wasn't expecting her to jump up and down with joy and say, "Wow, I'm so glad this is the last time I'll ever lay eyes on you, you hopeless asshole," but on the other hand, I didn't think she'd be, you know, crushed. But she looked pretty damn crushed. "I just don't believe you," she said. "You don't see me or even call me for two months, and then you come out here to tell me you're leaving town."

I didn't know what to say to that. She downed her drink and walked out into the kitchen. I followed her. She pulled a casserole out of the oven, and then she just stood there looking at it and started to cry. "Hey, I'm sorry," I said. I didn't know exactly what I was supposed to be sorry for, but I figured I had to be sorry for something.

"Fuck you," she said.

I just didn't get it. I'd been thinking that we'd pretty well run it out last summer. "Do you want me to leave?" I said.

"Yes," she yelled at me, "get the fuck out of my apartment."

So I started for the door, and I got about halfway there, and she said, "No, don't leave."

I turned around and she was just mad as all hell—her eyes shooting daggers—and she said, "Why do you always take me so goddamn literally?"

"Beats me, Connie. How am I supposed to take you?"

She gave me a little smile. "How about the living room floor?"

She didn't take any of her clothes off. She didn't even close the drapes. She wasn't wearing any underwear, and we had one of those—well, I guess you could describe it as a super-intense quickie. And then the minute—no, the very *second* we get done, she pushes me away, stands up, jerks her skirt back down, and walks out into the kitchen and makes us each a drink. None of that beer or white wine I've-been-cutting-back bullshit, but a real drink. I'm still laying there on the rug with my pants off.

I pull myself back together, and then we're sitting on two chairs like two normal drunks, drinking our drinks, and she says, "It's probably the best thing for you. I've thought all along you should get out of the valley. You've been going nowhere fast here."

I know I've probably given you the impression that I didn't like Connie much, and it's true—there were lots of times I didn't like her much. But there were also times when I liked her just fine, and that was one of them.

So what do you talk about if it's the last time you're ever going to see somebody? I asked about her kids, and she said what she always said—they were "making a good adjustment." And I asked her how things were going with her husband—if she thought they'd ever get back together again. "I don't know," she said. "It doesn't seem very likely—but who knows? If we're both willing to change." She asked me what I was going to do in Austin, and I told her about that airline, Braniff, and—well, you know all that crap about how you're going to get your shit together and start a new life.

Two things we'd always enjoyed doing together, and we'd just done one of them and now we were doing the other. Yep, the booze was just flowing down our gullets like a river, and she started telling me lots of things she probably never would have told me if she hadn't thought it was the last time she'd ever see me.

Like about the night she hadn't attempted suicide. "I wish I could say I don't remember how it happened, but I do remember. I opened the pill bottle, and I was just going to take one, and you know what happens sometimes when you're trying to pour capsules out of a bottle? You don't just get one, you get a handful? Well, believe me, Jim, I didn't think, okay, now I am going to commit suicide. I thought, oh, I just don't give a damn. And however many pills there were in my hand, I took them. Is that a suicide attempt? I don't know. I don't think so. I think it was a cry for help."

She told me she was seeing a lady psychologist up in Pittsburgh. She was driving up there a couple times a week, and it was helping her a lot. She was finally confronting her miserable childhood. "First I had to admit how bad it was," she said. "That was a big hurdle. And now I've got to dredge up all these ghastly things—like lancing a wound.

"I told her about all the men I've slept with," she said. "I lost my virginity when I was twelve—can you believe that? Then in my teens I was really promiscuous. I'd be embarrassed to tell you how many—I'm not even sure I could come up with an accurate count anyway. And you know what? A lot of times I would've had more fun blowing my nose.

"I told her all about us and she said it was a damn good thing I wasn't seeing you anymore—that she couldn't imagine two people more of a disaster together. She said I abuse sex the way I abuse alcohol. She said I should lay off both for a while, that a period of chastity in my life right now wouldn't kill me," and we both got a good laugh over that one.

She said, "I'm glad you came out tonight, Jim. This feels good—a good way to say good-bye."

We had dinner just at the right time—before we got so pissed we didn't give a shit. It was one of those pilaf things—with shrimp in it—and it was good. We were getting along just great, and she just kept saying nice things to me.

"I always trusted you," she said, "except when I was really loaded and paranoid—and then I don't trust anybody. And you never gave me any of that 'I love you, I love you' crap. I always appreciated that. And we had great sex, didn't we?"

"Yeah, honey," I said, "we sure did."

I sang her my sad song about driving west and grabbing a cheap motel, and she said just what I wanted to hear—"Oh, no, no, no. You're going to stay here and get a good night's sleep. Don't worry, I'll give you a good breakfast and shove you out the door bright and early."

So that settled that, and I went out to my car and got a fifth of Jack Daniel's out of my trunk, and she cracked open another bottle of gin, and we settled down to have us a little nightcap, and the next thing I know it's sometime around dawn, and I'm laid out on her couch, and that good old painful consciousness is creeping up on me again. I go lurching off to the can, and I drink about a gallon of water, and then something tells me to check on Connie.

She's in bed, out cold as a catfish, and I manage to notice the pill bottles sitting on her bed table. It's amazing how sensitive you can get to pill bottles.

Guess what? It's her good old pills. The Valium she used to take—you know, for the terrible anxiety she suffered from—and the Seconal for catching a few Z's and not attempting to kill herself with. I read the labels, and it was the same damn Dr. Andrew R. Hamilton who gave them to her before, and I thought, my God, what a quack. They ought to yank that bastard's license.

The lid was tight on the Seconol bottle and there seemed to be lots of pills in it, but I didn't know for sure she didn't have a couple of those mother's little helpers in her along with God knows how much gin, but she didn't seem like she was in a coma. No, she just looked like your standard-issue passed out drunk—drooling on her pillow and snoring away like a band saw—and I thought what the hell and stumbled back into her living room and crashed.

Well, when the Jim and Connie Show opened again the next afternoon, neither one of us was looking too good. And we discussed the matter and concluded that a little hair of the dog might be just what the doctor ordered. That first binge we went on lasted only four or five days, the best I can remember.

I've told this story before, you know—not in the detail I'm telling it to you, but hitting the main points—and I've had people say to me, "Wait a minute, Jimmy, there's something I'm just not getting here. How could you be on your way to Texas in October and still be hanging around getting loaded with that doctor's wife in December?" The folks who've ever had a real intimate relationship with the stuff inside the bottle never ask me that.

There's a certain amount of repetition that sets in at this point, so I'm not going to bore you with a blow-by-blow account, but I do want to give you, like they say, the big picture. Pretty soon we've got our life down to a nice little routine. First you've got your sex. And then you've got your happy hour when it all seems worthwhile. Then you've got your one drunken asshole delivering long lectures to your other drunken asshole who ain't saying much of anything. Then eventually your other drunken asshole opens his big mouth, so you've got your fight.

If you're lucky, the fight goes right around in a circle back to where it started, and you get to catch a few Z's so you can do it all over again the next day. But if you're not lucky, the fight keeps right on going. You know what? If the booze holds out, you can run a fight all night long and on into the next day. What did we fight about? I couldn't tell you. It's not like the passage of the years has dimmed my memory. We couldn't even remember from one day to the next.

Now if it was my turn to wind things up, I'd say, "Screw you, Connie, I'm going to Texas," and I'd go staggering out and jump in my car and drive away. And if it was her turn, she'd say, "Get the hell out of here. If you're going to Texas, just go, damn it," and she'd push me out the door. And then other times she'd be sitting at the kitchen table with the shakes, wrapped up in a blanket, crying her eyes out, trying to pull herself back together with a coffee and a pill. "Oh, God, Jim, this is insane! I can't go on like this. I've got to drive up to Pittsburgh and see my therapist. I've got to see my kids! I thought you were going to Texas. For God's sake, why don't you leave me alone?"

When I stumbled out of Connie's, I couldn't just get in my car and drive to Texas—because usually I'd be in fairly rough shape. So where I went was the Florence Hotel in Blantons Ferry. That's on the Ohio side just a short drive from St. Stevens. I stayed on the Ohio side. The last thing in the world I wanted was to run into anybody I knew, and I had like a superstitious dread of crossing the river back into West Virginia. I was on my way to Texas, wasn't I? Well, at least Ohio was one state west of where I'd started.

The Florence was an old rat's-ass dump down by the railroad tracks with one of those signs that says, "Furnished Rooms by the Day, the Week, or the Month." I'd driven by it a million times, and I'd always thought, Christ, that hole must be the absolute end of the line, so it seemed like the perfect choice. Two bucks a night, ten bucks a week, or thirty bucks a month, and what you got was a flop and a warm place to shit. "The Floss," the regulars called it, and if you were a regular, you could sit in the lobby and watch that old TV all you wanted just so long as you didn't bother anybody. And believe me, if you're the kind of guy who's flopped at the Floss, bothering anybody is not real high on your list.

I'd left town maybe not feeling on top of the world but definitely all filled with hope and high purpose, so how did I end up at the Floss Hotel? I did consider that question from time to time. I felt like something in me had snapped—like I'd been making a real big effort, and it'd been getting me nowhere, and I just couldn't hack it anymore. Like I'd been trying to do the right thing, but now I felt like doing the wrong thing, and so what? Who was I hurting? Of course Connie and me don't count, right? I can remember drinking with a kind of fury—like maybe this time, goddamn it, if I didn't chicken out or just give up, I could drink my way right on through to the bottom of everything.

Connie always had plenty of money, and she kept shoving it at me, and I kept taking it. A lot of times that was her way of getting me out the door. But I was spending my own money too, and I gradually pissed away everything I had and then I started spending the five hundred bucks Linda had given me. I kept telling myself I could always pick up some day labor like I used to in high school, but it's kind of hard to motivate yourself to go unload boxcars, you know, when somebody's shoving money at you.

I was still driving around with all my shit in my car. A lot of my clothes kept dribbling into Connie's, and seeing as she was a cleanliness freak, they'd end up washed and ironed. But there were still cartons and suitcases in my trunk, and in the backseat, with stuff spilling out of them, and I just couldn't get around to dealing with it. I couldn't get around to dealing with anything. I was leaving for Austin any day now, right? So what was the point?

Well, pretty soon the snow's flying on a regular basis, and it's kind of lousy weather for driving to Texas. I'd been lucky and hadn't run into any fellow Polaks wandering around in the great state of Ohio yet, and somehow the thought managed to cross my scrambled brain that except for Mrs. Constance Bradshaw, nobody in the world had the faintest idea where I was. So it's early in the day—for me that means around two in the afternoon—and I'm not totally shitfaced yet, and I've got some change in my jeans, so I call Linda. At work, right? In that dentist's office.

She's so glad to hear from me she starts crying—which naturally makes me feel just terrific—and she's telling me how worried everybody's been and how great it is to hear my voice. I'm standing in the lobby of the Florence Hotel, and I could have driven over to that dentist's office in about eight minutes. But I just can't bring myself to tell her where I am—because then I'd have to tell her what I've been doing—and somehow I can't tell her I'm in Austin either, so without even thinking about it, I say, "Guess what? I'm in Nashville."

"Nashville?" she says. "What on earth are you doing in Nashville?"

What am I doing in Nashville? Well, let's see— I stopped in to see an old service buddy—Yeah, Bill Johnson's his name. Nice fellow, just got married. Great to see him again. And I'm, ah, working in a gas station. It's not much of a job, but I don't figure on sticking around too much longer. Yeah, Nashville's okay. The country music's real good down here.

Poor Linda. It'd never cross her mind that I could lie to her. But she had to know I'd been drinking. Any fool could have figured that one out. She said she couldn't really talk, being at work and all, could I call home tonight? Did I have an address? Did I have a phone number? Was I ever going to write to Janice?

"Well, ah, I'm working the late shift. Four to midnight, you know. And I'm leaving in a couple days anyway. I'll call you from Austin. Tell everybody not to worry about me. I'm doing just fine— Yeah, Linny, I love you too."

The next remotely coherent thought I had, Connie was telling me that she was going to move back into the house with her husband and kids for the Christmas holidays. She wanted me to get lost for a couple weeks. She opened up her purse and peeled out something on the order of two hundred bucks and handed it to me. "What the hell's this?" I said.

"I know you don't have much money. Buy your family some Christmas presents." You see, I'd led her to believe that all those times when I was in the

Floss Hotel I was going back home and staying with my parents and working for Vick Dobranski.

I go, "Honey, I can't take this." It was the most she'd ever offered me at one clip, and believe it or not, I was ashamed.

"Sure you can. We've been over this a million times." Her standard line was that there was a trust fund in Baltimore and it paid her once a month. To get paid, all she was required to do was remain alive, and I was one of the main reasons she was still remaining alive.

So I took her money and moved into the Floss, and I thought, hmmm, maybe I could go home for *Wigilia*. Yeah, that'd be real nice. I could tell them I drove back from Nashville for it. That'd makes sense. It's only a day's drive. Of course I'd have to show up reasonably sober or Old Bullet Head would bounce my ass out the door, but I'd have a *reason* to stay reasonably sober, wouldn't I? If I tried real hard, I could do it. Sure I could.

I drank like a fish till the day before Christmas. My theory was I should get it out of my system. And then I had only—well, maybe only three or four shots before I went out to do my Christmas shopping. I had to stay reasonably sober, didn't I? So I drove over to the St. Stevens Mall and wandered around the stores for a while, not ready to part with any of my hard-earned cash yet, just planning what I was going to buy, and you know, comparing prices. And eventually it hit me that I wasn't going to make it through with only that pissy little bit of booze in me.

There's a nice tavern just off the highway, and I go sailing in there and have a boilermaker just so I can feel good enough to finish my shopping and get my sorry ass down to South Raysburg in time for dinner. Well, that first boilermaker tastes so good, I have another one, and then, guess what? The mall's closed, and I'm in the tavern dead drunk, and it occurs to me that there's no way I'm going home that night so I might as well have a few more drinks to console myself, because I'd really wanted to go home with some nice Christmas presents for everybody. It's just a damn good thing I hadn't told anybody I was coming.

The next I know it's sometime around midnight and the bartender's tapping me on the shoulder because I've passed out cold on the bar. "Merry Christmas, buddy," he says, "get the fuck out of here."

Making it from the bar to my car was a major effort, and as soon as I started to drive, I noted the fact that I had become one of those highway menaces you hear so much about. Concentrating real hard, I got into St. Stevens, and I got to Connie's, and that was the end of my road. Her Mustang was parked out front, and I thought, shit, she didn't go anywhere, but I walked around to the back, and her apartment was dark. I tried the one window I thought she might have left open, but it was locked, and then I thought about the air conditioner. It was me who'd put it in, right?

I pushed the window up, and I fiddled around until I got the wing nuts on the plastic sliders loose, and I gave the unit a push, and it made this enormous crash hitting the floor. Then I boosted myself up and through the window. I felt real bad missing Christmas Eve with my family, but, you know, there's a consolation to everything. Connie bought her gin by the case.

I kept meaning to clean Connie's place up—I'd been planning to do a real good job of it—and get the hell out of there and back to the Floss, but somehow I never managed to do it. And January rolls around, and I'm laying there on the couch watching something or other on the tube, and I hear a car out front, and then I hear the door unlock, and there's Connie with two suitcases. She takes one look at me and she just stops dead.

She looked like a million bucks. She'd had her hair cut again and even got her nails painted. Wearing a nifty little brown suit, shoes that matched, the whole bit. Even her purse matched. Looking at her, you'd think there was nothing the least bit wrong with her. But yours truly wasn't looking like a million bucks. It'd been awhile since I'd had a shave or a shower, and I wasn't totally loaded. Not quite yet I wasn't.

Well, her apartment just reeked of cigarette smoke, and she looked around at all the ashtrays piled up with butts and the beer bottles and the gin bottles and the pizza cartons and the fried-chicken cartons and the various other interesting items I'd been meaning to pick up, and she started screaming. I mean, she couldn't even get any words out, just opened her mouth and this horrible howl starts pouring out of her.

I figured I'd better do something fairly quick, so I jumped up and ran into the kitchen and grabbed a garbage bag and started stuffing things into it. And she's running along behind me, shrieking her head off, "Get out. Get out. Get out. Just get the fuck out," and I'm going, "I'm sorry, I'm sorry, let me just clean up a little here," and she's going, "You fucking asshole, I hate you, I hate you, I hate you," and it crosses my mind that if she suddenly laid eyes on some sharp object—like a carving knife for instance—I might not be remaining alive for much longer than another minute or two, so I take off out the door with my garbage bag—pretty much at a dead sprint—and I stuff the sucker into a garbage can and jump into my car and go tearing out of there.

I did feel bad about it, you know? I kept saying to myself, Jesus, Koprowski, you know what a cleanliness freak she is. How could you have done that to her?

I gave her a few days and then I called to see if it was okay to come back. As you can imagine, I was fairly sheepish about it. She sounded, I guess you could say, kind of grim, but she told me, yeah, I could come back. I turned up shaved and showered and not totally shitfaced. I brought her some flowers and told her how sorry I was. "Yeah," she said, "of course you're sorry. You're always sorry."

You know those nice gourmet dinners she liked to cook for her husband when I wasn't around? Well, they'd had themselves a real feast. Roast beef, carrots, potatoes, peas. A nice new jar of horseradish, the pink kind that's real hot. And I'm sitting there just enjoying the hell out of it—I didn't eat all that well when I was flopped at the Floss—and she's sitting on the other side of the table giving me the gimlet eye, and she says, "Jim, we've got to talk. You need help."

I'm going, "Huh?"

She told me they'd hired a new young guy at the medical center and his specialty was Vietnam vets—like he was doing research on the topic—and a lot of Vietnam vets had addiction problems, and he was real good with that. "You're just like me," she said. "You can't possibly get out of it on your own," and she told me how much it was helping her to see that lady psychologist up in Pittsburgh. "I actually have hope again," she said, and maybe this guy at the medical center could help me out too. "The VA would probably pay for it," she said. "He has a waiting list a mile long, but I could get you jumped to the head of it. I could probably get you in there in a day or two if you wanted me to."

"What? Your husband would get me in?"

"My husband has got nothing to do with it."

Well, I was just furious, but I was choking down the food and trying to restrain myself, you know, till I could see which way the wind was blowing. Now like I told you, back in those days I was the king of denial, and it never crossed my mind to think, hmmm, it seems to me I've heard this song before. Hell, maybe I'll give it a shot. I'm not exactly a Vietnam vet, but I sure have an addiction problem. What have I got to lose? Oh, no, that would have been way too sensible for me. What I was thinking was, hey, what's going on here? Connie wants to get me off her hands. So I thanked her for her concern about my sorry state and told her I'd think about it.

Well, I did think about it, and all of a sudden I'm starting to get this funny picture. Like, hey, wait a minute, you know what's kind of odd? She spends a couple weeks living at home with her husband, and then as soon as she moves back into her own place, she invites him over for dinner. It's kind of obvious, right? They're getting back together. So of course she wants to get rid of me.

But I still couldn't quite make it all add up. Why was her car parked out front the whole time she was gone? And when she came back, did she look like somebody who's just spent a couple weeks with her husband and kids just six blocks away? With her two suitcases and her purse, and her hair and makeup all nice, in her expensive little brown suit and her high heels? Hell, no. That's what you look like when you've just flown into the Pittsburgh Airport and ridden the limousine down to the valley. Coming back from where? Baltimore?

Okay, so I'm basically one of these dumb-shit types who believes anything you want to tell me unless I've got some reason to think otherwise. All of a sudden, I've got some reason to think otherwise. So the next time she tells me to get lost for a few days, I don't just get dead drunk. No, I stay in fairly good shape, and I drift over to St. Stevens about nine o'clock at night.

I've pretty well memorized all the cars that park on her street, but there's one I've never seen before, and it's an unusual car for the Ohio Valley—a dark green Volvo, and not your old beater either, but a bright shiny job straight from the workshops of those efficient snowbound elves of Sweden. I'd figured her husband for a Corvette kind of guy, but it could be I was wrong. And Connie's Mustang is parked where it always is. And the lights are on in her apartment. So there she is having dinner with her husband. Maybe.

But if by some odd chance it's not her husband, then good old Dr. Bradshaw should be at home with his kiddies, right? Well, I'd looked up the address in the phone book, so I drifted over there and had a look. Guess what? The house is empty. For Sale sign in front of it with the name of a real estate agent. I suppose that makes sense, I'm thinking. After Connie moved out, he probably wanted a smaller place.

The next day after I scrape myself together, I'm not sure how much sense it makes. I call the real estate agent. Tell him I've just relocated from Phoenix with my wife and two kids and I'm looking around for a house. He's just delighted to hear from me. Yep, that house is perfect for a family. And it's a real bargain. Yes, yes, it's a sad situation. Real messy divorce, you know. They're desperate to sell. The wife's here; the husband took the kids and moved out of town. They've dropped their price several times now, and if I made them a serious offer, they'd probably come down again. "Why, good heavens," I say—ol' innocent me—"and how long has that house been on the market anyway?" Since August, he says.

I look up Dr. David Bradshaw in the phone book and call the number. The girl answers, says, "Dr. Peterson's office."

"I thought it was Dr. Bradshaw's office."

"Dr. Peterson is taking Dr. Bradshaw's patients. Can I book an appointment for you?"

So I tell her that Dr. Bradshaw is the only physician in the Western Hemisphere—and I've tried many—who understands my bizarre medical condition, and I really need to see him. She says sorry, he's no longer at the St. Stevens Medical Center. Oh, I say, where is he? She isn't sure she can divulge that information. She has to check on it. Maybe if I called back— No, no, no, I really need to see the guy. I've been seeing him on a regular basis. She's getting really annoyed at me. "Why, I don't know what you're talking about. Dr. Bradshaw hasn't been here since August."

That night I drive over to Connie's, and there's the green Volvo. Does the asshole have enough sense to lock his car? No, of course not. I slip into the passenger seat. The glove compartment's not locked either. The car's registered to Dr. Andrew R. Hamilton. Am I surprised? Well, not by much. Yeah, it's that good old Dr. Take-one-at-bedtime-Do-not-use-with-alcohol Hamilton—yeah, it's the great Dr. Seconol himself. I'm out of his car like a ghost and around to the back alley. Then I'm standing in the same big black shadow I was in when I watched them yank Connie out of there on a stretcher.

The kind of girl Connie was, it'd never in a million years occur to her to draw the drapes. And I'm just totally blown away, and what's getting to me is not what's going on in Connie's apartment—no, it's pretty much what I expected—but the kicker is the guy. I'd been expecting Dr. Andrew R. Hamilton to be some perfect stranger, but no. Remember all the way back in The Italian Renaissance when that rat-faced little son-of-a-bitch doctor with the mustache came in with the nurse and saw us in the Night Owl? And Connie about went nuts? Well, that's Dr. Andrew R. Hamilton. I'd been so goddamned dumb. I'd thought his name sounded familiar.

I was so mad I walked across the alley and into the backyard and almost right up to the windows. I didn't give a shit if they saw me or not, but I had enough sense to stop just out of the light. They were in the living room having themselves a drink, talking and waving their arms in the air and generally yucking it up, so I must have caught them right in the middle of happy hour.

The kitchen table was next to the window, and I had a good view of it. She had a bottle of white wine sitting there, and some long white candles, and so she probably had one of her nice gourmet dinners in the oven, and they were going to eat what they wanted of it, and whatever was left, well, that was for me when I turned up in a couple days. And Connie was wearing an apron. One of those old-fashioned frilly things. I couldn't believe it. Connie in an apron? But then I thought, well, she'd figured me for a leather-dress-and-no-underwear sort of guy, so maybe she'd figured Dr. Andrew R. Hamilton for an apron sort of guy. Takes all kinds, right?

The longer I stood there and watched them, the madder I got. It was all fitting together in my mind—what had really gone down instead of all the lies Connie had been feeding me—and I was seriously thinking about walking up to the door, and kicking it in, and giving that rat-faced little doctor some interesting medical problems of his own. I was, you know, about three times his size. I was also thinking how much fun it might be to take Connie's head and ram it through the wall. It's scary how clear it was in my mind. But then I hit the point where I knew I just wasn't the kind of guy who could do something like that. I was almost sorry I wasn't.

I must have stood there for ten or fifteen minutes. I had time to smoke a couple cigarettes. I don't think I've ever been so mad in my life. Feeling this—this gigantic, unbelievable icy rage. And it wasn't just that she'd lied to me—I mean, she'd lied to her husband, so why shouldn't she lie to me?—but I kept asking myself, just who the hell *are* these people?

People like that, marriage obviously doesn't mean dickshit. Well, she'd told me over and over again it didn't mean dickshit to her, so why hadn't I believed her? And rat face in there, he's got a young wife at home, but she's a little on the plump side, so of course he's got to find somebody else to screw. Only stands to reason, right? And if that somebody else is married, well, who the hell cares? It's getting your rocks off that counts, right?

The way I'd always been taught, your kids come first, but they sure as hell didn't come first with these people. Connie's kids were probably back in Baltimore living with Connie's mother-in-law, or maybe her husband hired somebody to look after them, who knows, but is Connie in Baltimore making some effort at being a mom? No, here she is in St. Stevens screwing some pathetic drunken asshole who used to be a TV repairman, and screwing the doctor who gives her all the nice little pills she can choke down. Yeah, and rat face in there, the guy pumping the pills out, well, he's got a kid at home too. Would these people ever sacrifice anything for their kids? Oh, hell, no. They can't even sacrifice the next drink.

I mean, just who the hell *are* these people? It's been handed to them on a platter their whole lives, and so that's the way they think life is. It's not what they can do for somebody else, it's what they've got coming to them—and what they've got coming to them is anything they want, right when they want it. You have a few kids, well, shit, you can always hire somebody else to look after them for you. Yeah, trained professionals.

So who the hell *are* these people anyway? I don't understand these people. I'll never understand these people. I don't want to understand these people. And when it comes down to the crunch, I hate their guts.

And then I thought, yeah? So who the hell are *you*, Koprowski? You hypocritical piece of shit. You were taught to believe that marriage is a sacrament.

TWENTY-ONE

I went back to the Floss and naturally I got good and loaded, and the next day when I was scraping myself back together, I was still mad—like totally furious—and not just mad at Connie but mad at myself, and I kept thinking, okay, buddy, this is it. So I pawned my stereo. That gave me just enough for gas and smokes and booze and a hamburger or two. I'd have to sleep in my car, but there's a lot worse things than that, and I'd have to do a lot of praying that I wouldn't run into a snowstorm or two, but maybe luck would be with me. I'd hit Austin dead broke, but I knew Jeff would always lend me something until I got on my feet.

What I should have done was started driving west, but no, that was way too simple for me. I'd left a few things at Connie's, and I had to go back and get them. That's what I told myself anyway. But you want to know the real reason? I wanted to get one up on her. I just had to be sure that *she* knew that *I* knew.

I walk in and she's giving me shit because I didn't call first. Don't sweat it, I say, I'm just picking up my things and then I'm gone. "What the hell's the matter with you?" she says. I go, "When'd you start fucking that rat-faced little doctor?"

For a second she looked like I'd slapped her, and she just stands there looking at me. And she just keeps on looking at me. And I'm thinking, hey, she's not going to answer me; she's just going to stand there till I leave or something. And then she says in this absolutely flat, dead voice, "Last spring. It must have been late April, early May."

I've told you we had lots of practice running the good old drunken fights—you know, your full-tilt, no-holds-barred, pacing-up-and-down-and-kicking-the-furniture fights—and that's what I was expecting, but that's not what was happening. I mean, I tried my best. Yelling at her, calling her a rotten lying slut and every other damn thing, and she just stands there. Finally she says—kind of, you know, disgusted, "Oh, come on, Jim, don't be ridiculous. Do you want a drink? Of course you want a drink."

Well, it's like screw your mix and ice cubes, let's just get right down to business, so she pours some straight gin into a couple whiskey glasses. She sits down, so I sit down. And then it's really weird—like anything I ask her, she just answers me in that same dead voice.

"Jesus, Connie," I say, "all this time— Why the hell were you pretending your husband and kids were still in town?"

"I don't know. It just seemed simpler, and— It was to protect myself, I guess. To protect my privacy."

"Okay, so when did he really leave you?"

"We split up around the end of May."

"And that trial separation business you told me was a crock?"

"Yeah. He started divorce proceedings. I couldn't believe it. How fast he did it. Instantly. He took the kids and went back to Baltimore in August."

"Yeah, August. I figured that. Yeah, right."

She asked me if I wanted to hear the whole story. Of course I wanted to hear it. Wouldn't you?

Remember the night when that little rat-faced Dr. Seconol came in the Night Owl with the sleazy nurse? Well, Connie and her husband saw quite a bit of Dr. Seconol and his wife—all those hot-shit young doctors and their wives had these dinner parties damn near every weekend—so the first time she sees him, Connie's whispering in his ear, "Andy"—that's what she called him—"you breathe one word about the other night, and I'll be on the phone to your wife so fast your head'll swim."

He was kind of stunned for a second, and then he said, "Clear as a bell, Constance," and they both pretended to get a good laugh out of it.

Whenever they saw each other after that, Connie noticed the way Dr. Andy was looking at her. She was getting next to him, and she kind of liked that, and she admitted she played him a bit. "I knew I shouldn't," she said, "but I couldn't resist. Sometimes it's just too easy."

So comes the spring, and Connie's husband finds out she wasn't going to The Italian Renaissance, and the shit hits the fan. "And you just abandoned me," she said to me. "You told me to get lost, and you wouldn't answer your phone."

"Yeah," I said, "that's what I did all right."

So Connie and her husband had yet another one of their award-winning seventy-two-hour, nonstop, two-person encounter groups, and they worked out another set of agreements—they even wrote them down on paper this time— and they started seeing a marriage counselor, and she wept and pleaded and begged, and she swore on a stack of Bibles three foot high she was never going to screw around again. And everything was more or less going along okay until they had a big party at their house sometime in April. About eight couples, she said.

Nice sunny spring day, hot dogs and steaks on the barbecue, lots of booze going down, kids running around, some of the younger wives there with their babies—that Dr. Andy's chubby wife was there with their baby—and Connie's wearing one of her world-famous leather miniskirts. Dr. Andy whispers in her ear, "You look great in that skirt." She gives him a little smile—like, eat your heart out, stud—and he says, "Constance, I'd just love to fuck the living daylights out of you," and she says, "Okay, come in the garage."

So they go in the garage and he starts telling her how hot he is for her, and she says, "You didn't say you wanted to talk to me," and she takes her panties off and says to him, "Come on, man, we've got a good ten minutes before anybody misses us." That story, as you can imagine, sounded kind of familiar to me.

Well, when it comes to the moment of truth, Dr. Andy can't get it up. "Being a man, you probably don't know this, Jim," she said, "but most men are afraid of sex. You're one of the few I've ever met who isn't."

So she says to Andy, "You had your chance and you blew it"—or words to that effect—and puts her panties back on and walks back out to the party. After that, Dr. Andy just can't leave her alone. He's hauling her off into corners at parties to tell her how she's driving him up the wall. He's calling her up in the afternoon to say he's going to die. So she thinks, what the hell?

Remember that lady Connie hired to look after her kids for her? Well, that lady likes to take the kids out in the afternoon. Nice weather, you know. Great for going to the park, to the little kids' pool, and like that. So Connie and Dr. Andy start tearing off a few quick ones at Connie's house in the afternoon.

It was only a matter of time until her old man caught them. "Christ," she said, "it was like something out of a French farce. I've still got my skirt on, and I'm facedown on the bed, on my knees, and Andy's behind me going at it like Rover. He's so nervous it's taking him forever, and I'm thinking, oh my God, if he doesn't get finished soon, I'm going to have the world's worst yeast infection. And I hear a little click noise, and I look over and there he is standing in the doorway.

"What am I supposed to say—'Hi, hon'? Andy doesn't see him. I say, 'Andy? Uh, hey, *Andy!*'"

Her husband says, "Oh, for Christ's sake. Come on, get dressed and get out of my goddamn bedroom. We've got to talk."

As you can imagine, all Andy wanted to do was motivate his sweet little ass on down the highway. Her husband says, "You've just been fucking my wife. The least you can do is have a drink with me." So they sat down in the living room and had a drink. I told you I didn't understand these people. Do you?

Her husband asked them if they were in love with each other. He figured it had been Dr. Hamilton the whole time—you know, going all the way back to the night she'd come in stinking drunk after running around naked in the cornfield. Andy didn't have a good word to say on the topic, but Connie just laughed. "Love has nothing to do with it," she said. As you can imagine, her husband was just delighted to hear that.

Andy asked Connie's husband please not to tell his wife. "I'm not going to tell her," he said. "I like your wife, and I wish her all the best." Then he told Andy that they of course were going to have to appear in public together, and when they did, he hoped they would appear perfectly cordial, and Andy allowed as how that's the way he'd like to play it too. Then Connie's husband said, "I'm not going to go out of my way looking for it, but if life ever gives me the opportunity to fuck you over, I sure as hell will do it. Now get out of my house."

Connie's husband told her he was divorcing her and he couldn't stand to be under the same roof with her for even one more night, so who was going to leave? She said she would, but what about the kids? He said to let him worry about the kids, so she packed a suitcase and moved into a motel until she found her apartment.

Her husband called his dad back in Baltimore, and his dad pulled some strings and got him a job at some hospital or clinic or some damn thing, and he took the kids and went back to Baltimore. She was real bitter about that. "I'd been begging him and begging him for years to go back home, and he'd say, 'Oh, it's not as easy as that, Constance,' but then when *he* wants to do it, he's gone in a flash."

"Connie," I said, "there's something I really don't understand. I'm not just conning you here, I really *don't* understand it. How could that goddamned doctor—you know, after what you did—how could that son of a bitch just keep giving you more of those pills?"

She shrugged. "I'm very persuasive."

"Oh, I bet you are. Is that why you started seeing him again?"

"I never stopped seeing him."

"Oh, terrific. What the hell were you doing with me?"

"I thought—I don't know— Well, for the longest damned time you seemed really stable. Like a rock."

"But not lately, huh?"

"Your drinking scares the shit out of me, Jim. Mine too. It's like we're falling down a cliff together. And Andy— He's the only point of stability I have left now— Except for my therapist. But I mean in my ordinary life. The only thing I can hang on to. Can you understand that?"

I told her I could understand that. "Connie," I said, "what about your kids?"

She said, "I feel just terrible about my kids."

Hell, I knew she felt just terrible about her kids. That's not what I meant.

"Okay, so tell me the truth now," I said. "I mean, what's the point of lying about it? Were you really trying to kill yourself?"

"Yes, of course I was."

Could you think of anything to say to that? I couldn't. She asked me what I was going to do, and I told her I was going to Austin. "Jim," she said, "stop kidding yourself. You're never going to Austin."

"You're wrong, Connie," I said. "I'm going to Austin right now. I got a full tank of gas, and the minute I walk out the door, I'm headed on down the road."

We didn't say good-bye or wish each other luck or any damn thing. I had a little bit of gin left in my glass, so I knocked it back, and then I just stood up and walked out.

During my pleasant sojourn in the Floss, I'd managed a conversation now and then with some of the other regulars, and I had it on good authority that the best bang for your buck is port wine, and if you can fortify it with a pint of grain alcohol, then you're in heaven. Well, where I was didn't feel much like heaven, but I figured maybe I could get there.

The next few days are a blur. I kept trying to stay mad at Connie, but I couldn't do it. I ran the self-loathing number for a while, but the more juice I got in me, the more I shifted into the self-pity number. Port wine mixed with grain alcohol does not produce the world's most profound thoughts, so I'm just lurching along inside my head like— Shit, I wasted four years in the air force. That's when my drinking got bad. Shit, things would have been different if

Dorothy Pliszka had married me. Shit, I never should have come back to the Ohio Valley, what a mistake that was. Shit, it's not my fault Connie turned out to be totally crazy. Shit, it's not my fault I fell in love with a high school girl.

I stayed drunk till my money ran out, and then it was, like they say, harsh reality time. I pawned every damn thing I owned that was worth anything—my tools, my watch, my only pair of cufflinks—and I started looking for some dumb-ass job that even a drunk can do. I had a lot of faith in America, so I knew it had to be out there somewhere.

Eventually I found it—an Esso station out on Route 70. Yeah, so work was tight in the valley, but there's not a huge number of guys who'll drive out into the middle of nowhere to pump gas for minimum wage from midnight till eight in the morning. This was back before self-serve stations, right? So there had to be somebody on duty, and they didn't give a shit how drunk I was just so long as I showed up and managed to get a gas cap off and a nozzle shoved in.

But the money never lasted long enough. It's amazing how much you can drink if you put your mind to it. Well, all my life I'd seen these guys hanging around the State Store with their little routines—"Hey, buddy, I haven't had anything to eat for three days" or whatever the hell it is. I've always been an easy mark for those guys. "Hey, Sarge," they'd say. Back in the fifties they were Korean War vets, or if you saw an older guy, he was probably a vet from the big one.

So anyhow I'm outside the State Store in Staubsville, and I'm about a buck short of a bottle. And there's this suit and tie coming by, and I say, "Hey, buddy, sorry to bother you, but I'm a Vietnam vet, and I'm having a little trouble—" He doesn't even look at me, but he reaches in his pocket, and all of a sudden I've got enough for the bottle, and I think, well okay, that wasn't so bad, was it?

You've got to be Polish to know how heavy this is. A Polish guy will do anything—shovel out furnaces, sweep railroad tracks, dig ditches, clean toilets, you name it—before he'll take anybody's charity. Living off Connie made me the lowest of the low, the scum of the earth, but begging on the street? That's not even in the realm of possibility. So you can imagine how much I was liking myself. But hell, when you ain't got the scratch, they don't give you the bottle.

Hanging around outside the State Store was pretty good, but so was hitting the bars. I'd find some place where I was sure nobody would know me, and I'd always have enough change for a beer or a boilermaker, and I'd nurse it along and get to talking to whoever was in there, and when the time was right, I'd launch into my little story—"Hey, buddy, I did two tours in Nam, you know, and things have been kind of rough since I got stateside," and I'd throw in a few details I'd heard from Georgie, like all the thorns they've got on the plants over there. And guess what? Pretty soon there's drinks sliding down the bar at me. On a good night, there's lots of drinks. So I could get myself pretty well pissed before midnight when I had to drive out to the Esso station.

So, let's see here—you've got your small but steady income supplemented by your brilliant entrepreneurial activities, so how are you going to deal with the essentials of life? Like food, for starters? Yeah, well, first you got to get your priorities straight. Booze is number one, gas in the car is number two, smokes is number three, your flop is number four, and that puts food down there at the bottom of the list.

The cheapest thing you can get in a restaurant is either a bowl of soup or a bowl of chili. Be sure to get as many packages of crackers as they'll give you and throw in a little ketchup too. Pork and beans and corned-beef hash are two things you can eat straight out of the can. No matter how broke you are, you usually have a few cents to buy a doughnut. Try buttermilk. It's cheap, and it soothes the stomach and gives you a hit of protein.

In lots of places the Sally Ann lays out a feed for drunks. I liked the one up in Staubsville. Of course if you've got a car, you better park it a few blocks away because they don't like to see you driving up to get your free meal. The level of conversation ain't the greatest, but occasionally you'll meet some interesting characters, and you learn all kinds of useful things. Like one way to solve your smoking problem is find a public institution where they've got those big containers with sand in them—you know, sitting outside the door—and they don't let you smoke inside. The public library's your best bet. I used to hit three or four libraries, and I could pick up a dozen smokes with only a puff or two gone on them. If you think I enjoy telling you this shit, you're crazy.

No matter how different these stories start out, they always end up exactly the same, so you'll have to bear with me if this one is starting to sound like something you've heard before. I was losing weight fairly steady, and if I didn't keep the booze coming, I'd get the shakes—I mean, the serious shakes like a willow in a hurricane—and I was sick a lot of the time. Puking my guts out was getting to be a routine occurrence, and I was having those good old blackouts. But life was going on in that pointless way it does when you've given up completely. And from time to time I'd think, hey, the Pączki Ball must be about now; I wonder if the polka band's playing at it. Gee, I hope Mom and Dad and Linda aren't too worried about me. Oh, Christ, it's Janice's birthday. She's seventeen now. I sure hope she's okay. Memories, you know, of some other life going on somewhere else that used to really matter to me. And then I'd get this horrible sick feeling and the only thing that would fix it was another drink.

And you know what's the craziest thing? I drifted on toward spring, and sometimes I'd think it really wasn't that bad. There'd be long stretches of time when nobody stopped in the Esso station, and I'd sit in there and sip my port wine mixed with grain alcohol and watch their crappy little tube. I was really up on current affairs. I remember that poor son of a bitch Lieutenant Calley was on trial for the Mylai massacre, and I followed that with a kind of morbid fascination, thinking, yeah, well they've got to pin it on somebody, and one thing's for sure—they're not going to pin it on some *general*. But I didn't just watch the news. Hell, I'd watch anything. Old grade-B horror movies, reruns of Johnny Yuma, cooking along with Julia Child.

But even the best of times has got to come to an end, right? One night about four in the morning a car pulls in, and it's a couple young studs out catting around half loaded. One of them's Larry Dombrowczyk's little brother Eddie and the other one's Mike Sytek, and they're really amazed to see me. "Hey, Jimmy," Eddie says, "what the hell you doing out here? I heard you was in Texas or Arkansas or some damn place."

"Yeah, well I was," I say.

I sold them their five bucks' worth of gas or whatever, and I watched them drive away, and I'm going, oh, shit, this is horrible. Mike Sytek's dad had worked with Old Bullet Head at the mill for years, and you remember the night I took Janice to the Japanese restaurant? Well, it was Sandy Czaplicki and Eddie Dombrowczyk who'd dropped her off at my trailer and then picked her up later.

I just felt sick. So that night I worked the rest of my shift and when the manager came in, I quit. I knew my sister really well, and Linda was perfectly capable of borrowing the old man's car and turning up at an Esso station out in the middle of nowhere at four in the morning. And the kind of kid Janice was, some night it could just as easily be her.

The funny thing about not working is that nobody's paying you, and panhandling only gets you so far, and one day I'm down to like thirty-seven cents and that's not even going to buy me a beer. So what can I do about it? The answer to that one, naturally, is to go hit Connie up for a couple bucks. So what about my pride or my self-respect or any of that other good shit? Well, screw that, man. We all know that the next drink's the only thing that counts.

So I drive over to Connie's, and there's a sign in front that says "FOR RENT, NICE SUNNY ONE-BEDROOM APARTMENT." I walk around to the back and have myself a look, and I'm staring in through the clean shiny windows at a bunch of empty rooms. Naturally Connie left the place immaculate. Whew, I'm thinking, that was fast. She probably saw her chance to make her break, and she took it. I'm pissed off, of course, but I also can't help thinking, good for you, Constance. Good luck to you.

After that, panhandling got to be my main occupation, and grim as it is, you can keep running on it a fairly long time. I'd drive ten or fifteen miles in any direction and find the State Store, and I'd work it for a couple hours, and then I'd hit all the bars. I had my act down real good by then, and I sure looked the part. Some nights it wasn't worth warm piss, but other nights I could really score.

So one night I'm working this bar in Staubsville, and I'm talking to this older guy—a machinist, I think he said he was—but anyhow a working stiff, so he's careful with his money. But I've almost got him reaching for his wallet—yeah, and I'm right at the clincher where I'm saying, "So we're humping the boonies, and there's not a sign of Charlie. And then, ka-BOOM—trip wire rigged to a Claymore, and all hell breaks loose—" and all of a sudden, out of nowhere, I hear this quiet voice saying, "Come on, Jimmy. You was never in Nam."

It was dark in that goddamned bar, but to this day I'll never know how I missed seeing him in there. Georgie Mondrowski. He wasn't supposed to be up in Staubsville. What the hell was he doing up in Staubsville? Why the hell wasn't he down in South Raysburg where he belonged? He's walked over to the end of the bar where I'm standing, and he's pretty damn drunk, and he's stoned out of his mind, and of course he hasn't seen me in months, and he's giving me this real puzzled look, like, hey, something's wrong with this picture, and if you give me a minute or two, maybe I can figure out what it is.

"What's the problem, Georgie?" I say. "You forget who you're talking to, or what? I did two tours in Nam. You know that." And all the time giving him the old wink wink, you know, like, for Christ's sake man, can't you see what I'm doing here? This guy's about to sprout for a couple drinks.

Georgie is just not getting it. "No," he says. "You was in the war, Jimmy, but you was never in Vietnam."

"Oh, for God's sake," I yell at him, "sure I was," and he decks me. I mean just that fast. No warning. POW, he just punches me a good one.

I'm flat on my back and kind of, you know, stunned. I put my hand on my face, and it comes away bloody. And the bartender and some other gorilla have got Georgie in the old bum's rush, and whoosh, he's out the door. Then they're yanking me to my feet, and whoosh, I'm out the door.

When you've had the classic bum's rush slapped on you, they get you running real good, and the only way to stay on your feet is to keep right on running. So I'm lurching forward, trying to get my balance, you know, waving my arms, and I collide right into Georgie, and we sort of hang on to each other and go stumbling off, and he's crying like his heart's broke.

I've never heard anybody cry like that. Every time he tries to catch his breath, he just howls. He keeps trying to say something, but he can't get it out. We've got our arms around each other's shoulders, and we're staggering off somewhere, God knows where. I'm the one bleeding like a stuck pig, but he's the one who's crying. Finally he gets out what he's been trying to say—"I'm sorry, Jimmy."

"Hey, forget it, asshole," I say. "Don't worry about it."

Where else can you go but the river? We end up down on the bank, and he can't stop crying. I keep patting his shoulder and saying, "Come on, man. Come on. It's okay. I don't give a shit. You want to hit me again? That make you feel any better?"

But nothing I say makes him feel any better. He keeps trying to catch his breath, and then he goes off into another crying jag. Finally he gets so he can talk—you know, in little bursts—and every horrible thing is coming out. We're down there in the jungle, and we're blowing away Gooks right, left, and center. In Vietnamese, they say, "*Xin loi.*" That means something like, "Sorry about that," so you shoot first and think about it later, and if you've just wasted somebody like an old guy taking a crap by the side of the road, you go, "*Xin loi,* motherfucker."

He's telling me about this buddy of his, or that buddy of his, and how they bought it. He's telling me about the sharpened bamboo stakes covered with shit and how easy it is to get yourself impaled on them. He's telling me about the trip wires and the mines set right at the level so you'd catch it in the balls. He's telling me that Charlie knows how GIs are suckers for little kids, so Charlie wires up a satchel charge to a two-year-old and sends him toddling over. He's telling me the horrible stuff Charlie does to his own people who are playing ball with the Yanks.

Georgie's lieutenant doesn't much like to worry about prisoners. No, the main thing that lieutenant worries about is keeping his body count up. So they've captured this VC, and the lieutenant says, "Hey, Mondrowski, I think that man needs some *medical attention.*" Georgie goes over to where this VC is laying there, wounded, glaring up at him, and Georgie blows his brains out. "*Xin loi*, motherfucker."

He's telling me God knows what all. I can't remember a lot of it, and most of it I don't want to. Besides, it's his story, and if you want to hear any more about it, you ask him. But anyhow I'm sitting there listening to him, and I'm thinking, Christ, how could anybody live through that shit, and he's probably never told even half of it to anybody so it's probably a good thing he's telling me, and yeah, sure, I feel real bad for him, but the main thing I'm thinking about is my next drink.

He starts to get a little calmed down, so I say, "Hey, man, you want to go find another bar?" thinking, you know, he's probably got a few bucks.

He reaches in his coat and pulls out a pint of rye and hands it to me. I grab it and knock back a good one. I offer it to him, and he shakes his head. "You drink it, man. You need it." I feel like a piece of shit, but I kill the bottle. He's obviously gone downhill some since I saw him last—but that makes two of us—and I'm thinking, hell, he's got lots of reasons to be fucked up, so okay, Koprowski, what's your excuse?

He fires up a J, offers me that, but I shake my head. He's stopped crying, and a little while later he says, "You know, Jimmy, I keep having this dream. It's always the same dream. I'm back over there, you know, in country, and I hear this little rustle, and I waste the son of a bitch, and then I look and I see that it's my mother or my sister or somebody like that," and he drops his head down between his knees and starts bawling again.

I'm patting his shoulder, hoping he'll get straightened up enough so we can go to a bar. Eventually he pulls himself together, and he does another J, and we're just sitting there staring at the lights in the river, and oh, God help me, I'm really needing that next drink. I'm thinking, shit, this is horrible. How did I get so lost? How did it happen so fast?

"Hey, Jimmy," he says, "I knew you wasn't in Texas. I figured if you was in Texas, you'd send me a card."

"Yeah, that's right."

"Somebody said they saw you pumping gas somewhere."

"Yeah, I was doing that for a while."

"So what the hell you *doing*, man?"

"Georgie, that's something I really couldn't tell you. But what's happening with you, man? When I left, you were working for the city."

"Yeah, well, that one kind of went down the tube."

He stares in the river and then he says, "We had a big demonstration in Washington just a couple weeks ago. Just us, you know—Nam vets."

"Yeah, I saw something about it on the tube."

"Well, I was there. I chucked my medals over the White House fence. It was a big relief. I keep thinking maybe I can turn things around now, you know what I mean?"

"Yeah, I do."

"Jimmy," he says, "we got to stick together. We got to help each other out, you know."

"Yeah," I say.

"We can't spend the whole rest of our lives like this, you know what I mean?"

"Yeah, I sure as hell do."

"Jimmy, anything you need, you just ask, okay? You need a drink, you don't go begging in some goddamn bar. You ask me. Anything I got is yours."

"Christ, man, I appreciate that. Thanks a lot for saying that."

"You don't have to thank me. I don't have to thank you. You understand what I'm saying here? We're brothers, right? *Bracia.*"

He bends over and gives me a big kiss right on the mouth. "How you like that?" he says, "and we ain't even queer. Come on, man, you got to come home."

After that night I worked real hard at staying away from any place I thought Georgie Mondrowski might go. The last thing in the world I wanted was to run into him again. Why was that? Because he was one of the few people left who still gave a shit about me. Does that make any sense?

I don't know how I managed to keep on going as long as I did. Most of it's a blur in my mind. But I made it till sometime in the spring when I finally threw it away up in North Raysburg. It was getting to be nice weather, and I've always liked driving around. Yeah, driving was just about the only little speck of pride I had left. Like, hey, at least I'm not like those other assholes flopped at the Floss—I've still got a car, and I'm leaving for Texas any day now.

So it was early in the evening—anyhow the sun was still up—and I was out on the river road headed back into town, and there's a nice stretch there where you can really open her up, and I'd picked up a cop. Somehow I sensed him in plenty of time. I checked my rearview and he was floating along right behind me, and I thought, whew, that was close, because if my sixth sense hadn't been operating, I could have been really burning down that road. I drifted into town with my speedometer pegged right on the speed limit. Ordinarily what I would have done was flipped over to the island and then on into Ohio because I never drove through Raysburg—especially, you know, anywhere near South Raysburg.

We get into town, and I don't have a clue what I'm doing wrong, but all of a sudden the cop does his little WHEEUUR on the siren, so I pull over and check him out in the mirror. Just him, no partner, right? And it occurs to me that one of my taillights is missing—it's been missing for a while, and it's just another damn thing I could never get around to. So what? He's going to give me a ticket for it. And then maybe a drunk-driving charge on top of it—because I'm fairly loaded, and that's going to be obvious even if he turns out to be the village idiot. So I let him get out of the cop car and walk up to where he's just about to bend down and lean on my window and then I blast out of there like Evel Knievel.

What was I thinking? Who says I was thinking? I can remember I was really pissed off. Like that was the last straw, like something in me just snapped. Like screw you guys, I'm not going to take any more shit from you. And for a while there, I thought I'd lost him. I'm just driving the bat piss out of that old Chevy. I'm burning down alleys and powersliding corners and running red lights and jumping curbs, and people are pulling over and blowing their horns at me, and I'm just rocking and rolling and having a good time. I am, by God, brilliant.

I can't see him, but I can still hear his siren. Then I check my rearview, and yep, there he is, about a block away, coming up fast. So I go screaming around the next corner and go whipping into an alley—you know, sliding at some damn crazy angle—and I get this picture like a flash going off and it's burned into my brain forever. There's a little boy maybe nine or ten years old, and he's pushing his bike, and he's right at the end of the alley, and he's frozen, staring straight at me.

The kid had been headed to my left, so I stand on the brakes and haul the wheel over to my right, and then KABLAM, there's your screaming metal, exploding glass, the whole bit. It sounds like the whole world's coming down around my ears. At the time, I was a little vague about what'd happened, but I'd smashed into the corner of somebody's garage.

It could have been a brick wall, right? Or the poor bastard's car could have been parked in that garage, right? And then the chances are I wouldn't be here telling you this story. But I ripped out the corner of the garage, and went smashing through the garage door—and that took up some of the impact—and then I went on through to the inside. No car in there, just empty space, so I rammed up against the inside corner, you know, at a sideways angle, and that got me stopped. I mean, it was ridiculous. One of those Keystone Kops kind of crashes. Totaled my Chevy—totaled the garage too—but all I got out of it was a hell of a bang on the chest from the steering wheel and my big nose broke on the windshield. You see the bump there in the middle? That's it.

I jump out of the car. All I can think is, oh, my God, what happened to that little boy? But I run right into the cop, and he's so pissed off he just punches me right out.

I sort of remember being handcuffed and shoved in the cop car, but it's not real clear. Nobody'd ever heard of prisoner's rights in those days, so they just hauled my sorry ass down to the Raysburg cop shop. I was obviously impaired, right? And what you do with some slobbering idiotic drunk you've just caught after a high-speed chase that's endangered the lives and limbs of a vast number of Raysburg's citizenry, is you throw him in the drunk tank until he sobers up, and then you throw the book at him.

They dump me on the floor somewhere—that's all I know—and I pass out. I wake up and I'm in a cell, and not a very big one. Where I am is down in the basement of the police station, but I don't know that. There's not a breath of air, and the place stinks of shit and vomit. A couple bare bulbs burning away in the corridor outside, and that's the only light. I've got no way of knowing what time it is, but it feels like the middle of the night. And the first thing I can think of is—oh, my God, what happened to that little boy? I can't imagine anything worse than hurting a child.

I'm in there for hours. They've taken my wallet and my smokes and my belt and my shoes. Nothing but me and a wooden bench and a hole to piss in. I don't see a sign of anybody, and somehow I can't bring myself to start yelling. It's been—oh, I don't know, eight or ten hours since my last drink, and I'm not feeling real fine. I keep thinking, oh God, please, please, please let that little boy be okay.

This cop comes strolling down the hallway, and he stops to check on me, and his expression says, give me any trouble and you're dead meat. I was not in the mood to give anybody any trouble, believe me.

Well, at some point I started throwing up. I got down to the dry heaves. Every bone and muscle in my body ached. I lay there on the floor doubled up, and I kept thinking about that little boy. You know, that picture I had in my mind—frozen, staring down the alley straight at me. Scared shitless. I kept praying for him.

Oh, God help me, did I ever need a drink. Right, so how was I going to get one? Weren't they supposed to let you make one phone call? Wasn't that part of the deal? So where the hell was my one phone call? And who the hell was I going to call? Everybody must have pretty much written me off by then. Well, Linda I could call. She was the only person in the world I knew I could always count on no matter what. I didn't know what time it was, but after eight I could get her over at that dentist's where she worked.

The cop comes strolling down the corridor again, and I don't care if he beats the crap out of me, I've got to know what happened. "Excuse me," I say. "I'm sorry. Excuse me, but can you tell me what happened to that little boy?"

I don't think he's going to answer me, but finally he says, "He's okay. He jumped clear."

"No shit?"

"Yeah. Just quick as a cat. He's pretty shook up, but not a scratch on him."

"Oh, thank God," I say, and something in me cracks open and I start bawling.

Then he says—you know, like he's got to give me my due even though he'd just as leave not, he says, "And it's a good thing you swerved when you did."

I'm crying so hard I sink down on the floor. The cop looks at me for a minute and then he just walks away.

I'm huddled up on the floor, and I'm crying like a baby. I start saying one of those prayers my grandma taught me. *"Spowiadam się Bogu wszechmogącemu, Najświętszej Maryi Pannie, błogosławionemu Michałowi Archaniołowi, błogosławionemu Janowi Chrzcicielowi, świętym Apostołom Piotrowi i Pawłowi—"* That's the *Confiteor.* You know, where you confess to anybody who might have some interest in the matter—to Almighty God, and to the Blessed Virgin, and to the archangel Michael, and to John the Baptist, and to the apostles Peter and Paul—that you've sinned.

I get to the part that goes, *"moja wina, moja wina, moja bardzo wielka wina"*—that's, "through my fault, through my fault, through my most grievous fault"—and I get stuck there.

Then I prayed to the Holy Mother, "Please, help me. I can't go on living like this. *Módl się za nami grzesznymi teraz i w godzinę śmierci naszej*—Pray for us sinners now and at the hour of our death."

I really thought I might die. Right there in that hole before anybody found me. And if I didn't die, I'd have to stop drinking. And then I finally admitted the truth to myself. There was absolutely no way in hell I was ever going to stop drinking. I'd been lying to myself for years about all kinds of things, and especially I'd been lying to myself about drinking. Anything I promised myself—or the Holy Mother—was just going to be another pack of lies. There was nothing I could do about it. I was going to be a drunk for the rest of my life, so I might as well be dead.

Well, somehow I got through the night and they had a shift change. One of the Polish cops on the Raysburg force was Tiny Cieslak—you can guess why they called him Tiny—and I looked up and there he was looking down at me through the bars. "It's okay," Jimmy," he says, "I called your dad. He's on his way up here."

I was not real pleased to hear that. Old Bullet Head was the last person in the world I wanted to see. I figured he'd just tell them to throw away the key. Which was exactly what I deserved, but I had to get out of there somehow because I needed a drink. And I tried to pull myself together, because, you know, you don't want to look like a total broken-down wreck in front of your father.

I don't think I've ever seen him so pissed off. He was so mad he couldn't even speak to me. I don't know what the bail was, but he paid it. I was going to have to come back for a court appearance. I had all these charges against me—driving under the influence and reckless endangerment and resisting arrest and I don't know what all—but that was for some other day, and I can't begin to tell you how happy I was to get out of that jail cell.

We get out on the street, and I'm thinking, Christ, how fast can I get away from the son of a bitch so I can get a drink?

He said, "You think I don't have anything better to do with my money than piss it away cleaning up after you?"

I said, "I expect you've got lots of things better to do with it."

I got in his blue Chrysler and I realized I'd never seen this one. That's how long it'd been since I'd been home. He was staring straight ahead out the windshield. He wouldn't even look at me.

"I'm surprised you haven't written me off by now," I said.

"There's a difference," he said, "between being a criminal and being an asshole."

He drove over to the Island and parked at the Yacht Club. I didn't know what we were doing there, but I didn't ask. He bought us each a 7UP and carried them down to a table by the river. Boy, did that cold pop taste good. He offered me a couple Tylenol and I took them.

"Good thing that kid was a grasshopper," he said.

"Yeah," I said, "you bet."

It was about noon by then, and the sun was beating down. You've probably got a good idea what I was feeling like. Your basic scum on the side of the toilet bowl has more self-respect than I did, but it had been sixteen or eighteen hours since I'd had a drink and what I really needed, goddamn it, was that next drink. I was ready to do anything to get it. The last thing I wanted to be doing was sitting with my father staring at the river. I couldn't figure out what we were doing there.

"Some guys have got to hit bottom," he said. "You hit bottom yet?"

"I don't know," I said, but if I hadn't hit bottom, I'd sure hate to see what the bottom looks like.

All I could think was, for Christ's sake, Dad, whatever you're doing, get it over with. Don't you understand, I need a drink.

"You in withdrawal yet?" my father asked me. I just looked at him. How could he just say it like that? Just flat out like that? If you could say *withdrawal*, you might as well say *alcoholic*.

Well, he'd quit, hadn't he? He hadn't had a drink in years. I was twisting around inside myself any which way trying to find anything so I wouldn't look so pathetic, so I said, "I guess you've seen some hard times yourself."

"What would you know about it?" he said.

"Nothing," I said.

"You're goddamn right, nothing."

He was finally looking at me. We sat there for a minute or two looking at each other.

Just a few hours ago I'd been in hell, and like you do when you're in hell, I'd been praying my ass off. I'd confessed that I'd sinned, and it's true, I had sinned. And now that I was out, what was I going to do? Just forget all about it? Say, oh, well, it was all just bullshit and I don't believe any of that stuff anyway? Once before I'd asked the Holy Mother to help me, and she had helped me. And everybody and their dog had been trying to help me, but I'd pushed them all away. I don't know if I can tell you, but it was coming down on me, like the full weight of it. Here I was, this hopeless miserable asshole, getting offered another chance.

"Dad," I said, "I feel like a total piece of shit. I'd rather die than go on living like this."

"Okay," he said, "I'll take you somewhere you can dry out."

TWENTY-TWO

Where the old man took me was the RGH. I was already heavy into withdrawal when I got there, and they didn't give me nothing, just let me ride it on through. I was one sick puppy, believe me. Most of it's a blur in my mind now, thank God. You might not know this—I didn't know it in so many words—but withdrawal from alcohol is worse than withdrawal from heroin.

They kept me twenty-four hours. I came out of there, and I wasn't feeling any too wonderful. The old man picked me up and drove me straight to a center—a place up near the Pennsylvania line—and I was in for the thirty-day cure. What they offered you was three squares a day, a bedtime snack, as much coffee as you could chug down, and a bunch of other drunks to talk to. They had meetings every night and they strongly suggested you go to them. A doctor came by maybe once a week to make sure one of us hadn't decided to drop dead.

The first week I didn't sleep hardly at all. I watched a lot of shitty movies, and I played a lot of pinochle, and poker for bottle caps, and even chess, which believe me is not my game. Gerry, one of the guys who ran the place, kept telling me that nobody ever died from lack of sleep, but I wasn't so sure. I couldn't believe what a mess I was. Just walking around the building a few times damn near killed me.

They ran their meetings along AA lines. That's how they put it. They weren't real AA meetings for the simple fact that AA won't be part of anything where people are being charged for a service. But they talked about the Twelve Steps and like that, and you were encouraged to tell your story and listen to what the other drunks had to say. And they kept pointing out to us that our best chance of staying sober once we got out was to head straight for the nearest AA meeting.

For the first little while I just sat through those meetings like a stone. It's amazing how I could have been hanging on to my pathetic little scrap of false pride at that stage of the game, but I guess I was, and asking me to join AA felt like asking me to join the Mickey Mouse Club. Well, maybe it was the third or the fourth meeting, I don't know, but the light went on. And that doesn't even get close to it. It was more like Saul on the road to Damascus.

You've probably heard about the Twelve Steps, right? They've got twelve-step programs for every damn thing under the sun now. You want to quit using nose spray, they've probably got a twelve-step program to help you do it—it's ridiculous, if you ask me—but the reason it's caught on is that it works. But you've got to be brutally honest with yourself, and for most of us, that's a real hard one.

Step One is when you admit that you've got no power over alcohol, and Step Two is when you realize that the only thing that can save you is some higher power. I remember sitting in the meeting, and of course I'd heard it all before, but there's hearing it and then there's *hearing* it, and I finally got it—I'd already hit Steps One and Two in that crappy little jail cell in the basement of the Raysburg police station. The guys in the meeting probably thought I was bored or pissed off or something, but I had to get up and walk outside because I was, you know, pretty choked up.

The weather was real nice, I remember that. And I was almost to the point I could enjoy it again. And I walked away from the building and sat down under a tree and, like they say, contemplated the state of my soul. Naturally I remembered when Janice had given me that brochure listing all the meetings in the valley, and her little speech about alcoholism being a disease and like that, and how she'd talked to Father Obinski on my behalf, and I thought, okay, Janice, I'm a little late, but here I am.

When you're serious about trying to turn things around for yourself, thirty days goes by in a flash, and I wasn't ready. Gerry kept saying to me, "You know, Jimmy, when it's going to be really tough? When you first go home." He didn't need to say that. I already knew that. I couldn't imagine living in South Raysburg and not drinking. There's bars all over the damn place—not to mention that the PAC's only a couple blocks away from our house—so once I got home, I knew I couldn't stick around for very long.

Linda and I talked for hours. I felt real bad about how worried everybody had been about me. I'd just, you know, completely vanished off the map, and the only contact they'd had from me was when I'd called up Linda and lied to her about being in Nashville. So I told her the truth about that whole miserable time—what I remembered of it anyhow. When you're drinking as hard as I'd been, there's lots of it that just doesn't get stored very well in the old memory bank.

Naturally I asked my old man how he'd quit. It'd never crossed my mind that he'd been in AA, so he really surprised me. He'd been active in AA for years, all the time Linda and I were growing up. These days he put most of his free time into the church, but he still went to meetings every now and then. "How come I didn't know that?" I said.

"Well, I guess I didn't go out of my way so you'd know it. Back when I was active, we took the anonymous part real serious."

"Hell, Dad, how come you never said anything to me? You know, when I was getting really heavy into the sauce."

"What the hell was I supposed to say? I made things pretty clear to you, didn't I?"

"Well, you did in your way. But you could have—I don't know, grabbed me and really made me listen to you." You see what I was doing? I was still trying to find other people to blame it on.

"Oh, for crying out loud," he says. "Jimmy, I been talking myself blue in the face to you your whole life, and you never paid the least bit of attention to me. You're just as bad as I was. Hell, when I was growing up, you couldn't tell me a damn thing, and you're the same way—and besides which, I'll let you in on a little secret, bright boy. If just talking to somebody made them stop drinking, there wouldn't be any drunks left in the world."

I had to do my number for the judge—please note, Your Honor, that I am a veteran—and he must have liked hearing about the thirty-day cure and me planning to leave town because he let me off with a sharp slap on the wrist.

I had some long talks with my mom too, and Mondrowski came over to wish me luck, and even Patty Pajaczkowski came to see me, if you can believe that. Everybody was trying to convince me I could stay in Raysburg and still be okay, but I didn't believe it.

Linda told me that Janice had been real hurt by the way I'd just vanished and never wrote to her or called her—"hurt to the quick," she said, and boy, I sure wished she hadn't put it that way. But Linda figured she'd got over it. Janice was going out with that kid Tony and she seemed happy with him, and of course she was the star of the polka band. They'd played at the Pączki Ball and had been very well received. "Call her up, Jimmy," Linda said. "She'd be so glad to hear from you. She thinks of you as one of her best friends."

Well, maybe Janice had got over me, but I wasn't sure I'd got over her, and "one of my best friends" wasn't how I would have put it. I was still feeling real shaky, you know what I mean? And I didn't want to go looking for some excuse to fall off the wagon. And I thought, hell, if she's happy with that Tony kid, who am I to rock the boat? I figured I'd write to her at some point.

Then I hopped the Hound for Austin and sat there that whole long ride reading the Big Book—that's the AA book, you know, where they've got the stories of Bill and Dr. Bob and those other guys who started the first groups back in the thirties. It was like reading the lives of the saints.

Jeff Doren picked me up at the station, and we went to the Soap Creek Saloon. He drank beer and I drank 7UP, and we drank a toast to our old pal Ron Jacobson, just about the nicest guy you'd ever want to meet.

I stayed with Jeff for a few weeks until I found my own place—this little garage fixed up into an apartment over west of the university between Lamar and Guadalupe. Fifty bucks a month, if you can believe that. I told you Austin was a cheap place to live. And I went out and applied at Braniff. While they were thinking about it, I got on busting bags at the airport because I had to get some money happening, and I knew if I didn't find something to occupy myself pretty damn quick, I'd go straight down the tube.

Thank God for AA. I'm one of these guys who really did that double ninety you hear about—ninety meetings in ninety days—and if that doesn't get you heavy into AA, nothing will. Maybe it's because I was coming from a Catholic background, but for me it felt like joining a religious order. I drank so much coffee I thought I was going to turn into a coffee bean. To this day, I don't care much for coffee except for a cup in the morning when I get up.

Eventually they had an opening at Braniff, and I slipped right into it. It was a terrific airline. They'd had some tough times, but they'd just changed management, and they were making a real effort with the public. That's when we were flying those pastel-colored aircraft—kind of a joke, but fun too—orange and red and green and pink aircraft. They were a good outfit to work for. And I bought myself an old piece-of-shit Chevy pickup truck. Needed some work on it, and I didn't mind doing the work. So I was on the road again.

Anybody new to AA, for a while the most important person in your life is your sponsor. I was real lucky getting the guy I got—although he drove me nuts from time to time, which, I guess, is one of the thing's your sponsor's supposed to do. His name was Art, and I can't tell you his last name because of the anonymous thing.

Art was one of those guys who came back from Korea with a hell of a thirst, and alcohol had screwed his life up so bad he had an ex-wife and three grown-up kids who wouldn't speak to him. He was a trim guy for somebody his age, and he had a little gray beard, one of these goatee things, and if you saw him walking down the street, you'd think he was—I don't know what, a jazz musician maybe—but certainly not some kind of heavy dude in the Department of Public Works, City of Austin, which is what he was. After he'd turned his life around, he'd started a new family, so he had a pretty young wife and two little girls in grade school, and his house was like a refuge for me. A million hours I sat around drinking coffee or 7UP with him while he chewed me out or cheered me up or whatever.

I started off real optimistic. You think that when you get sober, everything's going to get better right away, but the same things that bothered you when you were drunk still bother you. The only difference is you're sober. And another thing—Austin didn't turn out to be the little slice of paradise I'd been dreaming about. You can't go and hang out in funky country bars, or cat around checking out the nightlife, or do lots of things you used to like doing—when you're not drinking.

Don't get me wrong here, Austin was still okay. A warm, friendly place in general, and there was still a nice laid-back feeling to it, and I did have a lot of good times there, but— Well, having fun is not the main thing I remember. There was one night after I'd been in Austin a couple months, and I was at a meeting, and somehow or other the whole— I don't know if this has ever happened to you, but there's a point where you know where you've been and what you've lost, and it's so heavy you can't even cry about it. I came out of that meeting and I walked the streets for hours.

I kept thinking about that flight to Goose Bay, Labrador. When you know that the whole world could end at any minute, the only thing to do is get dead drunk, right? It's kind of obvious. And when I got back to Carswell, that's exactly what I did. But now I had a new way of thinking about it. When you know that the whole world could end at any minute, the only thing to do is live a good life.

———

I think maybe AA made sense to me right from the start because it's so much like the Catholic Church—you know, repentance and confession and all that. Like there's Steps Four and Five. They're real killers, but if you can't get through those suckers, you can't get nowhere. Step Four is where you make your fearless moral inventory of yourself, and Step Five is where you admit to God and yourself and to some other person exactly what you did wrong.

Naturally the person I picked to hear all this shit was my sponsor. We set aside a whole evening for it, and we settled down in a couple easy chairs in his living room, and I said, "Bless me, Father, for I have sinned."

It's a joke, right? And we both laughed about it, but then he gave me this real long hard look and said, "You sure you don't want to be talking to a priest?" He knew I'd been raised Catholic.

"No," I said.

"Why's that?"

"I'm not really hooked up with the Church at the moment."

"You still think of yourself as a Catholic?" he asked me.

"Hell, man, I'll always think of myself as a Catholic. But that's neither here nor there."

"Okay," he says, "go ahead."

When I'd been making my inventory, I'd said to him, "Give me a little guidance here," and he'd said, "I usually tell guys to start with the Ten Commandments and the seven deadly sins," so that's where I'd started too.

Well, not only had I coveted my neighbor's wife, I'd fucked the hell out of her, and that's what we call adultery. And then there's all those times when I knew perfectly well I shouldn't get involved with Connie again and I went ahead and did it anyway. Why? Because I was letting my prick do my thinking for me, and, yep, that's what we generally call lust.

When I was telling my story, it was real easy to slip off to blaming Connie, and every time I did that, Art caught me. "Wait a minute here. We're not doing that woman's inventory, we're doing *yours*. Let's just stick to *your* moral defects."

I used to tell myself that Connie didn't believe she was doing anything wrong so somehow that made everything all right, but of course it didn't—because *I* knew it was wrong. And it was real easy to say, oh, well, Connie was on her way to busting up her marriage, and if it hadn't been me, it would have been some other guy, but it wasn't some other guy.

Another big one was sloth. That one surprised me when I figured it out because I've always thought of myself as somebody who liked to work, and even when I was drinking, a lot of the time I did keep busy with one thing or another. But for years—pretty much from the point I joined the air force—I hadn't taken any initiative about any damn thing whatsoever.

"Most alcoholics are like that," Art said. "When you're drinking, life's just something that happens to you."

"But am I allowed to be pleased with myself over the few little things I did right?" I asked him.

"Oh, yeah, you're allowed to do that."

"Well, you know that little girl? Janice Dłuwiecki? She had a real rough summer, and I'm glad I was there to listen to her problems and help her out and all that. And I'm real glad I never laid a hand on her."

"Do you think she was in love with you?"

Boy, did I wish he hadn't asked me that. "I don't know, Art. She was just a kid."

"Kids have feelings too."

"Oh, yeah, I know they do."

"Don't you think you owe her a letter or a phone call or something?"

"Yeah, I guess I do."

So we went through the whole works. You've heard my story, so you've probably got a good idea what we talked about. It lasted damn near four hours, and just like you're supposed to, I felt this incredible relief afterward. But Art wasn't a priest so there was one thing he couldn't do, and that was grant me absolution.

For those first few months in Austin I spent a lot of my time *not drinking*, if you know what I mean. And eventually you hit a point where you want something more out of life than just what you're *not* doing, so I went to the Y and got back into the weight room. And it seemed like everybody and their dog was getting into jogging in those days, so I started jogging too.

That was a real turning point for me because jogging led to running, and then running led to road running, and lo and behold, I was transformed into one of those wild-eyed, pain-in-the-ass fanatical fitness nuts. When you get your running over six miles, the endorphins start kicking in and you get that runner's euphoria, and believe me, there's not a drug in the world can touch that. Sometimes I'd think, hell, why should I bother to do anything else? I might as well just keep right on running on out to Dallas.

Austin's a fine place to run for three seasons out of the year, but summer in

Texas is just hotter than hell, and a man would have to be crazier than a coot to try to run in Texas in the summer, but I never told you I wasn't crazy, did I? I'd go late in the day or at night when I was hoping the temperature had dipped down below a hundred, and I made sure to keep myself hydrated, and it was a kick to have the sweat rolling off me by the gallon, and I only came close to dropping dead from heat prostration maybe twice.

Yeah, so there's the weights, and I had my stretching routine so my muscles wouldn't start shortening up on me, and there was the running, and eventually I got to the point where the thought of getting drunk just seemed ridiculous. The world looked so sharp and clear, you know what I mean? When you're drinking, there's always something in between you and the world. Depending on how loaded you are, it can be as thin as a piece of Saran Wrap or as thick as if you smeared your eyes with Vaseline, but it's always there. And it sure felt good to get rid of it.

Alcoholics can always tell you when their last drink was. It was one year and four months since my last drink. And there was this guy from Braniff I was working out with, name of Hal Sweeney— For years I held it against him, but hell, it wasn't his fault.

One Saturday we banged through the weights and then we went out and knocked off ten or twelve miles on the road, you know, egging each other on past that last thin edge of insanity, and we had ourselves a nice long shower afterward, and I said something to the tune of how I didn't really miss the hard stuff, I just missed the old suds. And he said he'd read somewhere that you should drink a beer for every six miles run—replace your mineral salts. "Hell, man," he said, "how long's it been since you had a drink? Over a year? Shit, you got it licked. All the running you're doing, you can have a beer now and then. It'd do you good. Beer's a *food*, you know."

So we're getting dressed, and we're floating along in that terrific high you get after a good run, and he's making jokes about how he figures that article he read got the figures reversed so he has six beers for every mile, and we have a good laugh about that, and naturally we end up in a little friendly neighborhood tavern where he was one of the regulars, and lo and behold there's a pitcher of that fine Shiner Beer sitting in front of us. Well, Hal Sweeney wasn't an alcoholic. That was the problem.

You better believe that beer went down easy. I'm thinking, my God, why did I deny myself this little bit of pleasure all this time? I must have been nuts. Beer's a *food*, isn't it?

Hal had a date, and so did I for that matter, so we strolled out of the bar into that last little bit of daylight, and the whole world looked just wonderful to me, and I thought about how it hadn't looked anywhere near as wonderful as that for a long time. Hal got in his car and drove away. I stood next to my car, checking out the world, and what I was supposed to do was drive away too, but I thought, hell, it's been sixteen months since I had a drink, and if I'm going to have a drink—and I'd already had one—I might as well explore the sensation. You know, purely from a scientific point of view—learn a little bit more about myself and my addiction, right? So I walked back into the bar and ordered another pitcher.

Halfway through the second pitcher I had one of those Zen satoris you hear so much about. I realized that getting loaded is the most intense pleasure known to man and all other pleasures—love, sex, food, running, looking at a nice sunset, you name it—don't even come close. There were a number of other patrons in the bar, and I felt impelled to share this insight with them, and they turned out to be a nice bunch of fellows with insights of their own, and then one of those nice fellows set us all up with shots of tequila.

Hey, you don't really want me to run you through this whole thing, do you? Oh, hell no, let's just jump on ahead here. So it's about a week later—although I couldn't have told you how long it was. I couldn't have told you that one and one makes two. I'm laying on the floor in the crapper in your classic hole-in-the-wall down by the river with my face mashed into the piss and puke and cigarette butts, and somebody's saying, "*Con permiso, señor,* I gotta take the leak."

Carlos his name was. Well, I rolled over so Carlos could take the leak, and then he looked down and took pity upon the sorry state I was in, and he helped me up and inquired if he could assist me in any way.

Carlos had a lopsided VW bug with a medal of the Virgin of Guadalupe swinging from his rearview and huge holes in the floor so you had to be real careful where you put your feet—especially if you're only wearing socks—and he got me crammed in there somehow, and we drove up and down Red River Street until we found my truck. By then I was having a dim memory of a young lady, name of Rita, who I suspected might know the whereabouts of my sports watch, my fine leather belt, my hand-tooled cowboy boots, and my wallet.

I asked Carlos for his address, and a couple weeks later I hunted him up and offered him some money, but he wouldn't hear of it. Who says there ain't any good Samaritans left in the world?

Okay, so had I bothered to call them at work and tell them I wasn't coming in? Had I called up the honey I'd been supposed to pick up at eight? Are you kidding? I'd vanished instantly into the Land of Piss-on-It. It scared the absolute shit out of me. I'd been Mr. Reliable at Braniff up till then, so I gave them a song and dance about the worst case of flu in my life, and they bought it. The honey, the next time I called her, told me to go screw myself sideways. And then, of course, I had to have a little chat with my sponsor.

"You got cocky, didn't you?" he's asking me, and I allowed as how I'd probably got a little bit cocky. "You thought you had her dicked, didn't you?" Yeah, I said, I guess I'd figured I had her about three-quarters dicked.

"You moron," he says, "you're an alcoholic. It's not fair that pal of yours can have a couple beers and walk away from it and you can't. Yeah, that's really not fair. But whoever said life's fair?"

He asked me if I'd been going to meetings, and I said I hadn't been going to too many of them for a while now. He wanted to know why not. "Shit," I said, "I was tired of hanging around with a bunch of drunks."

So now we're into Jimmy Does AA, Phase Two. Once you've fallen off the wagon, you know it's *possible* to fall off the wagon and that changes everything. All my optimism was gone. Before, I'd been like, hey, wow, I'm a new man. Yay, Alcoholics Anonymous—go, team go. Maybe everybody else is going to screw up, but not me. No sir, no way, for I am Koprowski the Superdrunk, and I have been reborn. Well, all that was over.

It was fairly grim there for a while. You're supposed to pray a lot in AA, so every time I turned around, I was saying the Hail Mary. And I was working out like a maniac. And I was back to a meeting a day—driving all over hell and gone to meetings. I was real glad I got along with Art's wife and kids because any spare time I had, I was over at their house drinking coffee and iced tea and lemonade and that Italian soda pop Art liked, you know, Chinotto. "Guys who fall off the wagon," he said, "they've usually screwed up on their Twelve Steps somewhere." He told me to go back over my Twelve Steps with a fine-tooth comb.

So I got out all my scraps of paper—when they tell you they want you to write it down, they're not kidding—and I went over it all with a fine-tooth comb.

Okay, so there's Step Nine. That's when you make amends to people you've hurt, and I'd been pretty thorough there. Guys I'd owed money to back in Raysburg, I'd sent it to them. I'd paid back Linda her five hundred dollars and Old Bullet Head every cent he'd spent on me. I'd told my mom and my sister I was sorry for the way I'd just vanished on them, and I'd promised I'd keep in touch—which is what they'd both asked for—and I had kept in touch. I'd called Georgie Mondrowski and told him how sorry I was I hadn't been more help to him, and he'd told me I'd been more help to him than I knew, and the best amends I could make was to stay sober. I'd even called up Vick Dobranski, if you can believe that, and apologized for being such a jerk-off. Connie I couldn't make amends to for the simple reason that I didn't have a clue where she was—and besides which I figured maybe the best amends I could make to her was that she'd never see my sorry ass walking through her door ever again as long as she lived. And that just left one person.

Well, I'd tried to write Janice three or four times since I'd come to Austin, but I'd always given up. That time I sat down and wrote her a six-page letter. I got it done, and I wasn't sure about it, so I didn't mail it right away. Then about a week later I read it over, and you know what it was? Six pages of real complicated excuses why I'd behaved like an asshole. I tore that sucker up.

The longer I stayed away from Raysburg, the more reluctant I was to go back there. Some part of me was convinced that the moment I set foot in West Virginia, I wouldn't just fall off the wagon, I'd get shot off, like rocket assisted. The first Christmas, I explained it to Old Bullet Head on the telephone. "Look, Dad, Christmas is a heavy drinking time, and I'm just not ready to face it." He said he understood perfectly. My second and my third Christmases, he was a little less understanding.

My sister wrote to me regular as a clock. I've never been big on writing letters, but I'd send her little notes or funny postcards, and I'd call her up maybe once a month. We'd talk sometimes for an hour or more, and she'd keep saying, "Jimmy, this must be costing you a fortune," and I'd say, "Hey, what else do I have to spend my money on?"

Naturally I heard all about the progress of the polka band. Their name got changed pretty much the way they'd got the name in the first place—it was just what people said—and nobody bothered to say "My Sister's Polka Band," and so they turned into "the Polka Sisters." And they were doing real well. Just like Mary Jo always wanted, they were playing for damn near every event anywhere around the Ohio Valley where people liked pretty girls and polkas. And they started getting invited to polka festivals way far away—Pennsylvania, Michigan,

New York, even up in New England. Everywhere they went, people seemed to like them. "There's even Polka Sisters fan clubs springing up," Linda said. "Can you believe that? We get letters, asking for our pictures."

Linda always kept me up to date on how everybody was doing. Mary Jo was happy as a clam. She and old Gene Duda were living on his pension, so any money she made with the band was pure gravy. And Bev Wright's famous brother got her a job at the Jamboree Shop, so she finally got out of Barnsville and moved into town. And Patty Pajaczkowski? Hell, you expect weird things out of her, right? But still Linda couldn't believe it. "My God, Jimmy, she's gone straight!"

Well, not straight exactly, but it seems that Patty had given up all unnatural substances. That meant not just drugs, it meant cigarettes, coffee, tea, Coke—you name it. And meat too. What turned her around on this, I don't know—maybe her lizard told her to do it—but Bev Wright had a little apartment over in East Raysburg, and Patty turned up and said, "I'm kicking the whole works," and Bev said, "Go to it, Patty Cakes," and Patty crawled into bed and turned green.

I didn't see her myself, so I can't tell you if she turned a pale delicate green or if she got as green as a bullfrog, but I've talked to a number of people who did see her, and they all swear it's true. So she lay there in Bev's bed—Bev slept on the floor; that's some friend, right?—oh, for maybe a month. Anyhow until she turned back into her normal dead-white self, and then she got up and said, "Thanks a lot, Beverly, I feel great," and she got herself a job working at that hippie health-food store down by the lower market, and since then, she'd been living on brown rice and strange bags of slime imported from California.

I didn't ask about Janice, but Linda told me anyway. Janice graduated from Central and started going out to Brooke College. Her playing and singing just kept getting better and better, and she'd developed an incredible charisma on the stage. That wasn't hard for me to believe. And she was still dating that kid Tony. Linda said she wouldn't be too surprised if the wedding bells weren't going to be ringing for them, you know, a few years down the road.

When I was going into my third year in Austin, Linda told me the girls were thinking of cutting a record. Wherever they played, people were always asking them if they had a record, and there was this wonderful studio in Youngstown, but the problem was, they couldn't quite get the scratch together. "Look," I said, "if it's not a million bucks, I'll pay for it."

I had to really work at talking Linda into taking my money, but she got a quote from that studio, and it wasn't all that much, and I'd been really socking the money away—hell, I even had some bonds and blue chips—and I said, "Come on, kid, I'll never miss it."

So life was rolling right along, and a lot of things changed while I was in Austin. Somehow it felt like the whole mood of the country had changed. Like what? Well, like you never heard anything anymore about student protests. And if you'd hear guys at work talking about drugs, it wouldn't be grass or acid they'd be talking about, it'd be reds or blow. And if you'd hear the Beatles on the radio, they'd sound like they were back with the pterodactyls. So what was a big hit? One I remember was Melanie and "The Roller Skate Song." Who knows why anything's a hit, but there's one thing you could say about that song—it sure didn't sound like the sixties.

Then if you're fond of the honeys like yours truly, there were a few things to notice. You remember hot pants? All they were was what we used to call short shorts, but real short, and real tight, and I've got to admit I enjoyed the hell out of them while they lasted. Bright red lipstick came back, and skirts got longer, and then there were those dumb platform heels. I always thought they were just about the most ridiculous things anybody ever invented. And the girls stopped trying to look like little kids, so if you saw a girl dressed like she was ten, she probably was. And— Well, I don't know. More than just the fashions had changed, but it's hard to— Hell, it's kind of obvious, right? They signed the Paris Peace Accords, so the Vietnam War was over—the American part of it anyhow.

Of course there were girls wandering in and out of my life the whole time I was in Texas. What? You didn't think I'd turned into a monk, did you? When I first got to Austin, I thought I wouldn't get involved with anybody—not until I'd got my shit together—but I didn't make it more than a couple weeks and there was this stewardess and she was just so damn cute. It wasn't like she was a party animal or anything, and she was real sympathetic about me being in AA, but like any other girl in her twenties, she wanted to go out—out to a restaurant, out to hear some country music, you know, just *out*, and the best I could offer her was a movie because they don't sell booze at movies. Eventually she stopped being sympathetic. "At what point," she said, "do you turn back into a normal human being?" I didn't have any answer to that.

And then there was that totally insane hippie chick I picked up at Barton

Springs, but that really didn't last very long either, and— Well, I'm not going to list them all. It's not like there were that many anyway. And you know what kept happening with a lot of those girls? The word "commitment" kept popping up, and when it did, I'd hit it on down the road just about as fast as I could get my ass in gear.

I've got to admit I did think about it. Like, okay, Koprowski, just what is it you want out of life anyway? You want a family, don't you? So one of these days you're going to quit running and settle down with one of these girls, and then the kids will start coming, and there you'll be in a little house somewhere with a honey and some kids, working at Braniff and living in Austin until you turn into an old crock, retired and drawing a pension. So what was wrong with that picture? Nothing that I could see. Except maybe I just hadn't found the right girl.

The next thing I know, I'm turning thirty. I didn't like that one little bit—*thirty*. It scared the bat piss out of me, if you want to know the truth, and I'd been feeling sour and depressed for awhile anyway, and I couldn't figure out why. I thought maybe it was just because I wasn't going out with anybody right at that moment.

So sometime early in the year, I decided it was about time for me to take stock of my life again, have another hard look at the Twelve Steps and like that. I drove to one of my favorite spots out in the Hill Country. I went for a nice run, and I drank about a gallon of Perrier water, and I cooked a steak on my primus stove, and I put some Merle Haggard on my tape deck, and I did my lonesome cowboy number. It'd been a long time since I'd gone off by myself like that.

One of the things I loved about the Hill Country is it looks so different from West Virginia. Lots of room—plenty of room—and you've got your basic beautiful nature stuff, little streams and rolling hills and spectacular sunsets and stars and all that, and not a sign of a blast furnace anywhere. Well, it did make me feel better being out there, and at the same time I ran smack into this thought I'd been having for awhile—shit, Koprowski, maybe you don't belong in Texas. It was a sad thought. I'd been trying like hell to belong in Texas, but all the time I was there— Well, to give you some idea, I'd be walking somewhere and I'd see a scruffy old aloe plant sticking up, and I'd think, come on, Koprowski, who are you kidding? You don't belong in a place where something as goofy as that can grow right out of the ground.

The reason I'd gone to Texas in the first place was because of Jacobson and Doren, but Jacobson was dead and Jeff Doren I hadn't seen in over a year. He was an alcoholic and a coke head, and he had no real desire to quit that I could see, and I was so far away from being able to Twelve-Step him—that's when you help other people—I just couldn't deal with him. I'd made a lot of other friends in Austin, but except for Art, my sponsor, I couldn't think of a single one of them I'd feel too bad about leaving.

But if I didn't belong in Texas, where did I belong? The Ohio Valley? It wasn't like I didn't miss my family, but— Well, drinking's so much a part of the Polish culture, it felt like asking me to go back to the valley was like asking me to make a little visit straight to Hell.

I lay there for hours in my little campsite under the stars and went over and over everything. If you don't know where you belong and what you're doing by the time you're thirty, maybe you're never going to know. I just couldn't shake the feeling that something wasn't right. Like something wasn't ever going to be right. It was like an empty feeling inside—that I kept bumping into at odd moments. I read somewhere in one of those AA books—I wish I could remember who said it, but naturally I can't—but anyhow, it's that some alcoholics get *spirits* confused with *the Spirit*. And the minute I read it, I knew it was true.

It wasn't just all those times when I used to get dead drunk and go stumbling into the church to pray. I mean that was part of it, but there was something else too. Drinking used to give me something that felt—well, you know, religious. Like right around the corner was an angel or something that was going to change my life. Drinking used to give me the feeling that life matters. That's how I felt when I started drinking anyway—you know, back in high school. Later on, after you've been doing it for a few years, the only feeling you get from drinking is that you're drinking.

But one thing I'd learned in Texas was that you could get those heavy mysterious feelings when you're sober. Sometimes running. Or sometimes just out of nowhere, maybe just walking down the street, and zing, there you are. My religious feelings were mainly going into AA, and somehow it never occurred to me to go back to the Church, but I started going to the library— You probably never took me for a reader, right? But there's been times in my life where I read a lot. So I read all the AA stuff and then—

Well, I read things I thought Janice might have read, and I'd wonder what she'd thought about this or that, if it'd helped her on her spiritual quest. I read some history books about Poland, and I read some books about the Second World War and even some religious books—like about these priests who'd died in the war and like that. I'd see something on the shelf, and I'd think, yeah, that's something Janice would like, so I'd read it. I guess it was my way of trying to stay close to her, if that makes any sense.

She'd pop into my head out of nowhere, or maybe I'd see a girl who reminded me of her—a blonde, or maybe a kid in pigtails—and I'd go, yeah, it still hurts, all right. It was like I used to feel about Dorothy Pliszka—only a million times worse because with Janice it was real. But I kept thinking about how little girls are with their crushes—they get over them—and I figured she'd got over me. I mean, Linda kept telling me how serious Janice was about that kid Tony, right? And so the best thing for me to do was get over her, and maybe if I gave myself a chance, I could do it. But hell, it'd been over three years. How much more of a chance was I supposed to give myself?

So I came back from my little camping trip, and I hadn't arrived at any profound conclusions, and about a week later I got a call from Linda. The record I'd paid for had just come out, and she was telling me how wonderful it was, what a terrific cover and how clean and crisp the sound was, a real professional job. And they were going to play at the Pączki Ball at the church at the end of February, and that was going to be their first public appearance since the record came out, and, oh, wouldn't it be wonderful if I could come back for it? And I made up some excuse the way I always did—how I'd used up my vacation time or some damn thing—and she sounded real disappointed the way she always did, but the minute I hung up the phone, I thought, hey, why not?

But of course I couldn't possibly get the time off, right? I just happened to mention it to my supervisor, and he said, "Sure. You want to take a week off? No problem." Nobody in their right mind wants to take their vacation time in February.

I was running out of time, so I figured I couldn't possibly get a hop anywhere back east at that late date. "Pittsburgh, huh? Sure. Just so long as you don't want to go on the weekend." People don't fly much in February.

I didn't really believe I was going until I got on the plane. I didn't bother to tell my sister because I didn't want to disappoint her if I changed my mind at the last minute. But I didn't change my mind at the last minute. I changed it after we were in the air.

TWENTY-THREE

So there I am flying into the Pittsburgh Airport on a Monday afternoon, and I'm just not ready for the Pittsburgh Airport. It was a pissy little dump back in those days—like an overgrown bus station—and the weather was miserable, cold with blowing rain, and it just depressed the hell out of me. I rented a car. I forget exactly what, a compact of some kind, and if I'd fired it up and aimed it south, I would have been in Raysburg by dinnertime, but that isn't what I did. I drove to the Holiday Inn and I checked into it. If you asked me why I did that, I really couldn't tell you.

They weren't doing a booming business so they gave me a big fancy room for the price of an ordinary one, and I dumped my flight bag into the middle of the floor and fell over onto one of the double beds and lay there for maybe an hour watching whatever little bit of daylight was left, and I watched it turn into nothing, and eventually I got up and slithered down to the dining room, and it took every bit of resolve I had not to drink my dinner. I kept thinking, so what did you expect, asshole? A motel room at the Pittsburgh Airport? I just didn't know what the hell I was doing there.

I went back up to my room and called room service and had them bring me a six-pack of tonic water. They probably figured I had a fifth of gin, but I didn't have any gin. If you're used to drinking, you like to have something to drink even if it hasn't got any alcohol in it, and I liked the bitter taste of tonic water, and there's no caffeine so you don't get wired like a Christmas tree, and if you've picked up a touch of malaria, well, it takes care of that too.

So I'm pacing up and down and bouncing off the walls, and I'm sucking back the tonic water, and I'm watching the latest installment of Watergate on the tube. I'd been following it real close. Hell, it was better than the World Series. Do you remember that shit? Is Nixon going to turn over the tapes or is he not going to turn over the tapes? Gee, wonder how they got all those big holes in the tapes? And of course it all comes down to the big question—are they going to get that sucker or not? Are they going to impeach his sorry ass or what? Like a lot of people, I really wanted to see him go down.

Eventually I ran out of news programs, so I was reduced to flipping through the channels looking for any show with some pretty girls in it. I kept thinking that maybe I should just fly back to Texas in the morning. The Ohio Valley felt like a black hole to me—like the minute I hit the gravitational field down there, I'd be sucked right into it and never be seen again—and I can't begin to tell you what was going on in my head. You ever get so scared you can't think straight?

So there I am pacing back and forth till God knows when—after four in the morning, anyway—and I figured, what the hell, maybe I could catch a few Z's, so I crawled into one of the beds, and then I tossed and turned for a couple more hours, having those horrible dreams you can't quite remember. I must have wore myself right out because when I did get to sleep, I was just gone.

I woke up and it was two in the afternoon. Checkout time was noon, but they didn't have a lot of customers—I did happen to mention it was February, didn't I?—and I'd put that "Do Not Disturb" sign on my door, and they'd let me sleep. I went down and had a nice big breakfast. By then I'd been at the Pittsburgh Airport for damn near twenty-four hours.

I shaved and had a nice long shower. I put on a western shirt and a clean pair of jeans, and my belt with the silver buckle, and my cowboy boots—so anybody who saw me would know me for a nice fellow from Texas and maybe they'd let me go back there. I climbed in that dumb little car and drove south—and driving, you know, has always been a good thing for me. I remember a lot more rain and a country music station on the radio. I wasn't feeling any too wonderful, but at least my mind was clear, and I thought, Koprowski, you fool, you're afraid to see Janice.

I didn't need any sign to tell me I was in West Virginia because, like always, I could feel it under my wheels as all of a sudden the road went from good to lousy. And there was the river—the big sad dirty Ohio—and I was following along it same as always, and it looked like nothing had changed and nothing would ever change. There's those lumpy hills all stripped and shit brown in the winter, and the Staubsville Mill blazing away against that pissy gray sky, and all

I've got to do is keep on driving south. Then there I am, pulling up in front of our house. I put on my cowboy hat because that's what you wear to keep the rain off your head out in Texas, and I got out of the car and walked up the steps.

I'll never forget this. It was one of the weirdest moments of my life. It wasn't quite dark yet, but the streetlights were on. The rain was blowing itself out, and the sky was clearing, and it was that beautiful painful blue you get sometimes just on the edge of the dark, and there was all this yellow light pouring out of our window, and I felt like— I don't know how to say this. Well, it was like I'd died and I was some kind of ghost.

I'd helped my father put that window in—although I don't know how much help I would have been. I was about ten at the time. Most of the houses in South Raysburg were built back in the twenties and they had dumb little windows, and then in the fifties a lot of the guys decided they needed nice big picture windows in their living rooms. Of course Old Bullet Head did it himself, and I remember being amazed that you could cut a bigger hole in your wall, and bring in a pane of glass without breaking it, and get it to fit into that hole in your wall, and finish it off so it looked just like an honest-to-God window. I remember thinking that you had to be a real grown-up man to be able to do something like that.

Mom hadn't shut the drapes yet. I don't know why I stopped and looked in the window. And I could see through the living room right on back to the dining room, and Mom was doing something in there. She looked kind of preoccupied, or sad, and it just felt so strange to be standing outside watching her—with her not knowing I'm there. Like if she was thinking about me at all, she was probably imagining me out in Texas. I watched her go into the kitchen and come back with some more stuff on a tray, and I finally figured out what she was doing. That was all the *pączki* she'd made, and she was getting ready to take them to the church.

It was my house—or it used to be—so why didn't I just walk in? Or I could have rung the bell or knocked or something. But it was like I was a stranger, like I'd never lived there, like I didn't even have the right to be there. And then all of a sudden I just couldn't stand it anymore, so I went charging right inside, and Mom jumped about a foot.

I'm going, "Hi, *Mamusiu*," and she's going, "Oh, Jimmy! Mother of God, I can't believe it." She's hugging me and saying all these dumb things and, you know, patting me like she's got to make sure I'm real. "Scare me half to death, why don't you?" she says. "You about gave me heart failure. What are you doing here? You haven't lost your job, have you?"

"No, no, no. I've just got a week off, and—"

"Everything all right? Look at you, there's no meat on you. Have you been sick?"

"Oh, no, Mom, I'm healthy as a horse."

"What's the matter? Aren't you eating?"

"Are you kidding? I eat everything I can get my hands on."

"My God, Jimmy, your sister's going to die when she sees you. Oh, where's your father? I've got to get my *pączki* over to the church. Here, eat one—no, no, take a hot one. Where the hell *is* your father? Jimmy, I just can't believe you're here. I saw you walking in, and I thought, who's that damn cowboy just walking right into my house?"

My mom's going on and on, same as always. "Your sister," she says, "she's got even crazier. I could just weep when I think of all the money that was spent on her education, and all she cares about is playing in that polka band with Mary Jo Duda and those other crazy girls."

And she's telling me about the girls Linda's age who've got married already, but fat chance of Linda ever marrying anybody when all she does is play her trumpet. "Your sister got one of those mute things because she was driving your dad and me nuts," she says, "and you'd think it'd help, wouldn't you?"

And does Linda go out on dates? Are you kidding? All she does is hang out with that little Dłuwiecki girl and Bob Pajaczkowski's crazy daughter, the tattooed lady. "I've spent my whole life surrounded by crazy people," my mother says, "so why did I expect it was ever going to be any different?"

I'm standing there munching on a *pączek* and laughing at my mother, and thinking, hey, this ain't so bad, and Old Bullet Head walks in. His mouth just drops open. "Look here, Walt," my mother says, "see what the cat drug in."

"Well, I'll be damned," he says.

I could count on the fingers of one hand the number of times in my life I hugged my father, and we didn't start out to hug each other, but it turned out that way. "Aw, you dumb jerk," he says. "It's great to see you. When'd you get in? What are you doing here?"

"I came back for the Pączki Ball."

"You didn't quit your job, did you?"

"Come on, Dad, give me a break. No, I did not quit my job. I didn't get fired either. I got a week's vacation."

So my father and I carried all the *pączki* out to his car—the latest one of his blue Chryslers—and he says to me under his breath, "You still on the straight and narrow?"

"Oh, you bet," I said. "I wouldn't trade my sobriety for a million bucks." It was a standard-issue AA line, but I believed it—or anyhow I was doing my best to believe it.

We got to the church, and Old Bullet Head wanted to play a trick on Linda. That's the kind of sense of humor he's got. So I had to wait outside, and he went inside to tell her some damn fool story he'd cooked up. She steps out the side door from the parish hall, and she's got this annoyed look on her face, and then she sees me and just bursts into tears. She flings her arms around me, and she's laughing and crying at the same time, going, "Oh, Jimmy, Jimmy, I can't believe it!" The old man's standing there grinning at us like an idiot.

"Dad, that was really mean," she says. "You know what he told me? He said, 'Hey, Linny, there's some strange cowboy outside wants to talk to you for a minute.' And I kept saying, 'What? What cowboy? I don't know any cowboys.'"

She leads me into the parish hall, and she's talking a mile a minute—still crying, you know—and hanging on to me like she's afraid if she lets go, I'll vanish instantly back to Texas, and it's like something's melted inside me. The minute I saw my sister, I knew coming back was the right thing to do.

We go plunging into your basic pandemonium. It's a couple hours till the festivities start, but it takes a lot of volunteers to put on an event like that, and they're all running around—guys from the men's club setting up tables, and the ladies from the sodality coming in with their doughnuts, and people coming in to do whatever—take the tickets, or sell you setups or beer, or doing anything else that needs to get done so you can have yourself a good time at the Pączki Ball.

They've got the hall decorated real nice with red and white crepe paper, and they've put in a little stage for the band—not real high, just a low platform to get them off the floor—and behind the stage there's the Stars and Stripes on one side and on the other there's the Polish flag, I guess to remind us we're Polish Americans in case any of us forgot it for a minute there. It's all so damn familiar, and I know everybody I see—guys shaking my hand, like Patty Pajaczkowski's dad and Larry Dombrowczyk's dad, going, "Hey, Jimmy, great to see you," and it's all too much—I can't take it in—and Linda's still hanging on to me, telling me how thin I am, and asking me if I'm okay, and not giving me a chance to answer her because she won't shut up long enough.

She keeps trying to lead me back to where the band's setting up, but we keep getting stopped. Here's Burdalski and some of the other guys from the PAC—Bob Winnicki and Franky Wierzcholek and I don't know who all—

coming in with kegs of beer, and they've got to do their "Hey, Koprowski, what the hell you doing here? You get lost or something?"

Eventually we get back to the stage, and Linda finally lets go of her death grip on me, and Mary Jo gives me a big sweaty hug and I can smell that she's already started in on the suds. And then Bev's giving me a hug, and even crazy Patty hugs me. "Well, stud, so tell me," she says, "how's things these days on the streets of Laredo?"

They were all dressed alike—in white slacks and white shoes and red vests with the Polish eagle embroidered on them and their name, the Polka Sisters— and the minute I'd walked in, I'd registered this tall willowy blonde, and walking toward the back I'd even got to the point of thinking, well, they must have got themselves a new band member Linda never told me about, and damned if it wasn't the same stupid thing I'd done on her sixteenth birthday—you know, not recognizing her—because that tall willowy blonde was Janice. And somehow I'd known who it was the minute I'd laid eyes on her, but I just hadn't *wanted* to know it, if you know what I mean. "Hi, Jimmy," she says, and I'm so blown away I can't say a word.

Of course I'd expected to feel bad seeing her again, but I hadn't expected to feel that bad. Like I've got a horrible pain in my chest, and my mouth's gone dry, and my stomach's in a knot, and I'm just, you know, stunned. And then, like your basic moron, I say the first thing that pops into my head—"What happened to your pigtails?"

Her hand goes up to her hair like automatic, and she says, "I kept them as long as I could." Her voice sounds hurt or something—I don't know what it sounds like—and she just looks at me with those huge blue eyes. It's obvious I'm not going to get a hug out of her.

I guess I must have been staring at her. The reason Janice hadn't had much of a figure when she'd been sixteen was that she was never going to be getting much of a figure. Well, she was a little bit curvier, but she was still this tall lean beanpole just like her dad. And it's not like she was wearing gobs of makeup, but in my head she was still sixteen and it was still 1970, and it really startled me, seeing her with that fire-engine–red lipstick a lot of the girls had started wearing again. And it wasn't like her hair was real short. It was down to her shoulders and curly around her face. I don't know one hairstyle from another, but it must have been whatever was big that month at Zarobski's because Linda had the same thing.

And there was something else too—just the way she was standing and looking at me or something—and I couldn't get it. She hadn't changed all that much, and at the same time she'd changed completely—like she was a totally different person. She still looked young, but nobody would think she was a little kid. No, not in a million years would anybody think she was a little kid.

Then she said—to nobody in particular—"Excuse me a minute," and she just walked away. Real fast. Like she was in a hurry to get somewhere. She walked all the way across the hall and out the door. She hadn't seemed the least bit glad to see me. Well, what the hell had I expected, the way I'd treated her? I was so ashamed, I just can't tell you.

There was this little pause—this little silence with the girls in the band looking at each other—and then they all started talking at once, like, okay, if there's anything weird going on here, we'll yuk it up and cover it right over. Linda's going, "Hey, Jimmy, don't you want to see what your money paid for?" and she leads me over to a table where there's a couple cartons of records, and she pulls one out and hands it to me.

I'm still thinking about Janice, but I'm pretending everything's all right— you know, for my sister—but when I see the cover, I've got to laugh. It is pretty funny. At the top it says "The Polka Sisters Present" and on the bottom "An Old-Time Polish Picnic." The picture's out at the park. Mary Jo is standing behind a picnic table with a great big grin on her face like she's just yelled, "Bingo!" and the table is crammed with food—*kiszka* and *kiełbasa* and buns and ketchup and relish and chopped onions and sauerkraut, and there's big plates of *pierogi* and *gołąbki*, and a bowl of sour cream, and of course a gigantic pitcher of cold beer. Janice and Linda are standing on one side of the table and Patty and Bev on the other, and they're smiling out at you and sort of pointing at the table like, come on, buddy, dive right in. Mary Jo just looks like Mary Jo, but the girls are dressed up in peasant outfits with the white blouses and the embroidered vests and the flowered skirts and the ribbons and flowers in their hair—they've even got Bev Wright dressed up like that—and they're wearing these white plastic boots to the knee like you'd buy at the El Cheapo Superior out at the mall. "Wow, terrific," I say, "it's the Polka Dolls."

"Oh, shut up, Jimmy," Linda says. And she drops her voice down so Mary Jo won't hear her. "Mary Jo drove all the way up to Pittsburgh to borrow those costumes," she says. "They were from some folk dance troupe up there or something, and she was so pleased with herself we just couldn't say no," and she's telling me how much fun it was to pose for that picture because as soon as the photographer got done, they ate up all the food on the table.

I'm standing there talking to my sister and somebody grabs me from behind and lifts me right up into the air. It's Georgie Mondrowski. He's got just huge—your basic man mountain—and he's trimmed his beard, but he still hasn't had a haircut, and his ponytail's halfway down his back. He's going, "Where'd you drop from, asshole?" and I'm patting his big belly and going, "You better start eating a little more, buddy, or you're going to fade right away." Boy, was I ever glad to see him. And Linda gives my hand a squeeze and says she's got to go warm up. "I still get so nervous," she says.

Georgie and I walked around the hall and filled each other in on the last few years. They'd started up a Vietnam vets group in Raysburg, and he was real big on that. "None of this VA bullshit," he says. "It's ours, just us." And he and some of the guys were doing their vets' trash removal service where, when you call them up, they'll quick as a wink clean out your attic or your garage or whatever, and it wasn't a lot of money but it was better than a sharp stick in the eye, and he was generally feeling better about things. And I was telling him how great everything was out in Texas.

People were starting to come in early to get themselves a good table, so I was shaking everybody's hand. Vick Dobranski and his wife came in, and I was surprised how friendly he was, like I was a long lost son or something, and he told me he wished I was still living in the valley because he was getting old and just couldn't keep on top of the work anymore and a lot of his customers were slipping away from him.

It was touching how everybody seemed so glad to see me, and I kept thinking, hey, this is nice. It's okay to be here. But at the same time I couldn't shake that sick, ashamed feeling in the pit of my stomach, and I kept thinking about Janice. Where the hell had she been going in such a hurry?

Naturally, the minute she came back, I saw her. I'd been watching for her, and I felt—well, like an electric shock when I saw her, like ZAP from all the way across the hall. She'd been in a hurry leaving, and she was in a hurry coming back. She walked straight over to where the band was set up. She walked right past me and Georgie, but I couldn't tell if she saw us. She took her clarinet out of its case and put it together and blew a scale through it and then put it down on this little gadget—I guess a clarinet stand. And I started drifting over in her general direction.

She looked out into the hall, and she couldn't really avoid seeing me. And I gave her a little wave—one of those things you could pretend you didn't notice if, you know, you wanted to play it that way—and she stepped down off the stage like she was killing time, just wandering around, and she ended up passing by close to where I was, and I said, "Hi, Janice," and she said, "Hi, Jimmy," and she didn't really stop walking, but she slowed down, and she said, "It's nice to see you. How have you been?" and Georgie gave me a wink and drifted away.

I walked along with Janice, and I said, "I'm good. I'm great. How about you?"

"Oh, I'm good too. Hey, thanks for paying for our record. That was really nice of you."

"Oh, I was glad to do it. I haven't heard it yet, but it looks like a real nice record. So, ah, Linda tells me you're going out to Brooke—"

"Yeah. I'm a sophomore."

"You like it?"

"I love it. It's a terrific school. Small, but really a good school. It's so quiet and pretty out there."

So we drift away from everybody until we bump into the wall, and then we prop it up. You know, just casual as all hell. I'm sweating like a pig, and it's not particularly hot in there.

"You look terrific, Janice," I say. "You look all grown-up."

"Thanks. I guess I should be grown-up by now. I'm going to be twenty next month."

"Yeah, I remember when your birthday is."

"Yeah. That's right. You would remember. You were at my sixteenth."

"Yeah, that's right, I was. So how's your family?"

"They're good. They're all good."

She told me her brother Mark was graduating from Yale in the spring, and he'd done real well there. And John and Anna had a kid—a little boy—and John was just finishing up his Ph.D. And she said, wow, did I ever look like I was in good shape. She'd heard from Linda I was working out like a fiend, and I said, yeah, I was doing that, and I told her about road running. And I don't know why it seemed important to say it to her, but I told her a little bit about AA. I guess maybe I wanted to remind her of how she'd given me that AA talk all those years ago, but if she remembered, she didn't mention it.

"I'm glad you're doing so well," she said. "We knew you'd make it. We were all rooting for you," and I gave her the standard-issue AA stuff about one day at a time and turning over your life to a higher power and like that.

I asked her what she was majoring in, and she said history, and I said that figured, and she said she was specializing in modern European history, and I said that really figured, and we both got a little bit of a laugh out of that one. "So, are you going out with anybody?" I said.

"No," she said. "I've been dating this guy out at Brooke, but I'm not really *going* with him—"

"Yeah? But I thought— Well, Linda told me you were going out with that Italian kid."

"Oh. Tony. Oh, yeah, I went with him for a long time. But he was always more serious than I was. I kept telling him I was too young to get pinned down, but— So I just had to break up with him. It was really sad. We're still friends. Maybe— I don't know if you can ever be friends with somebody you used to go out with— How about you? You going with anybody?"

"No, not at the moment. I mean I have been going out with some nice girls and all, but nobody right at the moment."

There was a little pause and then she asked me if I liked Texas, so I launched into my Texas-is-paradise routine. I must have gone on for ten minutes without taking a breath. I mean, the Austin Chamber of Commerce should have put me on a retainer. And I was telling her what a great airline Braniff was, and how I loved my job, and how I was making real decent money, and how I was just, you know, pretty much happy as a man could be. I listened to myself going on and on, and I just— Well, I felt like an asshole.

She told me she was glad everything was going so well for me, and she asked me how long I was going to be around, and I said about a week. "Maybe we could get together and have coffee or something," I said.

"Yeah," she said, "I'd like that. Call me."

So that was that, and Janice went back to fooling with her clarinet, and I didn't know what to do. For a while I wandered around talking to people. I was feeling almost exactly the same way you do when you're going into withdrawal— the shakes and the headache and the cold sweat and the sick stomach—and that was just crazy. I didn't know what the hell was happening to me, but all of a sudden I knew I had to get out of there. If I didn't, I was going to drink everything in sight.

I grabbed my jacket and my ten-gallon hat, and I walked straight down to the river. I must have told you how close the church is to the river. The rain had stopped, and it was clearing up a bit, and it wasn't a bad night for February in the Ohio Valley. Just like I'd done a million times before, I stood there and stared at the lights on the Ohio side, and— Well, it sure wasn't Texas. A barge was going by, and it had its big searchlight on, shining on the hills. It was carrying load after load of coal.

You know that line in the Bible—I don't remember where it is, probably in one of the Psalms—about your mouth being full of ashes? That's how I felt, and I thought, well, maybe I'm getting ready for Ash Wednesday early. I was pretty sure if I went back into the parish hall, I was going to drink. So obviously I couldn't go back into the parish hall. Right. So what was I going to do? Go back to the house and watch TV? Boy, that would make for a cheery evening, all right.

But then I thought, no, wait a minute. You're not going to do that. Because I knew what I was coming up against. I was avoiding Step Nine with Janice— just the way I'd been avoiding it for years—and either it means something or it doesn't, and if it means something, then you've got to do it. Even if you don't want to. Even if it's not going to be a barrel of laughs.

So I walked straight back to the church and through the parish hall and up to the stage. I don't suppose they had more than five or ten minutes before they had to start playing.

I said, "Janice, excuse me. Can I talk to you for a minute?"

She just looked at me kind of blank, and then she said, "Sure," and jumped down off that little stage. We went and stood in a corner.

"I know my timing's lousy," I said. "I'm sorry. I know you've got to play. And you're probably getting nervous—"

"I don't get nervous," she said, "but come on, Jimmy, what is it? I don't have a lot of time."

I was just stammering around like a goddamn fool. "Look— I just wanted to say— When I was drinking, you know— Well, if I ever did any harm to you when I was drinking— Hell, that's bullshit. I know perfectly well I hurt you. I just wanted to say I'm sorry. I mean, I just can't tell you how sorry I am. It's bothered me for years. I mean it's bothered me a whole hell of a lot. I never forgot you, you know, not for a minute, and I'll never forget you— I'll never forget how close we were. And I wanted to ask you to forgive me. If you can. And I just wanted to ask you if there's anything I can do to make amends to you."

Making that dumb little speech was one of the hardest things I ever did in my life, and I felt like I was hanging out on a limb about ninety miles. She closed her eyes for a few seconds. Then she looked right at me. "You're right," she said, "you really hurt me."

"I know I did, Janice. And I'm just sorry as all hell."

"Thank you," she said. "Thank you for saying that. It means a lot to me."

Somebody up on the stage—Bev, I think—was yelling, "Janice, come *on*," and she yelled back really annoyed, "Just a second, okay?" and then she said to me, "Jimmy, I forgave you a long time ago."

"Thank you," I said. What else could I say?

"But I'm serious here," I said. "Is there any way I can make amends to you?"

That was the first time she smiled at me. "I'll think of something," she said. "Talk to me at the break, okay?"

"Okay."

"I mean *really* talk to me at the break, okay?"

"Yeah. Right. I will."

Then she hopped back up on the stage, and I leaned against the wall breathing this huge sigh of relief. My knees felt weak. I felt like this huge weight had rolled off me. It's true what I'd said to her—I'd been carrying that weight around with me for years, and like with a lot of things, I'd never admitted to myself how bad it'd been. I was already starting to feel better—that pain in my stomach was gone—and I thought, just stick with the program, buddy. Because it works.

TWENTY-FOUR

I'm standing by myself off to one side, close to the stage. Mary Jo gets up to the mike. "Hi, folks," she says, "you all know me. I'm Mary Jo, the polka lady, and these pretty girls behind me here are the Polka Sisters," and she does her number about their record—how much fun they had making it—and if you want to buy a record, Darlene over there will be happy to sell you one. And Darlene Mondrowski waves her hand in the air so everybody will know where she is.

Then Mary Jo booms out in her great big voice, "But I know what you folks are waiting for. Okay, without further ado, here she is—our own polka princess—Janice."

Janice steps up to the mike. She gets a good round of applause and she takes a minute to look out at everybody and smile. You never saw anybody so relaxed on a stage. Then she says, "Are we proud to be Polish?"

Well, of course we are, and we let her know it too. And while everybody's clapping and whooping and yelling and whistling and stomping their feet, she yells out, "And if you're *not* Polish, you're sure going to be Polish tonight!" and she grabs up all that energy coming back at her and just flips it right into a polka. Counting in the tune—*"Raz Dwa!"*—and there's Patty and Bev— WHAM—laying down the beat, and Mary Jo squeezing out the intro, and it just yanks everybody up and onto their feet. Like one second there was nobody dancing and the next second the floor's crammed and people are laughing because it feels so good.

Janice is singing that old tune that says we're going to go from town to town, and we're going to dance, and we're going to sing, and we're basically going to party on till the sun comes up—

> *"Od miasteczka do miasteczka*
> *Hej, od miasteczka do miasteczka pojedziemy*
> *Będziem tancować i śpiewać*
> *I teraz hulać."*

It's a tune you could belt out real easy because it's a real upbeat tune, and I've heard it belted out lots of times, but she's easing it out like honey. Her voice is smoother than I remember—not as raw—but it's still got that wild old-country sound to it like when she was sixteen.

I'm hanging on every damn word—the way she caresses the word *"pojedziemy."* It's so gentle and so careful—like she just adores that word. All it means is "we will go," but she makes it sound so mysterious. Like go where? Go to the most wonderful and mysterious place you've ever been in your life.

Yeah, she's a great singer, but it's more than that. It's not like Polish is my language, you know. English is my language. But Polish is the first language I ever spoke, and it's a language I heard all around me when I was growing up, and I haven't heard a word of it all the time I've been in Texas, and it just gets to me somehow—hearing her sing, *"Hej, od miasteczka do miasteczka pojedziemy."*

They kicked into the drive. I was still staring at Janice because I was, I guess you'd have to say, just blown away. Then I heard one of the most beautiful sounds I've ever heard in my life. For a second or two, I thought it was a mistake. I'm not kidding you here, I just couldn't believe it could be coming from the band—like I thought somebody must have turned on a stereo by mistake or something. There's these big, fat, round, perfect notes just flowing along so easy, and I can't imagine what it could be. So I start looking around to try to figure out where that wonderful sound's coming from, and I see it's my sister playing the trumpet.

My eyes start streaming with tears. Just that quick, you know, and I can't do a thing about it. I'm so happy for her, I just can't tell you. And Janice is playing her clarinet—like a little bird flying around Linda's round, fat beautiful notes—and the band's laying down this terrific polka groove, Patty driving them along, Mary Jo pushing it with the bellows shake, and so relaxed, you know what I mean? So easy. And Bev is smacking out those big deep bass notes right on the beat where you want to hear them—feel them—if you're dancing. Yeah, well, I can stand there and cry like an idiot, or I can dance.

The nearest girl is Mondrowski's little sister. I don't figure she's going to be selling too many records during the first polka, so I say, "Come on, kid," and she jumps up just like she was waiting for somebody to ask her, and away we go.

I think I've told you that I like to step right along. So I lead her in a big circle around the hall. The band's really smoking.

The minute I start to move, I feel this tremendous energy go surging through me like four million volts, and I'm just swept right up into the whole shebang. It's all so familiar, you know what I mean? All these familiar faces, all these people I've known my whole life, and there I am right smack in the middle of it all again—hell, it feels like I'm in the middle of the whole damn universe—dancing like a madman and laughing with Darlene Mondrowski.

And here comes her big brother, my old friend crazy Georgie, and he's giving Maureen Wierzcholek a hell of a workout, and here's Larry Dombrowczyk with Arlene Orlicki, and she's doing her cute little majorette-style polka the same as always, and here's my mom and dad still taking it kind of easy because, you know, the night's young and if you're one of the older folks, you've got to pace yourself, and I can already feel that goofy frenzy starting to build up, like we're just going to get crazier and crazier right up to the stroke of midnight when everything stops dead—BANG, just like that—because midnight's Ash Wednesday and the beginning of Lent.

Well, Darlene and I danced the hell out of that polka, and we're coming off the dance floor, and we're both of us panting, and she's turned pink as a pig, and we're giggling like a couple fools, and she's headed back to her table in case somebody wants to buy a record, and I'm standing there catching my breath with the sweat just rolling off me, and lo and behold, Franky Wierzcholek is shoving a big plastic cup of beer at me. "Here you go, Koprowski." Yeah, a nice gesture, well meant, your basic friendly Polak thing to do, and you better believe it looks good, just like a TV ad, foam spilling down the side.

Right out of nowhere—he must have been watching me—here's Georgie Mondrowski. "He doesn't need that, Frank," he says, and he pushes the beer away. I've never been so grateful.

Georgie wraps his arm around me and guides me over to the table where they're selling setups. "It's on the house, man. You want 7UP, ginger ale—?"

"You got any of that tonic water?"

"You bet."

We're just grinning away at each other, and I say, "I love you, Mondrowski, you sorry asshole."

All that running I'd been doing had got me in pretty good shape to dance the polka, and I don't think I missed one that first set—like I was getting my workout right there in the parish hall. And the whole time, I kept thinking about Janice. I mean, it would've been hard not to, hearing her playing and singing and all that. And she'd turned into a great MC, remembering to thank all the million people you've got to thank, like, "This next one's going out for Ethel Warsinski and all the ladies in the kitchen. They're doing a great job the same as always. Let's give them a big hand."

Another thing surprised me—I didn't know she could be that damn funny. A couple times she really turned the goofball side of herself loose—like on that Walt Solek tune, the "Little Blondie Polka," she's really hamming it up, prancing around and flipping her hair like *she's* the blond-haired girl in the song, and jumping right to the edge of the stage and giving us these ridiculous looks, like making fun of ditzy blondes, and when she hits the Polish part, she's rolling her *R*'s like crazy, and the band's really got that Solek sound down—big bicycle horn mounted on one of Patty's drums, and Janice runs over and goes HONK while Patty hammers away on a cowbell—and me and Mondrowski and some of the other guys are whistling and yelling at them, "Go, go, go!"

Like I've told you, the downside of living in a place like South Raysburg is that everybody knows everybody. But do you know what the upside is? That everybody knows everybody. So who all did I see? Well, Franky Rzeszutko had closed the restaurant for the night because he wouldn't have missed the ball for anything, and there were the Czaplickis from the grocery store, and of course my Babcia Wojtkiewicz grabbing me and crying and talking to me in Polish, saying thank God for bringing me home safe, and I said, "Come on, Grandma, you've got to dance with me."

Janice's parents were there, sitting at a table right up by the band, and they got in a polka or two before the night was over. Old Czesław seemed real happy to see me and told me I had to drop out to the house while I was home, and I said, yeah, I'd sure do that, and then Arlene Orlicki's little sister yanked me out onto the dance floor.

And I got a chance to swap a few one-liners with all the guys like Burdalski and Dombrowczyk—you know, the boys—and after that first close call, I was ready, so the next time somebody shoved a beer at me, I said, "Thanks, but no thanks, buddy, I'm an alcoholic." For most people that usually does the trick.

Father Obinski stopped to chat with me for a minute—he was going around trying to have a word or two with everybody—and he was real pleased with the crowd. It was, you know, a fund-raiser for the church. He's not adverse to dancing the polka, so we were both of us kind of panting away, and I was thinking, hey, he's a nice fellow. I don't know why he used to put me off so much—maybe it's just because he wasn't old Father Joe Stawecki.

I loved seeing the tiny girls dancing with each other, or dancing with their daddies, and I was glad there was still a few young families in the parish. Like Dorothy Pliszka—I mean, Dorothy Green—and her little girl, cute as a button, and her daddy was teaching her how to dance. They'd had another kid too, a little boy, and there were a few other kids running around, nowhere near as many as in the old days, but still a few young moms left. And like always, lots of old folks. Old Gene Duda was dancing with the old ladies—my grandma and Patty's grandma—and you should have seen old Mrs. Zembrzuski, Shirley's grandma. She put some of the thirty-year-olds to shame.

So I'm munching a *pączek* and talking to people I've known my whole life, and I'm dancing every dance, and I've stopped thinking about having a drink— I mean, it's just gone completely out of my head. And all of a sudden it hits me. All the time I was in Texas I'd been lonely for Polaks.

Well, the word must have gone out that the Pączki Ball was where it was happening because the hall was packed—as crowded as I've ever seen it—and they opened all the doors because the place was getting kind of steamed. They ran out of tables and chairs, and still the people kept coming, not just people from the parish, but a whole bunch of other folks—a lot of them kids—from one place or another, and whenever they came in, Janice knew who they were and gave them a good welcome. "Oh, here's our friends from Mercersville. This next one's for them—and for everybody else who drove all the way here tonight from the great state of Ohio."

So we were coming to the end of the first set, and the band kicked into *"Oj Dy Di Daj."* It's one of those "Come on, girl, give me a kiss" polkas, you know, *"Daj mi, dziewczę, buzi daj,"* and the rhythm in the drive goes like this—

HUMP-ah diddle-diddle
HUMP-ah diddle-diddle
HUMP-ah diddle-diddle
Deedle eedle ee—

Well, you can get a hell of a good stomp going on that first beat—that is if you know how to do that old-country stomp, slamming it down with your left foot, and Old Bullet Head sure knows how to do it because he learned it from his old man who learned how to do it back in Poland.

So there's my father, swinging my mother along and stomping the hell out of the dance floor, and guess what? I learned how to do that old-country stomp from him, so all I need is somebody else who knows how to do it. I look behind me, and there's my *ciocia* Eva, so I grab her and away we go.

My dad and I are stomping that beat right together, and we're giving each other the eye—like I'm sending him a message that says, come on, old man, let's see what you got, and he's sending one back that says, more than you got, bright boy. He spins my mom, and I spin my auntie Eva—and they're both laughing—and we spin them back in to us and STOMP down on that beat, and hell, you would have thought we'd rehearsed it, that's how together we've got it. There's people forming like a half circle around us, clapping their hands, and Mary Jo is egging us on, yelling, *"Hop, hop, hop, hopla!"*

The drive kicks in again, and the ladies fall right in with us, and now we've got all four of us right together going, STOMP-ah diddle-diddle, STOMP-ah diddle-diddle, people clapping for us on the beat, and when Janice starts to sing again, my dad and I whip up our left hands to give the ladies a pivot, and my mom and my auntie Eva go spin, spin, spin, spin, spin, and then we're back doing the good old STOMP-ah diddle-diddle. "Haw!" my dad yells, and I yell back at him, "Yeah!" And you know what? My dad and I are the two happiest damn crazy Polaks in the whole damn hall.

We get to the end of that polka and I'm soaked, I mean right down to my underwear. The sweat's just pouring down my face like I've been in the shower. And Old Bullet Head's kind of moist himself. He's chugging down a 7UP, and I'm chugging down a tonic water, and he says, "Aw, Jimmy, you're not too bad, you know that?" and I say, "You're not too bad yourself there, old man."

My auntie Eva's laughing—"Never again," and my Mom's going, "Walt, I swear you're going to kill me yet," but I can see she's pleased with herself. I say, "We really got you hopping there, *Mamusiu*," and my father says, "Oh. God. I'm not goina. Be able. To get out of bed. Tomorrow."

I hear Janice through the PA system saying, "Wheww! I think after that one, we better slow it down a bit—give everybody a chance to breathe. Okay, so here's a nice pretty waltz. Linda's going to sing it for you."

I'm strolling along, looking over the tables to see who I can waltz with, and there's Dorothy, and I think, why the hell not? After all those years I spent moping over her, the least she can do is waltz with me. "You want to dance, Dorothy?"

She gives me a sweet smile and says, "Sure, Jimmy." Her little boy's clinging on to her, so she gives him a push, scooting him over to his dad, and then there I am, just the way I used to dream about, holding Dorothy Pliszka in my arms, drifting along to one of those soppy sentimental waltz tunes.

I'd always wondered if Dorothy and I would have anything to say to each other. I mean, there's all kind of things I imagined her saying, like, "Wow, Jimmy, we sure had a great time in high school!" Or, "I'll never forget you, Jimmy, not in a million years." Is she saying anything like that? Are you kidding?

I ask her how she's doing, and immediately she starts telling me about their house renovations. Seems like there was a slump in the market so they bought themselves a nice old house out the pike, but it needed a lot of work and the renovations are taking forever, and everything is coming in way over budget, and right at the moment their kitchen is getting done, and it's driving her crazy because they're eating all their damn meals out and it's costing them a fortune.

And I'm going, "Gee, that's too bad," and, "Yeah, those reno guys are always way over budget," but it wouldn't make any difference if I was just grunting at her like your basic ape because she's determined to tell me every single little thing there is to know about it. And I dial her out—and then I remember that's exactly what I used to do in high school. I'm not sure she ever noticed.

Well, the band played through the tune once with only the instruments, and then Linda started to sing. It gave me a shiver—I guess because she's my sister and because her voice was so sweet and clear, but it was also the words she was singing—"Nie mam nic"—and that means in English, "I've got nothing left."

Dorothy's a good dancer—real light and easy to lead—and so we're drifting along to this sweet sad waltz, and she's telling me how hard it is to get real top-quality counter tiles in the Ohio Valley, and Linda's singing—

"Nie mam nic, nie mam nic.
Wszystko mi woda zabrała.
Tylko mi dziewczyna
Na brzegu została."

I'm all choked up. Linda's always been a sucker for sad tunes, and waltzes are supposed to tug at your heartstrings, but this one's a real gem in the sad-waltz department. It means in English something like this—"I've got nothing left, I've got nothing left. The water took everything away. All I've got left is the girl on the riverbank."

Dorothy, of course, doesn't know enough Polish to be able to follow the words, so she's just yattering away in my ear, and I've given up on her. I don't give two shits about her house renos, but just because I've stopped saying anything back to her doesn't mean she's going to stop saying anything to me. Nope, no way. It's just like back in high school—on and on she goes to the crack of doom. Tiles and linoleum and kitchen cabinets and countertops. And Linda's singing—

"Dziewczyno, gdzie mieszkasz?
Ja cię tam odprowadzę.
Pod twoim okienkiem
Białe róże posadzę."

That means, "Young girl, where do you live? I'll walk you home. Under your window I'll plant white roses."

The waltz is over, and Dorothy says, *"Dziękuję."*

"Don't mention it," I say. "It's nice to see you, Dorothy. I hope you get your house fixed up right."

After all those years, that was it, huh? Yeah, that was it. In my mind I'd had her, you know, on some kind of pedestal, and that dumb little pedestal had just fallen over. She'd always been a nice girl, and she was still a nice girl—but not exactly the brightest bulb in the chandelier—and she was married and had a couple kids. I thought, well, good luck to you, Dorothy.

I was still full of that sad-waltz feeling, and I didn't want to talk to anybody for a minute, so I walked over to the end of the table where Darlene was selling records and I just stood there trying to get myself back together. Dorothy wasn't the one I was thinking about.

No respectable polka band would ever end a set with a waltz. No, you wouldn't want to leave everybody in that sentimental soppy waltz mood, so you've got to end on a good hot polka. The one they did was "Zosia." That's, you know, about the girl calling her boyfriend into the kitchen, and Mom says, *"Wy, Macieju, co robicie? Że tak Zosię całujecie?*—Hey, Maciej, what are you doing— kissing Zosia so hard?" The kids from out of town all knew it and shouted it back in the right places. The girl I wanted to be dancing with was up on the stage singing, so I danced with Sandy Czaplicki.

When it comes to dancing the polka, Sandy's just as crazy as I am, so we came shooting off the floor at the end of it laughing and gasping for breath and going, "Hey, wow. Far out!" We thanked each other, and I walked over to the side of the stage, and Janice was saying, "Thank you, everybody, see you after the break," and Mary Jo took over the mike to tell people that this was a great time to buy a record.

Janice was still high from performing, and you could see it—a lot of color in her face, like those real pink cheeks, that wonderful sparkle to her. She saw me waiting for her. "I've got to get outside," she said. "I'm sweating like a fiend up here."

I left my ten-gallon hat on the table—I wasn't feeling much like a cowboy—and Janice and I walked out of the parish hall and into the night.

It had cleared right up—not a sniff of rain left—and it was mild for that time of year, or maybe it just seemed that way because she'd been playing and I'd been dancing and we were both of us damn near melted. Janice said, "Let's walk down to Pulaski Park."

So we're striding down the street still high from all the music, and I'm going, "Hey, the band sure sounds great. You guys sound like real pros, all right," and she's saying, yeah, they've improved a lot, and telling me about all the places they've played while I've been gone, and about the new tunes they'd learned, and like that, but then when we get down to the park, all of a sudden we've both run out of things to say. I mean it's just that quick, BANG, and we're standing there in this dead silence. It must have hit us both at the same time—oops, we're alone together, now what?

What I'd wanted to say to her, I'd already said it. But I had to say something, you know what I mean? So I figured the best bet was just to keep on talking about the music. I told her I loved that last waltz they'd played.

She said she'd always loved it too. "My mom used to sing it to me when I was little. I taught it to Linda. I thought it'd be perfect for her. It's on our record. There's two waltzes on our record, one on each side. She sings both of them."

"Oh, yeah? What's the other one?"

"'The Linden Tree.'"

"Oh, right, I remember that. You guys did that at Franky Rzeszutko's—you know, that first night you played in there."

"That's right. We did, didn't we? You've got a good memory."

"Yeah? Well, about some things I do."

We'd stopped by the swings. I said, "You too old to swing now?"

"No," she said, "you're never too old to swing," but she didn't swing.

She'd brought a jacket with her, but she didn't put it on. We stood there looking at each other, and I could feel how nervous she was. It was like this vibration coming off her. I could see her shivering. "You're going to catch cold," I said.

"No, I won't. Why do you keep looking at me like that?"

I guess I'd been staring at her. She seemed almost like a stranger and— I don't know how to say this. The girl I was talking to just didn't match up with the Janice I remembered. Well, she did, and she didn't. It was weird. "You seem so different."

"I'm not that different. I'm older."

"But you seem different somehow."

"I'm still me."

"I don't know. Maybe it's your hair. When'd you get it cut?"

"Oh, the end of my senior year at Central. Mom said there was just no way I was going to graduate from high school in braids, and I thought— I guess I was tired of people asking me how old I was— I cried."

"You did, huh?"

"I felt like such a baby. Right there in the beauty salon. The tears just rolling down my face."

"Well, it looks nice."

"Thanks. I saved the braids. I keep thinking I should get somebody to make a fall out of them."

We'd had a nice little run for a minute, but then we hit one of those silences again. She took this enormous breath and just exhaled it, like—whew! "Oh, boy, this is hard!"

"Yeah, it is. I'm having a hard time too."

"Oh, Jimmy," she said, "I've wanted to talk to you for years. I *have* been talking to you for years—in my mind. And now here you are, and I don't even know how to start."

"I'm surprised you're talking to me at all, to tell you the truth."

"Oh, I was mad at you. Boy, was I ever mad at you! But I got over it. It took a long time, but I did. Linda told me what you were going through. That helped me understand it. You were struggling with your addiction—"

I had to laugh. "Janice, let me tell you something. For the longest damn time I wasn't struggling a bit. My addiction was one hundred and ten percent in charge of me."

She laughed too. "I'd almost forgotten how funny you are."

Then she stopped laughing and we stood there looking at each other again

THE CLARINET POLKA · 395

in this kind of miserable way. She was shivering so hard I wished she'd put her jacket on.

"Remember when we came down here and you got stoned?" I said.

"Of course I do. Whew. And you guys were so sweet to me. I hardly knew Georgie Mondrowski. I don't think I'd said ten words to him in my life. Oh, I was such a little kid! And did I ever feel privileged. Hanging out with you guys. I thought I was sooooo mature."

"Well, you were."

"No, I wasn't. Remember the night I ran away from home?"

"Oh, sure."

"Oh, boy, was I a brat. I can't believe some of the things I did."

"You weren't that bad."

"Compared to what? I was just— Oh, Jimmy, that summer was— It's like my whole life divided. That's how I think of it. There was everything before and then everything after. I really changed a lot over that summer."

She was shaking like a leaf. It wasn't just a little thing. "Put the damn jacket on," I said.

"Okay, okay." But she didn't put it on. She just wrapped it around her shoulders. "I was afraid you'd forgotten me."

"There's no way I'd ever forget you, Janice. I told you that. I'll never forget you."

"Well, I'll never forget you either. You were so nice to me that summer."

"It wasn't something, you know, that I had to work at."

"Thanks," she said, like I'd just paid her a compliment.

Well, we talked about this and that—I don't remember what—and I was thinking it was finally okay, that we'd got through the hard part and maybe tomorrow I'd take her out for coffee, and maybe we could end up being friends—or being *something*, I wasn't sure what. To tell you the truth, I didn't know what I wanted—except I knew I had to see her again.

Then right out of the blue she says, "Jimmy? When you came back to talk to me—you know, just before we started to play—that must have been really hard for you."

"Oh, yeah. It was kind of hard, I've got to admit."

"For all you knew, I might have told you to go straight to hell."

"That thought did cross my mind."

"Well, I've got something I want to say to you too. It's something I've wanted to say for a long time—"

"Yeah? So go ahead."

"There's, you know, things I'm sorry about too."

"Aw, come on, Janice, there's nothing you've got to be sorry about."

"Yes, there is. I listened to you, okay? Just listen to me for a minute." And then she started—well, I guess you'd have to say it was like a confession.

"Remember all the way back right after we first met?" she said. "That night when you drove me home and it was raining so hard? And we sat in your car and talked and you told me about that time you flew to Labrador? When you thought it was nuclear war?

"You'd never talked to me before, and I was so pleased with myself because I'd got you to talk to me—and we'd had a real conversation. A serious conversation. And I went to bed that night, and I lay there listening to the rain on my window, and I thought, oh, what a nice boy. I sure like him a lot. And I got him to talk to me—maybe I could get him to *like me* too. I didn't know what I was doing. I was only fifteen. It never once crossed my mind to say, 'Hey, Janice, come on. He's ten years older than you are.'"

I could see how embarrassed she was. "Hey," I said, "that's not a big deal. Lots of teenage girls do things like that, right?"

"I'm not talking about lots of girls. I'm talking about *me*. And yes, it was a big deal. I was like a kid playing with matches. Oh, I can't believe I'm saying any of this!"

"Look," I told her, "you don't have to say anything more. There's no problem that I can see."

"Just shut up, okay? I've been thinking about this for years, okay?"

I was feeling this kind of harsh buzz. Like I didn't know where any of this was going and it made me, I guess you could say, real apprehensive.

"Oh, boy, did I have a thing for you," she said.

I felt like somebody had kicked me in the stomach. "Yeah," I said, "I knew that."

"You probably didn't know how bad it was," she said. "I was just a kid. I was— Oh, this is so hard for me! No, don't say anything— I was such a little romantic. Such a little mush brain. I thought I was— I don't know what. I thought I was Zosia in *Pan Tadeusz* or—like the girl in that waltz. *Dziewczyno, gdzie mieszkasz?* And I was the *dziewczyna*, the lovely young girl, and you were supposed to be the lovesick man who follows me home and plants roses under my window—" She was kind of laughing when she said that.

"And we were supposed to go on together eating our hearts out in this lovely dove-gray-and-pastel-pink romantic mist forever," she said, shaking her head over how silly she'd been. It was like she was inviting me to join her in having a good laugh at herself. Well, the way she'd said it was funny, but I didn't think what she was saying was the least bit funny.

"And then I had to go and ruin everything," she said. She took a deep breath. "That night I kissed you— It just ruined everything. We couldn't go on after that. And I'm really sorry."

I didn't know what to say. She was right. That kiss had been like the absolute end of the road.

I guess she thought maybe I wasn't getting the picture. "It was really unfair of me," she said. "I wouldn't have kissed you if I hadn't liked you, but I was just being bratty. I wanted to see if I could do it. I wanted to see if—if I could really *get to you*. Do you see how bratty that was? It was really rotten of me. And I've regretted it for years. And I just wanted to tell you I'm really sorry."

Well, all of a sudden she wasn't the only one who was shivering. Even my teeth were chattering. "Hey," I said, "you don't have to feel sorry. You got what you wanted, you know."

She didn't say anything.

"You're not too young now," I said. "Would you go out with me now?"

She still didn't say anything. Not for the longest damn time. Then she said, "What are you talking about, Jimmy? How can I go out with you? You live in Texas."

"Aw, hell, Janice, maybe I don't have to stay in Texas."

She looked real annoyed with me. "You said you loved it out there. You said you had a great job, and— You said you were doing just fine."

"Yeah, well, it's true. I am doing just fine. But maybe I don't have to stay there."

"You're kidding me."

"No, I'm not kidding you. If I told you how much I'm not kidding you, you wouldn't believe me."

"Try me."

If you think I knew what I was doing, you're crazy. "I love you," I said.

She just stared at me. Then she giggled. I mean, really giggled. You know, hysterically. She slapped her hand over her mouth.

I didn't know what was going on. I felt sick, and, you know, deflated. I didn't think it was that funny.

She tried to say something, but it wouldn't come out. Then she did something really weird. She took my hand. I didn't know what she was doing, but I let her take it. She pressed it against her chest, on the left side, you know, just below her collarbone. Then I felt her heart. It was going about a million beats to the minute, and each one of those beats was so hard it felt like it was going to pop right out of her and up into my hand.

She said, *"Ja ciebie też."* That's what you say in Polish if somebody says, "I love you," and you want to say you love them too.

She said, "Oh, great. Oh, terrific. There goes all my cool right down the drain—and I was doing so well too. Oh, God, I think I'm going to die. Please tell me you're not kidding."

"I'm not kidding."

I took my hand off her chest and put my arms around her, and— Well, it's funny how you remember the damnedest things. I remember her jacket fell off her shoulders, and the sound it made hitting the ground—whump—and then we just hung on to each other.

"I wanted you to wait for me," she said, "but I never thought you would."

Well, hell, I hadn't been waiting for her. But then again, maybe I had.

"I know why you left," she said. "I know why you never called me or wrote to me or anything. There wasn't anything else you could do. I didn't understand it at first. It took me—maybe a year. And then I got it. I thought, oh, what if he loved me? That would explain everything.

"I couldn't let myself believe it. But I thought, okay, if it's true—if there's even a tiny little chance it's true—then he'll come back for me— Oh, you're crying," and she wiped the tears off my face. I hadn't known I was crying.

"Oh, God," she said, "this can't be happening. This can't be real. What if it isn't real?" She started crying too.

"I was so unhappy," she said. "I thought, I will *not* be miserable. I *refuse* to be miserable."

"You refused, huh?"

"Oh, yeah." And we must've both needed a good laugh because we sure got one over that dumb thing.

"So I kept my grades up," she said, "and I went out with Tony, and I said, okay, I'm going to be a polka star—and I am one—and I still wanted you to wait for me. I didn't dare think about it. And I knew maybe it wasn't true. And if it wasn't true, I had my music, and— Oh, my God, *polkas!* We've got to get back!"

So we just took off running like a couple idiots, holding hands and sprinting back up to the church. "What do we do now?" she said.

"I don't know. Ask me later."

"You want to go to Mass with me tomorrow?"

"Sure," I said. "What do you go to, the eight o'clock? I'll pick you up at seven-thirty."

We went running into the church, out of breath, and she was going, "How am I supposed to play? Oh, I'm so upset. But I'm so happy. Are you happy?"

I'll never forget this. We were in the hallway just outside the parish hall. Somebody saw us, and I heard all these girls' voices—Bev and Patty and my sister—going, "Janice, Janice, Janice." But we'd just stopped there, frozen, and I finally got it.

Hell, I thought, this is serious. This is just about as serious as it gets. Wait a minute, this is all happening too damn fast, and maybe that's not what she meant anyway. But I knew perfectly well that's what she meant. But it was crazy. We hadn't even kissed each other yet.

It was all worked out in her mind. I guess she'd always had it all worked out in her mind, except there'd been like this one important factor missing—and that was me—but there I was right on time and so far I'd fit right into everything just the way she'd always wanted me to, so who was I to come up with any objections? And what objections was I supposed to have? Like, hey, let's just wait one little minute here, kid. We've got to slow down on this one, and be adult about it, and think everything through, and make sure we're doing the right thing, and take it one step at a time and see what happens, and so on, and so on—all that crap. I didn't believe any of that crap. Sometimes adult is just another word for chickenshit.

She'd sure hung onto her dreams all right, but everybody knows that little girls' dreams can't come true. Oh, hell, no. They've got to grow up and get bitter and disillusioned just like the rest of us. But why shouldn't little girls' dreams come true? Although, God knows, it was hard for me to see myself as much of a Prince Charming.

But then, when you got right down to it, didn't I have a dream or two of my own? And here she was, not a dream at all but standing right in front of me, all sweaty and scared. My life's pretty much like yours, right? And most of the time you just stumble along doing the best you can, and you don't hardly ever get a chance to do exactly the right thing at exactly the right time. Well, that was one time I got the chance, and I knew it, and I took it, and it turned out to be the best thing I ever did in my life. "Janice," I said, "will you marry me?"

And she said, "Yes."

We go running into the parish hall, and the girls are yelling at her, "Janice, come *on!*" She jumps up on the stage, all out of breath and her cheeks pink

400 • KEITH MAILLARD

from the cold—and from all that adrenaline that must have been kicking through her—and they had their next tune lined up and ready to go, but that's not what she wanted to play.

Like I've said a million times, everybody in South Raysburg knows everybody else's business, but Janice got one jump ahead of the rumor mill and just flat-out announced it to everybody in the hall. She grabbed the mike, and she said, "This next tune's going out to Jimmy Koprowski—*od mego serca.*" That means, "from the bottom of my heart." If I'd had a chance to think about it, I could have guessed what she'd play for me. It was "The Clarinet Polka."

So that's how I ended up getting engaged during the break between sets at a polka dance to somebody I hadn't laid eyes on in three and a half years. Our daughter Sophie loves hearing that story. She just can't believe it. "You guys must have been absolutely nuts," she always says, and Janice always says, "If we hadn't been nuts, sweetheart, you wouldn't be here."

Yeah, we've got three kids. They're great kids. I mean, they're not angels—far from it—but we've got nothing to complain about. It was a rough road at times, especially when the kids were little and I was just getting my business started, and marriage, you know, is not always a bed of roses—anybody who's been married longer than ten minutes will tell you that—but that doesn't mean you never get *any* roses, and I've got to admit we've had a rose or two along the way.

So I don't know what else to tell you. Taking it one day at a time, it's getting on to damn near thirty years since my last drink. And I'd have to say what Janice's dad said that night we were sitting out on his back lawn—"God has blessed us." Yeah, He has—a hell of a lot more than I deserve.

So listen to me, you sorry asshole. Here comes the sermon. I don't care how much you lost. I don't care how far down you sunk. I don't care how hopeless you feel. I don't care about any of the shitty things you've done. There's a way back for you if you want to take it, and, believe me, you can get your life back. And you know what? You can even get a lot more than you deserve—because if we all got what we deserved, we'd every one of us be down there shoveling the coals where, you know, they keep things pretty hot.

So that's my story. Now you tell me yours. Don't worry if it takes awhile. I got as long as you need to take.

ACKNOWLEDGMENTS
AND NOTES

The Clarinet Polka is the seventh novel I have set either partially or entirely in my fictional town of Raysburg, West Virginia. In the course of writing these books I gradually became aware that I was attempting to create a large, complex portrait of Raysburg from many points of view and that to do so, I would be required to write in various languages, some of them alien to others and even in conflict with them. Although my own life had been profoundly touched by the Polish-American community in my hometown, I initially resisted writing about Polish Americans because I did not feel adequate to the task. Then two of my friends died within months of each other, and the struggles of their lives, completed in their deaths, convinced me—although I'd be hard put to explain exactly how—that this was a book I was required to write, no matter how I felt. Although neither of these two friends appears directly in the text and neither of their stories is told here, their shaping spirits hover over the work.

I cannot emphasize too strongly that the Polish community of South Raysburg as it appears in *The Clarinet Polka* is my fictional creation. Jimmy Koprowski, his family, the people of St. Stanislaus Parish, and, indeed, all the characters in the book (with the exception of historical figures like Richard Nixon and well-known polka bandleaders like Eddie Blazonczyk) are fictitious, and any similarity between the people, names, and events in this book and any real people, names, and events is purely coincidental. I hope, however, that the Polish community I have portrayed here feels *authentic*, and if it does, then it is only fair that I acknowledge my debt to at least the most important of my sources, both written and verbal.

Absolutely essential for background information were Norman Davies's superb books: *God's Playground: A History of Poland* (Columbia University Press, 1982) and *Heart of Europe: A Short History of Poland* (Oxford University Press, 1984). Władysław Reymont's fascinating four-volume novel *The Peasants* (Knopf, 1925) gave me a vivid picture of the world left behind by the immigrants who came to America at the turn of the century.

Of the many books I read about the Poles in America, the most useful were Helena Z. Lopata, *The Polish Americans: Status Competition in an Ethnic Community* (Prentice Hall, 1976); *The Polish Presence in Canada and America*, Frank Renkiewicz, ed. (The Multicultural History Society of Ontario, 1982); James S. Jula, *Polish Americans: An Ethnic Community* (New York, 1995); Paul Wrobel, *Our Way: Family, Parish, and Neighborhood in a Polish-American Community* (University of Notre Dame Press, 1979); and Eugene E. Obidinski and Helen Stankiewicz Zand, *Polish Folkways in America* (University Press of America, 1987). I don't claim to have read all of the monumental work by Thomas and Znaniecki, *The Polish Peasant in Europe and America* (Dover, 1958), but those parts that I did read were quite helpful.

Until I had completed a first draft of this book, I deliberately did not read any Polish-American fiction; when I finally did so, I was struck at once—and humbled—by the sense of entering into an ongoing conversation. I was somewhat disconcerted to discover that I was not the first to write about polka music, or even, for that matter, an all-girl polka band; Suzanne Strempek Shea, in her warmly detailed and heartfelt *Hoopi Shoopi Donna* (Simon & Schuster, 1996) had already beaten me to it. There are also, of course, real all-girl polka bands such as Renata and Girls Girls Girls and the Polish Peaches. The all-girl polka band in my book, however, has its own nutty character and is based upon no other polka band, either real or fictitious.

The edition of *Pan Tadeusz* I used was Adam Mickiewicz: *Pan Tadeusz or the Last Foray in Lithuania*, translated into English verse with an introduction by Kenneth R. Mackenzie (The Polish Cultural Foundation, 1986). Also useful was Stanislaw Eile's *Literature and Nationalism in Partitioned Poland, 1795–1918* (Macmillan, 2000).

Polka Happiness by Charles and Angeliki Keil, with photographs by Dick Blau (Temple University Press, 1992), gave me an excellent introduction to Polish-American polka music. Also helpful was Victor Greene's *A Passion for Polka: Old-Time Ethnic Music in America* (University of California Press, 1992). I frequently referred to Janice Ellen Kleeman's meticulous and passionate Ph.D. thesis, "The Origins and Stylistic Development of Polish-American Polka Music" (University of California, Berkeley, 1982).

My Polish town, Krajne Podlaski, is fictitious, but I have tried to be true to the facts as we know them, and I read a number of accounts of the years leading up to World War II, the war itself, and its aftermath. Richard C. Lukas's book *The Forgotten Holocaust: The Poles Under German Occupation, 1939–1944* (The University Press of Kentucky, 1986) was an essential source. I also relied heavily upon the many memoirs and first-person accounts I read; the most directly useful for my work were Christine Zamoyska-Panek (with Fred Benton Holmberg), *Have You Forgotten?: A Memoir of Poland, 1939–1945* (Doubleday, 1989); Leokadia Rowinski, *That the Nightingale Return: Memoir of the Polish Resistance, the Warsaw Uprising and German P.O.W. Camps* (McFarland, 1999); and Zoë Zajdlerowa, *The Dark Side of the Moon, A New Edition*, John Coutouvidis and Thomas Lane, ed., (Harvester Wheatsheaf, 1989).

The Story of Two Shtetls, Bransk and Ejszyzski: An Overview of Polish-Jewish Relations in Northeastern Poland during World War II (The Polish Educational Foundation in North America, 1998) was invaluable, as was Eva Hoffman's superbly fair and compassionate book *Shtetl: The Life and Death of a Small Town and the World of Polish Jews* (Houghton Mifflin, 1997). Also helpful was another excellent and moving book from a Jewish perspective, Theo Richmond's *Konin: A Quest* (Jonathan Cape, 1995).

Of the books I read on the Vietnam War, the most important was *Dear America: Letters Home from Vietnam* (Bernard Edelman, ed., for the N.Y. Vietnam Veterans Memorial Commission, W. W. Norton, 1985). I read all of the books written about the terrible events at Kent State in May of 1970; the best account of the shooting of the Kent State students is Peter Davies's *The Truth about Kent State: A Challenge to the American Conscience* (Farrar, Straus and Giroux, 1973).

I could not have written this book without the sound of Polish-American music in my ears, and for several years I saturated myself in that wonderful genre. I won't list everyone I listened to, but here are the groups and musicians who had a significant impact on my writing: Eddie Zima from Chicago, and of course the great genius of Polish-American music, Li'l Wally Jagiello; the Eastern-style bands of Frank Wojnarowski, Gene Wisniewski, the Connecticut Twins, Ray Buzilek, and the utterly astonishing Walt Solek; the sweet singers Marion Lush and Happy Louie; Lenny Gomulka and the Chicago Push, the innovative Prime Drive, the old master Eddie Blazonczyk and the Versatones, and my personal favorite polka band, the Dyna-Tones (Scrubby Seweryniak has a blistering version of "Zosia" on *Live Wire*, World Renowned Sounds 20067); from Pittsburgh, Henny and the Versa Jays; from the Ohio Valley, Bill

Binkiewicz and the Polka Barons; from Stevens Point, Wisconsin, Norm Dombrowski and the Happy Notes; and, finally, the female vocalists Theresa Zapolska, Regina Kujawia, Ania Piwowarczyk, Wanda and Stephanie, and Renata Romanek (of Renata & Girls Girls Girls), whose quotation of the first two lines of the Polish national anthem in her introduction to "Pod Mostem" (*I Love My Music*, Aleatoric, A4008) inspired me to have Janice do the same thing. Sources of early Polish immigrant music were *Polish Village Music: Historic Polish-American Recordings 1927–1933* (Arhoolie/Folkloric CD7031) and *Fire in the Mountains: Polish Mountain Fiddle Music*, vol. 2, *The Great Highland Bands* (Yazoo 7013). All the Polish song lyrics that appear in this book are traditional.

The tension between Polish and English is central to this book, so it seemed important to me that neither should be able entirely to defeat the other—even in matters of spelling. Writing the Polish phonetically so that it could be sounded out by English-speakers, therefore, never appeared to me to be a viable option, and neither did spelling every Polish word and name correctly as though the book were set in Poland. The method I have chosen retains the conflict between the two languages. I have spelled all the Polish dialogue, Polish song lyrics, occasional words of Polish, and the names of Poles from Poland correctly, using the Polish alphabet. Polish Americans, however, do not generally use the Polish alphabet when spelling their own names, so the names of all Polish Americans have been spelled with the English alphabet. Native speakers of Polish might find this system misleading. They should remember that Polish-American names usually retain their original pronunciation. Uncle Stas, for instance, pronounces his name Staś. Similarly, Pajaczkowski is pronounced as Pajączkowski, Wierzcholek as Wierzchołek, and so on.

I am, of course, responsible for *The Clarinet Polka*, and anything wrong with it is my fault alone, but it would have been impossible to write without the generous assistance I received from others. Frank Buturla took me to the Pączki Ball at St. Lads when we were in high school together and planted the seed that would grow into this book all these years later. He is one of those few people I could honestly say changed the course of my life, and I want to thank him for that, for his kind help with my work, and for his continuing friendship.

I also wish to thank Larry Dolecki, another old friend of my youth, who kindly met me in Wheeling twice, led me on a walking tour of the old Polish neighborhood, patiently answered my questions, and reminisced about growing up there. A number of his stories have found their way into my story; the joke about the bad-ass kid whose parents send him to school with the nuns, for instance, is his.

Barbara and George Maryniak not only supplied me with Polish words, phrases, and lines of dialogue but also spent hours transcribing the Polish lyrics from polka tapes and then translated them into English for me—and whenever I asked if they were getting tired or bored, usually replied, "Oh, no, this is fun." Barbara read an earlier, and much longer, draft of this book and offered a detailed and invaluable criticism. To Barbara and George, I offer a heartfelt *dziękuję*.

Many people in the Ohio Valley assisted me in this project. Wanda Kulpa and Verna Dolecki talked to me about Polish-American customs. Members of the Polish American Cultural Association whom I met, appropriately enough, at a polka dance, were wonderfully friendly and helpful, particularly Bob Sincavich and Frank Romanoski. Frank sent me a dozen useful items—everything from a videotape of the Onion Festival in Florida, New York, to a recipe for making *pączki*; he also arranged for me to meet Joe Handzel and Bill Binkiewicz, who regaled me with stories of playing Polish-American music in the good old days. Caroline Lakomy graciously invited me into her home, told me about her father's Polish orchestra, gave me a vivid picture of the old Polish community, and guided me through the Polish Catholic liturgical year.

When I knew nothing whatsoever about polka music, Chuck Stastny of the Polka Connection in Yankton, South Dakota, gave me excellent advice on where to begin. Karen Majewski sent me a copy of her Polish-American *Cute Girl Comics*. Ginger Eckert assisted me with matters of Catholicism, Barbara McDaniels introduced me to the great state of Texas, and Dr. Art Hister provided me with medical information. While I was doing my research, Pat and Fritz Temple provided me a home away from home. My old pal Will Hadsell was, once again, an inexhaustible source of Ohio Valley lore, legends, and obscure facts. My wife, Mary, trained her critical eye on layer upon layer of emerging text and was, as always, a marvelously supportive helpmate. Patrick Crean at Thomas Allen & Son in Canada and Sally Kim at Thomas Dunne Books in the United States provided encouragement and perceptive editorial advice, and my proofreader, Eliza Marciniak, read the final text, both English and Polish, with astonishingly sharp eyes. My colleague at UBC, Bogdan Czaykowski, corrected mistakes in the Polish and pointed out other errors of both fact and nuance; he also supplied me with invaluable details and was warmly supportive of this project. Ryszard Wójtowicz provided extremely useful background information, helped me solve a number of small but maddening problems, and, best of all, responded to this book from the heart.

I wish to thank the Humanities and Social Sciences Research Council for a grant that helped me to do the early stages of research on this book and the University of British Columbia for the study leave that gave me the free time necessary to complete my research and writing.

In these acknowledgements, it is only fitting that I should end where I began. Bill Barringer was not Polish, but he was certainly Catholic—even when he was trying his best not to be. No one could sing "Amazing Grace" with more conviction, and no one could have struggled more valiantly with the illness that finally killed him. If he were alive now, he would read this book with sympathy, intelligence, and insight. The last time I saw him, days before he died, he was only intermittently conscious. I shook his hand and said, "Have a good trip." He looked directly into my eyes, and I knew that he was suddenly fully aware. "Thanks," he said. "I'll see you later."

In dreams I'm young again, and I'm in a bar down by the river. All the boys are there—Frank and Ron and Augie and Larry and I don't know who all—and we're chugging down the beer and yelling at each other, and I can see him as he was then—laughing, red-faced, sweating, full of life—Prince George Cedric Hudacek, Pretender to the Throne of Bohemia and pretender to damn near everything else, the crazy guy who pulled me out of my bookish isolation, got me to like beer, took me to Mass at St. Lads, and, when I was sunk in gloom, cheered me up a million times—my classmate in high school, my roommate in university, my friend. "Hey, Maillard," he yells at me, "you're never late." He's right, and I'm pumping quarters into the jukebox. Every song on there is Polish, so I don't have a clue what I'm playing. All I know is that never in my life has music sounded so good.

I ja tam z gośćmi byłem, miód i wino piłem,
A com widział i słyszał, w księgi umieściłem.
 – Mickiewicz

Keith Maillard
Vancouver
February 28, 2002

READING GROUP GUIDE

1. Discuss Polish stereotypes and how they are dispelled, reinforced, or explained in The Clarinet Polka. How do characters like Jimmy, Patty, Linda, and Mary Joe acknowledge and deflect these attitudes?

2. Discuss the friction between first-, second-, and third-generation Poles in South Raysburg and how this friction ties into European ideas of class, and how it lessens during the process of "Americanization." What does it mean to "be an American" to each of these generations?

3. Describe the life/death cycle of an ethnic community as portrayed in The Clarinet Polka. Is there a fundamental contradiction between becoming an all-American boy or girl and preserving ethnic culture? Compare Raysburg's Polish community with other American ethnic communities with which you are personally familiar.

4. Discuss the effects of war on Czeslaw, Georgie, and Jimmy. Do you think that Jimmy suffers from a form of "survivor's guilt," having gone to Guam but not Vietnam? How do Georgie and Czeslaw come to terms with the horrors of war and their own survival?

5. The Clarinet Polka is a love story with a happy ending. Is this realistic? Discuss the love story's parallels with the folk-tradition polka lyrics that thread through the book. Discuss the archetypal pull on Jimmy, of the "bad" married woman and the "good" virginal girl.

6. What is the importance of Polish Catholicism, prayer, and specifically the role of Our Lady, in the Polish psyche? What are the similarities between Christian spirituality and the principles put forward by AA that enable Jimmy to come to terms with his alcoholism?

7. Some people feel that alcoholism is too boring or depressing a subject for a novel. Do you think alcoholism is realistically portrayed in The Clarinet Polka?

8. The author has used Raysburg as the setting for his previous books, including Gloria, which was set in the 1950s. Talk about the role of Raysburg in the book, and how the town is like a character in the story.

For more reading group suggestions visit
www.stmartins.com

Get a

Griffin St. Martin's Griffin

"and like that"

Is Jim's resentment of his father justified?

Are there things that "are ours" for older ethnic groups?

What's the significance of the "Clarinet Polka"?

Why should you be proud of something you can't help - like your ethnicity?

folksy, familiar tone

Why did he go back with Connie?

What was Connie after?

Where did you feel the book was going?

Czeslaw's response to Janice's music p. 204

What is the connection between the polka & Czeslaw's WWII experiences?

Was the friendship between Jim & Janice believable, well developed?

Teenage is a usually time for rebellion. Was Janice's rebellion due to her father's revelation or was it due?

Is your ethnic identity based on genes, or at